Every Day Scant-Less

By Monique Lynwone

ISBN: 978-0-9985645-0-0

This book is all about love and how people will do just about ‘anything, to attain it! But being that ‘love, can’t be bottled up, makes it a free spirit. And being free, means it can cast its spell on just about anyone it wants to. There is nothing like it, and there is nothing stronger, then this thing called; love!

I hope you enjoy this book as much as I did while writing it.

Special Thanks to God for giving me the love of writing as a gift. I am a song writer first, but love this change, of writing my first book. I would also love to thank this actor who was on the t.v show: Inside the Actor’s Studio. I didn’t catch his name because I came in on my lunch break and only heard him speak for a few seconds. “But I could pick him out of a lineup though!” Lol. He had said if one of your dreams isn’t coming true, make a new one; pertaining to your main dream and hopefully it will bring them together. That was great advice, so I thank him. I would also like to thank the ‘Beautiful Models, on my book cover; which I bought from: istock.com. ‘Plus, a special thanks to Hammadkhalid (hmd_gfx) from: Fiverr.com for making the cover. Also thanks to wonderful; Singer’s, Rapper’s, Television Shows, Movies and Comedians who I love, which made my story feel more alive 2 me. And to my family, thanks for putting up with my long hours of writing. And my daughter, for her help, love you for that. And to the people that I have met for whatever reason this past year; magically! I am thankful to you too, because I feel you made ‘me, want to be a better artist, and so for that, you will always be in my prayers. And last but not least a shout out to my mom and dad, love you both for believing in me. And thanks Google, and Oscar from best buys; geek squad along with Mike from Killer Book Marketing.com off you tube.

Chapter 1

Heels are 'click; clacking, up the stairs to Candis's front porch. 'Ding, dong; chimes the doorbell and a voice from inside the house yells "coming! After looking through the peephole she opens the door saying "oh, it's you!" It is Candis's best friend; Naquawna. "Girl, where have you been?" says Candis with a turned up brow. "I have been trying to reach you all night" she said with one hand on her hip. "Oh..., for real?" answers Naquawna with a surprised look on her face saying "well--, I've been kind of busy!" You know; running errands." Candis snorts "no I don't know 'busy, Beaver!" That's why I'm asking you". Naquawna laughs "busy, Beaver; huh?" "That's a new one" she cracks. Candis still laughing replies "and by the look on your 'face, I'd bet 'money, it was some, d*ck; involved!"

Naquawna busted up laughing saying "you do know a 'sista, well!" Naquawna is so excited about her new piece of "meat" if you 'will, until 'Candis, ruins the moment by saying "damn--; you just broke up with old boy!" Naquawna rolls up her eyes and throws up her hands while she's walking towards the kitchen spouting "don't hate the 'way; I play the game!" She puts her purse down on the counter and grabs an apple from the fruit basket still; chuckling. Candis blurts "heffa; please...! Ain't nobody; hating!" "Besides, I got more game then you anyway!" The girl's just stand there in the kitchen laughing with each other, while still trying to up 'one, on thy 'other, about who has more 'game, when it comes to men."

Candis and Naquawna have always been very competitive with each other. 'Though, competitive; it was mostly petty thing like; whose hair was the cutest?" 'Or in basketball, who could make the most 'baskets, in a game?" And when it came to 'track, they would always see who could run the fastest at the track meets. They've even gone as far as betting on who could find the cutest 'outfit, whenever they've gone out shopping. The two girls became best friends in 6th grade and no one could come between them. 'Although, not having the same taste in 'boys, did help in keeping their friendship; thriving.

Boys were the one thing the girls 'never, had an issue with. So at 17 years old Candis and Naquawna both went to their senior proms with their high school sweethearts. Sadly to 'say, they both broke up with those same 'boys, a year later; on-- the same day. They still laugh about it 'to this day. One of their saying from high school always was "that's how we roll"! Candis is the shy one. She likes to get to know a guy on the inside first. No 'sex, until marriage; or so she; hopes! Her method is..., to get to know a guy by asking him a lot of personal question, which seems to work for her. 'Whereas, Naquawna is the total opposite of Candis. She doesn't give a 'damn, about; questioning a man first. As long as the guy is 'fyne, as hell; has a fit body; drives a tight ass car; has money and a big "stick" she can play 'with, she's wit'; it! When Naquawna sees a man she 'wants, she will look him up and 'down, lick her lips; stick out her big tah'tah's and asks him for his 'number, and before the clock strikes 'twelve, she'll have him in her bed! 'Although--, Candis doesn't "approve" of Naquawna's life style; she 'does, like to hear her slutty stories from time to time.

Maybe deep down inside Candis "wishes" she could be as bold and daring as to see a man of her choice, get his number; hook up with him that same night; and start ripping the clothes off his 'rock hard; body while licking him; from head to toe! 'Okay! Maybe not his toes. Then she'd climbs up on top of his 'spaceship, and ride him until his 'bolts, start to drip; sweat! When finished she'd get up put her clothes on and while walking towards the door she'd say "I'll call you!" 'But; damn...! Why couldn't she just; do it?"! That is what creeps in and out of her mind sometimes when she's hearing; all about Naquawna's 'so called, "hot times"!

But then, on the other side of her brain, a voice always; infiltrates saying "you know exactly; why?"! And then she thinks back to all those church meetings; those religious classes; and yes all those fairy tale stories about "waiting" for her knight; in shining armor! Believing that "God" has made someone 'special; just for her! "Yes; all that gibber-jabber in her ear; growing up; that is "supposed" to mean; something; great! 'Plus, not to mention; how badly; her family would 'flip, if she was to all of the sudden; become an overnight; whore! So while Candis is still waiting; patiently for Mr. Right; to come along! Her best-friend Naquawna; is not! She is having 'Mr. Right now; in her bed! 'Even, if he's; Mr. Wrong! 'Ain't; that a bi$ch?!"

Naquawna still standing in the kitchen staring at Candis eating on her apples' moves her neck saying "so what makes you think you've got more game then me anyway?!" Candis looks Naquawna up and down slowly to be funny then she answers "well---, Quawna!" This will take about an hour for me to break it down for you, so let's go to lunch" she said laughing as she closes here refrigerator stating "I'm starving and I don't have a taste for anything in my house." Naquawna with high hopes adds "are you treating?" Ah--; no--! "You are! "You still owe me a treat from the last time we went to lunch" squawked; Candis. "When?!" asked Naquawna. "When we went to that Smoke House Barbeque place; remember?!" You ordered those hot wings but "claimed" you left your money in your other purse; so I paid the bill for you; remember now?!" "Oh..., yeah, that place!" recalls Naquawna smiling. "It 'was, finger lickin; good!" she adds. Saying "okay, then my treat!" But I get to pick the spot" says Naquawna. "Cool!" said Candis as she grabs her jacket and heads out the door.

The car doors shut on Candis's SUV, she has a tight truck with 22 inch rims on it with a Tequila Sunrise, orange and maroon 'candy; paint job, with a bumpin system; 'tah boot. Her car turns heads everywhere she goes because of how pretty the paint job is. One of her brother's friends, named Juan had painted it last summer for her for only $500.00 dollars. Juan is like family and that's why he hated to even charge Candis, but she wouldn't have it any other 'way, because she knew he had just started his company and needed the cash. And as far as Candis was concerned' business was business.

Hell, the paint alone cost more than the labor, so she felt blessed, that he even painted it for her 'for so cheap. "People would always ask her who did her paint job?" And she would always reply 'Juan, and give them his business card. It was the least she could do to show him 'some love, for the great job that he did on her ride. Candis turns up the beat and the girls are off to find somewhere good to eat for lunch.

Half way up the road Naquawna gets a text and Candis glances down at her phone saying "who's that? Before Naquawna could respond, Candis adds "probably one of your "many; men" she says with a laugh. "Ugh..! It's the stalker!" frowns Naquawna. "Who?" Bobby?" asked Candis. "Yes, says Naquawna sticking out her tongue implying "yuk! She exits out her messaging app on her phone and says "that's why I cut things off with him last weekend because he's a pest!" He always be calling and checking up on me all the time, and hell; we ain't even together like that!" like he 'thinks, we are! Laughing she adds "all he was good for; was eatin the cookie dough!

"I didn't even have sex with him; believe it or not!" and it was mainly because, his fishing pole was "not" up to par!" And I "did; not" feel like waste my time; at the fishing hole!" Candis cracked up laughing; sympathetically. Naquawna chuckling; too, grunts out "I remember one time, I had an appointment to get my nails done and Bobby just kept on begging to "you know?" taste the goods, thinking that once he did 'that, he would be able to slide into the oven!" But girl; please--!" When I got done Cumming; like Niagara Falls!" I got right up saying, "damn...; I almost forgot!" I have a Doctor's appointment!" And with my clothes up, and back on, I stood; saying "I've got to go boo!" And I grabbed my purse and went and got my nails done!" Candis laughing out loud says "you are a fool for that one!" Naquawna still laughing with her says "hell--, I thought of you 'Candis, when I ran that game on him! "Remembering" one of Candis's 'famous; lines, they both say it at the same time "you can lick it!" but you 'just; 'can't; 'stick; it!" They laugh in unison as they give each other a high five while cracking up. Then Naquawna spots an Olive Garden Restaurant. She shouts "that's what I have a taste for!" Some shrimp; fettuccini!" Naquawna shouts "get over!" Put your blinker on!"

They pull into the parking lot and park the truck, and as the girls make their way into the Restaurant Candis notices two handsome men waiting to be seated. The tall fyne one locks eyes with Candis, while the stockier one is talking to him about something that happened in football' you know; sports stuff. Candis couldn't really hear the whole conversation just bits and pieces of it. The taller gentleman had curly black, wavy hair that went a little passed his ears, with golden brown eyes and a sexy smile with a dimple. Damn, he is fyne thought Candis but couldn't tell by looking at him, what nationality he was. He looked to be a mixture of Puerto Rican or Latin and Black, or Jewish and Black, or who 'cares, she thought; he's--; fyne!

He kept on staring at Candis like he could read her thoughts, and it was like magic as they gazed into one another's eyes. She turned away from his gaze periodically acting like she wasn't that interested. It was a cute little game she liked to call; eye flirting. All she could think of 'was, that he was 'definitely, her; type! Well... from looking at him anyway. And although she hadn't really heard him speak too much, by just looking at him she was 'sure, it "wasn't" going to be a problem; unless he sounded like Mickey Mouse or something.

Naquawna was talking to the hostess at the time, telling her of how many people she needed to be seated for lunch, so she didn't see the eye contact between Candis and the tall 'fyne; stranger. For some reason Candis was glad that Naquawna didn't notice him because she was busy talking to the lady standing behind them. Naquawna was telling the woman how much she loved her shoes. But, being the "cock-hound" that Naquawna is; eventually she did spot him out of the corner of her eye. She then whispers to Candis "ooh girl, look over there!" Dang; he's cute!" I'm gonna see if I can have him for desert!" she winks. But before Naquawna could get her claws into him, a woman comes from the kitchen and grabs the tall one by the hand and gives him a big hug and a kiss on the cheek.

And as he stood there being hugged by the lady he just couldn't take his eyes off of Candis. Naquawna stops quickly in her tracks when the hostess says "excuse me, your table is ready." "Dang...! Sighed Naquawna. I wanted to get his number, he is 'just; my type!" So as the girls are walking to their table Candis is surprised to hear Naquawna say "that he's, just, her, type"! When it is a 'known, fact; that Naquawna only hooks up with black guys. And this man that Candis is getting looks from has to be mixed with something a little more. Candis thinks to herself "what, is up, with; that?!"

With her lips turn't up and her face on 'swirl, she thinks to 'herself, she must be running out of 'brother, to choose from; since she's pretty much slept with everyone in the hood! The girls are seated and then the waiter comes to the table. He says "hello?" ladies. "My name is Joel and I will be your server." "What can I get you ladies to drink?" Candis is first "I will have a margarita sour and a glass of water with lemon." Joel writes it down and then turns towards Naquawna who says "and I will have a margarita too, but with a shot of patron on the side" she smiles. She continues "um--, and can we order now too?" please?" asked Naquawna with a hungry look in her eyes. "Sure, says Joel. "Alright, then" says Candis. "I'll have the lasagna trio with a salad." "Okay, smiles Joel as he takes down her order.

"And--, I want the shrimp fettuccini, with a salad as well" said Naquawna. "Sounds good" he says as he puts his pen back into his apron. He smiles back at the girls saying "I'll be right back with your drinks." "Thank you Joel" cheers the girls; so happy to be out for lunch. As Naquawna squirms around getting comfy in her seat she says "so..., girl..., what did you think about that nice looking man and his friend who were at the front entrance?" "Oh--; him?" he was alright!" said Candis as she's putting her napkin in her lap trying not to smile. "Oh, batch; plaz!" Which means (Bitch Please)! "You know he was fyne!" I saw you, checking him out" said Naquawna with a big smirk on her face. Candis just laughs saying "no honey, he was checking; me out!" "Oh, really?!" smirks Naquawna, kind of jealous at the thought of 'not, being the one he was checking out first.

Then Candis in a peculiar voice says "so--, let me guess?" now you've moved on to Jewish, or Latin look-in boys; too?!" Naquawna; furrowing her eye brows retorts "he's not black?!" He looks black to me!"

she adds. Candis grunts "you know he ain't all--; black!" like you're use to dating!" she said grinning looking Naquawna right in her eyes to see her reaction. Naquawna blurts "how do you know?!" are you the nationality; police?"! Candis just laughs looking back at her saying "Whatevah! She wanted Naquawna to think she didn't care about the guy because she didn't want Naquawna to know how she "really" felt about him; seeing that this was the first time, that they had "ever" been attracted to the same type of guy. 'Besides, that would make Naquawna go after him even; harder because she was "scant-less" like that! Unbeknownst to Naquawna 'Candis, had already made up in her mind that she was going to get this man; one day; somehow! So Candis nonchalantly; changes the subject by saying "so anyways, "remember," we came to lunch to talk about your "lack" of game!" she said laughing while staring at Naquawna; jokingly. Naquawna replies "don't be looking at me all; crazy!" I'm doing just; fine!" Thank you, very much" she said while adjusting her boobs in her shirt.

Then the waiter brings their drinks, and after saying "thank you to Joel." Candis says "alright--, let's make a toast" she said as she raises up her glass voicing "to love, peace, and happiness!" "Here..! "Here..!" said Naquawna. Adding "and plenty of mad sex!" she said as their glasses chimed together. "Speaking of which!" Naquawna goes on to say, after drinking her shot of patron. She looks at Candis sideways saying "when are you going to 'finally, do the; do?!" "This is 'not, the sixties; and you are well in your late twenties; almost pushing thirty!" "Shut; up!" blurts Candis with some of her drink spilling from her mouth. Naquawna grinning says "no." Let's talk about; that!" Candis answers "what does my age have to do with anything?" She looks at Naquawna crazy while wiping off her shirt adding "as far as 'I'm concerned; having sex with everybody that you come into contact with; isn't cute; either!" at; any age!" Naquawna grunts out, "whatever"! Candis continues "and--, if you want to give away 'all, "your; goodies!" for free; without a commitment!" that's on you!" But don't rush me!" she said with her eye brows lifted and her head tilted to one side. Naquawna shouts "I don't sleep with everybody!" She continues to smile saying "just the ones, I think are fyne as hell!" Candis smirks "gurl; please!" "They are tossing you like a coin!" And what fun is 'that, if the men don't even have to; work for it?"!

Naquawna with a 'closed, lipped smile curses; shouting "Candis; 'stop; front-in!" You know damn 'well, that most 'men, are "not" going to wait around if you are not given up the panocha!" Look at what happened to 'you, and your 'last, boyfriend!" "He ended up cheating on you because you 'weren't, sleeping with him!" "So---!" and I didn't lose 'any, sleep over it either!" said Candis. Naquawna goes on to says "and you 'know, that cute ass ‘man, like the one we just ‘saw, in front of the Restaurant “isn’t” going to wait on a woman for ‘sex, when there’s so many ‘women, giving it up; for free!”

Candis yells, “see--; that’s just ignorant, talk!” because every man isn’t “meant” to have all my goodies; anyway!” “So if he’s not “meant” for me, I will find that out by getting to ‘know; him!” Get; it?!” Hint! “Hint! “You should try it sometimes; Naquawna!” Naquawna snaps; voicing “go on with that crap!” “And another thing!” ends Candis as she’s crossing her arms. “I’ve notice, out of all the men you’ve been, “screwed” by!” I don’t see any of them sticky around and getting ‘sprung; off of you; enough to marrying you!” like the men “I’ve; gotten!” and “don’t; screw!” get sprung off of me!” So, your; “f*cking” your way into a man’s heart!” isn’t working for ‘you, either; sweetie!” “You know what Candis?!” shouts Naquawna. Then she pauses because the waiter comes and sets down their plates saying “enjoy ladies!” “Umm- k! “We will!” thanks Joel!

Naquawna getting back to arguing says “well, like I was saying!” I, am, so “sick” of you, and this ‘high; ‘horse; you’re riding ‘on; thinking that you are ‘better, than everyone else!” Candis looks at her hard; spouting “my high horse!” B*tch...!” Don’t hate!” Naquawna shouts “all I’m saying is; you’re just ‘wasting, your young life ‘waiting, for a “prince; charming” that just doesn’t exist; anymore!” With a bite of her food she adds “these are different times; now!” Candis replies “the times may have ‘changed, but ‘not, as much as you think!” It’s just the “people” have just gotten; weaker!” That’s why; like I said!” Let’s just call it; like it is!” I have more “game” then you; do!” And I “refuse” to fall for that; this is the way of the world; bullsh*t!”

Naquawna just kept on eating having nothing else to ‘say, as she rolls up her eyes at Candis with a pissy; grunt to all of ‘Candis’s; ranting! The girls have had this conversation before on many; occasions but never this; heated! So ‘now, there happy ‘girl’s, lunch day ‘out, has gone; sour, as they both sit and eat in ‘silence! Until Naquawna softens her mood speaking out “well... I don’t know how you do it!” I get so horny” she says with a slight laugh. ‘Candis, slowly smiling says “oh, trust; me!” It’s very hard!” “But--, nothing a little “masturbation” won’t cure; before I go out on dates!” No penetration though; just clit-play” she continues with a laugh, saying “then, I’m all---; fixed!” That way..., I can get to know the guy better, without being such a “horn-dog”! Candis laughs so... loud, while telling Naquawna her secret weapon, on staying celibate, until she almost forgets where she’s at;

which happens to be, in a crowded Restaurant.

Candis then covers up her mouth with her napkin to muffle her voice when Naquawna laughs out "for real?!" That probably wouldn't work for me" she said with a sip of her water. "That's because you've never tried it before you've gone out on dates" chuckled Candis. "Maybe you should try it!" adds Candis. "So then, maybe you can keep your; legs closed!" Naquawna; mortified at how loud Candis is being about her business 'huffs, at first with her mouth open but then she laughs at the joke with her. "Trust me" says Candis guys masturbate before dates too. "So-- I've heard" she laughs. "They say it makes their erection last longer if they plan on having sex again, that day." "No way!" said Naquawna with a look of surprised; curiosity on her face. Candis just looks at her sarcastically because she 'knows, Naquawna always tries to play the dumb; role. 'Snickering, with this funny laugh Naquawna adds "oh, well, you know guys will use "any" excuse to bust a nut!" Candis laughs to herself thinking "and you are 'more, than "happy" to help them; do so!

Naquawna reflecting back says "take last night for instinct, since we're on the subject of sex." There's this guy that I have been liking for a while now." You don't know him, but he was out back by the shop last night and when I was getting in my car he asked if I wanted to go gets something to eat." And then...; as the evening 'progressed, we ended up having sex in the backseat of his Cadillac." "Dang!" said Candis. Naquawna twerks her face saying "I know it was kind of slutty of me!" but he was just so-o-o; sexy! Candis stares at her and then blurts out "I'm glad you said 'slutty, because I was thinking the same thing!" Naquawna slightly embarrassed shouts "oh, shut; up!" I have been liking him for a 'while, like I said!" And his body; gurl---!" she said with a sigh. "Damn!" Nothing; but; muscle!" Umm... mmm... umm...; umm... mmm!" she said blowing out a breath of fresh air with her eyes 'closed, just thinking about that 'hot; 'chocolate; of a man!

Candis just shakes her head saying "see---; making it easy for them!" as she laughed. Naquawna couldn't help but laugh too 'knowing, that Candis was partly right. But Naquawna still 'declared, that she just likes the 'thrill, of having casual sex. Naquawna looks over her shoulder to see who is laughing louder than they are and sees that the tall young man who was in front of the restaurant is still talking with that same lady he hugged earlier and she is laughing out loud with another person at another table from across the room. Candis takes another bite of her salad saying "it looks like somebody's having a good time down there." "Yep" replies Naquawna. "And I wonder if that's his woman?" She does look a bit older than him though." But 'hell, these days; who knows!" gawks Naquawna. "He might be a player!" Or even a jiggalow, or something!" Candis retorts "oh, my, God!

She laughs embarrassingly for her friend adding "you don't even know that man!" And who cares; anyway?!" We will probably 'never; even, see that guy again!"

But Candis was lying to herself because she definitely wanted to see him again, especially after feeling the magic between the two of them when they were looking at each other. But she didn't want to get her hopes up too high. She thinks to herself "could this be the man she's been waiting for?" Will destiny 'play, in her 'favor; for 'once; in her life?!" Or, is Naquawna right in saying "that there is no such 'thing, as a prince; charming these days!

She wonders even further; if it is 'true, that most of the 'men, now days, are wanna-be 'pimps; 'players; 'ballers; and 'shot callers! Who are living off of 'woman, and 'some; 'dope; deal-in! She gazes in a chain of thought 'thinking, could there be one special person out 'there, made just for her? And more 'importantly, will she know 'it's; 'him?!" when she finds him! Naquawna interrupts her thoughts saying "girl, let's get the bill!" I'm ready to go! Candis is still staring from afar at the tall stranger who is across the restaurant at the time of 'Naquawna's, interruption. She turns saying "oh. "Okay..., stuttering out of her 'fantasizing; gaze she gets the waiters attention. "Joel, can we get the bill please?" "Sure, one moment" he says.

"Woo- ooh- oo-we...!" I am; stuffed!" said Naquawna while rubbing on her stomach. "I know, me too" said Candis. "That was the bomb!" she adds. "Hey, I almost forgot to tell you" says Naquawna. "One of my friends told me that Jasmine is having a party this Friday." Do you want to go?" asked Naquawna as she's playing in her hair, checking it for split ends. "I'll drive" she adds. "Hells; no!" said Candis. "I'll drive!" I remember last time we went to a party and you left me, so I had to find a ride home." In fact, you left me; so you could go get some; now that I think back on it!" And it was for 'Bobby, at the time; your ex!" said Candis. "And now look at you; you ain't even with dude to this day!" retorts Candis as she stands up from her chair.

Naquawna just smirks not wanting to reminisce, about her past "mistakes". She stands up and leave the money on the table and they head towards the front entrance. On the way out Candis is looking around one last time to see if she spots, that handsome, ass, man, she's been salivating over the whole time. "But dang!" she says to herself. "He's gone. Walking toward the front she brushes it off saying "I've got to stop thinking about this man." I am tripping off of someone I don't even know." And, that I've only seen for the first time." She wonders "is this what they "mean; by" love at first sight?"

When she gets to her car she clears her mind and opens the car door. Looking back over her shoulder one last time to see if she would see him coming out of the place, or going to his car, but no such 'luck, he was really gone. Naquawna gets in the car and they close their doors and head back to Candis's house while listening to the XM radio jamming to a few stations like Shade 45 with Sway, the Foxx Hole and even the Starz channel. Candis says "these station are off the hook!" she says as she's bobbing her head up and down driving. Naquawna agrees and says "I can't wait, to go to this party on Friday" she said as she's dancing in her seat to the music as well. She adds "we haven't been to a rich 'be'yotch, party in a long time!"

Candis all surprised replies "what--?!" You mean to tell me, it's not a house party?!" "Hell--, no!" It's down town" said Naquawna. "Jasmine's family rented out the Grange Hall." It's her 21st birthday and my boy said they are trying to do it up; big!" said Naquawna swirling her neck to the music. "Everybody's talking about it, and all the homie's are gonna be there!" smiled Naquawna. "Good" said Candis. "Because at 'first, I was going to have to 'pass on it, if it was another one of those; ghetto ass house parties!" Most of them parties don't be nothing but a meat market; anyway!" Everybody looking to hook; up for sex!" said Candis with a "not; happening" look on her face.

Naquawna strikes a 'pose, while looking at Candis like; she's crazy! Then she; squawks out "hoe; please--!" I come up; at house party!" because there are so many "sticks" to choose from!" jokes Naquawna with a big laugh. "Yeah, you come up at a house party!" as your 'reputation, goes; down!" depending on how you look at it!" laughs Candis. "You are such a hater!" blurts Naquawna. "I know...!" says Candis sarcastically; my pussy's jealous of yours!" I want a 'cottage; 'cheese; 'snatch; too!" Candis laughs even harder after adding the words "as if!" Naquawna laughing back shouts "ooh--!" you are so; mean!" 'Even though, Naquawna couldn't help but laugh herself, as the two drove out of the parking lot and merged into traffic.

On the way home Candis stops to get a blunt wrapper and a 12 pack of Corona beer. Then afterwards the two girls finally make it back to her apartment and once they enter her place they both plop down on her couch. "What are you going to wear to the party?" asked Naquawna. "I don't even know" answered Candis. "I might half to see if I can get off early from work on Friday, so I can get to that 'Fashion Thug, Store before they close." Candis with a happy smile adds "you should come over that night, so we can get dressed at my house?" and maybe, you can do my hair for me" she pleads. "Okay... "That's cool, since you're driving" said Naquawna, adding "that would actually work out great because I only have 4 clients this Friday" she explains, as she happily snaps her fingers to the right.

Naquawna works at a small nail salon. She is tall curvy and busty with medium brown colored skin. Her smile is nice and her face is pretty. She started doing nails after high school, than she went to beauty school to get certified. Among her other talents she also does hair on the side, like braids, hair extensions, corn rows, weaves and hair color. Naquawna loves her job and would love to own her; own, business someday. Braiding hair is how she meets, most of her men. She likes that 'swag; 'look, from a man, with 'or without hair, she's 'not, picky!

Candis works at a hospital in the next town over, and she is cute as well. Medium height, slim, but with curves and a nice rack with brown coco skin. After high school Candis went to a two year community college to get her degree. Then she got hired as a medical administrator, working the front desk in the radiology department. Her job would entail, that she answers the phone, takes down appointments for the Doctor's and takes care of the paperwork in the office. Candis and Naquawna talk on the phone just about every day while they are both, at their individual jobs. Their friends always say to them that "you two girls "do; not" need a job where you have 'full access, to a landline phone all day!" Even their co-workers have commented on it, from time to time stating "that they are 'surprised, that they even get any work done, being that they are always on the phone; gossiping throughout the day. Candis and Naquawna pay it no mind when they are confronted about the constant "chattering" on the phone, saying to those hater's "that they are just jealous because they don't have a best-friend that they can talk to, while they're; at work!"

So back to Candis's apartment. Naquawna is now tired of lounging on Candis's couch and declares "it's time to get up!" and move around so we can work off some of that pasta!" She stands and walks over to the radio, turning it on to one of her favorite station's which is 102.5 where she hears the Madhouse Crew 'bumpin, one of Ludacris's songs called: Rollout! "Hey--!" yells Candis saying "turn that up!" She gets up off the couch and starts moving to the Hip Hop beat, then Naquawna states "Luda is so fine!" And he's got skills; too!" Candis smiles saying "yes he does!" She adds "and he really makes me wanna get on the dance floor, right about now!" "True that!" said Naquawna. "And I would definitely give him a whirl" she said, as she starts to grind thy air dancing. "Well...; that's a no brainer!" Laughs

Candis. "The question is; who "wouldn't" you give a whirl; too?!" Candis; laughing hard; swirls around Naquawna while dancing to the music laughing. Naquawna looks back at her and with her lips protruding 'outwardly, she proclaims "ummmm..., you; dogged; me!"

Then Naquawna's cell phone goes off, so she says "hold; up!" I got to take; this!" she said smiling as she jogs; gingerly back to Candis's room for a little; privacy! 'Plus, the music was way too loud in the living room for her to hear her call. "Hello--?" says Naquawna in a sexy voice. "What up; baby?" A man says on the other end of the phone. "You?" she answered with a big smile on her face. "What are you getting into tonight?" he asked. "I would love for 'you, to be getting into me, tonight" she said in a low soft voice. "Is that right?" he answered while rubbing under his chin. "Let's hook up around 7 o'clock tonight than" he said with the quickness. "Well--, it's Monday and tomorrow I have to go to work." "Plus, I'm at my girl's house right now" she said as she's pacing the bedroom floor. He says "so. "Why don't we hook up at your girl's house then?" I'll bring my homeboy with me" he said desperately. "Umm...?" I don't know?!" Candis is kinda picky when it comes to her men!" And, she's got to work tomorrow, too!" "But hold on, I'll go ask her." Naquawna puts the phone down on the bed and runs back into the living room where Candis is rolling up a blunt, on the coffee table. "Hey..., Candis..." says Naquawna with a sweet smile on her face. "Rayshawn... is on the phone... Candis cut in the conversation "that must be your new piece?"! "Yes..., it, is!" And he wants to know if he can come kick it; with us?" Candis says "where?!" Here?!" "I don't know that; fool!" "And I know...!" you don't know him that well!" laughs Candis. Naquawna laughing back says "ooh--, that's dirty!" Candis chuckles some more as she's closing up the 'blunt, with one last lick. Naquawna sighs "come on girl!" He's bringing one of his cute ass friends for you to meet!" Candis just looks at her, like she's 'really--, desperate. Then Naquawna begs "please--; yet again. Adding "I know, we have to go to work tomorrow, so we can shut it down early" said Naquawna trying to sweeten up; the deal.

"Yeah, you damn; right we are shutting it down early!" Those guys probably don't even; work!" adds Candis as she lights up her blunt. "Ooh--!" Now you 'know, you ain't right!" chuckles Naquawna. She says "he's gonna hear you!" he's still on the phone! "I don't care if he 'hears, me!" and his friend better be; fyne--; too!" grunts Candis. "I know?" I told him you were picky" said Naquawna scrunching up her nose with a 'half, smile. "Picky"! "You got that right!" "Unlike you; Naquawna!" "I want "quality" in a man!" "Not; quantities!" Candis laughing hard, adds "b*tch, I clown't; you! Naquawna grins back saying "ha, ha, ha; real funny!" Candis blowing out the smoke with a smile, says "my buzz is 'on, and crack-in!" This is some bomb ass 'weed, I got from those cute white boys down the street!" brags Candis.

Naquawna hits the blunt saying "yep..., it's some Kush alright!" She hits the blunt again saying "so is it cool, or what?!" "Can they come over?"! "Yeah..., I guess!" answers Candis as she coughs off the smoke she just inhaled. "Thanks you sis!" you won't regret it!" she said running back to the room yelling "I'll tell them to bring some drinks too!" Naquawna gets back to the room; hoping that Rayshawn has not hung up the phone. "Hey babe, sorry it took me so long!" Rayshawn replies "dang, where did you have to go?!" up the block?!" Then he says "so what's up?" What did your friend say?!" she said "it was cool!" But we can't party too late" she said while twisting her hair around her finger, thinking how she can't wait; to see him. Naquawna is so-- turned on, from just hearing his voice, until she can almost 'taste, his 'lips; through the phone.

"Ay!" I almost forgot to ask?" "What do you ladies want to sip; on?" "I know what I 'wanna, suck on!" thought Naquawna. But she wouldn't 'dare, say it out loud. She replies "umm... how about some hen-dog?" I love me some Hennessy." And can you get some HYPNOIQ to go with it?" I like to mix the two drinks together and watch it turn green." It makes my--, she pauses; then says "temperature; rises! "Is that right?" he said, while rubbing on the front of his pants, adjusting himself.

Rayshawn plays it 'cool, but all he can think about is Naquawna's 'lips, wrapped around his "special; toy"! So while she's rambling on "about how the drink turns green, and who turned her on to this type of drink?" and what party she was at, when she first tried it?" Rayshawn cuts in and interrupts her 'explanations, about the drink and says "so baby, not trying to cut you off, but what's the address?" "Oh..., okay" she says stumbling on her words. "It's on Clay tree Street." Apartment #70711." And it's the corner apartment." You will see a candy colored painted truck in the driveway" she said as she's licking her lips. "If you get lost, just call me back" she said. "True that" he said. "I'll find you though, believe that" he added. And hang up the phone.

Naquawna is so excited that the guys will be coming over. She runs back into the living room and says to Candis "O.M.G"! Meaning {oh my God}! "They will be here shortly" she voiced, while looking at herself in the mirror. "I'm going to need a rag, so I can freshen up a bit!" "Okay" says Candis. "Go on ahead, you know where all that stuff 'is, don't act like you're a 'guess, nig'gro! The girls laugh with excitement as Naquawna giggles her way down the hallway. Candis sits back on the couch (now high) and thinks to herself how it 'would be fun, to have some cute guys over to look at, after all--, it has been a long time since she's kissed someone. 'Okay, not that long; maybe like two weeks. But to be honest, she hasn't been really looking for a new man anyway. Especially after her bad break up with 'Ricky.

Ricky was this 'hot ass boy from 'Spain, who had a lot of swagger. To Candis he seemed to be "the one"! Not only because he was so handsome but also because he was so, kind hearted. What really drew her to him was how he stood out in a crowd, and how he would showboated in front of the ladies as being really, charming. She could tell he loved to 'wow, people by using his beautiful green eyes and his height to his advantage. Candis also loved the way his dark brown hair laid on top of his head and up against his skin, and she always liked to play with his facial hairs with her fingers because it was so clean cut around his nice looking lips and chin.

Her and Ricky met one day by chance at the hospital, where she worked at. He just so happened to work there too 'as a Phlebotomist. His primary job was drawing blood from the patients that came into the hospital needing blood work. But he also would be called up to different floors, whenever he was needed. 'Ricky knew, he was great at his job and everybody for the most part liked him. 'Plus, he also knew how to run game on all the nurses by joking with them all the time to get what he wanted. And that was how he got his name (tricky; Ricky) because he was such a smooth; operator. You 'would; think, that Candis would have known better, after hearing that nickname; that he was going to be trouble.

So when she's in the cafeteria eating lunch one day, he comes and sits down across from her at the table and starts to ask her all kinds of question 'like, "what department she works in?" And how does she like the staff that she works with?" You know, small talk. So that's when Candis starts to warm up to his flirtatious; conversation as she's looking in his pretty eyes, and while he's talking to her she starts wondering "could this be a longtime relationship in the making?" Or--, is he just a fool around; kind of buddy?" So as time goes on and after meeting in the lunch room several times together, and talking on a daily basis.

The two ended up exchanging numbers, and as the two became closer in their friendship they then started dating. When they were at work on many occasions they would sneak off and meet each other in certain private rooms in the hospital and fool around. Nothing 'buck wild, since they "were" on the clock and had to be ready to work at any given moment. But it was still fun and exciting, to say the least. 'Or, maybe it was just the 'thrill, of knowing that no one "knew" they were together, that made it; so--'much, more fun!

After about two weeks into their relationship 'though, Candis found out that Ricky had an ex-girlfriend who also worked at the hospital. She was this blonde chick named 'Kristal, who was kinda cute but had a short; temperament. Up at the hospital she worked in the accounting department. Yes, Candis knew going 'in, that it was a bad idea to start messing with someone on the job, but he was so-o-o 'cute, and he had already been broken up with 'Kristal, for about eight months. And word around the hospital 'was, that she had moved 'on, to a "brother" no doubt! So Candis wasn't trippin if Kristal found out about her and Ricky or not! She just didn't want Kristal fu*ken up her paycheck! 'Real; talk! "So... any; who! Things were great for about 4 months; until Ricky got caught; slippin!

"Ding, dong"! Went Candis's door bell. "Shit!" A voice said sharply. "They're here; already?!" blares Naquawna. Looking down the hallway at Candis she shouts out; meekly from the room; "get the door! "Sheez...; calm down" said Candis as she gets up off the couch with a laugh. "Just a minute" she shouts as she's walking towards the front door. Candis opens the door with "hello-?" "I'm Candis" she says as she lets them into her apartment. "What's up?" My name's Rayshawn." And this is my boy Jason." "Sup?" said Jason in a deep sexy voice, just the kind of voice she likes. They head towards the living room and in comes Naquawna all dolled; up with a black mini skirt on and a low cut pink shirt that showed damn near half her breast. She also had on a pair of Candis 4inch, pink heels to match. Even Candis, took a 'double take, thinking to herself (this b$tch is off the hook!) Candis couldn't help but chuckle; because she didn't even tell Naquawna she could wear all her; sh*t!

"Naquawna says "hey, baby" as she hugs Rayshawn in a seductive way with her arms up around his neck and one of her legs bent back; saying "I see you found us" she said as she's looking up in his brown eyes. Naquawna looks to her left and notices Jason taking a seat on the couch, so she says "hey, Jason... "What up; girl?" he answered. "Nothing, just chillin" she said. He places the Hennessey and the HPNOTIQ bottles on the coffee table. And then Naquawna asked "did you meet my home-girl?" She's pretty; huh?" Candis yells from the kitchen "girl--; shut; up...!" He just got here!" You are really---; trippin!" Candis then yells out "Jason, pay her no mine!" And you can bring the liquor in here, if you want too, so we can get this party started!"

As Jason heads to the kitchen, Naquawna and Rayshawn start kissing on the couch. Rayshawn slowly runs his hand up her 'inner leg, and up to her thighs to see if she is wearing anything under her skirt and of course she isn't. His eyes get as big as quarters when he says "damn!" Like that?"! And with a sly grin on his face he adds "I see you're already; ready for me; huh?" Naquawna laughs and whispers in his ear "you know it!" He grunts voicing "careful what you wish for!" Because, I'm ma put it on, yah!" Naquawna chuckles with a look on her face like 'what, but then she kisses him even harder. Candis and Jason quietly come back from the kitchen and they both walk into the living room, where Rayshawn and Naquawna are on the couch kissing and rubbing all over each other. They are so into each other at the time; that they don't even notice that 'Jason and Candis, have returned from the kitchen with their drinks.

Candis clears her throat saying "we hate to interrupt you two "love bugs" but here's your drinks." "I hope there not too strong" adds Candis with a chuckling smile. Candis can see how 'hot and bothered, Rayshawn and Naquawna are with each other, so she says "let's go into the dining room, so we can play some dominos." Still holding her drink she pulls her friend up off the couch by the arm saying "come on gurl!" Then the two start giggling after Candis whispers in her ear "to calm down because she would "really" like to get to know Jason a little better." Saying "after all, he is looking pretty tasty" laughs Candis. They both agreed and then Naquawna still giggling adds "and so is my new; piece!" As they walk to the dining room; arm in arm smiling behind the guys, they make hand gestures like "I'm going to get me some of that; tonight!" When they get to the dining room they all sit down and start to play dominos. Candis sits down for a second, then she suddenly gets up out of her seat to go and reload her CD player. The first song up; is a blast from the past called "Hurricane" being rapped; by: The Click/ E-40, and they are bang-in one of Candis's favorite songs with they; fine ass! Candis smiles because the boys; can spit!

The CD starts playing and Naquawna yells "that's... my... boy...! "Right there!" Talking about E-40 because she loves his story tell-in. Candis laughs from the kitchen because she knows how much they both love B-legit's voice as well. After she gets the music going she grabs some chips and some nuts from the kitchen cabinets and puts them into 'two, separate bowls. And then she heads back to the table before it's her turn to play her hand. When she sits back down Jason is giving her that damn-- you're pretty; kind of look! So she 'thinks; anyway, as she sits down slowly while giving him a shy smile. 'But, don't get it twisted; she is definitely; feeling; Jason because he is so handsome. Jason has beautiful brown eyes with long eyelashes. His skin is a nice rich Carmel color, which makes her want to just rub her face up against his and kiss it. His eyebrows are thick, like cutie-pie Drake's. And his smile is like pretty boy T.I.'s. He is a nice height with a nice build and his pants hang off his body, just right' in his Levis.

"Dang--, Candis thinks to herself, this is going to be 'hard, not falling; for this one! Even though Candis is trying to play it smooth, the longer they play dominos and the more she drinks, the more she starts thinking about how good his mouth 'looks, and wondering "if" he can kiss with it! Candis loves to kiss, that is one of her "specialties"! She always says "a man has 'got-tah, know how to kiss!" Or it 'won't, be a second date"! "Sorry!" So while they are playing the game she notices just how sexy he really is while he's sitting across from her, and her mind starts to wonder things like "how good is he with his hands?" And does he talk with that 'deep; voice, during sex?" And if so, she wonders how big; is he?" And does he know how to use it?" And of course during this time she couldn't stop wondering if he likes to eat the 'cookie dough?" 'You know, all the things that cross a girl's mind; when she's sizing a man up; on the real!

She thinks to herself all kinds of things about him as she's playing the game. When he talks she watches his mouth move; wondering "does he want to kiss her?" Because she damn sure want to taste his 'sexy, mouth! When it's his turn to play she takes quick glances at him while he's looking down at his dominos. Looking down at his hands she can't help but think about how it would feel to have his big, strong, manly 'hands, touching all over her body. She doesn't know 'why, her brain is on 'overdrive, with all these 'thoughts; but the sexual tension at the table is so 'thick, with lustful; curiosity, so 'thick, that you could cut it; with a butcher knife! And 'tonight, somebody's going to get "stucked!

Most likely, it's Naquawna, because she is squirming all around in her seat while rubbing her freshly manicured toes up and down Rayshawn's leg under the table. She tries to rub on his "package" through his pants with her 'feet, like a squirrel searching; for nuts. Then he unzips his pants when no one's looking, so he can feel her 'toes, on his body because he's freaky like that! Once she reaches his throbbing; 'packet, he tries very 'hard, not to let it show on his face, that he is getting very; aroused! 'Naquawna, feeling how 'hard, he is; wants him; badly! So Rayshawn keeps looking into her eyes from across the table, so she starts to lick her lips and pant; softly. With her eyes she tries to let him 'know, she wants 'him; right now! So with her eyes on him she puts a potato chip slowly into her mouth and licks and sucks the salt, off each and 'every, one of her fingers; intensively; while staring back at him from across the table!

Candis interrupts the moment saying "go Naquawna!" It's your...; turn!" "Hater!" 'Thinks, Naquawna to herself as she glances Candis's way with a smirk, but doesn't lose her stride, with Rayshawn. Candis smiles back at her because she 'knows, she's cock blocking on Naquawna right now. 'Plus, she could just "imagine" what is going on underneath the table and she just laughs to herself as she watches Rayshawn "trying" not to "burst" at the seams! Naquawna, focusing back on the game says "Oh." My bad...!" She puts down her last domino and yells out "domino; suckers!"

The night is going great and after a couple more games of dominos and a lot more drinks; were drank. Naquawna and Rayshawn start to get even "more" antsier with one another. Rayshawn brags about how he and Naquawna won the first four games, and how Candis and Jason won the last four. They were all about to play the tie breaker, when all of the sudden Naquawna says "she's got to go pee." She 'winks, at Rayshawn when she gets up from the table and then stumbles her way back towards the bathroom.

Candis, seeing everything go down with the two of them, throws her arms up saying; "whelp!" The game is definitely over, now!" She said with a laugh, because she 'knows, Naquawna is "not" coming back to the table; no time soon. So that's when Candis declares "good game partner" as she gives Jason a high five. Rayshawn not happy with that remark squawks "awe...!" Please!" We won four games too" he said laughing. 'Candis, not wanting to hear his 'mouth, puts her hand up towards his face and flops down on the couch laughing as she grabs the rest of her blunt. She turns asking Jason "do you want me to give you a charge?" "Sure" he answered and sat down on the couch next to her so she could blow some smoke into his mouth from the blunt.

Once Rayshawn seen the two of them 'cozying; up together, he slips away heading towards the bathroom conveying to them "I'm gonna go, check on Naquawna." Jason and Candis didn't hear one word he said because Candis was leaning in closer to Jason, with the burning end of the blunt in her mouth, and as she's blowing the smoke into Jason's mouth 'slow, and very close to his 'lips, she closes her eyes to avoiding the smoke from getting into them, and as she's blowing a steady stream of smoke into his mouth, their lips touch. Pulling back carefully she takes the blunt out of her mouth, to prevent the ashes from falling down on her tongue. Not being able to hold back her smile, she looks deep into his pretty eyes and in her 'softest; 'seductive; voice she asked "how was that?"

She smiles as she licks the bottom of her lip and with her mouth slightly ajar, she awaits his answer. "That was hel'la good" he said as he leans in towards her 'lips, while looking back into her eyes. "I haven't had a charge like 'that, in a long time" he said smiling. But, what she really wanted him to hear coming out of her mouth 'other than; how was that charge?"

"Was... "I'm drunk!" I'm high!" And I would love..., to kiss your fyne; ass right about now!" But she had to refrain from saying those 'extra, words because they would have; had to come, and take her players card!

As he's looking at her closely he says "you have got the prettiest eyes." Are they hazel?" She looks to the right of him hoping that he can't see her blushing as she reaches for the t.v remote off of the end table 'smiling, when she answers "yep, a little bit." Not wanting to be too conceited she adds "they change colors depending on what color 'shirts, I wear." When glancing at his eyes, her eyes then drift down towards his mouth and she says "you have a pretty smile." She turns the t.v channel to avoid any real eye locking stares from him and he smiles even 'harder, after hearing her say he has a nice smile. "Thank you" he said. They keep the t.v volume low because the music is still playing on the radio while they talk.

Candis is really high right now. And Jason is feeling pretty good himself. They make small talk then Candis says "so---, do you have to go to work tomorrow, too?" She didn't want to be too ghetto and ask "do you have a job?"! But, to her liking he said "yes. Telling her "that he works at Chevy Motors with his uncle, fixing on cars." She was shocked at first to hear him say that he worked on cars because he had such nice hands and no grease under his fingernails. She smiles looking down at his hands stating "that's a good job." I would have never guessed that you worked on car by looking at your nice hands." "Oh, for real?" he said. He touches her hand saying "I do get dirty at work." But I clean up well; though" he said smiling. Candis smiling back flirtatiously says "yes-- you do." She starts to 'blush, even 'harder, just hearing those words coming out of her mouth. "So what do you do, for work?" he asked. "I work at Treeberry Bay Hospital, managing my department in Radiology." He chuckles out "nice!" That's a real cool job too" he said smiling even; bigger showing all of his pearly white teeth.

He looks up at her hair and then down to her mouth asking "do you like what you do there at the hospital?" She has a sweet glow on her face when she answers "yes, I do." It's pretty rewarding 'knowing, I'm helping people get better." So while they keep making chit' chat'. Candis is getting more and more 'turn't up, by his conversation, and stimulated by his handsome face, because she's always been a 'sucker, for a pretty face. Thinking to herself though, at least he can hold a conversation. She looks at his mouth while he is talking; hoping he can pass the 'kiss, test. That is all Candis can think about 'now, after having touched his 'lips, for that brief second when she was giving him that charge.

It's just a matter of 'timing, she plots. She smiles inwardly 'thinking, when would be the best time to move in for the kill! 'Okay, so she didn't want to kill him! 'Personally, she just wants to kiss 'him, until his 'lips, started to go numb! "Ooh... yes...." she says to herself as she's moving one finger slowly across the top of her glass in a circular motion, while he talks. When he stops talking 'abruptly, because something has caught his attention on the Sports channel 'ESPN to be exact, where 'Stephen A, Smith was saying something about a football player. So for her to keep the momentum going while he watches his "sports; segment" she gets up and tells him she's going to make them another drink, saying "she'll be right back."

Walking towards the kitchen, when she opens up the freezer she starts to make their drinks. Then all of the 'sudden, he comes up behind her as she's putting ice into their glasses. She can feel his heart beating up against her back, because his body is pressing up against her butt. He wraps his arms around her waist and rocks side to side like as if to be dancing a slow dance with her. Candis is 'so, caught off guard but nevertheless; very turned on! So much so, that she almost drops the glasses on the floor. But then keeping her cool she sets the glasses down in the freezer, and while the freezer door is still open she turns around to face him asking "what are you doing?"!

She knows 'exactly, what he's doing, and she likes it! But she 'still, just wants to hear him say "why?" He's all up; on her!" 'You know. To hear him run his game! And say things 'like, how much he likes her!" Or, how pretty she is!" 'Yass, all that stuff, that turns us girls on. He looks at her real deep and with one motion of his mouth he flows out "I just love the way you smell." And when he pulls her closer into him, he whispers in her ear "and I bet you taste good--, too!" She smiles thinking to herself "yep...; that a do it!"

He can feel her breast pressing up against his chest so his 'happy hamster, gets even; harder! She lets him squeeze her tightly in his arms but says to him while he's holding her close "I bet you run those lines on all the women; huh?" Caught off guard he replies "naw. "I'm being serious" he says with a sincere grin on his face. He puts his hand on the lower part of her hair while rubbing it in between his finger he says "you are so sexy, to me." Candis 'not, wanting to fall for his charming 'words, to 'quickly, chuckles saying "yeah alright; Jason!" "Tell me, what you think I want to hear" she laughs. 'Even though, deep down, she wanted his feelings about her to be 'true, but she knew it was way-- too soon to 'tell, if he is a sincere 'person, at his word.

After seeing the skepticism on her face he replies "why are you being so hard on a brother?" Candis laughing softly replies "I'm not being too hard." "I'm Just, cautious" she said smiling shyly. She continues to say "but, I ain't gone 'lie, I do like the way your skin feels up against my face" she said when rubbing her cheek, up against his cheek; smelling his manly shaving cream. It was some kind of soft but not over powering musk cologne, that she inhaled; deeply off the side of his neck as he hugged her while talking to her in her ear. To Candis it seemed to pull her 'in, like as if to 'be, a love potion of some kind.

'Cautiously, she moves her hands up his back as they embrace, and when she brings her face around to face 'his, and without moving to far away from his 'face, with their cheeks rubbing softly away from each other, he kisses her. It is a slow passionate 'lip locking; meshing into one another; type kiss! Then the soft tip of his tongue slowly slides into her mouth and he's compelled to grab the back of her 'head, pulling ever so slightly on her 'hair, to pull her more into his mouth as they kiss. "Da'ah amm...!" "The boy can kiss" thinks Candis as she tries to hold back her moans.

While kissing him she moves her hands slowly up his back while holding on to his shoulders as her body 'levitates, to feel 'every; heart 'throbbing; 'lip numbing; taste of his mouth! He had her so 'wet, from just that 'kiss, and his hold on her body was 'just; right, like the neck of two swans wrapped in a loving embrace. "Wooh!" she sighs as she parts her lips from his. He smiles saying "that was real; nice!" But now, he chuckles "look how you got me out here" he said looking down at his 'Bazooka; showing from inside his pants. Candis gives him a sexy little grunt and looks him in his eyes not knowing what to say to 'him, or his 'third leg, as she stands there smiling wiping the corners of her mouth looking at him.

'Playing it off, she grabs the liquor bottles from off the counter while he's trying to kiss her on her neck. Chuckling she tries to stay focused over by the freezer while he's holding her by the waist and kissing her on the back of her neck. 'But eventually, she finishes up making their drinks all 'giddy, and 'bubbly, as they head back to the couch for round two of more smooching on each other. Candis takes a sip of her drink and so does Jason and they both sit down next to each other on the couch. But, without a 'second; thought, Jason leans in and kisses her again.

She puts her drink down on the coffee table while still connected to his 'hot; lips. Then he slowly lays her body down on the couch by pushing his body on top of hers while 'still, kissing her. Candis is not 'trippin; she is a "willing; participant" as she lies back with her legs slightly parted, with one foot on the floor and one leg on the couch. Reason being is because she's curious to 'feel, what he's working; with! "Even; if" she still has all her clothes on. Jason eases his body in between her legs and presses up against her middle. The feeling of him in between her thighs is so 'good, that she couldn't help but 'moan, out loud. Candis was moaning in his ear letting him know just how good he is giving it to her. "Oh... "Jason" she purrs, while kissing him even; harder! Wildly she grinds up against his "hockey-stick" as he's moving more and more into her; goalie!

If he can dry hump, on her this good! She can't 'wait, to see what the 'real, thing would feel 'like, one day! Trying not to be so-o-o 'hard up though, she grunts a giggle because 'hell, this is about the only thing she can do at this point. And it's been so long since she's been this turned on by a beautiful man that she really finds attractive in more ways than one. 'Plus, the drinks aren't 'helping, there making her want him even; more! 'Even though, this game of cat and mouse 'really, does excite Candis because she loves the chase from a 'man, when she knows he really 'wants, to have; her! She finds it "challenging"! 'And in truth, she's not trying to give him the 'pussy-willow, just yet! But she still wants him to 'feel; the 'heat; 'the passion; 'the lust; in every 'kiss; and 'grind; he gives her!

One thing about Candis 'is, she likes to get a man's "mind; first"! Then once they are "sprung" off of 'her, 'mind; 'fu^king; them! That's when she likes to takes them to the "next; level"! Which in her "mind; means" down thy aisle! 'After all, she does consider herself; a player! And with the love game 'she plays; it's her way; or no way! So while he's still lying down on top of Candis and still kissing her like she's the woman of his, "dreams"! He runs his hand across her breast wanting to squeeze her 'double; doses, but she can't so she whispers on his lips "no. "Not yet" she said while still kissing and grinding him because her spirit wants her to 'stay, in control! But her 'flesh, wants her to 'indulge, in the moment! She likes 'it; him touching her! And she doesn't really..., want him to 'stop. But she knows, she has to hold out, because it's 'all, a part of the chase!

Exhaling a sigh she sits back up on the couch trying to maintain, a little; "self-control"! She smiles out "I am so--; drunk!" Hoping he will get the 'hint; that it's "not" going to happen tonight! Looking him dead in his eyes she smiles as he puts his arm around the back of her neck on the couch. He tries to sweet talk her into given him some 'pooh-nanny, by saying to 'her, in her ear "come on baby" and with sympathy in his voice, he says "you got me so worked up!" And I want you so bad!" "Let's go back to your--, room" he said while rubbing on her leg softly. 'But drunk or not, she is "not" going to be falling for his 'begging mouth because she always thinks back to what her mother always told her "that boys will "say; anything" to get you to 'take; 'off; your panties!"

So as shy and willing as Candis may seem..., to Jason she is not going to be as "easy" as he thinks! In other 'words; a mark! (Meaning) a push over. 'Besides, fooling around with him with her 'clothes on; feels pretty 'damn, good! 'Not to mention, it makes 'things; 'less; complicated! 'Hell, if he plays his cards 'right, she might just make him (squirt) by jerking him off. She chuckles to herself just thinking about it. So while Jason is trying 'hard, and I do mean "hard" to run his game on Candis! Naquawna is in the bathroom, sucking on Rayshawn's "magic stick"!

Rayshawn is sitting on the bathroom toilet, with the lid down, his pants down, and his "lightning; cane" out! While Naquawna is kneeling down in front of him with her high heels still on, and her 'breast'stis'sis, hanging out! Rayshawn is sighing a sound of "Ahhhh! "Yeah...! "Baby" he moans. He pulls her hair back, out of her face saying "don't forget about my cohunes." With saliva dripping from her 'mouth, like an over flowing trickle of honey she replies "like this daddy" as she's in between licks. Leaning his head back in pure ecstasy he answers "yess... "Ooh... "Yass... His grunts turn into slow head shakes, do to all the 'gulpingly; goodness, she is doing to him as he's caressing the back of her head. Rumbling her cheeks like a vibrating sound, makes him moan even louder.

He pulls Naquawna's head slowly back by her hair while seductively; growling out to "hold up!" Saying "sh*t...! "I don't wanna burst yet!" He slurs out "play nice, and show me what you can do with these walnuts of mine?" 'Needless to say, a squirrel had 'nothing; on her! By the time she's done doing all the things he likes for her to 'do, he is so-- hard, that he has to stand up; to keep from; blasting! When he stands up with his 'big; 'hard; chocolate rod, which is still dripping of salty but sweet 'nectar, from Naquawna's mouth, he then tells her "to get up on the bathroom counter." Naquawna is thinking "oh... Hell... Yeah...!" He's about to eat my; kit-cat!" But; no!" Sike!"

This was only their second hook-up and he knows Naquawna to be a bit; 'hoe'ish, a mark if you will' considering that he 'already; hit it, on their first 'date, in his car; no dought! So in his mind, she doesn't 'qualify, for the "royal; treatment" which would include him licking all-, over--, her; body! But 'instead, she gets the 'pimp; special! So while Rayshawn's looking at her she starts to spread her legs 'slowly; 'like; come and get it; papi! 'Taste; me! But he starts to suck on her; apple seeds instead. He kisses her all down her stomach and while she is moaning in ‘anticipation, of his tongue; licking and sucking on her ‘flower; bud, he can tell that he has her very; wet! He grabs her legs and kisses the insides of her knees, and then takes his hard; brisket, and slaps it across her apple pie.

She moans even louder as she ‘squirms; eagerly for his tongue to taste her and with her eyes closing she pulls his shoulders closer towards ‘her, “wet; spot” so he can put his ‘lips, upon her. But to no avail. So when he gets through teasing her, with his fingers, moving them inside and out, of her, she just can’t take it anymore and she lets him ‘know, without a dought “that she wants all of him; now!” And that she is not going to wait; any longer!”

But Rayshawn’s the type of man that likes his women to beg; for it! He looks her in her eyes saying “you want this; baby?” Yes- she replies as she’s running out of breath. Panting; heavily and feeling ‘anxious, makes her temperature rise to match her breathing. “How bad do you want it?” Waiting for her to answer he begins to slap the side of her face playfully with his “slap; stick”! “Stop teasing me!” she blurts. “You already know; how bad I want it!” He voices out “naw--!” I don’t!” Tell me!” Like you need; it!” She looks up at him with a ‘begging; stare, replying “come on Rayshawn!” You know I want to feel you inside me right now!” He chuckles as he’s looking at her ‘begging; mouth, as she’s licking the tip; of his iceberg!

He keeps playing games with her like putting it in her mouth and pulling it out slowly. Then slapping her ‘playfully; ‘with it; while ‘stroking it; and ‘playing with it; until ‘she has; had it! Frustrated with all ‘his; teasing and ‘his; taunting, she decides to take matters into her own hands so she grabs his ‘candy cane, and gives it one, hard, suck, all the way down, to the back of her throat. Looking at him with wide eyes she holds him in her ‘mouth, until his knees start to ‘buckle; on him! He gets so... turn’t on by the suction of her throat! ‘So turn’t up, until he has to quickly grab his ‘cane, and squeeze it! Then, in a low rough voice he replies “awh...!” Damn...!” Baby...!” “Okay! Okay!” I’m ma give it to you!” Naquawna smiles up at him with a look of; that’s, what, I thought! “Now give me; my medicine!” she said. He exhales a deep breath and tells her “he hopes she’s ‘ready, for the jabbing he’s about to give her!” Then as he’s looking deep into her eyes he eases the head of his ‘bow, inside her inch by inch and she; squeals.

“Wooh-- wee...!” she says, while thinking to herself as he’s barreling into her like his favorite drill bit. Breathing through it, she has a moment of maybe she’s just not “ready” for all of this “pipe” he’s putting down! Her mind drifts to the conclusion that she’s probably “not” drunk enough! But as he starts to rub her ‘softly, she begins to relax more. “Awh... Gosh...” gasped Naquawna while squeezing his back and holding him tight as he’s going deeper and deeper inside of her; playhouse. He's so engaged; like a 'key, too a 'lock, until she almost slides into the bathroom sink. Rayshawn is so into the 'kitty- snatch; that he doesn't even notice her sliding into the sink because he continues to take her legs and put them both on top of his shoulders so he can go even; deeper!

He lifts her up off the counter so she won't fall all the way into the sink, and while doing so, she hits her head on the faucet. He doesn't give a 'damn, because at this point; he's in it; to win it! In the; zone! So as his hands are cupping her 'big; butt, he is bouncing her up and down on top of his "battleship" like as if to be saying "I am 'f-*king, the sh*t; out of you; horsey-back ride!" She tries not to be too—loud, by covering her mouth with her arm, while holding on to his shoulders but it's "not" working! All she can think about, in this position is 'he's trying to reach her 'tonsils, up in this mother f@^ker! "Oh... "Oh... "Sh*t--!" she mutters.

He can tell she's having a 'rough ride, so he slows it down. Naquawna is trying to play big girl, like she can hang with his, "showpiece"! But hell...! 'Not, tonight! Rayshawn; grunts thinking to himself "she talks, that talk!" But he 'knows, her ass won't be walking that same 'walk, when he's finished; with her ass!" He says "you like that baby?" I'm given you 'all, I got" he tells her in a ruggedly sexy voice. "You like it?!" he repeats, while looking at her. Naquawna just huffs and puffs as he's trying to 'blow, her house; down. She holds on to his lower arms, so she can take it all in 'slowly, but he keeps coming at her, at a steady pace. 'Slow, but 'steady, making it harder for her to catch up. "Oh... "Man... "You are trying to break me down" she said with a whimper, in her voice. Naquawna is feeling 'real, good... as she's taking all of his strokes as he slows down even more so she can catch her breath. Now he can hear her saying all the things he wants to hear. Which is "awh... "Yess... She moans even louder getting turned up to full blast as she smiles with her eyes closed because she can feel the vibes from his 'body, which are giving her chills up and down her spine.

So while she's getting off and Cumming back to back 'multiple times. Rayshawn tries to maintain his pleasure by telling her to hold on, once again asking her to switch; positions. Helping her down off the counter he says "turn around and face the mirror, so I can see your pretty face. Turning to face herself in the mirror is when he slides his 'log, back into her 'fireplace, from the back. But before he slides back into her, he checks to see if the condom is still on and then he slithers back into her 'kitty, of a cave.

Feeling the heat of her warm body he then moves his hands in front of her chest so he can hold on to her fruits with both hands. He loves her 'big; 'bow-dachas; 'fruit, spilling over in his hands. 'Vigorously, he starts 'twisting, on one of them, while licking her back as he's looking at her face in the mirror asking "do you like it this way, too?" "Talk to me" he says in a deep; masculine voice! "You like me all-- up inside you?" Because 'it's, all; yours!" He speaks to her in a stern voice saying "tell me!" Tell me if you like it!" But she couldn't say a word because she was "Cumming so---; hard!

And when he started saying even more; nasty, freaky, things to her and licking behind her ear; in her ear, and licking up the side of her neck! That's when her legs began to shake, and when she 'finally, could catch her breath! All he could hear was "yes...! "Yes...! "You--, are--, 'f*^king--, me--, so..., good--! "Don't! "Stop! "Please...! He gives her several more 'deep, long hard---, strokes and then he pulls his 'love-stick, out of her and takes off the condom and shoots his 'thunder, all over her throat, and on top of those pretty melons of heirs while he gives out a 'loud, growl' like as if to be (King, ding, dong,) of the jungle!

Panting like she's just finished a race, she licks her lips looking at him with a relaxed; posterior as she's breathing vigorously from such; satisfying pleasure! "Man...! "That was fantastic!" they both say while looking into each other's eyes. But before the two could say another word, Naquawna hears footsteps outside the bathroom door. It is Candis saying "she has got to go pee. Rayshawn yells "hold on!" I'm taking a piss." Candis laughs retorting "a piss! "Yeah; right!" she mumbles to herself "and what?"! Naquawna's holding it for you?"! She walked back to the couch laughing where Jason is anxiously awaiting her return. Rayshawn shouts "will be out in a minute" as he's wiping his; vanishing wand off with toilet paper.

Candis had already gone back to the living room so she didn't hear his last remarks. Naquawna smiling, pulls up her clothes stating "you were really on one!" He chuckles, and she adds "you were really trying to break a sista in half, up in here!" "Awe--, my bad" smiled Rayshawn with a half concerned look on his face, but a "conquering" I'm winning, look on his face as well. Grunting out a smiles he adds "it must have been that incredible hulk drink we were sip-pin on!

Naquawna not amused with his comment because she remembers he had already warned her earlier that he was "gonna" put it on her! So she turn't up her lips voicing "whatever; bruh! Running the cold water she gets a rag and puts it on her 'peach, and a sigh of relief comes over her face. Rayshawn looks at her saying "I thought you said that drink made you freaky?" She tilts her head to the side, with a look on her face that said a thousand words. He laughs saying "you just couldn't hang with the big guy tonight"! And with a proud look in his eyes he laughs again and kisses her on her cheek. He smiles in the mirror 'pimpishly, and with 'pep in his step, he tells her "I'll be out in the living room, so you go on ahead and get clean't up." Looking back at her he adds "and don't forget to brush your teeth" he says laughing as he hits her on her 'tuchus. "Shut; up"! "Rayshawn!" she shouts as she pushes him out the bathroom door and shuts it.

He walks away laughing and ends up sneaking up on Jason and Candis who are kissing on each other in the dining room, on a dining room chair. Rayshawn shouts "hey! "Hey! "Yaw need to take that back to the room"! Candis looks over her shoulder snarling "umm! "I see you're done; pissing"! Jason and her; bust up laughing because they know, there was more to the story; then that! Slowly Candis gets up off of Jason's lap, where she was sitting facing him, and when she stands she says "I'll be back" and heads to the bathroom to go pee. But what she 'really--, wanted to 'do, was check on her friend to see if she was 'alright, and--, find out all the 'dirty, details of what she and Rayshawn were doing in her bathroom? Candis knocks on the door saying "you alright mija?" The door opens with Naquawna saying "yep. "I'm alright" and in a slurred; tired voice she smiles. Candis sits down on the toilet to go pee saying "de-amm...! "Girl---! "What happened?"! "We could hear you two all the way in the living room"! Naquawna with her eyes bulged says "oh—hells--; to the no"! Adding "for real?"! Candis answers back "for real!

Naquawna with her right hand over her chest spouts "oh my Goodness! "Chil... "Rayshawn just went; crazy"! "He had me all twisted up on the sink, like I was some damn; blow up doll or something"! Candis starts busting up as she's getting up from the toilet laughing she states "so the player; got played!" I thought you were the; Mac?"! "Cuzen!" jokes Candis.
Naquawna with a 'smirk, blurts back "I, am, a; Mac! "Heffa! "I just couldn't hang with that crazy ass positions he had me in! "Or maybe; I needed a few more drinks" said Naquawna as she puts her hand up to get a high five from Candis. "Shoot, when Rayshawn and I first hooked up the other night and I was on top, it was cool" explained Naquawna. Candis answers "in his Cadillac?" "Yes! "Damn-mit!" retorted Naquawna. "Oh, Lord!!!" cringed Candis saying "you should have made him take you to a 'Moe, Moe' or hotel or something"!

"Oh... "Well... "Hell! "But, anyways' like I told you early. "I've always liked him and I use to eye ball him whenever I would see him around town, but we could never seem to hook up because he was always with his boys and I was either going to work or coming from work." But on this particular night, it just fell into place." And yes, I know--; it was reckless of me, to have sex with him on the first night." But, I just went with it anyway." You know me?" I love a good adventure" she laughs. "Plus, I was way drunk, feeling no pain!" You feel me?"! "Oh, shit!" laughed Candis singing the lyric from Jamie Foxx's "Blame it on the goose! "Got you feeling loose! "Blame it on patron! "Got you in the zone! "Blame it on the 'al-al -al-calc 'alcohol! They both sang it together with big grins on their faces laughing and dancing in the mirror. Naquawna freezes to the song, and while striking a pose in the mirror she says "but girl, he can f*ck; though"! "I'll give him that!" she said laughing reaching for her tooth brush.

After brushing, she spits in the sink and her and Candis chuckle while walking out of the bathroom. "Let's go check on these guys" said Naquawna. "I bet Rayshawn is telling Jason all my business about what just happened in the bathroom." Candis grunts "yeah---, and thanks tah you; and all you're screaming; and moaning and crap!" Jason ended up talking junk to me; saying stuff like "why" I can't be more like you?"! "And how we should go back to my room, so he can have a 'happy, ending; too"! "Chil please!" said Candis; belting out "sorry! "Not happening!

The girls crack up laughing some more and as they're approaching the living room they lower their voices. Naquawna says "where are they at?"! Rayshawn and Jason were on the balcony swapping stories like guys do. Rayshawn was telling Jason about how he had her all up on the bathroom 'sink, screaming; "it's too big! "Slow down! But then when it got good to her, she started saying "how good it was! "And to please... "Don't stop! Jason just cracked up laughing. Rayshawn continued to say "she's so easy man." He tells Jason "now all he wants to do is get paid because she works at the hair 'shop, so he knows--, she'll have cash every day in tips"! Jason gives him dap as they both laugh about Naquawna.

Then, Jason comments on how "he and Candis could hear her loud ass, all the way in the living room"! He adds "her friend is playing hard to get"! "But watch"! "I'll hit that' the next time I come swoop through to her pad by myself"! Rayshawn replied "bet that man! Jason smiling says "and--she's got a good job, too." Rayshawn replies "oh for real?" Where?" But before Jason could answer his question he spots the girls coming towards the sliding door through the crack in the curtains, around the same time Candis notices their shadows through the sliding door.

"There they are, outside on the balcony" said Candis. "Um-huh...; make me know it!" said Naquawna. "At first I thought they had left, and I was about to clown" frowned Naquawna. Candis grins "I bet they're smoking another joint out there." Naquawna slowly opens up the sliding door and goes outside on the balcony. Candis says "hey--?" can we hit it?!" "Fo' sho" said Rayshawn as he passes her the joint while looking at Naquawna's face with a crooked smile. It gets quiet for a few minutes while everyone takes their turn hitting the joint. It's late, so Candis tells them "to keep it down, so she doesn't annoy her next-door neighbors." She continues to say "after all, it is a week day" she snickers.

Candis moves a little closer to Jason with her back against his chest and his arms around her waist. They both stand there looking at Naquawna and Rayshawn while Jason kisses her on the side of her neck. It's funny to Candis how Naquawna is acting like she didn't just get 'boned, up in her bathroom, about ten minutes ago. And how Rayshawn keeps looking at his watch and staring out at the breath taking view from her balcony. Candis has a great view of the ocean from her apartment. You can see the water for miles in the daytime and at night the houses and small businesses around the ocean's edge are all lit up with beautiful colored lights. The water is dark at night but you know it's out there. And it is so relaxing when the stars are all out and on a real quite night, you can even hear the ocean's waves; crashing from her apartment.

Candis gets an idea so she can spend a little more time with Jason, while helping Naquawna get to know Rayshawn a bit better; too. She says "do you all want to watch a movie?" "I got a gang of movies" she adds. But before they could 'answer, Rayshawn's phone goes off. He looks at his phone to see who is calling him, and it's one of his other broads. But of course Naquawna doesn't know this, because she never took the time to get to know him, before she got to know his "dong"!

Naquawna gives him a dirty look saying "who is that?"! Then with an attitude she reaches for his phone and he takes a step back voicing "girl! "Quit, trippin! "Who is it Rayshawn?!" One of your other broads?"! She puts her hands on her hips and demands for him to tell her, if it's another girl that's calling him"! "Damn! "Gurl! "I don't ask you who's calling you on your phone!" he said, backing up away from her, playfully; grinning. She gives him the meanest look saying "oh!" It's like that; huh?"! "Okay! "Punk!" she shouts, in her pissed off (I'm not f*^kin with you no more) voice! Rayshawn turns his back to Naquawna and says to Jason "awe; man! "Let's go! "She's trippin! "No! "You're trippin!" shouts Naquawna with her finger all up in his face.

Rayshawn rubbing his chin says "let's bounce man." Because I don't wanna half to put hands; on this broad!" But if she keeps putting her hands in my face!" "Man--" he snarls. Naquawna shouts "what?!" "What's; up?!" "You gonna hit me?!" she asked as she stood there looking at him dead, in his eyes. Rayshawn looks at her and blurts "you would, want me to hit you, so I could catch a case!" But I don't hit women!" he shouts as he's walking towards the front door. Candis looks at Jason like dang-- their having a fight 'wishing, he didn't have to leave. But she knows he won't have a ride home, if he does stay. And--, she also 'knows, she has to go to work in a few hours. 'Hell! 'It's 12:15 in the morning! 'Forget a movie!

Naquawna follows Rayshawn out to his car still pulling on his arm, so he won't leave without talking to her. He grabs her by both arms with her facing him he says "you better check yourself"! "You're trippin"! "I don't owe you no mother f*^kin explanation"! "I'm a grown ass man"! Naquawna still high from the weed says "and, I'm not trying to hear all that sh*t"! "So, don't be f*^Kin; trying ta' play me; Rayshawn! "Yeah; okay!" he smirks. Closing his car door he states "I see you got your big girl panties on now; huh?"! "You weren't talking all that shit 30 minutes ago in the bathroom; though!" "Now were you?"! "That's because I had no reason too!" she said with both hands on his car, talking to him through his window.

Tired of arguing with her he yells to Jason "come on man...!" Or you're about to get left"! So while Naquawna is still arguing with Rayshawn by his car, with her lips; poked out, and her neck moving. Candis and Jason are getting one last hug and kiss in, while she puts his number in her cell phone and he puts her number in his phone. She smiles telling him "you better answer your phone, when I call you." "And don't let me go to voicemail; either!" she jokes, with a big 'smoochy, smile on her face. Jason closes the car door 'still, looking her up and down, then he tilts his head to one side saying "later; sexy! They drive away burning rubber; as Naquawna's giving Rayshawn the middle finger. Candis walks back into the house; all smiles! While Naquawna walks back into the house; pissed!

Naquawna is; heated when she shouts "I don't believe that fool!" "He's got me mixed up with the next; chick!" Candis chuckles voicing "okay"! "Homie don't play that!" said Candis, laughing at Naquawna's facial expression. Naquawna shouts "No! "Bi%ch! "I am so serious right now! "He'll get dogged out, playing with me like that! "I'll get his ass where it hurts!" "And trust me, he does not want me to get at his car, because you know how much he 'loves that; raggedy 'ass; Cadillac!" Candis laughs out "you ain't gonna do nay- thing!" You love--; that fool!" So, quit wolf-in!" Naquawna grunts with her arms folded; still too high to drive home, she says "that's what you think!" Then she sits down shaking her head shamelessly thinking about how she let 'Rayshawn, toss her like a salad, in the bathroom! Naquawna feeling nauseated asked "is it cool if I stay, until I sober up?" knowing that her friend won't say no, but being that it's on a work day she felt she had to ask. Candis says "chil... you know I'm not gonna let you drive your drunk butt all the way back home!" I'll get the airbed out for you" says Candis.

In a cheery voice Candis adds "what a fun night" she said smiling as she goes to the closet to get out her Coleman air mattress. When Candis pulls out the bed she says "I told you this bed would come in handy one day." "Um-mum" laughs Naquawna, saying "I remember when you bought it, wasn't it for that time when you and Ricky went camping down by the river?" said Naquawna; frowning looking at the bed adding "ugh, and I hope it's clean." "Ooh, no, you; didn't!" said Candis. "You just had to bring his name up!" frowned Candis. "Oops!" smiled Naquawna, knowing she had struck a nerve. She continues to say "so--, Candy--, do you still be seeing Ricky up at the hospital?" Candis's eyebrows shoot up; almost touching her hairline when she turns up her face in a displeasing manner replying "yes, I, do!" And it's awkward too, because all I keep remembering is slapping the dog-snot out his face when I busted him in the closet with his mouth on Natalia's boobs." "And to top it off!" it was one of the closets me and him uses to go in; frequently!

Naquawna blurts "what a jack-ass"! "I didn't trip with my girl Natalia though, because she didn't know that me and Ricky we're kicking it." "Nobody did." "Plus, Natalia always had the hook-up, on those 'screamin, chicken and beef tamales!" Remember?!" "Yes, I, do!" answered Naquawna. "She be hooking a sista 'up, for just $10.00!" giggled Candis. "They were pretty slammin" said Naquawna remembering back when Candis use to bring everyone some tamale's to taste down at her shop.

"I heard Natalia dropped his butt too, that same day after I slapped him in front of her!" bragged Candis. "So she says!" laughed Naquawna. "She's probably 'still, riding that pony because he is cute." "True; that!" returned Candis. Adding "but, I don't care, because I don't like him anymore anyway." "Especially after he had all our business all over the hospital!" "I remember!" said Naquawna. "What a scandal!" she adds shaking her head. "And you know big mouth Sherry was the main one spreading that mess all over the hospital; too!" said Naquawna while putting the sheets on the airbed. "You think?!" replied Candis. Adding "that's exactly why I don't like messing with people on the job!" she said snapping her fingers; queen style.

Candis concludes her thoughts with "once a man treats me wrong and it becomes too many times, that's when it's a wrap!" Cuz; I let it be;

known! "Once I'm done!" I'm done with yo; ass!" for real!" Naquawna agrees and laughs giving her a high five, long distance as they lay in separate beds. Then Candis switches the subject to thinking back on the night and smiling she says "but I really do like 'Jason, for a first time meet." And the boy can kiss; too." But, we'll see." He might be a player too, like Rayshawn" sighed Candis while getting cozy in her bed.

As Naquawna's getting comfortable on her mattress and pulling the covers up to her neck, she replies "do you really think Rayshawn's playing me?" "I don't know, but he sure was acting funny after that phone call came in" said Candis. "Yeah. "I know. "I just can't believe I was stupid enough to 'do him, in the bathroom" said Naquawna. She continues "but I thought he really did like me, and only me!" what a fool!" he really played me!" He would tell me, how much he was so--, into me." And how pretty I was." Just making me feel like I was special" she said in a mad confused voice. He took me out to dinner and everything that night.

Candis cuts in saying "but Quawana!" You really don't know anything about him!" other than; he's fyne!" has a tight car!" and has a big; toy!" Candis tries her best to say it in a nice way without making Naquawna feel like a dumb broad. Naquawna exhaling states "that's true!" "You're right" she confessed, adding "but he really don't know me that well; either!" she said with a plotting look on her face. She goes on to say "and let that nig play games!" I'll piss him off, by sleeping with one of his boys!" Candis lifts her head up off her pillow saying "as long as it's not Jason; heffa! They both laugh then Naquawna blurts out "well; hell!" you ain't gonna let Jason hit it; no way!" so, I'll just do him for you!" she jokes. Candis shouts "trust me!" I "do; not" need your help!" I got this!" beside..., you don't know what I might end up doing with Jason!" he just might be the one!" Naquawna laughs saying "the jury is still out on that one!" "That's okay; grunts Candis because it will still be interesting, to see how 'far, the love game will take us!"

Chapter 2

At around 7 o'clock in the morning Naquawna wakes up still; half-drunk as she gets up to gathers all her things. With a stretch she goes to the bathroom to go pee, trying not to wake up Candis. Taking a little bit of the mouthwash from the bathroom counter she swishes it around in her mouth so she can try and wake up. Then she stumbles out the front door heading to her car. As Naquawna is on her way home she stops and gets herself a tall cup of Mocalisous from Star Bucky. "Thank God, they have a drive-thru" she mutters. Because she 'definitely, wasn't getting out of the 'car; not as bad as she looked. "Ahhhh--" she says as she takes a sip of her coffee saying "now that; really hits the spot!" Putting down her coffee she looks down at her watch voicing "dang, it's already 7:50." "I have got to get my butt moving" she said out loud.

Naquawna has a 9:00 am appointment coming in to get his hair braided today. He is a middle aged Jamaican man named; Roger. Or let him tell it, (Raja) is how, he pronounces it. Naquawna met him at a football game in San Francisco one day when she went with some of her co-workers to see the 49ers play the Raider's. Roger just so happened to be sitting in front of Naquawna at the stadium and they just seem to hit it off, because Naquawna loved his accent and his Rasta braids.

So while they were all watching the game eventually as they kept talking, Roger found out through their conversation, that the people she was with all worked at the same hair salon together. Naquawna offered him 20% off on his hair 'if, he came in to her shop with her card. So that following Tuesday after that football game he surprised her when he walked into her shop, and the rest is history. 'Raja, has been coming down every fourth Tuesday, for two years now and that is one of the reasons why she doesn't want to be late. The second reason is because she just loves their conversations because he is such an educated man. He always flirts with her but she never takes him up on his advances because he's just "not" her type. She's more into the bad boys 'not, more so in their "actions" but more because of their looks. 'Mainly, she likes the way the 'so called, "bad; boys" dress and how they act all 'cool, with their; swagger. But poor 'Raja, he just doesn't have those qualities she's looking for, so she only flirts with him because he always ends up giving her a great tip. If he was a hottie, with some kind of swagger, he might stand a chance.

When she pulls up to her place she mumbles to herself "I, am, so--; hung-over! But as she thinks back on what a great time she had with Rayshawn last night, she smiles thinking it was 'all, worth it; hang-over and all! 'And even though, he pissed her off, she still had love for him and even more so because she can't believe how he dogged her out like he did. Part of her mind thinks; he's a jerk! While the other half 'thinks, how "hot" he looked; when he was mad!

She gets in her apartment and throws her purse and her keys on the chair. Her grandpa is in the kitchen making himself a bowl of oatmeal and she can smell the lingering hint of bacon that he had just fried. He says "hey granddaughter" as she runs past him. "Hi, granddaddy!" I'm running late, so I'll talk to you in a minute!" I've got to get in the shower!" "Alright" he said as he sat down at the table to eat his breakfast. Naquawna has been taking care of her 75 year old grandfather for about 4 years now 'do to the fact, that she lost her parents in a plane crash. Her parents were married for about 25 years and they wanted to take a trip to the Bahamas at the time. And since they had never gone before and heard so many beautiful things about the place, her father planned out the trip. Her father had also gotten such a good deal on the flight and the room; that they just couldn't pass up thy opportunity to go.

Well..., everything went great on their flight down and Naquawna had even talked to them while they were in the Bahamas. She even called her parents back to let them know that she would be picking them up, that following Monday at the Airport. But unfortunately the plane never made it back because the plane came down right after takeoff in a wooded area, with no survivors. Naquawna and her sister Sha'wanna were devastated, when they heard the news. After the crash her sister Sha'wanna and her family flew in from North Carolina where they were stationed at; at Ft Bragg. Her husband Officer Diller and their two kids Sha'lay and Danny Junior came as well. They ended up having to stay at the Sheraton Inn because Naquawna's place was way too small.

After the memorial service Sha'wanna said "she would take grandpa back with them to North Carolina, but Naquawna knew that grandpa was all she had left out there in Treeberry, and Sha'wanna had already had her hands full with her own immediate family, so Naquawna told her sister she would take good care of their grandpa from here on out. 'So-- after some serious 'thought, Sha'wanna finally agreed that it might be for the best if he did stay with her because it may be too much traveling for him to do at his age, being that Sha'wanna's husband is in the Military and they move around a lot. So, after they had the memorial service for their mom and dad, Sha'wanna and her husband Danny went with Naquawna to their parent's old house to get all of grandpa's belongings and some 'keepsakes, for themselves, and on that same day was when he moved in with Naquawna and the two have been living together ever since.

It is now 8:35 in the morning and Naquawna is just now getting out of the shower. She grabs her baby oil and put it all over her arms and legs. Walking over to her dresser she picks out a cute outfit to wear, black Capri pants and a yellow tank top. Sitting down on her bed she puts on her comfortable sandals. Then, with hair jam in her hands she grabs her hair brush and gels up her hair, putting it up in a high ponytail. In a rush she runs back into the kitchen to grab a granola bar and two pieces of bacon that her granddad had previously fried. Kissing him on the cheek she says "it's going to be hot today, so make sure you stay cool grandpa, and I'll call and check on you when I go on my break." "Okay sweetie" he replies. "Have a good day" he adds as he's walking to his recliner to sit down to watch one of his favorite shows called: The Price Is Right. Naquawna heads out the front door to her car and she now has fifteen minutes to get to work.

'Candis, on the other hand is still dragging around in her apartment but still; on cloud nine. She didn't get much sleep last night having; had 'Jason, running around in her head. And now--; damn...! Her period just came on, a day early. "Shit!" she says out loud reaching for her phone to call her friend and co-worker, Sherry who is already at work to tell her "that she will be a little late 'do to a "girly; problem"! Sherry chuckles "chil, no worries, it's quiet right now anyway. "So get here when you can" she said. Candis is relieved when Sherry said "it's cool." Stating back to her "I'll be there as soon as I can" then she hang up the phone.

Laughing to herself Candis thinks about Jason and hopes he will be calling her today. She keeps telling herself she is 'not, going to be the first one to call. With a charismatic smile on her face she gets into the shower so she can scrub her body down with some Victorious; secrets, soft body gel. "This smells so good" she says to herself as she inhales the floral fruity fragrances deep down her nose. After a nice shower the door opens to the shower and Candis gets out starting to feel a little better. Although she is still hung-over 'a tad bit, her mood has lifted. Her phone vibrates on the bathroom counter so she grabs it anxiously hoping it is Jason. "Darn! 'No such luck, it's her mother so she puts the phone down on her bed on speaker so she can finish getting ready for work. "Hey mom?" "Hey daughter" says her mother. "I know you're on your way to work but I was wondering if you could come by this Saturday and help me get some of this stuff; organized in my garage?" I have the junk hauler guys coming over later that same day, so they can take away all the things "we" don't need!" Her mother pauses, and in a sad voice she continues "all the 'things, "I" don't need anymore."

Candis had lost her father 3 years ago to prostate cancer and it is still; very painful for her and her mom to talk about. But her mother also feels like it is time for her to clean out some of the clutter that she has been putting off for years. Candis knows she's mindful of it, because she doesn't want to become a hoarder. Listening; strategically she catching bits and pieces of the important stuff that her mother is saying as she's running in and out of the room. When she comes back into her room she hears "I need to put the stuff I want to 'keep, on one side of the garage, and get rid of the other stuff." But I can't do it all by myself, and your brother is going to Vegas this weekend for another one of those "so called; conventions"!

And with an attitude in her voice, her mother goes on to say "and there is no reason; for your brother to have to go 'on; that many business trips in one year!" I don't care what nobody says!" It "can; not" be that serious!" says her mother in disgust. Candis laughs, listening to her go on about it, while she's putting her clothes on. He mom continues "and the way he does Dianna!" He; ne'vah takes that girl to Vegas with him!" "Now, you know she could find something to do"! Like go shopping or gamble when he's in them "so called; meetings"! Candis blurts out "I wonder why he doesn't take her with him?!" "Because he's probably doing something he ain't supposed to be doing!" said her mother. Candis laughs a hardy laugh as she's running around her room looking for her other white shoe.

The young lady they are talking about "Dianna" is Marvin's; fiancé. They have been together for two years now, and she is this sweet, cute 'black girl, who looks like she could work; for the geek squad with her sophisticated, corky ways about her. She has a nice small frame, wears glasses and has a pretty smile with beautiful long kinky curly hair. 'Dianna is known, to be very book smart, but Candis thinks she's a bit 'naïve, when it comes to men; and especially when it comes to her brother. But nevertheless they love Dianna and consider her family; all the same.

Candis's other line beeps, and it says 'private, call. Cutting it short she says "okay, mom!" I'll come by Saturday; love you!" I got to go!" "Okay" returns her mother. "Thank you baby! But Candis had already clicked over. "Hello?" she says, hoping that it is Jason this time. "Hello?" said a man on the other end of the phone. "Who is this?" asked Candis. "It's Jason" the person said. "Oh batch"! "Pah-leazz--!" laughs Candis. "I, know, it's you; Naquawna"! Naquawna cracks up laughing saying "I bet your heart was jumping out your chest when I said it was Jason." Candis hollers "no, because I knew it was your crazy ass!" Plus, I know his voice and it does not sound like, that!" besides, he's probably at work, if he went into work today at all."

Naquawna is still chuckling as Candis grabs her keys and locks her front door. She starts walking to her car and when she gets in her truck and starts the engine, Naquawna hears her car door close and the engine start and says "are you just now heading to work?" "Yes, I, am!" she fussed. "My dang, period came on early." And---; I'm still 'buzzed, to make things even worse!" It's going to be a long; day" she complains. "So much for kicking it 'late, last night; Quawna"! "Thanks!" retorted Candis.

"Well...! "Hell...! "You did say you have fun!" cracks Naquawna. "And Jason must have had your panties in a "bunch" last night, to bring 'flow; down!" laughed Naquawna. Candis blurts "honey; please!" You don't; even; wanna clown!" Because if I recall; correctly!" Somebody got their puffed pastry; blown; out in my bathroom last night"! Naquawna yelped out "oooooh"! And then they both started dying laughing.

Then when Naquawna hears "yes, I'd like a breakfast sandwich, with fries and a small coffee please" she laughs asking, are you at; Jack in the crack?"! "You know it!" I have got to get some food in my stomach before I; throw up!" said Candis with a burp. She knows Naquawna's already at work so she asked "are you braiding bumpy face 'Raja's, hair today?" Candis giggles while Naquawna tries not to laugh too loud when saying "yes. She adds "that is why I wore my pants today, because I do not want to give him any reason to check me out, more than he already does." She whispered that statement to Candis while waiting on him to come from the bathroom.

"Naquawna continues to say "only the fine ones get the skirt action!" she chuckled. "Girl! "Please...! "On a drunken night, you would probably let him; hit it!" laughs Candis out loud. Naquawna disagreeing grunts out "not, even; close"! 'Candis, eating on a hot French fry switches gears to "man--, we had a good time last night"! "I know" smiles Naquawna on the other end of the phone sighing "yes, we, did! Candis gets to work and flies into an open parking stall saying "okay girlly; I'm here at work now!" I'll call you later!" "Okay chil! "Later" said Naquawna. Candis hurries up into the Hospital so she can clock in. And when the elevator opens she heads over to her department; quickly. 'But, maybe a little 'too; quickly, she thinks to herself because Ricky's there. "Ugh! "Hells--; no! "I know, that is not Ricky, standing by my 'desk, talking to Sherry!" she mumbles. "Out of all the days of the week, he "would" be on our floor today, drawing blood; when I'm hung-over and feeling like; crap"!

"Hey---; Candis?!" says Sherry softly with her eyes shifting towards Ricky as if to say "look who's here today in our department?"! 'Candis, partially; smiling, thinks to herself "not today; b*tch"! But still manages to be polite when saying "hi, back to Sherry, when thanking her for holding it down for her." She explains to Sherry "how she was up a little late last night with some guess, and Sherry was more than happy to say in front of Ricky "I heard...!" I talked to Naquawna this morning when she called here looking for you." And she said you got a new; man!" And I heard he is gorgeous too!"

Ricky's eyes enlarged after hearing the unwanted conversation then he scratched his head voicing "whelp, I better go check on these patients." Sherry grins back saying "okay." Bye Ricky." Candis looks in the other direction after giving him a fake half smile. As he fades away down the hallway, Sherry and Candis give each other a fist bump. Candis sits down at her desk and proudly grins out "you know it"!!! (Meaning) "You know it doesn't take me long 'at all, to find me another man! "I be like; next! "On yo' ass! They both busted up laughing but not too loud because they are at work. You know; trying to keep it professional.

Sherry and Candis get back to work; answering phones and taking care of patients. After lunch it slows down to only 3 patients left on the books. Candis is so-- glad she is almost off of work, but still, no call from lover boy; Jason. It's cool though, she thinks because she wouldn't want him to be a pest, like calling her all day an stuff. Glancing at the hospital door for the next patient to come through she grabs a piece of chocolate out of the jar that sits on Sherry's desk, and then she starts telling Sherry "what a nice time she had last night with Jason."

The girl's 'chit chat, to pass the time and Sherry talks about her boyfriend that she has been 'shacking up with, for 4 years now and she asked Candis "should she be looking for a ring from him by now?" Or is it time for her to move on?" Candis replies "well..., you two should know by now after 4 years, if you are going to be able to tolerate each other for the long haul." Since you're already living together." So, I think it's just a matter of you asking him, where does he see you-all's relationship going in the near future?" she adds "you don't want to just keep living with him forever in sin; do you?"! "And what if you get pregnant?"

Sherry nodding her head giving it some serious thought answers "your; right!" because, what if I 'do, get pregnant?" "I am 'not, trying to raise the baby on my own! "So he is going to have to make a decision!" frowns Sherry. "Or, I'm ma have to make one for the both of us!" she said plopping another chocolate into her mouth. Candis laughing at Sherry's smirked face says "now--, you got your big girl, britches on"! The two girls laugh and joke and the time just flies and before they know it; it is almost 5:00 o'clock.

'Buzz..! 'Buzz..! Candis's phone vibrates in her pocket because of a text. "It's him! "It him!" she says jumping up and down in her seat as she's looking Sherry's way. "It's Jason!" she repeats; enthusiastically. He texted her "hello; beautiful! She melts, saying "oh my God! "What should I say?"! "Should I text right back?"! "Or wait a few minutes, like I'm busy?!" said Candis with a big smile on her face. She holds her phone close to her chest hugging it, like as if, it's him. Contemplating her next move she thinks; that it might be best, to wait about five minutes and then text him back, so she doesn't look like she's been sweat-in his call all day.

Answering the office phone to stall for time, makes it five minutes; exactly, and then she texted him back saying "hey, handsome"! "What you doing?" He texts back "I'm about to get off work." Candis text back "I'm about to clock out myself, once our last patient leaves." Candis sits back in her chair looking happy as a lamb in sheep's wool as she stares over at Sherry while she awaits Jason's texts. "I hope he's not trying to come by my house tonight and kick it, though!" frowns Candis. "I look a mess!" And I feel it too!" she adds. But sure enough, he texted "let's hook up tonight." "Damn!" said Candis. "What should I say?"! Sherry says "just tell him you're tired! "Sh*t!

Candis says "well I do want to see him, but just not tonight." Not the way I'm 'feeling, and cramp-in and junk!" "Sorry!" But I'm just going to have to lie." So Candis texted back "Aw, I can't!" I told my mom I would come over and help her with some stuff." She looks over at Sherry saying "that should do it!" Then to make herself feel better about the "lie" she just told, she tell Sherry "well, hell"! "I did tell my mom I would come over." So I'm 'kind of, telling the truth." Even though, it's really this Saturday, instead of tonight, but "technically" I'm still going to my mom's." He texted back "aw!" Alright!" since it's your mom's, I guess I can't complain." He ends the text with "call me later when you get back home, gorgeous!" After reading his text Candis puts her fist in the air and brings it down quickly shouting "yes! "See?!" That's how you do; it!" She continues to say "that way; I don't hurt his feeling by saying I'm too tired to see him."

Sherry just stares at her and being the "no; nonsense" kind of person Sherry is, she blurts out "had it been me!" I would have told his ass!" I'm tired!" I saw your ass last night!" And now; I'm ma need me; some me time!" 'Candis, staring back at her with her mouth parted thinks to herself "and you wonder "why?" your man of four years "still" hasn't put a ring on it!"

With a smirk of her lips Candis just goes back to texting Jason saying "okay, I'll call you later, pretty boy! Sherry sees the text and puts her index finger in her mouth as if to suggest; she wanted to throw up. Saying to Candis "hmmm...! "All this; lovey; dovey; crap! Adding "Chil; please...! Candis just chuckles as her and Sherry gather up their stuff so they can get ready to go clock out. When they get down stairs Ricky is clocking out at the same time and gives Candis a wink of his eye but she pays it no mind as she keeps on talking about Jason to Sherry. They clock out and walk out to their cars together chuckling about one of the patients that they helped today on their floor who was making them laugh about a Joke that was said on "Andy's" Watch What Happens Live Show! And after a good chuckle they both get in their vehicles and drive towards the highway.

Chapter 3

'**Now**, over at the shop; 'surprisingly, Naquawna gets a walk-in who wants his hair washed and cornrowed into braids, which would be going all the way back on top of his head. It is almost 5pm when he enters the shop, asking to get his hair done. Of course by then Naquawna is ready to go home. But this is too good to pass up because it is one of Rayshawn's friends named: Bubba Dank. And in the hood, he's known as "Big Dank" because he be haven that; 'sticky; 'icky; weed! This is so surreal to Naquawna because he has never come to her shop before and she can't help but wonder if Rayshawn sent him there to spy on her. 'Plus, she also wonders if Bubba knows all about 'her, and Rayshawn being, lovers.

She places Bubba in a chair and starts to comb out his hair while making small talk. "So how you been Bubba?" I haven't seen you since Cee Cee's house party last month." "Uh, I been alright." He adds "yep, that party was... crazy!" he said while getting comfortable in the chair. After his hair is combed out she takes him over to the wash area to lay him back so she can wash his hair. While at the wash area with a head full of soap, she is dying to ask him where his friend 'Rayshawn, is? But thinks, that would be too obvious. So after she washes and conditions his hair, she dries it with a towel and he walks back over to sit down in the braiding chair. Reaching for the hair oil to put in his hair and on his scalp, has her feeling more 'daring, so she 'casted, out her first lie, saying "oh, yeah...; your friend Rayshawn was supposed to get his hair edged up with the clippers today but he didn't make it in." "Ah, for real?!" said Bubba. "That sounds like him." "He's been having 'baby momma; drama, lately."

'Naquawna, damn near chokes on her own saliva when she hears that news. She coughs to play it off, then clears her throat saying "oh, I know!" He was saying something like that, when he called in earlier, to cancel." "His wife must have him on lock" said Naquawna through gritted teeth, fishes for more information, wondering if he was married. Bubba looks at her and laughs saying "his wife?!" "He's not married to her!" "She's just some chick he met last year at my house party" said Bubba. "I see, said Naquawna. "Is she black"? "Yeah, she's black and Filipino." "She's a bad little broad too" he said sucking air through his front teeth. "I met her a while back in Vegas, because she use to be a stripper, but Rayshawn took her out the game." I had her dance at my Birthday party one year with her friend Tammy, that's how Rayshawn met her." "But that fool got caught up!" Or should I say, caught; sympin!" he said laughing, stating "we had to take that fools player's card"!

Bubba continued laughing even harder, off his own joke, then he started to cough with a slight wheeze. While he was 'laughing, Naquawna's 'heart, was 'cracking, into tiny little pieces. But she "did" want to know the 'truth, she thought to herself. 'So through the pieces of her broken heart, she continued to comb the side of his head because she only had two more braids left. Naquawna began to stall, so she could get more info, but then his pager goes off. "Wow...! "They still make those?!" she thought. Pagers?!" Really?!" He takes his cell phone out and calls the number back saying "what; it do?"! "What; it do?"! He said to the person, on the other end of the phone. And whom-ever it was, on the other end of the line, wanted to know when he could come by?" Because he looked up at Naquawna asking "are you almost done?" Twisting up the last braid with care she answered "yep. "You're all done.

With a big smile on his face he gives her $80.00 bucks and a $20.00 dollar tip. He looks in the mirror admiring her work on his head and then he blurts "alright"! "I like this"! "You got skills!" he flirts. "I'll see you next time" he said as he's heading out the door grabbing one of her cards saying "Naquawna?"! "Right?"! Naquawna smiling, nods her head yes. The door shuts with a bell chiming; echo and with a pouting face she goes on to cleaning up her station. 'Cleaning up, was faster than usual because her nerves were 'shot, and her heart was; cracked! She was so 'crushed, and couldn't wait to call Candis and tell her what she had found out about Rayshawn. So when she finished cleaning up, all sad she walked out of the shop saying "bye to her boss." Voicing "I'll see you in the morning; Mrs. Lee" she said. "Okay, honey!" "See you tomorrow" said her boss as she's counting out the money drawer.

Naquawna hurries to her car and can barely open the door with the key because she is so distrait and upset. She sits down in her car and calls Candis trying to hold back tears, telling herself "she is "not" going to cry over that bastard"! Candis's phone rings but the number says "private, so Candis doesn't answer it, in fear that it is Jason and he will catch her in a lie because she is "supposed" to be at her mom's house. So after placing her phone down Candis starts to run her bath water and the phone rings again. Naquawna leaves a message saying "call me as soon as possible!" It's about Rayshawn!"

With her beer in hand she gets in the tub that she has filled with bubbles to relax all her stress, from the day away. As she sits in the warm water she takes a sip of her Corona beer as she envisions Jason's pretty face and how good his lips felt. Rolling the cold bottle of beer across her face, she continues to think of him. Then she puts the bottle up to her mouth; 'wishing, it was him! She closes her eyes for a nice meditating moment, and it's so... calm... and so... relaxing in the hot bubbling water. And as she starts to dose a bit, a light mist of steam floats up from off her neck and as her body calms, she almost starts to slips into a short dream and then the doorbell rings. "Sh*t...! "Who the hell is that?!" she said sharply. She sits there in the tub; stationary 'hoping, that they will go away. But the doorbell rings again. Then all goes; silent. Happy they've gone away, she goes back to laying her head back on a folded towel.

Relaxing again she sighs and then as soon as she closes her eyes, she hears a knock on her bedroom window. She's startled at first, then she gets out the tub; frantic! Drying off some, she puts on her robe and sneaks in her room quietly to peak out her window, in the dark. The nerve of someone to go to her bedroom window "just; because" she wouldn't answer her front door! She looks carefully out the side drapes and a sighs of relief comes over her face when she sees that it's only Naquawna. 'Happy, that it is not Jason or some nut case at her window she opens her curtains saying "what the hell?"! Naquawna shouts through the glass window "did you get my message?"! Candis opens her window saying "it cannot; be that serious?"! "Yes, it, is!" declared Naquawna. "Come open the door" she said in a crackly voice. Naquawna walks around to the front door and Candis lets her in the house; smirking "this better be good; heffa! "I was taking a "nice"! "And let me emphasize on "nice"! "Hot, bath"! "Until you came and interrupted me"! "Aw...! "I'm sorry!" said Naquawna exhaling in her saddest voice. Candis walking back to the bathroom still talking; 'mess, about

Naquawna's "intrusion" as she's putting on some clean underwear and a pad. She grabs her beer from off the tubs rim and heads back into the living room where she sits down, on the couch, in her robe spouting "so, what is so--; important?"! Naquawna still sitting on the couch with her head in her hands facing downward tells Candis 'how Rayshawn's friend Bubba came into the shop and told her all-- of Rayshawn's business!" And how he's with this Filipino and black chick who was a "stripper" out in Vegas"! "And how he lives with her, and she has a baby by him"!

Candis's mouth drops open voicing "are you serious?"! And with a crazy look on her face she retorts "that dirty; rat"! "Well, we figured something was up when his phone went off that night and he "all of the; sudden" had to leave!" said Candis. "Has he called you, since last night?!" "No!" said Naquawna sadly. "And I haven't called him either!" But she was lying. Naquawna called Rayshawn that afternoon on her lunch break after she checked on her granddad, and that's why her phone number is still on private. The reason why she called him was because she wanted to hear his voice. She didn't say anything to him, but she hung up on him twice. Candis calls her out on it, saying "mmm- hmmm!" "So you mean to tell me, you haven't called him; at all today?"! "Nope!" said Naquawna as she got up and walked towards the kitchen to go get a beer, trying not to smile. "Good!" said Candis. "And don't call his black ass! "Wait for him to call you!

Naquawna takes a drink of her beer asking "have you talk to Jason?" "Yeah," she replied. Even though she didn't want Naquawna to feel bad about Jason calling her, she still didn't want to lie about it, so she just played it down saying "he just text me today, before I got off work." Naquawna looking surprised says "what?!" Asking "what was he..., talking about?"! "He wanted to come by tonight". "But look at me, I am not looking or feeling my best today." So I told him I had to go to my moms and help her with some stuff." Naquawna laughs "is that why your truck is parked down the block behind that U-haul truck?"! Candis almost spits out some of her beer from laughing so hard. "I knew, something was up!" said Naquawna as they both laughed out loud. "Well, shoot"! "He doesn't need to see me like this!" "It is way-- too early in our friendship!" "Plus, I want him to miss me!" "Can't make it too easy for these boys!" smiled Candis as she took another drink of her beer. Naquawna frowning sighs "I know!" "Like me, making it so easy for Rayshawn; huh?!" "No." "But yes!" cracked Candis. "You run your game different from me and that's what makes us different!" "I don't judge!" said Candis.

"But-, on that same note!" You do need to find out a little more about these guys, you sleep with!" Naquawna shouts "see--! "You do think I'm stupid!" She puts her beer down on the coffee table like she's moping. Candis says "No!" "Not; stupid! "Per-say," she grins. "You're just a bit too 'quick, in the sex department with these guys." Naquawna blurts "who; are you to talk; Candis?"! "You let boys "lick" all over you!" It's damn nears the same thing!" "Not; really!" blurts Candis. "I choose---, who I let lick me!" Once, they've earned my "trust" of course!" she said laughing; snapping her finger with a twirl. "Whatever!" spouts; Naquawna. "And I choose--, who I let "do" me! Candis replies "I know!" So don't get mad when you find out that those guys are "boning" other girls too!" "Forget you Candis!" smirked Naquawna. "Don't get mad at me!" squawked Candis. "I'm just keeping it; one hundred with you"!

Naquawna's phone goes off and it's Rayshawn. "Speak of the devil!" retorts Candis. "Um... "I shouldn't even answer it!" says Naquawna with an angry voice. She's still mad but Candis can hear a 'hint, of happiness in her voice because he called. Candis laughs saying "girl!" Please!" I bet you would 'still; 'f*<k; him!" Even after what Bubba had just told you about him today!" "Uh..., not; even!" said Naquawna; turning up her nose. Walking towards the kitchen she turns her back to Candis when she answers her phone so Candis can't see her facial expression. "Hello?" she said in a pissy voice. "Hey, Baby?" answered Rayshawn. "What you doing?" he asked. "Not a thing!" she answers. "What do you want?!" she said in a crappy tone. "Damn...!" he said. Asking "what's wrong with you?!" She says "what do you want; Rayshawn?"! He answers "why you coming at me like that?"! "Answer the question?!" she said. "Why are you calling me?!" Is it because you need your d_ck; sucked?!" Your baby's "momma" can't do it for you tonight?!"

He shouts out "what?!" What are you talking about?!" And with an upset tone in his voice he adds "who told you; that; lie?!" "Don't trip!" she replies. "I got my sources!" "Well, your "source" is wrong!" And whoever told you that, is lying to you!" You're the only one I'm messing with right now!" he said, in his running game voice. Naquawna chuckles saying "yeah, right!" Then who was that on your phone last night, then?!" she asked stands there waiting for his answer with her hand on her hip. "That was a business call!" So see..., you were tripped for nothing!" he answered. "Sure--, it was a business call!" she said tapping her foot up and down on the kitchen floor listening to his; B.S. When he's done speaking she says "do I look stupid to you?!" Because I know the game Rayshawn!" He answers "naw, not at all." Smirking to his answer she grunts. 'But he knows, she only said all of that to him, to play hardball. But he can already tell that she is falling for the game; that is coming out his mouth. So he says "you know I got love for you." Candis can tell by the delusional; smile on Naquawna's face, that she's believing every word Rayshawn is saying, so Candis uses her hand signals to tell Naquawna not to fall for his "bullshit"!

But Naquawna keeps on listening, paying Candis no mind as he's saying to her, all the things, she wants to hear, in her ear. Rayshawn likes the way the conversation is going so he says "let's talk in person?" Where you at?" he asked. Candis, shushed; her telling her "not to say she's at her house, for fear that 'Jason, could be with him." So she tells Rayshawn "she's at the store getting a few things." He blurts out "aight!" I'll come through in about 30 minute so we can talk in person." She agrees and hurries and hangs up the phone with him. In a rush to leave, she says to Candis; that "she is just going to go 'talk to him, face to face." Candis laughs out loud "face to face"! "Humm...!" Is this with the big head?!" Or the little head?!"

Naquawna laughing out loud says "funny; b*tch"! "No, for real...!" I am going to get to the bottom of this!" says Naquawna as she grabs her keys and rushes to her car. Candis laughing shouts "I'm sure you "will" be on the "bottom"! "By the 'time, you two, get through "talking"! Laughing even harder Candis yells out "somebody's; sprung...!" Naquawna driving away flips her off while laughing and grinning to herself, and then Candis closes her front door and goes into the kitchen to get herself something to eat. She opens up the frig door and gets out some 'turkey lunch meat, mayonnaise, pickles, lettuce and Dijon mustard and puts it all on the counter. Then from her fruit basket she gets a tomato to slice and adds it to her delicious sandwich as well. Grabbing a paper towel off the role she wraps it around her sandwich and takes a big bite.

After biting it, the mayonnaise slides down the corner of her mouth and she licks it off with delight and then goes in for another bite. With a frown on her face though, she is dreading to have to go down the street to move her car, but there is 'no way, she is leaving her truck down there overnight because that 'truck, is her baby. In a slow dragging pace she goes to her room to get some pants, a tank top and a sweat jacket, to put on with her Nike tennis shoes. In her stride 'not missing a beat, she grabs her keys off the dresser and heads out the door and starts walking down the block to get her car while eating the rest of her turkey sandwich.

On the way walking down the street she passes 'Jake's, house and he's outside behind his car getting something out of his trunk. "Hey, what's up?" he said. Candis startled, jumps back shouting "sh*t! "You scared me! "Aw... sorry about that" he said. "I thought you were coming over to buy some herb." "No, I'm getting my car, it's parked down the street." "Well, after you get your ride, do you wanna smoke one?" "Sure" said Candis. "I'll be right back." With a slam of his trunk he says "hold on." I'll grab a joint and walk with you." We can smoke it on the way." He looks at her and politely adds "it is way-- too dark out here, for you to be walking by yourself." She smiles back at him saying "thanks for walking with me." "You are so sweet" she adds as she puts her hands in her jacket pockets.

Standing by his car she waits for him to come back outside from his house and then they start to walk as he lights up the joint. Jake and Candis have always had an attraction for each other, but they've never been alone with each other before tonight. Mainly because he always has people coming and going at his house because he sales, weed. "Jordan and his brother Jake had obtained this nice four bedroom house after their mom and dad moved to Texas. His parents moved and bought a smaller home in Texas but ended up getting more land, for there "would be; business". 'Both, of Jake's parents are retired now. Their mom use to be a Bank Executive, in the loan department in a popular bank. And their dad was a high-end 'Sales Rep, for a Quality Meat Company. One of the main reasons why his parents moved to Texas was so that his dad could raise the meat on his own land; cut it up 'butcher style, and sell it. His dad learned long time ago "that if you sell a product, make sure, it is of good quality!" is what he's always told his boys.

That's why his dad chose to raise all of his cattle grass; feed. And as for Jake and his brother Jordan, you could say, they took after their father by growing and selling; minus the cattle; adding; the grass! Jake has never been over to Candis's place either before, because she always goes down to his place to pick up her herbals. They walk, smoke, and talk about football teams. Jake is a huge 49er's fan, and Candis like them too. She tells him "how she's getting more into basketball too lately and that she's a Warrior's fan but also digs the Laker's." While they are on the subject he asked her "if she'd ever played basketball herself?" and she replied "she use to play back in the day and how she was pretty good." But she laughs thinking back on it, saying "it was all good at first, until I started breaking my long fingernail." "Then, I had to switch hobbies" she laughed.

While she was laughing he glanced down at her nicely manicured hands, to see what all the fuss was about, with her nails, and he thought to himself she had pretty hands. They finally get down to her truck and he takes her keys from her and opens the door for her. "Thank you" she said and then she unlocks his side, with the lock switch. He gets in her truck and being that it's his first time in it, he looks around the dash and touches the leather seats voicing "sweet; ride"! She smiles out "thanks, and at the same time he's leaning back in his seat, he asked "so, who's at your house?" "Um; caught by surprise, she answers "nobody." "Do you want to finish getting high at your pad?" he asked. Candis was; hesitant at first, but thought hell; why not?" We're friends, and she's not "really; officially" with anybody, so she agrees to his proposal.

They get to her place and she opens the front door and when they walk in her apartment she tells him to make himself comfortable, saying "she'll be right back." He sits down in the recliner and grabs the remote and turns on the television. Candis goes to the restroom and bushes her teeth and puts some sweet smelling lotion on her hands, and heads back out to the living room. When she gets back to where he is she sees that he has made himself at home and she smiles asking him "do you want a beer? "Sure, that a work." She brings him his beer and gives it to him and then she sits down lady-like on the couch with her beer.

"This is a nice place you got here, I didn't think these apartments were that big" he said. After thanking him she smiles "it's not a house though, like you and your brother have." But you know, it's a roof" she smiled. "True" he said. Candis takes a sip of her beer saying "you two, came up, when you guys got that crib!" "Thanks," he nods. "Luckily my mom wanted to move closer to her parents, or my brother and I would be in an apartment too." "The rent is so high out here in Treeberry" he said. She agrees returning "right?!" Adding "it's ridiculous!" People are so money hungry!" she concluded.

He gets up to look at a picture on her bookshelf asking "who is this?" You and your sister?" he asked. "No. "That's my best friend Naquawna." We were at Bay Beach and Boardwalk when her ex-boyfriend took that picture." "Your hair looks different on here" he said. "Oh. "I know. "I had Naquawna put big dookie braids in my hair for me that day." He laughs "is that what they're called?!" They both laugh and Candis replies "yep. "That is what they call them." He stood there looking at her, in her eyes and said "you look pretty, no matter how you wear your hair."

Candis didn't know what to say; nor did she see that one coming. Playing it cool she replies "awh--, you are too kind." With her hands in her jacket pockets she grins asking "so--, where's that joint?" He pulls out a bag of joints smiling saying "right here" he said as he dangles the bag in the air. Pointing to her sliding door she says "we can smoke it out there on the balcony if you want?" He pulls one joint out of his baggy and they go out to the balcony and Candis has a flash back of her and Jason out there smoking with their friends from thy other night. Looking at the time she knows she needs to call Jason, like she said she would 'but, as she keeps looking at Jake's pretty face, she thinks 'Jason, is going to have to wait because she's entertaining Jake tonight.

Hearing a noise outside has her a little on edge because she hopes "Jason" doesn't try and pop-up over her house while Jake is there. He gives her the joint and the lighter and tells her to fire it up. Smiling a cute smile at him she lights it up. For some reason he keeps staring at her while she hits the weed. With a cough she passes it to him thinking to herself he is too cute. 'Plus, she trips off the fact that he looks so much like 'Paul Walker, the movie star. Standing there looking at him, has her wishing she could call Naquawna, because she won't 'believe, that she has this fyne; white boy, over her house smoking weed with her.

Naquawna has seen Jake, a couple of times too. And on this one particular time when he was outside his house washing his car with his shirt off 'looking hot, was when Naquawna first seen him on her way up to Candis's place. Candis had told her that she buys herb from him sometimes but Naquawna didn't believe her at first; saying "that he was way too cute for Candis to try and get at!" "And that he probably only messes with pretty, "skinny" white girls!" Candis told her "that's probably true." But now; look! "What is he doing here with me?" she thinks to herself. Then her voice of reasoning says "we are just getting high together, and he probably has a girlfriend already; anyways."

So when they finish smoking the joint and go back to sitting down in the house Jake sees that Candis has a Wii game. "Dope...!" he says. "Let's play a few games." "Naw--!" said Candis. "You don't wanna see me, at no Wii!" He laughs saying "alright! "Show me what you got" and he hands her one of the controllers. The first game they play is tennis, and Jake is all over the place. He gets so into the game that he almost; trips on her rug. Candis tries not to laugh too hard, but they are having so much fun and she is 'so, forgetting all about her promise to call Jason. Jake casually tells Candis how he "use" to play tennis back in the day professionally. And how he has medals and all. He even told her how he got a full College Scholarship to go play tennis overseas but couldn't complete his deal after he fell on his wrist in a basketball game and broke it. Come to find out, he wasn't the only one devastated over his injury, because his parents took it hard as well. And to this day they think he does music beats, for a major record company, to make his money to pay the bills along with Bubba Dank. He and his brother even have a recording studio at their house and people do come by, to put down tracks but not enough to pay his bills on a regular basis. So that's what lead him into selling weed.

It is now 10:00 at night and Candis and Jake are on their 4rd game of tennis. She won the second game of tennis, but Jake beat her in the last two tennis games, so now they are moving on to bowling. "You are good; Jake"! "But I'm; better!" she shouts, as she throws a strike. When she jumps up and down with excitement after making her strike he notice her chest moving; wildly. With a grin he looks at her lady-lumps for a second but plays it off 'like he's not getting an eye full. Even she forgets for a minute that she still had on her low cut tank top shirt. But when she catches him staring at her in that 'flirtatious way, she refrains from jumping around so crazily.

'Candis, celebrates after she beats him in the last game of bowling and then they both plop down on her couch. He yells out "dawg; gone it"! "You got me"! She laughs back saying "finally...! Adding "it wasn't easy; trust me"! "You beat me at everything else!" she said wiping off her forehead. Catching her breath she asked him "are you hungry? "I've got the munchies" she said. He smiles "naw, I'm good." "How about another beer?" she asked. Without answering, he leans in close to her while still sitting on the couch next to her and gives her a quick kiss. She is baffled when she looks him in his eyes and with a smile on her face she says "don't you have a girlfriend?"

"Nope. "I'm a free man" he said. "Really?" she says looking deeper into his pretty greenish; blue eyes. He says "you are so gorgeous, Candis." She smiles and puts her head down thinking "oh shit!" What, am I, doing?!" He lives way too close to my house. Before she could think another word his face gets even closer to hers and he gives her another kiss. This one was softer and longer. Licking her lips she pulls back and looks at him saying "um-mm--; Jake?" He pays her no mind as he leans in and kisses her even harder. As they are kissing he gently runs one hand across the side of her head and then she kisses him back and starts to feel as warm inside, as her electric blanket.

Not knowing where this is going but liking it just the same she lets him kiss her. He's so pleased with her kiss because she does it 'so well, that he's compelled; to whisper on her mouth; to touch him. She brings her hand slowly up to the front of his chest to touch him 'knowing, that's probably "not" where he meant. So he takes her hand off of his chest and he kisses it before moving it down towards his jeans. He then indicates, that; that's where he wants her hand to go. Looking into his eyes as he leads her hand to land on top of his "private; part" is so she can 'see, 'what's up; "literally"! While her hand is on him, he kisses her again and with another hand he unzips his pants while still kissing all over her mouth, because now he really wants her to see, just how endowed he really is. Candis could tell that he was proud of his "package" and she could see why; after he pulled it out of his pants. Without smiling she was looking down at it and back up at him and when he asked her to touch it 'she all but laughed, because she just can't believe how guys always seem to want her to touch them, in some form or another.

So as she gazes at him, she slowly puts her hand on his body, even though she could have said "no. 'Sometimes, she just wants to amuse herself by seeing how far they are willing to go, to bust a grape. When he moves her hand down towards his "chestnuts" he starts to breathe heavier and that's when she uses her 'fingertips, to softly move her hand back up towards his shaft, just to see how he would respond to her touch. With hungry eyes while she's rubbing on him he asked her "do you want to put me in your mouth?" She plays along and softly saying "yes. "I do" as she's rubbing on his 'peter-piper, gently. Holding back her chuckle, she's thinking to herself, she is "not" about to put his pecker in her mouth! She laughs to herself, just thinking about it, because she doesn't "know; where" his 'cocker spaniel, has been!

Furthermore, she laughs "he must not know; bout me"! "Plus--, we ain't even a couple!" she grunt to herself. Then, on 'player mode, she pauses saying "wait, are you going to do me?" He answers "hell; yeah! She says "alright, then you do me first" she said. "Take off your pants" he replies as he's getting ready to go down on her. She knows she's on her 'monthly, so it's "not" gonna happen! But she just wanted to 'see, if he was down; for it! So she kisses him again saying "Naw..., it's cool. "You don't have to do me today." Besides, we're moving way too fast for all that." He's barely listening to her talk now as he growing; flushed in the face, from her touching him. His next words as he's looking at her with those; flaming eyes of his is "you wanna have some fun?" She grins out "this is fun, and--, we're not doing anything too; crazy!" He kisses her again saying "I know." That's the problem, let's get crazy!"

With a bursting chuckle she says "okay, wait here." 'Thinking to herself, she laughs because she 'knows, this is about as crazy as she is willing to get, when she goes back to her room to go get the baby oil out of the bathroom. But unbeknownst to 'her, he is right behind her walking quietly; back towards her room with her. He lays down on her bed with his pants down, rubbing on his 'hot Rod, while waiting for her. Candis walks back into her room from the bathroom heading for the living room with the baby oil in her hand, but she stops when she sees Jake laying across her bed. He replies "this, will make it even; funnier! She is stunned at first but ends up being cool with it because she is no stranger to boys wanting to 'play, by any; means; necessary! And if she wasn't into him; trust and believe; it would "not" be happening! In his mind though, he's really hoping for a little "mouth; action" from her in her room, but unbeknownst to him; she doesn't do that! She gets; done! But being the "tenacious" little "masseuse" that she thinks she is, she doesn't mind giving him a baby-oil, rub down being that she "is" into him and would love to see him; spurt!

Candis then lies down beside him on her bed, kissing him softly three quick times on his lips. He wants her to take her clothes off but she declines saying "I just want to do you; Jake!" "So just; relax" she said. "Okay, baby-doll" he answers. "If you're sure?" He continues to say "because I would love to show you what I can do to you" he adds as he licks his lip, looking at her. Candis kisses him hard answering "next time; k"? Then she begins to rub baby oil all over his stomach and down on his shaft. With his eyes closed she slowly rubs down on his 'coca-nuts, and he gets so erect, from her just kissing him 'until he has to pull off his shirt because he's becoming so--; hot!

Rubbing on his chest she listens to him moan in her ear and then she licks his mouth, as she's moving her hand down further, while massaging on him. When his man-hood starts to produce clear fluids, he holds on to her back with his other hand pulling her closer to him as they kiss. Looking at him she strokes him ever so softly, ever so slowly, with the oil slipping and sliding up and down his body with her hand. The harder he gets, the more; creative she gets. She slows down, so she can rub her thumb across the top of his helmet and he just loves that, and he makes sure to tell her that he does as he moans into her mouth while she kisses him some more.

Jake is a wild kind of kisser and she finds it magical, the way he plays with his tongue, in her mouth. As they're kissing she talks to him, asking him "Jake--, do you like my hands, on your body"? "Yes. "It feels good" he sighs. She goes further telling him "it's so--, big" she said while stroking him even; slower. With his eyes slightly closed he smiles when hearing her say that. Candis wants him to see what a good kisser she really can be, so she begins to suck his tongue while kissing him which makes him even; harder. He repeats the word "whoa..! "That's it! Over and over again moaning in her ear "whoa! "Yeah...! "That's it! "Baby-doll! "You are making me...! And before he could get another word 'out, of his mouth, his cobra begins to; spit!

He squeezes her even tighter around her waist as he's purging; all over his stomach. Candis loves it, as she watches him releasing the 'fire, from his pretty eyes when he Cums. If she smoked cigarettes, she would have lit one up, for the both of them. Instead, she gives him a big kiss and then she gets up with a smile and goes to get him a rag to clean off his chest and his stomach. After washing her hands she then sits back down on the bed with the cool rag for him to wipe himself off with. And with a satisfied smile on his and her face, he cleans himself off and lays sideway with his pants up and his shirt still off. "Wow! "That was interesting" he said. Now, feeling a tad-bit awkward he laughs, because he can't believe they just did that. Candis laughs too then smiles, thinking to herself "my, my, my, he is so-o-o cute"! She gloats to herself thinking "who's the real player now?" She's thinking those thoughts with Naquawna in mind and she can't wait to tell her all about her night, because that's another way, they compete as well.

She grins 'inwardly, because she doesn't want Jake to see how much she likes him, so she politely says "well, it's getting late". "I better get some sleep". He laughs "oh! "It's like that?"! "You're throwing me out?"! She laughs back with a sexy smile on her face saying "naw, it's not like that. "I had a great time" she said. "It's just that I have to get up so dang early tomorrow because I was late today for work, so I told my co-worker I would return the favor and go in earlier for her tomorrow so she could go to her Doctor's Appointment."

He smiles "it's cool... "I forgot you do work at the hospital" he says. "I be seeing you in your scrubs walking around looking like a surgeon and shit"! "You are good with those hands—though; that's for sure" he cracks. Smiling he puts his shirt back on and walks with her towards the front door. He gives her a big hug and a kiss saying "I'm gonna call you, real soon." And you owe me a rain check" he said. She laughs asking "what rain check?" He sticks his tongue out and flaps it up and down, while looking down at her "pizza; slice". "You are so bad" she says with a grins. But deep down she can't wait to hold him to it.

"Hey," she says. "Wait a minute." Don't forget your weed" she said as she; pointed to the coffee table. The sandwich bag of weed has about two joints left in it. He grunts "you can keep it, I got plenty" he winks. She says "thanks" and watches him walk off into the dark street. She closes the front door with a big sigh, then she runs back to her bedroom and lets out a quick scream, while flying down on top of her bed. She is so excited because she has always liked Jake but would always play it off, like she wasn't that attracted to him, other than, him being just a friend she bought weed from.

After brushing her teeth she gets ready for bed and tries to call Naquawna to tell her how much fun she had with Jake, but Naquawna's phone goes straight to voicemail. “Figures!” thinks Candis. Then she has a light bulb moment and remembers she ‘didn’t call Jason, like she said she would. Looking at her cell phone she notices two missed calls and they are from him, so she calls him and he picks up immediately saying “what’s happen-in?” are you just now getting home?” She didn’t want to lie, so she says “kind of, like a little bit ago.” Sorry to call you so late, but I just wanted to hear your voice before I went to sleep” she said. She rubs her pillow smiling thinking how easily those words just rolled off her tongue. “I’m glad you thought of me” he said. He looks at his clock saying “dang, it’s already 11:30.” “You must have had a lot of stuff to do for your mom?” his tone was skeptical.

She gets quiet not being able to have a quick come back to his question. He adds “see-- now it’s too late for me to come over and see you.” “I bet you’re tired now; huh?” hoping she would say “no. But Candis says “yes. “And I’m already in the bed too” she replies as she moves around in her bed to get more comfortable under her covers. “Maybe we could hook up tomorrow or something” she says. “Alright, I’ll call you tomorrow” he said. But then he tries one more ditch; effort to come see her by saying “are you sure, you don’t want me to come lay with you and rub that pretty body of yours to sleep?” Candis was so tempted but she had already played with Jake tonight, so she was; all good. So instead, she gives Jason a sad “I would love for you to rub me down, if it was the weekend and I didn’t have to get up so early tomorrow, because I bet you’re a ‘really, “good” ‘body, rubber-downer too” she said all; sexily.

When she said all of that to him he got as ‘stiff, as an icicle, hanging from a roof top, just hearing her talk like that to him. And as he lays back on his bed he touches himself while she talks to him softly some more, in his ear. Candis can tell he’s doing something on the other end of the phone and she’s “sure” it’s “not” folding; clothes. But she lets him have his fun as she talks to him, with pillowy words, in his ear. And when he’s finished pleasuring himself to her voice, he says “sleep tight; beautiful.” And she replies “I will, and they hang up. When she hangs up with Jason she lies back in her bed while still thinking about her time with Jake. Then she thinks out loud; shoot! “Jake lives way to close to the pad. ‘Thinking, now how am I going to kick it with ‘Jason, over at my house?” But then shaking her head with a grunt she laughs saying “I’ll work it out; somehow!” And that’s because she does considers herself a “gamer!” And she is “not” talk-in; Nintendo! Chuckling; off her ‘hood; ways she laughs.

Chapter 4

At 1:00 in the morning Candis's phone starts to vibrate on her nightstand "this better be important" she says under her breath. It's her brother calling from Vegas. "Hey, sis!" Sorry to wake you up." He sounds 'drunk, to Candis when he says "but can you post some money for me?" so I can Bail out of jail." She shouts "what?"! "Jail!" shouts Candis as she sits up in her bed asking "what are you doing in jail?"! He blurts "I can't tell you everything, until I get out." "I only get one phone call" he said in a slurred; voice. Candis replies "it can't be good, if you're calling me, and not Dianna!" "Does mom know?" "Hell; no! "And don't you tell her either!" He continues "you know I do not want to hear her; mouth!"

Before Candis is willing to say 'yes, to bailing him out, she asked "so Marv, how much is your bail?" "It's $35,000.00; dollars." She says "what...?"! "I don't have that!" He says "no, it's only 10% of that." "Just; which" he stumbles on his words. Then he pulls it together saying "which, is only $3500.00 dollars. "And as long as I show up in court, he explains; then you won't lose, your property." "My property!" she shouts. "Yes. "You might have to put your truck up for collateral for me" he said in a promising voice. "Boy!" You are really on one!" she retorts "And before I do a thing!" I wanna know "what" really happened?!" she said in her (I don't believe this sh*t) voice.

Marvin yells "damn, I got into a fight at the scrip---; club!" "I mean the strip; club!" He adds; "you remember Tammy?" "My old high school girlfriend?" Candis says "the one with the big lips?" "And no personality?" He grunts "Yep, and the big; ass!" he said with a deceitful drunken laughs. When he finishes laughing he says "whelp, anyway, she just so happens, to be a dancer out here." "You mean a "stripper" Marvin?!" said Candis not impressed. He groans "mmm... hu...! "Um, umm, um, umm, um...! "And she's a damn; good one!" he said ignoring Candis's 'rude, remarks. She blurts "you got in a fight; over a stripper?"! "That you use to go with in high school?"! "Marvin?"! "Oooooh---; who---; wee--!" she chuckled. "This is priceless!" "Mom was right!" He yelled "Candis!" Don't, even; go there!"

Candis interjects "that's why, you've been going on all those "so called" business; trips to Vegas! "Poor--; Dianna!" she belt out laughing even louder saying "wait till 'she; 'finds; out!" She is going to be; devastated!" Marvin jumps all over her words yelling "that's why I'm calling, your; dumb ass! "So she "won't" find out!" So I hope you can keep your big mouth shut!" "What...!" Ever!" cracks Candis. She chuckles some more stating "I, just can't; believe it!" You, cheat-in on Dianna, with a hoe; out in Vegas!" "Don't, call her "no" hoe; Candis!" She is just dancing her way through medical school!" he shouted. "Boy--! "Please-! "That is just a 'bunk ass; excuse; them hoes use"! "Knowing; it's "really"! "All, about, that; doll-la"! "F*ck! "You sis"! He yelled. "Say what you want to say about Tammy"! "But don't call her no, hoe"! "Because, nobody is perfect"! "Not even you"! He yelled.

With a smirk on her face she shouts "save it!" For David!" Candis still laughing while her brother pauses to eyeball the guard glancing his way says "well, are you going to do it or what?!" I've got to get off this phone the guard is now giving me hand signals saying "I have one minute!" She pauses thinking, then she says "I guess!" But you owe me; big time; Marvin!" and I do mean; big time; buddy!" She cracks on him one last time saying "I, am, going to have to chalk this up to being; another one of your; dumb-ass; decisions!" She is laughing so hard that tears start to form in her eyes. While she's laughing he blurts out "yeah! "Yeah! "Yeah! "Keep laughing Candis, because there will come a time when you'll need 'me, to bail you out"! She laughs back "dought it!" and cracks up some more.

The guard approaches him so he quickly says to Candis "just please call the Bails Bonds place for me." She shouts "all right!" she said in her (I'm tired, of hearing your ass beg) voice. "Thanks sis. "I got to go" and he hangs up the phone. Laying her head back on her pillow she stares up at her ceiling, still in shock at what has happen to her brother and she chuckles. She wants to call Naquawna so bad but it is now almost 2:00 in the morning, so she sends her a text instead saying "gurl...!" Marvin is in jail!" In Vegas!" "Over that skank Tammy!" Do you remember his old girlfriend?" the one with the big lips that we all use to call; tulips. LOL. "Well, she is a stripper out there." "Hit me up when you get up in the morning, then she hits send.

"Oh man" she sighs softly as she gets up to go to the kitchen to get the phone book so she can find the bail bonds place. Normally she would use her cell phone but she had already seen a place in the phone book's yellow pages a while back that a family friend told her they used so she wanted to use them as well for her brother. With practically one eye open she calls the number and they get everything going. It was easier then she thought it would be to get her brother bailed out, so now "hopefully" she can get some sleep. When she gets back in her bed, seeing that it is now about a quarter till three in the morning; her face sours because that only gives her five hour of sleep until she has to get up and get ready for work.

Wishing she could call in sick "so; badly" but that is off; the table because of her promise to Sherry. Chalking it up, she knows she is going to be so tired once again, at work; but as always she'll make it through. So with a big yawn she is 'finally, laying her head down to sleep. But Naquawna...; is still up. She gets Candis's text but she will have to call her back tomorrow because Rayshawn is over her house; trying to plead; his case!

Chapter 5

Rayshawn got to her house at about 1:30 in the morning 'after he got done, gambling at the shack 'so, he said. He knocks on her bedroom window with his pinky-ring finger and she gets up to see who it is at her window. When she sees it's Rayshawn she is so happy to see him deep down inside, but she acts 'cold, like she's still mad at him because of all that stuff she found out at work about him and some girl he has a baby by. 'Plus, his punk ass is 7 hours late as usual! But she still wants to hear the 'truth, from his own mouth about the girl and the baby. Or--, does she; "really"?!

Naquawna sneaks to the front door to let him in 'hoping, she doesn't wake up her grandpa. Even though it's her apartment she still doesn't like to disrespect her grandpa because he is very old school, believing in marriage first. She knows, deep down inside her grandpa is right when he tells her to have respect for herself, and how he always emphasizes on the fact; that a man should court a woman first, and then asks for her hand in marriage. He stands by that fact stating "that; that's how a man; truly proves his love for you!" 'But to Naquawna, "most; things" to be "learned" go into one ear and out thy other. She's the type that likes to do things; her "own" way! And as her sister use to tell her, on a daily basis as they were growing up, "some people just 'half, to learn the hard way" she'd say. So of course, hard; headed Naquawna rushes Rayshawn quietly back to her room and closes the door gently behind them.

He takes off his jacket and sits down on her bed, then she asked Rayshawn the big question. "So, tell me; who's that girl you're living with?"

and--, is that your baby?" Rayshawn has a stern look on his face when he answers "what are you talking about?!" Giving him a crazy look back she says "don't lie!" and don't play stupid!" because I'm already knowing; that you have a baby's; momma! He blurts "naw..., man!" you trippin!" that's my cousin, she just moved out here from Queens." "She didn't have anywhere else to go, so I told her she could stay with me until she got her own place."

Naquawna has a 'smirk-defied, look on her face like as if to be; confused. She asked "so... who's the baby's daddy?" Rayshawn puts his head down momentarily saying "some dude out there in New York." He rubs his hand under his chin and strokes his goat tee as he looks up at her to see her response. She studies his face hard then she blinks saying "and that's your story?!" Really?!" Flipping her hair to one side she adds "so why are people saying it's your baby?!" He looks at her saying "them people are just haters, that don't want to see me and you together" he said calmly. He stands and takes her by the hand and pulls her closer to him saying "you're the only one I'm digging on right now." He then gives her a kiss on the lips saying "you and me are like a 'book; with pages." "The rest of world just can't fade us."

Naquawna gives him a sexy smile and believes every word he just said, and in her mind, that was all she needed to hear. Believing him at his word, but she still; squints her eyes at him saying "you better not be lying to me 'Rayshawn, because I am putting all my 'trust, into this relationship, and I "do; not" want to get hurt! "Baby, I could never hurt you" he says as he takes his index finger and puts it under her chin and pulls her lips up to meet his giving her a convincing kiss, while licking his tongue; all in her mouth.

She then, just melts into him; like a wick to a candle. After kissing she looks into his eyes but can't see, all the lies and as he pulls down her nightgown, it falls slowly to the floor. When her gown falls to the floor she playfully pushes him back on her bed and climbs up on top of him like a caterpillar 'would, searching for food. Then she kisses him, like they've just met, all over again. His heart beats rapidly as he's unbuttoning his slacks and zipping down his zipper. He pushes his pants down so they can fall to the floor, and in a rush she slides up and down on his oversized; "log" grinding him, as he grows harder than a lumberjack's pile of wood.

But then remembering where she is; which is in her room; with her granddad down the hall, so she tries not to make "too" much noise. Lusting for her love he starts to nibble on one of her 'orchids, while he plays with her other one, which is peeking; at his touch. When the heat rises between the two of them and sticking his 'meat, inside her 'casing, is no longer an issue she reaches down between her legs and grabs the silky head of his 'meat and slowly puts him inside of her warm; crock pot. She lets out a soft moan and wants him to give her more of his slow groove as she grips him in every way, by bringing him into her; and out, while telling him what she needs from him.

The love making gets so wild and crazy as Naquawna is riding her lover! 'So crazy, that his legs are becoming numb from the loss of blood flow and circulation. "Baby," she whispers in his ear. "Baby, you make me feel so good, every time I make love with you" she moans. She rides him slow, and the deeper and deeper he goes, in between her moans she says "do you feel me?" She repeats those words as she's wiggling her rear while coming down on his 'nice; 'sized; chorizo. Naquawna tells him in a soft loving voice "no one can love you, like I can." He grabs her by the head with both hands and pulls her face closer to his lips, and he kisses her 'even; 'harder; as he goes deeper into her; like a worm; penetrating thy earth.

'With agitation, his hungry hands move down her body to her hips and as he moves them further down to her 'rumpus, he squeezes it as he's shaking it up and down on top of himself. With an adequate amount of rhythm, he shakes her body so it 'satisfies, the both of them. Naquawna is gushing with every shake of her rump, like 'splashes, of wet paint. And as the breathing between the two of them gets heavier and heavier and her 'nibblers, get harder and harder he then gives out a 'long; 'yelping; roar of satisfaction! When he bellows his last breath, she closes her eyes with her legs and her body still shaking after they have both; blended; together in the dark; of her room!

Naquawna lays there on top of him for a few minutes with her eyes closed and then she exhales fully as she rolls off of him. She just lays there with a big smile on her face in the dim, dark, light of her room, calmly thinking to herself how she just road the 'hell, out of "him" this time! But there was just one 'problem, she forgot to use a condom. "Sh*t!" she says, now realizing as she gets up out of the bed. Rayshawn whispers "where are you going? "I'm going to the bathroom" she says in a sweet but serious voice. Luckily her ½ bathroom was in her bedroom, so she didn't have to go down the hallway past grandpa's room to the other bathroom. She sits on the toilet to go pee, hoping to push out some of Rayshawn's "juices" from her body. 'Now, out of her 'daze, she still can't believe how careless she was to forget to use a condom; being, that she was so caught up in the moment.

When she gets up off the latrine as she's washing her hands she thinks about all the 'sexually, transmitted diseases she could get. And not to mention; a baby that she's not ready for. 'Beautiful; the baby! 'But not like this, without 'him, all to herself. She wipes her hands dry, trying not to think negatively, telling herself it's all going to be fine, and that she just won't forget to use one the next time. And while mumbling those words she walks out the bathroom and gets back into bed.

Rayshawn half asleep by now says "wake me up in two hours, so I can go home." She frowns "you're not going to stay with me all tonight?!" "I can't. "I have to make a run out of town with one of my boys in the morning" he said, rubbing his hand down her bare back. He assures her though, by saying "I'll stay overnight next time." She nods "okay, because she doesn't want to be too unreasonable. Smiling, she than reaches over him to set the clock for two hours. Once the clock is set she snuggles up against him and closes her eyes and falls into a deep sleep. Time, ticks, bye, but the clock doesn't go off in two hours. Naquawna accidently set the clock for 4pm instead of 4am. So when her cell phone alarm goes off, it is 7:00 am, the time she gets up every morning to get ready for work. Distress is on her face when she looks over at the clock that didn't go off, and she shouts "dammit!" It's 7:00 o'clock!" She scrambles to wake him and he jumps up yelling "what?!" "F$ck!" I told you to wake me up at 4:00?!" Throwing the covers to one side he grabs his clothes and starts putting them on quickly.

'Naquawna, feeling real bad says "dang! "I'm sorry! "What time were you and your friend supposed to go out of town?" He snaps "I don't have time for all these 'damn; questions!" He grabs his hat and starts to walk out of her bedroom but then he looks and spots her grandpa walking down the hallway from the bathroom to the kitchen. He backs up saying "your granddad's up"! She gets up off the corner of her bed and with a scared stare on her face she replies "you're gonna have to hide or go out the window." He looks at her like she's; trippin! "Climb out the window!" he said. "Ain't this a b*tch! He is hel'la mad and Naquawna knows it, but she is "not" about to have her granddad thinking she is an "unsavory; woman"! So Rayshawn had 'no choice, because he has to get home. So with a frown on his face he ends up climbing out the window 'cursing; all the way down to his car!

As he's driving away from her house he turns back on his cell phone, and with 'no, surprise he has 22 missed calls on his phone from his 'so called; "cousin"! She has to be at work by 8:30, so she's been calling and texting him since 5:30 this morning. He always drops her off at work and then takes the baby to daycare. 'His, so called "cousin" is on fire; right now!

She looks out the curtain and sees him pulling up. With a serious look on his face he gets out the car and goes inside the house and she's standing there in the kitchen with her arms crossed; not happy! The girl gives him a mean mug, of a look' and with anger in her eyes she blurts "um! "So, you're staying out all night; now?"! "Naw…, of course not baby!" I had to bail Flaco out of jail, when he called me late last night." "I tried to call you but my phone battery died." She smirks "let me see your phone! He replies "alright" and starts to feel on his pockets intensity. After not producing his phone before her, he convincingly says "aw, damn! "It must be in the car." "Yeah, right!" she said. "How convenient!" she adds as her anger engulfs.

Disappointed with his excuses she turns her back to him and finishes putting the baby's bottles and formula into the diaper bag. 'Him, not wanting to piss her off any further, walks over to the baby who is sitting in his car seat on the kitchen table and he smiles at him saying "how's my son doing this morning?" He quickly hides his phone under the baby's bottom as the baby sits in his car seat, because Rayshawn knows "Se'anna" his son's; mother, who is "not" his cousin; like he told Naquawna, will want to see 'if his phone battery is really dead like he said it was, when they get in the car. And since Rayshawn drops his son off at daycare, he can just retrieve his phone then.

Se'anna grabs all her stuff and the baby's bag and in a stern voice she tells Rayshawn "let go!" I can't be late!" They all head out the door with Rayshawn carrying little Ray junior. He buckles him safely in the backseat and then they start driving down the road and just like clockwork Rayshawn knows what she is going to ask next. Se'anna putting her lipstick on, turns to face him asking "so, where's your phone?" Rayshawn acts like he's really looking hard for his phone. He even feels on the car floor under his seat and tells her to look in the glove compartment.

When the 'search, is all said and 'done, she looks at him crazy saying "you must think I'm one of them chicken head b*tches; that you're 'use, tah f*ckin with?!" But let me tell you something!" If you; "ever"! "And let me make myself; clear! "Ever!" she says as she's moving her finger in his direction "stay out overnight, without calling and letting me know what's up!" You won't have a home… tah come home; too!" He pulls up to her job and before he could say a word, she adds "and you 'won't, be driving my car anymore; either!" His face hardens, then his eyes tighten, when he shouts "your ass is trippin!" Just because this car in your name; don't act like it's 'all; yours!" I'm the one who's making the payments on this ride!" She snaps "So!" And if it wasn't for me; you wouldn't have a car to make a payment; on!" She looks at him, with tight beaded; eyes, and a 'scrunched, up; face adding "and don't; even try to make this about the car note!" This is about 'you, staying out all night!" And it's; not like 'I can't, be staying out all night!" she said while moving her neck to the rhythm of her words. "So, don't; get it twisted!" You wanna play?!" We can play nig'ga!"

He looks at her; like the crazy bitch that she is! And he yells "whatever! "Se'anna! "Go on; with that; shit! She grunts with a smirk; because she knows; he knows; she's made her point; loud and clear! She kisses her son goodbye; shuts the car door and starts to walk away 'cute, towards the dental office where she works at, in Treeberry Hills. Rayshawn gives her the middle finger when she turns and looks back, and with a half ass smile on his face he drives away grunting; about her smart ass mouth. Glancing at his son in his interior mirror he says "you're the next stop buddy". Then he turns on his stereo and bumps Dr. Dre's: "It's all on me"! Featuring: Justus. While driving his son to the daycare thinking about the drama he just had with his baby's momma the song was fitting. When he gets to the daycare center he parks the car then opens the back door and pulls his son out of his car seat and grabs his cell phone and puts it in his back pocket. With a grin on his face he takes little Ray inside and gives him to his daycare provider 'Mrs. Becky, and before he leaves, he kisses his son on the cheek and tells the ladies "to have a good day, stating "that he'll be back by around 4:30." The ladies smile replying "okay, thank you, will see you later" they say as he's walking out the door. Rayshawn makes a call to one of his friends as he's walking back to his car but he doesn't answer so he gets in his ride and drives around for a while bumping his new Cd by: J. Cole.

While Rayshawn's turning corners, Ms. Naquawna is over at the hair shop, feeling like her 'tank, is on full, so she makes a call to 'Candis, while she's at work all perky asking "what happened with Marvin; gurl...?" Candis can't talk long so she gives her a quick rundown asking her "do you remember Tammy, my brother's old girlfriend?" We met her when we were in 'junior high." "You; member?" she asked in her George Lopez voice, saying "she was the one with the big lips; member?!" We had everybody calling her; tulips." "Well..., anyways that is the stripper he fought over." Naquawna can't really remember her that well, so Candis changes the subject after several attempts, at jogging her memory. Candis; snickering a bit, perks out "well..., on to more important things; like, what happened between you and Rayshawn last night?"! "Nothing!" said Naquawna followed by a chuckling; grunt. "Really?" said Candis. "Because you sure sound "perky" to me!" Like your 'sex meter, is off the Richter scale; right about now!" laughs Candis.

Naquawna chuckles even harder and then goes right into it; saying "well, I guess I could tell you what went down real quick." She continues to talk saying "when he got to my house I asked him about that girl and he said it was his cousin." I believed him because how else could he be able to come over and spend the night with me, all night, if he had a woman?"! "Oh...!" he stayed the night?!" All night?!" said Candis in shock. "Well... kind of" says Naquawna not wanting to push it. "He would have-, she says but he had to make a run with one of his boys and the clock didn't go off; it was a mess, but everything is cool; now!" said Naquawna trying to save; face. She didn't want to tell Candis the "real; deal" about how he had to climb out the window and how he was cursing all the way down. She figures she'll just tell her 'that part, at a later 'date, no need to ruin her moment.

"That's good, sis!" said Candis. "I am so... glad... for you, because I know how much you 'really, like him" she adds. Naquawna smiles returning "yep...! "That's my, boo! Naquawna trying to perk Candis's mood up as well yells "it's almost Friday! "Party time...! Candis with a big smile on her face; cheers along with her. Even Sherry was excited about this party voicing "how she could use a girl's night out because Bruce is always up underneath her." The conversation goes quiet on Naquawna's end of the phone then she whispers "my boss is back!" "I'll talk to you later" then she lays her cell phone down. The girls finish working at their own individual jobs. Naquawna bangs out cute hair styles for men and woman down at the shop. While Candis and Sherry answers phones and shift patients in and out of Doctor's, rooms. As the working day trickles; down, Rayshawn and Bubba also bang out their own business, over one of Bubba's friend's house named; Kennie. Kennie, is a tall lanky Asian kid, fresh out of College who buys herb from Bubba in big quantities. On most shipments he helps Bubba and Rayshawn to divide up the herb when it comes in on the days 'he's trying to re-up, that way, he can get the "family" discount on his weed.

Rayshawn and Bubba chuckle holding up one of the 20 dollar sacks saying "this should be plenty to sell at the party". Bubba thinks there might even be a few cokeheads there, so he makes sure he has some blow on him as well. Rayshawn, Kennie and Bubba chop up the herbals and bag it up while talking about the party coming up this Friday, and speak about all the girls they might see and try to get at when they get there.

In that same chatter Bubba starts to talks about "this nice looking broad he had do his hair the other day, and how he can't wait to see her again, when he goes back to redo his braids." Rayshawn laughs asking "who is she?" Seeming all interested in seeing if it's one of his; honeys that Bubba is talking about. But Bubba plays him to the left though; voicing "don't trip;

man!" I don't want you trying to get at mines!" Plus, you already got your hands full; anyway with Se'anna and the baby!" They both laugh as Bubba gives Kennie dap about the situation because he's siding with Bubba.

Then they ask Kennie "if he wants to go to the Mall with them?" but Kennie says "naw, he's already got plans." So after all the products are tagged and bagged they head out the door. When they get to the Mall they end up finding some tight outfits to wear on Friday night. Bubba all excited about Friday and not being able to keep a secret to save his life, eventually ends up telling Rayshawn which hair shop he went to; to get his hair done, as they both talked and walked through the Mall. And of course when Rayshawn heard that the girls name was 'Naquawna, he laughed out loud saying "man!" I'm already hit-tin; that!" "C'mon man!" blurts Bubba. "You trying to bone the whole city; bruh"! He and Rayshawn laughed; hard on the subject for a minute as they both are walking towards the food court to get something to eat.

Finding some of the foods they like, Rayshawn sits down at one of the tables with Bubba, after ordering a 'plate full, of food. When Bubba sat down with his stir-fried plate, loaded; with shrimp and pork he asked Rayshawn "so how's Naquawna in bed?" Rayshawn grunts at first, not wanting to talk about it but 'then, he gives him the rundown play; by; play telling Bubba, all about his "sexual; encounters" with freaky ass Naquawna! Bubba takes a big gulp of his soda and when he swallows; he replies "now, I won't be able to get those "images" of her, out of my head the next time I go get my hair braided." Rayshawn laughs and takes a 'proud, big bit of his subway sandwich as he continues to talk about her. I guess you could 'say, Rayshawn is the type of guy; who "likes" to kiss and tell!

Chapter 6

Days go by, and after a good rain, it's finally; Friday! It is about 5:00 in the evening and the sky has cleared up and the birds have quieted down in the trees. Naquawna is fixing her grandpa some dinner which consist of, a baked chicken, which is his favorite, mash potatoes, mixed veggies and cornbread. She plans on being at Candis's apartment by 7:00 tonight so they can get ready for Jasmine's party together. So while she's in the kitchen cooking, Rayshawn popped up, in her kitchen window and scared the; hell out of her! She let out a quick; scream and her granddad yelled from the living room "what's wrong?"! "Nothing!" I just burned my finger on a pot." I'm fine." "Be careful in there" he said. "Okay," she says as she opens the back door asking Rayshawn "what are you doing here?" With a whisper he smiles "I'm just seeing what you're doing tonight." She grins "nothing much. "I'll probably go to Candis's and hangout for the night" she says wiping her hands on a towel. "Alright, that sounds cool" he said.

"What you cooking?" he whispers as he's trying to cop a feel. Then laughing low he adds "you can't cook!" she laughs back saying "whatever punk"! "Yes I can! "Do you want a plate?" he nods yes, and she makes him a plate. While she's putting the foil on top of his plate she's asking him "what are you doing tonight?" he answers "I might go to the club with Bubba and Juan because it's Juan's Birthday. With love in her eyes, he takes the plate from her hand and kisses her and before her grandpa can make his way into the kitchen, to get his plate, Rayshawn 'disappears, as fast, as he had appeared; like a magic act!

Naquawna was feeling; great! She knew she had Rayshawn; sprung now. Hell... he was coming over to check on her and everything! 'Damn near, every night! To her, he just couldn't get enough of her good lovin. "Just, wait until I tell Candis how sprung he is" she mumbled to herself making grandpa's plate; smiling. Naquawna was practically 'floating, on cloud-nine when she took granddad's plate into the living room and put it on the dinner tray so he could still sit, and watch 'Wheel of Fortune, another one of his 'can't miss; shows. When she puts his plate down he pats her on the arm saying "thank you granddaughter." Seeing that she was is a rush he asked "are you going out tonight?" "Yep. "I'm just going over to Candis's house for a bit. "Okay. "You girls be careful!" You know there's a lot of crazy folks; out there" he adds with a chuckle as he's taking a bite of his potatoes.

As he's chewing his food he ends his statement with; "don't get caught up"! "Isn't that what you young people say?" she chuckles and gives him a kiss on the cheek, smiling she says "umm--, grandpa, are you trying to talk slang to me?" They both laugh out loud, and she ends the conversation with "we'll---, be---, careful. "Love you, and don't wait up. She grabs her clothes and her hair kit and everything she will need for tonight saying "night grandpa, see you in the morning." After she closes thy apartment door and gets in her car she mumbles "first stop; the liquor store" to get her and Candis's some drinks. Then she turns up her stereo and drives away bumpin "Bend-in Corners By: E-40.

When she gets to the liquor store she looks at the bottles behind the cashier saying "let's see... Grey Goose and orange juice for Candis, and Gin and juice for me." When she pays for the booze with her debt card, Ted comes out from the back room with a case of beer saying "it's party time; I see! Ted is the owner of (Lick um liquors) they always visit his store because he is so... cool, and--, he 'always, has jokes to tell. "Ok, Naquawna I got one for you!" he says. "Why did the man call her a potato chip?" Naquawna answers "I don't know; because she was salty?"! He laughs "no--; because she was 'Fri-ta-Lay!

He cracks up laughing some more when Naquawna laughs to the joke with him. She cheers "that's a good; one"! Then he belts out "one more; what do you call a cow; with no legs?"! "Um... chuck wagon?"! "Wait; a slab of beef!" she shouts. "No!" he laughs. "Ground; beef!" She chuckles, voicing "that's too; funny!" I'll have to remember those jokes" she grins. When she's done laughing she remembers she needs to get a berry blunt wrapper. 'So Ted, being the nice guy that he is, throws two free berry blunt wrappers in the bag saying "you girls have fun tonight and be safe!" Still laughing, off his jokes, he adds "remember!" Don't drink and drive!" And call me, if you need a ride!" he winks. Naquawna flips up a peace sign' with two of her fingers laughing "thanks Ted" as she walks out to her car. Over her shoulder she sees a familiar car pulling up next to hers, and it's; Bobby! "Oh God!!!!" thinks Naquawna hoping he doesn't see her. She hurries up and gets in her car. But before she could close her door and lock it. Bobby taps on her window. She looked at him 'as if, she was surprised to see him. "Hey, Bobby!" how are you?" she said. He grabs her hand and kisses it saying "I'm fine; now!" Now that I'm seeing yo' pretty ass!" Why haven't you returned any of my calls?" he asked as he gazes into her eyes. "Uh--, I did try and call you back one time, but it went straight to voicemail, so I hung up" she said looking over his shoulder to see who was in the car next to them.

Of course she was lying about calling him but she didn't care, she just wanted to tell him anything to get him to go on his way, so she could leave. "What you doing tonight?" he asked as he slid his tongue across the gold teeth in his mouth. "Let's go to a movie, or dinner or something" he said looking her up and down, like he hadn't "eaten" in a week! She smiles a fake smile, while in the back of her mind; thinking "oooooh...! "Yuk...! But he couldn't tell by her smile, what she was thinking and so she played him; saying "that is so sweet of you to asks, but me and Candis already have plans, thanks anyway, though." Not liking that answer he decides he's going to leans in and kiss her but she pulls back her head shouting "Bobby! "What are you doing...?"! He huffs "ah; what?"! "I can't get a kiss?"! "Uh... "No!" I got a boyfriend now."

With a mad demeanor on his face he pulls back, blurting "so!" He won't love you like I can!" "And you won't; 'f*ck; me!" like; he can!" she thinks to herself. But she smiles anyway, adding "oh--, Bobby--, you are such a sweet guy, and you will find the right woman who will love you, just for you. "I, just, know; it! Holding back her laugh, she smiles voicing "I've got to go boo! He smirks "yeah..., alright!" And with a snarly voice he adds "I'm ma still keep in touch!" Was his last words as he hit the roof of her car. She drives off saying to herself "hopefully not...! "Begley! "Begley! He reminded her so much, of one of the characters in a movie she use to watch.

Still laughing out loud thinking about that character she heads towards Candis's house. Before Naquawna gets there, over at Candis's place her fire alarm is going off, so she fans it with her apron to get it to stop sounding. "Finally!" she sighs, after the noise stops. Now, she is just finishing up, frying the rest of the pork chops, so they will have some food in their stomachs before they start drinking. Naquawna finally arrives, and walks through the door with several bags in her hands when she enters her apartment. "Hey, my sista!" said Naquawna. "What are you cooking?!" It smells good in here!" she said smiling, heading towards the kitchen. Candis answers "just some fried chops, baked pork-n-beans with onions and bacon, and a little potato salad." Naquawna high fives her with the words "hold it; gurl...!" You hooked it; up!" she cheers, saying "let me get a plate, right now!" She puts the bottles and her purse down on the counter then she washes her hands in the kitchen sink.

While getting her plate of food Naquawna says "chil, guess who I ran into at the liquor store?" Candis returns "who?" "Rayshawn?" "No!" "Bobby's ugly ass" she said with a stab, of her fork into her potato salad. Candis cracks up laughing saying "Ahhhh-ha---!" "You haven't seen him in a minute!" Naquawna; scowling her way says "and that's how I like it! She continues to talk and eat while she 'compliments, Candis on how good the food is. Then Naquawna pokes out her lips asking "so..., "playgirl" how's your cutie-pie; Caucasian boy doing?!" "He's doing; just finee....!" and yes, he does have a name; it's Jake!" "So make a note of it" she laughs. "Noted!" smirked Naquawna sarcastically. "I'm starting to really like him too, he's cool people" blushes Candis. "Plus, he respects my wishes" she adds. "Remember when I told him not to just pop up over my house?" but to call me first". "Well he came by last night after he called me and we smoked one and kissed a little bit and cuddled a lot." Naquawna rolls up her eyes spouting; "really?"! "Is that it?"! "Kissing and cuddling! "Chil; please! "I would have been; handled that boy by now; if it was me!

Naquawna turns up her nose and goes to the stove to get some more beans, to finish up eating with her potato salad. Candis laughs "naw--, Ms.; Quickie-pants"! "It's funnier; like this!" because I like, taking my time, that way I have the upper hand on how this plays out." Because I am not trying to get; played" said Candis. She takes a drink of her glass of water asking "what about you and Rayshawn?!" are you two going; "steady" yet?!" Naquawna smiles as she takes a bite of her beans answering "pretty much! Naquawna giggles voicing "lately it seems, after I've been; whip-pin it on him; these last few nights!" "He just be calling and texting me now, all... the time!" "And... he came over tonight just before I left the house, call-in himself; creepin up on me, while I was cooking in the kitchen." "I made him a plate" she grins. "Shut! "Up!" said Candis as she takes the bitten pork chop from her mouth.

"Whoa...! "You two are getting pretty serious, huh?!" adds Candis with a surprised look on her face. "Well... I wouldn't go that far" said Naquawna. "But it does feel good to be wanted." Now... what about you and Jason?" asked Naquawna as she clears her plate and puts it in the sink. "When's the last time you talk to him?" Candis smiles answering "he came by today, just before you got here." And he's on his way to Napa Valley as we speak." He looked pretty sad too, his grandma's sick" she said. "Awe... that's too bad." "Poor thing" said Naquawna all choked up because it's one of Rayshawn's best buddies.

"Yep, I know" said Candis. "I gave him a big hug and told him, I did not want to let him go." And while we were hugging he asked me "what was I going to be doing tonight?" "I told him you were coming over tonight and he pulled back from my hug saying "what are you two, gonna be up to tonight?!" "Are yaw'll gonna be playing dominoes again with some other dudes?!" Naquawna laughs and interjects in the conversation saying "you didn't tell him about Jasmine's, party did you?"! "Hell; no!" answered Candis, saying "you know we don't bring sand to the beach"! (Meaning) "We don't bring guys, to parties, when we're looking; for 'guys, at parties"! Naquawna gives her a high five with a snap; cheering "okay!" Naquawna remembers that Rayshawn asked her the same thing and she told him, she was just going over to Candis's place to do her hair. 'Candis, clapping her hands together simultaneously; while laughing and giggling in her seat says "that is the same thing I told Jason! The two girls dissolve in laughter and walk back to Candis's room laughing about their men, and how it wouldn't surprise them if Rayshawn and Jason told each other to find out what the "girls" were doing and report back to each other, what was said.

The girls get to Candis's room and she swings opens her closet looking to see what would look cute enough to go with the shirt she bought earlier, that day at the store. Naquawna sees the shirt and says "that is cute!" Did you get that today?" "Um-uh" said Candis. The shirt in "question" is a sexy low; v-cut, red shimmery top; that sparkles all down the front. And the sleeves which come down mid-way had that same shimmery red trim on the end part of the sleeves. The V-neck showed just enough cleavage to be sexy.

"Should I wear this with a sexy black mini skirt?" Naquawna looks at the clothes on the bed side by side answering "yes. "That will look cute together." "And wear your red 4 inch sparkly shoes; you know' the ones you wore to my sister Sha'wanna's wedding?" "Remember?" "Yes. "Good thinking, "I forgot all about those shoes" said Candis. "Plus, I could never find anything to wear with then, until now, good idea Naquawna" said Candis in a joyful voice.

Naquawna than turns to open her luggage saying "okay, Ms. Thing!" "Now, it's my turn!" "Remember that sexy, slinky dress I bought down in LA, at that cute little Kadazian boutique store?" "Well...; Vooh' la! "Here it is!" she said as she pulls it from her luggage. "What do you think?!" asked Naquawna with a big grin on her face. Candis's mouth flips open in amazement voicing "that's dope! She grabs the slinky, silky golden dress; wishing she had one; stating, "I love it!" Then she sees how low-cut it is, in the front and in the back and says to Naquawna, "how are you going to keep your boobs' and your butt, from not showing in that dress?!" Naquawna laughs "I know; right?!" She digs deeper in her bag saying "because I found some two sided tape to use, to keep it all; on lock!" "If you know what I mean?" she smiled. "Hell, that's how Jenny from the block does it!" "I learn all my tricks from the stars!" she adds with a 'twirk, of her neck.

Candis shakes her head with a laugh voicing "okay; tape"! "Will see after a couple of drinks, how well your "tape" holds up!" A laughing Candis laughs her way back to the bathroom and gets into the shower. Naquawna goes to the kitchen still laughing about what Candis just said and she starts making their drinks. After making herself a drink of gin and orange juice and Candis's Goose and juice, she turns on the stereo and gets her hair stuff out of her beauty bag and gets it all set up and ready to go.

Candis gets out the shower and goes into the living room with her robe and slippers on, ready to get her drink on, and her hair done. Naquawna says "look I brought you, these hair extensions, and they clip on." "Do you like 24 inches?" asked Naquawna. Candis damn near 'chokes, on her drink, and Naquawna laughs saying "in hair; fool! Then she pulls the hair out of the package to show her. Candis cracks up laughing "that is way--too long for me!" She puts the hair up to Candis's head saying "see--?" "It's not too long!" "Everybody in LA is wearing 24 inches!" "But we don't live; in LA! "Barbra!" jokes Candis. Naquawna replies "I know! "Suzie! "So let's just see how it looks when I'm done, and then, if you still think it's too long, we can cut it, to whatever length you want" suggested Naquawna. Candis smiles "okay, and goes to get herself another drink. Naquawna, with her curling iron in one hand, and her blow dryer in thy other; cheers "let's do this"!

After blow drying and flat ironing; Candis's hair, Naquawna gets the hair extensions ready. She lines the hair up, so it clips on securely, and when she's finished clipping on all of thy extension's on Candis's hair she also curls the ends and then tells her 'to look in the mirror. Candis gets up and goes to look in her long bedroom mirror and with her mouth open in an emotional state of disbelief, to sees how pretty she really looks, and she sighs "dang...! "Dang...! "Quawana"! "You really do know how to do hair!" I am so serious!"

Naquawna smiling with a humbling look on her face smirks out "oh batch; pah-leazz! And with Naquawna's head tilted looking at Candis she asked "so... how short do you want me to cut it?" Candis looks at her with a straight face and a gleams out the words "cut; what?!" Girl, please!" I'm rockin these 24 inches tonight!" And I gives a "damn" who knows; it ain't all my hair!" "Because I will be feeling too cute to care!" She gives Naquawna a big long heartfelt hug saying "thank you!" You are 'the best'est, friend; ever!" I mean that!" Naquawna is not really the type of person who takes compliments well so she blurts out "oh; stop!" Your buzz, must really be on!" But then she allows herself to take the compliment because Candis is giving her so much crap about it, until she finally breaks down and says "you're welcome, and you're my best'est friend too!" 'Naquawna so proud, of making 'yet, another person happy with what she loves to do, which is styling hair says to Candis "you should keep that look for a while, it suits you." Naquawna has always loved playing in hair since she was a little girl. But now that she's all grown up, she knows she has really developed in her craft, and considers herself a true hair artist. And after having other people, who have accredited her; in her hair art of work; makes her start to feel like; she might just be; pretty damn good!

'Now, feeling 'fabulous, right about now, Naquawna slams back her drink and Jumps into the shower so she can get ready next. When she gets out of the shower and dries herself off, she starts doing her own hair and Candis helps her curl the back of her hair into beautiful Shirley Temple curls. Afterwards Candis and Naquawna put their outfits on and dance around in the mirror. Naquawna shouts "I, am, buzzing!" she adds, "now, who's gonna drive us to the party?"! "I know..." said Candis. "Let's see if Sherry can pick us up, since she really doesn't drink like we do!" laughs Candis. "Good idea" said Naquawna.

Candis gets her cell phone and calls Sherry. "Hello?" said Sherry. "Hey, chocolate-bunny" giggles Candis. "You still going to the party?" Hell, yeah!" wouldn't miss it!" said Sherry. "Are you still going?" Candis answers "yep. "Why don't you come over to my place" adds Candis as she puts the phone on speaker. Naquawna yells "get your butt over here gurl, so we can all go to the party together!" Sherry laughs "um..., k". "I'll see you two in about 30 minutes." "I'm just now finishing up my makeup" she says. Candis and Naquawna scream out "yeah...! And they hang up the phone and start dancing to the song "all the single ladies" which is playing on the radio. Candis says "my hair looks just like Beyoncé's, all draped in the front, with a part down the middle with these long soft curls."

She starts doing some of Beyoncé's dance moves to the song with her hand switching back and forth. Naquawna laughs saying "now; Beyoncé'; she's got game!" The girls dance around and laugh and sip on their drinks while waiting on Sherry. They hear a car pull up and it's her, she arrives at about 9:45 to Candis's place and they both meet her at the front door, and all; scream together with happiness yelling "come on in, Ms. Thing!" Sherry looks at Candis's and Naquawna's outfits saying "I guess I'm under dressed." Candis and Naquawna both say "no, you look cute." Sherry has on a basic black dress that stops above the knees with some cute shoes that are a sparkling dark green to match her hand bag. Her hair is pulled to one side and clipped in the back so her hair drapes over her right shoulder and lays nicely against the side of her face.

But all Sherry could rave about was how cute Naquawna's dress was 'as, she kept asking her "where she got it from?" With all of the excitement over Naquawna's dress, Sherry didn't notice Candis's hair until Candis was getting her purse from off her dining room table. Then Sherry said "wooh--; child, your hair grew!" Candis laughs "I know, overnight even" she said laughing, slapping Sherry gently on the arm. Still smiling she says "naw, Naquawna put these hair clips in for me. "Does it look too long?" asked Candis while pulling lightly on a few of the long curls. "No, replied Sherry touching her hair saying "it's; pretty." Sherry glances over at Naquawna saying "you have got ta 'hook me up with that same hair style because I will rock; that, at my sister's wedding this summer!" "That'd a work!" said

Naquawna. Saying "just let me know when, and where."

Naquawna, pulling the glass from her lips switches gears to "who's driven tonight?" Candis looks at Naquawna and then she looks at Sherry. Sherry says "I'll drive, you two are looking drunk; already!" The girls all laugh thanking her for driving them as they get ready to walk out the front door to Sherry's car. Sherry says "what time does this party start; "officially" anyway?" "The invite that Naquawna got said ten o'clock" said Candis. "Oh..., Naquawna you got an invite?" asked Sherry. "Yes, Ma'am!" she said as she brushed her knuckles across her upper chest, like as if to say; she's got clout!

Naquawna continues to say "Jasmine's sister comes to the shop all the time to get her nails done by Mrs. Lee, my boss, and since Mrs. Lee wasn't trying to go to a night time youngster party Jasmine's sister, 'Cathy, gave the invite to me. "Plus, Cathy and I have always been cool." Ever since I braided her boyfriend's hair that time, they went to his college graduation party, last year." "And luckily, Cathy told me I could bring a friend, because that's the only reason why Candis is going!" she laughs. "But if I had a "real man" Candis's ass would be at home!" And, "he" would be on my arm tonight!"

"Ooh-; you dirty rat!" chuckles Candis. Looking at Naquawna sideways she retorts "but I thought you said, you 'don't; bring, "sand" to the beach?!" They all laughed out loud because, it was so--, true! Then Naquawna asked "what about you Sherry?" how do you know, Jasmine?" I know her mom Mrs. May, from the Olive Garden. "She told me to come by for Jasmine's "big night" even if, it was just to come by and get a piece a cake." Sherry puts one hand up in the air like she's testifying; spouting "and yes, and you already; know?!" I "will" go to a party; even 'if, it's 'just, to get a piece of cake!" She ended her statement with a 'dab. Naquawna gives her a fist bump and they all crack up laughing as they are driving in Sherry's car to the party.

When Sherry pulls into the parking lot of the party and sees that it is packed. She comments "the party must have started earlier than ten o'clock." After a couple of loops around the parking lot she finally finds a parking spot and the girls 'cheer, then they get out of the car looking all; cute! The ladies quickly finish up adjusting their boobs in their clothes and fixing their under garments pulling on them, where ever needed. Candis puts a last minute, lip gloss, over her lip stick and gets a tissue to blot any excess oil from off her face. They grab the gifts from the trunk and strut, 'confidently, towards the party doors. Naquawna is walking in front of the ladies and is the first to say a big sexy "hello, to the gentlemen on the door. The light skinned one looked Naquawna up and down and didn't care if she had an invite or not, but she flashed her invitation anyway.

Sherry was flirting as well with the darker brother who had a small gold tooth on the right side of his mouth and finger waves in his hair. Sherry had thought he was kinda cute, even though she already had a man. Candis walks in behind the both of them, since she was just a guess, without an invitation. But the bouncer's didn't trip though, they both just waved her through with no hesitation because they saw that they were all together. Sherry looks around the room and sees Mrs. May standing off to the side helping some other people finish up the decorations around the cake table. Sherry cheeses saying "I'll be right back." And she heads over to say "hi, to Mrs. May.

To her surprise Mrs. May looks up and gives her a big hug because she is so happy that Sherry has made it to her daughter's 21st, birthday party. She tells Mrs. May "she wouldn't have missed it for world and that she is so glad she invited her." They chat for a few minutes about how nice the cake and decorations look, and then Sherry tells her "that her friends are waiting. Reaching for her hand she says "bye, and with a final grab of Mrs. May's hand she goes back to where Candis and Naquawna are waiting for her over by the door.

The girls go put their gifts on the table by the DJ's booth and walk the room. Naquawna is like a kid in a candy store blaring; "look at all these fyne ass men; up in here!" Sherry chuckles because she can't believe how out spokenly; loud Naquawna is being while they are passing by a group of those so called "fyne; men"! They see an open table and hurry up to claim it. "Yippee!" said Candis. "And, it's near the dance floor" praised; Sherry, happy because now they can people watch. "This is a great spot!" Said Naquawna. "Thank you God!" agrees Candis. "At first I thought we were going to have to stand up all night, in our heels" she complained.

Sherry looking around the room says "Jasmine's family really has this place decorated nice; huh?" I wonder where the birthday girl is at" enquired Candis looking around the place for her. "Oh, look!" points Naquawna, saying "there she is, at the rear entrance talking to those people." "I see her now" says Sherry. "Yep that's her." "And nice dress" adds Candis. "But I think Naquawna has her; beat!" she grunts. They all crack up then a guy comes over to the table and asking Naquawna "if she wants to dance?" She listens to see what song is playing and then she answers "um... "Not yet." I don't like this song." "Plus, I'm about to go get me a drink from the bar. "Thanks anyway though" she said as she clutches her purse and stands. The guy replies "alright, maybe later" and he walks away.

Naquawna stands there fixing her dresses; shoulder straps, while asking Candis and Sherry "what they wanted from the bar?" adding "my treat." Candis says "I wanna try a long Island, this time." "And you Sherry?" says Naquawna pointing in her direction. "I'll take a Screw Driver!" Naquawna laughs "I'll take a screw driver; too!" "It just won't be in drink form!" Sherry pushes her lightly on the arm laughing "you are so bad; chil! Naquawna heads to the bar to get the drinks, and of course Sherry and Candis start to talk about work and how tired some of the guys are at the job.

Then, it just so happens to be a hot guy slowly coming into view over by the side entrance. When Candis gets a good look at him her heart drops, and she blares out "oh, my, God!!!" Sherry says "what?!" "What's wrong?!" Candis fumbles with her handbag saying "um...!" It's nothing!" Sherry says "are you sure?!" You look like you just seen a ghost!" "What to do?!" "What to do?!" thinks Candis to herself as she fidgets in her chair trying to play it off. Sherry with a mocked; puzzled look on her face, can tell something is up, so she says "is it an old boyfriend?!" Or what?!" "No!" No!" It's cool!" "It's nothing" she says shakes her head to those words to be more convincing. Candis looks to the right of her to change the subject saying "oh... lookie here!" "Here comes Naquawna, with our drinks."

Naquawna walks up to the table with their drinks and she's not alone. The guy who asked her to dance earlier is with her helping her carry back the drinks. Naquawna is all happy when she puts the drinks on the table stating "it is open; bar!" The girls give out a yelping; "yah-woo!!!" They cheer with a whole lot of enthusiasm to the news, but Candis and Naquawna are already way...; too intoxicated, when they yell out "yah...! "Woo...! For a second time adding "free drinks, lets toast to that!" And with their glasses in the air they toast. Sherry says "I may not know much, but I don't think that "free; drinks" for you two; right about now; is such' a good idea!" she laughs some more saying "and, I, am, "not" babysitting you two clowns tonight; either!"

Naquawna and Candis look at Sherry crazy and crack up laughing; mocking her, they say "okay, momma; Sherrita!" "Thanks for the update!" Sherry grunts "funny!" And don't come crying to me, when you two fall flat on your face, in them, high ass; heels!" laughed Sherry as she sipped on her drink with a frumpy; smirk on her face. She then looks at Naquawna saying "and by the way, Candis is trippin off of some--; dude!" Or, someone; who is way over there" she adds as she pointed to the left side of the room. "No..., I'm..., not!" frownt Candis as she takes a big drink of her long island ice tea.

Naquawna notices her slammin it back and says "you are going to be tore; up if you keep drinking that fast!"

Candis rolls her eyes ignoring her statement while she keeps her eyes on the hot guy by the side entrance, trying not to let Sherry or Naquawna know who she is looking at. And while everyone in the place is talking around them, Candis is scheming up away to get over there to see 'if it is, really him. She blurts out a laugh; out of the blue as a distraction; saying "let's all go dance!" The guy with Naquawna says "now that's what I'm talking about!" That's when Naquawna says "you guys...!" where is my manners?" I forgot." "This is Mike, everybody" she said with an open hand pointing in his direction. "Hello? "Nice to meet yaw'll" he said. Sherry and Candis return with "hi back, and then everyone gets acquainted.

Mike is a nice looking slim man who is about 5'9 in height. He has a nice dark brown skin tone and his hair he wears in a low afro. His eyes are small and his facial hair is non-existent just some soft peach fuzz like side burns and a mustache that is just starting to grow in fully. When he smiles he looks even more attractive. His body is average not to buffed, but not to small either. And as he's standing there Naquawna notices that he has a slight; bow-leggedness to his legs. He's not too bad to look at, and Candis thinks that's why Naquawna has him on standby just in case she doesn't find anyone else; tah kick it with, tonight.

The DJ keeps on spinning hit records back to back and when he plays this one hit called: Young, wild and; free. By: Wiz Khalifa. Featuring, Snoop Dogg' the room goes; nuts! Soon as Naquawna and Candis hear that song playing, they both grab Mike and head to the dance the floor, with Sherry not too far behind. The dance floor gets packed; quickly with people of all shapes and sizes trying to shake what their mamma gave-um! And during this time Candis is trying to make eye contact from across the room, at that guy while she's on the dance floor, but with no; such luck!

So she decides to make a bee-line over to see 'if it is; in fact' that handsome guy, she seen a while back, or is it someone who just looks like him. 'Either way, she's drunk enough to check it out! Bobbing her head and moving her body to the beat she tries not to be too; obvious, as she starts in, on her game plan. First she twirls around her friends and acts like she's on the dance floor to stay, and when they are 'gig-gin; locked into the music; not 'looking, that's when Candis sneaks off the dance floor by walking backwards while she's still dancing. She walks; quickly so they won't see where she is headed.

Making her way through the crowd she slips into the girl's bathroom and checks her hair and makeup. While standing there looking at herself all buzzed she almost cowards out; 'thinking, maybe she shouldn't approach him as she's looking in the mirror applying her lip gloss. But after she puts a piece of gum in her mouth she pushes herself into moving forward in her plan. Taking a deep breath with her eyes closed, she slips back out to the party. He is still standing by the side door checking out everybody on the dance floor as he's bobbin his head to the music.

While he's looking in the other direction Candis starts to sneak on the other side of him so she can act like she just got to the party. Steady--, steady- slow--, slower--, she tells herself as she's sneaking up behind him. Then; bam! She bumps into his shoulder from behind, like she didn't see him. "Damn...!" he said as he looked back to see who just bumped into him. She smiles "I'm soo...; sorry!" She then reaches down on the ground to pick up her handbag. He bends down to help her get some of her things off the floor that fell out of her purse and when she locks eyes with him as they begin to stand upright, he looks at her and says "do I know you?"

With an awkward look on his face he looks at her like he's thinking about where he's seen her at before. Candis blinks "no. "I don't think so" she said as she squints her eyes to be more believable. Then she says "wait a minute!" I take that back." I think I may have seen you one time, at a restaurant." "I can't remember which one though" she says as she flirtatiously moves her hair out of her face. He answers "yeah, now I remember." "It was at the O Garden" he said. She returns "where? He says "that's what I call the Olive Garden." "Oh--, that's funny" she said, with a blinking; eyelash; smile.

"You look different" he says. Candis knows it's probably her hair because it wasn't as long that day. But she just smiles anyway asking "is that good or bad?" He smiles back answering "it's not bad." "In fact; it's all good" he grins looking down at her cute outfit. As he's glancing down at her glittering; 'cleavage, and back up to her eyes he asked "so what's your name?" She answers "Candis. "And what's yours?" she asked looking at his dimple on his face. "It's Rafee'al" he smiled. "Nice to meet you" he said putting his hand out to shake hers.

When she shakes his hand, something 'electrifying, happens! It was 'as if, warm 'volts, of 'electricity; sparked, from his 'hand, and went all the way up her arm and 'entered; into her 'heart; like an invasion! She looks back into his 'eyes, to see if he can 'feel; the magic! Then trying not to shout over the music she says "I like your name." But before she could really get a deep conversation going on with him, or--, exchange numbers. A screaming; Jasmine runs off the stage after spotting her favorite cousin. She screams

"Rafee'al!" "You made it!" "You made it to my Birthday party!" He smiles and gives her a big hug. And all eyes are on the beautiful birthday girl, and her cousin over by the side entrance.

Naquawna and Sherry 'now, off the dance floor 'spot; Candis standing over there from all the commotion. Sherry waves over to Candis from across the room wanting her to come back to the table. While Naquawna is giving Candis hand gestures with a shot glass to her mouth 'indicating, she wants to do a 'shot; with her! Candis puts her index finger up as if to say "give me a minute." But then, it's too late, because Rafee'al gets swarmed by girls; when Jasmine starts to introduce him to all her "girl-friends" who have now; sauntered over to meet him.

'Yes, all the girls can see that he is a "hotty-potaty"! Poor; Candis, all she can do is just look on, while Rafee'al is being greeted; by all the young, sprung, hopefuls, yearning for his attention! He stands there all laid back, and very confident. He looks more; handsome than ever to Candis and she can't help but stare because he's about 6'3 in height with a nice muscular upper body from what she can see. She looks him up and down and her whole face starts to get 'hot, just imagining him with his shirt off.

He is wearing a white silk looking shirt, which is showing all of his muscles with just enough chest hairs, which is not too much; down the front of his opened shirt. And as he's standing there talking his face looks well-groomed from the top of his head to the nice but well maintained mustache that is on top of his luscious; lips. The mustache tappers down, both sides of his mouth, which forms, his sexy looking goat-tee. To Candis his whole facial look, goes so well with his golden brown eyes and his deep wavy black hair. 'And his smile! "Ahhhh--; she sighed!" is drop 'dead, gorgeous! 'With, or without the one dimple on the right side of his cheek.

She moves her eyes down to the black, nicely' fitted slacks which out-line his 'manly, body parts, and she can see that he has a nice rear as well. Plus, a nice package in the 'front, to go with it. With a slow motion of a blink, of her eyes she starts to drool over him, while he's talking to all the girls who are trying to; get at him! But then as she's standing there looking at how fyne; he really is! She begins to 'think, that she might not stand a chance of getting to know him, or at least 'not, tonight! Not to mention, she's also starting to see, that he might just be use to a lot of women throwing themselves at him, and the more she stands there she can't help but feel like she's getting smaller and smaller by the minute in the crowd of women.

But then her feline side once again gives way and with a 'pep talk, she thinks, to herself "should she work her way back over to where he is, to get the man of her dreams!" while scratching and clawing her way through a crowd of; estrogen?!" 'Or, should she simply bow-guard; the situation; by keep-in it; gangster! She laughs to herself thinking that thought. Then she pauses thinking she'll just chill, like the Diva she is, and wait for him; to make his move! Candis stands there in the moment, and then suddenly she hears a familiar laugh. She looks to see where the laugh is coming from and it's the lady from the O Garden. 'That same lady, that hugged Rafee'al that day when she and Naquawna were at lunch.

Candis's mind starts to put two and two together thinking to herself "now, I get; it!" They are all related!" It is a light bulb, moment for her. 'And then here--, comes--, 'drunk; 'ass; Naquawna; yelling "come---!" "On---!" "What's, taking you so long?!" Mike brought us back patron shots!" With a slurred; grin she starts pulling Candis away from the crowd by her arm. Candis gets mad because Naquawna is 'now, "another; person" who is cock blocking on her action; right now!

Rafee'al looks to the side of him, and sees Candis being pulled away by her arm, and a sad--, and way--, too drunk; Candis waves bye to him, as she stumbles away in her high heels. But she still manages to get one last look, into his pretty brown eyes; before; disappearing into the crowd. They get back to the table and Sherry asked "who was that you were talking to; Candis?" Candis just looks at Sherry like "nosey!" But smiles answering "um; him?" Don't trip!" He's just a friend." Sherry gawks voicing "he sure is cute." "No wonder you left the dance floor" said Sherry.

Candis trying not to light up in the face or draw too much attention to herself about her "business" smiles; changing the subject to "let's do our shots now!" since you guys were so 'adamant, about me coming over here" she said under her breath; sarcastically. They all do a shot accept; Sherry. She is "officially" the designated driver now. Sherry can be nice, at times, but she's also the type of person that likes to watch people get drunk, and then talk about how "drunk" they were, the next day. She means well, but she can be messy! 'A busy body, one might say.

Sherry sits there staring out at the crowd while they do their shots, and as she's sitting there looking passed Mike's head and in front view she sees this cute guy walking towards her. He smiles at her and behind him 'walking, is this long; legged pretty white girl with light brownish, blonde hair, and as she's approaching she yells out "Naquawna!" is that you?!" Then she screams "oh!" "My!" "Goodness!" "And Candis!" "Look at you!" The girls all scream in unison when Naquawna yells "Roxy?!" "Where have you been?!" "Long time no see!" said Candis. Roxy replied "I've been in

Vegas; girl!" "Making that money!" "You know me?!" said Roxy. Naquawna laughs out "yes, we, do!" You have 'always; been a paper chaser!" laughed Naquawna. They all laugh and hug and introduce Roxy to Sherry and Mike. "Let's go to the bar and get Roxy a drink!" said Candis. "Sounds good to me!" said Roxy. Adding "you know I ain't gonna turn it down" she said with a chuckle.

The girls walk over to the bar and do a shot. And then the DJ turns down the music and Jasmine's mom says a few nice words on behalf of her daughter's birthday. Then they asks everyone to join them in singing "Happy Birthday" as this huge cake is being rolled in. It is a beautiful pink cake with imitation and edible diamonds, all beautifully placed throughout the top and the sides of the cake. The frosting is made with whipped; butter cream, and has berries in the middle of the layers of the cake and the berries are mixed with real whip cream all throughout it.

Everybody claps as she blows out her candles. And yes, Jasmine's fyne, cousin is standing right there next to her with her friends. Naquawna's; "drunk" but not that 'drunk, when she looks at Candis shouting "hey?!" Is; that, that; dude?!" "From that time?!" "At the!" And before she could finish her statement Candis retorts "yes, it, is!" she said with a dreamy look in her eyes. Naquawna laughs saying "that's, why you snuck off the dance floor; heffa!" "You were trying to go get at "salsa; man"! She gives Candis a fingertip high five. Then Roxy looks over that way too, asking "who?" the tall one, over there?" "Yes! "Lord--!" said Candis blushing. "His name is; Rafee'al" she adds.

Naquawna and Roxy laugh at how Candis says his name, and they repeat it, just the way she does, but add more of a 'spin, to it "ooh... la-la!" "Raff--fee--'al!" laughs Naquawna and Roxy. Naquawna still clowning says "I don't know how this child is going to keep up, this is the third man she's added to her "list" of 'possible, for relationship!" Candis laughs out "what can I say?!" I'm on a roll!" "I'm kissing frogs and taking numbers; until my 'prince, comes along!" Candis concludes her statement with "but I'm not given up the 'draws; though!" Roxy grunt saying "what...?" Asking "what are you waiting on?" "A millionaire, to come swoop you up off your feet?" Candis chuckles saying "no. "And like I've been saying for years!" Don't be haten 'on; 'my; 'player; skills!" Roxy returns "ummmm--; okay then!" she said while her and Naquawna shake their heads to Candis's last remarks as they are all walking back towards the table, chuckling.

When they walk up to the empty table they see Sherry and Mike on the dance floor dancing. Candis jokingly blurts out "there's one of Naquawna's men right there!" "You a lie!" grunts Naquawna, saying "I just met that boy tonight!" "He's only my 'dance, and 'shot, drinking buddy!" Candis laughs "until he runs out of money!" Roxy laughing said "I heard that!" "That's how we do um in Vegas!" "Take, um!" "And break, um!" Candis laughs hard; spouting "ooh, that is too; scant-less!" Naquawna grinning with glee, reflects back on the hours before coming to the party thinking of Rayshawn she adds "naw, my man is at home!" "I got a text from him about an hour ago." "He thinks I'm still at Candis's house doing her hair" she brags.

Mike and Sherry walk up to the table and Sherry sits down to catch her breath saying that "she's all tired after dancing to 'four, back-to-back songs." Mike cuts in asking "you ladies want anything from the food table?" Naquawna smiles "yes, a piece of cake; please!" Sherry says "I want some of that spicy barbeque pork; she then clarifies; saying "some bulgogi." Candis and Roxy look at each other and hit their glasses together and pass on the food and keep on drinking.

And here comes 'Rafee'al, heading their way as Mike walks off, to go get their food. "Hey, Candis!" he says. Then a slow song comes on, and he asked "do you want to dance? He grabs her by the hand and she is breathless because he's all up in her face, asking her to come with him to the dance floor." All she can do is smile as she looks deep into his eyes answering "yes. They head to the dance floor arm in arm, and then 'Roxy, interrupts her fantasy saying "Candis?!" "Who are you staring at?"! Candis still sitting at the table puts her hand under her chin and pouts saying "why isn't he coming over to talk to me?" "He keeps looking this way" she frowns. Sherry says "who? "Your friend? "Yes...! "I'm going to go ask him to 'dance, the next slow song" she said, determinedly.

Naquawna jabs her saying "don't; you dare!" "You are way-- too drunk!" "Maybe you need to eat something first." "No, way!" slurred Candis. "I can't eat right now!" "What if he comes over here and I have spicy pork in between my teeth when I smile?" "He might think, I don't brush." Naquawna; drunk as well laughs saying "uh, sweetie; you are way--; over thinking this one!" She tries to convince Candis not to walk over to ask Rafee'al to dance because she's too drunk and will really look like a fool, or 'worse, fall flat on her face in her 4inch heels. Candis says "well, then you come with me." Naquawna is drunk, as well, but seeing that the party is almost over she says "she'll go with her."

So while the two are struggling to hold each other up, and are both walking in a zig-zag pattern, they start to giggle "Caddishly" like two school girls. Halfway through the crowd the lights start to 'come up a bit, and in walk's all the homeboys who didn't have an invitation to get into the party. It is 1:45 in the morning and the parties over at 2. Naquawna sees 'Bubba Dank, out the corner of her eye with two other guys she doesn't know, and then in walks 'Rayshawn, talking on his cell phone. Candis flares on her "you are so...; busted!" All Naquawna could hear from his phone conversation is "I'm here!" "Let's go!" "I'll meet you by the front entrance." Candis crouches down with Naquawna saying "don't let him see you!" "He's probably just here to pick up one of his homeboys or something" adds Candis. Naquawna smirks saying "Really?!" Then a real pretty girl with long wavy hair and light skin gives Jasmine a hug saying "I got to go." "Rayshawn's here." Jasmine replied "okay, my; girl!" "Thanks for coming!" "Call me later" said Jasmine with a hug.

'Naquawna, not being able to 'see; 'strait; or even 'breathe; screams "I'm 'gonna; 'beat, 'that; 'b*tches; ass!" Candis grabs her and pulls her back saying "that might be his cousin!" "Dummy!" "It fu^k-in; better be!" Yells Naquawna damn near in tears. Naquawna gets a real good look at the girls face as she and Rayshawn are walking out to his car. When Rayshawn gets to his car Naquawna goes back into the party in tears saying to 'Sherry; "let's go!" 'Sherry, looking real confused squawks "what's; wrong?!" After seeing Naquawna fighting back more tears, she cries out "I want to drive by my man's house, to see if this is really his damn; Cousin!" "Who?!" "Who?!" said Sherry and Roxy; simultaneously.

Sherry adds "I thought you said your man was at home? "Apparently; not!" shouts Naquawna. Sherry looks at Candis inquiring she says "what happened with you and Rafee'al?!" Candis's mood drops even further when she says "nothing!" I didn't even get a chance to talk to him." Naquawna closing her eyes, spouts; shit!" "I'm so-- sorry" she said while wiping the running make-up 'off, from under her eyes. Roxy walks them out to the parking lot and before the girls take off, Roxy gives Candis her number saying "let's all do lunch." They both hug and then Roxy hugs Naquawna saying "don't trip!" "It will be alright, chil!" "It's probably just a family member of his" she adds. 'Naquawna nods, with an 'attitude, but still "hopes" that Roxy's right. Mike, is still hanging around, through 'all, of the commotion, and with sympathy for Naquawna he asked Sherry "can I get a ride?" She says "Where too?" He answers "I just live up the hill." Staring at him hard she slowly replies "alright. After thanking her, he jumps in the backseat with Naquawna and puts his arm around her saying "it's gone be alright; home-girl!" Naquawna's drunk, depressed, and sniffling as she's sitting there, letting Mike hold her. Down on her luck she could use the comfort 'even if, it's from someone; she just met.

She tells Sherry "to turn left, up there by the stop sign, and then to make a right, after the light." Once Naquawna says "it's the house on the left, pointing she adds "see, over there, it's the one with the little white fence." Tapping Sherry on the shoulder she says "turn off your lights!" Candis is damn near passed out in the front seat, she burps, then says "are we there; yet?!" Naquawna cracks "shush!" A dog starts barking, and someone emptying the trash yells out "Ringo; be quiet!" Then the old man goes back inside his house and closes his front door. A car comes around the corner and it's Rayshawn. He parks in front of his house and gets out of the car and a girl, that; same girl, from the party gets out the car carrying a plate of food. He had walked around the car to help her by opening up her car door, since her hands were full.

The two walk up to the house and Rayshawn opens the door with his key. Naquawna tries to look inside the house while still ducking down from inside the car but she can't get a good look, so she decides to get out of the car to go get a better look inside his crib. Sherry snaps "you're gonna to get caught!" 'Naquawna, snapping; back shouts "I don't care, if I get caught!" Naquawna is drunk and out of control, so she says "come go with me Candis!" She begs her because she doesn't want to go alone. But Candis is so out of it, she is slurring; every other word. Sherry laughs saying "hell!" "You'll really get busted, taking her with you!"

Naquawna blows out breaths of air through her mouth, trying to get up the courage to get out of the car and go it alone. She spouts "okay!" "Shoot!" "I can do this!" Grabbing the car handle she gets out the car slowly, looking all around to make sure no cars are coming up the street. Grunting she looks back at Mike saying "that's all I 'need, is to get out this car, and get hit by 'car; in front of his house!" The living room window is on the right side of the house and the small kitchen window is on the left, by the garage. She scurries to the window where the kitchen is and as Naquawna is standing underneath the kitchen window to see if she can see through the sheer curtains or hear voices, she ends up hearing a woman's voice say "Ray?" Can you make the baby a bottle; please?"

Then she hears two voices at the front door as it is opening, and an older lady is standing in the doorway with Rayshawn. He says "thanks moms, for watching the baby tonight." Naquawna hurries and 'ducks, behind the garbage cans, which are on the same side as the garage; hoping she won't be seen. But of course that same dog next door starts barking again. She is hoping that once Rayshawn's mom or whoever she is 'leaves, he will stop barking. The lady gets in her car and Rayshawn wave to her, as she drives off.

The girl in the house yells out again "Ray?!" "Did you make the baby's bottle; yet?!" He closes the front door yelling back to her "just a minute!" "I was making sure your God mom, got in her car alright!" Naquawna goes back to the kitchen window 'knowing, now for sure, that he will be in the kitchen making a bottle, so she decides to tap on the window, so he can come outside and talk to her. 'After all, he comes to her kitchen window whenever 'he; feels like it! So she figures; why not do the same to him?"! 'After all, he 'is, her; man! "Right?"! Standing outside the window quietly she looks through the side crack in the curtains and taps softly on the window, but he doesn't hear her, due to the fact that the baby is crying for his bottle, and his cry, is getting even; louder as she taps.

So as Naquawna's getting ready to tap on the window again harder this time 'in walks that girl, his so called "cousin" with the baby in her arms, who looks 'just, like; Rayshawn! And Naquawna couldn't help but notice; that fact! Then the girl grabs the bottle out of Rayshawn's hand, and kisses him on the lips saying "such a good daddy." Naquawna's eyes; grow wide, with a 'gawked, look on her face of "oh! "Hell! "No! 'So disgusted, she turns her back 'to the window, and as the kitchen light goes off, she slides down to the ground because her legs have stopped; holding up her body.

She is so devastated because her worst nightmare has come true! She would have never believed it, if someone had a told her. 'Oh-! 'But wait! 'Someone did tell her, she's quickly reminded as she flashes back, to what Bubba had told her days before. "He was right about Rayshawn all along!" she muttered to herself as she 'sat, on the ground, under his kitchen window; drunk and unable to move. Naquawna's spirit is just; broken! And her heart is shattered into tiny little pieces. The once 'glamorous, golden dress' that she is wearing is now; ruined! It is a 'dirty; mess, of a dress, as she sits there in the 'muck, of his flower bed.

'Now, in her mind, the love that she has for Rayshawn and their future together has turned; into hate! In her drunkenness, she gets to her feet and under her breath through gritted teeth she Gers out words "that son of a b$tch!" "Lied to me!" She wants to bang on his front door so--; badly, and confront his 'ass, for playing her; for a fool! But she knows; he'll probably lie about the whole 'thing; between the two of them; and then side with the 'chick, in the house!

So instead, she decides "okay...! "Okay...! "You wanna play games!" "Let's play!" She runs back to Sherry's car mad as hell voicing "that lying bastard!" She is so mad she ends up chuckling a bit in 'spurts, to keep from crying anymore. With her fists balled up she begins to shake her head side to side trying to be strong, like she's seen people do, in boxing when they are warming up for a fight. Sherry yells "girl! "Forget him! "Let's go! "No!" "Hell...! "No...! "This mother f$#ker is gonna 'feel; me!" She bounces from side to side on each leg like she's about to do a 100 meter dash in thy Olympics. Then looking at Sherry she asked "do you have something sharp, I can use?!" Mike answers "I do!" "I have a small box cutter, like blade, on my key ring" he said pulling out his keys. "It's kind of small though" he adds. 'Sherry; tisk ing says "Mike; don't give her, that!" But it's too late Naquawna snatches it out of Mike's hand and runs up to Rayshawn's Cadillac which is parked in front of his house and scratches the driver's side from the front bumper, to rear bumper. But before she could scratch up the other side of his car, that 'same, 'damn, 'dog, starts barking again and then the neighbor's sensor light comes on. Naquawna gets scared that she might get caught, so as she's ducking down at the rear of his Cadi, she puts a quick; slash in his rear tire and the air starts to seep out.

'Now..., happy with what she just did' she runs and jumps back into the car. Sherry "not; happy" and mad as 'heck, speeds away shouting "you guys; are "not" about to get 'me; a criminal record!" With a shift of her eyes she blurts and "Mike?!" "Where can I 'drop; 'you; off; at?!" Mike is in the backseat; wiling out with Naquawna! Saying, "you are a crazy; ass woman!" "You really did that; Sh*t!" He finishes his sentence with a high five to Naquawna's hand, totally disregarding Sherry question, of "where to 'drop; him off; at?" Mike has Naquawna so hyped; from what she just did, and he 'knows it, so he whispers in her ear "let's finish partying at your house."

Naquawna all 'stoked, from the adrenaline running through her veins tells Sherry "Mike's coming home with us." Candis is missing everything that is going on because she is still passed out in the front seat. Sherry can't say if Mike 'can, or 'cannot, go over to Candis's house and Naquawna is using that to her advantage. Not amused Sherry rolls her eyes over at Naquawna saying "is Candis going to be cool with that?!" "You know how she is about just having "anybody" over her house!" "No offence; Mike!" said Sherry. He grins back "no problem. "It's cool" he said while rubbing on Naquawna's arm. They pull up to Candis's place and Mike and Sherry help to get Candis out of the car and into the house. After Sherry gets Candis's shoes off she lays her in her bed with her clothes; still on. Than Sherry closes her bedroom door and walks back into the living room where

Mike and Naquawna are in the kitchen drinking on some left over gin and juice. Sherry shakes her head saying "Naquawna?!" "Let me talk to you for a minute." She walks with Sherry to the front door and Sherry inquires "are you sure you can trust this dude?" Naquawna; slouching answers "yes. "He's cool. "Plus, we have a mutual friend that works with me at the shop." "I found that out from 'Mike, when he and I were talking at the table tonight." "He knows, Sang Lee, which is my boss's son." "They play in a band together and Mike is the bass player" said Naquawna; barely standing straight. Naquawna pleads her case by finishing up her statement with "he would have never even gotten in the 'car, if I didn't think that he was cool!" "I put that on everything I love!" Sherry smirks, voicing "okay!" "You just explain it to Candis when she wakes up!" "I 'won't, be blamed for this one!" Sherry throws her hands up saying "bye. And walks out the front door to her car.

Naquawna watches her drive away and closes the front door. Mike is on the couch drinking his drank saying to Naquawna "you are nuts!" "That man is gonna kill 'you, when he finds out what you did to his car!" "Boy..., please...!" said Naquawna. "He won't even know it was me, because I was at Candis's house all night kicking it; doing her hair and my car was outside to prove it!" "Which I'm 'sure, he drove by to check and see if I was really over here because he's sneaky like that!" Mike just laughs saying "what did he possibly; do?!" "For you to key up his car and pop his tire; yo!" "He lied to me!" she said. "He told me he lived with his cousin!" "And said that he didn't have a child!" "But that baby looked just like him!" she slurred.

Mike starts to write with an imaginary pen and a pad voicing "note to self; never lie to Naquawna!" He blurts out a big laugh, but Naquawna doesn't laugh back, instead she stand there looking at him 'not, amused; which makes him turn serious. He clears his throat saying "naw--. "But for real; for real?"! "And he has a kid too?!" he said while shaking his head. He takes another drink of his gin; juice and with a wink of his eye he smiles saying "you'll be aight!"

Mike has always been a really good listener. He lets Naquawna get all of her frustrations out about Rayshawn and while talking she even tells Mike "that Rayshawn's "lucky" 'that's; "all" she did to his car!" Adding "she should have popped all four of his tires and busted out his head lights, like Carrie Underwood sings about in her video!" Naquawna then sings part of the song to him, voicing "maybe next; time, he'll think; before he... cheats...!" Then she slams back another drink because she's so... damn; mad! And she keeps expressing just 'how; mad, she feels to Mike.

And as the minutes go bye; 'downing, drink; after drink, she is hoping to numb her broken heart, but it just makes her sadder and sadder to talk about it anymore. He encourages her "not" to worry about it, as he puts his hand on top of her hand stating "he doesn't deserve you anyway!" Naquawna cracks a sad smile at him while they sit on the couch side by side together.

Not only has Mike always been a good listener but he has always been the type of guy that girls could always talk to "especially" when they're having; "men problems"! To some women he is a great shoulder to cry on, but on the flip side, some think he's "too; nice!" for a long term boyfriend. But, Mike doesn't care what they think, because at the end of the day, he always seems to end up getting 'laid, for his "love" counseling; advice! I guess you could say he doesn't mind having a little "rebound; sex"!

Mike sit there talking to her as she is going more and more into a drunken, depressed; stage in her high. And when she starts back up with her tears dripping down her face, like a faucet. She sits there crying to Mike asking him, "why would he do me like this?!" "I thought he really loved me!" "But now I see that he has a family...!" "And a kid...!" "What if he's married?!" she shouted; crying even harder.

Mike puts his arm around her saying "some dudes are just 'players, and cheater!" He turns her face so she can look him in his eyes and he says "look at you." "You are a beautiful, independent woman, and 'dude, just couldn't see a good thing, when she was standing right there in front of him!" "But I can!" He takes her by the hand saying "I knew, you were special, the first time I laid eyes on you!" "And trust me, I would 'never, make the mistake he 'did, and lose you; if you we're my woman!" Naquawna looks up at him and smiles as she listens to his comforting words.

With an eye full of tears she leans over and puts her head on his shoulder and cries in his arms. Caressing her he puts his arm around her and kisses her forehead. She turns her head up to look in his eyes again and then he kisses her as tears are streaming down her cheeks. They start to make out on the couch rush-fully, and then 'Mike, being the good guy that he is, pulls back and holds her by her shoulders rubbing down her arms he says "Naquawna?" I don't want you to do anything you might regret tomorrow." 'Huffing; she snares and gathers herself then voices "the only thing I regret!" Is getting involved with that lying; bastard!" She gets up off the couch tugging at her dress; fixing it as she goes to turn on the radio, while kicking off her heels in a huff. After finding a good station she tip-toes; tipsily down the hallway to go get a sheet and a blanket from the hall closet. Walking back to where he is, she throws the blanket and the sheet down on the couch saying "you can sleep on the recliner!" "I've got the couch." She dims the lights and lays her head back on the back end of the couch, while listening to the slow groove music that is playing on the radio. Mike lays his head back next to hers, while listening to the tunes as well, as he talks to her; periodically about being with a real brother like him. Turning her head to look up at him she smiles, saying "I'm so glad I met you tonight." Mike puts his hand on her leg returning "I'm glad I met you too." He leans over and kisses her softly.

It is a slow groove night and a slow song starts to play, and it's a good one. It's a song by R. Kelly called: Bump N' Grind. And it's Mike's favorite song. But all she can think about is; Rayshawn! Even, after he played her, like a fiddle! Mike can tell that she's thinking of her ex, but he's relentless in winning her over, so he gets up off the couch and ask her to dance, while doing a cute little strip show for her as he unbuttons his shirt. He sings to her using this moment to get her to laugh. Grinning she gets up off the couch and he helps her by pulling her up by her hand, while singing parts of the song to her. The two dance a sweet friendship dance and as he holds her even closer he whispers sweet things in her ear.

Mike is 'really, having a nice time with Naquawna and as she holds him tight, he dips her back as the song ends. When the song is over, the DJ says a few words and then an advertisement comes on about some, window cleaner. She is still 'sad-dish, when they stop dancing, but as Mike is holding her by both her hands and looking into her eyes she starts to feel like there is hope in her moving forward; 'thinking; that there 'is, someone who likes her too. 'Until--, another beautiful song starts to play and this one is a doozey; 'because this one, is the one her and Rayshawn made love too in his car. It's by: Switch, called "Love Over And Over Again!"

With a deep sigh she just breaks down sobbing when she hears the music start up. He holds her close but all she can do is think about Rayshawn and how much she really needs him right now, as she's standing there with Mike in her 'golden, dirty; dress. Mike seeing the hurt on her face, kisses her; repeatedly. He starts to hope that it is 'him, she'll want, as he's listening to the song with her. So that's when Mike 'purposely, makes her fill wanted, and needed as the two hold on to each other; kissing in the living room, in the low light. He takes it even further when he feels that she is 'precipitating, what he is doing to her as he licks up her chest where her dress slits up the front revealing her cleavage. Softly he bites on top of her dress through her bra and she starts to cringe; with excitement, to every nibble of his teeth. Grabbing her by her neck he kisses her some more saying softly on her lips "can I make love to you?" she mumbles softly the word "what...?" because he's still kissing her. And he keeps kissing her as he tries to undo his belt. She sighs "I don't know, Mike." He begs her "please!" Naquawna glares at him because she feels so 'vulnerable, tonight. So while she's still staring; up at him, she says "I'm not on the pill." "And I haven't got a condom." He says "no worries. "I have a condom we can use. He grabs the blanket and the sheet from off the couch and throws them both down on the floor 'as if, he's making a bed. And when he gets down on one knee he takes a condom out of his back pocket and tells Naquawna "to come lay with him, on the blanket, on the floor, behind the couch."

Naquawna is still so angry about the whole night and wants to say "no, to him!" and to all men, from here on out! But her 'devious, mind is telling her "to go ahead, and do; it!" Along with her inner voice; concurring "that Rayshawn is 'probably; screwing that girl tonight in his house!" "So, why not?!" She kneels down behind the couch as her and Mike stare at each other on their knees. He says "are you sure you're okay with this?" she mumbles to him at first. Then she says "yes!" I'm sure!" She sounded more; angrier then willing, like it was because of what "Rayshawn" was 'making; her do; out of spite! He takes her by the hand and he pulls her down on the floor to lie beside him. Then he starts again to kiss her all down the front of her dress as he's pulling the dress down slowly from off of her body.

The song is almost towards the end as he's pulling down her undergarments on his knees kissing and sucking all on her melons while he's pulling down his pants and putting on the condom. He caresses her body slowly to the music and as she closes her eyes moaning to his touch, he slides his 'wet Willy, inside of her; excitedly! 'She moans, as he 'drifts, into the moment with; excitement! And as for him he grinds it out, as she drifts into a deep; fantasy, where it was all just a bad dream, and her and her lover 'Rayshawn, are now making; passionate love to one another, while the song is climbing up to the bridge playing (why don't you love me, love me; love me, love me, over and over again)! She moans; so loudly and in her 'own; 'minds; 'belief, as she sings some of the words in Mike's ear, she believes in her mind 'it to be, "Rayshawn" that she is making love too; in the dark; of the night; in the living room, behind the couch.

Mike ends up slipping out of her body, momentarily because he is so turned on by all of her sexual movements around his "Junk"! Then before entering back inside her, he thinks to himself; f*ck it! And he takes off the condom and puts his throbbing head back inside of her, without her even noticing. She is so far within her pleasure until she starts to lift her legs straight up in the air, bending her knees and as her back starts to arch from all of the releasing power going through her body she 'shakes, uncontrollably and 'cums, with 'every; 'last; 'bit; of her being!

He gives her a passionately long kiss as he's 'Cumming, to his; climax, right after hers. She passes out underneath him from drunken; exhaustion and he rolls off of her and covers her up with the sheet. He watches her sleep momentarily and then he falls asleep lying next to her. A loud cranking sound starts to play when Candis's cell phone alarm goes off at 7:00 o'clock in the morning. "Awe...!" Man...!" she says all; groggy. Candis is "not; happy" having been woken up from her slumber. It's kind of her fault though because she forgot to disarm her alarm for the weekend and now she is so-o-o..., so-o-o hung-over right now. Crawling out of her bed slowly she puts one hand on her forehead and groans, as she's starting to walk towards the kitchen to go get a drink of water.

When she gets to the living room she sees Naquawna's purse but no Naquawna. So now she wonders if she left with Rayshawn in the middle of the night and forgot her purse. She yells out "Naquawna?!" are you still here?!" A guy's voice answers "what?!" And it's coming from behind the couch so she jumps and lets out a quick; scream before seeing that it is Mike. "What the hell?!" she yells. Then she hurries back to her room to get her robe on because she was only in her bra and panties. Pissed she comes back into the living room yelling "what the hell; is going on?!" Naquawna now awoke and looking confused blurts out "what; happen?!" Asking "what are you still doing here Mike?!" "I thought Sherry dropped you off?" Candis just stands there in disbelief that her 'best friend, is on the floor "butt-naked" behind her couch with some dude she just met last night! "And--, he's, in, "her" apartment!" 'Although; "typical" for Naquawna to do a one night; stand! "But damn...! "In her house!" thinks Candis as she stares at her.

Naquawna becomes; stagnant because she knows that look on Candis's face means; that she's about to go; off! Mike starts to see that the girls are about to get into a heated argument so he grabs the blanket and his clothes to cover himself and heads towards the bathroom to get dressed, while the back of his rear is 'exposed, as he's walking past Candis. Naquawna wraps herself in the sheet that's left on the floor and stands up to face Candis who is shouting "come! "On! "Quawna! "Really?"! "What the hell were you thinking?"! "Umm... Naquawna replied slowly. Candis shakes her head saying "I can't believe you let a stranger stay here!" "What if he came in my room and raped me and killed us both?!" Naquawna just puts her head down answering "I know--?!" but he's not like that!" "How do you know what he's like?!" "You just met him last night!" And we know how your track record is; on that; shit!" Naquawna frowns "he is my boss's son's; best friend!" Candis yells "so!" That still makes him a strange to you!" "Did you have sex with him; too?!" Naquawna pauses looking confused but answers "no!" But Candis is not convinced, so she looks at her and smirks out "and you know Rayshawn is gonna find out, because this town is only so big!"

Naquawna puts her middle finger up saying "f*ck!" Rayshawn!" He's a lying dog; anyway!" "Besides, I only "slept" with Mike on the floor! "We, did not, do anything, but talk all night!" "Then why are your clothes off?" asked Candis. Before Naquawna could answer, Mike comes out of the bathroom with the blanket all folded up and tries to give it to Candis. Not wanting to touch it, she refuses it saying "just put it over there on the floor." Mike says "thanks for letting me sleep over; preciate it!" Naquawna says nothing. So he says "I'm gonna head out now." I'll be seeing yaw'll on the flipside" he said throwing up a peace sign. He gives Naquawna one last look saying "it was fun." "Hit me up later" he adds. Naquawna smiles saying "okay. "Bye, Mike. He leaves out the house and Naquawna voices "see?!" "I told you, we didn't do anything but sleep!" Candis still staring at Naquawna with a sarcastic 'disbelieving look on her face says "girl, you don't have to lie to me!"

"How was it?!" "How was what?!" shouts Naquawna with a bewildered, look on her face. "I was drunk!" He was drunk!" And we passed out, with our clothes off because it was hot up in here last night!" Don't you think, I would remember 'if I slept with him or not?!" Candis just laughs while she's pouring herself a bowl of Lucky Charms cereal saying "you don't have to lie; to kick it!" And with a bite of her cereal she adds "well, at least you were on the floor and not on my good furniture!" Naquawna, getting madder, yells "we! "Didn't! "Do; anything!

Just as she was voicing out those words Candis spots something behind the couch as she's walking passed Naquawna who is still standing there by the edge of the coffee table in a sheet. It looks like a bag of weed so Candis reaches down to pick it up, but then she sees that it's a used rubber with a knot on the end of it. After picking it up she drops it back on the floor yelling "Oooooh! "Gross! Naquawna gasped while looking back at Candis with her mouth wide open and with both hands over her mouth. "That, is not; mine!" shouted Naquawna. "He, must have jacked off or something!"

Candis looks at her like she's crazy as 'hell, if she 'thinks; that she 'thinks; that he would use a "condom" to rub his own; d*ck!" Candis; cracks on her saying "bi$ch!" "Yaw; did the nasty!" "And you don't even remember because you were just that; drunk!" Naquawna 'now, speechless just stares at Candis hoping it would jog her memory but then she still ends up; insisting "that it never happened!" Candis chuckles at her, and starts walking towards the kitchen sink to wash her hands. Afterwards when she goes back to sitting down on the couch she can barely eat the rest of her cereal. 'Naquawna, still denying the sex with 'Mike, picks up the rubber with two fingers and throws it into the trash. 'Totally, embarrassed she goes to the bathroom to get dressed and notices something running down the inside of her legs. "Yuk!" she spouts. Then she gets into the shower. The house phone rings and Candis being too tired to get up to get it, lets the answering machine pick it up. It's her mom saying "baby, you on your way over to the house?" she adds "the Junk Haller people will be here by 11:00 o'clock, see you in a few!"

"F*ck...!" yells Candis. Naquawna opens up the bathroom door shouting "what...?"! Thinking that Candis has found something 'else, her and Mike had left. "I forgot, I have to help my mom clean out her garage today!" "Oh..., sighs Naquawna relieved it had nothing to do with her and Mike. "Do you want me to go with you?" "Then we can get some lunch afterwards." Candis grimacing says "don't even try and be all-- nice; now"! "I'm still mad at you, for bringing; some "punk" over to my house that we "both" didn't even, know!" Naquawna grits out "I said, I was sorry!" Then she closes the bathroom door to finish up getting showered, and dressed.

When finished dressing she goes back out to the living room where Candis is and gives her a puppy dog eyed; look saying "I'm sorry!" "I was just so upset about Rayshawn last night and all the lies he told me." Candis says "I know, I vaguely remember but I think you messed up his car; badly!" "What?!" gags Naquawna. Saying "I did?!" "Yes, you did!" said Candis, stating; "I, know; I--, was tore; up!" "But you; were really--, tow-up!" because you went "ballistic" on that boy's, Cadillac!"

"Oh, my, God!" "That's right!" said Naquawna pressing her hands on each side of her face remembering; bits and pieces from last night. "Dammit!" he is going to be; pissed!" "He loves that car." "Oh well!" said Candis as she puts her empty cereal bowl in the sink. She then shrugs saying "but he knows you were at my house all night anyway." "So don't even trip!" she adds as she grabs a big glass of water. After downing her water she tells Naquawna "let's get ready to go to my mom's, so we can get this junk packed up, and over with!" Naquawna is still very upset about what she did to Rayshawn's 'car, even 'though, he "deserved; it!" in her eyes. But still she felt 'bad, because in her 'mind, she was not trying to be a heartless person. And to make her thoughts even 'worse, her mind is thinking; that she really "did" sleep with; Mike! Especially after seeing the "lubricants" running down her inner thighs. 'Furthermore, if they "did" do it! More than likely he "didn't" use a condom! Which makes her also very upset with herself for even going to such links. In her disappointment as she's looking at herself in the mirror applying her lipstick she 'vows, to "never" tell Candis this terrible mistake she made with Mike!

In the hallway, Candis is huffing out a sad song with a towel in her hand walking towards the bathroom to go take a shower. When she gets out of the shower and gets dressed she still looks like 'who; did it?!" And what for?!" She throws a girly baseball hat on 'Giants, and puts her hair in a ponytail. She even tries to fix 'two, slept on curls that have lost their luster on each side of her face, but to no avail. Yelling to Naquawna from the bathroom she shouts "you ready?!" "Yess, I, am!" returns Naquawna, looking at herself one last time in the mirror in her new Jeans. She only wishes Rayshawn could see her in them, because she 'knows, how much he loves to see her body, in a great pair of jeans. 'Thinking; back, if 'only, he would have picked her up last night before all this stuff went down, things would be different. 'And also, she wishes, she could turn back the hands of time, on what happened to his car. She looks at Candis saying "but, it is; what it is"!

Candis grabs her keys and Naquawna says "I'll follow you in my car, so I can go home after we finish up at your mom's house and eat lunch." Candis agrees saying "that's a good idea, then the girls get in their own cars and head to Candis's 'mom's house. On the way to the house Naquawna calls Candis right before they get on the highway on her cell phone saying "chil..., I might not make it to lunch." "So why don't we pull into that 'bugger; King, up the way real quick?!" Candis; smelling the grilled; goodness in thy air 'concurs, so they stop and get a small burger. They both go through the drive through still talking on speaker phone about last night 'laughing, about how Candis still can't seem to get the digits from 'Rafee'al. And how Naquawna and Rayshawn's 'drama, messed up her action with the man of her dreams last night!

Naquawna laughs back "you were way too drunk, to go over and ask him for his number anyways!" "So don't blame me for all of it, because you're the one who asked 'me, to go with you!" She finalizes her comment with "see, you should have done it, when you had the chance." Candis yelps out "what-evah!" "Mike"! Naquawna laughs back saying "that's not my, man!" They leave out of the drive-through with their burgers in hand, and while eating on their flame broiled burgers they hurry to Candis's mom's place talking and laughing on speaker phone all the way there about what she is going to do “next” to Rayshawn!

Chapter 7

'**Now--;** way-- over yonder on the other side of town at Rayshawn's house, it is a typical morning. The baby is up first, playing in his crib, and he has now, found out how fun his feet are, as he commits to sucking on his little toes. Rayshawn wakes up next because he is going to go play some basketball with some of the guy down at the gym. He goes to check on his baby and looks down at him in his crib smiling he says "hey little man, how you doing this morning?"! Seeing that little Ray is happily playing in his crib and his diaper is still dry, Rayshawn decides to get in the shower and let Se'anna sleep a little longer.

It is a beautiful sunny day in Treeberry Bay, and Rayshawn is now taking a long hot shower. The water runs down the top of his head and the steam slowly fogs up the bathroom shower's glass doors. He stands underneath the shower's nozzle as the water falls down on his head and passed his muscular chest to his most private'est parts. With water splashing his face he grabs the soap and lathers up from head to toe, while rubbing his body down with soap, until he's nice and clean. Rayshawn has one of those beautifully 'sculptured, body's, that just 'glistens, whenever it's wet or doused with oil.

His big arms are perfectly shaped on his strong physic, and his muscular legs look like he's ran in a few marathons. You can't help but think to yourself when you see him 'naked; that "(God)" is "truly" an artist! Rayshawn's body is all-- 'muscle, no, 'fat; 'lean, kind of like; "Superman's; body"! But not the one you've seen, in the comic books. This 'body, is like the "Supermen" you've seen in the NBA; the Slam Dunk; Contests! And 'even, in the NFL!"

Yes..., Rayshawn is 'so, the ladies, man and all the girls want to have a chance with him. With his nice brown eyes and his beautiful smile its hard "not" to see 'why, they "wouldn't" want to get; at him! And he knows it! 'But, being a "player" 'always, comes with some risks! And Rayshawn is going to see those "risk" first hand.

He gets out of the shower nice and fresh and brushes his teeth with the towel still wrapped around his waist. As he drops the towel on the bathroom floor he heads to the room to get dressed. Se'anna turns over when she hears the closet door slide open and she asked "are you going to go play ball?" "Yeah" he says. "I'll be back later." "Little Ray is up, but he's cool, he's playing in his crib" he said, zipping up his pants. "Okay, good" she replied and rolls back over to get a few more minutes of sleep before the baby starts crying for some milk. Rayshawn kisses her bye and slips out the front door with an apple, and a Gatorade drink in hand. He gets to his car, and his lip, just; drop! His half eaten apple gets thrown across the street as he's rushing up to his car. He is furious, and all he can do is 'curse, as he's looking at his car on a rear flat. But when he sees the scratch from one end of his car, to the other, he yells out even more; curse words!

Pacing back and forth he tries to figure out "who?" would do something like this to his car!" And for what reason?!" 'Of course, Naquawna and a few other girls comes to mind. But then he remembers Naquawna was at Candis's house all night and she wasn't mad at him when he seen her earlier, yesterday. His other females had no beef with him either as far as he could tell. This car; destruction; situation has him 'stumped, and with his fists on fire he goes into a rage! He knows it couldn't be a 'dude, over dope or money! "This is some shit; chicks do; for sure!" he mumbles.

Then there's 'Se'anna, which really gives him anxiety. How is he going to go back into the house and tell 'her, about; the car?!" 'Knowing; she is going to flip; out! So to ease his mind he calls one of his boys and tells him what has happened to his car and he ends up coming over with the tow truck. Luckily, Se'anna is still asleep and not in the kitchen, where she could see what is going on, right about now. Ernesto gets to the house in 15 minutes or so and puts the car up on the lift, and he and Rayshawn take off to Ernesto's shop where they fix the flat tire.

The whole time Rayshawn's mind is churning as he tries to think up an elaborate scheme to call his insurance company from the mall, saying "someone has vandalized his car." And since 'it's--, fully insured, it should, be covered. Ernesto laughs asking "what did you do; bro?!" "To piss off those women of yours?" Rayshawn shaking his head answers "man--, I don't know who-o--; did this sh*t!" "Because all of my hoes are cool with me right now!" "So you think; bro!" spouts Ernesto. "Somebody's not happy with you dude!" "You know how these women are, they find out sh*t and make you "think" it's all good!" "And then when you least expect it, they 'snap; on your ass!"

Rayshawn rubs his hands together, listening to what his friend is spitting to him and realizes he could be right. "Maybe somebody does--, know something" he tells Ernesto. With new thoughts in his head and his flat tire fixed he gives Ernesto a hand shake and a half hug saying "thanks man for coming through!" "I owe you; real talk!" Ernesto replies "it's all good!" "Just hit me up, when you; re-up on that herb!" "Know dought!" smiles Rayshawn adding "now, I'm off to the mall to work out my plan, so Se'anna won't blame 'me, for the car!" "I'll just tell her, I was going to buy her something at the mall after I left the gym" he said chuckling all happy about his plan. Ernesto laughs saying "aw--, man--!" "Will she believe that dude?!" "Hell, yeah!" "Remember, it's almost Christmas time!" "And she 'loves, gifts; so she'll believe it!" laughs Rayshawn as he gives him dap and gets into his car; heading to the mall.

Mean-time Candis and Naquawna pull up to Candis's mom's house eating what's left of their King Burgers. The girls get out of the car and go into the garage which is already open and looking like 'stuff, has been moved around already. She hollers out for her mom asking "where you at maw?!" "Naquawna and I are here!" Then in comes Candis's brother to greet them in front of the garage, doorway. "Hey, sis!" he says all smiles. "Hey, yourself bro." "When did you get back?" she said surprised. "And how was your "business" trip?!" she adds with a chuckle. Even Naquawna snorted out a laugh to the joke. "Funny!" cracks Marvin. Candis grinning blurts out "but let me tell you something that might not "be" too funny!" "Which is, when you 'gone, run me my money?!"

But before Marvin could reply, in walks Dianna saying "what money?!" The room filled with chuckles and laughter goes quiet; quickly! "Oh...!" "Hey---, Sis!" "I didn't know you were here" says Candis. "Sis, is what Candis always calls Marvin's "wife" too be. And she really 'does, like Dianna and doesn't want to hurt her by telling on her brother, so Candis just says "oh, me and Marv had a bet going on; on the game." "Oh, really?" said Dianna. "And what game was that?!" she said as she turned her attention towards Marvin. Candis has to think fast so she looks at Marvin for help, but he is stuck on stupid, so she just belts out "the Laker game!" "And he lost!" "So he owes me some money!" "Where's mom?!" says Candis quickly as she walks past Dianna so she won't have to keep; lying to her! "Mom...!" yells Candis walking down towards the hallway.

"When Candis gets to the doorway of her mother's bedroom she asked "what are you doing mom?!" Her mom is making up her bed when she looks at Candis with her face turn't up replying "what does it look like I'm doing Candis?!" Candis, holding back some rude thoughts, instead says "mom, why didn't you tell me that Marvin was here to help you clear out the garage too?!" "I could have stayed in my bed" she complained. "Well... if you must know?!" "After I called you and left you a message on your phone and you never called me back!" "I called your brother to see if he could help me but sometimes he is so; unreliable, so I just waited to see which one of you would show up first!" "And I'm glad to see that you both came, so we can hurry up and get this done!" laughs her mother with an (I tricked you both) smile on her face. While she's hanging up a few more shirts in her closet she smiles voicing "thank you dear." Candis can't believe she got played by her own mother. She walks off saying "you ain't right; maw!" Mumbling she says as she's walking away "I could be in my bed right now catching up on my; sleep!" She goes back to the garage where all the work is almost done. The Junk Haler guys are putting stuff on the truck, and Candis's mom comes outside when Marvin yell's for her to come see if she wants them to take both of the lamps or just the one. Naquawna is so glad to see that they are not going to have to do too much more work because now she has a major headache. Candis is on the same page 'even though, she didn't really...; do any work at all either. Candis looks over at Naquawna who is hunched over on the washing machine looking through her phone and says "honey, I am gonna need some hangover food, where are we going for lunch?" Naquawna looks up from her phone with a grunt thinking the same thing when Candis adds "that little burger didn't do nothing; but make my stomach; mad"! They both laugh then Naquawna says "what about the (All You Can Eat Buffet)?" "We can hit them up right before lunch ends, that way we can get dinner too, at the lunch price!" They both give each other a high five cheering "right?"!

Marvin and Dianna over hear the conversation so Dianna says to Marvin "let's go too!" "We haven't been to the Buffet in a long time and I could really go for some of their fried chicken." "It is; the bomb!" Marvin hesitates at first because he doesn't want Candis and Naquawna to start clowning on him in front of Dianna and slip up about the "stripper" jail; incident! So he says "I don't know babe." "I'm really not that hungry." Naquawna smiles over at Marvin saying "they'll have your favorite "chicken; strips"! And then she and Candis busted up laughing. Marvin says "see, yaw'll be on some dumb, stuff!" "And I don't have time for them games!

He looks at Dianna complaining "see, that's why I don't want to go with them!" Dianna gives him her pouty-ous lips saying "I'm starving, and you said after we helped mom clear out the garage, we would go to a place of my choice to eat!" "I even skipped breakfast, so I could throw down for lunch!" "Come on babe!" she begs. Candis mumbles under her breath, so only Naquawna can hear her say "I bet if we were going to Hooter's, he'd be hungry!" "No girl, he would be starving; then!" laughed Naquawna. They both laugh 'hardily, out loud and Dianna with a 'glazed, look in her eyes, smiled asking "what's so funny?!" "I want in on the joke too!" Marvin just glares at the two of them as if to say "keep playing here!" Which makes Candis laughs out "oh--, Marv..., we are just getting laughs off of the Junk hauler guys." But she just 'had, to crack one more joke. "I wonder if they take; tips?" says Candis. Grinning she asked Naquawna "do you have some dollar bills on you?" "So we can make it; rain on um!" Candis and Naquawna laugh so hard until they are in tears. Marvin can't help but grin as he tries to hold back his own laugh because even though he knows 'the joke is on him; it is still; pretty funny! Marvin's mom pays the Junk Hauler guys their money for taking all of her old stuff away, while Candis is sweeping up the rest of the sand, the paper, and pieces of broken glass left behind on the garage floor. She felt she had to 'at least, do something, since she came all the way over to the house. Her thought process 'was, even if she didn't help with the sorting of the junk in the garage she "did" do a small part by sweeping up.

Naquawna on the other hand didn't do much of 'anything, but stand around. And being that she feels like she is family, makes her comfortable enough to go into the kitchen's refrigerator and get herself a drink of orange juice, saying to Candis's mom "her sugar is getting low." After her drink she gives Candis's mom a hug good-bye and she goes outside to sits in her car. It is so hot outside so she leaves the car door open and sits with one leg hanging out. While sitting there she checks her cell phone to see if there's a call from Rayshawn. But no, and no text either. "Figures!" she says as she tosses her phone on to the dash board of her car.

Then she remembers she better call home to check on granddad. He picks up the phone and sounds fine so she tells him she will bring him home some food, so not to cook anything. Candis finishes up with the trash she swept up and then goes to ask her mom "if she wants to go eat with her, Marvin, Naquawna and Dianna, at the buffet?" But her mom says "no. "And that she is going to go to Beverly's to get some fabric so she can make some new kitchen drapes." Candis retorts "mom--, you can get that on the way back." "Come on, you got to eat something!" Her mom with a shake of her head says "maybe next time, you young folks go on ahead and go." "I've already planned out my day and I want to get these drapes done before Thanksgiving" she said clutching her wallet and keys.

Candis gives her mom a hug and so does Marvin and Dianna and they head out to their cars. Marvin blurts out "this is crazy!" "We are all taking separate cars". "No. "We all just have 'stuff to do, after we get done eating!" answered Candis. Marvin and Dianna get into the same car and Candis and Naquawna follow them to the Buffet in their own cars. Now, mind you, Candis and Naquawna are hung-over and looking a "hot mess!" Still cute, but not presentable enough to meet any cute guys. They finally get to the Buffet and can't; wait, to get in the door and eat. When they walk up to the door there's a long line but its moving fast. After standing in the line for a few and smelling all the food Marvin 'now, is talking about "how hungry he is!" 'Smiling, Dianna says "see-- aren't you glad we came?" "I got you!" she says kissing him softly. She adds "I know exactly what you need, even when 'you, don't know it!" she said as she gives him another kiss.

Naquawna and Candis are standing behind the two when they kiss so Naquawna pulls out a dollar bill and waves it so only Candis can see it; saying "I know 'exactly, what he needs too!" They both snicker; quietly with laughter so Marvin won't get so--, upset; thinking they're talking about him 'again, even though; they were! Naquawna says "Marvin, has got 'such, a complex!" laughs Naquawna under her breath.

The line moves up further and they finally get up to the counter to pay for their meals. Candis says "Marv, you treat-in?!" "Remember--; our bet?!" He looks back at Candis and rolls up his eyes saying "damn!" "You are milk-in, it!" Then he looks at Naquawna voicing "but I ain't treating you though!" "That's okay!" smirked Naquawna. "I got my own money!" she adds. "Good!" said Marvin. "Now let's go throw down!" he urged on. They get a booth that seats four people and then everybody scatters in all directions to get their plates filled.

When Candis gets back to the table she has her plate stacked with all kinds of delicious foods. On one side of her plate she has a salad fully loaded. And on the other side she has pasta with meat sauce and corn. She even waited for people to move out of her way to made sure... not to forget her three pieces of chicken; "wings" to be exact! Last to hit her plate was the 'faunally, a big warm dinner roll and on top of it, was a big dollop of garlic butter. Candis sits down at the table, and with her eyes closed she takes a big bit of the bread as the garlic butter is melting into it. Smiling because it's so yummy, she doesn't care that the butter is all over her mouth as she licks it off moaning happily and then her phone rings. It's Jason. "He must be back from Napa" she thinks to herself. She answers her phone saying "hey babe, you back?" "Yep. "I just got back this morning."

Naquawna gets back to the table with her plate filled to the rim, too. When she sits down she looks at Candis crazy when she hears her say "yeah, me and Naquawna are at the Buffet eating with my brother and his woman." 'Naquawna, mouths the words "who is that?" Candis covers the phone saying "Jason. Marvin and Dianna joyfully get back to the table and now it's getting a little too crowded. No elbow room to eat comfortably, so

Candis and Naquawna move over to the next table across from Marvin and Dianna. “How rude is that Candis?!” states Dianna. Candis returns “sorry, sis!” “But, I got ta’ take this call and I can’t do it all cramped up with everybody listen to my conversation.”

Dianna looks at Candis with a sour face as she takes a bite of her chicken, and it tasted so ‘good, that Dianna was ‘over, the fact that Candis had moved to another table. Jason asked “did you hear about what happened to Rayshawn’s car?” Candis blurts out “no! “What happen?”! She looks at Naquawna with an ‘awe; shit, look on her face then puts the phone on speaker but just low enough for her and Naquawna to hear.

Jason tells her how Rayshawn’s car was on two flats and all scratched up from the front to the rear of his car.” Candis plays like she is ‘surprised, when she tells Naquawna what Jason has just told her. Naquawna yells out “what?!” “Who would do something like that?!” “And why?!” she retorted ‘holding; back, her laugh. Candis chimes in saying “I know, that’s messed up!” She adds “where’s Rayshawn at now?” “I don’t know” said Jason, but we’re supposed to hook up later”. But of course he was ‘lying, because Rayshawn was listening on speaker phone right next to him as well, trying to narrow down which one of his broads messed up his car. Candis asked “is he going to be able to get it fixed?” “I think so” said Jason. “That is unbelievable!” said Naquawna in the background. Jason returns “alright than, I’ll let you get back to enjoying your meal, but call me later.” Candis replies “okay. “Later.

When she hangs up the phone she says “Oooooh…!” “Something is up!” “He never acts like that when I talk to him” said Candis. “I bet you Rayshawn was standing right there, because I could tell by the way he was talking to me that ‘someone, was telling him what to say!” “I know. “Huh?!” said Naquawna. She adds “should I call Rayshawn and act like it’s all good?” “Or wait to see if he calls me first?” “Yeah---. “When you get home, text him and say “hey, baby.” “Jason told us your car got broken into!” “That should ‘really, throw him off the trail!” said Candis. “Plus, did you hear Jason say, he had “two” flat tires?!” said Naquawna. “Now, you ‘know, that was a lie” she added. “They were probably trying to see if we would slip up and say ‘no, it was just one tire”.

The girls finished up their first plate of food and head back for seconds while talking about Rayshawn’s car. Dianna and Marvin were already done with their second plate and had moved on to desert. Candis is laughing hard over by the food section because she got the last two wings out of the pan before Naquawna did, and they were practically; fighting over it! Then, Candis glances up and a nice light brown image comes into view out of the side of her right eye. The brown image walks up to her saying "you two look like you were about to 'scrap, over those two pieces of chicken!" And like a Halo with a beam of 'light, over and around his head she looks up and sees that it is Rafee'al and she 'almost; drops, her plate, on the floor. Candis is so embarrassed at what he has probably just seen, which is the two of them fighting over the last two chicken wings, and laughing like two female inmates. She thinks to herself 'how ghetto was; that?!"

But then she manages to pull it together saying "um. "We get a little 'crazy, when we're hung-over!" 'Implying, that they "normally" don't act like this! Or, look this bad, on a normal day. He laughs saying "it cool. "I'm a little hung-over myself, that's why me and my cousin snuck over here to eat, so my auntie wouldn't be offended, if we didn't go eat at the Restaurant." Smiling he adds "being, that we are a little 'pasta-ed, out!" "I hear you" she said as she gives him a warm smile back.

And then here..., comes..., Jasmine "hey, Candis!" she says. "Hey, Jasmine" said Candis back. "Your party was off the hook, last night!" "I know, right?!" said Jasmine with a proud, cocky; smile. Naquawna has filled her plate back up and glances back at Candis with a 'work; it 'girl!" grin on her face as she walks back to the table, so Rafee'al and Candis can continue talking.

But Jasmine on the other hand, was being a cock; blocker! She stayed by her cousin the whole time Candis was there talking to him. Then Rafee'al glared at her; saying "Jaz! "I'll meet you back at the table" and he gives her the eye like; scram! Jasmine gives him a look back like "I know you are not trying to get at her?"! Then she turns and walks away smirking out; "whatever! 'Candis, now... having no reason at; all--- to eat anymore, just looks up into his beautiful eyes through the top of her shades. He beams when looking back at her, then says "would you like to hang out, or go to a movie sometimes?" Candis, trying not to be too 'quick, to answer says "okay. "Sure. "That would be nice." She continues "I like going to the movies." "Good" he said.

He looks down at her plate with the two wings on it saying "so, before you leave, shoot me your number." Candis, all; jumping up and down inside says "alright. "I sure will" she said all; calmly. They both nod at the same time and smile at each other and then not wanting to walk away too quickly from each other, say "okay, again. Then "bye, was said one more time. Then this lady that neither one of them knew walked passed and bumped Candis on the arm from behind because Candis was in the way of the salad bar. She caused Candis to move suddenly making her snap out of the 'trance, she was in with Rafee'al.

So as Candis slowly turns with a 'oops, kind of smile on her face, she then walks away slowly back to her table. Walking towards Naquawna 'her eyes are as big as silver dollars! And the smile on her face is as big, as 'homey, the clown's! Marvin notices her facial expression and says to Dianna "what's she so happy about?!" "Did they bring out more chicken?!" Naquawna hears what he said and starts busting up laughing along with Dianna, saying "you know you 'wrong; for that!" Candis is trying so hard to play it cool as she sits down real lady like in her chair, saying to Naquawna "is he looking over here?"! "No. "He's at the desert table." Candis wiggling in her seat about to 'burst, tells Naquawna "how he wants to take her out like to the movies or something." Naquawna is so happy for her friend, and she smiles with real sincerity telling her how "she's so-o-o glad' that she didn't mess this chance up for Candis in getting his number like she did last night, do to 'her, and Rayshawn's drama!

Dianna looks over her shoulder to see the man they are talking about and says "go on 'ahead; Ms. Candis!" Marvin chimes in saying "let me talk to the brother!" "I'll let him know!" "Don't be trying to run; game on my; kid sister!" "Play'yah!" Candis laughs "yeah...!" "You should 'know; all about; running game!" Dianna looks at them both and Marvin shuts up; quickly and goes back to eating on his peach cobbler and ice cream. Naquawna eating on her French fries gets a text, and it's from Rayshawn. "Damn--!!!" "We talked that fool up!" said Naquawna. "His ears must be ringing!" added Candis. The text said "what; up?"! Naquawna texted back "nay-thin!" "Just at lunch; with Candis." He text back "dang!" "You two are still hangin; since last night?"! She texted back "yep...! "We are hung-over so we are eating it off 'because we drank way to much last night at her house!" He texted back "true; that! Followed by "so when are you going home?" Naquawna texted in about 20 minutes. "Why?" 'Hoping, that he would say, he was coming over. "But wait, she's still mad at 'him, for lying to her; right?"! He texted back "alright, I'll come by your pad in 30 minutes; cool?"! She texted back "yeah, I guess!" But then, she erased it and sent "okay, boo!" "See you in a minute."

Candis just laughs, knowing this is going to take some "serious" acting on Naquawna's part 'to act like, she doesn't know about the 'baby, the 'broad, and the tore up Cadillac! Candis looks at her saying "good luck; with that; home-girl!" Naquawna blurting back says "shut; up!" "You are just so-o glad, you are going to hook up with dude!" "And that you don't have, all the drama I 'got, right now!" "But we'll see how Mr. "Rafee'al" turns out to be!" grunts Naquawna. "He might just have a woman; and a kid back home too!" she adds. Candis's happy smile; drops slightly, and she says "that's why... I'm not getting too close or getting my hopes up, until I know "all" about him!"

Naquawna laughs "but do you "really" ever "know" the mind of a man?"! "Look at what just happened to me!" They both stare at each other for a second, then Candis says "you're, right!" "Probably; not! "So that's why I put all my "trust" in God! "Because he will "never" disappoint me!" smiled Candis. Naquawna agrees and before she can elaborate more on the 'topic, here, comes, Rafee'al! Naquawna says "don't turn around now, but here... he... comes...! "Oh, shoot!" said Candis under her breath as she wipes the crumbs from her mouth and quickly takes a drink of water and swishes it around in her mouth to get all the food off the front of her teeth. He comes up from behind her and whispers in her ear "you got that number?" She jumps a little out of her seat to act like she didn't know he was coming up behind her. And as she's looking over her shoulder and up at him she smiles returning "yes. "I'll put it in my phone" he said. When she gives him her number, he notices the couple at the next table sizing him up. 'You know?" looking him up and down.

Candis blurts out "oh, and this is my brother Marvin, and his wife Dianna" she said smiling. Dianna lights up when she hears Candis say "her brother's" wife! They both say "hi, and Marvin shakes his hand. Candis looks at her friend saying "and you might know Naquawna from last night?" "She's my best-friend." He acknowledges her saying "nice to meet you, too." And Naquawna says "hi, back 'remembering that time she first saw him and thought he was handsome. As Jasmine is walking up to say "hi, to everyone. Marvin says to her "so-- this is the party girl!" who had everybody; drunk last night?"! Jasmine laughs back; cheering "you know it!" "Open, bar, and all!" Marvin shouts "Woooh...! "Wee...! "I guess I really missed out, then?"! They all laughed some more and then Rafee'al ended with "alright then folks!" He looks back at Candis saying "I'll be calling you soon" and he walks away smiling. Candis with a sweet grin on her face says "alright. "See you.

Rafee'al and his cousin Jasmine leave out of the restaurant and Marvin says "he seem like a cool dude!" "At first, I thought, I was gonna have-ta put hands on him, for trying to talk to my baby sister!" Candis smirks and the girls laugh as they get up from the table to get ready to leave, but then Naquawna remembers she needs to get a plate for her granddad, so she won't have to cook dinner tonight. So once she pays for a to-go box she fills it up with all of granddad's favorite foods, and they all walk out the door to the parking lot together.

Everybody hugs goodbye and drives away in different directions. Naquawna and Candis stay on speaker phone with each other until they both get home. Naquawna tells Candis that she will call her later when she gets done talking to Rayshawn. Candis laughs saying "talking to him?!" "Or, boning him; girl?"! They both laugh some more and then Candis asked "how are you going to pretend like he's "not" a dog?"! Naquawna laughs to herself because she's 'knowing; 'now, that she did in fact; have sex with Mike last night, so she thinks to herself 'who's; 'clowning; 'who; Rayshawn?"! So smiling to herself she tells Candis "I ain't; stud-den him no more!" "And I know 'exactly, what to do for his ass!" "And if anything!" she continues. "I'll just use him for sex, when I feel like it!" Candis belts out "oh! "God-od"!!! "That's not 'dogging; him!" "That is letting him have his cake; his ice cream; and-- some bootay!"

Naquawna shouts "hell, naw!" I've got a plan!" "You'll see!" she said. "I'll hurt him, just like he's hurt me, if it comes down to it!" Naquawna pulls up to her place and Rayshawn is parked outside waiting for her. Her heart; thumps when she tells Candis "he's here!" "I'll call you back!" Naquawna gets out the car and puts her fake "hi, daddy; smile on, when she really wants to slap the; sh*t; out of his ass! She gets out her car saying "Jason told us your car got broken into." Rayshawn says "naw, it got; vandalized!" "But I got it taken care of" he said as he eyeballs her facial; expression to see if she looked; guilty! He rubs down the side of his head saying "I just need to get the scratches buffed out and then repaint it!" With a hug she says "well at least you're okay!" "That's all that matters!" "A car can be replaced, but you are; irreplaceable!"

She can't believe how convincingly; smooth she said that. And he totally bought it too, because he hugged her back even tighter. They go into the house and granddad is taking a nap in his chair. Naquawna puts the food in the kitchen that she brought back from the buffet on top of the stove, and once again... she sneaks; Rayshawn back to her room. He sits on her bed and turns on the t.v. while Naquawna fiddles around in her room putting her clothes back in there proper places 'trying; to avoid, what is to come next! But the gig is; up! Especially since she knows "all" about Rayshawn, now!

And being the "user" that she's found him out to, be! He's probably thinking he's going to get; laid; right about now! 'But, nope! She pulls the brakes on that sh*t! Just listening to him talking about something he's watching on t.v. makes her think; hard, on what she could say, to cut this meeting with him 'short, because now, he's on her nerves! He grabs her by the hand and starts to kiss her saying "I missed you." "Did you miss me?" he asked. Trying not to give him too much eye contact because the eyes never lie, was what her granddad had always told her, so she closes her eyes when he kisses her again and she says "of course, I missed you." And as she pulls back from his kiss, with her eyes still closed she smiles up at him, but in her mind, she thinks "I'm, over; it!" She lets him hold her for a few seconds and then she tells him "I'll be right back." "I've got to go change my pad." He frowns "you're on your monthly; again?!" Laughing to herself Naquawna looking back over her shoulder at him answers "yep. "It came on this morning. "We could go to a movie or something" she said as she leaves the room area to go into the bathroom. She closes the door and opens the cabinets to act like she's getting something so she can stalls in the bathroom.

With the water; running she washing her hands and puts some night cream on her arms and hands. Still laughing to herself she takes her time so he can "think" on the movie idea. Even though to her a 'real; man, who is "really" into her; wouldn't give a 'damn, whether she's on her rag or not! He would still want to spend quality time with 'her, doing other things. So now Naquawna wants to see just what; lame ass; excuse he will come up with, for leaving! The bathroom door opens and she comes out all smiles waiting for his reply on the movie thing. While sitting there in her room Rayshawn had thought on it, and decided to say "yes, to a movie idea."

Naquawna is speechless. She says "oh. "Really?"! "Okay... call the movie theater then" she said handing him her phone. He replies "naw, you call and set it up and I'll be back to get you." Frowning she says "why do you need to leave, and come back?"! Frustrated he stands and walks towards the door, and 'her, not wanting him to 'leave, puts her hand on the door frame saying "let's go now!" But of course he makes up some 'punk-ass, story, about "how he's got to get his money from the house and change his shoes because he's still in his basketball gear." Ummmm!" she groans. Then she says "let me come with you to your house then!" "I can wait in the car, while you get your stuff."

She can't wait to hear this next reason why she can't go to his house; "knowing" what she knows about the girl and the baby. He puts his head down and shakes his head slowly really thinking on it, then he says "umm--. Than looking back at her he clears his throat saying "uh--; that ain't gone work, either because I've got to stop by Ernesto's house and drop off these tools he let me use today to fix my car, and he doesn't like people he don't know; knowing where he lives at." When he mentions the tools for fixing his car, Naquawna backs off, feeling guilty about what she did. "Alright; fine!" she said folding her arms looking sad at him. "I'll just wait, until you come back!" she frowns.

'Happy, that his lie 'seemed; to work, prompts him to give her a sweet kiss on the lips. Before leaving out of her room he ends with, "text me and tell me what time the movie you want to see starts!" "And make sure..., it's a good action flick too!" Naquawna walks him to the kitchen door and wave's good-bye 'knowing, he "won't" be back! But deep down inside "hoping" he proves her wrong. She turns her head sharply and in walks her granddad saying "who was that, you were talking to?"! "Um, that was just a friend" she said; mope fully. Her granddad grabs the food from off the stove saying "ooh-we... this sure smell; good!" She smiles "you are going to love it grandpa!" Her granddad beams saying "I can tell by looking at it, it's gonna be good"! Naquawna nods giving him a half smile. He says "you alright?" "Yes. "I'm fine" she said dryly. "He can tell somethings wrong so he says "you look just like your mother standing there." "I remember that same look on her face when she was sad and trying to hide what was really on her mind." He adds "I know it's hard to be a young woman now days, people expect so much from you." "And when you give them your heart sometimes, it gets stomped; on!"

Naquawna drops her head so her grandpa can't see her eyes welling up with tears as she listens to him talk." He says "was that the young man at the back door you were talking to, that has you all, upset?" She nods saying "he's always playing games!" Her granddad retorts "well a man is going to treat you; how you allow him to treat you!" Just like I use to tell your mother when she was a youngster!" I would tell her to respect herself because men come and go!" He went on to say, "I remember one day your mother came home 'crying, about some boy who broke up with her because she wasn't putting out!" And I told her, if a man will leave you because you "won't" sleep with him!" That same man will leave you; once you do!" Naquawna sadly listening says "poor mom, she really got her heart broken; huh?" "Well--, yes, at first she did, but then she stood her ground, and held out, and he married her!" Naquawna shouts "who?!" "Your knuckle; headed daddy!" That's who!" laughed her granddad.

They both laughed out loud and she could see what her granddad was getting at. 'Although, she had already; crossed that 'sexual, bridge with Rayshawn, already. But to her defense it wasn't the "leaving" her part, she was worried about. It was mostly the "committing" to just 'her; part, that she couldn't get passed. "You are my favorite granddaughter and I don't like to see you hurting!" he said. "That's why I wish your mother and father were still alive to help guide you through life!" But we all have to find our own way, through the good; the bad; and thy ugly!" And you know, I've always told you, follow your 'heart, and let 'God, be your guide!" He ends his thoughts with "the man for you, will be there' when you least expect him!"

Naquawna looks up at him saying "you're right granddad." And you always make me feel much better, when I talk to you, that's why I'm so glad you're still here with me" she said while giving him a long hug as the tears she was holding back start to fall down her face. Her grandpa looks her in her eyes smiling he says "you know I love you sweetheart, and life is 'really, not that 'bad, as long as you keep your 'faith, and trust your 'gut, in doing the right things!" She nods and he smiles; knowing she's going to be okay, then he reaches for his plate saying "but now; an old man's; got tah eat"! He kisses her on the cheek cheering "thanks again dear, for the food." And as he's walking back into the living room to go sit down to eat, Naquawna smiling back at him says "anything, for you grandpa!"

Naquawna has always loved her grandpa's wisdom because he could always lift her spirits when she's been down, ever since she was a little girl. Deep down inside she knows Rayshawn is probably "not" going to come back because she's heard these lies before. And as much as her granddad keeps telling her to do the 'right; 'things; in her life and how she will see the "rewards" in doing so! 'Despite, that fact; she always seems to get mixed up with the wrong men. And to her 'bad; judgment, she ends up sleeping with just about all of them, do to her "thinking" that they are all--her; Mr. Right!

When Naquawna finds the movie she wants to see, which is called {Iron Man}! She text Rayshawn the statist of the movie and the time it starts. So when an hour goes bye and he hasn't even responded; even after she's put away yesterday's dishes, she gets so mad because she got all dolled up for nothing! With her collapsed; spirit she starts to walk slowly back to her room. Once in her room she puts on her comfy; pajama's and takes off her earrings because after 2 hours go bye she is 'now, "knowing" that he's "not" coming back!

Sitting on her bed she ends up flicking through the channels and stumbles on a great show on the OWN channel. Naquawna keeps looking at her phone but no text back from Rayshawn, is found' so she heads back to the kitchen during the commercial to make herself some popcorn. 'Well, in truth she can truly say that this is "not" a big 'surprise; him "not" coming back; once again. But, one day he'll 'see, because she "won't" be sitting around waiting; forever! With her popcorn she walks back to her room and curls up in her bed to watch the rest of the show.

Candis shuts her car door and a breath of air leaves her mouth as she's walking up to her apartment, after "finally" making her way back home. Hours ago she had stopped by the 99 cent store, and as usual' she went into the store for one item, but came out with 12 things. With her keys still hanging from the door she enters her apartment and slips off her shoes by the front door and walks towards the kitchen to put all the bags down on the kitchen table. Candis was still feeling like she was in a 'fog; all loopy and stuff from the partying last night, and then Jake calls. "Should I answer the phone?" "No!" she said to herself out loud. "I'll let it go to voice mail". "I just can't do him right now" she thinks to herself as she's slowly pulling stuff out of her bags. He leaves a message saying "hey?!" "Candy?!" He elaborates, again saying "I call you candy because your lips are so sweet!" He goes on to say "I'm having a big barbeque party at my house today!" "Call me if you can make it!" He sings a bit of the song sung by Cameo Called "Like Candy!" Candis can't help but bust up laughing. He ends with "call me, when you get this message." Laughing he says "don't make me have to come looking for you; gurl!" Candis cracks a smile because Jake is just too cute, she sighs. But so is Jason and most 'definitely; Rafee'al! "What is a girl to do?"!

After putting everything away she headed to her room to take a nap. Grabbing her pillow and squeezing it tight as she lay's on top of her bed fantasizing about all of them and thinking which one of them, could really be her man forever; till death do they part!

Most girls know deep down inside that they want a man that will love them forever, and Candis is no different. She is 'truly hoping, to connect with one of these guys on a 'real; mental and spiritual; level! 'Knowing, that it's a game of chance, fait, destiny and 'yes, a nice dose; of chemistry! And--, as with any long term relationship "eventually" a kid may be born! So-- he has got to be 'good, "father" material!

Chapter 8

Rayshawn heads home and before he could get his key in the door, Se'anna swings it open with little Ray in her arms shouting; "are you alright?"! "The lady from the insurance company called and said she couldn't reach you!" "And she said that the car was vandalized at the mall!" "What happened?!" "Are you okay?!" She kept asking him, while checking his face for bruises. Rayshawn closes the door sighing "I'm alright!" "I just went up to the mall after basketball to see what they might have, for

Christmas gifts, for you and the baby!" "Awh..., baby!" "That is so sweet" she replies. Kissing their baby she adds "did you hear that little Ray?" "Daddy is looking for gifts for us" she said smiling kissing the baby while taking him over to his swing.

After winding up the baby's swing she walks back to the room where Rayshawn is at, taking off his clothes. Watching him get undressed she asked "so what happened to the car; exactly?"! "And when do we get it fixed?"! 'Rayshawn, stripped down gets ready to get into the shower to act like he has "really" played a long game of basketball and 'now, he is all; sweaty. He turns the water on and gets into the shower while answering Se'anna's questions, he says "someone just scratched the driver side up." "It was probably some kids." "The security guard said it's been happening a lot lately." "Damn...!" shouts Se'anna, and with her hand on her hip she states "probably some damn; bad ass kids!" With a frown on her face she voices "let me go see my car!" and she heads for the front door, and runs outside. When she walks around to the driver's side of her car and sees the long scratch, she can't; believe it! With her head tilted sideways she takes a deep breath and yells out "what the f_ck!" With her mouth wide open she is in total, utter, shock at how long the scratch is. Shaking her head she walks down the side of her car touching the scratches and almost wants to cry. For a minute, she has a moment of "was this a b*tch?!" "That did this to my car, because of Rayshawn?!" But then she just lets it go, remembering what the security guard had told Rayshawn, about all the other cars that got vandalized at the mall as well.

Walking back into the house she sees Rayshawn getting dressed and she just had to blasts on him "um--! "Hell! "Naw! "That look like some shit a broad would do!" She just had to say it out loud, to see his reaction. "Awe-!" "Here you go!" "I told you, what dude said! "We are not the only 'ones, who got their car; tore up!" He said it, twice; just to get her off his back! "Well--; they should have it on camera, then?"! "Right?!" shouted Se'anna staring at his face. Rayshawn has a surprised but stern look on his face because he 'knows, that is a true statement that could be a factor in him getting the car fixed. But he still convincingly said "yep! "And I hope they do, have it on film!" But he's lying, and he's hoping that the insurance company isn't going to want that kind of proof either, or he "won't" be getting the car fixed for free.

And Se'anna will want to know 'where, and 'when, the vandalism; "really" took place at?"! Rayshawn looks at her and sighs "sorry baby, for parking the car at the mall" than he gives Se'anna a hug and a kiss because he believes "sex" can solve any problem! He starts to take off her shirt as he's kissing and rubbing down the sides of her arms like as if she's a 'silky, piece of cloth. Loving his touch, and the kiss of his mouth makes her 'jump, up on him, and wrap her legs around his waist. With her arms she holds on to his shoulders, as he bounces her up and down with his hands under her bottom.

And with his 'mouth, he pulls up her bra with his strong teeth, and starts to milk her by suckling on one of her; "caper's"! It must have started to feel really good to her because the other side of her 'chest, got jealous and started to leak, real baby milk. "Ah, man!" "You're leaking!" he said grinning. But Se'anna doesn't care, she has a small window of time to get her some "pleasure" before the baby starts to get bored in his swing. So in a rush, she hurries up and takes off her pants and unzips Rayshawn's pants and jumps back up on top of her horsey.

Rayshawn, is loving every pounce she is giving him. After all, Se'anna use to be a cheerleader and doing the 'splits, was one of her "many" talents! Even at the strip club, they use to call her "elastic-girl!" because she could really 'stretch, those; legs of heirs! She runs her fingers across the top of his head as she straddles her long legs around his back. The ride is intense and very bumpy. He knows just how she; likes it; which is rough, then fast' and very bouncy. With a 'jilt, of her head she gives him a long lick across his lips and then kisses him; 'wildly, as her head moves from side to side as she's presses hard on to his lips, then soft on to them again. He starts to lift her up and down on his "cocka'doodle'do" with her legs stretched out as if she's doing the splits in midair.

Holding herself up on his shoulders she bites him on his left ear and 'her, breathing gets harder and harder, then she 'talks, in his ear "telling him how good he feels inside her!" Rayshawn is so hard, and turn't; up while he's; jabbing up the back of her 'velvet; walls! He's enjoying pleasuring her as he makes his strokes; longer and 'stronger, causing her to wiggles and jiggles her 'rump; vigorously up and down on him! Once she gets into a 'wild, and 'crazy; climax, she begins to reach 'higher; ground! And with her relaxed body, she leans her neck back into an 'elongated, back bend with Rayshawn trying to hold on to her so she doesn't fall on the floor.

'Carefully, he stumbles over towards the bed where he 'flops, her down while he's 'still; deep inside of her! 'Breathing; heavily; she is all over him while she's 'riding, his; whip! Se'anna is climaxing; 'so much, that he can feel 'her, on himself like a hot shower spraying down on the top of his head. Then once he hits her "G-spot" he can't help, but start to release himself! And when that happens, it is 'all, he want to 'do, inside of her! When he releases he becomes a 'new animal, and starts to 'roars, like a 'lion, in the wild!

'Exhaling, they finally finish and she lets down her legs, and he falls down on top of her, where they both rest in each other's arms. But the moment only last for about 5 minutes because little Ray's swing has stopped; moving and he awakes and starts to cry. Se'anna throws on her robe and goes into the living room to restart the baby's swing. So, rejuvenated 'now, after her love session she decides to start making dinner for her family. Rayshawn is back in the room passed out and he has forgotten 'all, about his movie date, with Naquawna! "Tisk! "Tisk!

Over at Candis's a yawn and a stretch, has her up with a 'happy go lucky, smile on her face so she decides to call Naquawna after her nap. She calls laughing saying "hey, puss in boots!" "What you doing?" Naquawna laughs "watching C.S.I. "Rayshawn and I are "supposed" to go to the movies, tonight. "Um-hum!" said Candis. Adding "dang...!" I was calling to see if you wanted to go to Jake's barbeque party?" "It's going to be a blast!" "Drinks, herb, and you know all kinds of 'ballers, are going to be there!" "Hopefully, some of them have a real; job!" laughs Candis. Naquawna grunts, saying "shoot, that does sound like it would be fun!" "But I'm already in my pj's and I just want to see if he is really going to come back. "Oh; hell!!!" squawks Candis. "You know he be; lying!" "He's told you that mess before!" "And you always end up waiting on him and missing out on having fun with the girls!" "I, know---," said Naquawna sad-ish. "But I think this time he really might keep our date." "Okay," said Candis. "I guess I'll have to call 'Roxy, since you won't go with me!"

"Umm--!" good luck with that!" retorts Naquawna. She adds "now, you know?!" "You can dress her; up!" "But you can't take her; nowhere!" "Ooh--!" "You know you ain't right!" laughs Candis. Saying "yes, we do know, she can be a bit of a "laptop; lush!" they both say laughing out loud. Naquawna chuckles "and you already 'know, once you get Roxy drunk, she'll be all up on somebody's lap!" Or..., she'll be dancing on somebody's table; or both!" "Laptop, laptop, laptop; lush!" they both sing out loud together laughing. "But she's 'still, our gurl!" cracks Candis.

Naquawna laughs "yeah she's cool." Then she tells Candis what had happened between her and Rayshawn and how she told him "she was on her ministration to postpone having sex with him," and Candis cheered "you go girl!" "I am so proud of you, for not having sex with that; fool!" "He needs to choose one, and not be playing you two women against each other!" Candis ends the chat with "well, I'll call you later!" "I'm going to see if I can reach Roxy before she makes other plans." Naquawna sighs "okay, talk to you later." Before Candis hangs up she says "hey, but if he fakes on you; you know where Jake lives; just come by." "Okay, she says "I will."

Candis hangs up from Naquawna and calls Roxy. The phone picks up with Candis saying "hey, hot momma!" "It's me, Candis!" "Hey buddy" says Roxy. Adding "guess who I ran into today at Wal-Mart?"! Candis says "who?" "Sherry!" said Roxy. "And she said you were off the 'hook; drunk last night, and so was Naquawna!" "Oh...!" Shit...!" said Candis. Not surprised, but a little embarrassed that 'Sherry, would run her mouth so, soon. Candis blurts "that heffa couldn't hold 'water, if a glass; asked her too!" Roxy laughed out loud voicing "you guys were lit; though!" And Naquawna was in tears over some dude "what ended up happening?"! "Ooh, chil, what a mess!" said Candis.

She adds "we 'were, on 'tilt, last night!" and I'll tell you all about it." "But the reason why I'm calling is, because I wanted to invite you to a "Baller's; Barbeque"! 'Candis, threw in those "choice; words" because then she 'knew, Roxy would 'really want to go, being the "dollar-bill; hoe" that she is! And of course Roxy; bites. She excitedly says "oh, really...?"! "And drinks too?"! "Yes, gurl!" "And all... the weed... you can smoke!" said Candis. "Sounds like my kind of party!" retorts Roxy. They both give out a "yah-hoo!" with laughter. Than Candis tells Roxy to come over to her house and they will walk to the barbeque from there. So after she gives Roxy the direction to her place, she hangs up the phone and starts getting ready for the barbeque.

Chapter 9

A commercial comes on and Naquawna still sitting at home 'waiting, gets an unexpected phone call and she doesn't recognize the number but she answers it anyway because she 'thinks, it could be Rayshawn using his friends phone to say he's on his way. She says "hello?" And an unrecognizable; voice says "hey?" back asking "is this Naquawna?" She says "maybe. "Who is this?" "It's Mike. Her lips and her eyes; turn't up in disappointment when she answered back "oh. "What's up?" she said in a flat tone. "Nothing much" he said. "I'm just finishing up a gig." She returns "a gig?" "What is that?" "It's a term that we use meaning a jam session" he said. Naquawna says "hmm…, I see." But she was not, as impressed, as he'd; "hoped" she'd be!

Not really caring she says "so you play music on a stage, for people?" "Yep. "We do all kinds of venues." "Weddings, birthday parties, you name it; we do it!" "You should come see us jam one day" he said. She pauses and then says "that could be arranged." He laughs "arranged; huh?"

He says "what kind of music do you like?" She rolls her eyes up thinking "what do you care. But to be nice she goes on to say "Rap, R&B, Pop, and of course Gospel" she said. They talk about their favorite artists and he tells her all the people he has opened for locally, when he's played in concerts at the fairgrounds, and at Planet Geminyiah.

Naquawna starts to see Mike in a whole new light. Even though he's not as fine as Rayshawn, she could see herself being his friend and maybe even using him to get Rayshawn jealous one day. He says "you want to meet up?" "Maybe get some coffee or a drink?" Naquawna not really in the mood says "no. "I'm kinda tired. He says "ah, come on!" I'll come pick you up, so you won't even have to drive." She thinks for a minute and then she says "okay. "What the hell!" "Why not. "Come get me" she smiles.

She gives him the address while thinking to herself, that she could even use him, to drive by Rayshawn's house in his car, to see if he is at home. With a new revived state of mind she jumps up out of her bed and gets ready saying under her breath "screw; you! "Rayshawn! "I am not, waiting all night for 'you, anymore!" she said as she's getting her clothes back on, to go out on her date with Mike. As Naquawna's getting dressed to go out for the night.

A Knock, knock, knock, sound; is coming from Candis's front door. It's Roxy. Candis opens the door saying "hey--! "Hey! "Hey! And lets her in the house. Entering Candis's apartment Roxy belts out "are you ready to party; hoochi momma?!" She laughs as she struts across the floor doing a cute little twirl to show Candis her new blue sexy top and light blue mini skirt that was clinging to her hips. Roxy then laughs at thy expression on Candis's face; voicing "but of course this outfit wouldn't be on hit, without my stylish white cow-girl boots!" You couldn't tell Roxy; shit!" She just knew she was the 'bomb, without; the prom!

Candis cracks up when cheering out the words "work it!" "Chica!" 'Candis was looking cute too, she had a sexy little summer dress on, even though the 'season, was; fall. In Treeberry, you can get away with summer clothes in the fall because it's always so sunny out there. The dress Candis has on is strapless and it fills out all her curves nicely. It has soft printed 'lavender, flowers along the top across her 'chest, and on the bottom edge of the dress, it has that same beautiful print. She also had on her 3 inch; strap around the ankle, white sandals with a medium heel on them which matches perfectly with her small handbag.

Candis likes the handbag the most because she can put her keys, her cell phone and her lip gloss in it, comfortably. Roxy brought with her, a bottle of Patron and said “let’s do a shot or two before we head out.” “Good idea” replied Candis. “Let me go get two shot glasses from the cabinet” she said. After doing two shots each, which soon turned into four, the girls were ready to go. Roxy says “I hope there’s some cute men over here today and no; Grenades!” Candis laughs out; “bi%ch!” “You got that from Jerry Shore” and they both laugh out loud. Roxy blurts out “I know, but that ‘was, ‘laughs, when those guys use to say that phrase, on the show, about the ugly girls that they would meet.” Candis agrees and laughs as she’s walking towards her balcony to show Roxy the view from her apartment.

Roxy is amazed at how lucky Candis is for getting such a great pad, for such a great price. So after she shows her the rest of her place, Candis turns on a night light in the living room and locks up the house, and they start walking down the street towards Jake’s house. They get to the front door of Jakes house and there’s a sign saying “use the side gate.” The music is bumpin and you can still hear people talking. Candis is starting to get butterflies because she doesn’t know who is going to be at this party. Roxy on the other hand is all excited as she starts to walk in front of Candis around to the side entrance so she can open up the gate.

“Holla!” shouts Roxy. “Now this; is a party!” she yells. Candis has a staggering; look on her face because she didn’t even “think” it was going to be this; nice! Soon as you walks in the backyard on the far left is where the DJ is posted up at. And in the middle of the yard is the dance floor. Then in the far right corner there’s a hot tub with half naked girls and guys in it, playing this water; shots; game! At the right side of that hot tub is a pool table. And near the dance floor is a stripper pole. The girls look back by the house door and can see where all the food is being placed on a long white table. The food tables ‘content, is a mixture of chips and dips and nuts, and the girls can also see two shrimp cocktail platters, sushi variations, barbequed hot wings, potatoes salads, beans, ribs, chicken, corn on the cob just all the good things, you would want to munch on, when you’ve got the munchies.

The drinks are being made at the bar next to the food table by some pretty brunet. Candis and Roxy walk all around the backyard like they are in a party; wonderland, which is full of ‘endless; possibilities! Candis looks to her left and spots ‘Jake, but he doesn’t see her yet because the party is so packed. This cute blonde is hanging on his arm laughing with him about ‘something, with two other people. Candis points in Jake’s direction and tells Roxy “that’s Jake right over there, standing with that blonde chick.” Roxy, ‘looking, squints her eyes to get a better view of his face, than voices to Candis “mmm, he’s cute!” Candis smiles proudly, but she can’t get to comfortable in 'believing, that she and Jake could "really" be a couple!" in a lifelong; serious relationship 'because, he sells narcotics!

Roxy, on scope mode, is listening to the music as she's looking around the yard 'admiring, all the hot guys at the party. And then this one particular man stands; out. He was looking at Roxy from way over by the bar and she was looking at him as well. Candis takes notice and says "let's go get a drink." Roxy mumbles under her breath trying not to let her mouth move too much when she says "oh--! "La! "La! "He is Fricken; sex!" "Look at his clothes." "I bet you 'he's, loaded!" Candis is listening to her talk but is still looking in 'Jake's, direction. She says to Roxy "go get him girl!"

When they get to the bar Roxy waits her turn in line and poses with one hand on her hip and one leg crossed over thy other. The hot guy at the bar that she was checking out comes over to her saying "hello, legs." 'She freezes up, thinking that he might be a past client, from Vegas. But he goes on to say "no, excuse me." "But you have something on your leg." It was some barbeque sauce. Apparently she had rubbed up against the barbeque platter that was on the table on her way to the bar and got some of the sauce drippings on her left thigh. "Damn, how embarrassing!" she said looking down at her thigh covered in sauce. But he didn't care, he acted like he wanted to lick it off of her leg, the way he was licking his lips; looking at her. But turns out, he was a complete gentleman, who got a napkin from the bar and wiped it off her thigh for her. Roxy thought it was nice of him, even though he was a little too touchy; feely. With the sauce off her leg she said "thank you. "No problem" he said. "My name is Steeli'o." "What is your name?" he asked as he reached down to grab her hand to kiss it. Roxy smiles but then gives him an inquisitive look; returning; "Steeli'o?"! "What kind of name is that?"! "Or better yet, what does that, mean?"! He frowns "it's my name!" "What are you talking about?"! "What does it mean?"! "You insult me?"! She lowers her voice saying "Oh. "No. "I'm sorry." "I didn't mean to offend you" she said as she grabs his hand with both her hands; pulling them up towards her chest like a clutched bag. After she apologizes he says "this is okay!" he said in broken English. And with the most; sexiest; accent she had 'ever, heard!" he makes her smile, just hearing him talk.

Roxy asks "where are you from?" "I'm from Italy. "Why?" "Why?" so many questions?" he asked frowning. Roxy just stands there like 'I don't know; I mean no harm. He reads her face and he smiles saying "let's go dance." She grins "okay. But before she could head to the dance floor, Candis is picked up off the ground from behind, with a big hug from Jake. "I see you got my message" he said to Candis with a wink of his eye. Steeli'o speaks over him saying "nice party man" as they give each other thy 'eye, implying; that there are a lot of beautiful women here.

Candis cuts in saying "Jake, let me introduce you to my longtime friend from junior high "this is Roxy. He says "nice to meet you." "And where's your other buddy?" asked Jake. Candis says "who?" "Naquawna?" "She had other plans tonight, but she will "definitely" hate that she missed this party!" Roxy laughs out "you got that right!" And then she grabs Steeli'o and walks off towards the dance floor with him arm in arm. Candis looks up into Jakes sexy eyes and 'beaming, she says "so--, you though I wasn't coming to your party; huh?" He grunts. She continues to say "because by the look of things, I can see that you have all your 'back up; babes here!" she said with a laugh.

He laughs back "nope, they are all just here for the ganja!" Candis sees the girl that Jake was talking with earlier eye balling her and Jake from across the yard. Jake turns and says to the brunet making the drinks "hey, Robin?" make her a Dirty Martini, and me a Black Russian!" They both crack up laughing at his drink selection and the way he said it, because Candis never drinks Dirty Martini's, she's more of a Patron and beer kind of girl. But she rolls with it anyway and tries the new drink and ends up liking it.

Jake puts down his empty glass abruptly; spouting "I'll be right back!" I got to go help Bubba get those other slab of ribs off the grill"! Candis sips on her drink, answering "ok, I'm not going anywhere." She stands there sipping on her drink through a straw looking at Roxy and Steeli'o dancing, while Jake runs around playing 'hostess, with the most'est! Then she thinks "where have I heard that name "Bubba" before?" Then out of the corner of her right eye she spots the same big guy that was at Jasmine's party, with Rayshawn that night bringing in some ribs and putting them on that long table beside the bar. Bubba doesn't know her, so she isn't 'sweating; him, seeing her! But she is curious to see if he is here with Rayshawn.

She watches Bubba leave and go out the other side of the gate, "not" the side where she and Roxy came in from, but on the other side of the house. On the other side of the house, is where the party is really; crackin! All the major gambling tables were over there, and so was the iron grill, where Jake was smoking all of his meat. Candis peeks through the gate and sees Rayshawn at the craps table with this really 'pretty, Spanish or Hawaiian girl, sitting on his lap. She really couldn't tell what nationality she was but she knew!" it "wasn't" his baby's momma! Candis gets; shuffled out the way, when the gate closes but she can still see, Rayshawn and the girl kissing.

She thinks to herself 'poor Naquawna, sitting at home waiting on this fool! When she could be out partying with us. "What; a dog! And then she looks to see where Roxy is and "sh*t! Where else?" she's on the damn stripper pole. This broad is hanging upside down with her 'udder's, halfway 'showing; nipples and all! She has one of her legs wrapped around the pole, showing her entire "ba'donka'donk" because she decided to wear a skimpy spaghetti thong, under her skirt. The guys are going crazy as usual and Steeli'o is the main one egging her on by stuffing twenty dollar bills anywhere he can, while copping a 'slight feel, on her body as if to be 'helping her, on the pole.

'What happened beforehand, was' Roxy got called out to a challenge by this Swedish girl who goes to one of the colleges out there saying "she is the best pole; dancer in this area!" And when Roxy heard that, she couldn't resist the $200.00 dollar bet to show the girl that "she" was the best! After Roxy won and got her money, she jumped back up on the pole, yelling "anyone else, want to lose their money?"! Candis walks over to where Roxy is and complains "Rox; you are all over the place, showing everything!" Roxy looks down at her tat ta's hanging halfway out and replies "oops! Then while stuffing her boobs back into her shirt, Steeli'o comes over to where the two girls are at talking saying "good show, bay-bee!" he smiles as he grabs Roxy by the hand and walks off with her towards the hot tub.

Jake sees Candis and rushes over to her saying "there you are!" "Come with me for a minute!" "I want to show you something" he says holding on to her hand. He pulls her by the arm towards the back door past the bar and into the house. Candis takes a quick glance around his house and sees some people on the couch smoking on a bong, and some other people are coupled up kissing in the hallway. The closer they get to his room they can hear sounds of moaning coming from the bathroom as they pass by. He quickly unlocks his bedroom door and closes the door behind them.

Smiling he tells Candis to sit down on his bed because he wants to show her something. She sits down on his bed looking around his room at all the psychedelic posters on his walls that are activated by the black light he just turned on. "Nice room, Jake" she glares. "Thanks" he grins. "It's my little piece of heaven." "This is where I come to think, and chill out." "You know, and get my head right." He reaches down and pulls out a huge bag of purple haired; skunk weed, from his bottom drawer. Candis is not really tripping off the big bag of weed because she is looking at her dress in the mirror. It looks so pretty when the black light hits it; making it all; trippy and stuff.

He gets her attention by saying "here!" This is for you!" She's 'taken back, for a second. Then she says "what?"! "What, am I supposed to do with all of that; weed?"! He laughs saying "you could sell it for me!" He's joking, but has a convincing look on his face when asking her. Candis laughing out loud says "no way! "I would be; way..., too paranoid; holding on to that much herb! He grunts back; laughing he says "naw, baby doll!" "I'm just playing with you!" "You want to smoke one though?" "Here, light it up" he said, handing her the joint.

Sitting on his bed she smiles up at him saying "is this "really" why you brought me back here; Jake?" "You could have smoked a joint with me outside" she said with a sexy, half smile on her face. He chuckles "it's one of the reasons why I brought you back here." He puts his hand on her leg and then strikes up a match to light the joint hanging from her mouth. When she hits it and passes it to him he turns his attention away from her gaze because he can hear an argument starting up outside his bedroom window where the guys are at gambling.

After mumbling somethings under his breath about the guys outside he gives her back the joint and walks over to his window and opens it saying "awh; Bubba!" "I thought you said you were gonna hold it down for me, until I got back?"! "I know; big; dawg!" said Bubba. "It's all good! "It's just Rayshawn; crying, because he's keeps losing his money at the crap table!" said Bubba as he tries to see who Jake has in his room. Jake cracks up asking "is that all?"! "Because that ain't nothing new" he laughs. "Bubba laughs too then asked "who you got there?" "Uh, this is my beautiful neighbor" said Jake. Candis waves from the bed, not wanting him to really get a good look at her, just in case they meet up again with Jason and Rayshawn around. Bubba gives him the thumbs up 'look, as he walks away spouting "playa! "Playa! "Handle 'yo; business! Jake shuts the window laughing saying "Dank's a fool!" "I've known him since Elementary." "Are parents are really good friends" he said passing her the joint. "They even moved to Texas together, his parents and mine." "That's why my brother and I, and Bubba, are thick; as thieves" he said, hitting on the joint. "We; tight! "Mostly because we are the only ones left out here in Treeberry, out of all our family members." He gets up off the bed as he's talking and puts a CD in. It's 'Keith Sweat, singing one of his jams and she has always been a big fan of his music. And 'Jake, being the player that he is, takes her by the hand saying "dance with me." Candis smiles saying "don't you have to get back to your guests?" Holding her close he replies "you are my guest. "And I want you all to myself, in my room."

Blushing she tries not to believe too much of what he's saying because she knows how guys ‘lie, to get what they want! Running that same game; ‘she does, but in a different ‘way, to get what ‘she, wants! ‘Can’t play a player, is what comes to her mind as she smiles up at him voicing “yeah. “Alright. “Jake”! “Tell me anything” she says smirking. He looks deep into her hazel brown eyes confessing “I wouldn’t lie about that.” “I have, always wanted to have you alone in my room, ever since I met you.” With smiling eyes she looks to read his face and even though she is high, she tries to keep her game face ‘on, like she ain’t trippin. But then he kisses her and in that moment she lets down her guard and kisses him back, not caring that there is about 50 to 100 people at his house, as she stands there, in the middle of his room, in the dark of the ‘black light, kissing him.

Making out with her neighbor is exciting, but risky. He tells her to lie back on his bed. And she says “Jake?” “I’m not ready for all that.” He says “ready for all of what?” “Sex” she says. He replies “no problem. “I just want to cash in on ‘that, “rain; check” you owe me.” She glares at him “you don’t owe me anything.” “And besides, I’m not into just going; down on people.” “You know?” “So---, she pauses hoping he’s getting what she’s saying which is “she’s “not” doing him! He looks at her long and hard with a smile on his face saying “Candis, that’s why I like you.” “You’re different.” “You think I don’t know about these girls out here?” “I know you’re a sweet young lady, and I just want to make you feel like a good girl; should feel” he says as he’s rubbing his hand slowly up her leg, saying “just lay back.” “I won’t hurt you.” “I promise” he says.

She studies his eyes and his face and then she says “what if someone comes barging in your room?” He gets up saying “see...; I’m locking the door!” “Now, you have nothing to worry about.” Candis thinks on it. Weighing out the pros and cons thinking to herself “well... if he tries to rape me, what could I pick up and beat him over the head with?” But then she remembers the ‘Jake; that was at her house; for hours! And who was also a real gentleman; all night! ‘Even though, he followed her back to her room, and was ‘pretty much, naked on her bed. ‘But aside from that, a pretty cool dude. And not to mention he has a gang of people over his house ‘and the last thing he ‘needs, is to catch a ‘case, from having ‘all, this, weed, lying; around in his room!

So she stops tripping and slowly lays back on his bed as he’s kissing her some more. Keith Sweat is still playing on the stereo as he starts to kiss down her stomach. She still has her dress on, not feeling safe enough to take it off. He pulls her dress up to her waist, past her belly button and starts to take off her; delicates. She says "Jake, I don't feel comfortable about taking them off." He looks up at her in her eyes, from in between her legs and without saying a word he slowly slides her panties over to one side so she will feel more; "comfortable"! With his eyes closed he starts to lick on her softly, gently, like a tickling feather up against her skin. And when he sees that she is starting to relax her legs more, he begins to lick her, like she's his 'favorite, ice cream cone.

Candis lays there moaning and moving to every lick of his tongue as she's holding on to his ears. While touching his head of hair, she gently rubs it and puts his head right where she wants him to be. Her climb starts to go up slowly--, then slower--, then it gets high--, then higher--, and as she's staying 'steady, in her climb; the higher--, she goes; the harder--, and harder her blossoming 'bud, becomes! And when he finally gets 'her, to the highest; skies, of her climax! Her head begins to 'shake, uncontrollably from side to side like a 'lightning; struck cloud, as she 'yells; out "ahhhh--! "Yes! "Jake! "Yesssss--!

When she was going through that 'stage, he could see and hear in her voice an undeniable; 'scream, of 'pure, bottled; up 'sexual; tension that was waiting to be; unleashed! Afterwards his confidence; sored after hearing and watching her climax. Jake is so pleased because he has 'done, what he had set out to do, which was; making her 'scream, at his command! So as he's getting up off the bed he smiles a big smile at her, as if to say "got; you"!

He grins at her and goes into his bathroom to wipe off his face and to brush his teeth. Candis is still; lying there in the moment; 'basking, if you will! But the energy from their connection is 'broken, when there's a hard; knock on his bedroom door! It's an angry girl's voice on the other side of the door yelling "Jake?"! "Are you in there?"! "Jake?!" she yelled; one last time, in a pissed off voice. Then she walked off; cursing! Candis already sitting back up on the bed, stands to fix her dress and her hair in the mirror. She laughs out loud saying "somebody's; in trouble--!" Jake comes out of the bathroom laughing back, saying "it ain't; me--!" He laughs out loud looking at Candis saying to her "that was fun"! And with a quirky; look on his face, he smiles. Candis just giggled a silly little laugh 'like, "I just had the best! "Nut! "Ever! Kind of laugh. Jake puts his big bag of weed back in his drawer after taking a few buds out saying to Candis "here you go, so you can smoke some with your friend." Candis says "naw--, you don't have to do that." Jake replies "don't get all weird on me." "Take it!" "You know I like you, or I wouldn't have done what I did, to you." He combs his hair while looking at her saying "see... like that girl, who just knocked on my door all crazy and shit!" He goes on to say "yeah, she's liking on me, but she don't know how to act!" "I haven't even kissed that broad and she's all on my nuts!"

He puts the comb down on the dresser voicing "I don't need a chick like that on my team!" "You know, what I'm saying?" Candis just looks at him 'with his fine ass; self and nods her head yes. He slides one hand down her arm slowly asking "are you ready to get back out there and finish partying with me?" She chuckles "let's do it! And as the room door swings open, to the right of them is that girl standing in the hallway waiting; for Jake! She looks at Candis like "you! "Black! "B^tch! "What are you doing, with my man?"! Candis looks her up and down and then back up to her eyes with a twisted; sista look on her face as if to be saying "I just got done...! "Be'yotch"! "By the 'man, on your; "wish-list"!

The girl walks up to Candis all drunk and as she's looking at Jake she yells "who the f^ck is she; Jake?"! Candis shouts "who the f+*k are you?"! The girl looks at Candis and with her neck moving she says "I'm Katey! "His b$tch! "Who are you?"! Candis says "I'm the chick that just left out of his room!" "And that's all you need to know!" Katey says "yeah! "And what were you doing in his room?"! "Hoe!" Candis get up in her face yelling "b$tch! "Slow your role!" "Don't let the drinks; be the reason you get your ass; whooped!" Katey glances over at Jake then 'back to Candis, with drunken; confidence she says "ain't nobody; whooping my; ass!"

Candis looks down at her because she's shorter than her and blurts out "don't let me make you another 'episode, of when keeping it 'real, goes; wrong"! "You Willy-Wonka; look-in; biscuit, eaten; b*tch"! 'Katey, not liking Candis's smart mouth attempts to charge towards her but Jake intervenes and grabs her saying "hey?"! "Hey?"! "Katey?"! "You're f*^kin; trippin!" "First of all!" "I'm not your man!" "And second, this is my neighbor! "One of my good friends! Candis just laughs at her as if to say "hoe! "You don't want 'none, of me!" Katey with her hands on her hips looks at Jake shouting "oh...! "Really?"! "Is that how it is?"! "I'm not your girl?"! "You're saying that sh*t; now; Jake!" "But we both 'know; who's bed you'll be in tonight?"! Jake shouts "get her drunk ass out of here"! Then her friend grabs her by the hand and take her away from the situation. Candis looks at her 'hard, as she's walking away like 'kick rocks; skeezer!" Before you get stomped!" Then with her arms folded Candis turns her attention to Jake saying "is she your woman or what?"! "Hell, no!" "She just likes me!" he said. Candis says "I can see that." "And apparently, she must like you 'a lot, to risk; getting her ass beat!" Jake says "I told you, I don't like her like that!" Candis grunts "but I bet you like her enough to have her suck on your "magic-mic" from time to time though; huh?"! He blurts out "what?"! "No...!" he says with a guilty look on his face.

Candis not believing him says "you're doing something with her, or she wouldn't be trippin that hard!" she said walking away from him with a look on her face like 'you be lying, just like the rest of these guys in this town. He yells out "Candis! "It ain't like that! And with his hands extended outwardly he yells "where are you going?"! While he's trying to get Candis to believe him, a group of people are pushed aside when Jake's brother; Jordan rushes up to him saying "bro!" "The cops are at the door!"

The brother's both rush to the front door and step outside. Jake, smiling says "hey..., Officer Thompson!' 'Luckily, he's a good friend of their dad's. "Hey..., Jakey!" he replies. "How long is the party going to be going on for?" "We're getting complaints!" say the Officer. "Awe...! "Complaints already?" said Jake with one hand over his heart and a sad smile. Jake grumbles "it's only 12 o'clock!" "I get that!" said Officer Thompson. "And if you turn down the music, it might get you a couple more hours."

The door opens and out comes Robin with two plates to give to the two cops because she knows them from the neighborhood as well. Officer Thompson says "awe--, Robin!" "You didn't have to do that!" Jake beams "oh, yes, we, do!" "You know you're like family to us!" She gives the other plate to his partner 'Officer Grady, who lifts up the foil off his plate cheering "yum...! "Ribs!" And with a big smile on his 'face, Grady says "thank you, young lady." The two cops walk off happy with their meals in hand. And when Office Thompson looks back as he's opening the cop car door he yells to Jake and his brother "two more hours; 'boys, and it's time to shut it down!"

Officer Grady nods in agreement and laughs as he's getting in the car. But when he 'sniffs thy air, he voices "is that weed, I smell?"! Grady laughing out loud says "they should have given us some of that; too!" The two cops drive off laughing and with Grady smirking he says "see... and you didn't even want to stop by them boy's house!" "Now look at us, we got us a home cooked meal!" Officer Thompson chuckles with him as they drive away. 'Yep, the cops know the boys smoke weed from time to time, so they don't bust them on it. But if they only 'knew, just how much 'weed, those boys sold in a 'day; it would make their 'dark; hair, turn grey! 'A smiling cactus, I mean' a smiling Candis, makes her way back outside to the backyard. She walks over to the long food table to make herself a small plate. After all of that 'moaning, and 'groaning, she did in his room, she felt like she had worked up an appetite. While filling up her plate she looks around the yard to see if Roxy is still kick-in it with Steeli'o, then she takes a dainty bite from one of the ribs on her plate. With the delicious sauce dancing around in her mouth she turns her head suddenly after hearing a loud “woo-hoo”! It was coming from over by the hot tub.

A small crowd was looking on as Roxy was twirling her shirt with one finger over her head like a ‘rodeo; cowgirl, as the crowd cheered ‘her, and two other girls on. Candis laughs ‘thinking, at least, she still has her bra on! As ‘Candis, is standing next to a girl she doesn’t know she says to the girl “Roxy’s; gone wild!” The girl to the right of her laughs back, voicing “yep! “Somebody’s hel’la; drunk!”

Candis can see that Roxy is doing her thing, so she decides to text Naquawna to see what she’s doing? She would call her directly but it is too noisy in the backyard to talk, so Candis text Naquawna saying “what’s up?” “Naquawna text back “nothing much, just chillin.” Naquawna texted her again; asking “so how’s the party going?” Candis replies “it’s off the hook!” “Wish you were here.” Candis adds “did you go to the movies?” “Yep” she answered. Candis thinks “poor thing, she’s probably too embarrassed to say ‘no, at this point because Rayshawn has her waiting at home; yet again!

“What did you go see?” texted Candis. “Hang-over 2” it was hilarious texted Naquawna. “Hey...?” I thought we were going to go see that movie together?” texted Candis. Then she says to herself “bump this!” “I’m calling her ass!” “She is lying about going to the movies with Rayshawn; because Rayshawn has been here the whole time; gambling! “I’m about to caught this heffa in a lie” she mumbles as she’s walking to the side gate entrance ‘where it is less noisy from all the music and the loud laughing and carrying on.

Naquawna picks up the phone and Candis can tell that she is not at home after hearing the clanking of glasses and all the chattering in the background. She says to her “where are you at?” Naquawna answers “hold on. She tells Mike, she will be right back and that she is going to the restroom to talk. When Naquawna gets to the bathroom where it is quiet she says “hey girlly!” “How’s your cutie-pie doing?”! Candis can’t help but crack a big grin when she says “he’s doing; just fine!” She cups her hand over her mouth with the phone saying “I told you sis, I got game!” “Jake ‘did me, tonight; in his room, with all these ‘people, in his house! Naquawna and Candis scream with laughter like they both just found out that they won a ‘sweepstakes, contest. Naquawna blurts out “you are ‘such, a hoe!” Candis laughs back saying “I know; right?”! Naquawna asked “was he good or what?”! Candis said “was he good?”! “That mother fu*kaka had my ‘toes; cracking!” “You, hear; me?”!

They were laughing so hard about how she sounded when she was climaxing 'out, his name, and then out of nowhere, Candis hears a deep familiar voice walking up to the party door entrance; behind her. It is 'Jason, with two of his friends saying "Candis"! "Is that you?"! She turns around; slowly and he gives her a big bear hug stating "I didn't know you were coming to this party! "Come on in!" "Let's kick it!" he says as he's opening up the gate to go in. Candis stuttering tries to think up a quick excuse but instead ends up saying "oh..., umm..., ahhhh..., I..., I'm waiting on Naquawna, she might need a ride!" "But I'll be in there" she adds. "So you go on ahead in there and save me a dance." "Okay." He nods and walks into the party with his homie's after giving her a quick peck on the lips.

"Oooooh...!" Snap!" said Naquawna after hearing the conversation. She continues to say "he knows; "Jake"! "B*tch"! Candis cracks "yah; think?"! And in a 'sarcastic, panicking; voice Candis adds "this town is way--; too small!" "I'm about to call Roxy! "I'm, out of here!" Naquawna says "isn't she already there with you, at the party?"! "Yes...! "She's in the hot tub." "Oh!" "Crap!" said Naquawna. "Let me guess?!" She's got her clothes off?!" Or at least her top!" Because you know how; "proud" she is about them implants; of hers!" Candis busted up laughing saying "you know you ain't right!" Naquawna retorts "I can 'joke, about it!" It's not like I'm 'dog-in her; out!" I got a pair myself!" Call that hoe!" says Naquawna laughing. Candis chuckles "I'm ma call her, but first' who are you out with?" "Rayshawn?" asked Candis wanting to see if she's gonna lie. Naquawna tisk-ed, saying "no, it's Mike!" He took me to the movies and now we are at some little night club 'like bar, up in Treeberry city, where they have open mic, poetry night and he "claims" he's going to do a poem for me. "Aw..., how sweet is that?" "See..., I am so glad you didn't wait around for that 'super, 'sorry; bastard!" said Candis. "So, any-who, now let me call Roxy on three-way and she better 'pick up, because I'm; out"!

When Roxy's phone rings her new friend "Steeli'o" answers it and they can hear Roxy in the background yelling "hey?"! "Don't be answering my phone!" He laughs and gives her a kiss handing her; her phone. She says "hello?" in Spanish. Repeating "oh, la' she said in a 'happily; drunken voice. "Hey..., it's me and Naquawna on 3- way! "Yea...! "Naquawna you're here, at the party too?" cheers Roxy. "No. "She's out with Mike on a date" said Candis, trying to talk quickly. Candis says "I'm going to have to leave the party!" "Why...?"! "We are having so much fun!" sighed Roxy, all disappointed with Candis for even suggesting that they leave. "I know Rox, but my other man 'Jason, just got here" said Candis. "Jason?!" replied Roxy. "Isn't that the guy who is throwing the party?" that I met earlier. "Umm..., no...; Drunky!" "That is Jake that you met earlier!" said Candis. Candis is now getting frustration because she is not trying to get busted. She shouts "tell her Naquawna, because she is "not" comprehending what I'm saying!" Naquawna says "Roxy?"! "Candis is leaving!" "Are you going with her?" "Or are you staying at the party?" "Oh..., okay!" "My bad," laughed Roxy. "I'm drunk; child!" she said giggling.

"But yeah, I'm going to go to Steeli'o's house for the after party!" "And I will texted you all the info, of where I am; okay?" "Cool!" says Candis. But then she says "Roxy?" what's really going on?"! "He is a stranger!" "Are you sure you're going to be alright?" because you sound way-- too drunk to be going to his house alone!" "No, trust me" said Roxy. "I won't be alone some girls from this party I met are going too." "And I got all of his info including his license because I told him 'that, was the only way I was going to be able to go to his after party." "And he knows 'that's, how we girls; roll!

Steeli'o politely snatches the phone from Roxy's hand and tells her "to eat the food that he's brought back for her to eat." He gets on the phone saying to Candis and Naquawna "that Roxy will be safe with him." "And that she will text them a picture of his driver's license." He adds "so don't worry, she will eat now, and call you when we get to my house." Roxy pulls the phone from his hand like she forgot to say something 'and with food in her mouth she shouts "Naquawna?"! "I am so-- glad you didn't have to see that Hawaiian chick who was sitting on your man's lap 'because girl, you would have wanted to whoop his ass!"

"Did you tell her Candis?!" "That; that---; his, sorry ass was gambling with some girl sitting on his lap, kissing all over him and sh*t?"! "Well, that's what Candis told me!" "I didn't see him, because I don't know what he looks like." "So--, I am glad you're out having fun with Mike, because that guy "Rayshawn"! Roxy; slurs "doesn't deserve you!" "What's she talking about Candis?!" asked Naquawna in a mad; as hell, confused; voice. "What are you saying?"! "You mean to tell me Rayshawn is there?"! "With another broad?"! "And you didn't tell me?"! "Oops!" said a drunk Roxy. "I'm sorry!" she adds. Saying "I thought you told her Candis!" Then Roxy's phone loses its signal and hangs up when Steeli'o grabs her phone.

"Wow...!" said Naquawna. "Are you f*cking kidding me?!" she gripes. Candis says "it's not like that!" Naquawna adds "is that why you called me?"! "So you could see if I was still; waiting at home for him?"! "Or let me guess!" "So you could see if I would lie, and make up some bullshit story about going to the movies with Rayshawn, when you knew he was there the whole time!" "Dammm!" "Thanks! "Homie!" shouted Naquawna sarcastically. "That's Fu*ked; up; Candis"! Then before Candis could get in a word. Naquawna hears the girl in the bar, on the mic saying "next; up!" "Mike"! "Doing a poem for his sweetheart who is here in thy; audience!" Naquawna grits "I got, tah go!" "Mike's doing a poem for me!"

Candis yells "I am so---; sorry!" "I just didn't want to say anything because you were out on a "real; date" with Mike"! "And you know?"! "I would tell you later, like the next day because I didn't want to ruin your night!" Naquawna sniffles out "whatever! "I got, tah go! "Mike's up on stage, I can hear him" she said holding back tears. Candis says "wait!" But the phone disconnects. Naquawna throws her phone in her purse and scrambles out of the bathroom to hurry back to her seat 'which is in the front row. Mike stalls by saying something funny to the bar tender like "how strong his drink was earlier!" "And to keep them coming!"

Naquawna gets seated and Mike all proud says "this is for my lady friend, this beautiful lady in the front row. All eyes go on Naquawna and she 'blushes, real hard wishing if only she could shrink down in her chair and vanish. Mike starts his poem as he looks directly at her. He says "I met her one night at a party. "I went there just to have some fun. "Then I met someone. "She was beautiful, as a midnight star, thus far. "I asked her to dance. "And she gave me a chance. "We danced on the floor. "Oh… but I wanted so much more. "To kiss her, to taste her, no other woman could replace her. "From her lips, too her thighs; as she seduces me with her eyes. "I'm hooked on her smile. "Her laugh. "And when she cries. "My shoulder she can rely. "I was made to love you, like no other. "Yes. "Naquawna! "I am; that brother! The crowd; cheered giving Mike a big round of applause as he walked off the stage.

When he walks back to the table Naquawna is sitting there with a big warm smile on her face 'like, thanks for that great poem about me. She stands before him saying "that was so sweet Mike" then she gives him a big hug and a kiss on his lips. Naquawna gets a little hot flash down inside her soul when she sits back down in her seat. It was so obvious that she was really flattered at the way Mike had serenaded her in front of a room full of people. 'Something; "Rayshawn" would never do!" she thinks to herself. She even felt a little better inside, after the 'blow, to her heart she was just dealt 'finding; out, that Rayshawn was at a party with another girl.

Mike gets them another drink from the bar and they sit and enjoy each other while listen to the duration of the show. Then afterwards he takes her home. As he's driving her home he reaches down and grabs her hand and holds it while they ride back listening to one of his mixed CD's and when a beautiful song comes on called: Mercy!" which is being sung by Shawn Mendes. Naquawna closes her eyes and listens to the words and can only see Rayshawn's face.

It is cold and foggy when they get back to town, so he parks his car and walks her up to her door. She says "I really had a great time with you tonight". Her grandfather is up getting a drink from the kitchen and hears Naquawna talking to a man on the porch. He opens the door to see who it is that she is talking too, and she's surprised when the front door opens, wondering what her granddad is doing up so late. "Grandpa?" sorry, did we wake you?" He says "no. "I was already up. "Come on inside you two, it's cold out there" he said looking at Mike. Naquawna looking at her grandpa returns "no. "He was just leaving. But Mike extended his hand to her grandfather saying "hello sir." "My name is Mike." "It's nice to meet you" said Mike with a smile. Her granddad shakes his hand back voicing "nice to meet you too, son."

Naquawna walks into the house thinking "oh, no. "What if, Rayshawn comes by tonight and sees someone's car out front?" But then, she thinks "yes!" that would be good for his 'ass, to see that 'yes, someone is over her house; who gives a 'damn; about 'her; too! So, she takes it a little further and she opens the curtains a bit, so passer buyers, can see inside her house, and at the same time she can see who drives by. Mike takes a seat on the couch and Naquawna sits down next to him, and she glances at every car that passes by, but tries not to be "too" obvious about it.

None of the cars ended up being Rayshawn's though; thus far. Grandpa heads back to bed after making himself a snack, smiling he says "it was nice meeting you son." Mike returns "okay sir, nice meeting you too. "Goodnight. Naquawna has never introduced any of her "so called" boyfriends to her granddad before, because she just never felt the need to. 'Even though, "maybe" it was because she had so many "boy-toy; boyfriends"! So, to introduce them all to her granddad would have been; "catastrophic!" to say the least.

Her and Mike sit and watch a movie on the BET channel and enjoyed each other's; company some more. So much so, that she even popped some popcorn for them both to share. Not really being in an affectionate mood, or wanting to lead him on, she ends up only letting him kiss her a view times. And that was as far as she was willing to go. Her mind just wouldn't stop thinking about Rayshawn being at a party with another girl tonight after all they've been through. And Mike knew she was preoccupied about Rayshawn because she had already asked him to drive by Rayshawn's house before he took her home earlier, and Rayshawn's car was not at home. All she could think about was who Rayshawn, would be sleeping with tonight.

Mike could tell that she was not her bubbly self because after they drove by Rayshawn's house and she seen that his car was not home; yet, her mood; changed. He made the best of the night by telling her how pretty and special she was as they sat next to each other on the couch. "And that poem" she kept on telling him. "You are so talented to be able to make up a poem off the top of your head like that" she said in amazement. "Thanks" he said.

She goes on to say "no really, that was some good free styling you did!" He knew by the smile on her face 'that; that poem "really" made her night! Because he showed her what guys do, when they are really trying to show a 'woman, that they like her. Mike leaves her house at about 1:00 in the morning but not before he gives her a big long kiss goodnight. Sad to say but Rayshawn never drove by or called Naquawna at all that night and she was disappointedly; pissed about it!

Naquawna went to bed and she tossed and turned all night. Roxy sent a text to Candis and Naquawna's phone at around 2:45 in the morning to let them know she was okay and where she was at. She also attached a picture of Steeli'o's Driver's license to show who he was. When Naquawna got Roxy's text she was hoping it was Rayshawn when she grabbed her phone off her headboard, to read it. But when she sees that it is "not" from Rayshawn, she just rolled back over and went back to sleep.

When Candis gets her text she's at home having her own issues, with all her lights off in her apartment 'avoiding, Jake and Jason's calls. She doesn't know 'what, she would even say to the both of them, if they were to come and confront her about trying to play them both. She lies in her bed with a worried smirk on her face 'thinking; that they are 'both, going to find out about her, because guys talk just as much as girls do. Guys talk about "what they are doing?" "And 'who, they are doing it; with!"

Her phone 'kept, going off, first Jake texted "where are you at?" And then 15 minutes, after that, Jason texted saying "let's dance!" asking are you back; yet?" "This is "not" good!" thinks Candis as she chuckles her way to sleep; voicing "way too much drama for one night!" Now down in the valley, drama free' is where Roxy's trying to be. While she's way out in Carmello Bay, passed Treeberry city. Roxy is having a ball!

Down in the Valley Roxy thinks to herself, now this is just my kind of crowd, all the cute boys you could look at, and all the drink and smoke you could handle! Some of the girls were even in the kitchen doing a line of blow on a big glass table. Roxy was not with that. She had seen; many of 'snow, blow; days, so she vowed to keep her nostril; empty! Steeli'o was sitting back in a big King on the throne like chair while everybody was dancing in the party room area. He only let the coolest people he could trust come to his house. So it was maybe only like 30 people there and everybody got along just fine.

Steeli'o's house is so big, with its tall vaulted ceilings and its grand hallways, which lead to the party room. In the party room it is laid out nicely with all kinds of games like pin ball, Pac man and even some of the newer machines with 'guns, attached to them, so his guess can play Warcraft; games. All of the games were lined along the walls. Two Ping-Pong tables were on one side of the room and a red pool table was in the center at the end of the room.

There were also 7 round tables with booth seating's with mirrors all along the walls. And in the middle of the room there is plenty of space for dancing. Steeli'o only tells Roxy about the home-theater in the downstairs room because he doesn't want other people to ask could they go watch a movie down there, or sneak down there, to have sex. So he had everybody stay up in the party room in one area which he called "The Refuge Room"!

Once everyone gets comfortable dancing, mingling and having fun, Steeli'o tells his main boys Jake and Jordan "to keep an eye out on his guests, so he can talk to Roxy privately." Steeli'o tells Roxy "to come with him, to the upstairs room so he can show her around." She smiles saying "what do you want to show me?" she asked with one hand on her hip laughing. He takes her by the hand and pulls her slowly up the stairs to his secret room. He says "close your eyes" and she giggles in anticipation to see the surprise he has to show her. When he opens the door he tells her to open her eyes, and low, and behold!" it's this lavished, pimped out, pleasure room.

It has all kinds of pleasure toys, around the room. And on one side of the room hanging from the ceiling is a sex-swing, with a giant pillow underneath the swing for easy access. There is also a black massage table on the other side of the room with all kinds of scented flavored body oils, on a small table against the window which she could smell from the doorway. In the middle of the room is a big plush, waterproof bed that has a half dome over it with all kinds of switches, and shower head holes, and lights. On his floor it is covered with this 'flat rock, like tile, all beautifully marbled, though out the room, with a drainage hole in the middle of his floor. 'Roxy; amazed, says "what kind of room is this?!" "It's called a fantasy room!" he said. "You can make love in thy rain, or in thy snow, and all of thy lights, heat up like thy sun!" "So, if you want to be making love on a Tropical Island, or in the Snowy Alps, all of thy sounds and pictures make it all come to life!" "The walls come alive and become like a surround sound picture movie theater and the surround sound fills thy room like you are 'really, where; ever you want to be!" "And I make 'all, your sexual; dreams come true!" he said. "Really--?!" said Roxy with wide eyes. Saying "so, this room can make "all" of my love making; fantasy's come true?"! He replies "yess, with just one touch of a switch; and me!"

A sly 'grin, forms across his face as he gives her a crooked smile. Roxy is speechless when she nods "hmm. She must admit she really does want to try it out and she even gives it some thought as she's checking out the bed, walking around it, while looking around his room. She says out loud "making love in a 'simulated, tropical forest!" wow--! "I would love that" she tells him. But then she thinks back to what Candis had told her "take your time, and go slow, with someone you really like!" "And most importantly 'no, sex!" Roxy, flashing back to those haunting words, saying to Steeli'o "I want--, too--. "But--, I can't!" was the look on her face.

She then says "well--, maybe one day, you can show me how it works, when we get to know each other better!" He tilts his head back, than when he moves his head forward again he tilts it to one side as he's looking at her, because he "did not!" want to hear that answer. She looks at him with a sexy blink and he smiles knowing that he has to respect her decision but he still ends up saying "awh; really?!" he said kissing her on thy lips saying "you know you want me to make love to you right now, while thy snowflakes are softly falling down, all--, over--, your body, as I'm kissing and licking every part of you" he said looking deeply into her eyes.

Roxy starts to feel like she could really get swept away by the room and all it has to offer. Not to mention his smooth Italian voice talking through her, making her body; eagerly; wanting to live out her 'fantasies, even 'more; 'now; in his room! Steeli'o has never been known to be a quitter, so he wasn't about to start now. He tells her to sit down on his bed and try it out to see how comfortable it is. He smiles asking "you like it?" "Yes, it is very nice" she said smiling back. She runs her hands across the blanket he has on top of his bed asking "is this Mink?" "No. "It's Chinchilla, and it's in a rare color and only 10 people in thy world have this same one."

"I ordered it straight from thy factory" he said rubbing her hand softly. She smiles saying "nice... "It must have cost you a fortune?" With a smile he puts his hand in her hair moving it from her ear voicing "it's just money. "Hopefully we live another day to make more, right?!" he said smiling at her as he eases his face into heirs and kisses her again. Steeli'o knows with his handsome face and his pretty eyes and his "swagger; ability" that he can talk a woman right, out, of, her; under garments! Especially when he pours on his strong 'Italian; accent!

While he's caressing her hand and her arm he says "at least lay back and tell me how you think my bed feels, up against your back." She thinks for a second as she flips her hair out of her face putting it behind her ear saying "okay--, no harm in that." Real slowly she lays down on his big oversized; fur covered; bed and her arms go up above her head to get the real feel of the bed and he kisses her endlessly all over her face, her mouth, her neck and down between her breasts. She kisses him back with passion like no other she's ever kissed before. He talks to her in Italian, telling her how much he 'wants, to "lay" inside her!

Then the door swings open to his room, and it's some drunken girl looking for the bathroom. He yells "get thy hell out of here"! The girl dazed and wobbling back and forth replies "sorry; dude!" "I just need to find the bathroom!" The mood now 'ruined, between Steeli'o and Roxy, prompts Roxy to say "I'll take her to the bathroom!" She gets up off the bed and looks back at him and blows him a kiss and heads down the stairs with the girl, to show her which bathroom to use. Roxy is kind of relieved that she and Steeli'o got interrupted because she really wants to get to know him and "not" just sleep with him and become another girl who got swept away by his "fantasy" room!

He walks back down the stairs 'disappointed, but looks for Roxy anyway and sees that the party is still going strong. He looks around the house but no Roxy is in sight. He starts to wonder if he scared her off, by coming on to strong with her, up in his room. But then he finds her standing by the dining room table eating on some strawberries with two other girls. Looking at him she says "hey, you?" He walks up to her and puts his hands through her hair saying "you are a sly one!" "You know how to get away from a man like me; huh?" Roxy puts the strawberry up to her lips and bites it stating "I don't know what you mean; Steeli'o"! Then she takes another bite of the fruit 'slowly, and then she licks her lips, before kissing him.

He kisses her back and looks her in her eyes saying to her "I'm going to have to keep my eyes on you." She laughs and pulls him towards the dance floor shouting "my song!" "My song--; is playing!" It is one of her all-time favorite songs called: "Big Pimpin" by Jay-Z. Featuring UGK. The dance floor fills up; quickly seeing that she is "not" the only one who loves this song!

The die-hard partiers are still partying; none stop! And some others are playing beer pong, while some couples are 'making out, in the table booths. Roxy is having the best time ever! And she hasn't had 'this, much fun in a 'day, in a really, really, long time! You would 'think, by her being; a "stripper" that she would party like this on a regular; basis! But quite the 'opposite, she is all about her 'money, and the partying is secondary! But tonight has truly been a blast to her. "I guess all 'work, and no 'play, isn't really; the best way!" she thinks to herself. And with a smile on her face she secretly gives a toast to Candis for inviting her to the "player's; ball"! Where she 'thinks, she's met the 'man, of her dreams!

'Cock- ka-doodle-do...! A Rooster crows down the street in one of Steeli'o's neighbor's backyards. It is morning and Roxy is passed out on Steeli'o's couch and he is laid out in his lazy boy recliner. The sun comes shining in through the living room window and wakes Roxy up. "Dammit!" she says aloud while she's rubbing under her eyes. She complains "my head"! And in a low croaky voice she says "Steeli'o--, do you have any aspirin?" He opens one eye and looks at her like "what are you waking me up for woman?"

Glancing his way she gives him a sweet smile repeating "I have a headache." He opens both his eyes and focuses on her saying "there is some aspirin in thy kitchen cabinet." Walking slowly to the kitchen she asked "do you have milk?" I don't want to take them on an empty; stomach." "Yes--, Roxy" he replied. "Get a glass of milk and take your pills!" Please--! Laughing from the kitchen she says "I take it, you're not a morning person?"

After taking the two pills she goes back into the living room and sits down softly on his lap. She blurts "I know what you need!" He gets a big grin on his face, until she says "breakfast"! His happy grin goes away quickly, and when she sees the disappointment on his face she blurts out "what were 'you--, thinking?"! He lifts up one of his eye brows to imply "what do you think I was thinking?" She laughs saying "come on..., get up." you will love it" she replies. Pulling him up from his chair she adds "they have the best; breakfast in town!" "Where is this place at?" he asked. She answers "Kappy's. "My treat.

He looks in her eyes and grins saying "are you trying to make love to me, with food?" She laughs out "yes, I, am!" and they both laugh and embrace and then go to start getting ready. Roxy goes to the bathroom to fresh-in up and he goes up stairs to do the same. After brushing his teeth he grabs his shades and runs down the stairs. Roxy spits out some mouth wash in the sink and meets him by the front door. As he and Roxy start walking out the front door, here come 'Elvina, his housekeeper saying "Ciao; Steeli'o!" she said with her strong; Italian accent. "You are up very early" she said smiling. He answers back something in Italian and Roxy just; melts. Then in English he says "we are going to breakfast." are you hungry?" Elvina says "no. "You two go ahead, I'm meeting my sister for lunch when I finish cleaning up here." She looks at Roxy and then back at Steeli'o and in Italian she asked "who is this pretty young lady?" Steeli'o returns "she's my future wife!" he said in Italian. They both laugh and then he says in English "this is Roxy." Elvina takes her by the hand voicing "nice to meet you." and Roxy gives her a warm hello greeting, back. Steeli'o then kisses Elvina on the cheek, saying "see you later" in Italian.

'Elvina, is this sweet little old lady that has known Steeli'o ever since he was a little boy. She has soft looking curly grey hair that sits on top of her head in a round bun. Her body frame is medium with a height of 5 feet, 5 inches tall. She has a cute smile and one dimple on each side of her cheeks, which are very noticeable when she smiles. Elvina she's the only one who can come and go as she pleases to Steeli'o's home. Steeli'o even bought her; her own house a while back, which is up the street from his, so she can walk to and from his place. He thinks of her as a second mother and only trusts 'her, in his house when he's out of town.

He opens the car door for Roxy and she sits down in his beautiful Mercedes Benz. The car is fully loaded all leather interior with a bumping system. The paint job alone cost him thousands of dollars but he knew just what he wanted, which was a deep ocean bluish, green, candy paint, it looked just like the ocean on a beautiful clear day. And the top coat was 'topped off, with a high gloss coating to bring out all the specks of light green. It also had custom made rims, which really brought out the cars personality.

Roxy says "your ride is so; tight"! And as she sat there looking at him she could just feel herself getting wet, just from riding with 'him, in the front seat of his car! She closes her eyes momentarily when he hits the gas; as they fly up the street; towards breakfast. Looking over at him while he's behind the wheel and seeing how hot he looks driving, makes her feel like a 'knotty; girl, who wants to have him in his car, in more ways than one. The place they are going to is not far away from where he lives, so when they pull up to Kappy's Café she kisses him before getting out of the car.

She gets out his car after he opens her door, and then the two walk up to the place and of course there's a line because the food is so--, good.

Roxy has the hostess put his name, on the waiting list, and then they go back outside and wait, while sipping on the complimentary coffee, talking to each other about life. Roxy casually asked him what he 'did, for a living?" and he said "I'm a Jack of all thy, trades!" She replied "what does that mean; exactly?" He answers "I'm a business man!" "I do a little bit of everything" he adds looking up at her from his cup. She smiles "everything like; "what"?! She continues "name one specific thing; that you do" she said with a sip of her coffee. He returns "I buy and sale houses." "Oh... "So... you're into real estate?" she said in an impressive; tone.

Nodding he smiles not wanting to talk too much about himself then he switches the conversation on her asking "so what do you do?" "What's "your" job?" he says tilting his head smiling at her. She pauses not wanting to say she's a "stripper"! So instead, she just says what he said, which is "I two, have many jobs" she laughed. He laughs back saying "ok..., so what is your "specific" job?" She chuckles and looks down at her feet and then "Steeli'o's" name is called, because there table is ready. Relieved to hear the hostess call them in to be seated, she grabs him by the hand and hustle him through the crowd and thinks to herself, how that; was a close call! And now she's hoping he doesn't asks her that again!

"Up on thy other side of town it is still foggy when Naquawna wakes up and gets breakfast started. When her granddad walks into the kitchen she smiles "pancakes and eggs today; grandpa"! He grins "umm... a treat. "You must of have had a nice time last night" he says grinning. Naquawna laughs as she's stirring up the pancake mix answering "yeah, Mike's a pretty nice guy." "He even did a poem for me last night Grandpa, at this poetry place in front of; everybody!" "I was so embarrassed at first, but flattered at the same time!" she said blushing. "You don't say!" said her granddad. He continued "see, that's what men did in my day!" "How do you think I got your grandmother to fall in love with me?" He went on to say "some of the guys now days just don't know how to sweet talk a woman or wine and dine her like we did in my day!"

He gets a big smile on his face when saying "see, I had game!" "I knew how to make my woman feel special!" Naquawna flips over his pancake with a laugh asking "were you a player back then; grandpa?" Let me guess, you had your penny loafers on, and your Pimped out threads, on 'all; creased up, to the tee; huh?" He just laughed, and laughed, saying "ooh...; I was sharp..! "Your grandmother couldn't keep her hands off me!" Naquawna shaking her head giving him his plate laughs out "okayyyy--!" too much information!" she said chuckling. He laughs some more adding "but she was a good woman!" "You couldn't get nothing passed her!" "She knew all the 'lines; that men could; think up!" "And she wouldn't do much of 'anything; until I married her first!" "And I've loved her till this day" he said as he blinked away the tears that filled his eyes. Naquawna could see how emotional he was getting so she comforted him, saying "granddad, now don't go getting all emotional on me!" she said as she hugs him from behind, as he sat at the kitchen table. He wipes his eyes with his napkin and with a sniffle he said "no, I'm alright, I won't get sad." I know I'll see her again one day, rest her soul," Naquawna tries to change the subject to a lighter note by asking "do you need to go shopping today for anything, like deodorant or under clothes?" "No, not yet." "I'm pretty good on all my toiletries" he said while eating. She answers "ok, just let me know when you get low." They both sit at the table eating breakfast and talking.

Naquawna's phone rings and its Candis. When Naquawna answers her phone she blurts out "what's; up?!" with an attitude that was very nasty, towards Candis. Candis blurts back "don't hang up!" "I just called to say, I'm 'very sorry, for not telling you right away when I first saw Rayshawn!" Naquawna pauses while listening to Candis's apology to her as she puts her plate in the sink. When Candis is done 'pleading her case, Naquawna grunts; "I guess; I might let it 'slide, this 'once, if I get treated to a pedicure today!"

Candis laughs out loud "ah; wow! "So now, I got to get your "toes" done!" just for you to be my "friend" again?"! "Yes; yah-do!" laughed Naquawna. "Because you dogged---; me out"! "I would have called you as 'soon, as I 'seen, Jason's black; ass with another broad"! Candis retorts "but I told you "why" I didn't think I should have called you right away!" "Especially, after I found out you were out on a "real" date!"

Naquawna shouts "that is no excuse!" "We are sisters and you dropped the ball on this one!" "Okay...! "Okay...!" said Candis. "I'll get your 'funky; little "toes" done!" "But from here on out!" "I don't want to hear; nothing about you and Rayshawn"! "Okay; fine!" said Naquawna. "Good!" said Candis. "What time, are we going to meet up at the salon?!" asked Candis. "I'll meet you at the nail place in an hour!" answers Naquawna. "But you call and make the appointment" said Naquawna. "Okay; heffa!" joked Candis. "See you in a minute!" she laughs, and then hangs up the phone.

'Now, on a 'perkier; note down in warm Carmello Bay; where the sun is giving off; rays! Roxy is sitting back in her seat looking at Steeli'o like she has 'found, her 'Mr. Right; 'all, in one night! They have both just finished eating there fabulous breakfast's, when he asked her "why she is looking at him like; that?" She gives him a happy smile when answering "because, you are such a handsome man." She asks "why?" "I can't look at you?" she said as she rubs his hand and scoots closer to him. He grunts out a flattering laugh when she moves up to sitting up, closer to him. They stare at each other for a 'few, needing very little words to say and when the waitress comes over to clear their plates Roxy says "I'll be right back." "I'm going to go to the ladies room." She gets up real slow and sexy while looking at him and then he watches her walk away with a smile on his face. In the bathroom she reapplies her lipstick and can't resist the itch to place a call to Candis. With her phone in hand she calls her saying "girllll...! "I think I'm in love!" Candis laughs "No... way!" Roxy shouts "plus, I did what you told me to do!" "No sex, until we get to know each other." Roxy shouts out "honey!" "Can you believe it?!" "Me waiting!" Candis, clapping her hands real loud on the other end of the phone says "you did?!" I am so; proud of you!" And watch, you'll end up doing more things together because you "haven't" slept with him!"

"Where are you at, right now?!" asked Candis. "I'm in the bathroom at Kappy's Café, we just got done eating breakfast!" "Ooh, nice..." said Candis. "I love that place!" Roxy cheers saying "and Candis, you should see his car!" 'Candis; curious says "bring him by the nail salon when you're done eating!" Because Naquawna and I will be getting pedicures done over there in about 45 minutes. Roxy cheers "alright!" "Bet, that!" Then before hanging up Roxy lets out a soft scream saying "I'm so-- excited about this man...!

Candis cheers "I'm so happy for you two!" And not to "toot" my own horn!" But I 'do, feel like 'I'm, a little responsible!" "Well, me and "God" that is!" for bringing this "love; match" together!" Especially since, I-- invited you to Jake's party!" Roxy cracks up laughing saying "You are so--, right!" "And you will "definitely" be my maid of honor if we do, get married!" They both laugh out loud and Candis ends with "I'll see you at the salon!" "Bye for now!" said Roxy hurrying out of the bathroom because she thinks she's been in their way-- to long.

When she comes out of the bathroom and sees Steeli'o at the counter paying the waitress, she shakes her head walking up towards him saying "no! "Babe! "It was my treat! "Remember?" But Steeli'o won't take a dime from her. So she blurts "well, I'll treat you next time!" He smiles and they leave out of the Café arm in arm kissing and hugging. Steeli'o, now; stuffed says "that was-- a great breakfast!" you were right." Roxy replies "I told you so. "And I just love their Eggs Benedict" she said. Smiling at him she says "and you just inhaled those pancakes, once they got to the table."

Steeli'o nodded his head agreeing with her as he grins.

She replies "see, now aren't you glad I woke you up?"! He laughs out "don't push; it!" I do love my sleep!" But yeah, that was worth it" he said tightening his eyes with another smile. They both walk down to his car and as he opens the car door for her to get in it they kiss. He gets in the car and when he closes his car door Roxy says "baby, can you drop me off at Treeberry mall?" I'm going to meet some of my friends there so we can get our toes; done." He saddens, saying "so, you are leaving me now?" "This is what you American's call "to eat and run?" "I don't 'want, to leave you" she said. "But I do need to go home and take a shower and all that good stuff." He rubs the side of her face with the backside of his hand while he's driving and says to her "you are so beautiful; Bella!"

She kisses his hand saying "and you are so handsome." "Talk to me in Italian" she says. And he does (Dio sei talmente Bella) which means (God, you are so beautiful)! Hearing those words makes her 'soften, like an ice cream 'cone, on a hot sunny day. They pull up to the salon and Roxy "makes; sure" he lets her out in front of the salon so the girls can see her get out of his dope; ride. He is such a gentleman to as he tells her; let me get your door for you. When he opens the door for her, Naquawna, Sherry, and Candis's mouths drop open in disbelief. Sherry blurts "well..! "Well..! "Well...! "Miss Thang has found her a "real; man" this time!" voiced Sherry with her lips poked out.

Roxy gives him a long kiss good-bye and then shake her rear into the salon, giving him one last look of her face, when she turns and waves; good-bye. The girls give her a cheerful high five and can't wait to hear all the juicy details. "Girl he is fine..! Blurts Naquawna and Sherry. "And the car is ban-gin!" said Candis. Roxy says "Humm... if you think the car is nice!" "You should see his crib!" Candis grinning real big says "yes, it was me, who hooked my girl up!" she said as she pats herself on the back. Roxy says "chil, and he is so--, sweet"! "I don't know if I can take; it"! "This is just too good to be true!" said Roxy.

Sherry asks "what does he do for a living?" "He told me he's into Real-Estate" said Roxy. "Real-Estate my ass!" said Sherry. She continues "but I guess they can make good money" she adds. "Or at least, they did back in the day!" finished Sherry, meekly. Sherry pauses from talking while her other hand it getting polished. And as she's looking Roxy up and down in her short skirt, and slinky; shirt it compelled her to asks "so... how was the sex?"! Naquawna shouts "Sherry...! "Damn..! "You get right to the business!" Roxy laughs back saying "we haven't had sex; yet!" Naquawna and Sherry say at the same time "say; what?"! "Yes!" says Candis. "Roxy is trying it, the old school way!" "Which means, to get a man's heart; first with real game!" "Without; sex!" shouts Candis.

Sherry laughs "good luck with that!" Then she looks at Roxy with a sour smile saying "now you know, you are not going to be able to hold out on that fine; hottie of a man"! Roxy shouts "just watch me!" "I 'tease, men for a living!" Remember?"! "I 'know, how to hold out!" "Ooh...!" "Tell; it!" shouts Candis. Roxy kicks off her boots and sits down in the pedicure chair in between Candis and Naquawna. Sherry who is getting her nails done, was already at the shop when Naquawna and Candis arrived and they had no clue that Sherry would be there today. It is a slow day at the shop 'being, that it is a Sunday, so the girls can talk freely about what ever happened last night, on everyone's outings.

Roxy takes the focus off of her and Steeli'o for a second asking "so..., Naquawna how was your date with Mike, last night?" 'Surprisingly, Naquawna produces a big smile on her face answering "I can't lie." "I really did have a nice time last night." "Mike, really showed me another side of himself." And she tells them how he did a poem for her and everything. She finished her story with "and..., he came in the house and met my granddad!" "And, he stayed for a while and watched a movie with me!" Candis shouts "what...?"! "You've 'never, introduce 'any, of your 'men, to grandpa!"

Sherry screeches out; "stop!" "Front-in!" "You know you we're thinking about Rayshawn 'all night, while you were with Mike"! Naquawna yells "dang...! "Sherry! "You are so negative today!" "Bruce must; 'not, be 'hitting; it that good!" The other two girls say "oooooh--!" in unison. Sherry; frowns over at her with both of her eyebrows up, blasting "b*tch; please!" "But my man didn't have some 'skeezer, sitting on his lap last night; either!" said Sherry. "Umm...," said Roxy. Saying "that's cold!" Naquawna says "no. "That's cool!" she adds "and I'm not living with a man going on 5 years either, without a commitment!" smirked Naquawna. "Maybe Bruce is bouncing somebody else on his lap too!" "Oh--, snap!" said Candis. Roxy pleads, saying "now, now, yaw; come on!" "We are supposed to be having a nice girls; day out!" she adds.

The salon owner Ms. Lesley tries not to get too involved with her customers 'conversations, but these girls come in on a regular basis so she says "girls...! "Girls! "Relax! "This is a time for relaxation!" she says as she hands them all a plastic champagne glass, and pours them a heaping glass of red wine. The girls settle down saying "thank you, Ms. Lesley!" "You are the bomb!" "Dot com!" Then the girls relax and sit back and sip on their wine and enjoy getting pampered. Roxy tells the girls all about Steeli'o's fantasy bedroom and how she can't wait to try it out. Naquawna says "I'll give you two weeks Ms. Thing!" because I "know" 'you'll crack, by then!" They all laugh out loud when Roxy says to Naquawna "do you want to put a bet on it?"! Candis shout "there--, you go!" make her put up!" or shut up!" Naquawna doesn't take her up on the bet though, saying to Roxy "you'd never tell us, if you really did it; anyway"!

'Sherry, now tired of hearing all about their do's and don'ts when it comes to sex, changes the subject to food, after seeing a picture of a Thanksgiving meal on the cover of a Martha Stewart's magazine. Sherry says "so what are yaw'll doing for Thanksgiving next Thursday?" Everybody just mumbles out what they might do?" And some say they don't know yet. Candis says "I'll probably go to my mom's!" Naquawna chuckles returning "me and granddad are going to your mom's house too!" she laughed. Sherry says "my in laws are coming down!" "I got to cook this year!"

Roxy comments "I'll probably be in Vegas, unless Steeli'o wants to do something, because my mom and dad are still not talking to me that much because their church members frown on what I do for a living". "Awe..., that's messed up!" say the girls. "Well--, once you pay off your house and move back here, they'll come around" spoke Sherry; shockingly, because she never seems to have a nice word to say about anyone. Candis hears her phone ringing in her purse and digs it out, and it is the call she's been waiting for, from Rafee'al! She picks up the phone right away but plays it; cool like; she's out with the girls having a great time and isn't even trippin; if he calls her or not!

When she answers her phone it's with a cute laugh like she had already been laughing off of something someone just 'said, like a joke. The girls look at her like, she's drunk. She laughs out "hello?" And a sultry; man's voice on the other end says "hello, Candis?" It's me; Rafee'al." "Oh. "Hi, she says all nonchalantly. Roxy hits her on her arm asking "who's that you're talking too?" Candis moves her mouth without vocalizing a word and Naquawna reads her lips saying "it's Rafee'al!" They all get a kick out of Candis playing the role like she's not trippin off this man, who she's been waiting forever to call her.

They listen in on her conversation when he says to Candis "did I catch you at a bad time?" "It sounds like you're at a party or something!" She replies "no. "I'm just out with some of my girls, getting our toes done." He chuckles "oh. "I see. "A spa-day; huh?" Laughing she says "yeah, something like that." He says "so what are you doing after you get your toes done?" Grinning she replies "umm--, I really don't have any other plans after this." She is smiling real big when she hits Naquawna on the leg. Then she asked Rafee'al "Why?" "What's up?" she said softly. He says "I just wanted to take you up on that promise, of going on a movie date with me." "I'd like to take you to go see Transformers."

He continues "do you like that movie?" "Yes..., I love that movie!" "I've seen them all!" she raves. "Okay. "Cool" he said. "Then let's go see {The Dark of the Moon} at 9 o'clock tonight then?" "Okay. "That will be great" she says with a big smile on her face. He tells her, "I'll call you 30 minutes before I come pick you up, so you can give me the directions to your place, that way you can get back to your "spa-day"! She chuckles returning "alright. "Bye Rafee'al" she says and he hangs up the phone.

Playing it cool when she gets off the phone 'doesn't, last, long, when she belts out a "hell!!!... "Yeah!!!... "My dream man and I, are going to the movies tonight!" Roxy and Naquawna give her a high five saying "honey... we are on a role this week!" Naquawna blurts out "and here you thought, you weren't gonna have a good day Candis because you didn't go to church this morning with yo' momma!" "But, now, look at you; going on your date!" said Naquawna hitting her on her leg. Candis gawks "oooooh...!" you dirty scoundrel!" yells Candis looking at Naquawna saying "you just had to bring that up! "I told... you I told my mom I would go with her next Sunday 'because I was way too tired to get up this morning and go!" Candis goes on to say "and I 'know, yaw'll ain't talking about 'nobody, needing to go to church; when we all should have went this morning!"

Sherry takes a sip of her refilled glass of wine laughing out "Amen to that!" still laughing she belts out "God is good!" Then they all say together "All day! "Everyday! 'Sherry, now buzzing gets up and starts to sing some of the song called "Triumph" which she heard from Hezekiah Walker featuring Susu Bobien who is the singer. Naquawna, Roxy and Candis try to sing in the background like "The Love Fellowship choir does, but failed; miserably! Mrs. Lesley even had to laugh out loud because the girls sounded a little off; key 'except, Sherry and Candis they sang like Angels.

When everybody settled down after Sherry sang parts of that beautiful song, Roxy looking over at Candis asked "so, what are you going to wear on your date tonight?" because I know you're going to be nervous, and excited, at the same time!" Candis smiles staring down at her painted toes 'still, laughing inside thinking about how crazy Sherry is, and as she looks over at Roxy she sighs saying "umm..., you are so right about that!" "I am, going to be nervous!" "And 'hopefully, I'll fine something cute!" "But you know how we do it?!" "I don't care if it's a 'sandwich bag, at this point!"

laughs Candis. "I'm just so glad that he really called me and asked me to the movies."

Naquawna jokingly blurts "yeah...! "Yeah...! "Yeah'a....! "Now--, we will "really; see" who will 'crack, and be on there; back "first" between you and Roxy"! Sherry and Naquawna bust up laughing so hard 'until, Sherry almost chokes mid sip on her wine. Ms. Lesley hearing Sherry coughing squawks out "no more wine for you; Sherry!" While at the same time Candis and Roxy shout out to Naquawna saying "whatever; haters!" "You guys don't believe we can hold out, because you two have "never!" held out to get a man. Roxy continues "and, you both have to give it up!" to get a man!" "But, "can't!" keep a man!" Candis, laughing; hard says "mmm... mmm...! But, we'll let Sherry slide on this part, because she has 'been, with her man going on 4 years, now!" "Even though the jury is still out on that, because she "still" hasn't gotten him, to put a ring on it!" Sherry with a sour look on her face retorts "no, you didn't; heffa!" The ladies all laugh and are having such a good time with each other voicing out loud, "how they feel truly blessed that they are out on this beautiful sunny day out in Treeberry 'sipping, on Napa Valley wine, getting laughs and getting their nails and toes done.

They all raise up their glasses for a cheering toast of "here...! "Here...! And as their glasses 'clink together, a car comes driving by the salon; slowly 'bumpin, there music; loud! So 'loud, that they could feel the "bass" through the walls of that raggedy; little nail shop! Everybody looks out the window at the same time and sees that it is Rayshawn 'bumping, 2 Pac's song: I Get Around! He didn't even notice Naquawna's car out front or at least he didn't indicate; that he did, by stopping to see where she was. All she could do is just look out at his car as he drove 'passed, with "her" not in; it! Sherry yells "and there's a girl in the front laying low!" Naquawna shouts "you lying!" Sherry replies "no, I'm, not!" "Unfortunately, for Naquawna Sherry did see a girl in the passenger's seat since she was the closest to the window drying her nails under the ultra; bar lights.

After hearing that news Naquawna wanted to jump up out her chair when she heard Candis says "it's probably that chick from the party last night!" "That 'sorry; bastard!" shouted Naquawna. "He has some nerve; high sighting around town with that broad!" "When he has "never" road me around in his car like that!" "Ain't that; some sh*t!" said Naquawna. Sherry turns to her saying "I'm glad you said it first; because I was about to say!" Naquawna shouts "not now Sherry!" "I am 'not, trying to hear your mouth!"

"Well--, I'm just saying!" said Sherry. "You know he ain't sh*t!" "But you still keep messing with him!" yells Sherry. Candis shouts "Sherry! But Sherry shouts back 'voicing, "Sherry, my ass!" "You know it's the truth;

Candis!" "You just don't wanna tell it, like I'm telling it!" "Oh, Lord!" said Roxy. Sherry continues to say "she sits at home waiting on that no good, dirty dog' and now look at him!" "He's on to the next hoe!" "That's the shit, I be talking about!" said Sherry; all pissed! "If you just wanna 'sex him, while he's doing another broads, than don't get mad if he's digging her more than you!"

"Because truth be told, it might be because you ain't got enough 'game, tah hold him!" "So my; advice is for you; is to keep your panties up!" and your d_*k sucking lips, closed!" "And if "not!" than 'Frankly!" that's on you!" shouted Sherry. She finishes with a wave; of her hand as if to say "girl bye!" Naquawna gets up 'with half of her toes still wet, with polish and rushes over to Sherry yelling at her she says "let me tell you something!" "You trifling ass; bit*h!" "Ain't; nobody trippin off of Rayshawn's sorry ass!" "And for your information, I keep a brother on my team 24-7!" "I just wanted Rayshawn to "see" that I ain't the 'one, to be fu*ck-ed with!"

Sherry pulls back her face shouting "but you 'are, being "played"! "And..., you be trippin hard; off that boy!" "Perfect example!" "If I'm not mistaken!" "Didn't you mess up his car one night?"! "Because you found out about his "real" woman!" Naquawna's all up in her face yells "naw, that wasn't the only reason why I did it!" Sherry talks over her adding "now--, you're flip-pin; out every time you see him 'out and about, because he's "not" with you!" Naquawna shouts "I don't give a 'damn, who he's out with!" "Mind--; yo' own, business!" Sherry yells over her, "but... at "his" convenience; he can call you at 'anytime, and you'll be 'right back, on his team!" "Like 'he's, yo; boo!"

"Shut the f*ck; up!" yells Naquawna. "You are such a "busy; body!" always up in other people's business!" Still taking over her' Sherry adds "damn; girl!" "You need to stop sweating that loser, and kick it with a brother who 'at least; likes you!" "Like maybe; what's dudes name?" she asked looking over at Candis. Then she remembers saying "oh, yeh; Mike!" Naquawna yells "I'm already knowing!" You don't have to tell me nothing!" You think you be knowing everything!"

Naquawna continues to say "just because you're living with "one, man!" "Playing; house!" "I'm a player; fool!" "That's what we do!" yelled Naquawna all up in Sherry's face getting even; louder. Sherry laughs out "you ain't nobody's; "player"! "If anything you're a broke down, wanna be player!" cause a real player wouldn't be sweat-in that fool!" "A real player; would have that brother sprung off of her!" "Not, the other way around!"

Naquawna yells "What-evah; Sherry"! "You're just a square!" "Thinking you know the game!"

Naquawna then puts her hand up in Sherry's face implying for her to "stop; acting!" like she's been a player once or twice in her life. Then Sherry slaps her hand from her face, and Roxy and Candis get in between them both to stop the fight from escalading. 'Roxy, being pushed and shoved in between the girls; squabble yells out "everybody... calm down!" But once, Roxy's feet get stepped on, she has had enough and moves out the way because her freshly painted toes almost got smudged! Still upset, Roxy walks away stating, "it's been real!" "But now, I've got to go!" Candis grabs her saying "Roxy, don't leave yet!" Then Sherry and Naquawna calm down, after hearing the girls say their leaving if they don't stop. Roxy all disappointed says "I'm about to get-on though, anyway, because I've got to get back to my grind." "Literally!" she said frowning. Reaching for her purse Roxy states "I have a house note to pay!" Sherry smirks "who doesn't have a house note to pay?"!

Naquawna mumbles to Candis "here she goes again." "Now she's on Roxy's case." Sherry hears her and rolls up her eyes at Naquawna. Then with a sour face Sherry, pays for her nails saying to Roxy "so... how are you and "lover-boy!" going to be together if he lives here, and you live all the way in Vegas?"! Roxy looks at her with an inquisitive smile answering "that's not going to be a problem, because I can fly home anytime I want to!" "I make my money out there and pay my house note out here, and when I'm all done paying for my house, I can move back here for good, and get a regular job!"

Sherry snarls at her "that sounds good on paper and 'all, but I guarantee you; you haven't told 'him, that you strip!" "Because men like 'that, don't marry hoes!" Candis gawks out "ooh!" Roxy puckers up her lips in anger and with a scrunched up face she retorts "F*ck; you; Sherry!" "That's mean...! "And for your information, I'm not no hoe!" Sherry stands there looking at her like um-- huh!" She adds "and no, I haven't told him yet" adds Roxy. "But I'll be done with that line of work before he finds out anyway!" "Trust; that!" Roxy looks over at Candis and chuckles stating "and if--, what I do for a living, ever comes up again!" "I'll just say, I'm a dance Teacher!"

"Technically" I am!" she replies as she shrugs her shoulders and pays for her pedicure. "I must admit that's a good-- one!" said Naquawna. And they all bust up laughing telling Roxy "she's a fool for that one!" The girls hug each other and say their good-byes, except Sherry and Naquawna they don't exchange hugs, and end up leaving the shop on bad, terms. Candis gives Roxy a ride to her place because she left her car there last night before they walked down to Jake's party. And Naquawna gets in her car, still very upset about Rayshawn so she decides to texts him a nasty message.

The message said "riding around with some skeezer in your car!" "Yeah! "I saw you punk!" And as the words to an old favorite song of hers comes to mind, by: The Ghetto Boys, she finishes the text with "I guess, you got ta' let a 'hoe, be a hoe!" But he never texted her back. So she drives by his house on her way home from the Salon just to see if he's home but his car was not there. I guess what Sherry had told her earlier 'went in one ear, and out thy other 'because some people just "love" the; drama!

Roxy gets dropped off at her car and says "thanks, and good-bye to Candis. Then Roxy heads home to get packed up so she can get back to Vegas. Roxy lives and works in Vegas from Tuesday thru Sunday with one of her friends, who is also an exotic; dancer. What happens is Roxy gives her a little money for utilities, and buys her own food so she can live in Vegas while she works. And in exchange, Roxy lets her friend use her house as a getaway home, away from home. It works out great because when Roxy is at work down in Vegas, her friend goes up and stays in Treeberry on her days off at Roxy's place. It is a nice arrangement that the two have been doing for two years now.

So as Roxy's packing up to head back down to work, she finds out through a text' that her friend will be using her place this Thanksgiving weekend, while 'Roxy, on thy other hand, is scheduled to work" says her friend looking at the schedule that just got put up down in Vegas. Roxy texted back saying "what a bummer!" With all her bags shoved into her backseat she slams her car door and high-tails it, to the airport.

Chapter 11

R&B music is 'thump-in, out of Candis's apartment from Jodeci, to Lauren Hill, and even Boys 2 men. She is starting to get ready for her date with Rafee'al. Standing in front of her closet for a few minutes she shuffles clothes from side to side looking for something to wear. After a bunch of clothes have been thrown to the side she finally pulls out a cute red 'tight; fitting dress that was found all the way in the back of her closet. She's glad she won't need to iron it, being that it's one of those clingy like dresses that; fits every inch of your body.

After blow drying her hair she slips on her red dress and loves the way it; looks on her. Bending over she reaches down on the bottom of her closet and grabs her black stiletto, platform sandals, and sits down on her bed to put them on. When she's dressed she starts to flat iron's her hair. Her hair comes out really nice but now she's getting kind of nervous as she's putting on a little makeup to bring out her eyes. Rafee'al had already called her to get the directions to her place, so it's just a couple more 'ticks, and 'tocks, before he'll be there. Walking to her living room she sits down on her couch nervously waiting for him and hopes he doesn't 'think, she's overdressed.

The doorbell rings and it is him. While walking over to her front door she pulls on her dress and fluffs up her hair and then opens the door with a smile. When he sees her he smiles back and has one big beautiful red rose in his hand. She blushes like a teenage girl about to go to prom. He says "this is for you pretty lady" and he hands it to her. She sighs "thank you" as she closes the door behind her. As they are walking towards his car she inhales the fragrance of the rose thinking; how sweet. Rafee'al's car isn't as modern as Steeli'o's car is. But it is still flashy and very nice. It is an old school 1961 white convertible, Lincoln Continental with suicide doors. "Wow...!" "It, is, a, beauty!" said Candis. And when he opened the car door for her, she felt like she could be one of those girls in a Low Rider Magazine. Or even, one of the girls in a Car-Show photo. On the inside of his car the interior is all black to match the leather seats and he is so proud when he closes her car door and walked around the front of his car looking at her as she sits in his ride. Smiling he sits down and starts the engine and points out 'the fact, that he's kept all thy original parts. The only things that were newly added, to his car was the rims and the stereo. And whether in the daytime or dark of night the rims really brought out the cars beauty. Candis says "this car looks like you 'really, put some time into it!" And it did! Whether on the road, or parked; it was clean! They get to the movies and Rafee'al is a gentleman all the way. They shared a big tub of popcorn and had two soda to drink on. When the two sit down together in the theater, it's a little awkward at first 'being, that it is their first date and all!

So as the small talk begins like, "where are you from?" "And how long have you lived here in Treeberry?" They slowly warm up to each other even more. Rafee'al even grabs her hand and tells her how beautiful her hands are and then the movie started. He had told her beforehand that "he was originally from North Carolina and that his family had a small dairy business." He said he 'moved to Treeberry about two years ago to come and help his auntie run her Olive Garden franchised business." Saying "he had an older sister" and then he went on to ask Candis about herself saying "so what about you." Candis told him "where she worked and how long she'd lived in Treeberry which was all her life". Then she told him "she had one older brother." she laughed saying "we both have one older sibling." "How ironic is that?" she said grinning up at him. And that's when the previews ended, and the movie had started.

During about the first part of the movie Rafee'al slowly put his arm around Candis and she leaned into him, like they've known each other for years. They laugh and chat about some of the scenes in the movie and eat there popcorn together. Candis is kind of thinking 'in that moment, while they are laughing, talking and eating that he "might" just be the real deal; the one! And in her heart she could just feel it because she wasn't thinking about 'Jason, and she wasn't thinking about 'Jake! Her whole mind, body and soul was into Rafee'al!

As the movie went on her and Rafee'al 'played, off each other's vibes and body language. He'd rub her hand softly when she placed her hand on his leg, when laughing at some of the funny parts in the movie. And with her head shifting to look at him, he looked back at her and quietly asks her a question, too low for her to 'hear, on purpose, so she would move in closer to ask him "what he just said?" She gets as close to his face as she can, and with her cheek up near his lips, he kisses her on the cheek. She turns her face to meet his response, after the kiss to her cheek, he kisses her again, but this time on her lips. He kisses her so-- long and so-- good, until every sound on the screen and in thy audience "is; silenced"!

All they could hear was the heavy 'breathing, through their noses and the 'beating, of their hearts. She is so into him as they kiss, that she even puts her hand on the side of his face and rubs down from his ear to his cheek as his hand slowly goes through her hair. When they finally release from the thunder and lightning of that; kiss!" he smiles asking "now what were we talking about?" She laughs back because she knows he was trying to be funny. Settling back in his seat he keeps his arm around her and she sits back and 'melts, into his snug embrace. While watching the movie 'cuddling, he kisses her forehead as the movie starts to come to a wonderful ending. They sit there a little longer watching the credits and waiting to see the final ending of the movie.

When they do get up, while leaving out of the theater the two talked about how much they both loved the movie, and all the action it had, and how they 'hoped, they would make a fourth one so they could come back and see that one. It's nice out when they walk out of the theater towards his car, so Rafee'al asked "do you want to go have a drink over at La'gaha's?" "Sure, she answers just so she can spend a little more time with him. They head inside and take a seat by the window and then all of the sudden, she sees Jason walking out from the movie theater with some black girl hand in hand.

She can't really get mad, because she's out with someone else as well, but she almost wishes she could let him 'see her; out with Rafee'al too, so he can 'see, that he's not playing her! "In fact, he's getting played! She thinks to herself "fool!" "You ain't playing me!" "Unless I 'let, you play me!" "And even then!" "I'm still doing it!" to get what "I" want!" "And then; poof!" "Your ass is; dumped!" She orders a Mojito to combat her nerves after seeing him out with another girl. And Rafee'al orders an Irish car bomb. The two learn a lot about each other, and pretty much close the bar. The cocktail waitress is wiping down tables and the bartender is cleaning glasses while Candis and Rafee'al are getting to know each other.

Rafee'al is really relaxed with her as he grabs her hand from across the table asking "how is it; that such a beautiful woman is still out here single?" She grunts "um--!" I guess it's because I kind of like to take my time when I date, so I can feel the man out that I'm dating." She blurts out a laugh "well not "feel" them out!" He laughs "oh..., so you like to feel them "up" first?!" "No, she said blushing. "I just like to see if the relationship is going to go anywhere, before I 'commit, to going steady with one person." He replies "I hear you. "I'm like that too. He picks up his drink saying "I can't just take anybody home to meet my family, unless I'm really serious about them."

He continues to say "so tell me about the things you like to do in your spare time?" "You know, like on your days off" he says as he's scooting up closer to the table to hear her better. Sighing softly, she goes on to tell him "how she loves to make things out of wood, like bird houses and book shelves and things." Then she gets a little sad when telling him 'how she use to make all kinds of things, with her dad as a little girl." Stating that "her father was a carpenter, who first introduced her to the wonderful things she could make out of wood." Pulling back from saying too much too soon about the passing of her dad, so she won't add a sad 'vibe, to their happy; mood, makes her say instead "and I love to bake in my spare time, too." "I can make a 'screamin, pound cake!" She added, as she took a small sip of her drink. He listens closely to her staring deep into her eyes as she finishes up with "and-- I like going on hikes and long walks on the beach." She giggles with her straw up to her mouth saying "just anything 'exciting, and 'new, I'll try!" Taking another sip of her Mojito she says "so--, what about you?" "What do you like to do?" "When you're not at the Restaurant "working"?

"Whelp--, I like to do outdoor stuff too, like sports!" "Paintball, with the guys, basketball, football, stuff like that!" He looks at her hard stating "and I love going to the shooting range!" She shouts "really--?"! And with a surprised look on her face, she swallows hard; 'like, he "likes" to play with guns!" "GREAT!" "NOT...!" she thinks to herself 'trying, not to gawk at him. After seeing the expression on her face he back peddles saying "not all-- the time, just sometimes when my friends want to go and try out their new guns to make sure they're firing properly." He smiles "I also like to hike and swim too."

He rubs his hands together 'cheesing, saying "and you haven't tasted my good cooking!" "I'm a pretty good chef, too!" "Not to toot my own horn!" "But I've been told, that I can burn in the kitchen!" She laughs saying "burn; in the kitchen?"! "Or, "burn; down!" the kitchen! They both laugh out loud. Then he cracks up saying "oh, you got jokes; huh?"! "Okay, we might just have to have a food throw down one day, so I can show you what I can do!" he said laughing. "Is that right?!" she answered. "This sounds like a challenge is being brought to my attention!" she said chuckling. He laughs a good laugh voicing "oh, we can make; it happen!" "I'll have you round as a ball!" "With all my good cooking!" She laughed so hard; envisioning all the unwanted 'pounds, she would be packing on 'do to his, "so called" good; cooking! So as they finish up their drinks with laughter, he scoots a little closer to her and gives her a nice kiss on her lips. Candis is so--, not use to a man taking 'charge, on the first date or even in her past, relationships; for that matter! So for that alone, she was really feeling him. He helps her with her coat and they walk out of the bar arm in arm 'noticing, that it has gotten even 'colder, outside. But she doesn't mind it at 'all, as she snuggles up under his long muscular arms to get warm. When they get to his car the leather seats are cold but he quickly starts the car up to get the heat; flowing, to warm up her body. As they drive away he looks down at her legs, and while smiling he says "you are kill-it in that outfit!" "Thank you" she said with a warm smile. He tells her to sit closer to him, so she can get warmer; faster, so she does. When she slides over he puts his arm around her while pulling her even closer to him as he drives with one hand on the steering wheel towards her house.

They pull up to her place and he opens the car door for her and with a smile he reaches for her hand to help her out of his car. Rafee'al walks her up to her front door to see if she is going to let him come in for a while, but 'Candis, can't; trust it!" She feels it is too late in thy evening, and she is not "that; strong!" to resist his charms at this point. So she just lets him give her a nice kiss outside up against her front door. He beams after kissing her, and with a big smile on his face he says “awe--, so you’re not going to let me come in?” She smiles back at him “no, it’s late.” “Is that the only reason?” because it’s too late?” he said grinning.

She opens her door and talks to him in the doorway as she smiles back voicing “that’s one of the reasons.” He chuckles again saying “what’s the other reason?” “You didn’t get a chance to clean up today?” “You’ve got dishes in the sink?” he said with his sexy ass smile. She grins saying “bye..., Rafee’al..., while laughing still looking at him with the door cracked. He chuckles “I can come in and help you do the dishes.” She still smiles saying “I had a great time.” “Thanks you.” He smiles back grunting “me too. And then he give her a quick peck on the lips and walks away backwards to his car, still looking at her, and her still looking at him, until he gets in his car and drives off with a toot of his horn.

Candis has a grin on her face that; “can’t” be erased! She closes her front door and walks back to her room feeling the ‘love, as she falls back on her bed with joy. And in her ‘mind, she “hopes” to “God” that; he’s; the one!

Chapter 12

A few days go by and Naquawna is tired of being; ignored by Rayshawn! So she thinks up a plan to make some flyers that say 50% off on shampoo wash and sets, color changes, haircuts, perms and weaves. Then she parks up the street where Rayshawn lives and walks down his street to pass them out. 'Ok, in "truth!" she does not have the money to loose on a bunch of people getting their hair done for next to nothing! 'So…, she only drops off 'two flyers, one to the lady next door to Rayshawn's house 'his neighbor, and the other flyer at his house, to make it "look" like a real; advertisement!

Naquawna sneaks up his street and puts the first one in his neighbor's mailbox which is on the curb. And when she gets to Rayshawn's house with the flyer, after dropping it in his mailbox, as she's walking away Rayshawn's door opens up and the girl inside yells out "what is this?"! Looking at Naquawna the girl is holding the flyer in her hand, asking her again about the flyer. Naquawna turns around slowly 'all, caught off guard, because she thought no one was home since she didn't see his car. So she says "oh, hi." "We are having a 50% off sale on most of our hair treatments." She just didn't know what else to say in that short moment of time.

Then Naquawna hears the baby crying in the back of the house, so the girl sighed "umm…, okay!" "Come in for a minute!" "Let me go and get my baby because I want to hear more about this sale!" she adds, "I've been looking for some place to go and get my hair done!" shouts the girl as she's walking towards the backroom. When she comes back with the baby in her arms she says "my name is Se'anna." "Hi, I'm Naquawna." And they shake hands. Naquawna tries not to look to jealous when she says to her "cute, baby." Se'anna smiling says "awh--, thank you, he's our little stinker!" she said as she kisses him on his cheek. Then Se'anna tells Naquawna to have a seat on the couch. Looking around Naquawna sits down nervously thinking this might not be a good ideal 'after all, because she knows Rayshawn could come home at any minute, and then; what would she do?"! Se'anna all excited starts asking her "how much is a perm?" and should she get a weave to go with it?" Asking "and how much would all that be?" Naquawna answers "not too much." $250.00 or so, with half off of that. Se'anna cheers "is that right?!" Saying "ooh… I can surely afford that!" she smiled. Naquawna halfway smiling back, starts to really feel overwhelmed with all the 'questions, and the 'cars driving by, and the baby screaming out playful 'baby, noises.

She gets so… overwhelmed with 'nerves, until she has to make her exit; quickly, by saying "that she's got to go and get the rest of the flyers passed out, so she can get back to work, or her boss will dock her pay!" Se'anna understanding says "ok. "Well--, I'll see you on Friday!" "Is 4 o'clock okay?" Naquawna trying not to show her true 'hatred, as she glances around the living room one last time answers "sure... "That would be fine." "Bye, for now" she says as she's walking out the front door. Se'anna waves bye to her and closes the door.

Naquawna, is practically; "running" up the street, to get to her car, so she can get the 'hell, out of dodge! And wouldn't you know it, here comes Rayshawn flying up the street playing his music loud as usual bumpin the song "Why"! By: Jadakiss. Featuring: Anthony Hamilton. Rayshawn could have 'sworn, he seen the back of Naquawna's car leaving from up the street but he paid it no mind and went on into his house. Se'anna was vacuuming their bedroom at the time and didn't hear Rayshawn come in. He sees a bright purple flyer sitting on the coffee table and picks it up and as soon as he sees the shop and Naquawna's phone number on it, he balls it up, and in walks Se'anna shouting "don't ball that paper up!" I just made an appointment with that girl today, for Friday!" She has a great special going on!" And you know I want to be looking 'cute, for Thanksgiving weekend since we're going up to your dad's house!" Rayshawn trying not to show his anger says "she came in the house?"! "Yeah!" "Why?"! "You know her?!" she said eye balling him crazy. "Naw!" But damn!" "She's still a stranger!" He goes on to say "she could have been some nut case or something!" and you just let her in our house!" Se'anna looks at him, like he's "really" over; reacting! She says "Ray was crying, and so I told her to come in for a minute." "Besides she wasn't even in here that long!" Trying to calm him; down she says "so, babe--, I'm going to need you to watch little Ray, for me on Friday, because my appointment with her is at 4 o'clock." She rubs the back of his head with her fingertips voicing "okay, baby?"

Not happy that Naquawna has come to his house has him just staring at the basketball game while the Warriors and the Lakers are playing. He's mad as hell but he nods his head 'yes, as he's glaring at the game while thinking about this 'broad, coming to his house! Naquawna gets to Candis's house just as she's pulling up after work. "Hey, girl!" says Candis. "You're off work mighty early today?" Naquawna answers "Yep. "I had some hair flyers to pass out, so Mrs. Lee let me off early, when I told her it was to "promote" her; business!" She continues "you know how; she is?" "She'll let me off for a whole week, if it's going to benefit 'her; into making more money!" she said laughing.

Candis asked "so where did you go to pass out all these flyers?!" said Candis as she's opening up her apartment door. She continues to says "because I don't see "no" flyer on my door!" "Where's, "my" discount?!" "Maybe I need to make a phone call to Mrs. Lee!" she said cracking up laughing. Naquawna busted up laughing with her saying "um, no, "honey...! "I only distributed them, over by Rayshawn's house!" she said biting on one of her fingernails.

Candis drops her groceries on the kitchen counter and looks at Naquawna and blurts out "are you; crazy?"! "That boy is going to go "off" on you!" "You are really playing with fire!" she said while pulling stuff out of her bags. Naquawna returns "he ain't gonna do sh^t!" "If he was so worried about what I "might; do!" then he would "stop" ignoring my calls!" "I am "not" going to be 'ignored, and "swept" under the 'rug, like I'm some "leftover; trash!" that he's "done" playing; with!" "Sorry!" said Naquawna rolling up her eyes.

Candis just shakes her head in fear for her friend. She asked "so what did you do?" leave it on their door?" Naquawna says "whelp!" I tried to leave it in his mailbox, but she ended up being home and caught me off guard, so I had to talk to her." Candis puts her hands over her nose and mouth in a prayer position voicing "tell me you didn't go in the house?"! "Yes, I, did!" said Naquawna. "And she needs a decorator!" because her 'crib, was; hideous!" Candis couldn't help but laugh, but a part of her; "doesn't" think it's going to be "too; funny!" when Rayshawn gets wind of it. Naquawna gets a cup and pours herself some green juice while telling Candis how his "girl-friend" plans on coming to the shop on Friday at around 4 o'clock." "And that her name is "Se'anna"! Naquawna says "you should come by too Candis, so you can meet her, and be my "question; helper"! "You know?" my wing girl, so you can ask her all kinds of question about her love life." Candis just looks at her like, she has really; snapped! Candis returns "oh...!" "Hell, no!" "You're my girl and all, but I'm not getting involved with that mess!" "Plus, I've got a date with Rafee'al!" she said while swinging her hair back towards her back. "What about Jake, and Jason?!" asked Naquawna with a flip of her wrist. Candis answers "what about them?"! Naquawna looks at her saying "don't tell me, you're putting away your "player's; card!" for Rafee'al! Waiting on Candis's answer Naquawna has a look on her face suggesting to 'Candis, that she just can't hang, with the game, no more! Candis replies "I thought I told you about Jason?" "I saw him leaving out of the movie theater with some chicken-head; broad when Rafee'al and I were at La'gaha's having drinks." "No. "You didn't tell me that" said Naquawna.

"You must have told Roxy, since you've been talking to her more lately, than you've been talking to me!" "No--, because I know I told you to!" said Candis. "You just don't remember, because you're so caught; up with 'Rayshawn, and all his; drama that you can't even; focused!" Naquawna still in denial replies "naw, that's not true!" "I just want some answers and since he's not given me any!" "I'm gonna see if 'old girl, will!" "What kind of answers do you really want to hear?!" asked Candis. "You already know he lives with; what's her name!" and, that they have a kid! "Plus, you know he's a cheating dog!" which you've 'seen, for yourself!" "So what else do you need to know about him?"! "Other than he's "not" trying to commit to one woman!"

Naquawna frowns; and then smirk out "that's harsh!" when you say it like that!" she said walking over to take a seat. She goes on to say "I just want to see how serious they are about each other!" "And see if she thinks she's with a "winning; man"! "Or..., does she already "know?!" he ain't; sh*t! "But she still stays with him 'anyway, because they have a kid together!" "Stuff like that!" said Naquawna. Candis mocks "if I didn't know you any better, I would swear you were trying to get to know 'her, and be her friend!" "Or, tell 'her, what a "dog!" Rayshawn is!" or both! Naquawna gets a sly mischievous look on her face while lifting up one of her eyebrows; smiling she says "whatever happens; happens!" "It's gone 'be; what it is!"

Candis just shakes her head while putting up her groceries looking at Naquawna; she voices "every day scant-less"! When her refrigerator door closes she says "you just better be careful, because you know he is not going to be happy if he finds out you went to his house!" Naquawna just drinks on her green juice and 'acts like, she's 'not trippin, one bit! The girl finish up talking as they make a mixed drink, with the green juice and vodka and then puffed on one, before Naquawna went on her way.

Chapter 13

The following day an alarm goes off, playing music instead of the regular beeping; sound. It is Friday morning and Naquawna has tossed and turned half of the night. She gets out of her bed and into the shower, and after shampooing her hair, and putting a leave-in deep conditioner on it, she gets out of the shower and towels herself off. Standing in front of the mirror she is thinking; hard about how she is going to wear her hair today. After combing out her hair and pulling it back, she ends up putting it up in a high ponytail after her hair had air-dried and wouldn't hold the curls like she wanted it to.

Then she put on a sexy yellow and black dress with some cute 2 inch white and yellow heels to bring out the yellow in her dress. You would "think" she was going on a date, the way she was dressed. Because in Naquawna's mind she is hoping Rayshawn will come by the shop and beg; her forgiveness; saying to her "sorry, I didn't tell you about my baby's momma, or return any of your calls!" "But it's "you" I really love!" And then they'd get back together and live happily ever after. So in her mind she wants to make sure she is looking her best, so he will want her even more, if he stops by the shop or drives by and sees her looking; sexy!

Naquawna all dressed up goes into the kitchen and makes herself a little breakfast, nothing major just some blueberry, raspberry, and blackberry oatmeal which is one of her favorite comfort foods. Once she adds honey and a slice of butter to her oatmeal she pours it in a coffee mug and grabs her keys and tip-toes out the house, so she won't wake up her granddad. On her way to work she gets 'mixed, feeling 'like, maybe she shouldn't go in to work today. And..., what if Rayshawn has told Se'anna "everything?" and they both come down to the shop and confront her at her job. She calls Candis and tells her, her thoughts and Candis replies "girl..., there is no turning back now!" "You might as well play this thing out!" she said. Naquawna answers "I know. "You're probably right. Then Naquawna blurts out "and don't you tell "nosey; ass" Sherry my business; either!" Candis laughs "I won't!" Naquawna grunting says "and I bet she's standing right there looking; dead in your mouth!" while you're talking to me right now!" "With her; nosey; ass!" Candis just laughs out loud, voicing "okay!" While playing it off. Then she adds "call me later and tell me what happened." Naquawna replied "fine!" "Wish me luck!" Bye chil!"

Naquawna gets to work and then locks her purse in her trunk and walks into her place of business, all quiet with her breakfast in hand. Mrs. Lee greets her with, "good morning"! Voicing "one of your discount customers just called." "She said, she will be here at 9:30." "Saying to me that she wants a new look" adds Mrs. Lee with a happy smile on her face. Still smiling at her she says "good job!" "Naquawna!" "You bring in more customers!" Naquawna smiles back but is 'quite, puzzled as she walks around her station getting ready to start working.

While she's getting all her combs and brushes out, she starts greeting her co-workers as they are all start; filtering into work. As everyone is walking around the shop preparing for the day; drinking their coffee or eating on their breakfast, Naquawna's mind starts to wonder "why" Se'anna is coming in earlier then she said she was, because she was the only discount person she talked to that had an appointment today.

Naquawna, nervously looks out the big glass windows to see who Se'anna will be coming in with at 9:30, "wondering" if it's going to be like she previously thought on her way to work, with them confronting; her at her job. Unsure she sits down and finishes up her big cup of oatmeal so she can be 'full and focused, for whatever, is to come of the day!

When she's done eating in walks this little older lady with grey hair down her back saying "hi. "I have a flyer. "Is Naquawna here?" Naquawna smiles with relief when she sees it's the lady next door to Rayshawn's house with her flyer, and "not" Se'anna and Rayshawn coming to jam her up. 'Happily, she walks up to the lady saying "hi. "I'm Naquawna. "I'm so glad you came in today" she said shaking her hand. "So am I" said the lady; smiling, saying "my name is pearl." Naquawna smiling back asks "what would you like to get done to your hair today?" While the lady is thinking on her question Naquawna leading with one hand telling her to follower her. When they get to her station she helps to put the little old lady in the chair in front of the big, mirror.

After taking a seat the lady replies "the reason why I'm here today is because I want a nice hair cut 'mostly, around my face but not to short." And maybe just a light trim in the back." "Okay, I can do that" said Naquawna. "Now--, what about color?" asked Naquawna. "I think I want to try--, a light auburn" answered Pearl. Nodding, okay to her request Naquawna goes on to show Pearl some hair cutting styles from a magazine to pick from, while she heads to the back to mix up the hair color.

When she returns with the bowl of hair color she says "did you find a hair style, you think you would like?" Pearl smiling up at her says "there are a couple of ones I like, but I'm going to keep looking" she said turning the page. "Okay, that's fine" chuckles Naquawna, take your time. So as Naquawna's touching on Pearls hair getting familiar with it, she starts to ask Pearl questions 'like, how long has she lived in the area?" Pearl replied "pretty much all my life." When I married my college sweetheart, we bought our first home when he got out of the Service." Pearl also told her all about her neighbors and how nice everyone is on her street was.

Naquawna was trying to act like she really cared but she couldn't help but feel a bit 'anxious, about her 4:00 o'clock appointment. 'Plus, Pearl wasn't telling her all the 'dirt, she "really" wanted to hear! She was hoping to hear some bad stories 'like, "how her neighbors are constantly; arguing, which leads to domestic violence!" Or, that the police are called to her neighbor's house, on a regular basic, do to all the 'loud, partying; and music being played!

'But the worst, Naquawna's mind was 'thinking, and 'hoping, to hear from 'Pearl, was that 'child protective services, had been over to the house on 'many, occasions; threatening to take the child away because of "suspected" drug; trafficking!" from Rayshawn! "But, ugh... that is 'just, plain; mean!" To keep thinking like that" thinks Naquawna to herself as she tries her "hardest" to stop "thinking" 'evil; thoughts!

Pearl, shifts Naquawna's thoughts back into reality when she shouts "there it is!" "I want my hair cut like that one there!" she says grinning; pointing at the picture in the magazine cheering "that is cute!" Naquawna looks down at the picture saying "yes, that would look cute on you!" Naquawna all happy, begins to smile. One, because the little old lady is so, cute! And 'two, because Pearl's 'kindness, seem to fills the room with joy.

Naquawna never thought this would happen but she was thrilled to see that her 'plan, had worked! 'Although at first, it was--, for revenge on 'Rayshawn, for ignoring; her!" 'But then, in the long; run she ended up being happier for it, because she gained a new customer, and 'hopes, that Pearl, will be a repeating; client. So after picking out a cute hair style, Naquawna with all her 'hair; 'bumping; "skills" makes it all; happen! And when Pearl's hair is all done, and cut to perfection, and the color is on point!" she is 'amazed, at how much younger she looks in the mirror. Everyone in the shop compliments her on her new look, and when she leaves out of the shop she is a whole new woman; "vowing" to be back in 6 weeks!

Tick, tock, tick! The time just slows... bye, as Naquawna keeps looking at her watch and the clock on the wall. She even called Mike, two times today, just to cheer herself up. Even though he had no clue as to what was going on!" just the fact that he is always so positive, no matter what is going on with him. Makes her 'feel, that much more important. In her boredom she also texted Roxy so she could have something to do, but Roxy had to get back to work herself, so she couldn't talk to her that long. Mrs. Lee, seeing that Naquawna is bored says "do you want to do a wash and set for me, while I finish up the next customer's nails?" "Yeah, sure" said Naquawna. "Anything beats sitting here, watching the second hand turn, on the clock on the wall." When she's done with Mrs. Lee's client, she sweeps up the hair off the floor and takes out some trash, and before she knows it, a Cadillac pulls up in front of the shop. Her heart; 'flops, into her stomach because she thinks its Rayshawn dropping off Se'anna, but she gets out of the car alone.

Naquawna breathes out a sigh of relief 'thinking, everything in going as planned. When the front door opens she is wiping down her mirror with Windex when Se'anna walks into the shop. "Hey, you!" says Naquawna. "I see you made it!" she adds. "Yass, I thought I was going to be late because my man had my car!" "Oh, really?" said Naquawna not wanting to be too nosey when she said "so your husband's watching the baby?" Se'anna taking off her coat to sit down in the chair grins "yes, but he's not my husband." We just have a son together." Naquawna happy to hear that said "oh, I see." So what did you have in mind for your new look, today?" "Well..., answers Se'anna 'fluffing up her hair, looking in the mirror, she says "I want a weave down to about the middle of my back, with some highlights!" "Umm-kay!" said Naquawna.

Naquawna then interjects saying "and I think color 4/30 would look good with your skin color" she adds. Looking at Se'anna's hair she continues to say "and I think I'll highlight it with, color 27, it's a strawberry blonde." Se'anna smiles "ooh--; that sounds pretty...!" I am so excited!" I am going to be looking so cute when I go out to Sac'mento, to see my man's; in-laws! Naquawna gets a fake smile on her face when asking "when are you going?" "This Thursday for Thanksgiving weekend" she said. "I can't wait!" she adds. "This will be my first time meeting his side of the family in person." "Wow..., how long have you two been together?" asked Naquawna while starting the coloring of her hair. "Um..., just two years." "We met at a party" she said licking her lips looking down at her phone.

Naquawna just listens and thinks back to what Bubba had said "which was the same thing, about how Rayshawn had met this stripper, and had a baby by her." Se'anna rambled on a little more about her and the baby and talked about how Rayshawn was such a good father, but how he needs to get a better job. Naquawna asked her "why?" what does he do for work?" She answers "he works on cars and sells them and does repos for a living with his friend Ernesto." And Ernesto's dad, owns the shop that she is referring too. Naquawna almost died laughing because she knows for a 'fact, that Rayshawn sells narcotics and gambles to make his money. And to her knowledge he has "never" had a real job! Naquawna holding back a laugh says "that's good money, though, selling cars and repoing them." Se'anna smirks "yes, but it is slow work, at their small family owned business, especially in this economy because no one wants to spend too much money anymore, unless they really have to, to buy a new or a used car."

Naquawna listens diligently to every word then she takes Se'anna over to the sink to rinse out the color. Then she shampoos and conditions her hair so she can; prep her scalp for the weaving. While massaging the conditioner in her scalp Naquawna wishes 'Candis, her "sidekick" was there so she could ask Se'anna even more questions about Rayshawn 'for her, because she has ran out of things to "ask" about him, at this point! So Naquawna finds other things to talk about with her 'like, cosmetics and the latest perfumes. And as time goes on, she starts to kind of "relate" to Se'anna, because she can see that Se'anna doesn't "really" know, the "real" Rayshawn either, as well as she "thinks" she does!

They walk back over to the chair and Naquawna dries her hair off with a towel and starts to blow dry it, straight. Se'anna is looking out the window at some passer-byer who are looking at her car and out of the blue she says "I am so glad I bought my car when I did!" And Ernesto gave me such a good deal on it back then, because 'now, I probably couldn't afford to get a new car with these prices!" She goes on to say "Ernesto would have had to charge me 'full price, for my Cadillac if I bought it today!" Naquawna had to pick her bottom lip "up" from off the ground!" because it was hanging so low. She catches herself; gawking in disbelief at how "sorry!" Rayshawn really is, because he doesn't even 'own, that; car!" like he "claimed" he did!" She stutters on her words asking "Oh...!" That's...!" That's, your car out there?"! "I thought it was your man's car!" "That's nice; girl!" said Naquawna through a phony smile.

Se'anna smiling back voices "thank you." "Yes, he wants my car, but I told him, when I get my BMW, he can have this one." She continues "that's another reason 'why, he needs to sell more cars, and do more repos or make better bets, on them horses that he be betting on!" She ends with "he goes to the race track a lot, and he's pretty lucky, but that's taking a risk, too!" every time he bets! "Whoa...!" thinks Naquawna. Because she didn't even know 'that part, about Rayshawn! He always tells her, he's going to the "gambling; shack!" so now after hearing about the horses, she 'thinks, he "might" even have a "gambling; problem" too! Naquawna has a flash back while she is talking to Se'anna, and she thinks back on the time she 'keyed; up the Cadi, that she "thought" was Rayshawn's! 'But 'now; she knows differently because it wasn't even his "damn; car"! She feels he has told so many lies and is living such a reckless life!" So much 'so, that, how?" he can keep up!" is any bodies guess?"! So Naquawna is now starting to 'see, that Rayshawn "really; is!" full of; crap! And she's also starting to second guess her feelings for him because Se'anna keeps talking about him, and 'everything, she "thought" that was great about him before!" Is "now" seeming to be, all; false!

At the shop it's getting late in thy evening and Naquawna has found out pretty much all she needs to know about "Mr. Wrong"! "Rayshawn"! She looks over by the register when she hears the register draw slam and catches Mrs. Lee looking at her like "less; talking"! And "more; work"! (Meaning) round it up, because it's after closing time. Naquawna knows that look on Mrs. Lee's face without her even saying a word, so she nods; okay, and puts the last track of weave hair in Se'anna's hair. After she layers her hair with the scissors she turns Se'anna around so she can see herself in the mirror, so she can see what she thinks of her new look.

Se'anna puts both of her hands over her mouth and lets out a surprising scream of; "I love it!" Then she jumps up and down while giving Naquawna a big; hug. Naquawna hesitates at first "not" wanting to be too chummy, chummy, with her, but then she gives in and hugs her back. Se'anna all cheery; pays Naquawna the money and gives her a nice fat tip shouting "you're the best!" I have found my new hair dresser!" And I will see you the next time, when I need to get my hair redone!" "Thank you so..., much; Naquawna!" she blared walking towards the door. But before she leaves out of the shop she turns yelling "have a wonderful Thanksgiving everybody!" All of the other hair stylists left in the shop cleaning up and getting ready to go home 'including, Naquawna yell back "you too!"

Naquawna watches her drive away with a smile on her face because she can't 'believe, she was able to pull; this one off! She really felt like she got more out of this hair appointment, then Se'anna did! 'And to think!" how at 'first, she wanted to 'f_ck up; her hair! 'But after thinking on it, she "knew" that; that would be putting her "own" reputation on the line! 'So now, she's "glad!" she did do the right thing on her hair! Even Mrs. Lee was proud of her because she had 'two, happy, new customers, come into the shop today, and Mrs. Lee made sure to tell all of the other stylists in the shop that night; "how they, could learn a thing or two from Naquawna's 'leadership, in bringing new customers into the shop!" After everyone complimented her, she graciously said "thanks, and went back to sweeping up her area. While cleaning out her brushes and her combs her mind started thinking back on the 'day, and when Se'anna came to mind she almost felt sorry for the girl because she was 'stuck, with Rayshawn's black; hearted ass! Naquawna and the rest of her co-workers finished cleaning up their stations and everybody walked out of the shop together.

Waving good-bye in the parking lot, Naquawna walks towards her

Chrysler 300; beaming at how fly her car looks in the dark, with the midnight black paint and gold flakes in the gloss as it sat there, on 30 inch, gold rims. Even her gas cover and her front grill was gold. So when she gets to her car, she starts it up, and as it's warming up, she steps out of it to go get her purse from out the trunk. Her car is backed in; in the parking lot, so when she closes her trunk and walk around to get back in her car, a man in all black with a hood on grabs her by the throat and throws her back on the front hood, of her car, and she didn't even have time to 'scream, it happened so fast!

The man said "bi$ch"! "Don't you 'ever, come by my house again!" Naquawna was pissed at first, because he called her a b$tch! 'But then, she was somewhat relieved to see that it is only Rayshawn! So she yells out "I don't know what the 'hell, you're talking about!" He presses his body up against heirs with his hand still around her throat 'although, "not" trying to hurt her, he says "you know what the 'hell, I'm talking about!" He gets all up in her face, blasting out "and about all those "b*tch; made; texts!" you've been sending me! "You need to stall, that sh*t; out! She yells "f^ck!" you; Rayshawn!" And then she tries to kick him, and fight him, so he can get up off of her 'because she is 'over; all his lies!

He doesn't let her go and while all up in her face he growls out "what's wrong; Naquawna?"! "You "need" some of me?!" is that why you keep 'f*ck-in; with me?"! "Screw you!" she shouts while laying back on the hood of her car trying to catch her breath after tussling with him. She blurts out "you are such a liar!" And I, hate you!" He laughs in her face because he 'knows, she's, far; from hating him. He tells her "you're the type that would rather have "negative" attention from me!" "Then no "attention" at all!" "Let me go!" she shouts. "Why?!" he asked. "Because you hate me?!" he said, sarcastically. "Yes!" she shouted. "Then why do you keep calling me?!" he asked. She ignores him at first. Then she says "I won't be calling you no more!" So you don't 'even, have to worry; about that!"

With a deep breath he then gets all 'close, up in her ear, and with his mouth touching her earlobe he mention "and out of all... the streets..., on this peninsula!" You 'choose, to pass out those 'sorry, ass 'flyers, in my; neck of the woods!" She just looks at him while he 'rants, and 'raves, about how 'she just wants, any attention; he's willing to give her!

He even pulls up her dress; midway while staring at her, as he unzips his pants just to see her reaction while asking "is this what you want?"! Rolling up her eyes she looks at him voicing "I'm, over it!"

"Especially, after seeing you with some girl in your car; riding all around town!" You don't give a 'damn, about nobody but yourself!" she said. He turns his face up at her and yells "I saw your car over there at that 'nail place, sitting in there with your nosy; ass friends, probably; gossiping and shit!" "That's why I didn't even stop!"

Naquawna tries to get up off the hood of her car but he still won't let her. So she pushes him saying "who was the girl?"! "I'm sure it's hard for you to remember, since you've probably been "doing" so--; many!" He grunts saying "so many; huh?"! "You think you know so 'much, don't you?"! "But that was Ernesto's chick in the front seat!" I couldn't let my friend's lady ride in the back, I'm a gentleman like that!" "And, her man was in the car in the backseat because we were out doing; ben'ness!

Naquawna yells "let me up!" I can't trust, or believe anything you say anymore!" He lays his body down on top of heirs even more pressing his third leg harder up against her middle and getting all up in her face saying "you know you love me!" she yells "no!" I, don't!" I hate, you!" But she was not convincing enough to Rayshawn and she couldn't even look him in his face when she said "she 'hated, him." So he begins-- to lift her legs... up slowly... and he slides her down to the edge of the hood of her car. Then he slowly snatches off her thong underwear and tosses them on top of the car's windshield.

Rayshawn then whispers in her ear "so, you hate me; huh?" "Is that what you're telling me?" he asked as he's looking at her as he's starts go down where her legs are, so he can kiss in her inner legs. She shouts "Rayshawn?"! "I am over this!" And I am, over; you!" He replies "I know." "I know. "You told me already, you hate me!" he said in a low seductive voice. With his hands on her legs he starts to lick her slowly. Still angry she closes her eyes and just lays there even though she "could" get up. Naquawna tries to hang on to the bitter taste in her "mouth!" that she feels for him. But as he's licking her to the best of his 'ability, she grows more and more "astonishingly; confused!" because he "never" does this to her. 'She's trying, not to like, the "sexual; way" he's slathering his tongue up against her!" but it's hard; not too. And the more he does it, she slowly starts to lose the fight, because her body's 'response, is telling on 'her, like she's really... been missing him 'deep, down; inside! And it's beginning to 'show, as she lays there 'liking; it! While his mouth is on 'lick patrol, his hands quietly move up towards her 'milk duds, and he gently; squeezes them to her satisfaction. He always makes her feel so--; stimulated! Especially when it comes to love making. 'Even though, she doesn't 'want it to be, as easy as he "thinks" it is, for him to get, back inside her, is why she tells him "he's wasting his time!"

But he doesn't hear her speak 'those words, because he's too busy listening to 'her body, as she starts to moan and move to 'his, every; touch! It's dark outside and cars are passing by on the main street. And by now she is so turned; on by his 'tongue, that her legs began to resemble the opening of the 'Trebbiano, flower. Caught up in his 'game, she now doesn't even 'care, who might pass by and see them in the parking lot 'doing, what they are doing!

Through all the moans, and heavy breathing that's being done she can still hear her car stereo playing in the background while she is being done; "righteously!" on the hood of her car. Its Biggie's and Lil' Kim's hit record playing: Get Money, and Lil' Kim's part is on, voicing; "you wanna lick between my knees baby"! While he's licking in between her 'knees, and she's 'Cumming, all down his; throat!

He lifts his head up after she climaxes; to the fullest! And he 'slowly, puts his 'Magic Wand, inside her 'Top Hat, and on her lips he says "you still hate me?" In her sexiest voice she snarls out "f*^k!" you; Rayshawn!" But the look in her eyes was saying something totally different and he knew; exactly what she 'wanted, so he laughed saying 'gladly, as he went in her ever so deeply. The music keeps playing on her stereo while he's talking to her in his gravelly voice, while holding her tight.

Just feeling him all over her body 'makes, it hard for her to forget how much she really loves him. He feels the love; that she is giving to him, and it makes him "stream" so--, hard!" into her. Without a 'though, of getting her pregnant! 'Or, him, becoming a father for a second time. 'Naquawna, lets him have his way 'once again, and she's lost 'all, of herself 'just, so she can please him!" and--, so he can pleasure her. 'Now, she is caught up in this; twisted, love triangle, like she's his 'puppet, on a string!

When they are finished she gets up off the hood of her car and grabs her panties from off the windshield wipers and puts them back on, and they get in the car and drive off. Rayshawn suggests they go to a drive thru window to get something to eat, so she does. When she pulls up she orders an almond berry chicken salad from Wheny's, and he gets a couple of burgers, a fry and a drink. And of course Naquawna pays for their food with the tip money she got from Se'anna earlier. Well, "technically" it was his money too, since he gave Se'anna the money to get her hair done.

They find a place to park to eat their food and she starts to pick his brain asking "so... how did you get to the shop with no car?" Chewing he replies "my boy Ernesto and I were sitting outside the shop watching you two." And when Se'anna left, I had him drop me off in the parking lot and I hid behind his car until your co-workers left. She says "but that car was still there in the parking lot when we just left!" "I know!" he said with a grunt. "That fool was supposed to leave, but he's stupid like that!" "I guess he wanted to watch!"

Naquawna shouts "what?"! "He was "watching" us?"! "More like filming us!" adds Rayshawn. Naquawna is outraged, she yells "you know what?"! "That is so--, childish!" Rayshawn laughs "I'm just joking!" But he really wasn't, he plans to keep that film on her 'just in case, she ever tries to say anything against him; like he raped her. He kisses her and makes her feel like she can trust him at his word. They talk and eat, and look; deeply into each; others eyes and that's when she starts to feel like Rayshawn has proven to her, how much he "really" loves her! But sooner or later she will have to wake up; to 'grim reality, and face the fact; that "Rayshawn" only care about "Rayshawn"!

Naquawna all 'happy, drops him off up the street from his house and kisses him good-bye. But as soon as he walks in the front door, Se'anna yells at him because he made her Godmother come all the way over to the house to watch the baby. She yelled "dang!" You couldn't wait 3 to 4 hours for me to get back from getting my hair done?"! "That is; ridiculous!" With pity on his face he grabs her by the hands saying "baby. I know!" "I'm sorry!" "But it was an emergency!" "Ernesto needed me to go on a 'real; dangerous, repo job with him!" And your God mom was the only one I could think of; to come through; so I wouldn't bother you while you were getting your hair done."

"I made us some extra money though" he grins. Then he continues to say "so now you can even go get your nails done." Reaching deep in his pocket he pulls out a wad of money and gives her $200.00 dollars stating "and, you can even get your toes done too, if you want too?!" She smiles 'now, thinking; that 'maybe, she had "overreacted"! After taking the money from him she gives him a big hug and kiss. He smiles saying "your hair came out pretty" he said as he ran his fingers in it. "Thank you baby" she replied. "I can't wait to go to your dad's house for Thanksgiving." "I hope they like me." He returns "they are going to love you and little Ray." All is forgiven now, so she goes back to sitting down on the couch 'all happy, as she finishes watching the rest of Judge Mathis. 'Grinning himself, Rayshawn "pimp; walks" his way back to their room, and 'gloats, over how much game!" he really has! He gets in the shower and gets himself all clean't up and as he's drying himself off, Se'anna hollers from the kitchen for his to come and eat dinner cheering, "its pot roast night"! So as the night dies down, then turn into days, the clouds 'open, up!" on Thanksgiving; day!

Chapter 14

By midafternoon Candis answers her mom's front door all; playful as she lets Naquawna and her grandpa in with a big hug and offers to take their coats. Naquawna leads her grandpa to the living room chair so he can relax before dinner. Once he's sitting comfortable she takes the pies that she has made and puts them in the kitchen. The house smells so good with that 'holiday smell, of the turkey baking, with all the spices that are lingering in thy air. The macaroni and cheese is on standby, but ready to go into the oven once there's more room.

Candis's mom comes out from the back room after hearing voices and gives an 'inviting hug, to Naquawna and her grandfather. While Mrs. Tomson is talking to granddad Naquawna; saunters into the kitchen telling Candis how easy it was to make her sweet potato pies. Candis just raves about how good they came out; stating "she can't wait to cut a piece after she eats her dinner." The door gets knocked on and it is Dianna coming over to the house next, and when she enters the house she has a small tray of her 'famous, 'Cajun; fried chicken. "Where's Marvin?" asked Candis. Dianna replies "he had to go into work today because one of the water mains; broke in one of the office buildings; that they were working on this week." "Poor baby" said Dianna sadly. She finishes with "he said he'll hurry up and get here as soon as he can though."

Dianna takes her coat off and sits down on the couch and Naquawna hands her a drink of eggnog and brandy. Mrs. Tomson standing proudly over by the window says "so what do you all think about the new curtains?" "I finally got them done right before the Holiday's." Everybody had a reply Naquawna said "they look 'really, nice! "Good job mom, you really out did yourself!" said Candis. Even Dianna said "they look like they were made professionally!" "Thank you" said her mother blushing; sweetly. Sherry chimes in via a text from Bruce's 'parent's house, texting Candis a picture of a turkey on top of a chicken having 'relations, and under the picture in the caption it read "happy gobble, gobble day!" Candis laughs out loud showing Dianna and Naquawna the text, then she 'forwarded; it, to all of her other friends. When Roxy gets the text of the turkey having fun on top of the chicken, she has just landing at Treeberry Bay Airport. She calls Candis saying "you are laughs!" "That text was hilarious!" she said. Candis replies "I would 'love, to take full credit for that joke, but that was not my doing!" That came from Sherry's crazy, butt!"

"Where you at right now?" asked Candis being nosy. "I'm here at the Airport, getting my bags right now" she huffs. "I thought you had to work; Vegas?!" said Candis laughing. "You should come over to my mom's house!" she adds. "I can't, Steeli'o wants me to fly with him to Italy to his mom's house for Thanksgiving." "And I am so..., scared!" confessed Roxy. "What should I do?" she asked Candis. Candis sighs "well. "Umm--; just go!" "If you're, feel-in; it!" said Candis. Roxy replies "that's the problem, I'm having!" "I think, it's too soon, but he keeps saying "no, it's not!" And he keeps telling me, that I will have my own room because his mom does not believe in couples "sleeping" under her roof, in the same bed; that "aren't" married!"

Candis laughs saying "ummmm--, she sounds like my mom!" Roxy agrees with her statement then adds "it does sounds like it would be a great; trip!" "And I have--, "always" wanted to see Italy!" said Roxy envisioning it. "But..., she says. Then she pauses contemplating her thoughts. Candis breaks the silence stating "I think you should just go!" she says as she's licking the vanilla frosting off the spatula. Candis puts the bowl in the dishwasher saying "this could be a chance of a life time." Naquawna over hears the conversation and says "don't do nothing!" I wouldn't do!" Candis laughs stating "which means; everything!" "And anything!" "Including the bathroom sink!"

Naquawna laughs reflecting on the time she hit her head on the bathroom sink while 'doing it, with Rayshawn. She hits Candis on the arm playfully shouting "you are; so trifling!" Roxy gets in her car which has been in the airport parking lot for days, still chuckling she says to Candis "you two should come by and have a Thanksgiving drink and a smoke with me before I leave to go to Italy." She continues to say "come on, you've never been to my house, you or Naquawna!" Candis look over at her mom asking "how long before dinner, mom?" "About 2 hours" said her mom. Candis chimes in "okay, meet us at 7 eleven and we'll follow you to your house".

Dianna standing up sharply says "I wanna come!" "I don't want to just sit here by myself. Roxy hearing her in the background says "it's cool, bring her to, she can be your designated driver because this is some "bomb; weed!" "Plus, the Champagne I got with 'me; will have you; stumbling!" she adds boastfully. Roxy ends the conversation with "and yaw'll already know?"! "I'm ma half to be 'faded, in order to get back up on another plane!" "I don't know how those flight attendances be doing it?"! Candis concurs saying "I know; right?"!

The front door shuts behind them as they are walking out the door towards Dianna's car. Roxy is still on the phone when the girls drive to seven 11 and park. By the time they get to 7- eleven Roxy is outside of her car pumping gas. After she pulls her receipt from the pump she signals them to follow her. The girls follow closely behind her because they don't want to get lost, trying to find her house up on all those winding tight roads. In the mist of it all Naquawna gets a text from Rayshawn saying "he misses her!" She shows Candis the text saying "see!" "I told you; it "ain't" just me!" Candis turns from the view of the text saying "I 'do not, wanna hear, "nothing" about him!" "Remember?"! Naquawna gives her a pinch on the arm from the backseat which causes Candis to yell "dammit!" That hurt!" You little rug-rat!" laughed Candis. Dianna cracks up laughing as well, voicing "that, is too funny!" I use to love that cartoon!"

They get to Roxy's house and pull in the driveway and when they exit their cars they all give each other big hugs. Candis is the first to say "this is a 'nice, looking house!" "Look at your yard!" she adds. They notice a couple of deer's on the side of her house eating flowers and Dianna states "how cute is that?!" Naquawna laughs out loud saying 'cute, will be; eaten!" if we ever have a major earthquake and run out of food!" She continues "honey please, folks will be eatin them!" "Sorry; Bambi"! Candis gives her dap, and cracks up laughing as Roxy's opening up her front door shaking her head with sadness, after hearing that, because she loves her deer's.

When the door swings open Roxy sees some luggage, and it's 'not, hers. She pays it no mind because she knows her friend was coming up for Thanksgiving weekend. Candis and Naquawna look around the living room at all the expensive pictures and the various vases that make her living room; pop! Dianna notices these beautiful Persian rugs on her floors and shouts out "shoot--!" "What do 'you; do, for a living?!" "This house is gorgeous!" she continued. Roxy laughing, answers "I, am, a dance teacher!" She winks at the girls and they all laugh; knowing that; 'that's, Roxy's 'story, and she's sticking to it! Roxy takes them out to the backyard and show's them the patio where her hot tub is and the small but nice size heated pool that is adjacent to it. You can see the pools lights glowing in the water and can tell how plush it would look at night time. As Roxy is showing them the backyard she can't help but notice some man's clothing on the ground by the hot tub. She comments on the bubbles that are still bubbling in the hot tub as well, like someone just used it and forgot to turn off the timer. But the girls didn't paid it no never mind, because they were so busy looking at her yard.

They all go back inside so Roxy can pop open the champagne bottle. Naquawna gets some glasses out of the bar cabinets at Roxy's request and she starts to pour. The ladies even tell Dianna to have one sip just so she can taste the bubbliness. Their glasses are lifted when they tell Roxy to make a toast. She says "to my girls"! "May we all keep moving 'forward, being 'blessed, in our; journey's in life"! "And in "hopes," along the 'way, may we find true 'love, and Happiness"! They all hit their glasses together and reply "good!" toast!" "Rox!" When they all taste the bubbling; Champagne and comment on how good it is. 'Naquawna; cracks "where did you get a $250.00 dollar bottle of Champagne, from?"! Roxy grinning says "from my boss!" He said he's been so proud of the work I've been doing!" They all laugh 'mischievously, when Dianna blurts out "hell, I need a boss like that!" Roxy pulls out the weed from a dish on her kitchen counter spouting "now 'this, is some real 'Humbo County, weed!" "I had this mailed to me the other day, and my friend got it out the mailbox for me this morning!" "Where is your friend?!" asked Candis. "I want to meet her!" Roxy says "she's back there sleeping probably 'all, jet lagged and stuff!" "I know she used the hot tub earlier though, because it's still; going!" said Roxy with a laugh.

Then they hear loud giggling from down the hall, and a man's voice saying "come here!" Roxy says "uh... "I see she's not alone!" "That little hoochi!" said Roxy lighting up the joint with a giggle. Once Roxy hits it, she passes it to the girls so they can hit it too. As the joint is being passed around the girls start to feel 'high, all except Dianna because she doesn't smoke. Roxy starts to feel high first after a few hits of the herb because she's a lightweight, and so is Naquawna. One thing that Candis and Naquawna always remembered about Roxy 'was, that she liked to play tricks on people! She has always been a real game player, so when Roxy says "let's go down the hallway and listen to my friend having sex with that guy in her room, it didn't come as a surprise to the girls. At first they said "no! Squawking at Roxy, saying "don't do that!" But then nosey Naquawna ends up leading the way voicing "come on, this will be funny!" And she won't even know we're outside the door listening!" she said.

Naquawna and the girl's tip-toe, down the hall and stand outside the door. They begin to hear slapping sounds like someone is getting slapped on their derriere. Then, as she starts to moan with every slap to her rump, the girls out in the hallway listening, look at each other and grin. The woman in the room tells the guy to 'slap it; even harder! And she gets even; louder, by vocalizing what she wants him to do! So after the slapping sound stops, the girl yells "tie me up to the bed post!" 'Candis, with her mouth open, whispers "she is a 'freak, of the week"! Naquawna laughing under her breath says "I am going to try that out on Rayshawn!" "But tie him up, instead of me!" The room goes silent, then they hear "get up here!" Now!"

Take me!" Then they hear movement as the noise grows 'louder, then 'heavier, and heavier! And when the bed starts to bang up against the wall aggressively, and then the breathing and the moaning get even louder. Dianna shaking her head in shame, for listening in, wants to go back into the living room, but she just keeps on 'listening, along with the other girls outside the door; giggling!

All of the sudden the girl in the room yells out "harder"! "Harder"! "Harder"! "Marvin"! She continues "is that all you; got?"! Roxy and Naquawna high as a kite laugh in each other's faces saying "well... we know his name is, "Marvin"! Then the guy "Marvin" says, "you want it harder?!" Okay!" Cuz, I can go; harder!" Candis looks at Dianna, and can't help but notice that she is listening 'now, even more; with her 'ear, up against the door and everything!" Then, Candis gets an "oh! "Hell--! "No!" look on her face. Followed with a look of panic and then she thinks back, to "Roxy!" Stripper!" "Her friend!" Stripper!" Tammy!" "Marvin!" "Jail!" Over a stripper!" "Oh!" "Shit"! And before Candis could say "come on yaw'll!" "That's enough listening"! "Let's go!"

Dianna busted in the room and almost broke down the door because she recognized Marvin's "sex; talking" voice! Tammy 'screamed, when Dianna barges into the room! And when the door busted open Marvin was lying on top of Tammy with her legs bound, and her arms tide to the bed posts, while he was going; all out!" to give her what she; "wanted"! Marvin turns and looks and yells "Dianna"! He gets up off of Tammy; quickly!" and falls off the bed. The first thing he says to Dianna is, "this! "This! "Ain't, what it looks; like!" He reaches on the bed for a pillow to cover himself. But as quick as an alley cat, Dianna lunges at both of them; knocking Marvin; right back on top of, Tammy!" while Dianna's punching anything, that moves with her eyes closed; tightly. 'Tammy, in return, had no choice but to start kicking her feet lose 'since, her hands were tied. Naquawna and Roxy break up the fight, after Dianna gets one more blow to the back of Marvin's head with her fist. Roxy, nervously tries to untie Tammy from the bed, who is 'now; huffing and puffing!" yelling "Marvin!" What the hell is going on?"!

She covers herself up with the thin robe that is on the floor asking "who is this chick?"! "I'm his fiancé b_tch!" yells Dianna as she's flashing her engagement ring in Tammy's face while trying to hit her again. Tammy pulls back avoiding a hit or a scratch to her face shouting "and so, am, I, you; whore!" shouted Dianna flashing the same ring back in Dianna's face. Candis is in the hallway not wanting to see her brother in his most 'scant-less; attire!" with no clothes on. So she goes to Roxy's bar to get another drink, while they are arguing. 'Candis, herself is also in shock, about the whole thing, and "hopes" her name 'does not, come up!" about the jail incident when she bailed Marvin out last month, because then Dianna will think 'she's, known about 'Tammy, all along! Candis slams back two shots of Patron and starts laughing to herself uncontrollably because she 'knows, her brother's "player's; card!" has 'finally, caught up with him!

Back in the room Tammy is skulking; at Marvin; looking him dead in his eyes she asked "are you playing us both?"! "No..., he answers as he's pulling up his pants. "I love you both!" he said. "You love us; both?!" says Dianna and Tammy at the same time. Dianna still being held back by Naquawna says "you said you had to work today!" You lied!" said Dianna as tears form up in her eyes. "And if I didn't come over here today, you would have come over to your momma's house like you weren't 'doing, a 'damn; 'thing; wrong"!

Tammy shouts out "Marvin!" You told me the same shit!" "You said--, you had to go to work, and that; that's why, you couldn't spend the whole Thanksgiving with me!" saying "and for 'me, not to worry about making you any 'food, because you were going to get a plate from your sister's house; on your way back to, work!" Since yo' momma!" Who you keep putting me off from "meeting" was out of town at her 'sister's, this year for Thanksgiving!" "No"! "No...! "Now see!" stutters Marvin. "I--; and before he could get another lie out of his mouth, Tammy halls off and slap the dog crap out of his ass. She yells "it's over!" "Marvin"! And she stomps off and goes into the bathroom.

Dianna looks at him and with a bitter look of anger on her face she pulls the ring off of her finger and throws it; hard!" and it hits him in his forehead; leaving a mark. He frowns; angrily at her, but says nothing. Roxy and Naquawna just look on at the situation in utter confusion 'thinking, "how is Marvin going to lie; his way out of this one?"! Tammy is in the bathroom getting dressed while yelling through the door "I wasted two f*^king years on you Marvin!" "You; dirty; bastard!" Dianna hearing her yelling from the bathroom blurts out "two years"! She looks at Marvin's face and says "we've been together for two years"! Tammy opens the bathroom door saying "well--, Marvin's been living with 'me, in Vegas for most of those two years"! "He even got into a fight over me and got arrested!" And his sister was nice enough to bail his sorry ass out!" But now, I wish she would have left him in there, tah; rot"! Dianna turns her attention towards Candis stomping towards the kitchen she yells "is that true?"! "You knew Marvin was with her; this whole time?"! Candis shouts "no...! "Hell! "No!

"Marv, just called me one night and said he needed to be bailed out; and that was; all"! Candis went on to say "he did not, tell me why"! Marvin blurts out "don't; lie! "Candis"! "You knew everything!" "Remember?!" I owed you money for a "bet" on the Laker's game"! "Recall now?!" is what Marvin kept saying.

He adds "but we both know it was "really" for bail money"! He continued to say "if you're gonna tell it!" then tell it all!" Candis blurts out "nuh-uh...! "Tell the truth"! "Marvin!" He yells "I, am; telling the truth"! Candis yells back "you wouldn't know the truth!" if I spelled; it for you"! Candis continues to yell "I never knew that you were seeing; no Tammy!" for no damn--!" two years!" so don't you 'dare; tell Dianna that lie!" "I thought it was a onetime 'thing; when you got in that fight in Vegas!" because I never heard 'anymore about it, after you deposited that $3500.00 dollars into my bank account"!

Tammy interrupts "which I paid half of!" ain't that a b*tch?"! Dianna gets light headed from hearing all of this bad news all at once, so she decides to sit down on the couch. While sitting there she begins to put her head down with her face covered; crying uncontrollably. Candis shouts "see what you did Marvin?"! Shaking her head she adds "you are not; right"! Naquawna goes over to the couch to comfort Dianna, while Tammy just looks at Marvin stating "I don't believe this"! Tammy continues "and not to be an 'insensitive; person but Marvin and I, were High School sweethearts!" "But my guess, is he never "really" grew up"! She looks at Marvin and gives him a (you will never hit this again!" kind of look)! Then she turns and looks at Roxy saying "sorry Rox, for bringing this "crap" to your house!" literally, she says as she's looking Marvin up and down. Disgusted with him she walks back to her room and closes the door.

Marvin goes on to picking up his shoes and the rest of his clothes that have been thrown outside Tammy's bedroom door. He looks at Dianna and sighs "I didn't mean for this to happen!" Dianna yells "no!" you didn't 'mean, to get; caught!" So angry, she can't even look at him, so she put her hand up instead as if to say "boy; bye"! Marvin walks out the door to his car which is parked up the street and doesn't look back when he drives away. He heads home before Dianna so he can grab some things to take to a hotel. But hearing his stomach grumble makes him have a change of heart, so he decides to 'still, go to his mom's house for Thanksgiving dinner. Roxy, Candis and Naquawna are still at Roxy's house looking at each other like 'ummmm...! 'Awkward! Naquawna says "what do yaw'll want to do now?"! Then they all look over at Dianna because she's their ride back to the house and she's not talking. Roxy hears a horn outside and it's Steeli'o parking the car. He plans on coming inside the house, so he can carry Roxy's bags out to the car, which she hasn't even packed yet. Roxy snaps back into reality shouting "oh, my, God!" I've got a plane to catch!" She throws her hands up in the air turning back and forth looking at the girls saying "I got to go get packed!"

Steeli'o gets out of the car and knocks on the door which is still ajar from Marvin, who had just left. Steeli'o opens the door even further saying "hello--? "Roxy--?" Your Chauffeur is here." He looks in the house from the door entrance and sees the three ladies in the living room getting their purses and getting ready to leave. He smiles saying "hey ladies" with a nod of his head, and a wave of his hand. He continues "how are you all doing?" They all say "hi..., we're fine!" and you?" they say. Candis smiles voicing "Roxy's almost ready." He grins "I remember you from thy party that night." "Yep, it's me." He asks "and which one of you is 'Nea'quawna?" Naquawna lifts her hand up answering "that would be me. He says "I've heard a lot about you ladies, and it's all good." They laugh stating "we hope so."

Naquawna then points saying "and this is Dianna, Candis's; she pauses and before she could say sister in law, she has a brain freeze but recovers by saying "her play sister!" She just didn't want to say the wrong thing, right now, after everything that had happened. Steeli'o says "nice to meet you too; Dianna!" Then he yells towards the back hallway "sweetie, we got a plane to catch!" I'm coming!" yells Roxy as she bolts out the back room stumbling in her 'heels, with three pieces of luggage. When he sees her struggling to pull the luggage down the hallway, he rushes over to help her and gives her a big kiss and carries her luggage out to the car.

Roxy gives the girls all a big hug and especially Dianna. Looking at Dianna she says "don't you worry about a thing!" "You will grow from this!" Whether you forgive him or not!" I believe that you will find love, and happiness again!" You are a beautiful person Dianna!" Don't let some jerk!" "Sorry, Candis!" she said. "I know it's your brother," she continues to say. "Some jerk!" harden your heart for love! Remember, out of all those 100,000.000's of sperm!" "You made it; to that egg!" You are a strong woman and you can make it through; anything!"

She gives Dianna a big hug and kiss on her cheek. Dianna nods clutching Roxy's hands and with tears streaming down her face she says "thank you, Roxy. "Thank you. "I needed to hear that. "You have a great trip to Italy!" cried Dianna all choked, up. They walk Roxy out to the car and say to Steeli'o "you take good care of our girl"! He smiles "I will take good care of "our" girl! He kisses Roxy on the hand and they drive away smiling. The girls get into Dianna's car, not saying a word and then Dianna spills out "screw your brother!" I'm still going to your mom's for dinner!" The girls sigh with comforting relief, knowing that she is going to be alright, and 'thinking, that; that is a good idea because she shouldn't be alone right now. They reply "good, Dianna because it wouldn't be the same without you there!" The girls pull up to the house and Dianna asks them "how her makeup looks?" They both say fine, but she checks it for herself one more time in the car's mirror. Dianna gathers herself and blows her nose, and clears her throat, and the girls say "are you ready?" she nods "yes. And Naquawna says "okay. "Lets' go eat!"

They walk into the house and Candis's mom is just getting the turkey out of the oven she says "you girls are right on time for dinner!" I tried to call you Candis, but you didn't answer your phone!" What good is it, to have a cell phone, if you don't answer it?!" Candis just rolls her eyes up by the kitchen sink as she's washing her hands voicing "sorry; mother...! Dianna asked "can we help you with anything maw?" and she says "yes. "Please put that macaroni and cheese on the table for me baby, under those two pot holders, so it doesn't burn my table cloth."

Naquawna helps Mrs. Tomson put the turkey on the carving platter and then she says "where's your brother?" he said he was on his way." "I'm going to need him to carve this bird" said her mother. "Your father use to do such a good job carving the meat" said Mrs. Tomson sadly; reminiscing. She than sighs "God, rest that man's his soul!" She gets a little teary and Candis say "now momma, don't you go getting all upset right now!" Her mother wipes her hands on her apron sighing "I'm fine!" Candis hears a car pull up and retorts "umm!" and here comes Marvin!" She sees him pulling up in the driveway from the kitchen window. Dianna and Candis glance at each other like 'okay! 'Here we go! 'Emmy; Award time!

Naquawna goes into the living room and wakes up her granddad and tells him it's time for dinner. He is startle at first, not knowing if he's at Mrs. Tomson's house or at home because he was in such a deep sleep. "I was dreaming about your grandmother" he said with a smile in his eyes. Naquawna helps him get out of the reclining chair saying "her spirit is probably here because if we weren't at my momma's house for Thanksgiving with grandma, we were at Mrs. Tomson's place. "Remember; granddad"? She walks with him towards the dining room table talking about old memories. He smiles "yes, your momma always had the best Holiday; spreads!" he said as he sat down looking up at her. He says "you know your mother learned all that good cooking from your grandmother?" Naquawna kisses him on the cheek saying "I know." "That's who I got it from." She gets a little choked up thinking about her mom and dad when she sits down in her chair, but shakes it off to stay in a good mood. Dianna takes a big drink of some wine and then very politely asked Naquawna's grandfather to pass her the bottle. He says "sure honey." Then Candis 'watching, says "slow down; chil!" You know you don't really drink!" And you don't want to be sick in the morning!" "I, don't, care!" said Dianna gritting the words out through her teeth. And then she gulps another glass full down.

Naquawna exchanges glances with Candis like "why are you letting her, drink?"! Candis just throws her hands up and makes face gesture like 'duh?"! "I can't stop her from drinking"! Then in walks Marvin not, saying too much and giving 'very, little, eye contact. He kisses his mom on the cheek and says "hi, to granddad" as he takes a seat beside him. Dianna was sitting across from Marvin which was something she never; did! She always sat right next to him 'almost, like she needed to hold his hand, at all the Holiday functions.

Mrs. Tomson noticed the change in their seating ritual, but didn't make a fuss. She just thought the two were having a "disagreement" about something or another and she went on to say Grace. "Heavenly; Father". "Thank you so… much, for bringing my family and my extended family together on this beautiful; Thanksgiving Day"! "And Thanks for this food, you have blessed us with!" in Jesus name we, Pray; Amen." "Alright!" Momma!" blurts Marvin as he takes another drink of the 'strongly, spiked; eggnog! "The food looks spectacular!" he goes on to say, after he swallowed his cheek, filled drink of Brandy; strait. Mrs. Tomson smiling says "oh, boy, now hush!" as she blushes with a humbling; sincere look on her face of 'thanks…

His mom sitting down at the other end of the table tells Marvin "now, you carve the bird, son!" That's your job from now on!" she said in a scratchy voice with one hand over her chest. He looks at his mother seriously and knows she is referring to his father who always carved the turkey and the hams on the Holiday's. He gives her a caring look, and nods and starts to carve the bird. Everybody passes the steaming; delicious, smelling dishes around the table. And it is a treat! Dinner rolls, macaroni and cheese, mustard greens and collard greens mix with smoked neck bones. Giblets sautéed in the gravy which is 'drizzled, over the corn bread stuffing.

And to add to the meal, some homemade cranberry sauce, with a splash; of orange liquor. Candis made some of her delicious fried corn on the cob, drenching in butter and a small dish of string beans, smothered in cream of mushroom, with French onions, heavily; layered on top. And of course it wouldn't be the same without Naquawna's garlic mash potatoes; they were the creamiest! Her potatoes were so fluffy it was like eating a real live cloud. But the topper, was 'Dianna's famous fried 'Cajun, chicken wings. They were the first to go because they were so flavorful. Ooh... how... they... ate! They ate so much, until they had no more room for desert! 'With, thy exception of Dianna and Marvin. Those two drank... and drank..., until Marvin's mom took notice saying "Dianna!" You haven't touched your; food!" Are you not hungry?" Dianna stands up slowly; growling "no!" I'm not!" I can't; eat!" she said looking down at her plate. And as she slurs out her words, she reaches for the wine bottle. Mrs. Tomson with a puzzled look on her face says "Marvin?!" Help your wife!" I think she's had too much to drink!"

Dianna, mutters "his wife!" That's a joke!" Marvin walks over to Dianna trying to get her to leave the table and go with him outside to get some air, so his mother won't suspect anything is wrong other than, Dianna's had too much to drinks! When he reaches for her arm saying "let's go outside and talk." Dianna turns into someone from the exorcist when she yells out "get your hands off of me!" "You f*^king!" liar! "Don't touch me"! Mrs. Tomson, Naquawna's grandfather and the girls drop their forks all at the same time at the mere 'language, coming out of Dianna's mouth! Candis and Naquawna try to help soothe the situation by saying "we'll take her outside for you, Marvin." But Dianna is "not" having; it! And she begins to fight 'anyone, coming towards her! In her mind, she is going to be heard and she doesn't care "who" is offended!

Dianna yells out "do you know?!" what I gave up!" I gave up everything; for this man!" I was the "perfect" wife; to be!" "But it just wasn't good enough for him!" because he; is..., trash!" she slurs. Mrs. Tomson shouts "That's enough!" Dianna!" You are drunk!" and you need to go home and sleep it off!" Dianna ignoring her words shouts "home!" What home?"! She continues with tears welling up in her eyes "you mean the house?!" that your son has probably "screwed" his "other!" wife, to be in!" And--, he's probably done; her!" In our; bed!"

Marvin yells out "you know what?"! He continues pointing "you are "not!" going to disrespect my 'mom, in her own, house!" grimacing at him she says "You're...; right!" Because you've got the "Thorne!" on that one! Mrs. Tomson now confused about the other woman says "what is going on Marvin?"! "Why are you two fighting?"! Dianna slurs out "tell her, Marvin!" All eyes go in Marvin's direction waiting to hear what he could "possibly" have to say, to justify the cause of his woman's anger! Marvin stares at Dianna for a few seconds wanting to just 'choke; 'her; 'out!" for 'ruining, thanksgiving dinner! But he couldn't find the words. Dianna yells "what?"!

"You can't talk; now?!" Then, I'll tell her!" As she's moving back and forth tittering on her heels with a glass of wine in her hand she looks at Marvin's mom with 'purpose, and shouts out "I--, busted in on Marvin 'screwing, another; b*tch!" "Your language!" shouts Candis. "Sorry, Mrs. Tomson!" says Dianna. "But he has been cheating with his 'stripping; "whore!" for two years! "Two...!" Years...!" blurts Dianna as her voice gets even louder. She continues to say "he 'even, bought her the same "ring!" that he gave me! "Who--; does that?"!

She starts to whale up, all over again with tears as big as crocodiles as she's looking into Marvin's mother's eyes. Mrs. Tomson looks over at Marvin with disappointment and can't believe what she is hearing. His mother says "Marvin, is this true?"! Dianna puts her hand up to block his face then she blares out "don't; even; lie!" Dianna adds "even Candis, and Naquawna were there!" And the kicker is!" adds Dianna; bitterly. "Luckily, sweet old Candis; bailed him out of jail one night in Vegas, after fighting over that prostitute"!

Marvin yells "she's "not" a prostitute!" Dianna yells back "uh-huh...! "You can speak now; huh?"! "You keep on defending that; skank"! Candis blows out a breath of air through her mouth to calm herself because she knows her mom is going to think that she's known about Tammy all this time and didn't say anything about it. And sure enough her mom looks at her asking "Candis, you knew Marvin was cheating on Dianna?" Candis blabs out "no!" not, at, all!" Mrs. Tomson shaking her head in disappointment yells "Marvin, how could you?!" do that to Dianna!" and after all I went through with your father, when he had that affair on me long time ago!"

Her eyes get watery when she says; sadly "now, you are making me bring up bad memories about your 'father, on, what, "was!" a good day! His mom stands up from her chair and as her napkin; falls to the floor she leaves the table and goes back to her room to gather herself. Marvin turns to Dianna and with tight lips he girts out "b*tch!" don't you 'dare, try and turn my mother against me!" He goes on to say "yes. "I was with Tammy, and you, at the same time!" And-- yes; it was wrong!" But I have loved Tammy, since High School!" And--, when Tammy moved away, and I met you, and I fell in love with you too!"

I never ever planned on running into Tammy when I went to a business meeting out there in Vegas!" "But, I must 'admit, I was glad to see her, and she was glad to see me, because she wanted to rekindle things." Dianna cuts in saying "yeah, and your weak; ass could of said, I got a woman right now"! He shouts "I did...!" but she kept after me!" She even 'Googled me, to find out where I worked at, and started sending me naked pictures!" And, I didn't even ask for then!" "So once I lost contact with her thinking she got the 'message, because I was with you!" "Then when I went to Barney's bachelor party she ended up being the dancer there!" "You remember my friend from work?" "Barney?" She smirks at him, not caring. He continues "and you, even encouraged me to go; to his party!" Dianna didn't want to hear it! She just kept, on, saying "weak; ass, mother f*cka!" was what she would say, whenever he would try to "justify" why?" he cheated!

Marvin starts to get sick of hearing her talking mess about him in front of granddad and the 'girls, so he blurts out "weak, ass"! "Weak, ass"! "Really---?"! "Dianna?"! "You want me to tell you, why?" I "really" cheated?"! He yells; angrily, because now, he's pissed! And doesn't give a damn; if he hurts her feelings or not! He yells "the real reason "why?" I cheated, is because 'she, has a wild side!" And she's... better in bed, then you are!" "Okay?"! "There!" I said it!" he yelled. Dianna, yells back, and gets all up in his face when she blasted out the words "of course, she has a "wild; side"! "She's ah, f*cken; stripper"! "You, Jack ass!" And everybody's probably "seen" her "wild; side"! "So you're stupid ass couldn't; possibly 'think, you're the only one she's screwing!" Because let me tell you something; honey!" You're not that good in bed; yourself!"

'Marvin, mad as hell, after hearing; that' has to 'refrain; with everything he's got; to keep from 'throwing, his drink in her face! Naquawna's grandfather gets up from the table with an 'embarrassed, look on his face for 'Marvin. Then he scooted out of his chair and walked slowly back to the living room to sit down to wait for Naquawna, so she could take him home. Still arguing, Marvin puts his hand up in Dianna's face yelling out for her to "go...!" Home...!" adding "I am tired of arguing with you!" Then frustrated he asked Candis "if she could take Dianna home?"!

Candis now in the kitchen getting some peach cobbler and sweet potato pie to take home, gives him a look of (are you kidding me)?"! But when Dianna comes in the kitchen Candis; sympathizes with the situation answering "I guess. With Dianna still out of control drunk, she gets even louder retorting "hum--! "Telling your sister to give me a ride home!" "Why?!" So you can go back over to your "whore's!" house! He yells back "no!" I'm staying here tonight at my; mom's house!" Dianna shouts "and so am; I!" Because I do "not" want to be at "that; house" anymore!" Where you and your "concubine!" have been!

Then she starts to cry all over again. "Marvin throws his hands up in the air shouting "then I'll go to the house then!" He walks into the living room to ask Naquawna to drop him off at home, with Dianna running behind him yelling "I hate you Marvin!" You sorry bastard!" She reaches out to grab him by his collar and missteps and falls on the living room floor and ends up twisting her ankle. She keeps yelling out; obscenities while she's down on the floor. And then Marvin's mother, who has had; enough! Rushes into the living room yelling "get out"! "Everybody get out"! She continues "Dianna?"! "I am, sorry!" But you and 'Marvin, have got to go!" I am not going to have, all this bickering and arguing on Thanksgiving Day!" Marvin trying to calm his mother down sides with her saying "you're right mom!" His mother ignores him and points towards the door and without any; more; sympathy!" she blurts "get out!" You two, have ruined my Holiday!" 'Marvin, holding his head down after realizing, that there is no getting through to his mother starts to walk towards the door. Naquawna sneaks back to the kitchen to get her and her granddad two plates to go, plus desert and gives Mrs. Tomson a big hug good-bye. Mrs. Tomson gives them her deepest apologies for an upsetting dinner as she walks them out to their car. Marvin gets into Naquawna's car still trying to apologies to his mother. Smiling at his mother, Naquawna says "we'll take Marvin home so he doesn't drive drunk." "Thank you; sweetie" says his mother as Candis is coming over to kiss her mom good-bye. "Love you mom." "Sorry for all the drama tonight" smiles Candis.

Dianna comes hobbling over and tries to save face by sobbing "I didn't mean to ruin the Holidays for you Mrs. Tomson!" She continues to say "but Marvin is a dog!" "He treats women like toys!" And then he just throws them away!" She leans to one side to eases the pressure off her hurt ankle and continues to bash Marvin, but Mrs. Tomson just pats her on the shoulder smirking "good night; dear!" We'll talk about it later, when you're "not" so drunk!

Candis waves to Dianna to come on, and get in the car, once she's done putting all the food in the backseat. Mrs. Tomson starts to walk back towards the house while Dianna is still left standing there with her shoes in her hands. Slowly she limps over to Candis's car and plops down in the passenger's seat and they drive off to Candis's house together. Naquawna blows her horn at Candis and turns up the beat in her car, and is now on her way to dropping Marvin off bumpin Young M.A's song called: Ooouuu!"

Then when that song goes off Naquawna is singing some of the song that is being played in her car which is called: Shawty is A 10 by: The-Dream featuring Fabolous because she is in such a great mood! 'While Marvin's relationship; is shattering! 'Hers, seems to be thriving because Rayshawn has been texting her all, day, long!

Chapter 15

Rayshawn and Se'anna got to Sac'mento at about 3:30 in the afternoon, and as soon as Se'anna got out the car, Rayshawn's little sister came out to greet them. Rayshawn's little sister is 14 years old, and her name; is Brandy. When Rayshawn introduces her to Se'anna she smiles, saying "hi, while extending her arms out to carry the baby into the house. Brandy "loves babies" is what she stated to Se'anna as the two are walking up towards the porch. Rayshawn grabs the luggage from out the trunk of the car and hurries up to the house. His father gives Se'anna a nice welcoming hug and then sees Rayshawn and gives him a big manly hug, and as he looks Rayshawn up and down he voices "you look good son"!

His father who is named; Big Ray, says to Se'anna "you have really been taking good care of my son!" Se'anna smiling, sweetly returns "awh--, thank you Mr. Ray." He replies "we are family!" You can call me Pops!" Or, Big Ray!" She nods saying "okay. And then sits down on the couch with Brandy and the baby. Big Ray, walks towards the couch with a big smile on his face to meet his grandson for the first time. When he gets near him he takes him from Brandy's arms and holds him up like a proud grandpa and kisses him on his cheeks. Big Ray says "he's a handsome little guy, ain't he?!" he said looking at Brandy with a smile.

Rayshawn hearing his father yells from the kitchen "he takes after me pops!" His father laughs out "he gets his cute looks from his momma!" They laugh again, and Se'anna chuckles, saying "thank you." She adds "I tell Rayshawn the same thing all the time!" and they both chuckle some more. Rayshawn yells "awe--!" Yaw wrong, for that!" he said while he's still in the kitchen eating on some tri-tip that his father had smoked earlier. Rayshawn seeing that he has a little time alone in the kitchen, decides to give Naquawna a quick text while his family is in the living room getting acquainted.

He tells Naquawna how much he misses her, and then texted her asking "so how is the food at Candis's mom's house?" Naquawna had texted him back saying "I'm over at Roxy's house, and Marvin just got busted cheating with a stripper"! "Now, we are on our way back to Candis's mom's house to go eat." "Miss you"! Then she concluded her texting with "Dra'mahh"! He texted back "dang!" Poor; dude!" He ends with "I'll holla at you later, baby! Rayshawn walks back into the living room saying "that tri-tip is on; hit!" Pops!" So when we gone eat?" His father answers "I'm waiting on my lady friend to get hear then we can eat." Rayshawn grunts "aw--; naw!" Don't tell me you went and got yourself another chicken-head?"! Brandy starts to laugh so Rayshawn looks her way asking "sis, is she a hood, rat?" or, what?!" Big Ray jumps into the conversation before Brandy could respond shouting "hell--, no!" she ain't no rat!" I got more game than that!" he chuckles. "She's not as beautiful as your mother, but she's sweet, and she's good peoples." "You'll see, when she gets here!" he says nodding like as if to say, he's got good taste in women.

Rayshawn looks back at him with a half-smile saying "okay. "Now, if she's sweet; and good peoples, that must mean; she's a little plump around thy, edges" he says laughing. Se'anna clicks on him saying "Rayshawn that is not; nice!" Inner beauty is what "really; counts"! Rayshawn chuckles saying "not in this family!" Then he laughs even harder. Brandy gives out a big "ah-ha ha... herself, but still agrees with what Se'anna had said. And then the door gets knocked on, it's his father's; date. Rayshawn anxiously opens the door to see what she looks like 'and to his surprise, she is kind of thick, and round in some areas, but is still a very cute looking older lady who looks to be about 58 years old; he guesstimates. He also couldn't help but notice that she was all bust, hips, and butt. She wasn't a knock out doll, but she was pretty. She gives everyone a nice "hello, and says "sorry I'm late, to Ray" as she gives him a kiss.

With a cute little stride she walks over to the dining room table to put the food she made down on it and then makes her way back to the living room. Big Ray takes her coat and introduces her to the family saying to them "this is Zailda." Rayshawn and Se'anna say "hi and reaches out to shake her hand but she grins back saying "I'm a hugger." I want a hug" she said as she reaches out to hug everyone with a sweet smile on her face. While no one else is looking Rayshawn looks at his father like 'okay; dad! 'Way tah go; Idaho! 'Was what he was thinking. And with a half cracked smile on his face he gives his dad; dap. They all gather together sitting in the living room talking about sports and looking at the football game waiting on the turkey which has only 10 more minutes to go, before it's done. Zailda and Big Ray sit next to each other on the loveseat like two teenagers in love. 'Brandy, thinks it's; grouse!" 'Se'anna, thinks it's; cute!" And all Rayshawn can think is "how is his dad; hitting all that; boot-tay?"!

The timer goes off on the stove and everybody gets up and head to the table after they've washed their hands. Big Ray is not much of a traditional man "meaning" he'd rather eat steak and potatoes on Thanksgiving. But of course he makes an exception for his family and makes a turkey anyway. Zailda takes the foil off of her homemade enchiladas that are already on the table. Se'anna's mouth waters when she tells Zailda 'how deliciously; good her enchiladas look. Zailda smiles returning "they are a family recipe from my step mom who cooks the best Mexican food, I've ever tasted!" Big Ray starts to carve the turkey after Zailda said Grace. The doorbell rings and Rayshawn looks at his dad 'like, you want me to go get that?" Then he asked "are you expecting more company dad?" Ray answered "naw..., but I got the door son. "Yaw go on ahead and start eaten."

He goes to the door while they start eating, and when he opens the front door thinking it's one of Brandy's friends who lives up the street. To his disappointment, it is Rayshawn's cracked; out mother, who is asking for a plate and wants to see her daughter; Brandy. Ray steps outside saying

"Bonnie, we are having dinner right now, this is a bad time, I've got peoples; over!" Bonnie gets loud "I, don't, care!" "I want to see my child!" Rayshawn hearing bits of 'muffled, words all the way in the dining room, wants to see who's at the door getting loud with his dad, so he gets up and struts to the front door and opens it saying "dad, you alright?"!

Bonnie was so tore; up and broke down when he looked at her standing there. She had a green scarf on her head and no makeup on. Her lips were 'dried, cracked and crusty and her teeth were rotted out in the front. Bonnie was so frail and under nourished that Rayshawn didn't even 'know, that; that was his own mother! Bonnie looks up at her son and with almost a whisper she says "Rayshawn?" "Is that you?" my baby. His head tilted when she said "my baby!" Then as she extends her arms to hug him, he hesitated and looked at his father like "who is this?"!

His father has tried for 'years, to avoid 'their kids, from ever seeing their mother like this. He has even gone as far as continuously; relocate when she's found out where they've moved to, "especially" when they were little. 'But now, that they are somewhat grown, except Brandy, he feels he has no choice but to let them see their mother because she's not going to go away this time. Ray bows his head down in shame for his ex-wife and as he extends his hand in her direction he says "this is your mother, son!" Rayshawn not wanting to believe it, says "what?"! "My mother?"! "That's not my mother!" "You told us mom lives in Europe, furthering her "fashion; designing" career!" "I've seen pictures of mom". He points at Bonnie saying "and this ain't her!"

Rayshawn looks at his father and then cracks a skeptical smile laughing out "funny; dad!" That's a good one!" "Who is she for real?!" A smoker?!" Is she looking for some dope?!" "No, son!" This is really your mother!" Rayshawn steps back and looks 'hard, at her. Then he belts out "hells--! "No!" She looks like one of my; patients!" He; gawks at her while walking back into the house towards the dining room table. Shaking his head not wanting to believe it, he keeps on walking away. But then when Bonnie yells out "little Ray, Ray, rascal!" Rayshawn turns and looks back, because that was what, she always called him, since he was a little boy. And he knew, no one knew that name but his mom, and his family. Rayshawn turns and looks back and as he's 'looking, at 'her, his face goes; pale! Time; slows down, and he can feel his heart; as it beats. He just stood there with his hand rubbing across his chin; mumbling; softly the words; "wow--! Wow--!" Wow!

He just never 'thought, out of all his years of selling 'dope, the one person; that meant the world to him 'his mother, would be 'smoking, the very; dope!" that he sold. As he walks back slowly towards his father looking confused thinking that to himself, but still; in denial he says "aw...!" Dad!" "You really went all; out with this joke!" You even told her my nick; name and everything!" Huh?" Big Ray tells Rayshawn to come back outside, then his father says "son, I, am, so-o-o, sorry!" I did not, want you kids to "ever!" see your mother like this." Rayshawn just shakes his head slowly like a person 'dazed, that couldn't speak.

And when his mother started to talk to him, he turned on his father and in anger he states "how could you?!" You lied to us; pop!" And in an elevated voice; of sadness he went on to say "you're telling me; that my "mother!" has been a crack-head?!" this whole time?!" Bonnie interjects saying "now, wait a minute; now!" I, am; "not!" Nobodies; crack-head!" I, am, just, going through; some hard times; right now!" she confessed, as she adjusted the scarf on her head. Brandy is sitting at the table eating but she gets curious to see what's taking her dad so long, so she says "I'll be right back!" to Se'anna and Zailda and she excuses herself from the table. Practically; sneaking she walks towards the front door to go see who is talking outside to her brother and her father for this long. When she gets to the living room she slowly pulls back the living room curtains while still trying 'not, to be seen. It works for a second but then; oops! Brandy opens the curtains too far and 'buck-eyed, Bonnie, on geek mode, spots her in the window and waves to her to come outside, after seeing her peeking through the curtains.

The door opens and big Ray and Rayshawn try to tell Brandy to go back inside of the house saying to her "that they are coming!" But Bonnie, with a rotted; tooth 'smile, stops her from leaving by saying "Brandy--; you sure have 'grown, into a beautiful young lady!" Brandy, not knowing what to do, or say after seeing the distaste, on her father's face; cautiously says "thank you... Then she looks at her father and Rayshawn and says "come on; your foods getting cold. Bonnie grabs Brandy by the hand in a desperate attempt to get her attention she says "Brandy, it's me!" Your mother!" You don't remember me; do you?!" Brandy swallows hard, and then looks at her dad asking "who?!" "Who is this?!" My mom is in Europe!" Right dad?!" she said looking to her father for reassurance. He nods his head up and down slowly and reaches for Brandy's hand saying "let me talk to you for a minute baby." Brandy looks over at Rayshawn's face to see if he's holding back a laugh. But after seeing that her brother is almost fighting back tears and her dad is looking like someone just told him, he's about to lose his house. Brandy slowly starts to believe that this is "really" true!

Like someone kidnapped her mom in Europe and she just 'escaped, and that's why she's 'looking, so back! Well--, at least that's what she's 'hoping, after seeing her mother looking like; this! Brandy snatches her hand back from her father and crosses her arm asking "is this my mother for real?!" "What happened to her?!" asked Brandy as her eyes swell up with tears. The tears fall down her face and all her high hopes of a mother she was so "proud; of" that she bragged about, to all of her 'friends, had 'right before her; eyes disappeared! 'Not to mention, the mother she could talk to about 'anything!" like boys, fashion, and life itself. And also her dreams of all the fashionable clothes from her mom's collection 'that she was "hoping" to be wearing; one day! All came crashing 'down, like a ton of; brick!

Bonnie could see that Brandy is about to have a full on cry, so she whimpers out to her saying "I'm, sorry baby." "I've been trying to see you 'kids, for years!" But your father wouldn't let me!" Ray shouts "Bonnie"! "Don't you dare"! "Make me out to be the bad guy; here"! He raises his voice and continues to say "you chose--; to be a crack-head!" and be in them streets!" over, raising these kids with me!" 'Brandy, didn't 'even, want to hear that she was a crack-head! That made it even worse! She was 'more, excepting to the thought of her mother being ill or having a hard 'time, for the reason; of her condition!

But Brandy just couldn't wrap her head around the fact; that her mother was in the streets this 'whole time, doing "drugs" when she could have been home with her and her brother! 'So, in all of the 'commotion, with her mom and her dad, putting the blame on each other; arguing and pointing fingers; at one another! Brandy gets a blank stare on her face because she has heard; enough! And with all the noise, and all the yelling; back and forth, she takes off; running. She runs, and runs, and runs, all the way up the street "not; daring" to look back, as she ran straight up to her friend's house; crying.

He father yells for her to come back, and while looking over at Bonnie he blurts out "see!" look what you've done!" That's why, it was best for you to stay away, until you got your shit together!" Rayshawn still in a state of numbness himself, puts his hands on top of his head asking his dad "do you want me to run up there and get Brandy?!" "No. "She'll be back." "Let me go call Betty and tell her Brandy's on her way up to her house!" "And tell her why?!" he states as he's giving Bonnie a dirty look walking back into the house with Rayshawn to go get his cell phone. Bonnie, still standing outside puzzled; hears a baby crying 'so she sneaks in the house while Ray is searching for his cell phone.

She ends up in the dining room where Se'anna, little Ray, and Zailda are sitting at the table eating, not really knowing, what was fully going on outside. Bonnie peaking from the dining room wall then when they see her she says "hello?" What a cute baby" she said smiling walking up closer to the child. Rayshawn comes in to where his mother is standing over by the baby and he says "my dad said you need to wait outside." Se'anna interrupts with a smile saying "babe..., hold little Ray please, while I go use the bathroom." Just then, Bonnie inhales with a surprised look on her face, saying "is this your baby, son?"

Se'anna not putting two and two together that; this could be Rayshawn's mom, says "yes---, this is little Ray the 3rd" she said proudly as she scoots her way to the restroom. Zailda, trying not to be 'rude, offers a warm hello, and notices that Bonnie could use a 'bite to eat, being that she looked so--; thin. Big Ray had already told Zailda about Bonnie and how she abandoned the kids, but on 'Holiday's, how she'd "always" seemed to find them no matter where they moved to.

Zailda offers Bonnie some food and she gratefully accepts and sits down to eat. When Ray finds his phone and calls Betty; afterwards he walks back to the front door but doesn't see Bonnie. Happy that she has 'left, he closes the front door and goes back into the dining room to go eat. But 'then, he sees her sitting down eating at the table. He says "Bonnie, you've got to go!" "This is a 'disruption, to our Thanksgiving dinner!" "And now I need you to leave!" he said sharply. Bonnie shouts "I just wanted to see my kids; Ray! "You are so... selfish!" He blares out "I'm selfish?!" "You left when those kids were both in diapers! "First, when Rayshawn was little, then I'd take you back, after months of being gone!" Then, when you did come back!" You tell me you're pregnant with Brandy!" I give you the benefit of the 'dought; that she is mine!" Hoping that you would change!" But sure as the 'grass; is green!" "You were right back to 'being, the same old Bonnie!" running them; streets!

"I just got so--; tired--; of you breaking those kids; hearts!" And hearing them cry; where's mommy; all the time?!" Asking me; when she coming back home?!" So... yes!" I made up some lavish story about how you went to Europe to become a famous designer!" Rayshawn interjects "but dad, I seen the runway pictures, of mom"! His dad says "yes. But that's when she was a beautiful model!" She looked just like 'the beautiful Dianna, from the movie 'Mahogany, back in the day!" She was so talented and beautiful everybody wanted to sign her up for modeling!" But she just couldn't keep that "coke" out of her nostrils!"

While the commotion is at full; peek between Bonnie and Ray,

Se'anna come in from the bathroom and sits down next to Rayshawn and whispers under her breath "what's going on?" 'Rayshawn, in a very sad and emotional voice says "this is my; mom; man!" She's a smoker!" Rayshawn gets up 'sharply, from the table and walks out of the dining room and goes into the living room where he walks around in circles wanting to punch something. Se'anna gets up from the table and follows behind him with the baby in her arms. Even though she is confused about the whole story, she still wants to be there too comfort him.

The front door swings open and it's his sister coming back home because her friend had to leave to go to her in-laws house for Thanksgiving dinner as well. Brandy can still hear her dad arguing with their mom, but then she sees her brother standing against the wall being; consoled, by Se'anna. So when Rayshawn sees that his little sister has come back home he rushes over to her and gives her a big hug as they both shed tears of sadness, over the condition of their mother.

While that is going on in the living room, Big Ray is in the dining room and he is so-- 'tired, of arguing with 'Bonnie!" that he starts to escorts her to the front door with her plate in hand! But to his 'dismay, she is "not" leaving as easily as he'd hoped! And to make matters worse 'Bonnie; still not wanting to leave, turns her attention towards the quiet and meek; Zailda saying to her "so you're Ray's 'new, tumble weed, I see"! 'Zailda, with her eye brows; lifted answers "excuse me?"! Bonnie blurts "you heard me hoe!" Are you the one keeping my 'kids, from me, too?!" Ray shouts "don't even answer her Zailda!" "She is in; need, of a 'hit; from the pipe!" "Kiss my ass; Ray!" yells Bonnie.

"I see you got yourself a 'chunky, monkey; this time!" huh?" said Bonnie, maliciously. He talks over her comment stating; "just leave, Bonnie before I call the police"! She continues to say "I bet she really puts a 'dent, in your mattress!" laughs Bonnie trying to instigate a fight with Zailda. Once she said that about Zailda; Zailda was fed up when she looked at her hard; while swirling her neck she yelled out "look here; bones...!" I'm putting more than just a 'dent, in his mattress!" I'm 'taking, really; good care of him as well!" "Something you're sorry ass could 'never, do!" So keep it 'movin; twiggy!"

Bonnie gets mad about the way she is talking to her in front of Ray, so she extends her arms forward to grab Zailda by her long hair, but Big Ray intercepts; instead and grabs Bonnie by her arm shouting "that's; it!" You're out of here!" Zailda looks at Bonnie with a half-smirk on her face and shouts out "bye; cavity central!" Zailda chuckling after saying that to her, take a bite of her food while, Bonnie is getting thrown, out of the house. Rayshawn, Se'anna, and Brandy are still in the living room when they see their 'father, throwing their 'mother, out of the house. The two really didn't have too much to say about the whole thing anymore. And maybe it was because, they really don't even "know" this woman!" that was; their mother!

'Yes, their father lied to them but he's always been 'there, through the 'good, and the bad. Brandy looks at her 'mom, one last time as the door closes behind her, and her mother yells out "I love you kids!" "I always have!" Big Ray locks the front door, and he and Zailda walk back towards the dining room arm in arm as he shouts out to his kids "come on yaw'll"! "Let's go eat!" "I'll tell you all about your mother at the dinner table!" "Because she is "not" going to ruin this day with me and my family!"

They all walk back to the table in a somber mood, while sadly embracing; one another. And after their dad explains from the beginning to thy end, about their mother and their relationship. The family 'finds, some closure. In fact, it has actually brought then closer together. They eat, laugh, and then play a few board games after dinner. And all is peaceful, at Big Rays house, until Rayshawn's phone goes off!

Chapter 16

'Now, just like a wild fire; peace seems to be 'spreading, as Roxy and Steeli'o's plane lands across the globe. Roxy tell Steeli'o how she can just smell the freshly baked bread in thy air as she steps off the plane. With her feet on new ground the sun feels so warm and inviting, like it is shining just for them. Roxy holds on to Steeli'o like they've just gotten married and they're out on their honeymoon in a romantic; paradise! Once off the plane they board a boat that Steeli'o 'owns, and had requested waiting for them with his cousin Vinnie; driving it. He gives Vinnie a big hug and Vinnie says "hey-- cousin!" It's been a while since you've come home." Steeli'o replies "I know. "I've been busy" he said as he glances at Roxy; implicating that she's been keeping him "occupied"!

Vinnie smiles returning "I completely understand "why"! And the guys laugh. Roxy, smiles, knowing that they are talking about her, so she puts her shades on and looks over the; borrow of the boat while 'enjoying, the beautiful view of the city. Steeli'o introduces her as his lady and Vinnie welcomes her with two kisses on her cheeks. They head to a beautiful villa where Steeli'o's sister lives. They stop to pick her and her husband up before they go to their mom's house to go eat. When they dock to go up to Steeli'o's sister's home, they are greeted by her husband; Spartique. 'Gi'la, is Steeli'o's 'sister, her and her husband 'Spartique, have been married for only 9 months and the wedding was a party to remember.

Her brother 'Steeli'o, spared no expense because Steeli'o 'knew, that this would have made their father very happy, since he wasn't there to walk his only daughter down thy aisle. Their wedding was; extravagant!" and the people in the town are still talking about it to this day. It even made front page news in the daily papers. And so did her dress, which was also on the front page of many of the Glam Magazines. When Spartique opens the door to their home Gi'la runs to meet her only brother with a hug and kiss on each cheek. She then turns to Roxy and gives her the same heartfelt greeting which made Roxy feel right at home.

Gi'la pulls Roxy and her brother into the house arm in arm and tells them "to have a seat." She went on to say "and can I get you two anything to eat or drink?" They both smile saying "sure. So while waiting on their drinks Roxy looks around the living room and sees all the beautiful things in Gi'la's house and says to her "this is nice!" On all of the walls there is simple but very beautiful art paintings on them. Roxy continues to say "what a beautiful home you have Gi'la." Roxy being a first time home owner herself; wonders what kind of 'job, her and her husband have, to be able to afford all these nice things? 'Heck, she could hardly keep up with all the bills that come with owning her own home, let alone furnishing it with such 'lavish things, she thought. But Roxy just keeps those thoughts to herself and would wait until they've all had a few cocktails to get the "real; deal!" on the finances.

Beaming from ear to ear Roxy tries not to stare at Gi'la as she's putting down a tray of goodies. On the tray that she's putting down, it has some sweet treats, like figs, meats, cheeses and bread on what looks to be a crystal coffee table. "Yummy, this looks so good" said Roxy. Gi'la smiles with a "thank you, and Roxy can't help but stare at her because she is so pretty. Gi'la has light brown eyes and soft looking brown hair; with just a hint of strawberry blonde in 'streaks; throughout her nicely straighten hair. She is tall and slim like a runway model. And her cloths just draped on her body like a well fitted manikin in a store window. 'Gi'la, to 'Roxy, was very pleasant to talk to, right out the 'gate, because her and Roxy started talking about shopping the second they met. Gi'la told her about all the fun things they could do out there, and she just fussed over all the girly; things, they could shop for downtown.

The guys laughed when hearing them talk about shopping saying to one another "hold on to your wallet; man!" Gi'la slaps her brother on the arm laughing "don't tell my husband that!" Vinnie just shakes his head with a grunt, and takes his last bite of cheese and pops it into his mouth while dusting the crumbs off of his hands on his pants. He chews his food saying "we better get going guys!" "Your mom and my parents are all waiting on us so we can eat" he added. Before they leave Gi'la's place, she grabs one of her best liquor bottles out of the cupboard to toast her brother's return home and insist everyone take a shot. It is so lemony and delicious as it smoothly goes down their throats with a warming sensation. Roxy commented on how fabulous the drink taste, and says to them that "she will be buying; that drink, when she gets back to the States, so her friends can try it.

Chuckling, Vinnie rushes everybody out of the house so they can get on the boat, since he is in charge of seeing that everyone gets to momma's house safely. Happily and playfully they all are with each other 'laughing, and 'drinking, on the boat ride over, all except Vinnie. He is the sea Captain, so he is only allowed one shot. The two happy couples head to momma's house with Vinnie leading the way.

The boat ride is so beautiful and all of the houses are nicely arranged on the mountain side in the nooks and crannies of the cliffs. As the day goes on, the sun is slowly slipping into her 'night gown, as she 'begins; to set. And as the beautiful ray, of colors, from the sun, lay on 'top, of thy ocean, and drape, across the 'sky; is when the sun 'falls; beneath thy other side! "Roxy feels like she could live here forever" she says out loud. "I'm never going back to the States" she said smiling. Steeli'o smiles at her and gives her a long kiss, while they're enjoying the sun; setting. After docking the boat they go up a beautifully, lit stairway to Steeli'o's mom's house. And as soon as the door opens to momma's house Steeli'o is the first to give her a great big hug and a kiss; as he tells her in Italian "I have missed you; my mother"!

His mom speaks full Italian and very little English. She glances at Roxy asking her son in Italian "Chi e' questa Donna che hai portato alla mia casa?" Meaning "who is this woman, you have brought to my house?"

Steeli'o pulls Roxy by the hand up, to meet his mom, answering "this is my girlfriend momma." But he says it; in Italian "Cio' e' la mia mamma Della ragazza." Roxy gives her a hug and a kiss on both cheeks and with smiling eyes she tells his mother "how happy she is to meet her, and what a beautiful home she has." Steeli'o translates, what Roxy has just said to his mother and she smiles welcoming Roxy into her home. Vinnie's mom and dad are at the house too, so everyone hugs and greets each other in the living room.

Steeli'o's, mom's house, is a fortress, it sits off a cliff overlooking the water and all of her fruits and vegetables she grows in her own backyard. His mom who they call 'momma Milian, is a fabulous cook. She makes everything from scratch. Her sister Rosie who is Vinnie's mom owns her own Restaurant in town. I guess you could say 'good cooking runs in the family. Steeli'o had always made sure that his mom had the finer thing in life, after their father died. As a young boy around 16 years old Steeli'o got involved with the drug trade after his father passed. Some of his dad's old Butcher friends 'who called themselves looking out for Stevonno's family, ended up giving Steeli'o a job.

Stevonno was Steeli'o's father's first name, and he was a very well known; fisherman. Lorenzo was his dad's best friend and a very well respected Butcher. One stormy night on Stevonno's way back from a fishing trip, the news reporter had stated "that his boat had capsized and the wreckage was found on the shores of Spain." The family was 'broken up, over the loss of their father as you can imagine. And the 'devastation, was what lead poor Steeli'o to drop out of school; just so they could keep their home. It was a small two bedroom house where he and his sister had to share a room when they were little. 'Though small, their home was a loving and inviting place to grow up in. After his father died, Steeli'o got a job at the Butcher Shop where he started off making small deliveries to the underground Butcher's Market's. He was transporting meats, at first, but then as Lorenzo started trusting him more, he started moving hashish that came in from Maraco. Once he made a name for himself by expanding Lorenzo's empire from northern Europe to Spain. That is when Steeli'o 'moved up, in the business, because Lorenzo felt he had gotten older, and wiser.

But then when Lorenzo got sick, Steeli'o got workers to help him move Lorenzo's products for him by mules and by boats. This went on for a while until Lorenzo died and then he left Steeli'o the "Butcher's; Business!" and that is how Steeli'o got the "money" to start flipping houses. And to this day that is why his mother thinks he's a self-made Millionaire do to his 'high; demanding, real-estate business! But little does his mother 'knows, that; that is just a quarter of his income. 'True, he's always loved buying and selling beautiful home, which made it easier for his mom and his sister to get such nice houses from him. But as for Steeli'o's "other; source" of income, there is his 'colleagues, who mostly stemmed from the very 'rich, who bought his diamonds, to the super 'rich, who also dabble in big; weed, and diamonds.

But, Steeli'o has no problem selling to the average income worker, either. To Steeli'o's 'credit, he stays away from harder drugs such as Heroin and Meth saying; to his colleagues "that; that!" is too 'much, of the devils; drugs to him!" And that "he; like" his customers 'happy, when they get high!" "Not; dying" while their high!" His sister and her husband are 'clueless, as well to his double life. Roxy doesn't even know "how" deep he is "either" in the dope and diamond trade. But deep down, she really doesn't "want" to know the "real" dirt about him!

'Although, she does recall "meeting; him" at a "Baller's; party"! Which was just 'that, men and 'woman, who were 'balling, out of control with drugs, diamonds, and money! So Roxy continues to "thinks" or "wants" to 'think, that he's only selling a little blow or pot on the side because she doesn't "really" want to ask him too many personal questions, because she's loving the "lifestyle" she's having with him, and figures; no need to rock the 'boat, sort of speak! 'So--, as Roxy and Steeli'o's family are now sitting down to feast on all that beautiful food, out in Italy. Back in the States the back door of the 'precinct, just opened up over on the south side of town past; Treeberry, and in walked 'Detective Mahavez, with a sour look on his face because he has to work, on Thanksgiving Day. One of the guys named 'Office Kitpatrick, says "hey, man?"! "They got you too; huh?"! "I guess that's what happens to us guys who aren't married with kids!" he laughs. Mahavez laughs back and sit down at his desk cracking up he says "yep!" and I guess we'll be working Christmas too!"

They both agree and chuckle and in walks the Captain asking "so what's going on?!" "I heard the case is going cold!" he adds. "No!" says Mahavez as he stands up from his desk and directs the Captain to his strategizing board on his wall. He point on the board saying "he just landed in Italy." Talking about Steeli'o. He continues to say "and we're keeping a tight tail on him to" he adds. "Plus--; said Kitpatrick interjecting "we just got confirmation that he's at his mother's house having dinner." "What about the other four?" asked the Captain with a sip of his coffee? "The two brother's Jake and Jordon are in Texas at their parent's house." "And the two black guys Rayshawn and Bubba dank are in Sac'mento, but not at the same house together."

Kitpatrick comments "I'm sure business will be going on tonight as usual, with those two outside of Sac'mento, up in Plasma City, because that's where Bubba's at right now, up in a Motel. Mahavez confirms to the Captain "that he, and Kitpatrick are going to be driving up that way in a few minutes to relieve Lenny and Officer Flank, who have been up there for two days now staking everything out. The Captain listening nods, asking "so--, what about the stripper?" he asked as he put his coffee cup down to eye ball her picture up on the board. He continues saying "is she in on the drugs and money as well?" "Naw" said Mahavez. "It seems like she just met dude, from what Candis has told me." "All, righty; then!" "Let's get this case cracked; and closed! Declares Captain Watson as he slams back the rest of his coffee.

He looks over at Mahavez before walking back to his office and says "you might want to call that girl, so she can at least "think" you're thinking about her on Thanksgiving!" Officer Kitpatrick laughs voicing "he's going to call her right now; Captain!" Mahavez gives Kitpatrick a dirty look like; shut the hell up, man!" Then he sits back down at his desk to get the paperwork ready, so they can check out a company vehicle. But before him and Kitpatrick head up to Plasma City to relieve Lenny, and Officer Flank, Officer Mahavez goes to the men's room to call Candis where it is quiet.

Candis picks up on the second ring saying "hi baby, in 'her, happy that he's called her; voice! He returns "did you have a nice thanksgiving; beautiful?" "Well. "No! "Not; really!" "If you count all the drama that went on at Roxy's house, and then traveled all the way back to my mom's house!" but other than that, it was cool!" she said while cleaning under her finger nails with a file. She sighs then says "I'll tell you all about it later, because my brother's "girlfriend" is over here 'passed out, on my couch. Dianna hears her, and slurs out some choice words 'like, "I ain't that mother F*^#ka's woman no more!" she adds "that sorry chump!" Candis retorts "okay...! "Okay...! "Dianna!" go back to sleep!" said Candis chuckling a little under her breath as she walks back to her room, so she won't have to hear "Dianna 'grovel, over Marvin and the mishaps, of thy evening" she tells Rafee'al. {Better; Known; As!} "Officer Mahavez!"

She ends her story with "See?" that's what kind of Thanksgiving we had!" Rafee'al laughs out, voicing; "sounds like my house on the Holidays"! Candis asked "so are you still at your folk's house right now?" "Naw, I had to go into work tonight, that's why I'm calling you because I wanted to see 'you, but I can't tonight." Candis lets out a disappointing sound of sadness then she sighs "okay--. He says "but I'll make it up to you, though." "Well--, at least you called" she said. "I guess I'll go to bed now, since I can't see you." She pauses for a moment then says "hey, how about I come by your job?" "I have a kiss with your name on it." "Are you at the O Garden?"

He had to think; quick "uh, no!" he answered. "I'm at the corporate office up in Sac'mento." "Wooh--; really?" said Candis in an impressive tone because she's never heard him say that place of business before. She just thought he worked in the area; locally. But sadly, after hearing that she can't see him tonight, in a draggingly; sad voice she sighed "okayyyy... "I guess that would be way too far for me to drive" she replied. He laughs saying "yep. "That would be a long drive, even though, I am worth it!" She laughs at his "cocky; joke" but at the same time her mind wonders for a second, "thinking!" is he with another girl, up in Sac'mento?" "But just "saying" he's at work?" The phone goes silent for a few seconds and before she could respond back, his partner Kitpatrick busted open the bathroom door asking "are you ready; bro?"!

Not knowing that Mahavez is on the phone with Candis, Kitpatrick decides to hold back on his next question, after suddenly; seeing Mahavez put his index finger up to his mouth, to let Kitpatrick know; to shut up! But Candis has bat ears and hears the man's voice and says "hmm, who is that?" "And where are you guys getting ready to go?" she asked being nosey as usual. He answers "uh, that's just a co-worker wanting to go get a bit to eat." Candis returns "see, if you were closer, I would have brought you two a plate". He smiles saying "I wish I was closer." Then I could taste you." "I 'mean, taste you're good cooking; that is." He chuckles and continues to say "instead, of going to get this greasy fast food were about to go get." Kitpatrick jokes around in the mirror doing kissy; face gestures to implicate, that Mahavez is laying down his "macking; game" hard, on Candis, when he's "supposed" to be getting on the highway so they can relieve Lenny and them. Candis not wanting to keep him from getting some dinner says "alright, well... I'll let you go, so you can get you some food, but call me tomorrow, k?" He nods his head answering "most definitely" while he's looks in the mirror admiring his good looks and his gift of gab with the ladies.

His partner looks at him and shakes his head when Mahavez hangs up the phone with Candis. Kitpatrick still looking at him says "man--, I hope you're not getting too caught up with this girl for real, because that would "really" compromise; this case!" "Naw..., man!" I'm cool!" I know this is just business" he adds. "Besides, she's messing with the white boy." "Remember?" "Jake?" "So when we close this case and I break it off with her; that will be my reason." I got it all planned out" he explains while combing his hair back with his pocket comb. He checks his smile in the mirror and replies "now let's go close this case!"

While walking out of the bathroom Kitpatrick is 'still, not convinced that Mahavez has it "all" under control, so as they are getting ready to sign for the car he says "you know, we can always put in a 'stand in, man for you." "Because she is pretty, and I can tell you are really starting to like her." Mahavez looks at him out the corner of his eye and turns his head slowly saying "dude!" "You like her, huh?"! Kitpatrick 'stops, on his words "no...! "Not, even; man"! Mahavez holding back his laugh says "you want to be the stand in man, for me; huh?"! Kitpatrick not being able to hide his feeling says "no, bro!" You got it all wrong!" Mahavez stares at him saying "naw, I think I got it; right!" He continues to say "somebody's likin the; "chocolate!"

"Have you ever had a piece of "real; chocolate" in your 'mouth; Kitpatrick?" laughs Mahavez trying to be funny. Kitpatrick turns a slight shade of red, in his cheeks when he responds back saying "all..., man...!" Come on bro!" I just think you might be getting a little "smitten" off of 'her, that's all!" Mahavez still chuckling at his last statement voices "I don't know, though, man!" You might stand a 'chance, because she does like white boys!" "And apparently; Latino's too!" "I think it's safe to 'say, that she might just hold the "crown" for being an "international; lover!" he said laughing, stating, because she "does" seem to like 'all... the colors of the rainbow!" His laughter gets even louder when he looks over at Kitpatrick's "embarrassed; face" knowing for a "fact!" that Kitpatrick couldn't hold a candle, to his good looks and his smooth talk when it comes to 'Candis!" but he humors himself anyway saying "go ahead man!" I bet you could even; hit it"! Kitpatrick shuts the door on the vehicle, and steps on the gas at the same time, he's giving Mahavez the bird, as they fly up the freeway ramp, towards Plasma City.

Most of the ride up Rafee'al is giving Kitpatrick shit, about all the things he could do with Candis and how he just needs to just put his Mack-in; game on!" And how Kit can even have 'her, once he's through with her." Kitpatrick still denying his attraction to her, but deep down inside he's thinking he might have a shot, once Mahavez dumps her and she's on the rebound. When they get to Plasma City they radio Lenny and Flank to go on ahead and leave because they are pulling up to the Motel where Bubba is at.

While the two Detectives are staking out the Motel, a woman knocks on Bubba's door and he lets her in. There seems to be a small crack in the curtains, so Mahavez takes a closer look through his binoculars. Once they are focused he can see that it is only a smoker buying a hit of dope and she's not paying with cash. Kitpatrick snatching the binoculars saying "let me get a look." Smiling he says "oh--, yeah--, fat boys getting some head." They both laugh but then Mahavez replies "now see--, that goes to show you, a big dude like that, would have to have big money!" or sell dope, to get that type of action on a regular basis!" said Kitpatrick.

Bubba is lying back on the bed while the lady is pleasuring him with her mouth. Ten minutes go by and then a Cadillac pulls up in the parking lot. "It looks to be only Rayshawn in the car" says Kitpatrick. They were hoping it was also going to be another man with Rayshawn who is one of the main trafficker's under Steeli'o. But he always seems to stay under the radar. So much so 'that, the department started calling him "Mr. Invisible!" His real name is 'Marky'os! 'Marky'os is Steeli'o's 'main guy, or right hand man if you will. They are like brothers because Marky'os's father was Lorenzo, which was Steeli'o's dad's best friend.

His father was the one, who started Steeli'o in the business when Steeli'o's father died. And just like history can repeat itself in the books, in life' it can do the same too. So when Marky'os's father died he was too young to take over the business, so it went on to Steeli'o. But when Marky'os got older Steeli'o gave him a job so he 'too, could take care of his; family. Steeli'o 'knew, that he had put in his 'time, of slanggin, in them 'streets!" so now, he just handles the money coming in. But the diamonds, he likes to inspect on his own. Plus, he also likes being a shot caller, so he can hiring people he can trust, to do the dirty work!

Steeli'o sits back behind his "Real-Estate; Empire" like; Mr. Untouchable!" which literally makes it somewhat 'impossible, to convict him on any drug or diamond charges. But, the Department is 'adamant, about bringing all of these men to; Justice! Rayshawn has just parked at the Motel where Bubba is, and after removing his stereo's face cover and putting it in his glove compartment he gets out of his car and goes up to the Motel door. When he taps on the door Bubba lets him in the room with a smile on his face while he's zipping up his pants. Rayshawn smiling back rubbing his palms together trying to stay warm; states "are you ready to make this drop?"! Bubba; shushes him saying "be quiet, I got a smoker in the bathroom." "She just got through "pleasuring" a brother!" he said with an excited; smile. Rayshawn shouts "awe--, come on, man!" This is a big drop!" "We don't have time for this shit!" "Get rid of her!" Bubba knocks on the bathroom door saying "come on Bee!" "You got to go!" She flushes the toilet returning "okay. "I'm coming." Rayshawn closes his eyes mumbling; "I don't believe this fool!" The bathroom door swings open and the lady; "Bonnie" is still whipping off her mouth when she looks up and 'sees, that it is Rayshawn.

She gawks at him saying "what are you doing here?"! "What?!" he answers. "What am, I, doing here?!" "What the hell are you doing here?!" Bubba looks at them both saying "damn; dawg"! "You two know each other?!" Bonnie says "yes. The same time Rayshawn shouts "no!" He shakes his head with complete 'shame, while staring at her 'like; you better not 'dare, say you're my mother, right now! He turns his back to her and says to Bubba "get her out of here dude!" Bubba pushing her out the door nicely saying "alright Bonnie, don't come back tonight." I got business going on." But hit me up tomorrow if you need any more of that "candy" he winks.

He closes the door and Rayshawn grabs him up; quick by the throat and throws him up against the door yelling "what the fu_k?!" "Man!" "You let a crack-head come to a 'drop; room!" "You're slippin; Bruh"! Bubba yells back "Damn...! "Man...! "I was just getting a little 'fellatio, while I was waiting!" "Everybody doesn't has in house p*ssy like you, man"! Bubba not knowing where all this anger is coming from gets pissed and pushes Rayshawn off of him shouting "plus, those guys won't be here for another hour anyway"! He continues to say "I was gonna to get rid of her before you got here!" "But it just got so good!" he said flashing back in his mind. He adds "she can really suck a mean one!" Rayshawn throws his hands up voicing "I don't want to hear that man!" "That's nasty!" "You having that smoker sucking on your d*ck!" "Dang; dude!" "You, can't be that; desperate?"! Rayshawn; smirks out a frown, then he seriously; looks back at Bubba stating "well, maybe you "can" be that; desperate!" Bubba shouts "forget you man!" "I can get pussy!" "Don't let the fatness; fool you!"

Rayshawn shouts "but; "not!" when we're 'making; a very 'important; drop!" Most, of Rayshawn's 'anger, was because it was his own 'mother, in the room; suckling on his friend! It could have been anyone 'else, and he would have been cool with it! 'But now, he is just so 'mad, and ashamed at what his "mother" has become!" that it is starting to affect his confidents, in business. "Bubba; still" not knowing why, he's so mad, brings up their past drops, saying "how they use to screw woman all the time waiting on drops!" Telling Rayshawn "remember that time you had that girl with the nipple rings, playing with your "golf club" on one bed?!" And I was on the other bed getting road like a 'Shetland pony, by that Asian chick!" Bubba all hyped, cheers out saying "that's; the Rayshawn I remember!" Rayshawn grunts "but that's when we were small time!" "Now, we're big time!" and I'm not trying to have no hoes, mess up this 'money, for me and my family!" he stated.

Rayshawn went on and on until Bubba could tell, that he was "not" going to get any resolution from Rayshawn's 'bickering; mouth!" all because he had a lady-friend in the room. So after a while Bubba gets tired of hearing his mouth, so he sits down griping out "alright--; bro!" "Calm down!" She was just an old friend who sells weed for me sometimes." "And that's why Bonnie wouldn't have been a problem, because she's cool!" he said. "How do you know she's not going to take your weed and by rocks with it from somebody else?" asked Rayshawn. "Because she 'knows, she won't 'even, get a second chance to burn; me!" and she'll be losing; 'badly, if she ain't on my team!" grunts Bubba. After his speech, Rayshawn just went back to focusing on the plan at hand, as they sit down at the little table in the room and get the dope ready for pick up.

'Rayshawn, more 'quiet, than anything now, just couldn't bring himself to telling Bubba that; 'that, was his mom. But one day, he 'might, unfortunately have to tell him, because in time, Bubba will probably find out somehow. There's a soft knock on the door and the two get their guns cocked and ready just in case some bullsh*t jumps; off! Bubba looks out the curtain and sees it's the two Cuban boys that Steeli'o had given them pictures of, so Bubba opens up the door and lets them in the room. Kitpatrick is in the car snapping pictures while Mahavez is out of the car trying to hear and see the deal go down at close range. Mahavez plays it off by acting like he's getting a soda from the vending machine and then he reaches down and puts a small tracking device under the bumper of the Cuban guy's car. In the room, one of the Cuban guys introduces himself as Crispytoe. And his friend says "his name is Forerito. After everyone said there "hello's, Rayshawn said "don't take this personal man, but I need to pat you two down, that's just how we do business!" In the room the deal goes down after Rayshawn pats the two men down and has them empty out their clips, from their guns. They place their empty guns on the table and Bubba and Rayshawn counts the money they hand them, with a money counting machine. After they see that the money is all there, Bubba reaches under the bed and gets out all 10 kilos, of cocaine and gives it to them in a duffle bag.

Then motel door opens and Crispytoe and Forerito get back into their car and get on the highway heading south. Headquarters keep an eye on the tracker that was put on their car to see where the Cuban boys end up going, hoping it leads to a bigger dealer. Rayshawn lays back on one of the beds after the deal is complete and texts Steeli'o saying "it's a wrap!" Which to Steeli'o means we made the drop!

Chapter 17

Steeli'o, lying in bed by himself texted back "bravo!" good buddy!" Then he gets up out of his bed in a good mood and sneaks down the hallway to where Roxy is sleeping, and quietly opens her door and climbs into bed with her. She turns over quickly saying "Steeli'o!" you can't be in here!" what if your mother finds out?!" "She will hate me" she frowns. He smiles kissing her all down her neck voicing "she won't find out." "I'll only been here for a few minutes" he says as he leads with his tongue all the way down to her stomach. Roxy of course doesn't want him to stop. But even though she wants him terribly, it can't be like 'this, at his mom's house, with his sister and her husband in the next room.

She thinks "how will he act in the morning?" and will everyone 'know, by the look on her 'face, that they had sex in his momma's house?" "Oh, hell, no!" she thinks to herself." this will ruin what we have built up together so far, if we have sex here. So, before he could slide her panties off and get one, soft, lick, in, she says in a soft panting voice "Steeli'o; wait!" I want us to make love for the first time in your room!" "I want the snow falling down on my body while you make love to me" she said steadfast, while pulling his head up from underneath the covers so she could 'look, into his eyes.

He stops, and listens, but then says "no." no, Bella!" we can make love here too, because we are in 'Italy; where all thy romantic; beginnings 'start, between lovers!" He takes her by the face and kisses her 'dramatically; hoping to persuade her into his; love making; wishes! She 'gets, so... warm and wet as he is grinding up against her in her undies, forcing her to want him really... badly now. Between the 'ragging, hormones in her body to the masculine smell of his hair, it is 'seemly, getting; harder to tell him, no!

But like an angel on her shoulder 'tapping, on her 'temple, she could just 'hear, Naquawna's voice clear as a bell; blurting out!" don't do anything, I wouldn't do! And in the forefront of her 'mind, she remembered the bet she made with the 'girls, a bet she "can't" 'lose, for herself! And so now, as the heat is 'on, she can see more than 'ever, that 'this, is going to be "harder" then she ever; anticipated! But Roxy has a few tricks up her sleeve to, so she decides to pull out her "own; playbook!" because 'she, just like Candis is 'use, to telling men; no! It's just harder with someone you are getting to know and really like. So with a sly smirk on her face, she decides to kicks it up a notch and grind him back, while kissing him and loving him with her night clothes still intact. He starts to 'really, beg her now, asking "please, just let me rub you with my fingers." But she still says "no. "It's too soon for all of that 'especially, in your mother's house." He gives her this 'big, sad 'look, pleading; like he will just 'die, if he can't have her right this; second! But Roxy doesn't 'break, as she's kissing him even 'more, knowing that she can give him 'plenty, of 'affection, without; penetration! It kind of reminds her of 'work, except she wants the happy ending with him.

She bites him on the ear and wraps her legs around his back and squeezes her body into his 'so intimately, until he almost; releases in his pants. He pulls up off of her saying "shit; woman!" What are you trying to do to me?!" She plays; dumb smiling at him answering "I'm just trying to make you see, how much I really do want you, too. She moves her bent leg back and forth showing the inside of her thigh and a peekaboo of her 'pretty, pink panties. He kneels back down on the bed with his one leg bent, while his other foot is on the floor. And with hungry eyes he watches her leg moving back and forth, and when he leans back over to kiss her, he hears a door creaking from down the hall.

Roxy panics; thinking it's his 'mom, so he decides to leave her room through the sliding door because he knows his mom would 'not, be too 'happy, if she caught him coming from Roxy's room. That's one thing momma Milian 'did not play!" and that 'is, to allow 'anyone, to play; house in her 'house, that isn't; married! With a "stiffy" Steeli'o creeps back to his room so he could rub one out, while thinking about Roxy in her sheer, pink lace, teddy and matching panties. 'While she, on thy other hand lies in her bed with a big smile on her face after playing with herself, with him on the phone together.

When they are done, she sighs, thinking of a familiar quote from a cutie pie rapper named: Ice Cube, and she says to herself (Today, was good day)! Roxy grunts to herself because now she is starting to see how much fun "real; love" can 'be, when you 'wait, before making love to someone you "really" want to be with! She turns over in her bed and softly says out loud "I'm still in the game"! And then her phone goes off and its Candis saying something to her about what had happened earlier.

Chapter 18

Daylight peaks its bright light through Candis's living room window and onto the couch where Dianna is at, sleeping. When the sunshine hits Dianna in the eyes she doesn't wake up 'happy, she starts her day off with a cup of coffee and a pissy mood! 'And as we all know, there is no greater 'hater, then a woman scorned! Candis can hear her in the kitchen getting a drink of the coffee, that came on 'automatically, by way of, the coffee timer. Hoping that Dianna leaves by taxi or uber, Candis covers up her head with the blanket because she doesn't even want to deal with Dianna right now! Her thoughts are, that her "brother" should be dealing with his own; mess!

'And then of course, in walks Dianna into Candis's room. She sits down at the end of her bed asking "Candis?" with a scratchy voice. "Are you sleep?" "Well, hell!" thinks Candis. "I'm up now!" Candis pulls the covers down from her face answering "not anymore. Dianna smiles asking "do you want to go have breakfast?" "I'll pay for you, because it's the least I could do for having put you through all the drama yesterday" she said rubbing her hurt ankle. Candis explains "you don't owe me 'anything, Dianna." "I'm the one who is sorry about what happened between you and my brother." "I wish we would have never went over to Roxy's house yesterday."

Dianna with her head down says "well everything happens for a reason." "And even though it hurts like hell; I needed to know the truth!" The girls hug and then Candis feeling; hungry says "sure..., let's go eat breakfast!" "How about Rosanna's?" said Candis? "Okay" replied Dianna, adding "their food is pretty, spectacular! "And you know we will have got to get a piece of that 'award winning; cake to go!" said Dianna with a smile. The two share a laugh and then get ready so they can go eat.

In the next town over 'Sherry, who is up bright and early today; just so happened to texted Candis as she is driving with Dianna to Rosanna's for breakfast. Sherry texted "Girl..., what's; crackin?"! She adds "Naquawna told me what happened at 'Roxy's, house!" call me." But before Candis could text her back Sherry calls and Dianna answers the phone because a police car is driving behind them. Sherry says "what's; up girl?!" thinking it is Candis. She continues "I heard it was a mess over at your mom's house yesterday!" Dianna speaks up "you heard right!" Sherry pauses asking "who's this?" Dianna returns "it's me; Dianna." "Candis is driving, so I'll put the phone on speaker for you two." Sherry is silent because she almost said too much about what she heard about Dianna and Marvin. So then she plays it off asking "where are you two headed to, this early in the morning?" And I bet it's a "meal" involved; knowing you; Candis!" Dianna laughs "no, it was my idea." We're just going to Rosanna's for breakfast." Sherry says "ooh... I want to go!" Candis and Dianna look at each other and Dianna shrugs like, it's 'cool, I ain't trippin! Even though Dianna 'knows, the only reason why Sherry wants to come is so she can be nosey and hear all the dirt that happened on Thanksgiving. But Dianna assures Candis that she ain't gonna be talking about it to her. Candis tells Sherry "come on then." And we're hungry, so hurry up!" Laughing Sherry blurts out "you don't have to tell me twice!" I'm on my way" and she hang up the phone. Candis says to Dianna "you don't have to talk about anything that happened yesterday around Sherry because you know how she is?"

Dianna looks at Candis after she gets out the car and closes the car door and while they're heading towards the restaurant Dianna replies "I already 'know, how messy Sherry is!" And I'll give her 10 minutes after we sit down before she starts asking me, what happen between me and Marvin!" The two walk up to the café and are seated by the waitress and then in walks Sherry waving towards the girls as she heads over to their table to take a seat. She sits down, a little out of breath voicing "chil... I was flying on the highway and Bruce really thought he was coming with me!" I told him, just us 'girls, were going to breakfast." And he said, I wanna go eat to!" So when he got in the shower, I grabbed my purse and said 'not, today pal!"

Sherry laughs along with Dianna and Candis and then her phone rings; its Bruce asking "where are you?!" "You left me?!" "That's messed up babe!" he shouts. Sherry smiles at Dianna and Candis and with a wink she says to Bruce "honey, I did not think you were serious!" because I told you only us; girls were going!" Plus, I know how much you hate listening to us gossip!" she said as she winks again. He yells "I wasn't even going to be listening to that; crap you all were going to be talking about!" I just wanted to get me some steak and eggs!" Sherry sees the waitress coming towards the table to take their order so she just blows Bruce off saying "okay, babe!" "I'll bring you back something then." She finishes with "Love you!" Bye!" And she hangs up in his face. He holds the phone out looking at it 'like, I know she didn't just hang up in my face?

Sherry orders first, "I'll have the eggs Benedict with hash browns and toast." Then Dianna orders the pancake special with ham and eggs. Candis has French toast with sausage, and egg whites with a side order of fruit. Once the waitress walks away with their order, Sherry after taking a sip of her water says "so..., Dianna; what happened at Roxy's house?" "Was Marvin really 'balls; deep up in some stripper?!" Candis's eyes; bulged out at the 'mere; gall of Sherry's bluntness! Even Dianna's mouth opened in utter shock at the 'nerve, of Sherry being so hurtful! Dianna looks at Candis while shaking her head shouting "I stand corrected!" It took her only; 5 minutes "not" 10 before she asked 'me, about me and my; ex"!" Sherry looks at Candis 'not knowing, the implication of Dianna's remark so Candis just waves her hand 'like, never mine, not wanting to go into it. Then with a turn't up nose Dianna blows Sherry off saying "I don't want to talk about it!" Sherry asked "why?!" Talking about it 'helps, in the healing process!" Right; Candis!" said Sherry looking her way. Candis rolls up her eyes saying "I guess?" but none of us are psychologists" she adds. "That doesn't matter!" said Sherry. "We are all living 'life, and learning in life, what; works!" And I think talking about it; after it happens; helps!" "So, Dianna; Sherry continued "how did you feel?!" in that moment? She adds "I know you were pissed!" Dianna looks at her half-cocked because she can see the fakeness, so Sherry glazes over her expression and says "I would of had (murder was the 'case, that they gave me)!" if that had of been; Bruce!" because I would've kilt his ass!

With her eyes turn't up Dianna blared out "well, I'm not trying to go to jail behind his ass!" Plus, his sister was there, so how would that; look, me doing that to her brother?" "See, Sherry!" that's your problem, you don't think!" just like you asking me all my personal business, right now!" You have 'no, home training!" "Screw; you; Dianna!" yells Sherry. "I do have home training!" Don't get mad at me, because Marvin's been sticking his "dipstick" in another chick!" for two years! Dianna sits back in her chair with an 'angry bird; balled up face, and with her arms folded she belts out "wow!" I see you know more about my business!" then I 'thought, you did!" she said, while looking over at Candis.

Candis replies "I didn't tell her nothing!" And you were at my house all night!" "Remember?!" Dianna blurts "then it must be that ghetto ass Naquawna running her mouth!" Sherry sits up in her seat voicing "it doesn't matter 'who, told me!" "I was just 'generally; concerned when I heard about what had happened to 'you, despite; what you think!" The waitress comes with their food and when she leaves Dianna yells "cut the crap!" "Sherry"! "You could care less about what I'm feeling!" You are just a nosey ass person that loves to gossip about other people!" Candis eating a piece of French toast almost chokes holding back her laugh. Sherry yells "well at 'least, I own; it!" because, I don't have a problem with being nosey; it works for me!" And you are just jealous anyways, Dianna, because I know how to stand up for myself!" unlike you, who just lets people run, all over you!" And this is 'why, you got caught slipping; when it came to your relationship!" "See me!" continues Sherry. "I would have known something was different, and I would have started my 'own, investigation and before that bastard would have known what hit him!" "I would have been stepping out with a 'new man, on his; ass!" "Not, the other way around!"

Candis tries to interject by saying "now; Sherry!" But Sherry continued on, "I don't care, women need to be up on game!" "And if the man you're with; ain't acting right!" drop his ass! "And move on to next man!" "Or..., without a man!" Candis laughs out "I know that's right!" Dianna just chews the food in her mouth saying "yeah, that sounds good and 'all, until it happens to you!" Then you'll 'see, it's a whole different ball game!" And not to mention; I was engaged; to be married to this man!" Had my ring and all!" she said as she's giving Sherry a smug look like 'top that, you live in skank!

Sherry mumbles under her breath "and you weren't the 'only one, with that "same" ring, either!" Dianna stands up quickly in Sherry's face and gets loud asking "what did you say?!" Candis stands up with them voicing "stop, we are in public!" Sherry blurts "you heard me!" I didn't stutter!" Dianna shouts "you're just jealous because you are a live in; whore!" I was a fiancé!" There is a big; difference!" Sherry yells "yeah, okay!" and in being a "fiancé"! "You either make it down the aisle!" or in your 'case, yah; don't!"

Dianna screams "that's why nobody likes your fat ass"! "Sherry"! "I don't need you to like me"! "Dianna"! "And nobody 'else, for that matter!" "But I'll tell you what?!" I got a man, who 'does, like me; though!" yelled Sherry; angrily. Candis shouts "can you both; shut; up?!" and finish eating! "Talk about something else"! "Please...!" adds Candis looking around the café embarrassed because all eyes are on them. Dianna gives Sherry an evil look shouting "roach"! Sherry shouts "Rat"! Dianna "Hippo"! Sherry "Scarecrow"! Candis cuts in because she's tired of hearing them both go back and forth like two kids. Candis blurts "Sherry, you always have to have the last word!" Let it go!" And that's when Candis shuts Sherry and Dianna up for good after changing the subject to shopping. She says "we should go to the mall after breakfast, I know yaw wanna go get a few things" says Candis all giddy. "I need me a new pair boots" she adds. Sherry gives it some 'thought, while Dianna plays in her food not really 'caring, to go shopping. Candis smiles "I've been thinking about going up to Tahoe and staying at that nice little cabin we all stayed at, a year and ½ ago." "Remember how much fun we had?" said Candis all happy. Sherry nods "yes, I do." We did have fun" said Sherry. "Yep, and that's why I wanna take Rafee'al up there so I can show him our 'kick it; spot!" She smiles just thinking of him adding "because he's never been to Tahoe." Dianna with a sour; patched, half smirk on her face retorts "yes, I remember that 'place, very; well!" It's where your brother "Marvin" had 'proposed to me, in the snow cave!" 'Dianna; disgusted throws her napkin on her plate; angrily indicating that she is 'done, with this whole 'meet and greet, breakfast! She stands shouting "I'm ready to go!" Then she signals to the waitress 'rudely; with a snap of her fingers! Candis mortified shouts "Dianna"! Then with sympathy in her eyes over the whole 'Marvin snow cave thing, she said "I'm sorry!" I totally forgot."

Candis looks over at Sherry for some help in convincing Dianna to stay, but Sherry just keeps on eating her hash browns with a dumb founded look on her face 'like, she could 'careless, whether she stays or leaves. Dianna pays the waitress her portion for her breakfast and she walks away saying "I'll see you around Candis!" With an uptight facial expression on her face she walks out of the Café. Candis is speechless as she watches Dianna walk out the door with no regards to their friendship. She turns to Sherry saying "luckily, I drove my own car down here, or I guess I would be on the 'transit bus, with her!" Sherry laughs out "now, chil, you know I would have taken you home."

Candis finishes up the rest of her breakfast voicing "and that heffa said she was treating!" "Now what if I didn't bring my purse?!" and I pulled a 'Naquawna, saying that I left my money at home! Sherry laughs "oh, yes!" Naquawna is good for leaving her purse at home, when it comes to going out to eat!" And to top it off, she always expects for other people to pay for her meal!" They both cracked up laughing, then the waitress comes back to the table to leave the bill, and that's when Sherry remembers that Bruce wanted steak and eggs, so she gets his order to go. The two ladies tell the waitress thank you and leave a nice tip on the table for her.

Walking out to the parking lot before leaving Candis says "don't forget to tell Bruce, we are doing another trip to Tahoe." "Let's go up right before Christmas like on the 15th of December" said Candis. "That way we can leave Friday after work and stay until Monday" says Candis. "That will give us the weekend, so we can hit up the clubs, and then recuperate on that Monday when we get back home." Sherry returns "sounds like a plan to me!" Sherry then asked "who's all going"? "Well for one, we 'know, Dianna won't be going" grunts Candis. "That's for sure!" laughs Sherry. "It will be more than likely you, Bruce, Roxy, Steeli'o, Naquawna and Rayshawn "if" she can get him to go." If 'not, then Mike might go with her." But who knows with Naquawna's 'player; haven, ass!" "That's enough people for that big cabin; right?" asked Candis? "Yep, that's perfect" answers Sherry closing her car door talking with her window down. "I can't wait to go" she adds while starting up her engine. "Me either" cheered Candis.

Sherry then looks over her shoulder saying "girl let me get this food home to my man before it gets cold, so I don't have to hear him gripe about it!" Candis chuckles saying "call me later." Sherry nods then drives away with one hand waving out the car window then she stops; abruptly, in the middle of the street, because she thought she let her purse! 'Now, way across the globe back over in Italy, Roxy and her man's 'sister, are having the time of their lives shopping, eating, and running; from store to store!

Chapter 19

First thing in the morning, when Roxy first woke up she got in the shower, washed her hair and dried off with an oversized towel that was folded nicely, on top of the bathroom chair. Hearing a soft knock on the bedroom door she hears a family members, voice say "breakfast is ready!" come and eat!" It was Gi'la. Roxy answers "okay, be there in a second." Roxy gets dressed and puts her face together 'real quick, making sure not to overdo her makeup because she wants to look like a natural beauty.

Closing her bedroom door she rushes to the dining room, but no one is in there and as she turns to look in the kitchen Steeli'o comes up and hugs her from behind. She turns to face him with a big smile and they kiss. While in his embrace they 'looked like, a familiar famous painting and then in walks his mother with a 'smile, because she's so glad to see how 'happy, her son is. So she just watches them, and when the kiss is over his mother says "we are out in the yard eating breakfast in the sunshine." Roxy smiles and after Steeli'o translates what his mother had said, Roxy replied "oh, how nice! As she and Steeli'o walk behind his mother towards two beautiful French doors the two can't keep their hands off one another.

And when she opened the doors to Roxy's amazement a lovely table setting is spread out, with the best dish ware, filled with nothing but 'deliciousness, on them. The food pastries were all made from scratch and you could tell that they were homemade 'just, by; looking at them. The croissants were light and fluffy looking and the rich filled pastries made her mouth water. Even the cold cuts looked like she just got them from the butcher's that morning. There was all kinds of different cheeses, from sharp cheddar's in white and orange, to the nutty flavored cheeses that just melted in your mouth. Roxy's favorite was the sheep's milk cheese from Spain, which Steeli'o kept 'plopping, into her mouth slowly. Some of cheeses Roxy couldn't even pronounce, "but who needed to know the 'correct pronunciations, when you've got all this yummy food going down your mouth and into your tummy!" she said to Steeli'o with a giggle. Fresh prosciutto wrapped figs and salted olives made her mouth dance a slow dance as she filled up her plate with a sigh. His mom even had coffee brewing and you could just smell the coffee for miles. Steeli'o leans in closer to her ear and with his lips nibbling on her he asked her "what would she like to drink?" saying to her "we have cappuccino, espresso whatever your heart desires" he said. She grins saying "whatever my heart desires; huh?" Then she whispers to him "other than you, I guess I'll have is a 'big cup, of latte macchiato and two more biscuit cookies" she said with a slight closure of her eyes. "And also, some of those prosciutto wrapped figs" she said after spotting them at the end of the table. Gi'la sneaks up behind Roxy and with a hug she whispers in her ear "hurry up and eat, so we can go shopping!" Roxy smiles and with an excited grin on her face she replies "I sure will." "What girl doesn't love a great shopping day?!" right?!" thinks Roxy to herself.

The whole family sat down to eat after Vinnie's mom said grace. As the two families are eating they are all talking amongst each other about their travels and work related things at the restaurant. Personal things were also spoke on, that were going on in their town, and abroad. After eating that wonderful breakfast Steeli'o sat back in his chair with his arm around Roxy asking her "what she wanted to do today?" Gi'la speaks for her "we planned on going shopping today, so I can show her all our beautiful shops." Steeli'o frowns "she doesn't want to go shopping!" Looking at Roxy he asks "do you Bella?" Roxy smiles "sure..., I would love to spend some time with your sister shopping."

Gi'la grabs Roxy by the arm pulling her up out of her chair all giddy and ready to go. The guys look at each other and reach for their wallets smirking with a look on their face of "I knew, this was going to happen! Spartique joking with his wife voiced out "girls gone mad!" Shopping mad!" adds Steeli'o. Gi'la laughed and kissed her husband on the lips after he gave her some extra money to shop with. Steeli'o gives Roxy a small wad of money as well, in which she replies "I can't take this from you!" But Steeli'o's sister intervenes grabbing her by the arm saying "no, problemo!" "Roxy!" He just wants you to buy yourself something nice to wear for tonight."

Roxy kisses Steeli'o on the lips while 'confusingly, she shouts "tonight?"! While smiling Gi'la pulls her out the front door and down towards the boat. At the water's edge Gi'la says to the water taxi "to Milan!" please!" for some girl's day out; shopping!" Then she laughs at the cabby because she 'knows, she's not really going to take the taxi to Milan, although he wishes because that would be a nice chunk of Euro for him. Instead, Gi'la and Roxy are going to board a Chartered yacht. "It is so--, the way to go!" she tells Roxy. And with a gleam in her eye she adds "me and my girlfriend's do it this way 'all the time, when we go on long--, shopping sprees!" With Gi'la leading the way; her and Roxy bored the Yacht, and there are other people on there going to Milan as well. And to Roxy's surprise it is "definite" a party; going on! The girls have a glass of wine and relax and enjoy the sites. Gi'la points out all of the 'neat; coves, that people love to go in and hang out at' on their boats. And as they are traveling through the water she spots one of the houses on a hillside that her brother helped to design and then sell, and she pointed it out to Roxy. Roxy smiles and can't believe how talented Steeli'o really is. Putting her wine glass up to her lips taking a sip she starts to feel so relaxed in this beautiful atmosphere on the yacht, and she also feels so comfortable with Gi'la and the other people around them, 'so much so, until she 'wishes now, that she would have bought her first home 'out here, instead of in Treeberry.

So while the girls are coasting on the water enjoying the day together. Back over at Gi'la's mom's house Steeli'o has made a few business calls and now him and his brother in-law have decided to head out to play a few holes of golf. When the two men get to the golf course Steeli'o sneaks in a text, now and again saying "how much he misses Roxy." She just laughs to herself and texts him back the same. When they finally dock Roxy and Gi'la are having the time of their lives running from shop to glamorous shop. They don't even think about eating lunch because they are so caught up in the moment of all the pretty things to buy and wear. But as the sun starts to cool and the clouds start to roam the sky, Gi'la decides to take her to this nice little place for some great food and wine.

The ladies didn't want to eat too heavily because they plan on going out tonight with their men. So Roxy and Gi'la both order a small Filetti with some side dishes. The steak is a beautifully prepared piece of meat with two sides which are 'specially prepared, by the Chef. As the women are eating Gi'la takes this time to talk to Roxy about her brother. She asked her things like "how they met?" And how long they've been seeing each other?" Roxy with a big grin on her face tells her everything she wants to know, including her love of thy 'arts, once her job was mentioned and what she does there.

Roxy tells Gi'la "that she shows, people; how to dance. Gi'la replies "like a choreographer?" Roxy nods "yeah, something like that." Gi'la was so impressed about Roxy's job that she told her "if she was to come back again soon one day to visit, how it would be great if she could come show the kids at the school; that she teaches in her P.E class; another form of 'exercise, through dance."

Roxy tell her "how she would love to do that one day when she comes back to Italy." But on that same thought, she giggles to herself; imagining the look on Gi'la's and the kid's faces, if they were to "really" see her style of dancing! The waiter comes over to the table to clear their plates and suggests desert? And the two laugh; welcoming the thought with "of course we would"! They decide on the Tortino al cioccolato and the waiter, who was still chuckling, walked away so he could hurry back with their desert. When it came to the table it looked so-- good as the warm chocolate oozed out of the cake as they cut into it. Too Roxy's surprise, it looked like a 'molten; chocolate cake, like the ones she's eaten back home, at Chili's but this one had peaches on top. "Yummy...!" Moans the girls as they take bites of it, wishing 'now, that they had ordered their own separate piece. After eating at that particular place it was time to head back to her mom's house. Gi'la turns to Roxy when they leave out of the Café and she laughs mischievously saying "we'll, go back to my mom's, after I stop at one more shop!" Roxy cracks up laughing because she 'can't believe; that there is someone who loves to "shop" more than her!

Back where Steeli'o is, it is also getting late where he and Spartique are at playing 18 holes of golf, so they decide to pack up. On their way back to the house the guys both get separate text from their lady's saying "thanks, for such a 'great, shopping day!" and that they are on their way back to the house as well." When the girls fly back to the house, the men are out back smoking on a stogie and drinking brandy. The ladies both hustle over to meet their guys with big hugs, smiles and kisses. Gi'la then whispers in her husband's ear to see if they are still on for tonight. When he gives her the go ahead the two girls then, run off to go get ready for a 'night, out on the town.

Once Roxy gets out of the shower she tries on her new dress and as she's looking at herself in the mirror she 'hopes, he likes the dress on her, just as much as she does. Standing there all dressed she curls her hair in the front and leaves the back slightly curled, but it was more; wavy. With a lot of hairspray and a rat-tail comb she tugs on her curls and 'finally, gets her hair to lay the way she wants it to. She grabs her handbag and walks down the hallway and in the living room is where she finds Steeli'o standing by a chair up against the fireplace.

His mouth drops when he sees her because she is just that stunning in her new dress. And as she walks closer he smiles looking at her in her blue dress with a shimmering soft glow on her face as the light catches it off the stone fireplace, which is 'burning hot, showing off, her beautiful skin in the light. She gives him a twirl asking "you like it?" He walks over to her and puts his hands out so she can grab his, then he pulls her closer to him and in his deep; accented; voice he said "Yass--, I like; it!" Then with his arms up on her shoulders he embraces her and gives her the 'most; 'seductivest; 'kiss, she had ever felt from 'him, to date!

The two are so caught up in a romantic lip locking kiss until they don't even know his sister and her husband are standing there waiting for them so they can all leave. With a cough from Gi'la they get startled out of their kiss when Gi'la replies "look at thy lovers" she said in a loving tone. Roxy laughing shyly; blots her mouth off while trying to fix her lip stick back. Still grinning from ear to ear Roxy beams "so where are we going?" Steeli'o grunts "it's a surprise." And then they all head out the front door arm in arm. Once their boat docks in Positano, Roxy notices a beautiful vertical building facing them right on top of this sandy hill. Roxy didn't 'know, that; that was where they were taking her to dine, until Gi'la said "this place has the best seafood you could ever imagine!" And the wine selection is incredible, too" she adds.

They all go inside the place and are seated by the window and as usual Steeli'o ordered them some drinks. Before eating though, when the music started to play they all got on the dance floor laughing and dancing, and the world just seem to spin between Steeli'o and Roxy as they laughed and loved on each other in the middle of the dance floor. Gi'la had never seen her brother so happy. To her, he has always been so caught up in his work and would only go out with what "seemed" to Gi'la to be 'lose; women, who he would never take home to meet his mother. Gi'la thought he would never settle down with a nice girl such as Roxy and that is why she is so happy for her brother right now.

After dancing they went back to their table out of breath laughing from all the dancing they were doing, and ordered their food. The ladies had eaten earlier so they had a seafood salad fully loaded and Steeli'o had pasta with all the seafood mixed into it with a side order of greens. His brother-in-law had a fried seafood bowl which was Spanish; style served on top of black beans, red rice and a cabbage vinaigrette salad. They all ate, talked and watched people come and go in and out of the Cove Restaurant.

As the evening got dark they moved on to another place, this time it was in Venice. They took a quick small plane ride on that same plane Roxy and Gi'la were on earlier. "Whoa--!" chimed Roxy. "Another romantic place" she said in a soft voice. She laughs "are you guys trying to make me 'not, go back home?"! They all laugh out loud as they are exiting the little plane to go get on the canal boat ride, so they can ride through Venice. The boat tour 'guildsmen, were singing beautiful Italian songs to them, as they glided them through, and on 'top, of the Nile. "It is so romantically; relaxing" said Roxy as she laid back in her man's arms. As the night went on she started to really fall in love with everything about him. Like how he holds her and speaks to her in this loving way, to make her feel like she is as 'precious, as a 'gem, or a flawless diamond.

"The night just couldn't get any better than this" she thought, and then said it to him out loud as she turned her head up to kiss him. The couples ran around the town once they got off the canal boats, but it didn't stop there because they were popping in and out of different tavern's, laughing, drinking wine, kissing and hugging all throughout the night while enjoyed each other's company. 'By the end of the night, it was almost morning so Gi'la wanted to stay in Venice. She says to her brother "let's stay in a hotel here." Roxy over hears her asking her husband the same thing and she swallows nervously because she doesn't feel that would be 'wise, her staying in a room alone with Steeli'o tonight. She could just imagine, the two of them in the hotel room 'alone, staring each other 'down, with lust in their eyes, and then before she 'knows it, the two end up being 'glued; together, like two magnets that couldn't stop sticking to each other.

'Heck, they are in a lovers 'paradise, and it has all been so romantic. And for Roxy that has been the hardest thing right now, is for her "not" being able to 'take it, to the next level! Plus, he's been so sweet, and good to her in letting her come all the way out here to see these beautiful places, and meet his mom, and his family, which makes her 'feel, almost 'obligated, to lay with him. But then she snaps out of her reasoning for letting him have his way with her tonight, and instead she stands her ground; being the diva that she 'knows, she can be!

So with her deepest breath she inhales to speak, but before she could make up some story about why she didn't think that; that would be a good idea to stay in a hotel together. Steeli'o sees the brooding; look on her face and says "no. "Momma would be hurt, if we didn't come back, being that it's our last night here and all." "Yess... "I guess you are right" frowns Gi'la. "Momma would be upset because she takes things to thy heart." Roxy, sighed a sigh of relief and Steeli'o could see the relief on her face, so he grabs her by the hand and she can't help but feel he gets it, as she looks him in thy eyes and laughs saying "well--, we dodged that one!" they both laugh and Gi'la who is looking at the two laughing; wondering what's so funny; laughs along with them because she's drunk.

The girls go to the bathroom together before getting back on the boat, and Gi'la who is way tipsy now says "Roxy, I really... like you!" You and my brother are so cute together." Roxy, sighed "awe--, thank you." I really like you too, and your family is very kind." I will truly miss you all" she adds. After the two wash their hands they give each other a big hug and Roxy 'thanks her, for the best shopping day; ever!" in Milan. The two ladies head out of the bathroom still talking about the great deals they found in each of the shops earlier that they had visited, while the guys are talking outside near the boat area about guy stuff. When the ladies get to the boat their men help them into the water taxi so they can get back to the plane. On the small plane they climb aboard and make their way back to Steeli'o's boat which is waiting in the harbor. Everything is going by so fast, since they are all drunk and having a great time. And the laughs just kept on coming when they got off the plane and boarded Steeli'o's boat. All is quiet and calm on the water as they sail back to their mother's house in the dark. Since it's a clear night and the moon is out Steeli'o takes this time to show Roxy how to steer his boat and use the throttle. As she gets more comfortable in the 'ends and outs, of how things work he then shows her all the bells and whistles on his big boat as they skim; across the water.

The jokes and the laughter die down 'somewhat, when they get back to Steeli'o's mom's house because they don't want to wake her or the neighbor's up. And now Gi'la and Spartique are stumbling and chuckling as they walk to the side of the boat because Spartique has drank way too much and is 'now, throwing up on the side of the boat. Gi'la who is helping him, then trips while trying to hold her husband up, as she's helping him off the boat. They are all talking and laughing about his drunken condition but it starts to taper off as they are getting closer to the house, so they don't disturb people who live by their mom.

It doesn't work for long 'though, with everyone saying "shhhh…! "Keep it down!" Shhhh!" You'll wake momma!" When the door is finally opened because Gi'la couldn't get the key in the hole, a sad aw…; sounded from everyone's mouth after seeing his mom standing on the other side of the door in her robe and slippers. They felt so bad because they just 'knew, that they had woken her up. Roxy was the first to put her hand on her shoulder saying to her "sorry we woke you." But his mom just smiled with her eyes saying "no--. "This is fine" she said in broken English. She walks with them to the living room asking them "are they hungry?" Steeli'o replies "no, momma, we are fine!" You go back to bed!"

Roxy then grabs both of his mom's hands saying "I wanted to thank you so much for your kind hospitality and wonderful food." "And with joy in her eyes she says, and I want to give you something." Steeli'o and the rest of the family say "no!" No!" That's not necessary!" But Roxy doesn't listen as she rushes back to her room to bring back the most 'beautifuliest; Chrystal vase she had ever seen. And in her heart she just 'knows, it will look so nice on their mother's mantle over the fireplace. When she comes back to where they are at, his mother is in 'awh, at how beautiful the vase is, and she 'knew, that it had to have come from Paris.

Gi'la smiles saying "so that's who you bought that for?!" "That was very nice of you" she said reaching for Roxy's hand. Her mother gives Roxy a big hug and two kisses on the cheek saying "ho guadagnato un'altra figlia!" (Meaning) "I have gained another daughter!" And after saying that his mother said to her son "you be good to her Steeli'o" she said as she places the Chrystal vase on the fireplace so she can look upon it beauty. "I will, momma" he said. "She's a keeper" he replied as he gave Roxy a loving embrace. They all give there last good-byes because Roxy and Steeli'o will be leaving the house early in the dawn of the morning because of Steeli'o's urgent business matter that came up last minute.

Gi'la hugs her brother and tells him "we will be coming out to

Treeberry to your house next year for thanksgiving with momma". Then Gi'la embraces Roxy like she's her sister now saying "and we look forward to seeing you as well, next year at my brother's house for thanksgiving." Roxy smiles humbly saying "I'll be there." When all is said and done, they all head back to their own rooms to get some much needed sleep. Steeli'o lies in bed with Roxy for a while after his mother went off to bed. And as they lie there he softly rubs her back and she drifts off into a deep sleep from such an exhaustingly; long day.

At the crack of dawn, Steeli'o sneaks out of Roxy's bed and tells her to get packed. She says to him "I thought you said our flight doesn't leave until noon?" He kisses her saying "I know, I have one more place to take you." She laid there on her back 'smiling, with the covers still up on her neck. Then with a sigh she rolled over and forced herself to roll out of bed and get into the shower so she could get packed. It is now 5:30 in the morning and Roxy feels so bad about not being able to say bye to everyone. Steeli'o tries to comfort her by saying "my mom and sister know we are leaving early so I can surprise you with this one last trip." And that's why they said goodbye to you last night." "Okay..." said Roxy as he opens the front door of the house.

His mom hears the door open and comes down the hall to give her son one more hug and kiss saying to them both "I'll see you next time you come to visit." "Hopefully at Christmas" she says. "Love you both" says his mother. "Thanks for everything, and please tell Gi'la and Spartique much love too them both as well" says Roxy. She continue saying her heartfelt thanks as Steeli'o hustles her out the door. Roxy yells out one more last thing to his mother, voicing "and when you come to the States, I will show you as much love as you have shown me!" Momma Milian squeezes Roxy's hand one last time, and then Steeli'o pulls her away down towards the sidewalk.

His mom stands there in her doorway still waving as they head out of her sight, down the stairs. In the distance they could see the water taxi, and knew it was ready to go, once they got down to the dock. After getting off the water taxi Roxy spots a helicopter in a distant field and was so surprised to see that they were getting on it. So when they board the helicopter and fly away, after about 15 minutes of flying is when Steeli'o decides to cover Roxy's eyes with a scarf before it's time for the aircraft to land. Roxy is so excited even though she doesn't know exactly where he is taking her. With the aircraft bobbing through thy air for miles, after a while of flying he finally pulls the blind folds off of her face and she looks around but doesn't really know where they are. But then she thinks she spots a familiar building from what she's seen on t.v.

She Looks over at Steeli'o and back at the buildings then back at him and then she starts to jump up and down in her seat saying "No! "No! "No!" "Are you kidding me?!" It's Rome!" Oh...!" Baby...!" she says kissing him all over his face cheering "how did you 'know, I wanted to see Rome?!" "Well you are Catholic" he jokes sarcastically. She laughs "yes, but I think any person, no matter what their religion, would 'love, to see Rome!" She gets a little teary eyed and he hugs her saying "don't cry, Bella." I even got us a tour, so you can really enjoy the place." "But first, let's go get some breakfast" he said. The aircraft lands and they get off running towards the shops. When they got to an eatery the happy couple sat side by side, so close, to each other while eating breakfast that you would think they were wearing the same outfit. The place they ate at was a nice peaceful place in the middle of Rome, and Steeli'o treated her like a princess all day showing her the sights. After eating they went on their tour and Steeli'o knew just as much as the tour guide man, if not 'more, about Rome because he had visited Rome on many of occasions as a young boy and as an adult.

Steeli'o may be caught up in a life of crime but he is no stranger when it comes to "God!" 'Meaning, he knows right from wrong. Roxy marveled at all of the unique and spectacular monuments, and of course the most; Holiest too many, is the 'Vatican City's, Cathedral. Roxy even found out that it is said that one of Jesus's Apostles, Saint Peter's burial site is there. And with a big grin on her face she even got to see this stunning architectural Gallery with all of these fantastic painting and beautiful sculptures in this grand; building. All of the Chapels and the Museums were just; impeccable from walls to ceilings. And before they left they even got a quick glance of the famous Coliseum and they could just envision what went on back then in those days.

Roxy felt so blessed, thinking this is truly a dream come true of hers and she couldn't have asked to be with a more beautiful man inside and out on this trip. The two were falling 'hard, for each other as they felt the warm spirit of Rome; flowing through their veins. Once the tour was over her and Steeli'o walked through the streets kissing like they have been living there all their lives together in this exquisite; place of history. With all her mind, body, and soul she did not want to let this trip end, but she 'knows, she's got to get back to work, back to the USA, and back; to her reality! So, taking it down a notch, Roxy gets one last look at the city as she's standing outside the aircraft. While holding on to Steeli'o with sadness in her eyes she slowly boards the aircraft. Steeli'o comforts her by putting one arm around her saying "we'll come back, real soon" he said in her ear. Roxy feeling over dramatic says "look at me, getting all choked up, when it's you who should be feeling much sadder about leaving here then I do, because your whole family's here." Steeli'o nods agreeing with her saying "sure, but I'm always here." I fly back and forth a lot because of my mom, and my Real-estate business."

In part, that was true, but Steeli'o left one thing out, he also flew back and forth to check on his Cocaine and Diamond business as well! Because he practically runs his hometown, and the people in it, do to those "so called" businesses! Roxy's; conscience, is now more than ever starting to bother her on the plane ride back home to Treeberry because, while Steeli'o; lays sleeping on her shoulder, she is wide awake thinking about how great he and his family is. And she also thinks about, what will they think of her, when they find out she's a stripper?

Roxy knows she has to tell him 'but when? 'She can't say anything 'now, because it would ruin the whole trip! 'And then there's 'Christmas, which is coming up, and all of his family wanting to get back together again 'then, and she'll just mess that up, too! 'She goes back and forth with herself thinking when would be the right time? 'Maybe, she could just stop dancing all together, and then she'll never have to say anything! 'But then how is she going to make her mortgage? Steeli'o turns his head so he can snuggle up against her breast, and with one eye open he looks up at her saying "bay'be?" you're not going to try and get some sleep?" She gives him a sexy convincing smile; voicing "I will." I'm just not tired right now."

He gives her a kiss saying "suit, yourself." And then stuffs his head deeper into her side boo. It is dark when they land back at Treeberry Bay Airport. Steeli'o drops Roxy off at her place and carries her bags in the house for her. He ends up meeting her friend Tammy who is leaving out the house at the same time to catch a late flight back to Vegas. So Roxy rushes with Tammy out the front door out to her car, so Tammy won't slip up and ask her when she's going back to Vegas in front of Steeli'o. When she gets back into the house Steeli'o holds on to her tightly because he doesn't want to leave. With her eyes sweeping his handsome face she tells him to stay the night, but he can't because he says he has to get back to his house to take care of some property business early in the morning. He kisses her goodnight and promises to see her later. They share a long lingering embrace and then he leaves. Roxy watches him drive away waving from her front door. Then as soon as she closes her door she gets a text, it's from

Candis. "This girl must have radar, how does she know I'm back in town already?!" said Roxy locking her front door. The text says "you and Steeli'o are invited to a 'winter; cabin, party up in Lake Tahoe on Dec. 15th! "Save the date!" And don't; fake!" The same text went out to all the girls, the only thing different was the men's names, and of course Naquawna had two men options. "What is a girl tah do?!"

Chapter 20

'**Whelp**. 'Now it is Tuesday morning. And with Thanksgiving over, the girls and the guys were all back at work; or, on their grind. Naquawna's work place was 'slow, even for a Tuesday. She wanted badly to go home but one of her co-workers beat her to it, by calling in sick first. Plus, Mrs. Lee is still on vacation so Naquawna really has to stay at work since she's in charge whenever Mrs. Lee's out of town, or out of the building.

The front door swings open and it's her boss's son Sang Lee, who is normally all smiles when he comes to visit, but today he enters the shop all upset, wanting to know 'if Naquawna has seen or heard from Mike?" She tell him "no. "Why?" What's wrong?!" she asked. He answers "he didn't show up for practice last night, and no one can seem to get him on his cell." "Where do you think he could be?" asked Naquawna; worried. "I don't know man?" said Sang. "But that ain't like him, we talk almost every day" he says looking down at his phone. She starts to feel bad now because she blew Mike off when he called her earlier yesterday morning, so she could sneak off to be with Rayshawn in a motel. "Aw, man..., I hope he's alright" she said softly while biting on the side of one of her fingernails.

Then with one hand over her mouth she thinks for a second and says "I hate to say this, but should we call the Hospital?" "Awe!" Damn!" Do you think he got hurt?" Like in a car accident or something?" he asked. "Well-- you never know" she answered. "He might be laid up in the hospital, or even worse, in a ditch somewhere" she said nervously. Not wanting to jinx the situation she quickly recants her thoughts saying "let me stop thinking the worst!" she said as she paces the shops floor. Reaching for her phone she starts to call Candis who is working today at the Main Hospital. As the phone is dialing she says to Sang Lee "if anyone knows if Mike's in the Hospital, it would be her!"

Candis picks up her phone saying a joke "Motel 6!" Can I help one of you "happy; hoes" get a room?!" Candis then laughs; quietly because she's still at work. She knew it was Naquawna because she called her on her cell phone instead of on the hospital line. Naquawna laughs back to, but the laughter is cut short and Candis can hear the seriousness in Naquawna's voice when she says "hey, is Mike up there at the Hospital?" "I know you're not supposed to give out that kind of information, but Sang Lee and I' haven't heard from him in about 24 hours." Candis being optimist says "chil I'm sure he's fine, he's probably just busy doing his music thang!" Candis cups the phone over her mouth laughing "or maybe, he's up in a Motel like 'you were; yesterday!" "Spla'douw!" laughs Candis. "Not; funny!" retorts Naquawna. She continues to say "no." But for real." Even Sang who knows him like a brother, says that; that ain't even like Mike!" He would never miss a gig and not call!" Sang remembers he knows a few people who work at Treeberry Valley Hospital so he decides to call there and while doing so he says out loud "something just doesn't feel right!" he said as he's waiting for the other line to pick up. Naquawna agrees with him and tells Candis "to check the Hospital's computer records up there on her end, to see if he's registered up there just in case." "Nope, no Michael Ellis is coming up on the computer here" she said. Naquawna is relieved but still puzzled. Then Sang looks over at Naquawna hard in her eyes and says he might be at Valley Hospital because my ex-girlfriend just texted me asking "if I'm okay?" "Saying, because it looks like your friend Mike is up here in ICU, critical; and in a coma."

"Oh!" My!" God!" blares Naquawna loudly. She stands there with one hand over her mouth and the other hand clutching the phone with Candis listening in. "Damn, are you serious?" asked Candis. "And you can't even leave the shop!" rants Candis. "I know, Candis!" I know...!" I know...!" was what Naquawna kept on yelling. 'Paused, looking out the window she stands there in shock. Naquawna tries to ease the information into her brain to keep herself calm, when Sang Lee puts his hand on her shoulder saying "I'm going up to the Hospital, just come up there when you finish up with your last client." My mom won't 'trip, she loves Mike." He finishes with "and I'll call her and tell her what happened to Mike so she knows."

Naquawna not really hearing all of the words coming out of his mouth because she's still in a fog says "yeah. "Okay. With Candis in one ear saying "I'll go up there with you when I get off, if you want me to?" And Sang Lee in her other ear asking "are you going to be alright?" Naquawna looking over at him directly answers "okay....!" Yes!" I'll be fine!" And to Candis she says "I'll meet you up there!" And she hangs up the phone with Candis 'still, out of sorts. Sang still standing there looking at her hoping she'll be alright, prompts her to say "just go!" I'll be up there in a few, after I close up the shop!" she said trying to hold it together. He grabs his keys from the table next to the register answering "okay. "Cool. "I'll see you up there." He adds "don't worry, he'll be fine!" you know Mike!" he's a hog!" he said sharply. "I hope so" smiled Naquawna sadly. When he leaves out of the shop Naquawna tells her other co-workers "she'll be right back." saying that she's going to the bathroom." Some of the co-worker's nod, and some say "okay, with sympathy; knowing how upset she is about Mike.

When she gets into the bathroom she looks at her face in the mirror and braces herself with both hands on the sink and the tears just seem to flow down her face. She just can't bear the thought of losing Mike. 'Even she, can't believe how sad she is 'feeling, right now! 'I mean, I 'likes, Mike" she says to herself. 'But, damn!" 'I didn't think I liked him 'this, much!" 'To have all these 'tears, coming down my cheeks" she mumbled. Sniffling she says 'but now--, crying over Rayshawn!" 'Hell--; yeah!" 'Now, that's a different story!" she thinks to herself. 'But, Mike!" she repeats as she's wiping the inside corners of her eyes. She then thinks 'I just can't be falling in love with him; too!" She blows her nose muttering "oh, my, goodness!" how did this happen?!"

She stands there with her hands over her face and in the dark; inners of her mind, she starts wondering 'is he going to die?!" Or, never wake up?!" And then she thinks further 'will they have to take him off of 'life support, if he doesn't get better?!" Dropping her head she can't bear the thought of not being able to see Mike's bright personality, that lights up a room whenever he enters it! 'Or the fact that she can always call on him for 'anything!" from her car breaking down, to her shattering!" bad days. No one has proven themselves more 'loyal, to her, than Mike.

The bathroom door gets knocked on from one of her good friends and co-workers named: Frenchkah, asking "hey, are you alright in there?" Naquawna flushes the toilet playing it off like she just finished using the bathroom. She clears her throat, so she will sound normal, not like she's been crying when she says "yes. "I'm fine. "I'll be out in a minute. Frenchkah smiles on the other side of the door returning "okay. "I was just wondering because 'Tahzey, is here for her nail appointment." "Alright, thanks" said Naquawna. "Tell her I'll be there in a minute."

Naquawna gives herself one last glance and blows her nose and washes her hands and walks out of the stall to greet her client: Tahzey. "Hey, my friend!" says Tahzey. Naquawna smiles as much as she can trying not to show her worries when she answers "hey, yourself!" She tells Tahzey "to pick out a nail color" while she's getting her nail tools and clothes out. So as she's starting to do her client's nails, she makes small talk. But eventually Tahzey can tell that something is bothering Naquawna and so she confides in her about what she heard 30 minutes ago about Mike being up in the hospital.

Tahzey gives her; her deepest sympathies as they talk about it while she's doing her nails for her. Then to lighten the mood they change their tune to a happier subject like to "whom" Tahzey is dating now?" She tells Naquawna it's a freshman at her college that she has been seeing for a month now, and Naquawna looks down at her phone to see the young man's picture saying to her "he's cute. Smiling back a big smile Tahzey answers "thanks. When she's all done with her clients; nails and they are dried to the 'fullest, she walks Tahzey to the door. Cashing out the register Naquawna finally closes up the shop, and walks out to her car with Frenchkah by her side. The drive to the Hospital is nerve-rattling for the most part because she has 'never, been involved with anyone who has; had a major car accident before. Candis is already standing outside her car waiting to meet Naquawna in the side parking lot of the Hospital. So once Naquawna arrives at the hospital, when she gets out the car they both meet at her car and hug.

Her friend can very much tell, that she has been crying by looking at her blood shot eyes. So in comforting her, Candis says "he's going to be fine." "Come on sis" she adds as they walk up towards the Hospital arm in arm. Naquawna is still sniffling as they are walking into the hospital when she says, "I hope he's going to be alright." You should have heard how I blew him off yesterday, just so I could go be with Rayshawn." She shakes her head adding "I feel so guilty right now, because Mike has always been so-- good to me." Candis feeling the hurt in her friend's voice says "Mike won't even be tripping off of that." The point is, you're here for him now."

They go up to the waiting room area, where all the friends of Mike's are waiting in the visiting section, and Naquawna starts to notice all these groupie girls sitting around crying. She mumbles to Candis under her breath saying "um!" look at those four girls over there crying; hard, in a circle" growls Naquawna. Candis looks and then over walks Sang Lee to greet Naquawna and Candis saying "ahhhh; man!" good, you two made it! Half winded he says "the Doctor said he can't tell us too much until Mike's mom gets here." She's flying in from Georgia." "Mm... "Really...?" says Naquawna, nervously moving her leg up and down while she's sitting in one of the chairs. Then she looks around the room asking Sang "who are all these girls crying over Mike?" are they his other women? Sang laughs "no. "Mike ain't like that. "Some of these girls are backup singers." And the rest of them, just like to hang with us and rock out when we practice and do shows". "Mm-huh!" said Naquawna not knowing what to "really" believe!

Then, while they are still talking, a flash of 'bright colors, come running passed them and it's a lady in high heel boots, a long jean skirt, and an; out dated, fuchsia ruffled top. The woman in question has on fake eyelashes that are caked; up with mascara. And the eye shadow she is wearing; is on overkill. She yells to the nurse at the desk "where's my baby?!" Is he going to be alright?! The nurse answers her with "will get the Doctor, and let him know you're here, so he can answer your questions." The Doctor comes out from another room saying "hello?" You must be Mrs. Ellis?" I'm Doctor Weber" he says shaking her hand. "Yes, nice to meet you" she says, vaguely hearing his name. She jumps right into questions "so what is going on, Doctor?" "Well, he says cautiously, not wanting to send her into hysterics. "Your son Mike, seems to be in a state we call "prolonged; unconsciousness." "What?!" she voiced. Asking "what does that mean in English?" asked his mother. "It means he's not responding to stimuli" says the Doctor. "He's not what?!" she says, responding to the medicine!" she said franticly. "No...! No...!" No...!" said the Doctor. Giving up on beating around the bush, he blurts out "he's in a coma!" She takes a deep sigh. He sees her face and says "we don't see any brain activity, but there's no bleeding in his brain either, so that is a good sign." She nods happy to hear that news. "We just need for him to rest, so his body can heal itself" said Doctor Weber.

She nods and sighs with tears still streaming down her face asking "can I see him?" The Doctor says "sure you can" and he walks her to his room. When Mrs. Ellis sees her only child lying up in that hospital bed, she loses it. You would 'think, it was his 'funeral, the way she was laid across his stomach crying over him. The Doctor leaves the room telling the nurses "to keep an eye on him, and his mother as well, because she seems to be taking the news; understandably; hard!" So while Mrs. Ellis is in the room tending to Mike. Sang, Naquawna and all of the band crew, are gathered around the Doctor and his staff wanting to get some answers. The Doctor explains to the crowd "that his mother is the only family member here; that can tell them what is going on with her son."

The Doctor; feeling overwhelmed is trying to get some kind of order in the small waiting room, but Naquawna isn't buying it, so she sneaks back to the room to see Mike on her own. By the time Naquawna gets to his room and opens the door Mrs. Ellis who has cried herself to sleep next to her son in a chair, doesn't hear Naquawna when she walks in. Naquawna walks over to Mike slowly and quietly so she won't wake up his mother and with a sympathetic look on her face she reaches down to grab his hand. His eyes flicker slowly as if he knows she's there, so she stares at him while he sleeps as she softly strokes the top of his head.

The nurse comes in the room to take a forehead temperature reading and thinks Naquawna is his 'sister, or his 'wife, so she doesn't bother them. But when the door closes behind her, Mike's mom wakes up. At first she thinks it's the nurse checking his vitals. But then she sees Naquawna stroking Mikes head and kissing him on the mouth. His mom blurts out "who are you?"! Naquawna pulls back with a surprised look;

returning "hi. "I'm Mike's, she had to think for a second, then she just blurts out; his girlfriend!" "Mike never told me he had no girlfriend" said his mother 'eye balling her, looking her up and down like she's 'not; impressed! Naquawna gets a drab look on her face answering "well, I don't know why he hasn't mentioned anything about me yet!" because we have been dating for a while now! His mom looking; disinterested says "well, he's resting now, so you can go on ahead and run along." and I'll have him call you, when he wakes up" she adds with her lips poked out.

Naquawna's face hardens when looking back at her and she replies "I'm, not; leaving!" because he would want me to be here when he wakes up! His mother shouts "you 'are; leaving!" I don't know you!" and Mike has never mentioned you!" for all I 'know, you could be the reason why he's in here!" shouts his mother. "What?!" yells Naquawna with her hands on her hips. "Why would I, want to hurt your; son?!" His mother answers "I don't know?!" Why is 'spring, before summer?!" said his mother. Naquawna just looks at her like she's got a screw loose, when asking her "what does that have to do with anything we are talking about right now?"! Mike's mom looks back at her and replies "child--, go on now!" I'm tired, and I want to get me some rest, and I can't do it, with you in here!" Naquawna returns "I won't even be bothering you!" I'll just sit over here in this other chair.

Mrs. Ellis replies "now, I was trying to be nice, but now I see you want me to act a fool up in here!" Mrs. Ellis gets up from her chair and walks over to Naquawna pointing her finger towards the door yelling "get your; 'raggedy; 'ass; out of my 'son's; room!" Naquawna is in 'outrage, as she stands there with her mouth wide and her eyes; bulged. The nurse on duty hearing the yelling comes running in the room asking "is everything okay?!" Naquawna looking at Mike's mom with an evil eye shouts "yes!" its fine!" I was just leaving!" but I'll be back tomorrow!" she adds with a tight; lipped sarcastic look on her face. "No, your ass won't; be back in here!" said his mother. Then she turns to the nurse on duty saying "she is no relation, to 'me, or my son!" And I do "not" want her in here!"

Naquawna 'now, more; pissed then embarrassed, blurts out "I, am, related to Mike!" And to really piss off his mother she adds "we are engaged!" His mother shouts "what?"! And looks down at Naquawna's fingers asking "where's the ring?!" Naquawna thinking fast answers "the ring is at home because I'm afraid to wear it to work, because I deal with chemicals everyday"! "Yep, you deal with chemicals alright!" laughs his mother. "Because you done lost your 'damn; mind, if you think my son is marrying you!" Now get your trifling; behind' out of this room, before I call security!" Naquawna gives her a wicked smile and winks at her saying "see you tomorrow; maw!" And then she walks out the room chuckling; an evil laugh. Naquawna mad as all 'get out, grabs Candis by the arm voicing "let's go!" I've met his mother, and I 'don't; like her!" As the two are walking out of the hospital Naquawna adds "and if she 'thinks, that 'Mike, is going to choose her over me!" She is in for a 'rude; awakening"! She said with a twirl.

Chapter 21

'**N**ow--, speaking of; twirls! Twirling nipple rings and loud music are 'booming; out of the strip club over in Vegas, while Tammy is on stage dancing to the song: Big Bootie Hoes, being played by Two Live Crew! And I don't even need to tell you but the men are all going crazy! She jumps up on the pole and slides down, upside down, with her legs as flexible as a rubber band. A slightly large figured white man, with a tan brim hat on and a cigar hanging from his mouth walks up to the stage and puts a $20.00 dollar bill in her thong underwear as she's sliding down on the pole, upside down; slowly. Tammy blows him a kiss when she lands on the floor. Crawling to her knees she unsnaps her lime green bra, and gives the boys a shimmy shake of her; maracas.

Tammy twists and turns on the stage floor as she takes her lime green thong panties off and then she spots 'him, glaring at her from a corner table in the dark; it's Marvin! She just keeps on dancing looking in his direction, but not directly at him, while she teases; him with her knotty strip show. Tammy was so turned 'on, by all the men in the room that were cheering her 'on, and showering her with money, and gifts. One guy even gave her a $100.00 dollar bill, so she let him kiss her in the middle of her inner thigh. When it happened, she giggled, and she could just 'see, Marvin from afar getting; angrier and angrier from across the room as he 'fidgeted; there, in his seat staring at her. She gloated with pride because there wasn't a 'damn thing, he could do about it!" so fulfillment crossed her face as she ended her first dance set.

When Tammy is finished with her routine as she's picking up all her slinky under garments, she glances in Marvin's direction one last time before leaving the stage. Roxy was in the back getting ready to go on stage after Tammy finished up her second set, so when her phone rings and its Steeli'o, she can't answer it because the music is cranked up so loud, and he would want to know where she was at. So she thinks of a quick plan and decides to text him instead; saying that "she's at a Baptist, church with Candis, and that she will call him back in an hour or two." He hates-- to be texted by her on his phone, and she knows this because he always says he would rather hear the person's voice on the other end of the phone.

'But tonight, he will just have to deal with it!" thinks Roxy as she puts her phone down and rushes to the stage. Roxy passes Tammy in the hallway on her way to the stage and with a chuckle Tammy says "girl--, Marvin's ass is here!" Roxy gives her a big grin replying "you 'keep; them, coming back for that; snatch!" huh?!" They both crack up in passing, while hearing the stage announcer saying "and coming to the stage!" Here is your favorite girl!" On the; Rocks!" It's!" Foxy!" Roxy!" The boys go cray-cray as Roxy starts off her show in a skimpy little sheer red lace outfit. 'But, instead of walking out on to the stage, she crawls out like a sly fox or a slinky cat. The men start howling like dogs and some even bark like wolfs as she gets into her act.

Roxy climbs up on some manmade boxes and props that one of the stagehand guys had made for her for her routine. 'Purring, she laze on her back and lifts up her bottom, as she goes up and down, with her inner legs showing all of her goodies as she grinds the air slowly to the music. The men near the stage sway their heads up and down, and side to side, with every 'movement, of her hips. Then a regular to the club named 'Barley, who is drunk as a skunk, puts his hands on her thighs slurring "just one touch; baby"! He reaches out to touch her with shaking hands and Roxy 'shoos, him away with her hand then the bouncer come over and escort Barley back to his seat. Roxy caught off guard by Barley's 'protests, almost made her forget where she is in her routine. She stands on her feet but is still moving her body to the slow music as a beautiful black man walks up towards the stage.

When he gets up to the stage he pulls out a stack of two hundred dollar; bills, in 'ones, and slides them in between his hands like he's dealing cards, so the money will 'lands, all over her 'body, from her head to her 'toes, as he makes it 'rain, all over her! She just twirls her hips all around like an Egyptian snake and then bends over shaking her ass in his face as the money 'falls, to her feet. 'He was so handsome, she though as she smiled back at him while working the stage. Roxy doesn't remember ever seeing him in the club before. 'But then hell!" who's really trying to remember these guys; anyway?" she thinks to herself.

Then her mind flashes back to Steeli'o and then all the men in the room just become 'green paper, as she dances thinking about her 'lover, that she hasn't make love to, yet! When her show is done she runs sexily off the stage with her clothes and her money in hand. When working at the club, when the girls finish up their stage dancing, they can mingle around the club with the men who might was to buy them drinks, or pay for lap dances from them, so they can keep the money flowing, into the club.

So, now that they have finished their dance set, Roxy and Tammy hang out in the lounge talking about things going on at the club and then of course their men start to get mentioned. Roxy ends up telling Tammy "how much she's missing Steeli'o tonight." Stating that "she doesn't know how long she can keep up this charade of being a "dance; teacher." Tammy grunts "just tell him chil, while the relationship is still new." Then before Roxy could elaborate on the subject in more detail, Marvin walks over wanting a lap dance from Tammy. She looks him up and down and then says "naw--; I'll pass!" 'Marvin; desperate flashes a $100 dollar bill asking "please--! "Tammy! "Please! She thinks on it for a minute as she's watching Roxy slam back some gin. Then Tammy takes a drink of her Brandy and looking at him she replies “I don’t need your money; that bad!” She gets up to walk away and he grabs her by the arm softly; blaring “but I need; you!” so Please!” he begs. She blinks her eyes slowly and then rolls them up to ceiling, as if to say ‘she’s heard these lies before.

But, Marvin ‘desperate, to win her back, goes down on one knee begging “please!” Just let me talk to you for the $100 dollars, then!” You don’t even have to dance for me” he said holding the money; begging her! Roxy looks at her and shakes her head ‘like; girl, you might as well talk to the man him and get paid. With a sharp; grunt Tammy slams the rest of her Brandy; voicing “you got 20 minutes Marvin!” He nods “okay. She says “and let’s go over here by the ‘couches, so it looks like I’m working!” “Alright” he said happily. But before walking over to the lap dance area she snatches the money out of his hand and walks towards the couches pulling him by his tie.

Roxy chuckles and orders another watered down drink before she has to get back to working the room. Bobbing to the music she takes the drink from Shelly who is one of the barmaids who made her drink previously and she sit there making small talk at the bar with her. Roxy laughs at a joke that Shelly has said to her and she almost falls off her stool. As she catches herself from falling back, over walks a handsome, ‘tall, glass of water. ‘Okay!” Not water; but you feel me! He walks over to Roxy saying “hello, beautiful” as he takes her hand and kisses it saying “I loved your show.” She smiles up at him and gets a quick blush of redness in her cheeks when she tells him “thank you.

He looks her up and down lustfully asking “may I?” Then, while holding her hand, in his hand he twirls her around to get a better look at all of her “assets”! “Nice!” he said after taking the tooth pick out of his mouth. Still blushing Roxy clears her throat trying not to act like she is so taken by his ‘lustful; compliments when she answers back “I try. “Yeah” he says. And it’s working for you, too” he adds nodding his head, looking down at her face and her body. They both share a laugh and then he sees that her glass is half empty and he offers “can I buy you another drink?” sure” she said.

She was glad when he asked to buy her another drink because now she won’t have to go back on the floor ‘just yet, and be pestered by those same; dirty old ‘men, who always want her to give them a lap dance. This way it looks like she’s still working the ‘floor, so her boss won’t trip. Roxy moves side to side on her stool, with her arms out in front of her, snapping her fingers to the music ‘thinking, this is nice! ‘Just chillin. ‘Not being ‘drooled, all over. Plus, this guy, she is talking to is; hot! And he has money, and to Roxy he’s a change of scenery! And since he’s new to the club and not bad to look at, or-- talk to, she felt more at ease sitting and talking with him. He never tells her his name, and she doesn’t ask him either. Most of the girls never ask the 'tricks, their names anyway; unless they really want to tell them. Some people think, it keeps the business part of the job 'less; complicated! Roxy is sitting there feeling the music and loving the company. He casually asked her after she finished her 4th drink of gin and juice "if he could have a lap dance from her?"

So being that he was such a gentleman and not a "cock; hound!" like some of the rest of these guys in here, Roxy didn't mine. She stood from the bar stool and stumbled to her feet, and then the two of them walked, arm in arm across the room. Roxy twitching her fanny trying to look cute while walking in 5 inch heels to the lap dance section of the club, sees that all eyes are on him and her, and as she's walking through the club 'her co-working, stripper pals, are eyeballing the trick on her arm shouting "I see you found a 'new-bee, to the cat club!" "Don't hurt him Rox!" says one girl. "Send him my way; when you're done with him!" says her friend Pepper. While, Oniqueka yells "you don't know what to do wit; all--; that!" being that, Oniqueka was "not" a big fan of Roxy's, is why she said that. The girls cracked jokes and liquefied, into laughter as they swayed up and down, and all around on their 'men, of money!

Roxy is feeling so Horney right now from all of thy attention she is getting from this guy, and she can't help but think of her man 'Steeli'o, as she's starting to lap dance for this, trick! She closes her eyes and thinks of Steeli'o in the heat of the moment and then the soft touch of the hot; black; stud; which she didn't even get his name, starts to touch her on her arms. He rubs with both his hands up and down her arms softly, and when she turns her backside to bend over up against his "crotch" he's as stiff, as blown glass. He lets her feel how 'hard, she's making him 'get, as he's rubbing his 'frankfurter; up against her "buns" while she's bent over shaking what her momma gave her.

Roxy knows she's 'really, not even supposed to let him 'touch her, in this 'intimate, of a way. But being that it's his first time at the club, and she's too drunk and turn't up to really care, makes her think "what's the harm in it?" Plus, she's probably not going to see him again anyway because most of the guys they meet from out of town hardly ever come back to the same clubs in a year's time when there is so many clubs out here to visit. All of this crosses her mind, as he's touching her 'all, over her waist and her hips. But the kicker is, when he starts kissing her on the back of her neck as she rocks side to side to the beat of the music that's being rapped: by Petey Pablo called: Freek A Leek. He even goes as far as running his hand up her stomach and on to her breast, and in that 'instant, her mammilla's went; hard. She tilts her head up and back, trying to see his face, while her back and her rear were still up against the front of his pants. They kiss and he squeezes her breast softly and she feels herself starting to get 'slushy, when he slide his hand down her shorts and starts to put his fingers, where they shouldn't, be.

The club is so dark that no one can see what the next person is really doing in the lap dance area, unless they are really looking; hard. Most of these guys are only interested is getting their own jollies; off so Roxy doesn't think anyone is paying that much attention to her and him, so she lets him have his fun, as she's getting her money on. Slowly she lifts her arm up over the back of her head and rubs the back of his head while he's down in her pants. Breathing heavy she turns her head to the right to get another glance at his pretty face and as she's moaning quietly he kisses her again. She's breathing even harder and is really into it now, but as soon as the song ends, she 'flicks, like a light switch!" gasping; "No!" wait a minute! "Hell...!" "No! "Wait a minute...! "Wait a minute...!" she said quickly, as she's snatching his hand out of her shorts. But it is too late by then, because one of his friends catches a glance of the 'touching, in a "no" "touching; zone"! And his friends yells out "get; it!" Ray-dog!" While another one of his boys starts up with this loud 'Rottweiler bark, from a couple of lap dancer's down from where he and Roxy are.

It is crazy how Roxy had lost her since of 'loyalty, to Steeli'o in that quick; moment! She hurries and stumbles away, quickly shouting "thank you!" "Thanks for the dance!" "But I got to go!" she said rushing away. He yells "hey! "Where you going?"! "I want another dance!" Come on--!" he yells. All crushed with his feelings he stands there holding up a wad of Benjamin's in her direction but she keeps on running.

One of her co-workers Pepper see's the wad of money and jumps on him. He played with her for a few minute but he wanted; Roxy! Through all the muck, and smoke, the men and women could still hear the club's owner yelling "last call for alcohol!" he said as the lights started to lift a little. Tammy looking around the room at all the tricks having their moment, had seen Roxy running off towards the back, so she tells Marvin "to meet her out back by her car, so she can go see if Roxy's alright."

When Tammy gets to the back dressing room she hears Roxy getting in the shower spouting to herself "damn it!" "Damn it!" She sees Tammy and says "I'm so tore up right now!" Tammy laughs "oh, is that all?!" I thought something was wrong when I saw you running off like that." Tammy gets in the shower stall next to Roxy's and they talk eye to eye because the stall doors only go up to their necks. Roxy with a big 'sigh, says

"I kind of got carried away tonight with that guy that I was lap dancing with." Tammy replies "that's only natural to start feeling a little turn't up!" "I get stimulated all the time" laughs Tammy. "Especially if the guy I'm dancing with, is fine as good, wine!"

Roxy not being able to laugh over her guilt, cuts in saying "no!" this is different!" "I would 'never, let a client touch me like that!" "Let alone, feel me up and rub all on my chest!" Tammy smirks "let, it, go; gurl!" "No, you haven't heard the worse part yet!" She closes her eyes really tight voicing "and then, I let him put his hands down my shorts and 'do, things, to me!" Tammy blares out "wooh!" "Chil!" "You did go too far!" "Somebody's... cheating on their man--!" laughs Tammy. She continues to joke "maybe you and Marvin need to hook up!" Roxy belt out "oh! "My! "God! "See...! "Now I really feel dirty!"

Tammy chuckles as the water is running down her lathered up scalp. Then she tells Roxy "don't be so hard on yourself." "It happens to the best of us." "What you really need to do, she continues to say "is call up your man when we get to the house, and have a little 'phone sex, session with him, before you become one of those "girls" who starts sleeping with the 'clients, because you're so 'Horney, from missing yo, man!"

Roxy nods her head returning "you are so; right!" The water shuts off and they get out of the shower and as the two women are drying off, their boss walks in. Tammy says "can we get some privacy, Burt?!" Burt chuckles "it's not like I haven't seen you two girls naked before. "You're like daughters to me.". "Um--; grouse!" spouts Tammy. While Roxy laughs slightly, looking up at him 'hoping, that him coming in there, isn't so he can tell her, about how she went 'too far; tonight, in the work place. But Burt with a big smile just hands them an envelope saying "here's your Christmas bonuses ladies!" adding "I'm giving them to you girls early because Roxy and I won't be working after the 15th of this month!" "Really...?" "Why?" asked Tammy as she shifted her focus to Roxy? "You remember?" "I'm going to Tahoe with the crew." "Candis and them." "Oh--, yeah, that's a week away" answers Tammy. Stating "well--, you know where I'll be?"! "Right up in here, with these 'fools, breaking me off; my money!" Burt and Tammy chuckle while Roxy's putting lotion on her legs. He catches himself gawking at Roxy as she's running her hands up and down her legs with the sweet smelling lotion on her hand. Still looking at her he slaps the rest of the envelopes in his hand back and forth on the side of his leg voicing "I'll be at my daughter's house, for the Holidays." Roxy returns "that sounds fun!" Tammy chuckles saying "who cares?!" Then she laughs saying "I'm just kidding!" Roxy knowing it's late tries to hurry up and get dressed and tells Tammy to hurry up as well, so they can get to Tammy's house where it is quiet enough for her to call Steeli'o back.

Burt watches as the girls get dressed and then he goes to finish up passing out the rest of the checks as Roxy and Tammy head out the back door. When they get outside three guys are waiting around in the parking lot standing by a Bentley. Marvin is waiting for Tammy at her car which is on the other side of the parking lot with his headlights on. One of the guys standing by the Bentley says to his buddies "they're taking that buster home with um?!" Talking about, Marvin? Another guy by the Bentley yells out to Roxy "hey...!" "Let me talk to you for a minute!" He jogs towards them looking at Roxy as she's getting into Tammy's car. The guy walks around to the car window and gives her his card that says "Rappin, Ray!" "Call me, if you ever wanna play!" After reading his card, she looks at him with 'focus, so she can remember his pretty face.

Then with a flattery type smile she says "I don't think that's a good ideal, me, calling you." "Why?" he says with his big brown eyes staring back at her. "Because we're really not supposed to get involved with the men that come into the club." He smiles "that's not going to be a problem, because this was just a onetime shot for me." "Plus, I don't really come to Vegas that much" he said with a grin. She smiles up at him returning "well, I also have a boyfriend." "And I'm sure... you have plenty of women knocking on your door." He laughs saying "well, I'm not gone lie. "The ladies do give me play. "But none of them 'lately, have been as hot as you" he says licking his lips. With a girlish grin she looks up at his pretty face smiling and he smiles back at her and she replies "you are cute!" "I'll give you that!" "Thanks" he grins. "You're a fox yourself; Ms. Roxy!"

Then he hears his friend start up the car, so he starts backing away towards the Bentley stating "all you have to do is call!" And he sings the rest of the words "and I'll be there...!" She laughs and waves bye as he walks back to his car. Tammy chuckles and then long "ummmm---!" comes out of her mouth. And then she puts the car in drive and tells Marvin to follow them home. Tammy figures 'hell... she's already slept with Marvin, and "technically" she "was" his fiancé! So she figures 'she'll just get a 'nut, on 'him, tonight! When the girls get home Roxy bolts to her room. She calls Steeli'o's phone and when he picks up she sighs "can you believe it?!" "I just got back home!" "Who knew?" that some of them black churches, went 'on--, for so long?!" They both laughed then out of nowhere Roxy hears moans and moving furniture coming from Tammy's room.

'Roxy, still 'stimulated, from the whole night and 'all, starts to ease into her seductive; voice over the phone. And with her shoes kicked off and her light off she tells Steeli'o how much she really misses him and that she was thinking about him 'all, night. They both lay in their beds miles apart, he in Columbia on business and she in Vegas but telling him she's in Treeberry at home.

As Roxy starts to touch herself she can't stop her mind from going back and forth 'picturing, that nice looking black guy she had met earlier tonight named 'Rappin Ray! And Steeli'o, on the other end of the phone plays along with the phone sex game that Roxy is giving to him. While the sweet talk is happening she smiles on the other end of the phone when his breathing gets harder and harder. And before long as she takes him on a 'mind ride, that she made up on the 'fly, her cooing; him 'all up in his ear, makes him end up; with a happy 'ending, and so does she.

Laying back in her bed she laughs out loud when the two are done pleasuring themselves. Roxy also chuckles because she's kind of relieved when she tells him "damn, I needed that!" He lays there in his bed trying to catch his breath; up, to meet his heartbeat when he confesses "yes, me too. All relaxed she says "honey, are you going to be able to go to Tahoe next week, on the 15th"?" He replies "anything for you bay'be" as he closes his eyes while she's talking to him because now he's in a 'sleepy, state of mind. The next morning Officer Mahavez is woken up, out of a dead sleep by the Captain!

Chapter 22

That next morning when Officer Mahavez was woken up out of a dead; sleep at home it was when he had just gotten back from Vegas, where him and his crew were doing some undercover work late last night on the case. So when his boss calls him saying "there is some drug activity dates being switched around, the 'Captain, with anger in his voice yells "what the hell's going on?!" "Your dates don't match the wire taps we've been listening to!! Mahavez sits up in his bed abruptly and wipes the sleep from his eyes stating "that can't be right, sir!" "Unless--; they're moving thing around because of the Tahoe trip!" He continues to say "don't worry Captain!" "I'll keep a close eye on them and check in with you from time to time, while I'm up in Tahoe. "Alright!" says the Captain. "You do that." "And make sure you get close with those guys, too!" "Make them think you're one of them." "If they smoke weed, you might have to hit it" said the Captain. Mahavez gets quiet. Then the Captain asked "have you ever gotten 'high, before, son?" He awaits Mahavez's answer after reassuring him that this is off the record. Mahavez answers "well--, once or twice in college, sir." Captain returns "okay, good to know." so it won't come as a surprise to you." The Captain finishes up with "just be safe out there, because this is 'still, a dangerous case!" "Thanks sir" he replied. "I'll be careful" he said and then hang up.

Later on that day after Rafee'al wakes up again from his nap, he receives a call from Candis telling him "they might have to cancel the trip do to the "tragic; accident" that happened to one of their friends, name Mike." Naquawna was in the background saying "no." "Let's still go, because everybody has already put in the time, to take off from their jobs!" "Okay" said Candis. "If you're sure?" Candis then reassures Rafee'al who is listening in on the other end of the phone; that they are still going to be going up on the 15th of December as previously planned. He laughs asking "are you two sure?" He cracks up because he's listening on the phone to the two women go back and forth on the pros and cons of the "trip" in Naquawna's kitchen. Candis laughs back saying "yes, we're, sure!" 'Naquawna, getting more and more upset as she's puttering around in her kitchen trying to remember where she last saw her mixing bowl; cheers, when Candis finally agrees to help her look for it.

While helping her look for her favorite mixing bowl Candis asked her "did you tell Rayshawn about the trip?" Naquawna smiles after finding her mixing bowl cheering "there it is!" Then to answer Candis's question she says "no. "I haven't talk to Rayshawn since last night 'or, today for that matter" she grimaced. Rafee'al still on the phone laughing at the girls, stops when Candis asked him to meet her for lunch. She says to him "I'm, starving!" And Naquawna has to cook a pot roast for her granddad so she can't go anywhere right now." Even though, Candis "really; believes" that; the only reason Naquawna is making the pot roast, is 'just in case, Rayshawn "happens" to stop by again so she can feed him. But she keeps that thought to herself asking him "so what do you say babe?" "You hungry?" he answers "sure, but I'd rather get some steaks and potatoes and make you an early dinner, at your place.

Candis and Naquawna look at each other at the same time and give each other fingertip dap. Which is like a quiet; high five. Candis smiling returns "sure, that sounds even better." "Okay. "Coo." he replies. "I'm getting in the shower right now and I'll meet you at your place in 45 minutes" he added. Candis smiling while doing a cha-cha dance in the kitchen said "okay, sounds good; snuggumes. Naquawna looks over at her and snickers "dam-mmn--; home-girl!" "You got him cooking for you now, too?!" She continues to say "you know he's only doing this "cooking; shit!" at your house, so he can; hit it?!" Naquawna laughing, dances around the kitchen slapping her hand in the air back and forth like she's slapping someone on the butt. Candis cracks up laughing too, then jokes saying "Whelp!" "I've, gotts-dah-go!" adding "I've got a lunch date!" Oh, my bad!" "An early; dinner date!" Naquawna laughs back saying "a lunch date!" that will probably turn into a "d*ck; down!" Candis giggling, sneers out "I'm weak!" she said laughing as she opens the back kitchen door and heads out to her car. She hurries and gets home so she can clean up a bit, and get in the shower before he gets there.

When Rafee'al gets to her apartment with bags in his hands, he sees that there are candles burning and soft music playing as he's walking into her place looking around. He tells her "this place is nice you got here." She smiles 'guessing, he must have 'thought, she lived in a pig pin because she'd never let him come in before. She chuckles thinking that thought as she opens the blinds a little more so he can see the beautiful water from her balcony. "Wow!" that's a tight view you've got there" he said as he walks over to get a closer look while opening her sliding door. "Thanks sweetie" she said taking the bags from him. "Do you want a glass of wine or a beer?" she asked?

Rafee'al not wanting to break cover says "no, at first." But then he remembers what his boss had said which was "do what they do, to fit in." So he changes his answer to "yeah, I'll take a beer." Trying not to smile too hard she says "coming right up." She takes the grocery into the kitchen while Rafee'al is standing on the balcony looking out at the ocean. And when she brings him his cold beer outside he asked "do you every catch a glimpse at the whales when they come through here?" She answers "no. "But some people that live here in my complex say they have." "But I haven't seen any of them yet." "I see dolphins all the time, though" she adds. "And I could have sworn; I've seen a shark fin sticking up out of the water a few times too."

He laughs saying "you don't have to swear." I believe you." "But was this 'before, or after you've smoked a fat one?" She hits him playfully on his arm as they laugh their way back into the kitchen. In the kitchen sink Rafee'al washes his hands and tells her to sit down and watch a "chef" go to work! Cracking, back she laughs "oh, is there a "chef" leaving to go to work?!" she asked looking around the room to complete her joke. He laughs back saying "awh, you're funny!" huh? And they both stand there laughing while Rafee'al pours her another glass of wine, then he starts preparing the food.

'Rafee'al, is a confident undercover cop who knows how to get the job done in 'any, situation. But the problem 'now is, he never; planned on a woman like Candis. She is smart, sweet, funny and very attractive. Rafee'al tries to keep in mind, that this is 'still, a job. But the more he gets to know 'Candis, the more he has to keep his wits about him. He has had "many; women" fall in love with him and he has always been able to keep his distance, whether it 'be, a real 'date, or a job related date. He's kind of the type; that likes to love them, and then; leave them. It's just what he's been use too. That's why with this particular job going as smoothly as it is, he is starting to second-guess his own feelings, because he can't seem to really figure Candis out.

On paper he gets who she is, but in person she's a whole; different kind of woman. At first he thought she was just a simple; pot smoking, college like, party girl! But as he's starting to find out things about 'her, he can see that she's got a little more 'substance, to her; then he initially thought. One of the things he likes about her is, the fact that she's a positive person who seems to like to have a good time. He also can't overlook the sexy way she looks and acts around him. And the fact that she has "some; morals" and loves God, is somewhat surprising to him too. But nevertheless Rafee'al tries to stay focus.

The two start to play around in the kitchen and he slaps her on her butt with a hand towel 'after, she threw a sliced cucumber at the back of his head while he was seasoning up the steaks. So while she's standing there at the sink washing off the potatoes, he splashes her with water. So she laughs and chases him around the kitchen and he uses that moment to love on 'her, when she catches him. After she is done making the salad she turns to him asking "which dressing do you want to try?" "The choices are, blue cheese or Italian?" He replies "Italian of course" and then he leaned over to kiss her. She ends up leaving both of the dressings on the table because she likes a little blue cheese on her steak. The two walk out to the balcony hand in hand sipping on their drinks while enjoying each other's company waiting for the potatoes to finish baking.

To Rafee'al's surprise there is a couple of pretty good 'surfer's, out in the water riding big waves. He comments on how brave they are because he has yet' to try surfing. He even tells Candis they should try scuba diving one day. Candis laughs hesitantly returning "um- hu," but in a no; kind of voice. But then she thinks back on the time when she had told him how she likes doing anything; exciting and new. So she recants her initial statement; saying "that she's open to the idea but tells him, "that maybe they should try 'snorkeling; first, like on a warm tropical Island, so they can work their way up to the 'big; cold, ocean." He chuckles returning "yeah, like graduating from a little pond, to a big pool?" Candis nods back while looking at him and she giggles when he says "I like the way your mind thinks."

The timer then goes off on the stove and the potatoes are done. Rafee'al clicks on the stove so he can heats up the iron grilling pan, to fry the steaks on, so the meat and the potatoes can be hot at the same time. Than he asks Candis "how she likes her meat?" And she laughs thinking of a dirty thought and he catches it as well, commenting back he says "that came out wrong." She giggles again answering "I like my steak medium but well done." "Me too" he said. He goes on to say "I will eat my steaks on the rare side sometimes, as long as it's not too bloody." He reaches for her hand and tells her to take a seat after she's done putting the dishes on the table.

The porterhouse steaks are cooking up perfectly. And he had pulled the baked potatoes out of the oven prior to the steaks being done and had filled them with butter and sour cream and chives. Candis smiled with pleasure while looking and smelling his good food. After closing the refrigerator she puts the nicely made salad in a big bowl so they could get as much as they wanted. With cooking tools in his hand he smiles at her saying "we make a great team" then he puts her steak down on her plate. "This boy can cook" thinks Candis. And she lets him know just how good everything looks, smells and taste by all her moans and groans over his food, as she affectionately touches his arm.

They both sit at the table talking and looking into each other's eyes while eating and drinking wine and beer, and it's as if they've known each other for years and without a thought, or a care in the world, they hold hands across the table. 'Rafee'al, loving the moment they are having together smiles, but still remembers he is on a job. So he asks "so... how are we all getting to Tahoe?" Candis smiles but shows no teeth because she's eating, and with a sexy grin on her face she answers "we are all going to try and go in a van." "Or--, we might rent a small mobile home." She then squints her eyes while thinking, saying "that might even be better!" she says as she's holding her fork out with a piece of steak on it. "We, all, should take a mobile, home!" Rafee'al laughs agreeing he returns "that actually sounds great. She says "yes, that way it will be more like a real road trip!" "And--, we can take our time 'driving, play cards, even dominoes" she added. "That way, when we drink, we already have a bathroom on board, so we don't have to keep pulling over on the side of the road at those rest stops." Rafee'al nods his head up and down while he's chewing on his food in agreement, voicing "right." Right."

She even tells him "how he is going to just love the Cabin." She adds "the owners have done some 'nice, upgrades to the property." Then she ends with "I'll show you the property I'm talking about on-line, later." He smiles "yep, I can't wait!" This should be very interesting, because I have never really met any of your other friends" he states. Candis says "I know right?!" "But trust me" she says. "I'm sure, you're going to like them because they 'are fun, for the most part." And I just know, they are gonna love you" she said looking deep into his eyes. Rafee'al trying not to read too much into her words and her deep eye contact says "well, if you say so."

Candis laughs and scrapes her plate, although there was really nothing left on her plate to scrape off other than the bone, because the food was so good. So when the food has eaten, and the wine has 'sunk, into her brain, she starts to get a little flushed in the face when thinking about Naquawna's comment of 'dinner, and a d*ck, down!" And as her face, is starting get warmer she grins over by the sink because 'now, what are they going to do, now that dinner is over? She turns to him saying "I'm going to do the dishes since you cooked such a fabulous meal." Her thought was, she'd stay busy until something would come to mind that they could "platonically" do together.

Rafee'al sits back in the chair with his hands clasps together around the back of his head chuckling he says "yeah, I did cook a fabulous meal, didn't I?" Candis takes the dish towel and pops him on the side of his leg laughing "you are so cocky, aren't you?!" He laughs back "naw--, just confident. Then he jumps up from his chair and grabs her by the arm, pulling her into him, he gives her a long passionate kiss. Candis forgets all about doing the dishes, as they stand there in the kitchen loving on each other, in the moment. When they come out of their hug and kiss she jokes "you didn't make me dessert!" He kisses her again and chases her into the living room shouting "you 'are, dessert; woman!" She gets pushed back on the couch laughing and giggling as he tickles her and kisses her on her lips, neck and her cheeks. Then staring at her he says "we could go out and get dessert, if you want too." "How about some cold stone ice cream?" She jumps up voicing "you don't have to ask me twice!" and she runs to get her coat.

As they're walking out the door he jokes "I don't think I've ever seen you move so fast." Laughing she; nudges him saying "I'll drive." "You just relax sweetheart" she says as they are walking towards her truck. When they get in her truck Rafee'al comments on 'how nice her car is." And after thanking him, she grunts to herself because at this 'point, she doesn't even 'care, if Jake, sees her or not! In her mind she is showing off her 'new; man, to the world! 'And, anyone who doesn't like it!" can kiss her; grits!

Chapter 23

The next day at around 6 o'clock am bright and early in the morning Rafee'al B.K.A. 'Officer Mahavez, walks into work whistling a new tune 'and is all; smiles. Officer Kitpatrick his partner and good friend says to him "someone sounds like they had a great night!" Rafee'al laughs while fixing his gun holster answering "yep, I cooked dinner for her last night." "Now, she loves, me!" he said smiling as he sucked air through the front of his teeth. 'Kitpatrick, grunt saying "it must've been a late-night, because you never called me back and we had movement in the case." Rafee'al gets serious; quickly saying "oh shit!" "What happened?!" Kitpatrick sighs "no worries, Lenny and I got two boys in blue to handle it." Kitpatrick then elaborated on it saying "what happened was, the two golden boys had the cops called to their house because the girl 'Katey, claimed one of the brother's tried to force her into giving him "fellatio!"

Rafee'al retorts "I knew I seen patrol lights from Candis's house last night. He continues to say "so what are you saying?" "Both the brother's Jake and Jordon tried to get that girl to go down, on them?" "No, just the one brother 'Jordan." "But she dropped the charges because she likes Jake" said Kit. "From what I gathered, she was "doing; Jake" at the time, and I guess Jordan was trying to get in on the action too." But he got shot down, so the two boys ended up fighting, so Katey called the cops. But come to find out, she didn't get sexually assaulted after all' because Jake protected her.

"Well at least dude protected her" blurts Rafee'al. "That's a damn shame!" he adds shaking his head. "His brother ain't got 'no, Mack-in; skills!" "You don't force no woman to do 'things, she doesn't want to do with you!" said Rafee'al. "And this proves my point, those boys are spiraling out of control!" and it's just a matter of time before they get locked; up and loose mommy and daddy's house!" Kitpatrick returns "I know bro." And before he could keep speaking on it, in walks the Captain saying "okay, men!" listen up!" he says as he's calling everyone to order. "We have got a lot of cases to close this week!" "And as you all know Mahavez and our crew will be leaving in a few days for Tahoe." "We will all hang back, to make sure other things are getting done on our end, while Lenny and Kitpatrick cover as backup in close range to hear all microphones, and to get all the needed video surveillance."

He continues "this is one of our biggest cases!" so guys, handle this one with extra care." The Captain; shuffles some papers around and goes on to talk about another case that got solved yesterday by the ladies. "Officer Jackson and Officer Frankel got it done!" he said proudly. "And without any help from you men!" he added. Everyone claps for Officer Mary Jackson who is a tall slender built, big hipped; black woman. And they also clapped for Officer Stacy Frankel, a busty' curvaceous; Jewish woman. These female 'Officer's, have been partners on the force for four years now. And not only are they both 'beautiful, young women inside and out, but they are also brave as well. Most of the guys on the job joke around though, about them, behind their; backs saying 'that they are way too; pretty to solve "any; real" hardcore cases!" But this time, they ended up showing up the 'men, and letting them 'see, that they have 'beauty, brains; and bronze!

The girls stand up smiling, while taking a slight; bow in front of their peers, as they are 'all, applauding them on a job well done. The Captain gives more recognition to other cops in the squad who are doing big thing too and then before the meeting is augured he tells everyone "to get out there and make him proud!" He ends with "and be safe!" They all cheer each other on while yelling "alright!" Captain! And then they disperse. Kitpatrick and Rafee'al talk privately on their way down to the evidence room so Kitpatrick can try to find out how far he got with Candis last night. Rafee'al chuckles at his attempt saying "a real player never tells, what he's doing!" Kitpatrick laughing back says "well..., I'm not talking to a real player!" "So do tell!" said Kit still laughing. Rafee'al looks at him crazy, than Kitpatrick with a grunt says "just like I thought, you didn't get far!"

Rafee'al laughing back at his remark; retorts "and--, you're--; all-- up in my business!" "Get some!" shouts Rafee'al. Kitpatrick blurts "this girl is not going to fall for your, crap!" like those other women you've been with in the past!" "I can just tell" said Kit laughing. Rafee'al stops what he is doing and puts the box on the table asking "Kit, why are you so interested in what Candis "is?" or "isn't?" going to do with me?!" He continues to say "yes, she's a nice girl!" and-- she's not too bad to look at! He pauses than says "and yes, we do have good times together." "But I don't mix business with pleasure!"

Kitpatrick blurts out "and that's his story and he's sticking to it!" He pats Rafee'al on the back with a sarcastic smirk on his face and walks out of the evidence room laughing. Rafee'al catches up to him asking "why do you keep trying to 'jinx me; dude?!"

They both walk down the corridor semi-arguing and then when the two women Police Officer's pass them in the hallway they smile playing it off. Kitpatrick looks back at their backsides and comments on how nice Officer Jackson's rear is. Rafee'al looks back and agrees and then he laughs saying to Kitpatrick "you should ask her out man!" "Hell..!" ask someone;

out!" "So you can stay 'out; 'my; business!" Kitpatrick laughing; shout "alright; then!" "Tahoe"! "You just concentrate on staying "focused" in Tahoe while sleeping in the same room, with Candis!" pre-tending when you waking up, that you're "not" falling for her!" "Yep!" "This is "definitely; not!" going to be mixing business, with "pleasure!" cracked; Kitpatrick with a snort. Rafee'al, playing him to the left; sighs out "alright; already; man!" give it a rest!

When they get in the car Kitpatrick starts fiddling with his paperwork when Rafee'al starts the engine of the car. And as they drive down the road a voice enters Rafee'al's head, it's Candis's voice, and her laugh comes to mind and he thinks back on what a great time they had last night. He has to stay in control of the situation and not fall in love with Candis because he 'knows, it's the right thing to do.

In his mind an undercover detective has to be a solo job for him right now, because he doesn't want to risk bringing a family into his circle just; yet. 'Plus, he's not ready for all the stuff that comes with being a family man. He has his whole life ahead of him 'and he's just 'too; fyne, to only be with just one woman right now" he says to himself as he's looking at his face in the car's interior mirror. Rafee'al convinces himself of all these things so he "won't" fall in love. He's a creature of habit and he 'likes, how his life, has been going on so far. You might say, that it's his 'pep talk, to himself as they drive up the road to the next stake out spot.

Rafee'al still thinking happy thoughts, yawns when Kitpatrick starts rambling on about what he ate for dinner last night. By the time they get to where they want to be, which is driving past Bubba Dank's house they see that same woman standing outside arguing with Bubba. Kitpatrick says "isn't that; that same crack head lady?" Rafee'al looks, then tightens his eyes to see her better then he voices "yep, that's Rayshawn's mom alright!" he said. "What the hell is she doing here?" "I thought she lived up past Sac'mento?" adds Rafee'al as he turns up the street going further so he won't be seen. When he pulls over and park's the car he and Kitpatrick blend in perfectly because they are in their street clothes, sitting in a Nissan Maxima rental car.

They blended in; so well, until two smokers ended up approaching there car asking for some 'Dee. (Meaning dope). Rafee'al thinking on his toes answers "I just sold my last rock man!" Do you know where I can re-up at?" asked Rafee'al. The one smoker says "show-do." And points up the street towards Bubba's house. The smoker's name is Jeffie. After introducing himself he jumps in the backseat and takes them up to Bubba's house. When they pull up in front of Bubba's house Jeffie get out the car and knocks on the door. Bubba looks out the window saying "I know you didn't bring no narks to my house, fool?"! Jeffie; geeking and 'tweaking, lies "naw man." "That's my cousin." He wants to get some 'Dee, from you man!"

Bubba asked "how much?" "Big weight" said Jeffie. "Bet!" said Bubba. Asking "where's the money?" "He wants to meet you and buy it from you himself." Bubba frowns "hell, naw--!" If he doesn't trust you with his money!" "Then how can I trust him in my house?!" Jeffie desperate to get high sighs "awh, man!" Forget it then!" I was just trying to bring you some big business!" Bubba knowing that rent is due, and funds will be on the low-side; since he plans on taking a trip to Tahoe with the guys; prompts him to take the risk, so he can double up and take this vacation.

He tells Jeffie "alright, tell dude I'll holler at him." "But you're gonna do the transaction" says Bubba. "Like what?" said Jeffie? Bubba says "you're gonna take the money from him." "And 'you're, gonna give him the dope!" "That way it's on 'you, not me!" Jeffie pauses for a minute 'thinking, about the risk! But, because he wants to get high so... bad, he agrees; to do it. Jeffie runs back to the car where Rafee'al is, saying "okay, it's cool, but only one of you can come into the house with me." "And, I told him you were my cousin, so just play along" explains Jeffie, scratching his arm like a junky.

"So how much do you want to get?" Rafee'al already prepared with a wad of money in his pocket answers "a brick." His partner Kitpatrick looks at him like 'don't get robbed, when you go in the house man!" Jeffie smiles with a gleam in his eyes, just thinking about his finder's fee, which he 'hopes, will make a nice big rock or two. Rafee'al steps out of the car and casually 'pimp, walks up towards the front door 'acting, like he's bought dope; many of times before. Bubba opens the door and looks him square in his face asking "what up, man?!" Who, you?!" Rafee'al extends his hand to give him a cool brother hand shake answering "I'm Rafee'al, man." "Alright, cool... said Bubba. "You ain't five-0, right?" he asked? "Naw, man" laughs Rafee'al. Bubba grin saying "you know we got to ask that?" He continues to say "and now, I'm ma half to get my lady friend to pat you down, because I don't know you; partner!" Bubba then yells for Bonnie to come out from the back room "so pat dude down for him." Bonnie comes out from the back room, where she was getting high and cleaning up at. She sees that Rafee'al is cute as hell, so she replies "gladly!" to patting him down as she's looking him up and down reaching out to touch his body. When she rubs her hands up his back to see if he's wearing a wire she feels his piece instead and takes it and puts it on the table after pulling out the clip.

Bubba doesn't trip because he knows everyone's packing heat now days. The kilo is in the back room so Bubba makes Bonnie go to the back with Jeffie so she can make him bring it out. Rafee'al shows Bubba the cash and Jeffie come back with the kilo and passes it to Rafee'al. Rafee'al stabs the brick with a bold point pen that is sitting on the table next to his gun and takes a taste of the cocaine with his pinky nail. After tasting it he nods his head saying "this is some good coke, man" and he hands Bonnie the cash smiling.

"Hell--! "Yeah! I got the best stuff in town!" laughed Bubba. "You better asks somebody!" Bubba, still laughing; jokingly says "oh, yeah!" you 'did, ask somebody!" that's why you're here!" Everybody laughs out loud and then Bubba shakes Rafee'al hand saying "if you need some more man!" Jeffie knows where I be!" Rafee'al answers "right on man!" When the transaction is over Rafee'al takes his gun from off the table and when no one is looking with his other hand he sticks a circular, sticky device 'like microphone, which is about a quarter of the size of a contact lens, and sticks it under the edge of the dining table. He then puts the coke; wrapped in a paper bag under his arm under his jacket saying "thanks for the business, man!"

Bubba answers "alright, I'll check you out!" Then he head gestures; shifting his head to Bonnie saying "to give the man his gun clip back" and then he closes the door behind Rafee'al and Jeffie. Rafee'al was happy as hell that he got to stick that 'transmitting microphone, under the table. He is so happy, that it makes him want to give 'Jeffie, a nice amount of 'blow, for him "unknowingly" helping him to get this, job done. When Rafee'al gives him a lot in a folded piece of paper Jeffie is happy as can be when he gives Rafee'al dap on his knuckles after receiving such a nice amount of the blow.

Walking away with the folded; blow in the paper, Jeffie stuffs it in his pocket and then hurries up the street practically; skipping so he can go 'rock up, his reward. Kitpatrick was 'amazed, at what a natural Rafee'al was at buying dope. He laughs at Rafee'al as they drive away and with a staggering look on Kitpatrick's face he says "way to go man!" "You seem to have the dope game; sewed up!" And they both crack up laughing as they get on the highway. Rafee'al is all stoked about what just took place too, as he confesses to Kitpatrick "how he use to have some in-laws who really did sell dope back in the day, so he was no stranger to what goes on in the dope game!" He went on to say "that's why he's so passionate about getting some of the big dealers; off the streets, due to the fact that he lost his sister to crack, when he was just 13 years old and she was only 18." As they are driving on the highway Rafee'al continues to tell Kitpatrick "how she died at the hand of a deal gone bad, over at her dope dealing boyfriend's house, where they both were found shot." They never found the trigger man who robbed and killed them, but Rafee'al is still secretly trying to solve his sister's case with the 'help, of some of the guys and gals in his department. Ironically that is what drew Rafee'al into law enforcement.

At first he started out as a Highway Patrol Officer which he found very rewarding. Then an opportunity came up for him to become an undercover agent do to his background in Criminal Justice and work history passing some tests. Once an opening came up for the job he took the undercover position with no hesitations. And this dope case with Bubba and Steeli'o has been ongoing for 3 years now and now he has finally gotten in with one of the top street seller's 'which is; Bubba.

Lenny who is also another one of Rafee'al's and Kitpatrick's detective friends, decided after this big move in the case that they all would go and have a drink at a local bar that night to celebrate after they get back and shared their progress in the case with the Chief. The guys always met down at this particular bar where an old Navy Seal; friend of theirs owned the place. 'To say; he was a bad ass; was an understatement! 'He was (skits)! He has every medal you could receive, in his field of expertise. He even got a Medal of Honor from the President himself one year when Obama invited him to the white house. His name is; Zeek! Zeek is a solid; built, kind of man, who has a 'bold head, by 'choice, because he likes to shave his head, with his machete.

As a Native Indian, living in the states all his life, when he bought the place he made it so he could live upstairs at the very place he worked at and owned which is called "The Tark"! So after work that night when the guys walk through the door Zeek was glad to see the guys because it's always a good time, filled with laughs, drinks and sh*t talking. Rafee'al sitting at the bar throws his first drink back blurting out "now, it's just a matter of tying everything up in a bow, with this Tahoe trip coming up!" They are all in agreement with him and then Zeek pumps them up further saying "you guys got this!" Then he pulls his 6 ½ inch, Buck Nighthawk Blade out and sways it around saying "I wish, I was still out there in the field!" I would be 'slaying; evil, left and right!" They nod their heads siding with him, while drinking there drinks; rooting him on as he's doing a martial arts routine with his blade in hand. Rafee'al tells the guys "he's getting anxious as he's counting down the 'days for the trip, because a lot is riding on 'him, "really" fitting in with these guys." Zeek says "you being anxious, is just the blood running through your veins because you're getting closer to thy enemy!" They agree and talk more about the case with Zeek, and then he puts his blade away and goes to get the guys some 'beer food, from the back kitchen. While Zeek is in the back getting food Lenny offers his opinion saying "Zeek is right!" "We are getting down to the 'knitty- gritty, in this case, and everything will change once it's over!" Kitpatrick says "I wonder what we'll be assigned to do next?" The guys ramble on talking about this and that, but in Rafee'al's mind he couldn't help but have a heavy heart when thoughts of 'not, being able to see Candis anymore once this case comes to a close; is what entered his mind. He didn't even know 'why, he was even thinking on it, because he knew this was going to be the end result.

Kitpatrick watching Rafee'al day-dreaming in his glass; cracks a joke saying "well, man, this might be your last chance to hit that!" before we half to close this case! Lenny laughs saying "hell--, this has to be a record for you Rafee'al!" "I don't think you've 'ever, waited this long for sex with a woman!" "You might just be losing your touch; my boy!" laughed Lenny. Rafee'al chuckles saying "that's funny!" Lenny still laughing orders another round of shots for the men when he sees the waitress coming to clear the empty glasses off another table. With a grin Rafee'al comments back on Lenny's allegations, and calmly states "it's not always about having 'sex, 'fellows, because this woman, is truly into me!" "And she's the one who wants to 'wait, and I believe; it's because she really does; like a brother!"

"Man; please!" Get out of here with that!" laughs Kit. "Maybe it's because she doesn't trust you!" blurts Kitpatrick. Lenny adds "well... you could have a point." Or--; maybe she's taking her time with him, like he said" voiced Lenny. Rafee'al smiles "yep, that's what she's doing!" she's taking her time!" because she 'knows, I'm worth it!" Rafee'al still laughing with a big grin on his face, looks right at Kitpatrick and pops his collar boasting "it ain't 'easy!" being 'Ma'ha'vezy!" They all laugh and get up from the table to go over and play a few games of air hockey.

While taking turns on the tables Zeek comes over and starts telling them one of his "many" highly dangerous; opts stories as he places some food down for the guys to snack on. He goes into details; play by play about what went down, on a mission he had gone on way back in the day, explaining "how he was lucky he even survived!" and made it back alive! The guys listened enthusiastically as he painted a picture in their minds as the story began to unveil. With wide eyes and big smiles the men chopped it up for a while exchanging war and cop stories and then when it got late, they decided to call it a night.

As they started heading out the door Candis gives Mahavez a text and they all laugh out loud some more chuckling voicing "well, lookie here!" "We sure talked her up!" Rafee'al pops his collar once again beaming "I told you!" "She's into me; dude!" "Whatever!" blares Lenny! "I've got someone into me too!" "My wife!" "And I'm about to get into 'her, when I get home!" He laughs "see, guys, I'm the one with the "real; game" here!" said Lenny bobbing his head side to side like a bobble-head doll. He continues to say "the reason being; is because I got a woman to fall in love me; enough to marry me; who sticks it out with me 'year, after; year, no matter; what!"

Kitpatrick and Rafee'al could only 'wish to be so lucky in love, as they envisioned going home to their empty beds tonight. But they still give Lenny sh*t about it, calling him a 'whipped, one woman; wonder!" as he's walking away towards his car. 'Even though, they didn't want to agree with Lenny's wisdom, on love and staying committed to one person in a relationship. They still had to admit the benefits must be 'great, for those who 'do, stay commitment! Standing over by his car Rafee'al yells out "see you boys in the morning!" and they all get into their own cars and drive home. The next day is here and it is dump-in!" outside from the rain, and Naquawna is "not" happy!

Chapter 24

Like I was saying ‘the next day is here, and it is dump-in outside from the rain. Not only is the weather on ‘freakish; ‘blast!” mode! But so is the fumes that are ‘flying, out of the ‘top, of Naquawna’s head! All she can think about is all the bad things that were said to her yesterday by Mike’s mom! It is early in the morning, when she heads up to the hospital ‘armed, with a ‘tongue, sharp enough; to cut up; in an argument! And on her left finger she’s wearing a fake engagement ring.

Once she gets up to the hospital, she sneaks up to Mike’s room, with a bouquet of flowers in hand, to cover up her face from the nurses on duty. The coast is clear when she walks past the front desk because they are talking amongst themselves. Closing her eyes she takes a deep breath and then she opens the door to sneak into his room. Her spirit, ‘jumps, with delight when she sees that his mother isn’t there. So with a sigh she puts the flowers down on the side table by the sink and opens the curtains to let God’s light into the room.

Looking over at Mike she smiles and starts to talk to him as if he’s just lying there sleeping or taking a nap. Touching his face she tells him about “how she needs him to wake up, so he can come with her to Tahoe ‘and how, it just wouldn’t be the same without him there.” While holding his hand she kisses him on his lips saying “I am so glad you’re okay.” When she leans down to hug him she whispers in his ear “you are going to be just fine, honey.” Then the room door creeks and slowly opens, and in walks Mike’s mom yelling “oh! “Hell--; to the no!” She puts her plastic cup of black coffee down on the nightstand and quickly shoves Naquawna out of the way, while she is standing there at Mike's bedside. Naquawna puts her hands up in the air like she's being 'arrested, indicating to his mother that she's not there to start any, trouble. And her body language was, of a person who wasn't even mad anymore.

Naquawna decided to play nice because she has this 'fake, engagement ring on, so she figures 'there is no way, his mother is going to ask her to leave; now! And she hopes she's right, because she even took off work today, just to see if he would come out of his coma, after hearing her voice. Naquawna trying to be the bigger person smiles at his mom saying "see..., look, this is the ring that Mike bought me" she said as she flashed her left hand for his mother to observe. Mrs. Ellis, still; not impressed; with her, or, her 'so called, "ring" shouts "you, and that 'brass; ass; ring need to leave before I call the security guard!" Naquawna tightens her eyes glares at his mother and with a shady; smile she returns "you must not know about me!" She gets closer to Mrs. Ellis and growls "and you "don't!" wanna keep; pissing me; off; either!" "Trust me!" stated Naquawna staring her down with her hand on her hip pointing her finger, saying "I am "not" leaving; this room; old lady!"

'Mrs. Ellis, staring her down; blinks 'hard, after hearing old lady; she shouts "and you must not know about me!" gloats, Mrs. Ellis with confidence, being that she use to be the 'Taekwondo; "Queen!" back in the day. So she 'dares, Naquawna to step to her! So with confidence she walks over to where Naquawna is standing over on the other side of Mike's bed still talking mess, and when she steps to Naquawna looking her square in the face; irately; pointing she says "you might have my son; fooled!" "But I can see right through that 'fake; smile' and those 'fake; boobs' that you are 'nothing, but someone to play with!" like one of his instruments!" Trust, and believe!" I've raised him better! 'Naquawna, gets; pissed! I guess you could 'say, his mother 'struck; a 'nerve!" because Naquawna 'snaps, and bum rushes her and they both fall to the floor. With all the strong arm; roughness from the tug by Mrs. Ellis; Naquawna's arm gets tangled up in the heart monitoring cord and it becomes dislodged.

So when the buzzer goes off, the nurse on duty rushes into the room to see what's happening and then she sees the two women; squab-in on the floor! The nurse nervously hooks the heart monitor back onto Mike's chest and then runs to call Security. Mike starts to have very rapid eye movements during this time but his mother and Naquawna don't even notice because they are on the floor fighting. When his mom gets to her feet, she starts to bounce around like she's a 'prize fighter, in a rink. And as soon as she lifts her leg to get 'one good, round house kick to Naquawna's face, Mike wakes up yelling "stop...!" Naquawna with half her weave on the floor and his mother's shirt; torn down to her bare bra 'stopped; 'fighting; 'immediately!" and they both rush to his side pushing and shoving each other out of the way, to get to him first! His mother anxious says "I'm here son!" "Are you okay?" He sighs "where am I?" But before she could answer him, he gets a glazed look on his face like he doesn't really know who she is. Naquawna attempts next saying "you're in the Hospital!" "How do you feel?!" she said? He glances over at her asking "who are you?" She answers "it me; Mike!" Your," and she remembers his mother is in the room too, so she says "your Fiancés!" "Remember--?" she said looking at him to see if she could convince him, along with his mother. The Security guard comes running in room asking "is everything alright in here?"! Mrs. Ellis so happy that her son has woken up from his coma looks over at Naquawna and in a stern voice she replies "yes!" "We're fine!" 'Even though, she only said everything was "okay" because she didn't want to upset her son any further because he keeps going in and out of consciousness.

As the Security guard exits the room, in walks the Doctor saying "excuse me ladies, but I need to get a good look at him now!" said the Doctor as he looks at Mike's eyes, ears and throat with an Otoscope. Mike still not knowing what's really going on, 'or, who all the people are in the room says to the Doctor "what happen?" The Doctor answers "you've been in a car accident." "Do you remember any of it?" Mike shakes his head "no. And when his mom approaches him while the Doctor is still standing there she says "hi son." "It's me." "Your mother." "Do you recognize me?" He looks at her really hard trying to jog his memory but ends up saying "no," to her, as he faintly slips back into a deep sleep.

His mom starts to cry; hard asking "why?" can't he remember me?" I'm his mother for goodness sakes!" The Doctor reassures her that this is normal and that he should make a full recovery. Doctor Weber wants Mike to be left alone now to rest because he 'knows, all about the fighting, the name calling, and all that stuff that has been going on between Naquawna and his mother. So he escorts the ladies out into the hallway saying "you two can come back in the morning, but for 'now, Mike needs total peace and quiet!" Naquawna and Mike's mom nod in compliance with what the Doctor is saying, and agree to leave the Hospital.

When they leave out the hospital Naquawna goes over to Candis's place and hangs out with her, telling her all about what had happened at the hospital today. As for Mike's mom she goes over to his place and cleans up around his apartment, so when he gets released from the hospital he can rest peacefully in a clean environment. It was a hard few days not seeing Mike, so now it's time for Naquawna to go back up to the Hospital to see how he's doing before she leaves to go on the Tahoe trip that she has already committed too. When she gets to his room 'this time, she is very polite with his mother because she's going to be gone for a few days and doesn't want to seem like a "terrible" fiancé to his mom. So what she tells her is "that she has a hair show out of town, but she will cancel it, if his mother thinks that she should." His mom not 'caring, whether she stays or 'not, says "no, you go on ahead and go." "Don't miss your hair show because I'm sure 'Mike, wouldn't want you to do that." "Plus, I'm here so he won't be by himself." Naquawna smiles saying "okay, if you're sure?" His mother is watching her when she kisses Mike on the lips while he's sleeping, and with a sad look on Naquawna's face she slowly walks backwards out of the room looking at Mike saying "I'll hurry back though sweety." Naquawna with her bags already packed and in the car hurries back home to meet Candis because she's picking her up there.

Naquawna hated to have to leave Mike when he "really" needed her the most! But she had her other "wingman; Rayshawn!" who was needing her as; well! 'Perhaps, if Mike's mother wasn't here to watch over 'him, she "might" have a change of plans! 'But then again, just thinking about all the "fun" she could have 'rolling around, in the bed with 'Rayshawn, makes her; feel; feenish! And that's why she just "can't" pass up thy opportunity 'even; if 'Mike, was or his death bed!

Chapter 25

Beep… beep… goes the horn when Candis; pulls up to Naquawna's house with Rafee'al already in the RV. Sauntering; out her front door with a slight; skip, Naquawna comes out to the vehicle dressed like she's going to the club with high heel boots on, and a mini skirt. Candis smirks her way; saying "I hope you know it is going to be snowing; up in Tahoe?!" "I know," retorts Naquawna, adding "I brought some snow gear with me too; you know?" Plus, it's not like it's going to be snowing in the RV; right?!" Candis looks at her like; unbelievable! Then she looks at Rafee'al like "please, excuse my 'ignorant ass, friend!" At this point Rafee'al and Candis have gotten to know each other's 'mindful; thoughts, without even speaking. You could say they were already finishing each other's sentences.

Naquawna climbed aboard with her luggage, which Rafee'al helped her with, and then she made herself a drink, to 'start off, this road; trip! The three, slowly turn that big rig around and head to the Library to pick up Roxy, Steeli'o, Sherry and Bruce. It just made more since for the rest of the group to meet up at one spot, so they could all get on the road faster. Everybody climbed aboard saying "hi, and hello?" While looking to see who is driving and then they got on the road.

Rayshawn and Bubba 'were; "supposed" to ride up in the RV too, but decided at the last minute it would be best for them to drive up in a rental car, because they had a few business stops to make along the way. Naquawna 'of course, was butt hurt about it, when he called her at the last minute saying "he wasn't going to be in the RV with them. She even asked him "why?" she couldn't ride with him and Bubba? So after arguing about it with her for a few minutes, 'he assured her, he'd be there by the time she pulled up to the Cabin." Naquawna hangs up the phone all sad, so Candis gets Rafee'al to drive the RV for a while so she could have a drink with her friend. They all discussed a plan before they took 'off, that the guys will take turns driving up to Tahoe and the ladies would take turns driving back from Tahoe.

Everybody was having so much fun cracking jokes, drinking, laughing and playing cards. Naquawna even got her mind off of Rayshawn not being there because she ended up having so much fun as well. After a while, she even started wishing Mike would have come instead of Rayshawn. Stating to Candis "that at least, he would have been in the RV with me!" She continues to say "but I guess I should be happy because 'at least, he's coming!" "I mean hell, I'm just glad he could get away for once!" she ended. Bruce and Sherry were looking and listening to all of Naquawna's complaints. And Sherry with a snobby look on her face would look Naquawna up and down from time to time without her seeing her, while shaking her head at the clothes she was wearing. So many things were going on around them on their road trip, inside their RV, and, outside on the road as they were driving.

One instance was they almost witnessed a five car, pile up accident is the fast lane traveling alongside of them. Then a guy broken down on the side of the road who was putting gas in his car got a little; too close to the slow lane and his arm just about got clipped by the RV's, outside mirror. And Rafee'al who was driving at the time 'swerved, just in the nick of time to avoid the man. Naquawna screeched because she almost toppled over in her heel when the RV shifted to the left. After all of that had happened everyone was conversating on the crazy events that were; popping up like some weird movie, they felt like they were in.

Bruce and Sherry sat back at the RV table observing everyone and laughed at how many dumb things kept coming out of Naquawna's mouth. The two, Sherry and Bruce are such a 'cute, care bear like couple. 'So Bruce, being thy outgoing fun kind of guy that 'he is, says "he wants to teach everyone a game called; spoons!" "It's kind of like musical chairs except you put spoons on the table and pass cards around clockwise." "And whoever gets four of a kind in cards first, needs to grab a spoon." "And the one left without a spoon loses that hand and get an (S) under their name." "So the first person to spell out SPOONS loses the game" said Bruce.

They all get excited about this new game and want to play. The game starts and when they start playing it; it goes slow at first because every ones trying to get the concept of the game. 'Then, once it started to kick in; on how to play; it! It got--; crazy! People were diving on the floor, trying to get a spoon. Even falling off their seats to get one. 'At one point, Bruce and Steeli'o were even going to 'fight, over who had the same spoon; first! "Boy, this game is fun!" shouted Naquawna. But as the game went on, she started complaining because she started losing. She tried and tried to win, with all her might, but when the game ended, Naquawna was the looser so she didn't want to play anymore. In a drunken tantrum she went on to claim "it was because everyone was playing against me!" And that's when the game changed to something more 'calming, like spades. They figured with all the movement of the RV and the craziness going on with the first game, it might be best to wait until they get to Tahoe to play dominoes. Steeli'o and Roxy were having a good time playing spades too, even though' Steeli'o was tired as a dog from flying back from Cuba yesterday, just to make this trip with Roxy and her friends.

Roxy rubs the side of his head smiling; sympathetically at him because she knows that he's tired but she can't help but notice 'how hot as 'hell, he looks' with his hair all slicked back sitting there with his snow gear on. 'Roxy, on the other hand wasn't tired because she slept through most of her flight back from Vegas because 'she knew, that these; girls were going to want to party; 'hard, up in Tahoe! Bruce decides to take over the wheel the rest of the way to Tahoe; giving Rafee'al a break.

So when they get back on the road after switching places, Rafee'al gets handed a cup of the 'bubbly, and joins the partying. The RV is so roomy that they even start dancing smack dab in the middle of the kitchen/dining area of the RV. Candis and Rafee'al get a little wild and crazy too, laughing and hugging all over each other while trying to do that 'Juju on that beat; dance, in a moving vehicle. Then Candis pulls Naquawna and Roxy up out there seats too, so they will get up and dance with them as well.

As Roxy shakes her hips in Steeli'o's direction, with her index finger she tells him "to come and; get it!" 'Meaning, her! Sherry wanted to dance to but Bruce begged her to stay up front with him to keep him company while he drives; so she did. The RV is 'rockin; now, like a real party is going on. And they are all really having a good time together. Friendships are being bonded, and memories are being made while Rafee'al is getting closer to Steeli'o and the crew. Even Rafee'al is surprised how laxed he really is with this group of friends. And the cool part about it is, that everyone seems to be warming up to Steeli'o and Rafee'al 'being, that they are the new comers to the group.

Who knew?" that; this would be the beginning of a great road trip? When they finally get to the cabin it is still light outside and the snow is starting to fall once again from the sky. They pull up to the cabin with a hardy; cheer of "yeah''''!" "We finally made it''''!" Naquawna gets out of the

RV first running up to the cabin door in her high heel boots, and almost slips and falls on her butt. She opens the front door; shivering, but once she gets inside she hurries to turn on the heater so she can get the place warmed up and get changed into her pants. 'Why--?" she didn't get changed in the R.V bathroom first?" Is puzzling to many! Especially to Sherry, who held back from saying anything else; mean about her. 'Instead, she just heads into the Cabin with Bruce, stating to him "that even the "dumbest; Broad" isn't as dumb as Naquawna!" Bruce chuckles under his breath and carries their bags inside, not saying too much on the subject because he didn't want to get Sherry started. When everyone finally gets into the cabin they see that it is looking more; beautiful then the pictures they seen online. The floors are a deep mahogany wood throughout the place, and even the kitchen cabinets had been switched out to frosted glass.

The living room was still huge with an extra-large sofa that wrapped from wall to wall, and the fireplace is about as big as the 60 inch plasma TV on the wall. The kitchen, has brand new pots and pans in it, and when they go out back to see the yard the fireplace is on the outside as well with a pizza oven on the side. There is also a pool in the backyard with a hot tub that flows next to it, which fits about 10 people. The heated pool is in the center of the yard with a diving board and rock stones all around it for a river; waterfall design; type look. In addition the owners of the property also added a nice covered gas grill that was all nestled in a brick like casing to protect it from harsh winters.

All you could hear is "ooh's...," and awe's...!" when they looked around at all the nicely upgraded amenities in the cabin. Even Candis commented on it saying "how it wasn't 'this nice, when we came up here two years ago" she said to Rafee'al. Sherry agreeing said "that's for sure!" Sherry continued saying "so now, who's sleeping where?" asked Sherry. Candis and Rafee'al get first pick of their room, since she booked; the place. So Candis picks the master bedroom which has a sliding door and stairs that lead down from a grand balcony to the pool and hot tub from their room.

Sherry, Naquawna, and Roxy roll the dice for the other room that looks just like Candis's but is on the opposite end of the Cabin, but still looks out; over the backyard where the pool and hot tub is. "Can we get a drum roll please!" jokes Rafee'al as the dice are being rolled. Sherry rolled a 3, Naquawna rolled a 5, and Roxy rolled a 6. "And the winner is...?" "Roxy"! Sherry and Naquawna are disappointed but went on ahead and took their bags to their standard sized rooms with no balcony or sliding doors.

While everyone's doing their own thing, getting settle in' they hear a ding... dong... at the door. Bruce is downstairs so he goes to open the door and sees that it is Rayshawn and Bubba Dank. Naquawna runs down the stairs 'drunk, and jumps up on Rayshawn and wraps her legs around him because she's 'so happy, he really came. He grins "dang; girl!" "You trying to break a brother's back!" She laughs out loud "baby; stop!" "You know I'm not 'that, heavy!" she chuckled. He puts his stuff down by the door entrance and he and Bubba take a look around the place. Rayshawn, all excited about the cabin is about to take his stuff up to his and Naquawna's room, when down the stairs comes Steeli'o to greet him and Bubba with a big home-boy "you made it!" like, hug.

The guys are talking in code about all the business they will be doing later on tonight. And as Steeli'o is standing there talking to the guys here comes Roxy skipping down the stairs in her winter boots, jeans, and a low cut warm fitted red fuzzy shirt, feeling as 'cute, as she looked. She is so--, happy and hasn't got a care in the world. 'Until; bam! Rayshawn and her lock eyes and she miscalculates the last step and stumbles. Steeli'o turns to try and catch her fall and when he grabs her she is inches from hitting her knees on the hard floor.

He pulls her up by her hands asking "you alright bay'be?" "I'm good" she says shaking. Once he sees she's okay he then turns towards Bubba and Rayshawn saying "this is my lady guys; Roxy!" Bubba with a cool smile says "what up?" But Rayshawn, can't even look her back in her eyes. He rubs his nose with his hand, and moves it down to his mouth and further down to his chin and then he slowly manages to get out the words "what's, happen?" His hand ends up under his chin and on to his neck, where he grabs his necklace and turns his attention to Naquawna while picking up his luggage he asked "so where are we laying our heads at?" Naquawna all happy grabs him by the arm and escorts him up to their room. Steeli'o states "okay guys, will talk later about that; thing...! 'Meaning, the drug pick up.

Roxy's hands are still shaking because she can't believe 'out of all the 'guys, at the strip club; that she could run 'into, this one; guy 'here, ends up being one of Steeli'o's best-friends! Steeli'o sees her quivering a little and puts his arm around her asking "you sure you're alright?" thinking it's all because she almost, bit it!" at the bottom of the stairs. She plays it off; even more by saying "yeah, I'm fine." "It's these damn boots, they are so slippery" she said as she lifted up her foot to look at the bottom soles.

Roxy is on the borderline, of going into shock!" And--, she can't even tell Candis about this because as cool as she and Candis are with each other, Naquawna would still find out, because it would be just too hard for her to keep that kind of a secret from her best-friend. After Roxy's "convincing; act" on Steeli'o believing her nerves were shot because she tripped, she then headed to the kitchen to get a 'strong; 'drink; 'made; "strictly" for an actress! Because she 'knows, she will "really" be playing the role for these next few days. And as for Mr. Rayshawn, B.K.A "Rappin Ray" to Roxy. He is just as shocked as she is to find out that not only is she his boy's; girl! But, that she's also a stripper in one of the hottest clubs in Vegas. And Rayshawn's guess is 'that; Steeli'o has 'no; 'clue; about it! Steeli'o takes a seat on the couch saying to Bubba "are you sleeping on the sofa bed?" because you know?" we're all out of room's man" he laughs. Bubba returns "well, that's cool." "Or--, maybe I can sleep in the RV?" Candis over hearing him 'laughs, answering "no you're not sleeping in the RV" she said as she, Roxy and Rafee'al are coming from the kitchen with their drinks in hand. Bubba laughing says "awh..., come on now!" "Give a brother a break! Candis grinning replies "I'm just kidding!" Me casa es you casa" she said putting her face down slightly praying that he doesn't recognize her.

Then Bubba notices Rafee'al and he stand to his feet and extends his hand towards Rafee'al voicing "my man"! "My man"! "What up player?!" said Bubba. He adds "I didn't 'know, you knew the homie's?!" 'Candis, being her 'first time, meeting Bubba in the light, since the first time she "really" met Bubba "officially" was when she was standing in Jake's room under that awkward black light, says to them both, "you two know each other?" Bubba answers "yeah--, you could say that?" "We did some business a while back" he grins. 'Rafee'al, not wanting to really 'elaborate, any more than that, said "yep, me and Bubba's cool!" Rafee'al switches the conversation quickly asking "so what are we all planning on eating tonight?!" "I'm starving!" he said, taking his beer to the face; guzzling it. 'Even though, Candis lets the "we did some; "business" a while 'back, role off her back. In the back of her mind she couldn't help but wonder what kind of "business" would they; possibly be doing together?" because Candis knows for a "fact" that Bubba is a dope dealer!

'So now, she's wondering; is Rafee'al selling drugs now, too?" 'Or, even 'worse, is he doing drugs; secretly?" Candis trips for a second because she still doesn't really know a "whole; lot" about Rafee'al! 'Plus, she "still" hasn't even been to his house; once! After a few minutes of those thoughts, she moved on in her mind, so she doesn't let it ruin her fun. Instead she says "let's go out to the RV and bring in the food we brought up with us, that is out there in the refrigerator." Roxy concurs saying "and don't forget about the meat, that's in the cooler guys; please." The men answer "alright" as they go out to the RV to carry all the heavy stuff back into the cabin. As the guys are getting the food from outside, Candis takes a gulp of her drink and whispers to Roxy how she seen Bubba that night at Jakes party but he doesn't remember her. Candis smiles saying "thank God"! 'Roxy, hel'la surprised to hear that, looks at Candis like "oh; snap!" Commenting to Candis "are you kidding; me?!" But Roxy "doesn't; dare" convey to Candis how she met Rayshawn on her job down in Vegas. Instead she just listens to Candis saying "how she plans on keeping her distances from Bubba by trying not to get caught standing under any black lights that might jar his memory of her." Steeli'o, Rafee'al and Bubba come back into the Cabin laughing and cracking jokes. Roxy and Candis start putting the food in the refrigerator and then Sherry and Bruce come down to help get some food going. The guys of course want to barbeque, so the ladies get the meat seasoned and the men go out back and get the grill going.

The snow has stopped falling and the sky is a clear blue. Candis looking around while they are all in the kitchen asked "where's Naquawna and Rayshawn?" She adds "they need to get their butts down here and help us with the cooking!" "Or they ain't eatin!" she said laughing. Candis then goes over to the staircase and yells for 'Naquawna and Rayshawn to get down here and help!" She gets no reply but ends up hearing Naquawna; faintly 'moaning, from where she stood at the bottom of the stairs. Candis listened for a second and then went back into the kitchen laughing saying "Naquawna's gonna be a minute!" Sherry replied "let me guess?!" "That hoe, is upstairs screwing; already?"! Candis just shakes her head 'with her hands up; like 'you ain't heard it from me!

Roxy chuckling says "let that girl have some fun!" Then she looks at Candis voicing "we're the ones who are gonna be in trouble tonight, because we will be sleeping in the same room with; our guys!" Sherry laughs "oh; please!" Yaw'll still on that, kick?!" Candis blurts out "shush...!" "They're gonna here you." And then in comes the guys into the kitchen to get the seasoned up tri-tip and skirt steak to put on the grill. As Bubba and the boys hang outside, the ladies get the potatoes boiling, so they can make a big bowl of potato salad. Sherry slices and dices the veggies for the salad and Candis marinates the chicken in teriyaki sauce, onions and garlic for tomorrow's lunch.

Roxy has a sweet tooth, so she makes a batch of 'double, chocolate, pistachio, cookie dough, to bake for later. 'For sure, they will all be hitting up the buffets, while they are at the Casino's, but these girls like to cook and eat home cooked meals and so do their men. 'Plus, they can save money doing it this way and party harder in the clubs, buying drinks and gambling in the Casino's with the money they save on "not" eating out as much. When the girls are done prepping the food, in comes Naquawna with a silly smirk on her face asking "was someone calling me?"! Candis looks her way chuckling "heffa!" go on wit, that!" "You know we were calling 'yo; ass!" laughs Candis. Rayshawn comes down the stairs next, smiling playing it off as usual grabbing a beer from the frig he says "smells good in here ladies!" He pops his beer open and heads out the back where the rest of the guys are drinking and chopping it up, about how great they're favorite teams are playing this year. "Go Niner's!" yells Rayshawn as he walks outside towards the grill; chugging on his beer. The guys joke around asking him "where have you been?" Knowing 'already, by the look on his face what he's been doing. Rayshawn chuckles answering "my girl wanted a piece of me!" "A big piece!" he said laughing while lifting up his beer. Rafee'al laughing the loudest; spouted "you are a 'fool, for that; dude!" Bubba laughs too, and Steeli'o shakes his head voicing "yeah... my lady better want a piece of 'me, tonight; too!" He continues joking "or, I'm gonna have to, keck her ass; to thy curb!" They all laugh in agreement then Steeli'o ends with "this waiting shit; sucks bro!"

Rafee'al takes the rest of his beer to the head and tosses the bottle in the recycling bin to the left of them but says nothing about his and Candis's relationship. But, Rayshawn doesn't let him off that 'easy, he cracks on him saying "and I 'know, you ain't hitting that; player!" cause Candis ain't; having it!" They all laugh even harder and then the girls walk up and 'Candis, who heard her name asked "not having what?"! Rayshawn plays it off for Rafee'al by saying "not, having anybody sleep in the RV!" he said looking at Bubba. Bubba frowns, saying "that ain't what was said!" Don't mess up my sleeping arrangements; man!"

Rayshawn looks at him like 'shut up; fool! But the girls pay it no mind and walk over to the hot tub; chuckling. Candis over by the hot tub glances at Rafee'al when telling her girls "let's get wet!" Rafee'al almost choked on his beer after hearing Candis say that while looking in his direction. She turns the bubbles up on the hot tub and the ladies go upstairs to get their bathing suits on. The guys stand around talking secretly about 'business, pretty much in street code. 'Well--, that is, Bubba, Steeli'o and Rayshawn are talking.

And as for Bruce they know he won't pick up on it because he's not into their life style. He's more interested in book like things and technology. So to them he's more of a square, and a smart square, is not a bad thing. Because that's what Sherry loves about him the most, is his beautiful mind, he can remember numbers and things that other people can't. 'Rafee'al, on the other hand has 'both; worlds, working in his favor because he's up on game when it comes to street life, and street slang. And he too is very book smart when it comes to remembering certain codes and laws and things 'that many, aren't privy to; decipher.

Whereas Bruce has never really even seen as much as a piece of rocked up; cocaine. And Rayshawn and the rest of the guys know this because Bruce keeps asking in between their conversation "what are yaw'll talking about?"! Then from time to time as the men speak on what they will be doing at around 10:00 pm tonight he asked them "where are you guys going to be going?" Rafee'al is acting drunker than he 'really is, so he can filter in the things he wants to retain, that they are talking about. So while the men are all standing around the grill laughing and talking, the girls come running down the stairs with their swimsuits on. Roxy goes first into the hot tub, then Candis and Naquawna slides in third "literally" and bumps her knee on the hot tubs edge because she was trying to be the first one in. 'And then poor-- Sherry she gave up halfway down the stairs on winning the race 'figuring, she'll just get Bruce to pay for the first round of drinks since she's the one who came in last.

While they were upstairs the girls made a bet that the first one to get changed and down to the hot tub wouldn't have to buy a round of drinks when they get to the club tonight. 'And well--, Sherry lost! So while the girls are chilling in the hot tub, the guys are making their own 'silly little side; bet, to see who will take their clothes off and jump into the 'cold pool, in their boxers. Everyone egged Bubba on wanting him to go first, since he was the biggest. They joke around saying "you got the most blubber, Bubba!" Then someone yells "we'll give you a $100.00 dollars if you jump right now!" Bubba laughs out "hell--; no!" I'm not freezing my balls; off!" "Are you crazy?!" "You do it first Steeli'o!" yelled Bubba. "You're the warm blooded one!" Implying because he's Italian.

The girls laughing; yell out "why don't you 'all, jump in?"! Then the girls start to count; one, two, three and the guys all start trying to push one another into the pool. They run around like crazy frat boys for a minute and then they all target Bubba. Being that Bubba's a big boy, with a cute baby face, they figure it's probably going to take all of them to push him into the pool because he's so stocky, and he's about 6'0 feet in height. He's quick, but he can't out run, all of them at once. 'So Rayshawn, who is not only showing off for 'Naquawna, starts to show out in front of Roxy as well and ends up catching Bubba off guard and pushes him 'sideways, into the pool.

Everybody dies laughing 'except; Bubba, he is cussing all the way down as he falls into the pool! The girl's gasps while laughing; 'hoping, he can swim. When Bubba gets out the pool mad and going strait; off!" Rayshawn yells out "awe..., man!" stop crying!" "We're all just having a little fun!" he said as he pulled out a wad of money for the girls to see, when he gives Bubba his hundred dollar bill; smiling he voices "here man!" "Stop bitchin!" Rayshawn takes a quick glance at Roxy, while Candis and Naquawna are talking, and Roxy takes a quick glance back at him and then; splash! Rayshawn gets caught; slippin and Steeli'o ends up pushing 'him, in the pool. Rayshawn could only laugh at this point yelling "damn...! "You got me!

Bubba laughs out "that's what yo' ass; gets!" "Now--, who's bitchin?"! 'Bruce, laughing the loudest is backing up from the pool area shouting "hey, now, don't push me in guys, because I'm not a good swimmer!" Sherry vouching for him voices "that's; real!" So 'don't; even, push my man in the pool!" because he cannot swim!" And if you do, it will be considered 'a homicide!" They all crack up laughing and laugh get even louder as Rayshawn's getting out of the pool, because he's bagging on Bruce about 'not, being able to swim! Rayshawn cracks on Bubba saying "he doesn't need, to know how to swim, because his fat ass will probably; float!" Steeli'o not wanting to get pushed into the pool is now laughing his way over to where the girls are in the hot tub. And as Rayshawn is getting himself all dried off with the help of Naquawna he hollers over at Steeli'o saying "oh..., I'm ma get you dawg!" "When you least expect it!" Steeli'o just laughs returning "you should have seen your face, man!" "And I only did it, he said laughing, after I seen you put your phone down on thy table." Rayshawn grunts "yeah, luckily!" because I would have lost all my contacts."

Rayshawn and Bubba go inside to get some dry clothes on, and Steeli'o and Bruce go add some more meat to the grill. Bruce takes the cooked meat off the grill and puts it on the dining table after he and Rafee'al sample; a piece. "It smells so good!" says Sherry. "Nothing like barbequing in the winter time!" she adds. Out by the hot tub Sherry who hardly ever drinks says "I am so 'toasted, right now!" The girls lift their drinks shouting "wooh...! "Whooo...! "Party, over, here...! Then, Sherry feeling 'bolder, than usual starts in on Naquawna asking her "so--, Naquawna, you know everybody could hear you screwing Rayshawn upstairs earlier, right?" "You on the pill?" Naquawna answers "what?!" "Who's; everybody?!" "And what does 'me, being on the pill or "not" have to do with anything?!"

Sherry answers "well Candis said she could hear you guys from the bottom of the stairs!" Candis; tissed her tongue up against the roof of her mouth as if to say "damn! "Snitch! Naquawna with a long face retorts "if you must know?"! "No! "I'm not on the pill!" Sherry asks "why...?" "You trying to get pregnant by Rayshawn?" Naquawna says "naw...!" and are you on the pill?" Sherry answers "nope...! Naquawna replies "why not?" "Are you... trying to get in pregnaded, by Bruce?" Sherry smirks saying "you don't half to get an attitude!" "We are just talking 'girl, stuff!" Sherry continue to say with a frown on her face "I tried the pill, long-time ago but I had to get off that sh*t!" because I was tired of convincing my breast!" and my uterus that I was pregnant for five years strait!" "While still; drinking, and partying and "not" producing a child after 9 months!" "Or..., releasing the breast milk or colostrum from my titties!" But the kicker was, when my sister said to me "do you really think you're not going to have consequences for tricking your body like that?"! Candis blurts "awe..., sh*t!" You know how Keyera is?!" She is all about the "natural; stuff!" Sherry laughs out "yes, she is!" Sherry adds Keyera has always said "there is two things she "does; not" want to piss; off!" And that would be, her "uterus"! And the "IRS"! The girls bust up laughing and then Roxy says "well, I remember my mom had really bad periods, so they made her take the pill." "Yeah... that may help for severe cases I've heard" said Candis. "But let Sherry's sister tell; it!" all you need" says Candis and Sherry at the same time "is some red raspberry tea, and some cinnamon sticks!" Sherry just shakes her head laughing about her sister stating "you, got-dah love her!" She wants to save the 'world, one uterus at a time!"

They all crack up laughing about all of Keyera's 'special remedies, and then the guys yell out from the kitchen "come and get it; ladies!" Sherry laughs "come get what?"! Implying that she's hungry for more than just "food" now, as she smiles at the girls with a wink. Roxy gives her a high five because she was thinking the same thing about her man. In the cabin the men had all the meat 'and the food, all spread out on the dining room table and the ladies couldn't; believe it! Sherry mumbles to the girls as they are walking up towards the table "these boys are really trying to knock some 'boot, up in here tonight!" The girls snicker holding back a full laugh saying to the guys "awh..., this is so... nice!"

The ladies than kiss and hug their men and make their plates. As everyone is gathered in the dining room eating and sitting on towels because the girls are still in there bathing suits, the guys talk about going to the casino to gamble afterwards. The ladies comment on 'how they want to go to the club which is in the casino that the guys want to gamble in, so they all agree and plan on doing; just that. Looking across the table, it is so-o-o...

uncomfortable for Roxy as she sits on Steeli'o's lap on a towel in her sexy yellow swimwear. It wouldn't bother her so much 'if, Rayshawn wasn't watching her every 'move, like she's still at the strip club, with his hands all over her. Naquawna, is sitting across from Bubba, who is telling everyone how great she is at doing hair. And he flat out flirts with Naquawna right in front of Rayshawn. But Rayshawn doesn't even bat an eye, as if to let everybody know he ain't sweat-in; nare-bitch!" because that's just how confident he is, in his game, with his women. Rayshawn just sits back and listens to all the conversations going on while he's eating on his barbeque.

Roxy glances at him as he eats but tries not to let him see her staring. She's slowly finding herself 'having; somewhat, of an attraction to him, that won't go away as time goes on. Then Steeli'o kisses her out of her chain of thoughts saying to her "bay'be" in Italian, can you get me some more potato salad and steak?" Roxy smiles saying "sure, repeating his words back to him in Italian as she gets up and walks to the area where all the extra food is spread out in dishes. Rayshawn gets up to; to go get him some more meat and when Roxy turns to walk back to the table she bumps into Rayshawn in the kitchen. Startled she says "oops. "Sorry" she said glancing up at him as he looks down at her, with lust in his eyes he replies "that's alright" as his eyes move down towards her chest.

He doesn't even want to 'move, to let her pass bye 'like he wanted to say something else to her like "what's up with you?" But she can see Naquawna looking hard from the table. So Naquawna clears her throat saying "babe, I could have gotten you some more food." When he turns his attention to Naquawna, Roxy starts to squeezes by him, while he's still standing there explaining to Naquawna "that it's alright." Saying "I got it" he said, as he's licking the barbeque sauce from his fingers looking at Roxy's rear. Roxy gulps when she hustles passed him, fearing that he might try and touch her on her butt, or rub up against her as she passes him.

Rayshawn sits back down at the table with a grin on his face because he can feel that Roxy is digging 'him, just as much as he is digging her. After everyone gets full off their dinner they all head to their rooms to get showered and dressed to go out. "Everything is going as planned" says Rafee'al in a text to Kitpatrick. Rafee'al tells him how he believes the guys will be picking up something tonight from what he has gathered in their street slang. Kitpatrick replies "we are standing bye." Then as a joke Kitpatrick texted a picture of a girl's pair of panties, asking "I bet you're still waiting?!" aren't you...?" "Lol." Rafee'al laughed back texting "mind; yo; business...! "Lmao! When finished he deletes all the text messages just in case, Candis was to go through his phone, like most girls do, when guys are sleeping or not looking.

Candis comes out of the bathroom all dressed to kill, so he puts his phone in his back pocket and grabs her by the hand saying "you look so sexy in that dress!" He kisses her and they end up on the bed where he lazes on top of her, kissing all over her lips and behind her ear. He is really trying to get her to make love with him before they go out. And Candis is so turned on by Rafee'al and his sexy face and his body until she is practically coming out of her clothes. He slides his hand up her dress to pull off her panties and she lets him, just because she's tired of telling him no. She's not "really" going to do anything, and in her mind she just wants to play out a "fantasy" that she's; seen on TV. But the door gets knock on, its Naquawna yelling "come on!" "We're all ready to go; Miss. Thang...!" Rafee'al blows out a "tah; sound. Than says to Candis "I'm starting not to like your friend. He and Candis laugh as they get up off the bed and fix their clothes. Candis; grinning opens the door and through tight lips she whispers to Naquawna "cock blocker"! Naquawna smiles like "mmm-- did I interrupt something?" Hoping that Candis was finally getting some long overdue; pito! Candis takes a deep breath and smiles but says nothing else as she's applies her lipstick; keeping; Naquawna; guessing!

Bruce and Sherry were the last ones down the stairs because they were bickering a little bit about Bruce wanting to go with the guys to a strip club. So as the couples are walking out to the RV Naquawna says to Bruce and Sherry "why are you two mad--; now...?"! Bruce shouts "she doesn't want me to go to the strip club, with the guys!" Bruce continues to say "I thought we were up here to have some fun?"! Candis says "who's going to a strip club?"! And then she looks over at Rafee'al who then puts his hands up 'like, I ain't said; nothing! Roxy with a dead stare looks over at Candis like the 'cat, who swallowed the canary 'thinking, to herself "this sh*t ain't; funny!" because a strip club is being mentioned. Then Bubba finally owns up to it, saying "I'm the one who said that I wanted to check out some of strip clubs out here, to see if they're just as nice as the ones we went to out in Vegas!"

Naquawna yells "who, went to a strip club; in Vegas?"! She looks over at Rayshawn who answers "I don't know 'what, he's talking about!" Bubba; who is now smirking; stops talking about it all together, but ends with "whatever man!" "Ya'll can play dumb if yaw want; too!" but, I'm bringing home a honey tonight!" I know that; much!" He was talking to Rayshawn so Roxy was relieved to see that it wasn't "Rayshawn" who was trying to throw her under the bus by bringing up the strip club, so she felt a little bit more at ease; thinking she could trust him now with her "knotty" little secret. 'Plus, she can tell that Bubba doesn't even remember her because he was so far up one of her co-worker's skirts that night, to even notice anyone else in the club.

The R.V door closes and they finally get on the road to the Casino. Pulling up to the Casino in an R.V is so funny to them because they usually arrive in 'style, like in a town car or some kind of souped-up SUV. But---, the R.V is still on fleek, because they all fit together in one vehicle. And just in case they get too drunk to drive back to the Cabin, they can all post; up in the RV until someone sobers up enough to drive back. So when they get to the Casino and park, they all step out of the R.V looking 'tight, as they are all walking up towards the place. When the doors open; Cha-Ching!" sounds are ringing and chiming as they entered the Casino. And unfortunately, so is the 'smoke, which hits them as soon as they open up the doors. With a sniff and a cough everybody scattered to see who could find the best machines to payout. The couples stick together at first, gambling in the same vicinity of each other, and then after a while the guys decided to go handle some business.

'Well..., that is, Rayshawn, Steeli'o, and Bubba decided to get down to business! Steeli'o says to Bubba "what do you think about Rafee'al coming with us?" Bubba returns "Rafee'al's cool!" 'Plus, they know Bubba has done business with Rafee'al once before. Rayshawn adds "he might as well come with us, because Bruce and Sherry are pretty much doing their own thing anyway." He laughs adding "Sherry is pretty much putting Bruce on lock down to make "sure—" he doesn't sneak off and go to the strip club! They laugh out loud as they are watching Bruce, walk away pouting. And then, they tell Rafee'al "that he could come with them, and that they'll meet up with the lady's at the club by 12:00!"

Candis over hearing asked "where are you guys all going?" "To the poker room" answered Steeli'o. Candis; smirks "umm, I don't want to play poker" she said, kisses Rafee'al bye. Roxy says "she's not feeling it either" so she kisses her man too. Normally the guys would have the lady's come with them to the crap tables or the blackjack tables for luck. But this is more than just a poker game. 'This, is going to be; big business! Naquawna kisses Rayshawn as well, but before he walks away she turn and grabs his hand before he can leave and says to him "so let me get this straight!" "We are all hooking backup at midnight?" which will be, upstairs in the club, right?" The guys all say "yes, at the same time and then they part as the girls watch them walk away.

The ladies drop a few more coins into the slot; machines while walking from table to table. They also play a lot of blackjack, along with some slots, and linger around the crap tables to sip on free mixed drinks. Naquawna ends up winning a grip of money at the roulette table and refused to play it all back, so she says to Candis and Roxy "I wanna go check out some of the souvenir shop right now." The girls are cool with it so they end up going in to some of the nearby souvenir stores in the Casino to buy keepsakes to bring back home for friends and family.

Naquawna even snuck off while Candis and Roxy were at the register making a purchase so she could call the Hospital to check on Mike. When she calls, his mother answers his hospital room phone and she tells her "that she is still at the hair convention out in Atlanta." She goes on to say "how she won first place in thy "original; styles" category and is about to enter in the "who could braid hair the fastest?" contest next. His mom still doesn't like Naquawna but she puts up a 'front, for her son saying "that's nice!" Then she hands Mike the phone and Naquawna cheers out "hi baby!" "I miss you!" Naquawna is still playing the role because she knows his mother can still hear her through the phone. And poor 'Mike, still not really knowing either one of them says "hi, in a slow; groggy voice.

Naquawna says "I miss you, boo! "I'll be home soon!" "So you get plenty of rest; okay?" He repeats her words back to her like a parrot would, and then his mother takes the phone. Naquawna ends the call with "I love you! But she freezes as her mind flashes back to 'Rayshawn, who she "really; loves!" but, she makes her words sound as sincere as she possibly can 'knowing, that his mom is still listening in. She quickly hangs up as Candis is walking up towards her and while shaking her head laughing, Candis says "now you know you going; straight to hell!" Naquawna chuckling hits Candis in the arm blurting "I do, love mike!" "But---, just not, like I love, Rayshawn!"

Roxy walking up hearing Naquawna's confession says "oooooh...!" "Naquawna's; in love...!" "What do you love-- so much about Rayshawn?" asked Roxy? Even Roxy couldn't believe she just asked that question. Candis blurts out "Oh!" "God!" "Don't get her started!" Naquawna looks at Roxy and ignores Candis's comment voicing "thanks for asking Roxy!" "Well, first of all, I love his eyes." and second of all I love his smile" she says with a sophisticated smirk on her face. "And thirdly; I love his body." "Fourth--, let me see" she says looking up towards the sky. "Oh, yeah--, and-- I love the way he looks at me when he's sticking his big--!" "Oh! "Come...! "On...!" yells Candis laughing. Candis retorts "I told you she's a Horney frog!" Roxy laughs saying "Isn't it called a Horney toad?"! Candis blurts out "Whatevah!"

while still laughing.

Roxy cracks “well... at least she knows what she loves about him; you can’t ‘knock, her for that!” Naquawna laughing a drunken laugh about her last remarks says “I’m... just joking; around!” “I love him for more reason than that!” Candis groans “um... hum!” sure, you do!” said Candis followed by “okay...!” “Enough already about him!” says Candis as she pulls the girls by the arm cheering; “speaking of nice bodies!” “Let’s go in here” she says pointing at this sex-toy; shop in front of them. Candis smiles looking at the window display saying “I wouldn’t mind getting some of those black handcuffs for Rafee’al.” They then chuckle running pass these little old ladies who are also heading into the sex-shop to buy some toys too; they presume. Roxy looking over Candis’s shoulder asked “is that a toy from Bedroom Kandi?!” She gawks and hurries to get a closer look. Naquawna picks out a sexy two piece that comes with vibrating accessories, and pays for it with the money she won from the roulette table. Candis and Roxy don’t buy anything because they are still on virginity lockdown. So while the girls are picking up toys and looking at lingerie. The boys are four doors down is the Poker room, where stogies and drinks are being passed around in a hidden room.

Chapter 26

All seems normal in the Poker room so Rafee'al starts to think that these guys aren't going to be doing much of anything tonight but partying and gambling! But then a beautiful Russian lady comes out from a secret wall looking right at Steeli'o. She steps to Steeli'o slowly asking in Russian "who the fu*K is this?!" talking about Rafee'al? Steeli'o glares at her saying "calm down!" he's cool." He's with us." 'Claudia, is an ex-girlfriend of Steeli'o's who has always hooked him up with the best diamonds. She does it because she still loves him deep down inside. But she has soon found out that he has a new lover, which is Roxy. She makes no apologies on how she feels about him and she always flirts with him whenever he comes bye for a pick-up.

Claudia sits down on his lap and whispers in his ear in Russian "how she wants to screw him, in his house, in the valley, in his bed of wizardries!" He slams his drink down on the table replying "it's "called" a fantasy; room!" "Not a wizard-trees room!" She grabs him by the face and kisses him voicing "who--; care!" He pulls back from her kiss saying "come on Claudia!" let's stick to business!" With a half-smile on her face she gets up off his lap grinning after feeling his 'hard; erection on her leg. Looking at him she replies "at least he misses me!" He doesn't want to, but he; kind of chuckles a little bit along with the guys when she walks away. When she comes back bringing the case full of uncut diamonds, Rafee'al leans in real close to get a good view with his hidden camera, sunglasses which are on top of his head. Kitpatrick is outside in a van with Lenny getting all of the footage recorded, just in case the glasses get broken or lost.

Once Claudia gives Steeli'o the diamonds she tells him "the other 'stuff, won't be in for a few days." "So he need to lay low and that she will call him when it comes in." Rafee'al listens but acts like he's not that interested as he flickers with his chips and cards looking around the room at the other card games, that are going on, at a couple of other tables in the room. 'Rafee'al thinks, the stuff they are waiting on, is more than likely; drugs. But he just doesn't know which ones yet; that they are waiting on. After receiving the diamonds Steeli'o hugs Claudia and says "thank you" in Italian. And she replies "ciao, I'll call you when the package gets here." He nods and they get up from the table and leave with the case. The small case that they are carrying looks like Casino chips are in it, sows 'not, to draw unwanted attention to themselves through the security; camera's. Bubba takes the case from Steeli'o when they get outside and stashes it in the R.V so they can head over to the club to meet the girls. Their thoughts and feelings of confidence in hiding the diamonds in the R.V, is because 'who, in their right 'mind, would want to steal an R.V?

It is 12:05 when the guys get to the club. The music is loud and the girls are over by the bar. Roxy and Naquawna are up on a small stage with three other girls dancing wildly. While Candis is on the side taking lots of pictures 'of the madness, for tweets and Instagram for later. But also to show them later on how tow-up they were, when they've sobered up. When the guys come into the club Roxy and Naquawna run off the stage to greet them like 'screaming, love starved; groupies.

The guys are 'beaming, letting everyone in the club 'know, that the true 'players, have just entered the building! 'Candis, more collected in her new relationship, walks over to meet her man; too. He meets her halfway in the middle of the dance floor where they share a kiss and a slow dance. "Perfect timing" he says to her in her ear as they slow dance with each other in the middle of the floor sows 'not, to be; interrupted by Naquawna or anyone else for that matter.

Bruce and Sherry walk in late because of course they went to one of the late night shows and ended up at the buffets to throw down on all the food they could get their hands on. "Dang...!" says Sherry's to Bruce "now, I'm ready to go get in my bed!" But Bruce ain't hearing it!" he heads straight for the bar as Sherry takes a seat by the dance floor looking at all her friends slow dancing. She looks over her shoulder to see who 'Bubba, is talking to, as he's standing there by the bar with some cute black chick trying to buy her a drink. When the slow song fades out, and a fast jam comes on, the dance floor is pop-pin.

All the friends are dancing by each other having a good time. And even Bruce drags Sherry up out her seat, so she can burn off that food they just ate. Rafee'al and Candis are on the dance floor too, grinding up on each other like two dogs in heat. While Steeli'o and Roxy are just holding each other swaying side to side looking into each other's eyes; loving, on one another. Naquawna and Rayshawn are dancing like no one can 'tare, them apart like they are; inseparable. But when Naquawna turns her back to rub her butt, up against Rayshawn's middle-leg, a really pretty curvaceous black girl starts to grind on Rayshawn back, pushing her big; breast up against him while dancing to the beat with him. Candis and Roxy look over at each other like "what the Fu^k?"! Naquawna not knowing what's happening turns around to face Rayshawn still dancing, and sees this chick, all up on her man and she loses; it! After she tells the broad "to back; up off her man!" and she doesn't! The girl says to Naquawna "stop; trippin home-girl!" "Me and Rappin Ray; go way back!" "Ain't that right?!" she said rubbing the side of his face with the back of her fingers. Naquawna retorts "Rappin; who?!" "B*^+h?!" "You got my man mixed up with somebody else!" The girl says "naw--! "I'd know that 'body, anywhere!" said the girl as she winks at Rayshawn while licking on her lips.

Naquawna knowing that she's '9 deep with friends up in the club yells "hoe!" step; back!" up off my man!" "Or it's about to be some; funk!" The girl not backing down because she's 11 deep up in the club shouts jump "b+*ch!" "Bring it!" Rayshawn gets in between the two ladies saying "come on; now!" "We're all trying to have a nice time!" "Don't nobody wanna go to jail, up in here, tonight!" Naquawna yells "yeah...! "Skeezer! "So go back to the "hole!" you crawled out of! The girl yells "I got your skeezer!" "And let me tell you another thing!" "He 'loves, the 'holes, I've got him 'crawl-in, in and out of!" "Ba lee-dat!" smirked the girl as she walked away blowing Rayshawn a kiss.

Then to piss Naquawna off some more she shouts "I'll call you later; Ray!" "Is that number 'still, (841) 121-2345?!" She was letting Naquawna know "I got the right mother f*^#er; b#^ch!" Naquawna shouts "he won't be answering; hoe!" "I got this on; lock!" The girl flips; Naquawna off as she disappears through the crowd smiling. Naquawna not happy turns her attention to staring straight at Rayshawn like; 'that hoe, has your number!" Naquawna all pissed; off mad!" says "are you screwing her too; Rayshawn?!" "Or is it Rappin Ray?"! "I'm confused!"

Rayshawn replies "she's just a groupie, trying to get at me!" Naquawna screams "everybody can't be a groupie; trying to get at you!" He replies "I'm telling you, she's no body!" "She heard me rapping one time and she wanted me to rap at her birthday party, so I gave her my number. She grunts with a smirked; face when he puts his hands on both her shoulders voicing "forget that broad!" "Let's go to the bar and get a drink!" Naquawna just stands there not moving yelling; "punk! "That bi*ch called you; 'Rappin Ray! "What the hell are you using some 'fake ass name for?" anyway?" "What?" so you can pick up on girls, and no one will know what your real name?!"

Roxy looks at Rayshawn waiting to hear his answer and he glances her way 'kind of embarrassed, because now he knows Roxy can see him as being more of a 'dog, then a player! But in Roxy's line of work, she is use to men fighting over women all the time at the strip club. In fact, she's had a few men fight over her, more than she can count!" and it kind of a turned her on, seeing how Rayshawn handled the situation. So she tries to help him out by saying "go on Naquawna, and get a drink with your man!" "Don't let that broad ruin your night!" Rayshawn looks at Roxy like 'thank you. But it was more behind those eyes of his, than just a mere; thanks. 'And in reality, Roxy and Rayshawn are treading on dangerously thin ice, because there is 'no way, they could ever be together 'sexually, or any other way because it could 'cost, someone their life! There are just some 'lines, you can't cross and this 'one, is a big one! The club is still going on, and so is the crew; out there, dancing on the dance floor. It's like everyone got there second wind, as a round of shots were being passed out and slammed back on a snowboard over by the bar.

Roxy said what they were drinking off of was called "a ski-shot! And tonight, Steeli'o is celebrating more than just him being up in Tahoe with Roxy and their friends. He was also celebrating because he got 'even; better, cut diamonds this time, so that means, more money coming to him tomorrow, and more clients in the future. But he is 'especially, happy about having his woman bouncing up and down on his lap right now, in the club' because he considers 'her, his trophy. He slaps her on her 'donkey booty, and orders another bottle of champagne.

The song "Everybody in the Clubs getting Tipsy; which is being done by J-Kwon comes on, and it's back to the dance floor they all go. It went on like that 'all night, until 4:30 in the morning. Bubba ended up driving everyone home in the RV because he didn't have that many drinks, because he chose to smoke weed instead. So when they all got back to the Cabin everyone crashed. Bruce made it up to their room with the help of Sherry who had been babysitting him all night because he was so drunk on drinks.

While Rafee'al and Candis drag themselves up to their room because they both we're way too drunk to even enjoy each other, and remember it! Also, the night-life took Rafee'al on a ride, because he knew he had 'this, waiting period, going on before the big; drop 'was to happen, so he went on ahead and partied a little 'more, than he usually did.

He even hit the blunt with the guys in the parking lot before they came home and now his buzz has really; snuck up on him. By the time he and Candis got up to their room, they both ended up taking off their clothes. Candis changed in the bathroom and Rafee'al changed in the room area. And after putting her swimwear on 'herself, and 'he, got his swim trunks 'on, they both sat down on the bed laughing and kissing on each other all drunk and stuff. But the plan was--, to go down the backstairs from their room to the hot tub but they 'never, made; it! 'Instead, they both passed out on the bed together kissing and making out. Rafee'al fell asleep first, because he was so high and hadn't smoked weed like that since college. 'As for Candis, her eyelids were soo... heavy and as she laid beside his warm body, she started to get even sleepier. But once her face made its way up on to his chest, she was out like a light.

So now, that left Rayshawn and Steeli'o, the two best buds, and their women are still up and in the kitchen eating on some left over barbeque. Naquawna and Roxy all 'high, have stripped down and are now running outside to go get in the hot tub in their bra and panties. Steeli'o said to Rayshawn while they were eating in the kitchen "my Roxy, she is a wild woman!" Rayshawn chuckles thinking to himself "if he only knew just how 'wild, she really is!" Steeli'o continues "did you see her all over me in the club?!" "Ah...; man...!" I am going to get something, tonight!" he said with a hearty; bite of his steak. Rayshawn laughs at him saying "yep.., she's about as crazy as Naquawna!" "Look at um out there in the hot tub." "Damn near naked!"

And as soon as Rayshawn said that, Roxy flung her bra into the pool. She must have thought she was at the club! Then, she dares Naquawna to do the same thing saying to her "everybody's asleep; so don't be a chicken!" A convinced and very drunk Naquawna takes her bra off as well, and sling it into the pool to. Steeli'o sees them topless and, gapes! He stops eating, and rushes out to the hot tub to cover up Roxy, with Rayshawn not too far behind him. Steeli'o reaches for a towel yelling "my God; woman!" "Cover up your teats!" "There are other 'men's, here!" "I don't want them looking at you with no clothes on!"

She laughs a drunkards laugh while standing up in the hot tub so Rayshawn could see her full chest and while looking right at Rayshawn she says to Steeli'o "oh, papi, no one is looking at my breasts" she said nonchalantly as she runs her fingers down her hair to squeeze out some of the water. But Rayshawn 'is... looking, and he is 'looking; so... hard; that he starts to get a woody and Naquawna notices it and stands up to show her bazookas in front of Steeli'o 'just to see what Rayshawn would say to; that! Rayshawn looks at her and shouts "hey...! "Hey...! "You two have had way--, too much to drink!" Steeli'o looks at Naquawna's large breasts as he's helping Roxy out of the hot tub. And 'Steeli'o aroused himself places a towel around the front of Roxy and walks her past Rayshawn who is standing there with his mouth open and his hand in his pocket to hold back his; stiff-dog! 'Roxy, slurring some of her words says "bye Naquawna-ahhhh!" see you in the morning!" Then her tongue 'slips, and laughingly; she adds "good; night Rappin Ray!" She starts to laugh even more as she looks at him with lust in her eyes. Naquawna shouts "that's not funny!" "Roxy"! Roxy covers her mouth like a kid in trouble and giggles her way up the stairs.

Naquawna now aroused by Rayshawn's "package" licks her lips and tells him to get into the hot tub saying to him "she's; thirsty!" She doesn't even have to repeat herself because before Roxy and Steeli'o could get halfway up the stairs, Rayshawn has become 'butt naked, and climbs into the hot tub with a full on erection brought on mostly, by Roxy. When Steeli'o and Roxy make it up to their room, he jumps in the shower and she opens the sliding door out on her balcony so she can watch Rayshawn getting his "poker; face" sucked! Rayshawn is sitting there getting pleasured while sitting halfway out of the hot tub, and he looks up when he hears the sliding door open and sees Roxy up on the balcony with her breasts still out.

She looks directly at him as she starts to rub on both of her cantaloupes in front of him. And Rayshawn begins to licks his lips from 'afar, while watching her. Once Roxy sees that she's got his undivided attention she moves her right hand slowly down inside her panties so she can rub on herself as she's looking at Rayshawn and he's looking up at her. With Naquawna clueless as to what is going on because she is facing the other direction, Roxy begins to get herself 'off, the more; she looks at him.

He looks up at her and makes 'sure, she can hear him talking dirty to her 'too, while Naquawna's thinking he's talking directly at her. So then Roxy slowly puts one leg up on the rail so he can get a good look at her inner thighs as she's playing with her; clicker. And with her other hand she puts one finger in her mouth and sucks on it wishing that it was him. As Roxy starts to 'cum, to her climax, he can tell, so he gets even louder and more sexual when he's tugging on Naquawna's hair, while she's 'chugging, his 'beef, down her throat!

The shower stops and as Steeli'o is toweling off he yells out "where are you bay'be?!" She wants to yell back, she'll be in there in a minute, but instead she softly chants "I'm coming! "I'm coming! "Literally" she 'was; Cuming! When finished she goes back inside the room where Steeli'o is and says "she was outside looking at the moon." Then she drops to her knees over by the sliding door so she can pretend that it is 'Rayshawn, she is servicing. Steeli'o looks at her and just drops his towel, not complaining at all as he stands there 'enjoying his, unexpected; treat!

Rayshawn still looking up towards the balcony can see her silhouette through the blinds and as Naquawna climbs up on top of his 'mountainest-peek, he's imagining Roxy riding him in the nights luminous; moon light. 'Yes, Roxy has broken half of her bet with Candis to hold out on any type of sex. But this was just too "hard" for Roxy to pass; up! 'Wink!

Naquawna is thinking he is so turned on tonight, because of her new perfume. But his deceitful thoughts; are solely on his boy's woman. So as Naquawna's riding him into the night, the moon becomes further and further away as she lays her head on his shoulder with a well; fulfilled; sigh!

A door creeks at the cabin's front door and unbeknownst to Naquawna and Rayshawn 'Bubba's big butt, is tiptoeing around in the kitchen with some girl he found at the club tonight named; Mandy. And after he fixes her a plate of food as she's eating on the food, he tells her to bring her fine self and her plate outside with her, to the RV. She is so taken by Bubba's 'smooth, street talk and gift of gab as he's telling her all about the money, cars, and traveling he wants to take her on, while mentioning; that he's got the best herb in his city. 'You know, just saying anything; and everything; to get her "chips; wet"!

After they smoke a blunt he places her up on top of the R.V dinner table and she becomes his main course. He plays with her "pink; pulse" with his tongue and then after he's done "playing; her" like a 'piccolo, he tells her to sit on the edge of the bed, while he stands in front of her so she can 'blow, his 'trumpet! When he's halfway 'faded, he climbs up on top of her on the bed and the RV starts to shake like an; earthquake. In her ear all that is heard is his heavy breathing while he's on top of her. When he gets a good groove going, that is when the sweat starts to roll down from his face. The trickles of sweat lands on her chest, and on her face, and then one drop almost lands in one of her eyes. Not wanting that to happen anymore she turns her face to avoid any more drops to her eyes and then she slaps him on his ass a couple of times, to really get him 'done, and over; with!

When she screams out his name he just can't, hold it, back; any longer!" and then it's; bam!" man, down! He gets up off of Mandy 'if, that's really her name, and rolls over on his back to catch his breath. Through, huffing and wheezing he offers to walk her out to her car informing her 'that, he's about to call it a night!" She stands and looks around for her clothes admitting that "she's tired too, and for him to call her the next time he's in town." 'But she's not going to hold her breath, she thinks to herself as she's looking down at his protruding stomach. Mandy pulls up her clothes, and gets her purse and hurries out to her car. And good thing for Bubba to, that she left because if Steeli'o would have found out that he had someone in the RV other than himself, around all those "trillion; dollar" diamonds! Bubba might have gotten 'not only, his meat; beat! 'But his ass; beat as well!

'Although, this is no secret to his friends because they 'know, Bubba has always been a sucker for a pretty face; a big butt; and a sweet smile. What happened earlier was he had called Mandy as soon as they all got back to the cabin. Then once he knew she was 'down, to come over he told everyone he was going to go to bed. So when she pulled up to the cabin, Bubba was standing outside, and while the two were outside talking he seen Steeli'o going up the stairs with Roxy to bed through the curtains, so that's when he made his move to the kitchen with Mandy. And that's how they ended up; doing the do, in the 'badah-badah-boom, R.V; room!

'Next day unfolds, and it is now 9:30 in the morning. "Rise and shine!" yells Bruce as he plops down on Candis's and Rafee'al's bed. Candis yells "get; out!" As she pulls the covers up over her head. Rafee'al laughing turns over to snuggle up underneath her. He then mean-mugs Bruce voicing "yeah; dude!" "Get out!" "We're busy!" Bruce, pushes his glasses up on his face asking "busy doing what?!" Because he's already heard from Sherry, that Candis doesn't put out. Candis pulls the covers down from her face and looks at him like 'he's; stupid!" And then she yells out "none, of yo; business!" She then yells to Sherry "to come get her nosey; ass; man; out of their room"! Sherry, already; up and dressed when she hollers to Bruce from the bathroom, says "babe, I told you not to wake everybody up!" "We can go to breakfast by ourselves!" "You were supposed to ask Rayshawn, for the keys to the rental car!" Not Candis, "yah doe-doe!"

Rayshawn hears all the drama from his room and yells back "hell... naw!" "Ain't nobody using my rental car, I need it today!" "We got ben'ness to take care of!" Sherry yells back "forget you; Rayshawn!" "You are so, stingy!" Naquawna chimes in yelling "no... he ain't!" "That car is in his name, so he will be responsible if anything happens to it!" Sherry retorts "oh girl, please!" "Ain't nothing going to happen to that car!" "I know, because yaw'll ain't using it!" shouts Naquawna. "Have Bruce rent you a car, if it's that serious!" she continued.

Sherry snaps "shut your dumb ass; up!" "It is way too early in the morning to be hearing your mouth!" said Sherry finishing up curling her hair. Naquawna returns "what? "Fatty?"! Sherry shouts back "you heard me!" Then she slams the bathroom door and finishes up her hair. Steeli'o now awoken, yells "thanks guys!" "For waking us; all up!" And with his strong accent he begins to curse in Italian. Bruce jokingly says "umm--, go back to sleep; little-Italy!" They all crack up laughing then Steeli'o retorts back "I got your little Italy!" "And trust me!" it's not; little! The girls laugh out "ooh...! And even Roxy chimed in voicing "that's for sure!" Roxy chuckling some more kisses him and shakes her tail into the bathroom shower.

Steeli'o jumps up out the bed hoping to have a morning "recap" but when he opens the bathroom door Roxy blares out "no, Steeli'o!" "Not yet!" "I was drunk last night and I don't know what came over me!" "So please..., don't be mad!" He just stands there looking at her through the glass shower door as she's washing her body down with soap. He answers "ah, bay'be, you're killing me; with this shit!" She steps out of the shower with her towel wrapped tightly around her body saying "babe, you know I want you more than anything." "But I feel that the 'time, is still too soon" she said looking at him as she dries off her body.

Out of frustration he yells "what do you mean; too soon?!" "You had my 'dee'ck, in your mouth; last night!" Her eyes closed; mortifyingly; tight!" as he continued to say "so, I thought we were moving; forward in our relationship!" She hardens her face asking "are you kidding me right now?!" because she couldn't believe he just said that to her, she walks passed him not wanting to say anything else to him about last night, even though "technically" he had a point! She pulls up her panties and while looking for her bra, she vents "I just got caught up in the moment; okay?!"

He answers "I got caught up in 'thy moment, too!" "So can we move on to making love 'now, or what?"! Roxy screams "oh, my, God!" are we 'really, having this conversation right now?!" she said 'while snapping on her bra in front of him. "Yes, we are!" he yelled back. "I feel like you are playing with my emotions!" or playing me for a fool! She sighed hard; voicing "babe, you know I love you!" "That is why I got so caught up last night and did what I did." "Was it right for me to lead you into believing we could go further?!" "No!" "So for that, I am sorry" she said standing there in her bra and panties; posed, looking all; sexy.

He stands there looking deep into her eyes trying to read them, and when he feels that she is telling him the truth he smiles saying "come here" as he holds out his arms for her to come, hug and kiss him. After they kiss she laughs a little to break up the bad vibes between them stating "I think we just had our first fight!" "Yeah, and you won!" he grunted. She smirks out a chuckle and bats her eyes then finishes up putting on her makeup.

As he walks past her on his way to getting in the shower he squeezes her, on her rear, with two hands and she jumps with a giggle. The rest of the house mates are up and pretty much dressed 'all except, Candis and Rafee'al, they are still hugged up in bed. A Horney and impatient, Rafee'al decided he's going to do a little 'undercover work, on his own. He slowly goes down under the covers to where Candis is lying there still dressed in her swimsuit. He begins to slowly take off her bikini bottoms. And with a soft voice she asked "what are you doing?" He says, not a word. So she says "despite what you feel about me letting you sleep in the same bed with me, I'm still not ready for all the stuff that comes with that." "I know" he replies. "I'm not going to 'deflower you, if that's what you're worried about" he explains in his deep morning voice. "My intentions are only to make you feel as good as I can."

She smiles sweetly returning "you don't have to do that Rafee'al" as she looks at him for a second and then glances backup towards the ceiling and back at him while holding on to his shoulders thinking to herself 'oh-my- God-, please don't!" 'Because them I'm 'really, going to be sprung off of you" she thinks to herself. He replies "true, I don't have to, but I want to." In an attempt, to get him to wait, so he doesn't ruin their friendship 'and or, courtship she adds "I'm not going to be able to do you back." He stops, already having one of her legs out of her bathing suit bottoms and he asked "why?" She answers "because I don't do that." "Plus, I have to sing at my church two Sunday from now." He pauses for a second, then he says to her "and what?" doing that, will mess up your singing voice? "Well--; yes. "Kind of" she said 'in as much, as a convincing voice as possible. But even 'she, wanted to slap herself on the forehead for even saying it out loud.

But, oh, well, she likes to see how much game she has, too! 'And--, to see how much he really likes her, and how 'far, he's; willing to 'go, to prove; it! With a grunt like; chuckle he proceeded onward not listening to another negative word she had to say. All Rafee'al wants to hear 'now, is the sound of her; climaxing. With her eyes slowly closing she has lost the fight in this round in stopping him from doing what he wants to do, in pleasuring; her. But she has won in the fact; that she 'thinks, that he must "really" like her, to want to just do her as she lies back in that big cabin bed getting 'licked, like a princess in a palace!

While Candis is trying not to let the whole house hear her squeal, Rafee'al has forgotten 'all, about his "camera; sunglasses" which were left on record all night, on the nightstand. So when Kitpatrick and Lenny get back into the van with their coffee and bagels they see the whole love session unfold from beginning to end. And even though, Rafee'al is underneath the sheets, it doesn't take a rocket scientist to figure out what he's "doing" to Candis!

Lenny gulps "wow... he is really taking this "undercover case; seriously"! They both bust up laughing but then Kitpatrick pauses saying "what the hell is he thinking?"! "He's going way too far in this investigation! "He doesn't even have to do all that!" "See, like I've been saying, this is how you become too; attached!" said Kit. Lenny sighs "Uh, let the guy have a little fun!" "He's been waiting a 'while, for this girl to crack!" Kitpatrick laughs "I think it's safe to say, by the width spread of her legs; I'd say she's; cracked!"

The two guys laugh it up and the laughs gets even louder when they see Rafee'al come up from the sheets with a stiffy and Candis not doing anything to relieve him of it. 'Candis, awkwardly lies back when he's done satisfying her, but she wants to please him like he has just pleased her. She sighed stating "awe..., now I really feel bad" she said looking down at his "stiff" position. Rafee'al doesn't trip though, being the gentleman that he is, he shows her that he's a man of his word. He looks at her lying there all satisfied and he smiles thinking to himself "anything for the case!"

He goes to get into the shower 'knowing, that he will have his way with her; eventually, so he ain't; trippin! She rolls over with a big smile on her face because he is 'really, a 'great, cookie dough; eater! Candis starts to realize 'now, that maybe it "wasn't" such a good idea for them to share the same bed, because she's going to want him to play with 'her, like that again tonight! And she must admit, it is kind of selfish of her in a way, because she really can't go against her "own; beliefs" of trying to wait until marriage, just to please his; manly urges!

But she also can't seem to tell the boys 'no, when they ask to taste her. In her defense she's "never; asked" them to do her!" but they always seem to end up doing; her! So technology the guys know up front, that she's not going to be 'sucking, 'f*cking, 'Gutting, or even; giving up the 'butting!"

until she has a ring on her finger and the 'papers, to back it up! 'It's a dirty game, but 'Candis, is in it; to win; it; too!

She lies back thinking to herself how sometimes the way she uses men to her advantage is so..., wrong! 'But feels..., so... good, when they know what they are doing with their tongues. Naquawna knocks on the door asking "you two up?"! "We're all going to breakfast in about 30 minutes, so get dressed!" Candis yells out "okay, from the bed, too tired to get up and unlock the door for Naquawna. And besides.., Rafee'al's fine ass has just gotten out of the shower and Candis wants to view his sexy; body all by herself. He smiles at her when he enters the room with a towel around his waist, and all she could do is give him a sweet smile back, thinking about how much, she really wishes she could jump his bones right now.

He runs his hands through his wet hair pushing back all his beautiful curls, as he stands there looking like a hot; runway model. She's just in ahhhh... thinking about his towel falling to the ground 'and her, getting an eye full of his luscious; bod. For some reason he is even finer 'now, that he's all soaking wet. 'Or.., grunts Candis to herself, could it just be 'perhaps, the handy work he just did on her body with his mouth! She chuckles thinking about it and he hears her and says "what's so funny?" She looks at him with love in her eyes replying "I'm just thinking about how fine you look, standing their 'all, watered down" she flirts. He laughs, but his chuckle fades when Candis picks up his sunglasses and puts them on her face, voicing "you look so good, right now, I'm gonna have to give you; shade" she said. He was about to rush over and snatch the glasses off her face because he knows now, that they are probably still recording everything that is going on in the room. But being the smooth operator that he is, he just walks over to her, playing it cool, he gives her a long kiss and slowly takes the shades off her face.

Candis with her eyes still closed from his kiss doesn't notice when he reaches for the covers and snatches them off of her, so he can get a better look at her hot body. She quickly opens her eyes with a scream, of embarrassed laughter because her bikini bottoms are still off. He laughs "get up and get ready princess, I'm ready to go eat breakfast" he says. Poking her lips out with a smoochy face she flirts some more laughing "two can play that game" then she hurries to her knees and snatches his towel off. He doesn't even flinch as he stands there 'proudly, displaying his beautiful; stallion.

With her eyes wide she can't help but stare at his lower body parts hanging there, growing harder right before her eyes. She thinks 'wow, it's so big and pretty. He replies "oh... you want play; huh?!" don't start nothing you can't finish!" he said as he pushes her playfully back down on the bed, kissing her all over her face. They play around 'wrestling some, and he kisses her some more, while he lays his naked body alongside heirs. They are so emotionally invested in one another 'or at least, Candis thinks so. And she also feels like the kissing and the caressing from the both of them, is all that they will 'need, for now, when they're together.

In the cabin downstairs everyone's ready to go eat. The guys want to take the rental car so they can go drop off the diamonds. But of course no one else knows this plan but them. So that means the girls are stuck with riding in the R.V again. Once Candis gets showered her and Naquawna head out the door walking towards the R.V talking, and when they open the door they see Bubba all sprawled out butt naked on the R.V bed. "Ewe...!" squeals the girls at the same time. Naquawna staring; shouts "Bubba, get your butt up, so we can use the R.V to go eat breakfast!" She continues "you'll be riding with Rayshawn and the guys in the car." Bubba yells "okayyyy...!" close the door! Candis feeling sorry for him as he hurried to cover himself says "no worries, take your time." Naquawna walking away with Candis shouts "take your time!" You didn't even want him to 'sleep, in the RV at first!" What gives?"! She adds "and why are you so "giddy" all of the sudden?!" stared Naquawna.

Candis just lets Naquawna's comments 'role off her back, while she's walking she smiling out the words "I'll tell you later, get in the RV. When Bubba gets out the R.V Candis honks the horn for Sherry and Roxy 'to come on, so they can go. Rayshawn, Steeli'o, and Rafee'al go in the car and wait on Bubba to get showered and dressed in the cabin, because he didn't feel like squeezing into that little half shower in the R.V.

Bruce, standing outside the rental car proclaims "that he'll ride with the ladies over to the buffet place because he doesn't want to sit in between two guys." So on the road they go, and through all the hustle and bustle of the 'morning traffic, they finally get to the buffet and park next to each other about a street away from the Casino. Doors slam on all vehicles and everyone strolled; hungoverishly, towards the Casino doors. Hearing all the slot machines; pinging, makes them want to start gambling again, but the sound of their stomachs growling takes precedent over the urge to drop a few coins in on their way to breakfast. They make their way through the crowd of people who are still drinking and gambling on all sides of them, and then once they go up a flight of stairs they see the buffet place on the left. Everyone pays to eat and sit at a big table.

The girls end up talking in codes 'about what happened!" or "didn't; happen" last night with their men! Candis flips her tongue up and down discreetly at Naquawna and Roxy when Rafee'al gets up to go back to get more food. With her mouth she was implicating that she got licked by Rafee'al this morning, and that it was; the bomb! Naquawna went next, telling them 'all, about her "bobbing" for something!" in the 'hot tub, last night, and it "wasn't" apples! Then, looking over her shoulder Roxy sneaks in 'her, 'own; forbidden story about how she ended up on her "knees," late last night; but wasn't "praying" at the time! Sherry laughs at all the girls; affirmations about their men but was not happy with her own situation last night as she complained "well at least you all's men were up for it!" Bruce was passed out snoring as soon as his head hit the pillow.

The girls just laughed 'and hooped and hollered, and then when the guys got back to the table they switched the subject to "so what are we all going to be doing today?" "Shopping, gambling or both?" asked Candis looking at Rafee'al while he takes his seat. Sherry still not satisfied says "well, the question is?!" What are the guys doing today that's so... important, that Bruce can't go with them?!" Rayshawn answers "he can't come with us because Steeli'o's looking at some property up on one of the mountains today, that he might be interested in buying." Sherry snorting with a grunt, simmers down answering "umm... that's right, you did say he was into Real-Estate" she said looking at Roxy.

"Well, Bruce would love to see the property too!" she snaps. "That way, the girls and I can go get our massages" she adds looking around the table at her friends to confirm. Rayshawn blurts "we don't have enough room in our car for Bruce!" "Well why does Rafee'al get to go?"! Before Rayshawn could answer her, she points her fork at him shouting "that's messed up yaw'll!" Candis keeping the peace says "Bruce can come with us Sherry." Or he can gamble while we go to the spa." "I'm sure the guys won't be that long; right?" said Candis looking at Steeli'o waiting to hear his reply, as he's walking up to the table with his food. "Naw..., we won't be that long." "A couple of hours; tops" said Steeli'o with a reassuring nod of his head and a look in his eyes.

So after breakfast when the boys get up and leave, all except Bruce, the girls decided to go get their massages. At the spa doors Bruce and Sherry depart from one another saying "that they will meet up in 2 hours or so" and kiss each other bye. Bruce wanders around the Casino and gambles a little bit. And after he's spent what he intended to spend on the slots and crap tables now all "bummed" that he didn't win a nice amount of his money back has him feeling; down!" so he figures he'll go walk off some of his breakfast. Practically out of breath he makes a full 2 laps around the

Casino, and out of pure boredom he then heads straight to the bar.

As Bruce is sitting at the bar a beautiful woman comes up to him and asked "if she could buy him a drink?" He politely answered "no thanks, and he wasn't 'about, to offer to buy her one, in fear that she would stick around all day and Sherry would come to where he was and confront him about the woman. The lady sits down anyways and fingers her long brown hair with her hands, smiling at Bruce as she throws her long hair back towards the middle of her back, then she sweeps her bangs away from her eyes and winks at him.

Bruce blushes, then sees the halter top that she has on showing off her cleavage as she sits there crossing her legs with a cigarette in her hand wanting Bruce to give her light. Bruce nervously looks around as he lights her cigarette thinking to himself "is this a trick?" 'Thinking, "did Sherry and the girls put her up to this?" But no one came out, and no one laughed, so he sat there enjoying her company. Bruce "loved; Sherry" no doubt about it!

But this girl was gorgeous. While sitting there, listening to her talk he would often flash back to his high school days, and then his college days 'thinking, if the guys could only see him, now!" See, Bruce was always a 'introverted; like, quiet chubby guy, since junior high school to college. Which worked in his favor because he was always first in his class, but never could seem to get the hot; chicks! 'In fact, he never even had a girlfriend until Sherry, who he met on a blind date through Sherry's sister's old boyfriend. Bruce couldn't 'say, it was love at first sight, but he was very happy 'having met Sherry, because she was not only beautiful and sharp with her tongue, but she also made him laugh. But this girl, sitting next to him at the bar, now; she, made his 'heart, skip about a beat, with her cocoa brown skin and her long brown legs. He could barely focus on anything she was talking about, other than, her telling him "she had a room at the casino." He couldn't understand why 'she, was talking to him out of all the guys in the bar. So when he finishes up his drink and starts to get up out his seat to leave, she halts him with her hand saying "don't go!" She looks over at the bartender smiling "another round for me and my friend please." Bruce just looks at her sitting there looking like a 'hot-tamale, in her chair as he stares her up and down; with flattery.

His eyes went from her boobs, to her face and then back down to her chest and down to her bare legs. Reaching out she touches his arm saying "stay a while." He replies "no, you don't understand. Wiping his hand across his mouth he adds "I, um...," um...," I do..., um, have a girlfriend!" he says uncomfortably. She laughs at him, saying "sweetly, is that all?" It's not like you're married or anything" she said as she switches her other leg to cross it over thy other. "Well..., I'm kind of engaged" he says stumbles all over his words. She returns "there's no such thing as "kind of; engaged!" Either you've proposed to her already or you haven't!" she said as she puts her cigarette up to her mouth and blows the smoke passed his face.

The bartender brings them another round of drinks and questions her saying "do you want me to run a tab for you, Ms. Charlotte?" "Yes, just bill it to my room" she glares. "I'm up on the 55th floor in the Penthouse Suite" she said while moving her 'bobbing, crossed; over leg; sexily up and down. Bruce takes a gulp of his drink, acting very impressed to hear that she's in the Penthouse Suite. Smiling he says "hum..., I bet that's a nice room?" She smiles back with her glass and her cigarette in the same hand answering "it sure is." "Would you like to see it?" Bruce, is now "reallyyy" drunk when he replies "I don't know if that's such a good idea, Charlotte." "I told you, I've got a girlfriend!" I'm engaged!" Charlotte winks at him saying "I won't tell, if you don't tell." Bruce just stares at her as he's swaying; slightly in his seat reading her eyes and looking down her entire body thinking this might be his last chance at a beautiful woman before he "really" ties the knot one day with Sherry. Charlotte puts her hand on top of his hand voicing "you only live once!" He slams back his drink in one gulp and replies "nope, that's not true!" "There's another life after this one!" he blurts as he slams down his empty; glass on the bar. "Well..., I could be your last; dance!" she said as she twirled around on her stool laughing with her arms straight up in the air. He is in la-la land as he is watching her jiggle and wiggle as she twirls around in her chair, all drunk and happy; laughing! When she stops spinning, her legs are parted right in front of him and he can't help but see up her 'short; miniskirt, and noticing that she is nude, underneath. Wetting her lips with her tongue she stands to fix her skirt and stumbles into him with a chuckle, and he grows; hard instantly.

Charlotte starts digging through her purse for some lipstick and pulls out a card with her room number on it. She slowly puts the card in his upper shirt pocket and tells him "if he has a little bit of time, he could come and see how beautiful her Penthouse view is." Standing, after she puts her card in his pocket, causes his mind to flip-flop because he knows he has at least an hour or so, before the girls are finished at the spa.

Looking at him 'contemplating, what he should 'do, leads her to says "you are more than welcome to come up by using the 'side, private; elevator." Bruce just can't believe this is really happening, that this beautiful tropical woman is asking him up to her room to see her; "view"! He thinks as he's looking at her 'that, if he's going all the way up to her 'room, he's going to want to see 'more, than just her; "view"! She walks away smiling giving him one last lingering look at her tempting; invitation. Bruce sits back in his chair and summons the bartender for one more drink; thinking, should he go or should he stay?" It didn't take him long to decide, do to his heavy drinking and his curiosity, which finally got the best of him. He looks over to his left and heads for the private elevator. The elevator door opens, and up he goes to Charlotte's room.

When he gets to the 55th floor, the elevator door closes behind him and he is greeted by a sexy Charlotte in the middle of the room, taking a bubble bath. She tells Bruce to take off all his clothes and get in. Bruce is speechless, but manages through the shock, to say "I'm just here to see the view!" She stands up in the bathtub with all the bubbles running down her beautiful body and while striking a pose she says "I, am, the; view!" Having said that, after looking at his face she knows 'now, she's got his 'undivided; attention, so she bends over and touches her knees and shimmies for him. He stands there looking at her and a bead of sweat forms across his forehead and his palms start to get hot. She chuckles not wanting to scare him off because she can tell that this is probably his first time with a woman of her, statue. So Charlotte says "go ahead baby, go over to the window and get a good look at the "view"! "It is beautiful!" she beams.

Bruce curiously walks over and looks out the window and stares down at the city and the captivating lake over yonder and sees just how beautiful it really is. While looking past the lake at the white covered mountains which are covered with snow he hears Charlotte moving around in the water. She can tell that Bruce is hesitant, so she gets out of the bathtub and walks over to him 'dripping wet, and grabs him by his face and kisses him in front of the big window. 'Nervously, his glasses fall immediately to the floor and break. Luckily they split right in half, so he can fix them back with tape easily. Ms. Charlotte not caring about the glasses, just keeps on kissing him and pulling his clothes off.

Bruce is so... stiff, she could hardly pull his "nozzle" down when holding on to it, as she drops to her knees. He glances down at her in amazement when she begins to 'siphon him, like he's in need, of life; support!" But she doesn't make him 'perk, just yet because she wants to play with him a little longer. So gently, but with firm control, she persuades him into laying down on her bed. See, Charlotte is more of a man eater, because she likes to play with men for money, but she doesn't want to keep them!

Plus..., Charlotte "use" to be a 'man, so she feels she knows firsthand what a man would "like" in the bed. And being that she paid so much; money for her surgery's and seeing that everything is working properly makes her so; happy. Charlotte smiles at Bruce with one hand on her ass, while lying sideways on her bed and then she slowly turns her butt over for Bruce to play in. He doesn't know what to think at first!" but is quickly; obliged, to 'conform, to her freaky; ways!

She yells out things to Bruce like "you, are, in charge; of all--; this; ass!" With his glasses; 'broken, and his view half; sighted!" he feels his way around her sexy; body. His lack of sight, to him, "isn't a problem" it's her demands on him; that he "can't" keep up with! But eventually he does everything she asked; of him. Bruce has never had 'back door, access before because Sherry is "not" into that type of intercourse.

She would always tell Bruce "that; that is "not" for her!" And that only "porno; girls" did stuff like that!" He flashes back, on those words that Sherry had said, but he keeps on 'romping on, "knowing" he should be "using" a condom! Ms. Charlotte has him bending her over on every piece of furniture she can find in the penthouse, and Bruce is galloping around the "room" to give her what she wants! 'With his eyes wide open, he is doing things he has "never" done with Sherry!" all, in one day!

But 'Sherry, is all he can think about after he's 'poured; out his "content"! Bruce gets up off of Charlotte because now the thrill is gone. He asked to use her bathroom so he could wash off and while he's in her bathroom, Ms. Charlotte goes through his wallet and takes his last $1200.00 dollars and stashes it under her pillow. He comes out of the bathroom 'parched, asking "for a glass of water?" Smiling she gets up and gets him a drink and while doing so she says "not to be rude; Bruce, because it's been nice!" but now you've got to go, my boyfriend will be here soon."

'Bruce; dazed and coming down from his drunken high retorts "your boyfriend!" you didn't say you had a boyfriend?!" He looks around for his clothes hurrying to get dressed and just when he gets his zipper up he hears the elevator starting to rumble, indicating that someone is coming up. Bruce looks at her and she looks at him, and she starts yelling for him "to go down the fire escape!" He shouts "what?!" "It's the only way!" she shrieked, as she throws his shoes and shirt on to the fire escape's medal floor. Bruce, being 'somewhat, afraid of heights; squawks out "this is ridiculous!" She frowns saying "sorry!" Then closes the sliding door and the curtains with him on thy other side.

When the elevator door opens, it's her roommate asking "how much did you get?!" Charlotte jumps on the bed and pulls the twelve hundred dollars out from under her pillow cheering "look"! And as the two jump around on their bed together; cheering, Bruce is working up the 'nerve, to get down the fire escape in one piece. Charlotte and her roommate named Antauwnette have always liked playing tricks on men. Which one would consider; them being "Pimped" right out their money!

The Casino manager's know all about it, and that is why "only" "preapproved; men," from the girls are able to get up to the penthouse floor. The girls always kick the men out through the fire escape so they won't even 'think, about coming back 'once, they 'realize, they've been; rob! It's not just money they take, if the men don't have cash, the girls are more than happy to take their credit cards and drain them in the lobby's ATM machines without a trace. The fire escape isn't as bad as it sounds. It's just five floors down on a sturdy ladder and then it leads to a regular elevator. The biggest problem to people like "Bruce" is the height, of the building.

So as he's looking down from this high; skyscraper type 'building, 'outside, in the windy 'cold, air; nervously he is trying 'not, to slip on the icy ladder. So..., let's just call it; like it is! 'Bruce, will be much, more, "careful" next time, when talking to stranger's!" because now, that the drunken "sex" is over; he is now left; feeling used. 'Sure, he had a wild time but at what cost? Now he has to fake; it with Sherry like everything is still fine with the two of them. Once he gets out of the elevator he heads over to a different bar to calm his nerves. Slamming back a shot of Hennessy seems to do the trick. But then when the bartender looks to him to pay for his drink he notices; he has no more cash, in his wallet. Bruce knew he had gambled some of his money but he still had cash left. A thought quickly enters his mind "Charlotte"! Now he really feels like a 'fool, knowing 'now, that she had to have robbed him. 'Angry, he pulls out his credit card and hands it to the bartender. His anger grows even more as he's walking around the casino, just wishing he would see Ms. Charlotte now, so he could give her a piece of his mind!

So while Bruce is walking around the Casino thinking "negatively!" the girls... on the other hand, had; had a wonderful time at their spa place. They leave out all relaxed, and ready to go gamble, and get a meal. Sherry starts looking around the Casino for Bruce as the girls are walking through, putting their last bit of coins in the slots. Since Bruce and Sherry have a cheap mobile carrier, they can't seem to reach each other through text or calls. But finally she spots Bruce across the room looking a little haggard. She waves to him to get his attention and when he gets closer to her she blares “babe, I almost didn’t recognize you!” where’s your glasses?”

Bruce, not even noticing he’s not wearing them because he is so distraught about his missing money answers “uh, I broke them, when they fell on the floor.” Sherry asked “where?!” “And how?!” “This is all carpet in here!” she adds looking down at the floor and back up at him like; come again! Bruce yells “the whole Casino floor isn’t “all” made, of “fu^king!” “Carpet! “Sherry”! Sherry yells back “damn!” Why are you, so mad?!” “Did you lose all of your money gambling, or something?!” “Yes… I, did!” he yelped. And as he’s looking at Sherry, over her shoulder he can see Ms. Charlotte sitting at a different bar, drinking with another guy. His palms begin to sweat and he gets an even madder; twitch on his face; just looking at her!

Sherry sees the anger on his face growing so she points asking “is that the table where you lost all your money at?” Bruce doesn’t answer he just nods real slowly looking over at Charlotte with an evil eye.

He is so mad, he wishes he could go over there to where Charlotte is and get his money back! ‘Or better yet, have Sherry beat the; sh*t out of her; for him! When Charlotte turns to take yet another victim up to her room she spots Bruce and gives him a sly wink. Candis sees the wink and says “ooh--; look, she’s a pretty transsexual!” Bruce shrieks out, “a what?!” Candis says “you can’t tell?” “Look at her small Adams apple.” Roxy says “are you sure?” Adding “she is really pretty though.” Naquawna answers “oh yeah, she’s probably been snipped and tucked because she really looks like a girl!”

‘Bruce; gags, and runs to the nearest garbage-can and throws up. The girls are laughing so hard; thinking that Bruce must have had way too much to drink today while they were at the spa. ‘But unbeknownst to them, it wasn’t just the liquor; and if they only “knew” the real; reason, why Bruce stood over that trash can hulling like a dog, he would never hear the end of it! And if Sherry knew the ‘real; his penis would ‘definitely; be on the ‘chopping; block! As he’s hurling Sherry with sympathy in her eyes says “awe…, baby, you alright?” She rubs his back to make him feel better while he’s leaning over the trash can. Then she says “she doesn’t even care that he lost all his money gambling.” She gives him a hug saying “honey, don’t even trip about the money.” “That’s what we came up here to do; spend money and have a good time.” Roxy and the two girls; cheer Sherry on, regarding her last statement to Bruce as they walk through the Casino arm in arm. Even though the ladies had cheered at how sweet Sherry was being with her man, she didn’t give them the same regards when it came to their men. In fact, after Sherry seen how sickly Bruce looked she gave the girls a concerning look saying “my boo-boo needs something to eat!” “So you-all’s men are going to have to 'fin; for themselves because Bruce and I, are 'not, waiting for them!"

The girls give Sherry a "say what?!" Kind of look. But keep it moving through the Casino, think-in to themselves "that she is really on; one! So while they are all walking through the Casino looking for a food spot, up on the hill the wind has picked up on the mountain as the gravel crackles under Rayshawn's rental cars tires.

Chapter 27

The guys finally make it up the mountain to a spectacular house, overlooking the lake which sits way back on the hill. No one knows about this house already being "owned" by Steeli'o. And he likes to keep it that way because when he doesn't want to be bothered or found for a while, he can retreat to one of his favorite spots up here in Tahoe. He even keeps a Realtor's lock on the front door to make it look more "official" like it's still on the market. 'So playing it to the max, he uses the combination on the lock box to get the key, and then they all go inside the house.

"Wow...!" says Bubba. "I hope to be able to buy a house like this one day!" he said with high hopes. Rayshawn grunts "yep--, it's always good to aim high!" Bubba gives him a friendly push laughing "forget you man, I'm balling out of control right now!" Rayshawn laughs "you mean you're "growing" out of control!" "Look at your gut; dude!" he cracks. Rafee'al hearing the two go at it laughs while he's looking around the house voicing "how dope the place is." "Shhhh..., be quiet!" said Steeli'o. "I hear someone coming up the hill."

Rafee'al knows he is out of range, so he thinks it might be his back up trying to get a closer signal to the house. But when he hears doors slamming he knows it can't be Kitpatrick or Lenny. The door gets a quick knock on and Steeli'o opens it and everyone acts casual, as the three men enter the house holding a suitcase. Rafee'al at the time, is the only one who breaks out into a cold sweat when he sees the brother with the same tattoo on his neck that his sister had a picture of in her hand right before she died. The police at the time had said it was more than likely the killer's trademark, but they didn't know for sure. Rafee'al walks over to the window to play it off stating "man, this altitude is something else!" ain't it?!" Rayshawn answered "I know, my nose is all dry and sh*t!"

Then, when Rayshawn gets a harder look at Rafee'al's face he adds "you look like you need to get you some water; dawg!" So while Steeli'o is making the sale of the diamonds over by the lit up glass table with these two European guys, the one brother with the dream catcher's tattoo on his neck is just standing there looking around the room making sure, no one, pulls out any weapons. Steeli'o making light conversation says "I would offer you guys a drink, if I lived here, but this is a rental!" "Rent to own" he laughs. They all laughed back wishing they could get a bid in for the house, or even a realtor's license like he's got, because he keeps finding these great houses to meet them in, to do business. Steeli'o never meets his business partners at the same place twice, and that's the beauty of him being a realtor, because he always keeps them guessing, where the next drop will be. It's just better to him doing it this way. I guess you could say, he sleeps better at night not telling his clients where he lays his head. When the deal is done Steeli'o walks the men to the door and then closes it behind them.

Rayshawn hears their car start up and leave down the mountain as he's looking out the blinds at their tail lights. Happy that the deal has been made 'successfully, they all make a toast with some left over cognac that

Rafee'al had found in one of the cabinets, when he was getting a glass of water. They get ready to lock up and walk out to the car, and once the door is locked back with the lockbox on, as they are walking towards the car, before they could reach for their weapons, someone with a ski mask on, yells out "stop!" "Everybody put your hands; up!" The masked man said "don't make me have to kill you!" Then he tells Steeli'o to give him the suitcase.

Steeli'o slides the suitcase to the man on the slippery; icy driveway and as the man is picking up the case, he points his gun at Steeli'o with shaking hands and then he pulls the trigger. When the gun goes off Bubba jumps in front of Steeli'o to block the bullet from hitting him. And as Bubba falls to the ground the man takes off running. Rayshawn fires his gun and misses. But Rafee'al being a great shooter pulls his piece from his ankle and shoots the guy in his right arm; forcing him to drop the suitcase of money.

The masked man jumps back on his snowmobile and gets away down the mountain. He doesn't get to keep the money though 'thanks, to Rafee'al's sharp shooting. But when the suitcase hit the pavement, it opened and some of the money blew out onto the ground, and some even blew down the side of the mountain. When all this was going on Steeli'o was helping Bubba make it back into the house at the same time that Rayshawn and Rafee'al were running down the hill to catch the man on the snowmobile while they were firing their weapon. But they just couldn't catch him.

Rayshawn hunched over with his hands to his knees trying to catch his breath shouts, "shit!" "Man!" "What just happened?!" Rafee'al picking up the rest of the scattered money breathing heavily answers "that was shady shit; man!" They cursed, and fussed, about the masked man who shot at them as they walked back towards the house. When they get back up to the house Steeli'o looks at them 'like, it's not looking good 'meaning, Bubba's condition! Bubba is all sprawled out on the couch gasping with every breath asking "how bad is it; man?!" "I don't wanna die up here!" Steeli'o tells Rafee'al to get some more towels from the kitchen as he's telling Bubba at the same time "you're going to be just fine!" Don't talk! Just relax!" Steeli'o shaking his head in gratitude sadly says to Bubba "what were you thinking; man?!" "Jumping in front of a 'bullet, with no vest on!" You crazy; f#^k!" sobs Steeli'o. He looks Bubba hard in the eyes promising "we'll find this guy don't you worry!" he said holding back more tears.

Steeli'o keeps firm pressure over the wound to try and stop the bleeding yelling "did you call 911?!" Rafee'al tries to get a signal on his phone and so does Rayshawn. Kitpatrick, hearing the gun shots from where he was down on the other side of the mountain tries to get closer but he can't get through; do to the storm. And by now Bubba has lost way too much blood, so they ditch the idea of a 911 call, because it wouldn't help him now 'anyway, and would only cause more problems, and make for 'more, unanswered question from the police.

Watching Bubba deteriorate right before his eyes makes Steeli'o so mad that he ends up throwing his keys and shattering, one of his priceless; vases on his counter top. Steeli'o looking over at Rayshawn yells "what the f#^k; man!" "You're slipping!" "How could somebody come out of the 'trees, and you not see them coming, first?!" Rayshawn can't answer him, angry himself he shouts "I thought everything was cool!" Because I watched them leave down the mountain!" he said, talking about the guys who bought the diamonds. Steeli'o paces the hardwood floor with his hands through his hair and then after Bubba passes, he pulls out his phone to call in a favor from his cousin Vinnie saying in Italian "get some of the guys up here to come get the body and take Bubba back to his house. He adds "and make it look like a robbery gone bad."

He continues to say "clear out his safe, and make sure there are no drugs left in there, or in his house!" "I want to make sure his family doesn't know he was dealing drugs!" "You got it?!" Vinnie answers "got it!" Then he jots down all of Bubba's info and then hangs up the phone. Vinnie is at Steeli'o's house in the Valley and has been staying there ever since Steeli'o left for Tahoe. After Steeli'o hangs up the phone with a tear in his eye he shouts "let's go!" The guys say their goodbyes to Bubba one by one trying to be strong for their own mental state of mind, and then Steeli'o locks up the house. On their way out to the car Steeli'o looking down at his blood soaked clothes says "I've got to go buy me some new clothes before we go back to the Casino to meet thy others." When they get in the car and drive down the hill, the car is silent, all thoughts are on their longtime friend Bubba. Then with a cough Rayshawn breaks the silence saying "those Europeans who came to the house must have brought that guy up with them, with the mask on to rob us!" "Because we didn't hear nothing once they left down the hill" he concluded. "No. "Can't be" said Steeli'o. "We have been doing business with them for a long time." "So why now?" To not only rob me, but to try and kill me; too?" He continues "he already had the suitcase full of money" said Steeli'o, as he sat back in the passenger's seat thinking of who would want him dead?" Rafee'al sitting in the backseat was 'thinking, the same; thing, which was "why?" did someone want Steeli'o; dead?" And right before this big; drop was supposed to come in.

The guys make it to the bottom of the mountain and see a clothing store, so they stop. Rayshawn verbally gets Steeli'o's sizes from him and then picks out some clothes for him so he won't draw attention to himself wearing bloody clothes into the store. After Steeli'o changes his clothes in the car they meet up with the rest of their friends who are still eating at this little sushi place. Roxy had called Steeli'o earlier 'wondering what was taking them so long, saying "that they were ready to go back to the cabin, so for him to hurry up and get to the sushi place or they're leaving. When they get down to the sushi spot, the guys try to walk in 'like; everything is fine. It works for about 2 seconds and then Sherry asked "where's; Bubba?!"

The men had already hashed out a plan so Steeli'o chimed in first "uh, he had to get back home, something about work!" Rayshawn jumped in "yep, you know that 'brother, he's trying to make him some extra money!" "It's Christmas, time!" he's got gifts to buy" jokes Rayshawn with a 'forced, half smile. The girls all chuckled after he said that 'but not Sherry, she grunted "well, when you talk to Bubba, tell him we found his dates 'panties, under the dining table. Sherry continues "he is so...; kidding!" "How's he gonna have someone up in the RV?!" "And ain't no telling "what" they were doing!" Or, on "what" furniture!" The guy's smile at each other thinking to themselves at least he 'got some, before he checked out.

But Sherry was 'not, amused, she just kept; rambling on about 'Bubba, and his "sexi-paide"! And how she and the girls had to use 'bleach wipes, to wipe everything; down! Sherry also shouted "the nerve of him!" "He didn't even 'rent, the RV!" "Right?!" Candis?" she said looking at Candis with a piece of ginger on her chopsticks. They all kept chuckling and laughing while listening to Sherry 'kap, and 'case, on Bubba! Then finally, fed; up Bruce shouts "shut; up!" already!" "You are giving me a headache!" Sherry looks at him 'like he done; lost his damn; mind! 'Talking to her like that! She quietly finishes up her food, with a grunt; rolling up her eyes at Bruce, but not another word about 'Bubba and his R.V adventure, came out of her mouth. When they finally get back to the cabin, it's still kind of offsetting not having Bubba there. They try to act the same way, but they need a pick me up. And that pick me up, came in, when Roxy started; running down the stairs shouting "let's all go get on the Gondola!"

Roxy had her ski pants on and all her snow gear; standing there she cheered "or, we can all go snowboarding!" Looking at Steeli'o with a big smile on her face she jumped up and down up against him, like a kid; wanting to go to the playground. Steeli'o needing to blow off some steam, after one of his best friends and main dealer's got kilt today; sighed answering "alright!" "I'm down!" Sherry who has never skied, retorted "I'll be at the bar; drinking or 'sipping, on something, hot!" Candis all happy says "um--, I want to learn how to ski!" she said looking over at Rafee'al smiling. Rayshawn being the crazy adventurous man that he is, laughs saying "okay!" "Let's do it!" He was glad to go to, mainly because he didn't want to mope around the cabin or dwell on what a terrible morning they had; had after losing his best friend as well.

So as Rayshawn's glancing at everyone's excited faces he thinks the idea does sound pretty good, him riding down an icy mountain 'thinking, that; that would really help him take his mind off of everything. 'Naquawna, on the other hand was "not" feeling it! She told Rayshawn "she is not trying to fall down on some cold, ass, ice, and break a limb; or, a nail!" Finishing her statement; with "I'll be with Sherry and Bruce; at the bar!" Rayshawn tries to talk Naquawna into getting on the slopes but she's not having; it! She looks at her nails and then back at him and with a smirk on her face she belts out "I'll meet you at the bar; babe!" "Rafee'al has never gone skiing or boarding either, so this will be 'interesting, to see them all on the mountain" says Sherry to Naquawna with a laugh. They all head out the cabin to go buy what they will need in order to 'play, up on the snow packed mountain. And when they arrive at the sports shop they get things like ski pants, gloves, goggles and helmets. Up against the wall is where the big ticket items are that they will be needing like skies, poles and snowboards.

Once Candis sees the price of some of the stuff they will be using she states "good thing we can rent most of this stuff, because this sport can be pretty expensive to buy all at one time!" They all commented as they were walking and talking inside the little store. Even Rafee'al never planned on all of these expenses, and 'neither, did his job. But the department kept his cash flow; flowing through the credit card that they had given him before he had left to go on his trip. They use the R.V to all go in, to get to the mountain called Heavenly, to ski on. Up on a small area of snow Bruce, Sherry and Naquawna watch Candis, Rayshawn, and Rafee'al take a quick lesson on how to snowboard and how to 'stop, on their boards without crashing! "But, falling!" is the name of the game" says Naquawna with a gruntful laugh. With a giggle she tells Sherry "this is why; I'm heading to the bar...!" They give each other a high five and 'right then and there, is when Bruce realizes for the first time, that this is about the only thing these two girls have "ever" agreed on!

The three friends wish the couples good luck up on the mountain, and Naquawna after wishing Rayshawn good luck kisses him long and dirty saying "you be careful up there baby, don't break nothing" she says as she's looking 'down, at his 'private; dancer. He laughs then replies "you just keep it hot for me, because when I get off this cold board, I'm gonna wanna put my 'slap; stick, into something warm! He slaps her on her 'big; cannon's as she's walking away; briskly 'giggling, so she can hurry up and catch up to Bruce and Sherry who are about to get on the gondola.

Right before they close the door Naquawna climbs into the gondola 'wishing, she could fire up a Dub, but decides to wait until she get down after seeing 'now, how high they are rising up off the ground. "Whoa..., look over there" says Sherry looking at the lake. Bruce, placing his taped up glasses on his face to see how high they are going up, comments with a surprised tone but he is "not" that impressed, after having; had seen, that same view before, up off the 55th floor! But he plays it off, like it's his first time seeing it. The first stop is just gorgeous so they take some picture through the glass from inside the gondola. Inhaling deep, Sherry says "I think I should have had me a drink before I got on this thing!" she said complaining while gawking over at a younger couple in front of them sipping on a bottle of Jagermeister.

When they get to the top, all the chills, and squeals, are all worth it after exiting the gondola and seeing how beautiful the view was from up on top of the mountain. It looked so much like Christmas with all the white and green of the trees all beautifully created along the big lake. And as they look around at all the people hanging out sipping on something or another, like latté's, hot chocolate, and some even having liquor drinks, just to stay warm, they walk over to the bar to get a shot of something from Mexico; like Patron! "Yippee...!" yells Naquawna and Sherry as they get a table to sit at while waiting on Bruce to bring back their drinks.

'Now, while they are at the bar about to get faded, the other couples 'plus one, who is the odd ball, man out "Rayshawn" are now on the ski lifts. Roxy and Steeli'o decided to ride apart from one another to make sure their friends knew how to get down the mountain safely. Rayshawn, Steeli'o and Rafee'al were in back of Candis and Roxy on the lifts which caused the girls to have to go first. Roxy started Candis off on a semi-small slope, so she could build up her confidence because Candis is scared as hell, and all that is going through her mind is "God; please--!" don't let me get hurt, on this big; beautiful mountain of yours!" Then she says a quick prayer and then down they go. "Wooooh...!" yells Roxy. And, "oooooh...!" Sh*t...!" yelled Candis. The wind and cold ice; crisped Candis's face and her legs began to wobble. She could feel all of her senses flowing through her body down to her feet as she moved on that icy cold snow. With her nose cold and running, she felt like she was a bird in flight while gliding down that high mountain. When she got towards the bottom she fell slightly sideways because she couldn't stop her board as well as she did in practice. Roxy hugs her yelling "you did it!" "You did it!" girl!

Candis still a bit dazed from her fall, giggles with pride because she tried something, she was very much, afraid of trying. It reminded her of the time when she was in 5th grade and her father had taught her how to swim and how frighten she was then, but how she loves to swim to this day because she took a chance. Thinking back on it, makes her miss her dad in that moment. Then Roxy shouts "let's go again!" She smiles pulling Candis up by her arm. And Steeli'o, up top seeing that the girls made it down with no problem says "okay guys!" "Just try not to fall, that is thy main thing!" "And don't forget how to stop" he says with a quick demonstration.

Rafee'al goes down first because he's not worried, in fact he's rather excited because he likes to challenge himself. 'Plus, Candis is watching him so he 'can't, wimp out 'now, after seeing how good she did. He pumps himself up and plays it cool 'like, he can handle; anything!" including 'her, then he gets ready to go down. Rayshawn is going down next, he's also kind of hesitant at first but you wouldn't know it though. He even says his own prayer, thinking about his son and Se'anna and how they would both be alone if anything was to happen to him. 'Not to mention, him lying about being on this trip; would be front page news! But funny, Naquawna never even entered his mind as he prayed for a safe outcome. I guess you could say Rayshawn is starting to believe that life is way too short, because he just can't stop thinking about Bubba dying up on that mountain today. And how 'now, he's riding down a mountain that could very well take his life too. He clears his mind and gets ready to take this mountain; down, and 'ride; it like he 'rides; his women!

When Rafee'al starts to go down his legs are a little shaky at first because the snow is so icy and hard. But once he gets in his groove he looks like he's skied in his life before as he feels the wind on his face and the thrill in his heart. When he makes it down safely 'he thanks God, with a kiss from his lips and two fingers up towards the sky. He too, fell back on his board when he stopped, but he was pumped when Candis came over to help him up with a big kiss. She was so happy that he had made it down in one piece, and she told him so, as they both rejoiced on the white powdery snow. "Here, comes; Rayshawn!" Points; Roxy yelling. Rayshawn is screaming and hollering down the mountain like a black bear is chasing him, but let him tell it; this was just his way of releasing his held back tears for his friend because he won't be driving back home with him 'or, the fact that Bubba won't be laughing and joking with him anymore. Everyone grieves differently and this was his way of saying 'goodbye, to his longtime friend; Bubba Dank!

A lady standing next to Roxy and Candis hearing Rayshawn howling and screams as he's flying down the mountain, laughs out saying "oh..., my...!" "You can 'barely tell, that this is his first time on the mountain!" "He is just "not" excited enough!" laughed the lady jokingly. Candis and Roxy cracked up with the lady along with Rafee'al. And when Rayshawn stops at the bottom of the hill, they all run up to him jumping around him; cheerfully because they could see how proud he was. 'Roxy, looking back up on the mountain for her man yells "okay guys!" "Last, but most "definitely" not; least!" "Here comes my man!" She stood there watching him in amazement as he showed out, doing one of his skills which was a half-pipe on a rail on his way down.

Roxy, was cheering him on, with the loudest; scream! She didn't even 'know, he was that 'good, on skies, and it's probably because he doesn't like to talk about what he can do; he like to show people; what he can do! 'And in that moment; she 'knew, she had found her black diamond, buddy! So as he was coming down the mountain 'her mind was thinking, once Rafee'al, Rayshawn, and Candis felt confident enough to board on their own, it would be off, to more "advanced" slops for her and Steeli'o.

'Roxy, anxiously waited for him to stop on his skies then she ran up to him with a big hug and a lip smacking smooch to his face. So happy from his ride down the mountain, he picks her up off her skies and spins her around as they hug and kiss. Roxy all excited shouts "babe, I didn't know you were that good on skies?!" He smiles big, and all hyped, he blurts; "yeah...!" "I needed that!" "Woo--!" he yelled out. Steeli'o gives Rayshawn and Rafee'al; dap as he and Roxy walk away arm in arm along with Rafee'al and Candis. Rayshawn all pumped shouts "let's go one more time before they shut down the slopes!" They all cheer "hell; yeah!" And head back up on the lifts.

So while their getting their "skiing" on, Sherry and Bruce are doing another shot of patron while Naquawna is on her cell phone over by the bathroom talking to Mike, or her granddad. She comes back to the table but never says who it is she was talking to. But come to find out' it was Mike, because after her fourth shot, she pretty much told on herself. Naquawna sits back down at the table and tells Sherry "how Mike's mom, just went on an interview today because she likes it "so much" out here in Treeberry that she can't 'think, about leaving her one and only son to 'fend for himself; especially, after his horrific; car accident!" Sherry and Bruce just listen to her talk all--; about it. But then the more Naquawna 'talks, the more she starts to wear on their; nerves. The two of them lose interest and they start to feel like two deer's caught on the freeway; 'wishing, she would just run them over already!

Sherry eventually tells her "to give it a rest" as she sings the words, "b*tch; don't kill my vibe" by Kendrick Lamar, which is being played from her cell phone at the table. 'Naquawna; annoyed now, gets up to go to the snack bar because she is still drunk, so wants to eat something, as well as brush off, the playful; read she got from Sherry! 'Even though, Sherry was "not" a 'member, of hooked on phonics. Time goes by and everyone finally meets up at the bar after Steeli'o and Roxy get done doing a crazy black diamond run. The ski buddy's all enter the bar at the same time all loud' and all smiles, telling Bruce and Sherry how much fun they had on their boards and skis. Getting comfortable in their seats Rayshawn orders another round of shots saying "this is for homie's who ain't here" he says as he looks at Steeli'o and Rafee'al as they raise up their shot glasses and drink.

Naquawna holds on to Rayshawn telling him "how she wishes she could have seem him flying down the mountain" then she gets up on her tippy toes and gives him a kiss while she's sucking on a lime. After leaving the bar they head back to the gondola and Rayshawn's crazy butt fires up a blunt because they are the only ones riding on it. Bruce coughs, and complains about the 'dangers, of second hand smoke, and they all laughed, but kept passing it around; anyway. Rafee'al sided with Bruce but still had to hit it, so he could keep his 'cool brother; cover in check. It is just about dark, when they walk down from the mountain and get back in the R.V and the rental car. The girls decide to get shrimp, broccoli, butter, real cream, garlic and all the ingredients to make fettuccini. And of course, it was Naquawna's idea because it's one of her favorite dishes.

The guy's head back to the Cabin in the rental car and the girls head to the store. At the Cabin the guys get changed and one by one come down the stairs and sit around talking waiting on the ladies to get back. Rafee'al still undercover and still "technically" working says "so... how did you guys all meet?" He looks at Rayshawn and Steeli'o after he takes a long neck; beer out of the refrigerator. Rayshawn answers first "hell, I've known Bubba since Elementary!" "We use to play basketball together on our junior high team." He continues "see... everybody thinks that Bubba has been fat, all his life' but he use to be a tall bean pole when we were in school." "But after he lost his scholarship to play basketball he just stopped playing ball and started doing other things".

Bruce sitting with his face in his laptop says "what other thing did he do?" he asked as he looked up from his taped up glasses. Rayshawn answered "you know?" things like, retail jobs. He couldn't just say "selling narcotics"! 'Not to square ass Bruce. Bruce answers "Oh, I didn't know Bubba was into retail?" "What does he sell?" Rayshawn rolling up his eyes, answers "he sales; beats on-line, and to local artist. 'In Truth, Bubba 'did, sell beats but it was mainly a hobby of his, and a 'cover, for where his "real" income was coming from 'if, his parents asked; along with Jake and Jordan's parents. "Cool!" smiles Bruce. Adding "so that brother is an artist?" "Yep" said Rayshawn, trying to cut it short.

Bruce all curious says "I'll have to check out some of his stuff!" You got his website?" he asked, itching his scalp wanting to pull it up right then and there on his laptop. Rayshawn looks at him like 'come on man!" you ain't no; rapper!" But instead of saying that out loud, he grunts, looking at Bruce; smirking he says "naw, but I'll have Bubba get it to you, when we get back home." Bruce gives him a slight smirk back, returning "yeah, okay!" And then he goes back to doing what he was doing on the web.

Steeli'o, chuckling; blows Bruce's inquires to the wind, saying "well, anyways." "I met Bubba at a party out in Hollywood, it was niceee... too!" "Jake and Jordan had introduced me to hem, and all I remember that night was Bubba talking about how 'tight, his beat sounded at thy party as this new Rapper, was rapping to it!" "I can't remember thy guy's name right now but he went platinum off thy song, and Bubba still gets 'royalties, till this day from that beat!" "Man..." said Steeli'o with a shake of his head thinking back. He continues to say "those were thy day's... man!" And we've been friends ever since" he said getting a little choked up when clearing his throat.

Steeli'o trying not to get sad puts a big grin on his face when looking over at Rayshawn he spouts "and then, I met this; pimp!" wanna be over here!" he said laughing; pointing in Rayshawn direction saying "at Bubba's house one night with two females on his arms!" "Yep..." says Rayshawn laughing, thinking back adding "and Steeli'o took one of them females from me to that night, and... took her home with him!" said Rayshawn laughing out "so come on now 'playa, don't get it twisted!" Pimp; who?!" laughed Rayshawn saying "and I was mad as hell that night too!"

They all laugh and then in walk the girls with all the bags of food. The men play it off and change the topic back to race car. And the girls put the food on the counter and go get changed and put there comfortable clothes on. When the ladies get downstairs and back in the kitchen Rafee'al comments to the guys on 'how it looks like a 'mess-hall, cooking station as he laughs and gets two beers out of the frig. The girls screech out for him "to shut; up!" And then Roxy throws a dish towel at Rafee'al telling him "to get out of the kitchen, before they put him to work!"

He goes back into the den area where the guys are at and says "those girls are crazy!" Naquawna and Sherry are peeling shrimp and Roxy's cutting up garlic" he said. Rafee'al hands Steeli'o his beer with a chuckle saying "yo' girls gonna to be stink-in man, she's chopping up; all-- the garlic!" "But my girl, has the easiest job, she's only cutting up the broccoli" he said with a lift of his beer smiling. Rayshawn laughing out loud says "and I guess they'll be flipping a 'coin, to see who's making the sauce!" The girls yell out from the kitchen "we can hear you!" And the boy's just laugh and crack more jokes the whole time they are in the kitchen cooking. Steeli'o even yells out "we'll be eating at the shrimp-shack tonight!" boys! Followed by Rayshawn's comment of "no... it should be called the 'crawdad-house of many shrimp!" Everybody had a joke to say and the girls didn't want to laugh but it was pretty funny all the names they came up with.

But by the time the food is done, the girls have the last; laugh because the men were quiet as a mouse, while enjoying; the deliciousness. All that was being said was "this is great ladies!" And "ooh...!" wee...!" "You ladies surely put your foot in this meal; for real!" "Thanks" say the girls as they are chuckling with their mouths full. Sherry with a funny grin on her face blurts "and we left "you; guys" the dishes! "See, if yaw would have kept your mouths shut, and stopped crackin on us, with your 'shrimp la la's, and your crab-craw-dad's!" We might have done the dishes too!" But now--, she says looking at the ladies laughing "I guess we get to see what; "clean up" looks like; in the mess-hall!" "Thanks guys" said the girls laughing all the way to the den to go watch the Atlanta House Wives. The guys unhappily begin to clean up the kitchen, while hearing all the "Bloops; giggles; and; oh, no; she didn't!" Coming from the TV set which went on for about an hour.

When finished with the kitchen the men flopped down next to them towards the end of the program, and after all was said and done, they all started heading off to bed one by one. 'Although, the morning was depressing after the death of their friend. The snowboarding did help the guys get some normalcy out of a tragic situation. But, it also made the guys exhausted by the closing of the end of the day and with no strength left to do anything else they passed out in their beds after that great meal.

The snow is falling and the fireplace is still; crackling while they all sleep. Some people can sleep like a baby, while other's like Rayshawn, toss and turn through the night. He started dreaming about pushing Bubba into the pool and laughing, and as he's laughing the dream turns dark, and now he has blood all over his hands and his face. In the dream he thinks it's Bubba's blood, but it isn't, it's Rayshawn's blood because he was dreaming he had been shot. When he looks down at his stomach where he had been shot, he jolts himself out of his bad dream. Which causes Naquawna to get startled out of her sleep asking "baby, you alright?!"

Touching him she asked "what's wrong?!" He laid back down and in a cold sweat he said "yeah..., yeah..., I'm fine." "I just had a bad dream that's all. With his heart still racing he closes his eyes trying to catch his breath. She asked "what was the dream about?" "Nothing..., nothing..., just go back to sleep" he said not wanting to talk about it. He looks up at the ceiling wondering; what the dream meant, and 'hoping, it didn't mean that he was going to be the next one, to get shot. Naquawna hugs him with a concerned look on her face and then she tries to go back to sleep.

As for Rayshawn for the rest of the night he barely got any sleep at all. 'It's the next day when the sky cracks her cold, blue, light outside. Rayshawn very early gets a text from Steeli'o telling him to get up, so they can go pick up the drop. He quietly gets dressed, so he doesn't wake up Naquawna. Rafee'al is up using the bathroom and hears movement in the hall so he opens their room door and sees Rayshawn all dressed and looking like he's ready to go somewhere. He whispers to him "you heading out?" "Yep. "We got to make this pick up." "You wanna roll?" Or crawl back into bed with Candis?" said Rayshawn smiling. Rafee'al chuckles at his comment, and knows, it would be 'great, him staying in bed with Candis, but he can't, because he's on assignment. So he says "I'll meet you at the car." Rafee'al grabs his clothes and his shades and gets dressed downstairs because Candis is 'not, that deep of a sleeper. In the car Rayshawn complains "Dammm...! "It's early and cold as hell!" He continues to say "I'm not use to getting up this early!" "See, in the car business, I don't have to be at work until like 9:30 in the morning and sometime 10:30 if Ernesto's dad is out of town picking up new cars from the Auction!"

Rafee'al asked "so that's what you do for a living?" Steeli'o answers for him, "nope!" That's what he tells his "woman" he does, so she doesn't dump his black; ass!" Rayshawn laughs back "you're trippin!" "I do work!" "It's just not steady work!" "So that's why I make my money other ways to feed my family!" Steeli'o laughs "but he knows..., Se'anna could hold it down by herself, if she had to, because she's a dental hygienist." Rayshawn blurts "dang; man!" "Just shoot; me down!" Steeli'o returns "no..., bro!" "I said that shit because I just don't understand why you're still fu#king with Naquawna?!" "Knowing, she's going to end up causing you problemo in thy long run!" Rayshawn groans "yeah... maybe, but I'll leave her alone before that happens!" Rafee'al inquires asking "so you got a family?" "How many kids you got?" "One son" said Rayshawn. "And he's a cute little dude, just like his daddy" he chuckles.

They pull up to that same Casino and enter from the back door this time. Claudia walks up to Steeli'o and grabs him by the hand saying "you guys, wait here!" she said as she looks at Rafee'al and Rayshawn with a serious look on her face. Then she walks with Steeli'o to the back room. Rayshawn turns sharply and looks at Rafee'al when he blurts out "and he's talking about; me!" and my down falls; with women!" Huh?" he chuckled. Claudia grabs Steeli'o by the head and kisses him; like crazy! While looking at him she slowly gets down on her knees while she's unzips his pants. With her warm tongue she licks him first, all the way down to his navel. And once she makes eye contacted with him she slowly starts to 'swivel, on him, like a vacuum 'vac, with no off; button!

'He loves it, just the way she takes what she wants; which is him! Then she jumps up on top of him and he can't stop her. He holds on to her backside; tightly like he remembers she likes it. She kisses him as she is riding up and down on his "roller coaster"! Then when she looks him in his eyes with this certain look, he knows she's about to go 'there, by the look on her face. It's almost like her soul has just left her body and is flying above them. He looks into her beautiful eyes, as she's "climbing!" thinking to himself, it's like a beautiful butterfly, 'fluttering; its wings, in midair, in slow motion, while flying above him, in their love making spell! But once she focuses back on him, she can hear voices in the other room; growing louder as the two are climbing to their 'magical moment, together; like an amusement park ride! And Claudia is even "more" turned on, then Steeli'o could ever imagine!" because it is her new boyfriend's voice she can hear talking and walking, back towards where they are, and he is calling out her name.

Claudia begins to climax... even; harder, the closer her new man 'gets, to the door. And by the time she climbs down off of Steeli'o, her man is standing a few feet away from where they are. Then Rafee'al yells to him "hey man?!" what kind of sculpture is this over here?!" Which gave Claudia and Steeli'o just enough time to fix themselves and walk out from the back, with the package. Claudia with a big smile on her face says "hi, my love!" "I thought I heard your voice" she said giving him a kiss, while looking at Steeli'o. Steeli'o gloats as he watches her then he says "thanks again Claudia" as he smiles looking at her thanking her for 'more, than just the package.

When the guys get back in the car Steeli'o belts out "thanks bro!" Talking to Rafee'al, he adds "that was close!" You gave me just enough time to get that 'dog; off my bone!" He kept on telling them how "she just jumped his 'meat, out of nowhere!" And how he couldn't even stop her, it was like she was; possessed!" Rayshawn and Rafee'al looked at each other and laugh real; hard saying "all--, come on man!" "And you weren't trying to make her stop; either!" "Oh..., how they laughed...! 'Rayshawn, with tears of laughter said "and you're talking about me?!" getting caught up with Naquawna?!" "You're the one who's gonna get caught; up!" Steeli'o shook his head laughing because he knows; damn well, it could happen!

But in his defense he replied "I ain't gonna lie, I needed that man!" because Roxy is still--; holding out on me!" She did a little "son'thang-son'thang" as you say; one night and that's been; it!" "I think she's trying to hold out until marriage or son 'thing like that!" "I tell you guys, these girls, are a piece of work!" Rafee'al jumps in laughing out "they can cook; though!" They all chuckle saying "there's truth to that!" Then Rafee'al talks about "how Candis seems to be on the same page." Rayshawn answers "yep!" Yaw don't know?!" "Roxy, and--; Candis!" have some kind of bet, to see who can hold out the longest!" "I overheard Naquawna and Sherry talking about it yesterday!" He grunts "they didn't know I was listening!"

He smiles again saying "can't get nothing passed; these ears!" Rayshawn's phone buzzes while he's still laughing he cracks "ah, no!" "It's probably Naquawna!" he laughs. "She's probably up by now; looking for me!" "Needing her "feeding; tube"! He said laughing continuously. But when he looks at his phone and sees that its 'Se'anna calling, he straightens up saying "yaw be quiet!" "It's my woman!"

"Hey, baby; what's going on?" "You know I miss you two!" "How's my son doing?" "He's fine!" Ray. She cuts it short, asking "so when are you getting back home?!" "Ernesto promised me that this would be a three day, "repo; tops"! He answers "I know babe, but we ran into heavy snow." "And we even had to get chains" he explained. She listened as he continued to say "and then the car wasn't at that house we went to, to go repo it at!" "So we are staking out another house from one of the dudes references that he gave to Ernesto's dad." "So it shouldn't be too much, longer" he said. She groans out "okayyyy...!" believing him at his word. 'Well...!" kind of.

Se'anna drove by the shop a day ago to see if Ernest's shop was open and it was closed, so she could only 'conclude, that Rayshawn was telling her the truth. But little does she know, Ernesto and his whole family went down to Baha Mexico for Christmas and won't be back until New Year's. Rayshawn smiles at how cleverly he planned out his trip. He then tells Se'anna, "how much he misses her and how she better be ready when he gets back, because he's got all this "sexual; tension" built up inside from him "not" being able to love on her! 'But if she only...; knew...; just how much sex he was "really" having! 'Her weave, would be 'falling out!" by the; bundles!

Holding his phone close Rayshawn says his 'I love you's, and then hangs up the phone. He brags out loud when he hangs up, telling the guys "now, that's how you do it!" My brother's!" Steeli'o laughs, and Rafee'al says "now, "that's" an Emmy award!" if I've ever heard one! Rayshawn still laughing 'tells them, "how he timed everything; just; right!" They pull up to the Cabin and park the car and go straight into the R.V to open up the packages. It was so... much compressed hash that all Rafee'al kept saying was "how are we going to get this back home without anybody smelling it?!" Rayshawn nods adding "that's a good question!" because Bubba and I was supposed to take it back together." "But now; damn...!" he says. "I guess, I'm going back solo."

Steeli'o backing out of the situation says "man, I would ride back with you, but Roxy would be upset and sh*t!" Plus, I have that client coming in to look at one of those houses over in Treeberry Grove." Steeli'o switches up asking "what about you; Rafee'al?" Will Candis trip out, if you don't ride back with her?!" "Hell... yeah!" But I'll talk to her though, and I'll tell her I have some paperwork at the corporate office I need to pick up." I was going to pick it up on Tuesday, but I'll just get it done tomorrow so she won't trip". "Plus, I'll get a co-worker of mine to drive me back because it's going to take some time to get all the papers printed and faxed" he said with a convincing nod. Rayshawn chuckles as he's looking at Steeli'o he says "I like this guy!" that sounds like something I would tell Se'anna!" Still chuckling Rayshawn asked "so where do you work at exactly over in Mento"? "I remember Bubba saying he sold you a kilo up that way before" said Rayshawn. "Yep, that he did" said Rafee'al. He went on to say "but for my "legal; job" I do the books for my auntie's restaurant." "Oh--, yeah!" "The O garden!" said Rayshawn. "I remember Naquawna talking about you meeting Candis there."

Rafee'al taking the focus off of himself nods saying "yep. "Yep. Then he picks up some of the hash saying "this is some strong smelling hash" he says putting a block size piece up to his nose. "Yes, only thy best money can buy" smiled Steeli'o. They pack the hash deep down in where the spare tire compartment would be in the rental car and cover it with these big zip-lock baggies filled with coffee beans, which Rayshawn had already had in the trunk to mask the strong smell once they got the, hash.

After packing up all the hash in the trunk the guys decided on telling the girls 'tomorrow, at the last minute about the new "driving" arrangements. Reason being, is so Naquawna won't 'beg, Rayshawn all day long to ride back with him. And then; cokes Candis into making it a double date having her ride back with them too. The guy's lock up the car and go back into the house and when they enter they see Naquawna at the top of the stairs asking "where did you guys go?!" And more importantly, where are the doughnut?!" Frowning she adds "I thought you would at least bring back something sweet!" Rayshawn chuckles voicing "I got something sweet for you, right here!" He walks up to her and takes her by the hand and pulls her back upstairs to the room. Steeli'o and Rafee'al chuckled at the two, and then they both went back to their own rooms and crawl back into their own warm beds. Thankfully, their women were still passed out when they got into bed.

'It's about 1:00 in the afternoon when everyone starts to get up, get showered, and eat lunch. It's their last night at the Cabin, so they plan on having a party. Candis and the girls go back to the store to get the things they will need to get their last party bash; off and running. Roxy even said she wanted to get decorations to give it that 'real, party; like feel, so they did just that. Naquawna wanted to test her game by asking Rayshawn if she could use the rental car but Rayshawn played like he couldn't find the keys and Steeli'o helped him "pretend" to look for them because they surely didn't want anyone driving around town with all that hash in the trunk. Naquawna and the girls eventually give up on finding the keys to the car and end up taking that big R.V; back to the store once again. The men tell the ladies they plan on keeping it simple tonight on the grill, cooking hot links, hot dogs and homemade hamburgers with two slabs of ribs in honor of Bubba Dank.

But that part about 'honoring Bubba, was the guys secret about the ribs because the guys knew they were Bubba's favorite. Rayshawn still kinda felt like Bubba was still here at the house, in spirit' and so did Steeli'o as they talk secretly about it. With heavy hands the guys put all the hard liquor up on the counter in the kitchen and the beer went in the Frig. Whatever didn't fit in the Frig like beer, soda's or bottled water, went in the ice cooler. The girls get back from the store quicker this time, because they are egger to party and have fun with their men tonight. After Roxy takes her time putting up all the cute party streamers and party banners on each side of the staircase rails, the party begins!

The music came on first and then the grill got to smoking. 'Speaking of smoking! 'Now in truth, Steeli'o would 'never, get high on his own supply! But he just had to get his boys and their ladies to try out his new stuff. So he told Rayshawn "to act like it was his stash that he brought up from home, if anybody asked." The girls hit the hash from Rayshawn's pipe and then clown't on him saying "we see how it is, now!" Rayshawn! "You've been holding out on us!" He laughs with a wink "I just wanted to save the best for last; ladies!" They all laugh and then the doorbell gets rung. Everybody looks at each other 'thinking, it might be the police because 'they are, playing their music; pretty loud. 'Or, could it be the smell of the herb 'lingering, all outside the cabin. Rayshawn opens up the door with the song in the background bumpin; welcome to My House by: Flo Rider. And with a big drunken smile on his face he yells out "it's my vanilla brother's; from another; mother!"

'Candis; gawks! And if she wore 'dentures, they would have; fall-in; right; out of her mouth! After seeing that it was Jake and Jordan at the front door giving Rayshawn hugs, Candis looks at Naquawna, and Roxy looks at 'Candis, then Candis turns her back so her body, is out of Jake's view. She stands there; motionless about to be 'sick, then she takes a big; gulp of her drink. When she swallows the liquor she flips out the words "wow...!" Really?!" she said sarcastically. Naquawna, Roxy and Candis are all huddle up together near the kitchen talking and can't believe what is happening. Naquawna asked "what are they doing here?!" "No! "The real question is, who told them where we were?!" adds Candis. And at the same time Candis had asked that question to the girls. Jake had said to the guys that "Bubba told us a few days ago, you guys would be partying before you leave Tahoe so that's why we came up."

Jake whisper's in Rayshawn's ear "and he also said yaw'll might be needing some help transporting those packages that would be coming in soon." Jordan looks around the house glancing at all the people then he asked Rayshawn "where is big Dank?" Rayshawn plays it off answers "Bubba had to get back home, something about work!" I'll fill you in on it later." Rayshawn with his pipe in hand walks the brother's over to meet Rafee'al and Bruce who are at the table getting ready to start a game of dominoes.

After they said their hello's Rafee'al glances over at Candis when Rayshawn introduces Jake and Jordan to the ladies. Rafee'al 'knows, this is an 'unexpected; turn of events in the house for Candis and he watches to see just how she plays it off because he knows all-- about her and Jake. When Jordan, sees Candis 'excitedly, he spouts "hey..., we know Candis!"

She's our pretty neighbor from up the street!" he said while shaking her hand. Jake, still crushing on her, looks at her; deeply while he's being introduced and then he puts his hand out to shake heirs saying "long time know see; Candis!" He smiles at her as he looks her up and down; lustfully with his eyes. She smiles back as he's holding her hand and stoking it with his other hand longer than he should, then he hugs her. Rafee'al finds himself getting quite jealous almost instinctively but he holds back his fighting words of "get your hands off my woman; man!" Candis notices the displeased look on Rafee'al's face and she was 'stimulatingly; glad, to see that he was jealous. Rayshawn gives Jake a look and then says; "her man's here partner" as he shuffles his head towards Rafee'al indicating to Jake; who she's with. Jake nods out of respect saying "ah..., okay!" So, after that was established Rayshawn moved on with a hit of the pipe; beaming "and this is my lady-friend; Naquawna!" And right over here is Steeli'o's little "some-um- some-um, named Roxy!" Roxy interjects "you mean his lady!" Not his little; something... something...!" she said laughing as she takes the pipe out of his hand and hits it, and blows the smoke in his face.

Rayshawn's quite; turned on, but 'focused, says "I'll deal with you later, smarty pants!" he said with a grin; taking the brother's over to the kitchen counter to get them a drink. The party is going; fabulous! Even some college kids in a group of 12 staying in a couple of houses next door came over to party with them. They had a keg of beer to contribute so they carried it into the house and that's when some of the people started playing upside down 'keg guzzling, games. Some people were even gambling up against a back wall in the den area. The music was loud, the grill was grill-in; and the drinks were pop-in!

"This party is off the hook!" said Sherry to Bruce, Rafee'al, and Candis as they sat at the table playing a quick game of domino's while they got their sip on. Steeli'o and Roxy were drinking and making out by the fireplace all hugged up kissing holding on to each other while talking, laughing and keeping an eye on the grill. While other people were dancing in the living room area and pretty much anywhere they stood. So while everything is crack-in!" drinks, music, and the herb is being passed around on the dance floor! Rayshawn and Naquawna find themselves sneaking off to the laundry room. When the two get into the laundry room they close the door quickly. Naquawna with a bottle in her hand sits on top of the dryer and playfully turns it on; giggling. The talking between the two of them stops and they start to kiss, and as the dryer gets; hotter, so do they.

Rayshawn pulls her halter top down while they are kissing, and she unzips his pants. He slides her pants off while she is still sitting on top of the dryer holding on. The music is up so loud until no one can hear them 'or, would even care that the dryer is on. 'Except, Jake and Jordan who start to look for Rayshawn because they want to get some more of that 'hashish, he let them smoke on earlier. 'To all their friends, Jake and Jordan are known for doing "pranks" on people. And when they 'think, someone is having 'sex, anywhere; even at a party; it's fair game. After running around the house looking for Rayshawn they end up at the back of the house which looks like an added on room but in fact is a laundry room. Jake listens at the laundry room door at first and then he gets a sneaky grin on his face and he slowly opens the door. He and his brother crawl down on the floor to sneak a peek at Rayshawn in action. Rayshawn has done this to them before on 'many occasions, when they've been with girls out at parties, or just chillin at their house, so to 'them, this is 'payback, as far as they're concerned.

Naquawna's eyes are closed; tightly and Rayshawn's back is to the boys as they are watching Naquawna bounce up and down on Rayshawn's "cork n bottle"! "Naquawna's 'bon-bons, are bouncing all over the place!" like a big bowl of 'yummy, jello" whispers Jake. 'Jordan; nods with a big smile and starts to get even harder just looking at them as she arches her back almost lying back on the dryer while wrapping her legs around Rayshawn's waist. Being that this is the last night that Naquawna and Rayshawn will be spending together in 'Tahoe, makes her want him even more because she doesn't know 'when, she'll be able to see him when they get back home. But to really add 'fuel, to her already 'fired; up, body!" and the fact that there is a house full of people, in the next room; it has her even more sexually aroused. And since the music is up pretty loud, she feels like she can scream as loud as she wants to, so she does with Rayshawn's encouragement.

He touches her in all of the places he knows will heighten her vocal pleasure, while telling her "to just let, loose!" Saying to her "nobody can hear us!" "It's just you and me baby, go ahead; let it out!" "Ahhhh...!" yeah...!" She purrs out loud. And in amazement Jake and Jordan look at each other like "this b*tch is so-o-o...; loud!" 'Jordan, bites on his fist, to keep from getting too, excited! She reaches the 'tippy-top, of her love making pleasure and gets louder, and louder, and louder, and while he's sucking on her "milk; duds" the dryer; stops! And then shortly after, that the music stops because someone in the other room has tripped over the stereo core and unplugged it. But Naquawna is still; yelling out; nasty things; like "how good he feels as he's banging up her walls!" "And how much of a good lover he is!" "And to never stop 'f^%king, her!" ever!" And while she's talking dirty to him, and he's very much into it! 'So much, into it!" that he holds; out so she can keep 'Cumming, at her request! He moves his body so... athletically, to give her all of him by using all of the strength from his legs, to his calves, all the way down to his feet, so he can put his; back!" into it! But then he starts to get a 'cramp, in his right leg but he 'refuses, to stop 'driving, and 'driving, and 'driving, his Cadillac!" up, into her garage! 'Rayshawn; didn't hit the 'brakes, until 'he; himself 'finally, went; out with a bang!

He jerkily; laid his body on top of her chest as he 'bursted; deep; up inside her. Naquawna just held her arms around his neck and her legs around his back and she didn't want to let him go, as the sweat ran down her face and his, because the laundry room was very still hot. With a sigh of her mouth and a smile on her face she turns her head and notices the door is a little; open. Tightening her eyes to get a better focus, she sees movement on the floor out of her peripheral vision so she sits up; quickly in front of Rayshawn's body to cover herself. Rayshawn asked "what's wrong?!" He turns, in her eyes direction and sees Jake and Jordan on the floor trying to sneak out and he laughs at first, saying "awh... you caught me!" But then he sees the look on Naquawna's face so he says "man...!" That's messed up!" You nosey little bastards get out of here!" Jordan cracks up saying to him "It was good for us 'two, man; thanks!"

Laughing, Jake nods in complete agreement stating "dude; you've got yourself a real...; screamer!" The two look at Naquawna and Rayshawn with a grin; and while laughing out they say "and you two are way... better than the latest; porn!" we've seen! Naquawna yells "shut--; up!" and get the F^#k; out!" Jake and Jordan both end up running out of the laundry room laughing with noticeable; hardware! And they head straight to where Steeli'o is, which is out back by the grill, flipping the meat. The boys wanted to go tell Steeli'o what they just witnessed. But Steeli'o already knew, because he was in the backyard by the grill and could 'still, hear Naquawna's knotty; nasty; screams! The music went back on once the cd was changed but it was too late by then, because everyone in the house had heard her as well. Candis and Roxy are use to Naquawna's "escapades"! Saying to each other "that Naquawna likes it when people can hear her having sex." Or, in this case; she likes letting people 'know, when she's being "plowed; righteously"!

Roxy takes a big gulp, of her drink after getting another image in her head of what Rayshawn "might" be like in bed! Or, anywhere 'else, for that matter, after hearing Naquawna's; bellowing! 'Plus, Roxy still can't get that image of him out of her mind, on that night when he was out in the hot tub being sexed by Naquawna, while she was masturbating up on the balcony and him watching her; intensely! Naquawna and Rayshawn 'all done now, come back to the party all sweaty and oily looking, like they've been having sex all day long. Jake and Jordan are still out back by the grill with Steeli'o talking about the next fast car they want to buy. So when Rayshawn comes out back to where they are, Jake starts laughing; tauntingly; blasting "ahhhh...!" "We got your ass this time; bro!" Rayshawn laughing back gives them dap; grinning he says "I told you man!" "I make um; holla!" Jake and Jordan laugh excessively shouting "and she can definitely holler; dude!" "She was loud as hell!" said Jordan while pulling on his pants. Steeli'o laughing just shakes his head thinking back on how he made someone "holler" today too, meaning; Claudia.

But then he 'shushes, the guys when Roxy walks out to where they are all at, standing by the grill talking. Steeli'o says "what's up; bay'be?" She walks up to him asking "do you have a lighter?" Because Candis and I want to relight the fireplace for a little more "ambiance". He pulls a lighter out of his pocket and she kisses him and walks away switching from side to side with a slight glance at Rayshawn 'hoping, he likes what he sees, too.

Jake and Jordan smile as she's walking away, and say "damn; dawg!" "She's hot!" Steeli'o chuckles "yess..., she's my future wife!" Rayshawn almost chokes mid-sip on his drink when he hears that, especially when he thinks back on the time he saw Roxy for the first time at the strip club. And not to mention the other night up on the balcony. 'But, for some 'reason, he just can't bring himself to 'snitching, on the real "Roxy"! The one that he 'knows, and has "played; with" in person, and from afar; if' he counts the masturbation! 'Even though, "self-consciously" his reasons go deeper than that, because he does, kind of like Roxy, and from one player to another he thinks she's got some game; herself, for playing Steeli'o the way she has. 'So for now; her secret is safe with him.

Everyone is dancing again having a great time. Even Bruce and Sherry are dancing all over each other with the lights dimmed low throughout the house. When Rayshawn gets a call on his phone he lets it go to voicemail because it's Se'anna calling. Not only is he way too; drunk to talk to her, but the music is also being; cranked up, from their speakers. And--, yes, then there's that other thing 'which is, "Naquawna" who is now, sitting on his lap. So after the call he gets up saying "I'll be right back" he tells Naquawna so he can go to the bathroom, so he can hear the message Se'anna has left him.

With the phone up to his ear, he hears crying in her voice but before he could get all of what Se'anna is saying, because of all the crying, and high pitched; verbiage, she was using. Sherry looks at the TV that is still on but down low and reads the bottom words on the screen that says "Breaking News!" Then Bryant Gumbel is sitting there saying "tonight, Bubba LL Banks' was found dead is his home by his housekeeper, Bonnie!" Sherry screams and points at the television saying "is that 'our; Bubba?"! Rayshawn; runs out of the bathroom when he hears Naquawna yelling for him "to come see the news!" Steeli'o hurries and turns off the music and stares at the tube, as did Roxy holding his hand in shock at what they were seeing. Everyone in their circle of friends was; devastated! Candis started crying as Rafee'al held her tightly in his arms consoling her. But Jake and Jordan really took it hard because they were like brothers to Bubba, and they just 'knew, that Bubba's mom and dad were going to be so--; broken up, over the loss of their son. The mood had taken a bad turn in just a matter of minutes.

Rayshawn's dad calls him in the middle of the madness saying "did you see your "mother" on the news?!" "Talking about she was his housekeeper!" He continued to laugh "housekeeper; my ass!" More like the; crept-keeper!" Rayshawn chuckled out a laugh with his dad for a bit because it was 'funny, but then reality; really set in and his high; was; gone! He ends up talking to Se'anna in the bathroom because he knew she needed him to comfort her, just as much as he needed her, to comfort him. They shed some tears on the phone together and she said "luckily your mom was okay." He answers "yeah, I know." But don't worry babe, I'll be home tomorrow" he said. "Okay, good" she sighed. She then asked "so, you guys repossessed the car already?" "Yep...," he said in a tired voice. She sniffles out a smile saying "okay baby, I just wanted to hear your voice and know that you were okay." "Love you" she said softly. "Love you too" he said. And then Naquawna opens up the bathroom door shouting "come on!"

Se'anna says "was that a girl's voice I heard?!" He shushes; drunken Naquawna with his index finger up to his mouth, and replies "naw, that's the t.v!" Naquawna starts playing games saying "come 'on, down and bring your 'auto; parts!" like she was really doing a commercial. But Rayshawn is not impressed, he hurries up and hangs up the phone. Naquawna chuckles and he pushes her aside as he walks out of the bathroom yelling "you play too damn; much!" You know who the hell I was talking too!" "Damn...!" she said. "Sorry--!" she voiced 'all taken back, because she 'thought, they were really; growing closer! But "apparently" he is still more into his baby's momma than she was lead to believe! Sherry snickers a bit over hearing them two arguing and as she's giving Bruce a kiss she mumbles in his ear "looks like girl number 'two, is starting to see, that she is "not" girl number 'one, after all!"

The party had fizzled out as you could imagine as the crowd of people pack up their party streamers and their big keg and headed next door. After the girls 'sadly, talked about Bubba, and commented on how funny. They went on to say how much he will be missed as they sat at the dinner table. Naquawna, not wanting to be sad anymore though, eventually changes the subject to hair products, since that's her job and she pretty much eats, sleeps and dreams about hair and nails. When the girls get tired of talking amongst themselves, and Candis lies her head down on the dining room table because there is no way to bring life back into this 'depressed party, the girls decide to retire to their beds.

'The guys though, sit out back by the fire pit smoking stogies and hitting hash out of this 'hookah bong; that Jordan went out to his truck to bring in. Bruce ended up going to bed shortly after the girls went up being that he was so tired from the party. So now the guys felt they could talk freely about what had; really happened; to Bubba, amongst Jake and Jordan. With tears in his eyes Jake couldn't believe; what he was hearing! His mouth was so wide open, with disbelief; that it looked like one of those tunnels that a toy train could pass through. Jake says "he had just called us the other morning when you guys were at the Casino about to get the Diamonds." "I know" said Steeli'o talking in a low voice. He continued "we left thy next morning and it happened up on thy mountain at one of thy houses on my Realtor's list." "Awh...!" Man...!" voiced Jake. And "damn...!" said Jordan. Jake adds "so they were trying to hit you, Steeli'o?" blurts Jordan, asking "aren't you trippin about that man?"

"Hell--; yeh...!" I'm; trippin!" I don't know who?" would want to hurt me?!" I haven't done anyone; wrong!" I'm a good; business man!" he said with a heavy sigh. "We'll find out who it is!" said Rafee'al. "Don't you worry man!" he said. Which it was a true fact; that Rafee'al was serious about, because he didn't want to get kilt either in the crossfire, job or no job! And whomever, it is that is trying to kill Steeli'o is interfering with a federal investigation, so they do need, to get it handled! Yes, Rafee'al wants to be as tight with these guys as much as possible but he's not going to jump in front of a 'gun, for none of them! He plans on talking to his police buddies who were up on the mountain that day when he gets back to headquarters because he figures they should know something by now. The guys all sad, yet again 'slowly, walk up to bed, and Jake and Jordan sleep on the couches in the den.

When it is morning, it is a sad but a beautiful morning at best. The sun is out and the snow is lightly; falling. Everyone has packing up their belongings; quietly, but then all you can hear throughout the house is "drama!" coming from Naquawna. She is upstairs yelling at the top of her lungs "why can't I ride back with you?!" Yelling "you don't even "know!" Rafee'al that well! "And maybe Candis want to ride back with her man; too!" Rayshawn yells back "see?!" "It's your; mouth!" "Plus, I don't have to worry about Rafee'al asking me a bunch of dumb-ass question, while I'm driving; back home either!" She shouts "oh, so now you think I'm a dumb-ass?!" He says nothing else because he knows there's no getting through to her at this point, and she "ain't!" getting in his car; so he's done wit; it!

After packing up the rest of his stuff, he carries her bags downstairs for her, and then takes his bag out to the car and puts it in the backseat with Naquawna still; barking in his ear. Naquawna walking right behind him on his heels says "if you put your stuff in the trunk, you'll have more room for me and Candis to ride back with you guys!" He just lets her talk her non-since as he goes back into the house shouting "Ralph?" you ready?!" Rafee'al holding Candis in his arms at the top of the stairs says "yeah, give me a minute." He kisses Candis who has a sad look on her face, but understands' that Rafee'al doesn't want Rayshawn to have to ride all the way back home by himself. Plus, there's the paperwork at the office thing, so Candis can't get mad about him wanting to do his job for his auntie's business. And, Candis is actually glad to see that her man is getting along so well; with Naquawna's man. So with that in mind, she looks at Naquawna spouting "girl, let it go!"

Naquawna who is pissed; shouts back to Candis "ain't that a biTch?!" "Why can't we ride back with them?!" What kind of sh+t is that?!" Rafee'al holding back his laugh takes down Candis's bags and makes sure she has everything she needs, and then he and Rayshawn say "bye to Steeli'o, who is helping Roxy bring down all her crap. Rayshawn witnessing Steeli'o stumbling with all the bags laughs saying "damn; girl!" You act like 'you're, one of the 'housewives, with all them; bags you got!" They all laugh at Roxy, when she replies "I'm ma; Treeberry housewife; in the making!" and don't you forget it!" She continued to laugh "I just haven't had the wedding; yet!" she sassed; out, glancing Steeli'o's way. After hearing that from Roxy, Steeli'o's eyebrows shot up sharper than a pencil head, because he was surprised to hear her say that. Candis chuckled too voicing "umm..., tell it!"

Naquawna catching the tail end of the joke asked "tell, what?" They all disperse and leave Naquawna wondering what they were talking about because Rayshawn is ready to leave and doesn't want 'any, more drama from her at this point. By the time the crew all pile in the RV, Rayshawn and Rafee'al are already on the highway heading towards Sac'mento. Rafee'al laughs out loud as they are going up the highway saying "you have Naquawna; mastered!" "You knew everything she was going to 'say, before she even; said it!" Rayshawn laughs even louder voicing "that's why I didn't want her to ride back with us; man! "She would have drove me; crazy!" "And I already have "crazy!" at home waiting on me! "But even she's not as cuckoo as Naquawna is!" Rafee'al laughed as hard as Rayshawn did, keeping in mind; that he was still on the clock "job wise," so Rafee'al takes this time to get to know Rayshawn a little more, while they're driving up the highway.

He asked Rayshawn "so, are you and the mother of your kid ever gonna get married?" "Or are you cool with the way it is now?" Rayshawn didn't see that question coming, so he paused before answering; then he said "hmm--, that's a good--, question!" "We've talked about it, but I haven't bought her a ring or anything like that." "Plus, I guess I'm just playing my "players card" to the 'fullest!" before I 'do, tie the knot one day" laughs Rayshawn. "Why you asking; man...?" You starting to get that; marrigin-itus; fever for Candis?" "I wouldn't blame you, though, she is a good catch!" smiled Rayshawn with a wink. They both laugh when Rafee'al comments on the word "marrigin?!" Is that even a word; man?!" said Rafee'al and they laughed some more. Rafee'al still laughing blurts out "spell; it!" And they both laugh even; harder. But before Rayshawn could take a gander at trying to spell the word "marrigin-itus fever!" for jokes; sakes; immediately behind them is a Highway Patrol car's flashing lights.

Through all the laughs Rayshawn thinks he didn't realize how fast he was going; and just that; quick, he is getting pulled over. Rafee'al on the other hand wasn't trippin that hard because he figured it was his team trying to recover the hash and charge Rayshawn for transporting drugs. But Rayshawn was cool as a fan and Rafee'al couldn't figure out 'why?" knowing; that they have all this hash in the trunk. The Officer comes up to the car on Rafee'al's side and Rafee'al knows him. He met him a while back when he use to be a Highway Patrol Officer himself. Plus, this Officer also knows Rafee'al is undercover because Kitpatrick is the one who sent him to bust Rayshawn on this stretch of highway. The Officer immediately wants to see Rayshawn's license, registration and proof of insurance. Rayshawn calmly says "okay, no problem, but this is a rental car" he says looking up at the Officer, asking him "why did you pull me over anyway?"

The Officer looks at him and in an insinuating tone he asked "is there a problem?" like as if, Rayshawn is getting smart with him so he tells him "to get out of the car!" Rafee'al replies "sir, is that necessary?" he said those words so he sounded "more" like a civilian, instead of a cop himself. So in keeping with the 'act, the Officer tells Rafee'al "since you have so much to say, you can stand over here on the gravel outside by the car as well!" As the Officer is walking back to his patrol car he says to Rayshawn "what is that smell, coming from your trunk?" Rayshawn answers "what smell?!" knowing that the coffee beans should; mask any odor. Then, the Officer, with his hand over his gun tells Rayshawn "come open the trunk!"

At first Rayshawn refuses because he knows his rights. But he also knows the law, and the fact that the Officer can impound his car and get a warrant to search it, makes it a no brainer for Rayshawn. Rafee'al trying to show that he's a true friend yells out "he doesn't have the right to search your car man, not without probable cause!" Rayshawn pissed says "I know man, but I'm tired, and I just want to get home. So with shaky hands and a scared; face, Rayshawn opens up his trunk. The Officer had his gun drawn and ready, just in case someone was in the trunk. When the trunk is slowly lifted up the Officer is surprised to see that there is nothing but a spear tire and loose pieces of plastic with coffee grounds sporadically placed on the inside of the trunk's floor. Rafee'al's eyes were as big as silver dollars as he stood there looking. Rayshawn believes that Rafee'al is spooked because they are about to go to jail, but he winks at Rafee'al like; it's all good!

But little did Rayshawn know, Rafee'al's eyes were big because he had messed; up! "Royally"! 'Dropped the ball, one might say, and now he is going to have a lot of explaining to do with his Captain about the missing drugs. The Officer had no choice but to let Rayshawn go. He even called Kitpatrick from his patrol car to make sure he had the right guy. When Rayshawn and Rafee'al got back in the car Rayshawn sweating as they are driving away says "somebody is really looking out for me, man!" Luckily, Jake and Jordan decided at the last minute, to take all of that hash back with them!" At first, I was offended!" said Rayshawn. "But then it did start to make more since because they had a truck with a camper shell on it, which would blend in on the road better than this ride we're in!" And not to throw in the "race card" but they 'would, have a better chance of getting it back home because they look like clean cut white boys!" "And as you can; 'see, look who ended up getting pulled over?!" He laughs out loud voicing "I guess I'm looking like "Gangster; Gee!" up in this rental car or something!"

Rafee'al laughs and gives him dap saying "damn we got lucky; dawg!" "I just knew we were going to jail" said Rafee'al shaking his head.

But as he turns to look out the window all he could hear is crickets from everyone at the station who thought, he couldn't do it. And Kitpatrick laughing thinking he was too soft on Candis and got side tracked and lost the stash. Rafee'al, still thinking on it, scratches his head asking "so--, when did they load up the hash into their truck?" Rayshawn answered "Steeli'o helped them put it all in their truck at about 5:00 this morning." That boy be getting up; early!" cracks Rayshawn talking about Steeli'o. He adds "I think he has sleep issues!"

Rafee'al chuckles saying "dang..., they left that; early?!" "Yep..., they were on the road by 5:30." I was just turning over" smiled Rayshawn. Rafee'al was pissed because that's about the time he was spooning with Candis and heard a car but thought he was just dreaming. Rafee'al adds "I thought the hash was still in the trunk because you put all of our luggage in the backseat."

Rayshawn laughs out loud; saying "yeah, that was to guarantee that Naquawna wouldn't be riding back with us, when I told her that there was no place for her to sit." Rayshawn continued to laugh even harder; just thinking about how cleaver he is; when he wants to be! Even Rafee'al had to give him credit because he fooled; even him, about the hash switch. Sitting in the passenger's seat has Rafee'al so mad because he knows Jake and Jordan are home or somewhere by now with all that hash and there was no way he could give Kitpatrick or Lenny a heads up on; who?" now, had all that hash! Rafee'al is just going to have to take this loss, and be on his 10 toes for the next one, especially since 'now, he's in pretty tight with all these guys. And he has to admit with all of the things they have been through in such a short period of time, he felt confident that the guys would trust him on their next big shipment!

'So--, although mad, Rafee'al smiled inwardly thinking this could be a good thing 'them, getting pulled over together and 'him, witnessing the death of their friend and not telling a soul, not even Candis. In his mind they would have no 'choice, but to think of him as a loyal brother. Plus, they've taken him to their drops, and to their pickups, in such a short time of knowing him, thanks to Bubba telling them he was cool! Rafee'al sits back in his seat and Rayshawn cranks up the music as they float up the highway playing Meek Mill's song: Levels!

Rayshawn drops Rafee'al off at the O garden's main Office in Sac'mento and he tells Rayshawn he will get a ride home from his co-worker who he had called earlier to confirm with, in front of Rayshawn in the car which was really Kitpatrick. Rafee'al did it this way not only to show him where he worked, but also to establish more trust. Secretly Kitpatrick is standing in the elevator waiting for him so Rayshawn won't see him when he drops him off. With a 'dap, to Rayshawn's fist, Rafee'al all happy gets out the car thanking Rayshawn for the ride. Then Rayshawn drives off bumping his music.

When Rafee'al opens up the office elevator doors Kitpatrick is standing there with his phone on speaker while the Captain is yelling at him. Rafee'al can hear the anger in the Captain's voice so to calm him down he blares out "this is a good thing though; boss!" "Because now, I've bonded with these men!" The Captain yells even louder "what's so good about you losing the drugs?!" "Tell, me, that!" Kitpatrick just scratches his head, feeling sorry for his buddy because he is getting so-- chewed; out!

By the time Rafee'al explains his "belief" in them taking him on the next big pickup, his Captain has calmed down 'somewhat, responding with "you better be right; Mahavez!" Or you're off this case!" The Captain yells at Kitpatrick as well saying that "him and Lenny should have done a better; job in watching who had left that house at 5 am this morning!" Deep down the Captain knows Rafee'al could be right in his theory about the gained; trust! 'And in fact, who could he "possibly" get to replace Rafee'al?" being that he's gotten so far in this case thus far. After hanging up with his Captain Rafee'al smiles; confidently knowing that no one can do what he's done, in this short amount of time. Even Kitpatrick jokes about it saying "you know they ain't gonna replace you; because they need you to close out this case!" Kit continues to say "hey, I almost forgot to tell you, and this is on a "sadder; note," and I hate to even bring this up, at this time; but, they found out that your sister was pregnant when she was killed." As Rafee'al is getting the papers he needed to copy he looks over at Kitpatrick; shocked, he shouts "my God!" are you serious?!" said Rafee'al. "How did you find that out?" Kitpatrick answers "actually, Officer Jackson found that out." I think she has a thing for you" he said as he slaps Rafee'al on his back shoulder as they start to walk down to the copy machine.

Rafee'al frowning asked "do you think that might be a motive, for why she was killed?" "I don't know, but I was thinking the same thing" sighed Kit. "Wow!" said Rafee'al. "So did Officer Jackson say 'who, she was pregnant by?" "No, but they have DNA from the fetus, so now all we have to do is find her killer or the baby's father to find out what happened" said Kitpatrick; somberly. Rafee'al runs his copies and then locks up the building.

When they get to Kitpatrick's car he sits down and tries to think back on who his sister could have been dating back then. But he was so young and naïve, and into his own issues of growing up when he confessed to Kitpatrick saying "I don't even remember any of her boyfriends; really!" "And our dad was so strict, so she had to of hid that part of her life from our family!" especially the pregnancy.

Rafee'al rubs his hands back and forth on top of his legs trying to keep warm in that cold car as he talking and thinking back on who his sister might have gotten pregnant by. With his head filled with questions they ride up the highway back to town bumpin the song: The Other Day Ago with E-40 featuring Spice 1 and Celly Cel! Back in Treeberry the RV comes to a screeching halt and everyone gets dropped off at their cars, which are parked at the library. Steeli'o and Roxy say good-bye to everyone with a hug, and Bruce and Sherry do the same, because they are so happy to be back on snowless; ground!

Naquawna gets dropped off at home so her and Candis can talk "privately" about all the sexual things; they 'did, or in Candis's case did "not" do! Candis laughs at how crazy Naquawna is for having sex on top of a dryer. And Naquawna tells her "how nasty the two brothers were for watching her and Rayshawn while they were doing, it!" The girls, filling thy R.V with laughter when Naquawna reflected back on the time "that Ernesto stayed in the parking lot to watch as well while she and Rayshawn were having relations outside on the hood of her car." It was the first time Candis was hearing about that story. But in Naquawna's defense it was because Candis told her "she didn't want to hear nothing else about Rayshawn!" But here they 'were, once; again "talking" about Rayshawn!

Naquawna smiling; happily because she's home, jumps out of the R.V, but before she could make her way up to her front porch, she throws up in a nearby bush. Candis rolls down the passenger's window yelling "are you alright?!" Wiping her mouth she returns "yes." I think I'm just a little car sick." Candis gives her a look like "are you sure that's the reason?" Naquawna can read her facial expression so she replies "no--; bi#%h!" It's the RV ride home!" "I'm not; pregnant!" Candis grunts "okay... and with a smirk on her face laughing, she yells "I'll holla, and she drives off with a toot of her horn.

Chapter 28

The next day after their trip, when everyone is at their own homes, the breaking news crew comes on saying “that the Homicide of Bubba happened somewhere else; ‘not, at his home as they previously reported.” Stating; “that now, the case is under a full; investigation!” Rayshawn and Se’anna are watching the news while lying in bed when he gets a phone call from Steeli’o after he sees the same news feed, so Rayshawn gets out of bed and takes the call in the kitchen. Standing by the fridge Rayshawn says "man, I hope we don't get charged with tampering with evidence, because we didn't kill him!" Steeli'o says "I was worried at first too, but we should be cool, because we didn't move thy body, my peoples did, and trust me they were very throe."

"Alright?" "Alright, then." "Cool!" said Rayshawn as he's closing the refrigerator after getting out a cold drink. Se'anna yells from the room "come on babe!" "Are you bringing me some orange juice too, or what?" Steeli'o can hear her in the background so he says "okay bro, I'll let you go, but we need to hook up tomorrow to get thy hash from Jake and Jordan's house so we can divide it up four ways." "Alright, bet!" said Rayshawn. "But what about Rafee'al should we see if he wants to sell some of the hash too?" Steeli'o answers "maybe, since we don't have Bubba's spot." "Okay then, hit me up at around noon" said Rayshawn. When Steeli'o hangs up the phone Rayshawn heads back to the room with a glass of orange juice for Se'anna and then he gets back in bed. He's a little more confident about not being implicated in Bubba's cover up, so he decides to have a nice love session with his woman as the 'lights, go 'dim, in their room.

Now over at Sherry's house; Bruce is "not" so lucky! He gets off the computer after Sherry says to him she's going to take a shower so they can have a "little; fun" in this 'sexy; teddy, that she found up in Tahoe. But when she gets out of the shower and noticed this heavy; smelly discharge, running down her leg followed by a rash, in her inner thighs she screams out "Bruce!" "What the 'f#^k; is this?"! Bruce drops the remote that he has in his hand and rushes to the bathroom where she is, shouting "what's wrong?!" She shouts "look!" And as she's showing him her private area his responds is "oh, wow!" "Maybe it's from those ski pants you were wearing; remember?" "You said they were making you sweaty and itchy." "No!" This is not from no damn; ski pants!" I know my body!" she belts out. Then in an even angrier voice she yells "Bruce!" I swear!" If you've given me any kind of 'infection; it's over!" He frown voicing "awe, come on sweety!" You know damn; well, it's not no; infection!" She yells "then pull down your briefs!" I want to see if you have the same; rash!" He blurts "are you kidding me?!" I don't have no damn; rash!" He continues to shout out, other words as he's walking away trying to blow off her request. Sherry gets even madder because she has to grab him by the arm to make him; pull down his pants.

Bruce is a bit hesitant, and for good reason too, because he 'knows, he slept with that girl in Tahoe, and that's why he stands there for a minute; thinking back. Then he realizes that he hasn't been itchy, and he feels fine, and the last time he checked his penis was when he went to urinate and it looked normal. So after arguing about not pulling his pants down, he pulls them down with confident saying "see?!" I'm fine!" And he stands there all proud, looking down at himself. Sherry looks at him and can't see anything wrong with him, and a part of her sighs, with relief but then she takes an even closer look; lifting up his tea bags, and with a sharper look down there, she then looks back up at him and with a disgusted look on her face she yells out "you have the same rash I got!"

When she moves her hands from his 'plum size walnuts, his penis falls and starts to drip, so she screams "ewe...!" And with a mortified look on her face she yells "mother f^&ker!" I work; at the hospital!" So I've seen this sh^t; many of times!" So you better start talking!" I wanna know who the hell!" you slept with?!" Bruce; stunned; himself thinks, how could he possibly have contracted VD from that girl, the one and only time he ever!" cheated on Sherry! 'In denial, he yells back "hell...!" No!" This is from that trip!" An allergic reaction, of some kind!" I would never; cheat on you; babe!" And you 'know; that!" Sherry goes into hysterics "I don't know sh*t!" You lying; bastard!" "Who is she?!" "Who is she?!" "Bruce!" "That hoe at your office?!" Bruce backs up when she starts swinging her hands on him, all over his chest, while trying to hit him in his face. He yells back "no! "No! "And if you keep on hitting me!" I'm calling the police; and they will get you on domestic violence!" She yells "call the police!" I'll get your damn phone for you!" Still yelling she stomps off to the living room to get his phone, to throws it at him! Then she yells again "tell me Bruce!" Or I'll call that bi%ch right now, from your office!"

He grabs the phone from her saying "it's not her!" "Oooooh...!" she retorts. "So it is; someone else?!" Who, is, it; Bruce?!" she said getting angrier and angrier! Then not being able to hold it back any longer he yells out "it was a girl up in Tahoe!" he said flinging out his arms shouting "okay?!" you happy now?!" Sherry shouts "WHAT?!" He adds "but she only gave me head; that's all!" I didn't even have sex; with her!" Sherry shouts "in Tahoe!" Then in an even louder 'ghetto 'er voice!" she shouts "when was this?!" because I was with you the whole time!" In a meek voice with his head; dropped he answered "it happen when you and the girls were at the spa." "Oh, hell, no!" she said standing there looking at him paralyzed; with guilt. And for a split second, she could hear Dianna's voice saying "you'll never know; what you'll do; until it happens to you!"

She is trying not to cry because she is so freaken; heated! And he can tell; so with sad eyes he says "sherry! "I am; sorry!" I was drunk and the lady asked me to come up to her room to see how great the view was." And when I got up there, I didn't know she was going to do me like she did." Sherry just couldn't believe what she was hearing; it was like going through a tunnel, with the sounds muffled. And when she came out, on the other side all she could see was 'fury, when she called him "a dumb-ass!" son of a bitch! She gets up in his face yelling and screaming for him to "get; out!" Saying "I have; never!" cheated on you! "Get out!" And take all-- your sh^t with you!"

Bruce, not wanting to leave shouts "this is my place too!" And, I have nowhere else to go!" He voices "yes, I made a mistake!" I know that now!" but I do love you Sherry; and I'm sorry!" But Sherry just kept throwing all his stuff out the front door shouting "hurt me!" Hah!" Hurt; me!" No!" You some---; bi+ch!" You've done more than just; "hurt me"! "Cheating on me; was the 'hurtful; part!" "But the worst; of it all!" is you not being 'smart enough, to uses; protection!" "And now--; you end up bringing me back; Lord, knows; what!" That's the 'humiliating part; that your dumb-ass didn't think about!" "You nasty; bastard!" Tears start to fall down her cheeks as she looks him; hard in the face 'yelling, at the top of her 'lungs, so he can 'feel, her pain and 'know, that he has 'fu*ked; 'up; royally! She went off on Bruce so 'badly, calling him everything in the book; but a child of; God! 'Until Bruce 'knew, there was no reasoning with her tonight or maybe; ever! He grabs his car keys and his laptop and tries to pick up most of his stuff from off the front lawn with Sherry still yelling and throwing things. He knows he really doesn't have anywhere to go and stay tonight, so he has no choice but to get a room at a nearby hotel. Sherry slams the door behind him and calls her gynecologist so she can get in to see her first thing in the morning!

Chapter 29

It is cold outside, on Saturday morning but all the guys decided to meet at Jake and Jordan's house anyway to divide up the hash, and go to Bubba's funeral today too. Rafee'al was surprised when the guys cut him in on the hash but technically they had no choice because Rafee'al knew way too much about their business. When they get to the church Candis and Naquawna are already there sitting down. 'Sherry, didn't make it because of her "situation" with Bruce. And Steeli'o came to the funeral solo, and walked up to the girls asking "where was Roxy?" implicating to them how she never returned his call." And that he even drove by her house before going to Jake's place." So when Candis hears that, she tells him "that Roxy went out of town to her sister's, because her sister's water broke." Soon after Candis had told him that, Roxy called him saying "sorry baby, I was on the plane."

He didn't grill her about 'not, letting him know because he was feeling a little shady now too, for having had sex with his ex-girlfriend; Claudia. So he says to Roxy "no problemo bay'be." "I was just worried about you" he said. Roxy says "awe... I miss you pumpkin." She tells him that she'll be back on Tuesday, and he replies "okay." He adds "love you." She was a little taken back because he said it so, straight up. She smiles saying "I love you too." At the time of her saying "that she loved him" she was sitting in a rental car about to go back into work. Now, she is feeling crappy for lying to him about being at her sister's place. 'Yes, Roxy's sister really did have the baby but it was days ago and Roxy just left the hospital that morning. She felt so guilty, about lying to him, so she sent him a picture of the baby to make it more; believable.

Her boss comes out to her car and taps on the window asking "are you alright; honey?" She rolls down her window smiling, saying "yep. "I'll be in there in a minute. It's no secret to the girls at the club that her boss favors her the most. She even gets extra bonuses for no reason at all, but he tells her it's because she's doing such a spectacular job at the club. Burt even told Roxy not to tell the other girls that he pays her more than them because he doesn't want to cause "jealousy" or bickering amongst the women. He opens up her car door for her and she steps out looking like a 'Vegas Show Girl!

Burt licks his lips as he's standing up close to her; dreaming of a chance to be with her he smiles. She smiles back at him then she scoots him out of the way with her bum, so she can shut her car door. Feeling how she's flirting with him, he then grabs her by the arm and escorts her into the club like she's his prize possession. Of course she loves all of thy attention he gives her, but at what cost? 'Sometimes, prize possessions can become 'problematic, because people usually become obsessed, with them, like Burt is, with Roxy. Roxy walks to the back of the club to get a hat from her locker so she can wear it, during her next routine. The show starts and as she's walking out on the stage, she can't help but feel in her 'gut; that it is getting about that time for her to come clean and tell Steeli'o everything before Christmas, or risk losing him forever after hearing him say "he loves her. All the girls at the club take their turn up on the stage, while making Burt proud, as the club members; spend their money; on his girls; buying them drinks, and tipping them out!

'But now, back in the town of "Treeberry" there is still, a funeral today. After the church said a few words and "shouted" in the name of; Jesus! Everyone sadly; gathers together outside at the burial grounds. The funeral was beautiful because Bubba's mom and dad really sent him off; in style. Some people even stayed to eat over at the church hall. But once the visiting with friends and family members was slowly departing, the couples started walking out to their cars when they were approached by two plain clothed Detective's. Even Rafee'al was caught off guard because he didn't know 'these, particular guys and his department wanted it that way, so he would have more of a natural responds along with his friends.

The Detective's take the guys to the side to talk. The first Officer says "we know that Bubba was up in Tahoe with you guys, and Rayshawn responds first "yeah, but he left Tahoe to go home to take care of some business." The other Detective says "you wouldn't happen to know what kind of "business" that might have been would you?" "It might have been 'music, from what we were told" said Rafee'al. The Detective responds "we've checked his computer and he hadn't logged on for days."

"Well, he also works sometimes off his smartphone" answered Steeli'o. The Detective clips his pen on his writing pad, saying "that might be true, but we can't seem to find his phone, any idea where it might be?" Rayshawn blurts "his phones missing?" Rayshawn asked that question with a sincere look of concern on his face because in truth, Steeli'o and the guys really didn't know where Bubba's phone was, and that's 'not; good! The Detective's walk away saying "you boys stay available, just in case we need any more questions answered." They respond back with "for sure; Officer's!"

Naquawna then walks over to where the guys are standing asking "what are they trying to say?" "That we had something to do with his death?" A horn blows and it's Se'anna coming to pick up Rayshawn because she figured he might need a ride since he got dropped off by Jake. Se'anna didn't attend the funeral telling Rayshawn "that she just can't 'do them, anymore because she gets too upset and would rather remember Bubba the way he was." Rayshawn had forgotten; that she had said something earlier about wanting to go to the flea market today, so they could buy a big rug for the dining room, but when she pulled up, his memory came back; quickly!

Naquawna is 'pissed, when she hears the horn and sees who it is, and they can see it, all over her face. But all Rayshawn could think about 'is how lucky he is, that he wasn't posted up with his arms around Naquawna when Se'anna pulled up and blew. Se'anna didn't even notice Naquawna because she had on such a big hat covering up most of her face. And the scant-less part about it is, Naquawna had stopped taking Se'anna's calls down at the shop saying "that she was way too busy, to do her hair any longer, but that she could recommend a shop in the next town over for her; if she'd like?" 'Now, Se'anna tells all her friends "how Naquawna is such an 'unprofessional; "be'yotch!" for not keeping up with her client's; hair."

Rayshawn gets in the car and Se'anna gives him a big kiss on the lips then she gets out of the car and walks around the vehicle to get in on the passenger's side so Rayshawn can drive. 'All eyes, are on Naquawna right now, and she couldn't even hide the fact that she is 'second; best, in the relationship!" 'If, she could even call it that! She was so mad when she walked down towards her car; that steam, was coming out the top of her hat. Candis sighs "gurl--, don't even trip off of him!" Naquawna doesn't say a 'word, just her lips were balled up in anger. And then she gets a big lump in her throat and leans over, down by the side of her car and throws up. Candis shouts "hoe!" Twice in one week!" Oh--!" Hell; no!" You need to get a pregnancy test!" Naquawna grunts "pah-leazz...!" I'm fine!" But Candis; insisted. So she and Naquawna decide to go to the store to get a test, but before leaving the burial grounds Candis says "bye, to Rafee'al with a hug and a big kiss. He had told her already that he was going to go with the guys to hang out.

So Steeli'o starts up his car and he and Rafee'al follow Jake and Jordan in their car back to their house. After they pick up the hash from Jake and Jordan's house, Rafee'al and Steeli'o head to Steeli'o's house. The reason being is mostly because Steeli'o wanted to 'floss, how nice his pad was. His thought were, he'd show Rafee'al how a self-made man is supposed to live. So when they pull up in the driveway and Rafee'al sees how big the house is, he is in awh... because it looks way bigger in person then on the surveillance; camera. In truth, Rafee'al was 'very impressed, but "not" that envious, as Steeli'o would have 'hoped, he'd be, because Rafee'al believes is 'honest; hard work. Vinnie comes down the stairs and introduces himself to Rafee'al, while Steeli'o is walking him around, showing him the house. With a big grin Steeli'o laughs out loud in front of Vinnie saying to Rafee'al "let me show you where all thy 'Italian; Stallion; magic happens!" "Which; technically" is all over thy house, but mostly up in thy room" he tells him.

Rafee'al, all glossy-eyed sighs "damn..., you doing up it big; man! He gives him a fist pound saying "I got to give it to you bruh, you know how to live!" This pad is on; fleek!" Steeli'o nodding; feeling the love replies "yess, but erry-thing has a price" he says as he's looking down on the ground thinking back on how he almost lost his life a couple of days ago, and in his 'place, someone 'else's life, got taken. Rafee'al sighs "I know man, problems always seem to find those of us; who 'choose, to live on the wild; side!" Steeli'o returns "I know!" It's crazy; but it is so--; true!"

He continues to say "sometimes I wonder how different my life would have turn't out, if I would have went to school to be an Architect?" I've always wanted to do that, and I use to talk to my father all thy time about it when I was younger." And when he died-- he starts to choke up but finishes "I had to grow up fast and become a man quick, for my family and I never got to fulfill that dream." Is that why you got into real-estate?" asked Rafee'al. "Yeas, I think it keeps me connected to my dream of one day designing my own home." You know?" doing it; thy right way!"

Rafee'al smiling says "you can do it bruh." You surely got the money to pay for school; by now." He continues to say "it's just a matter of you finding the time." "Yeas, I know" answered Steeli'o. "That's thy problem" he adds, "I have no time" he laughs, because I'm, always on thy move!" Moving sh*t from city to city!" Steeli'o chuckles as they head down the stairs saying "see?" like now, me having to take 'you, to go drop off your 'hash, at your place!" Rafee'al laughing back says "yep, I see what you mean." He continues to laugh saying "you should just get an 'Am-Track; stamped on your back; so you can keep it moving!"

Steeli'o cracked up laughing so hard that tears came to his eyes. He says to Rafee'al "you are a funny 'dude; man!" You always make me laugh!" Steeli'o than blurts "I take it, one of your dreams is to be a comedian?!" "Awh-ha-ha-ha!" that's funny!" laughs Rafee'al stating "not all brown folks can be comedians!" But that would be cool though" he said laughing about it, thinking about all his favorite comedian's, jokes. When he's done laughing he adds "but no; seriously!" One of my--; dreams, has to do with cars!" I've always been into cars!" he said grinning. "You mean like working on them?" asked Steeli'o. Rafee'al interjects "yeh, I love old cars and I like to fix them up." But I'm also talking about, fast cars!" "You mean like race cars?" asked Steeli'o smiling. "Yep, said Rafee'al. "But I've never really got to race in a real legitimate 'race, like you see on t.v!" But I'm pretty good though" he brags, thinking back on those days. "I use to tear them boys; up in my neighborhood, down this long stretch of highway, they could 'never, catch me!" I remember one time" he says with a gleam in his eyes, when I outran this Highway Patrol car and got away clean!" I was so far ahead of him, until he couldn't even get my; license; plate!" Steeli'o grinning shouted "no sh*t?!" Rafee'al laughs as they head outside while he's still telling him all about his glory days, and then he ends his story with "I really wish I could have started racing cars when I was a youngster, because maybe by now, I might have a few trophies sitting on a mantle, in my-- dream house too!" he laughs.

Steeli'o asked "why didn't you?!" What happened?!" Rafee'al shakes his head side to side as they are getting into Steeli'o's car and in truth, he doesn't want to say "because his sister got kilt." So instead he just says "my mom was always telling me it was too dangerous!" And--, I didn't have my dad to back me up, to say it was ok because he was missing in action." He had left us a long time ago and started another family, so-- you know; it just didn't happen!" The mood kind of shifted into a somewhat sad but guy bonding moment. And in fact this was totally off the record as far as Rafee'al was concerned, because he really wasn't working the case at that particular time, as he dug up his own buried dreams, that he rarely spoke about to anyone 'since, he's been undercover.

See, Rafee'al was a good kid but he always had a wild side to him and it always seemed to get him into trouble. When he was racing one night not only did he almost kill himself, but he almost killed a pedestrian that he didn't end up seeing; until the last minute. When the incident happened he had swerved; on a dime, but crashed head on into an overpass; stone wall. And when he walked away with only a sprained neck he vowed to 'God, he would find a better way to feed his 'need, for speed! At the scene of the accident is where he met 'Hank, who was a Highway Patrol Officer; that same Highway Patrol Officer; that he had outran mouths back before his accident. 'And Hank, remembering that chase, took him under his wing and told him that he would make a great Highway Patrol Officer by 'using, his racing skills and his brain. Rafee'al didn't even get charged for reckless endangerment; "mostly; because" he didn't hurt anyone, and secondly because Hank was just a cool ass; cop! And to this day the two men Hank and Rafee'al have been best buddies.

Steeli'o's car stops and he, Vinnie and Rafee'al get out in front of Rafee'al's apartment so they can drop his half of the hash off. Rafee'al's apartment 'failed; slightly' in comparison to Steeli'o's house! But his old school; car, now that's; another story! Rafee'al's car caught Steeli'o's eye and as he walked around it, admiring it, he made Rafee'al an offer on his car 'as if to think; he could buy anything he wanted! But Rafee'al said "naw; man! "This is my baby!" I've put a lot of work into just the engine alone" he said as he starts the car up, so he can let Steeli'o and Vinnie hear how quiet the engine sounds. Even Vinnie said he would love to have a ride like that back in Italy, claiming; it would be a 'panty dropper, for sure!

They finish looking at the car and then go into thy apartment. Steeli'o and Vinnie politely say how nice his bachelor pad is. And Rafee'al said "thanks guys" and offered them a drink. The guys sit down to talk, one on the sofa, and Vinnie sat on a chair. They started talking about the Tahoe trip and then Steeli'o says "I'm glad Bubba is finally at peace." "Me too" said Vinnie. Adding and it was some 'work, too getting him back home!" "We had to drive him back home in a pine box, in that small van, and he was starting to wreak!" "Plus, he continues to say, we never found the bullet in his body 'or, on the ground."

Steeli'o; cringing says "we need that phone too!" "So you might need to check the van again" said Steeli'o. "Damn," says Rafee'al we still have no clue who this guy is. Steeli'o grunts "at first I thought it was my business partner; Marky'os!" (Also known, as) Mr. Invisible, to the department." thinks Rafee'al remembering that name. "But he checked out" said Steeli'o. "And all the guys I deal diamonds with, through Claudia; checked out too." So as far as I can tell, Claudia definitely needs me alive, so I can't think of anyone else; offhand who would have a problem with me" he said yet again. They all pause thinking and talking about the hash while Rafee'al is stashing his part of the hash away in his sofa cushions. And when all of that is done Steeli'o with a big sigh belt out "whelp!" "Enough about depressing stuff" he says as he stand and stretches his arms. He continues to say "my cousin Vinnie, who has done such a great job cleaning up our mess, deserves a night out on thy town; on me!" "It is almost Christmas and Vinnie will be going back to Italy before New Year's, so--, as a thank you 'Vinnie, where would you like to go?" "I will spear no expense!" my cousin.

Vinnie had never been to the Bahamas's or Hawaii so he says "how about somewhere warm?!" The guys say "naw... save that for a romantic trip with your girl one day." Vinnie laughs "you're right, that wouldn't be a fun 'trip, not with you two; knuckle heads!" laughed Vinnie. They all laugh together then Steeli'o cheers saying "you need to get laid, my friend!" "So I'm going to take you to Vegas!" Rafee'al with his head tilted back and his hands over his face blurts out "awh-- man"! "Now, you, know...; Candis and Roxy are gonna be; pissed!" They all take another shot of the 1800 and then Steeli'o says "that's why we're not telling the girls!" "Besides, Roxy won't be back until Tuesday." "And we'll be back Monday night, so... it will all work out; great!" "I also remember hearing that they have a party plane that leaves right out of Treeberry" says Steeli'o. "Yeah... I've heard about those flights too" said Rafee'al. The guys take another shot and say all together "let's; do it!" Rafee'al asked "what about Rayshawn?!" "Naw...," says Steeli'o. "He's on lock down; for sure!" "Besides he just got back from Tahoe, so she ain't gonna let that guy out of her sight. Rafee'al chuckles "did you see how his woman came to the funeral and snatched that fool up?!" "Heck; yeah...!" said Steeli'o. "He's getting to close to getting caught." "You can only live a double life for so long" said Steeli'o shaking his head.

Rafee'al's eyes drop to the floor when Steeli'o mentions a double life and he changes the subject back to 'Candis, saying "maybe I should just tell her I'm going to Vegas, so she doesn't think I'm sneaking around. Steeli'o looks at him like go on ahead. But after his fourth shot Rafee'al too, decides "not" to tell her; either! They board the plane and all thy excitement of Vinnie going to Vegas for the first time has him 'acting, like a 'French whore, in a whips and chains, costume store. When they land in Vegas they go up to their room first. Their room is on the top floor because Steeli'o knows the 'high Rollin, Casino; owner. He didn't even have to make reservations, and he called it in from the plane and had everything set up for them when they landed. They headed up to their room when they first got there, so they could check it out. Up in the room the guys make themselves more drinks, and decide to also eat, before heading to the clubs, so Steeli'o orders room service. Steaks, shrimp, BLT's, crab cakes and other fine entrees came rolling into the room on a serving cart.

Vinnie is overjoyed when he finds out that they also have a full open bar, just because the owner knows Steeli'o; personally! Rafee'al has to admit to himself, that this 'guy, has it all! 'The life, 'the girls, 'money; 'power; he's thinking; what more could a man want?!" 'So now--, while the guys are getting twisted; off the drinks and eating on all this good food, soon it will be time to go out on the 'town, to get; faded! But in the meantime 9 hundred and 89 miles from Vegas over in Treeberry, Candis is over at Naquawna's house waiting outside Naquawna's bathroom asking "well..., what does the test say?!"

Chapter 30

Naquawna is in the bathroom trying to pee on a pregnancy stick and when she reads the results she opens the door saying "give me the other test!" This is some; bullsh%t!" Candis chuckling; sarcastically voices "It's some bullsh%t alright!" Naquawna with a dumb founded look on her face sighs out "this can't be happening!" Candis smirking her way says "so-- are you going to tell Rayshawn?" Naquawna not hearing her just stares at the test; hoping it turns negative. Candis tries to make her feel better by saying "you're granddad will be happy though!" "No, he, won't!" "Because I'm not; married!" frowned Naquawna. "Well, just wait awhile before you tell anyone because there is a 10 to 25% chance that you might miscarry, and there's no need in getting everyone all "mad" or, over "happy" at the good news until you've reached at least 12 weeks!" Then, speaking of mad, simultaneously as those words came out of Candis's mouth, Mike's mom was knocking on the front door. And before Naquawna could get to her granddad and tell him "not" to open the door, he swings open the front door saying "hey there, pretty lady?!" "How's it going?!" he smiled.

Her granddad is kind of 'gaga; over Ms. Ellis so he lets her in the house with Mike following behind her like a little puppy dog. Candis chuckles saying "well, I see you're "extended; family" is here!" Naquawna; overwhelmed says "Candis?!" don't leave!" "Please... don't leave!" Candis would stay but she tells her how "she 'can't, because she already promised her mom she would meet her at the church after the funeral." Candis says "you can come to the church with me though" she smiled. Naquawna mutters some choice words then says "and throw-up all in the pews!" "I don't think the church folks would like that very much" she concluded. "Not to mention, your mom all up in my business wondering why I'm 'so sick, with that look of, "are you pregnant?!" on her face.

Ms. Ellis comes into where the girls are at talking by the kitchen's back door; asking "are you sure you can't stay and eat with us Candis?" "No..., sorry, but thanks anyway" she says as she waves good-bye and goes to get in her car to head to her mom's place. Mike sits down on the couch because he gets light headed if he stands for too long, since his accident. Everyone was happy when Mike was released from the hospital after Naquawna had gotten back from the Tahoe trip. The Doctor had said that he should make a full recovery, but that he still needed to be closely monitored. So Naquawna thinks, that's why he and his mother have been coming by her place, more often. Ms. Ellis puts the food down on the table that she had made back at Mike's place while asking Naquawna "how was the funeral?" She starts grilling Naquawna by asking her every little thing that happened at the service. And she even asked her things like "how did she know Bubba?" "And how did he die?" Naquawna looks at her and thinks to herself "damn!" his mom is nosey!" Naquawna gets so fed up with all the drill sergeant questions until she finally says to his mom "I'm a little tired, so I'm going to go lay down for a while." "Mike overhearing her says "ok babe" as he's sitting there on the couch watching the game. "I'll leave your plate in the oven" says his mother as she's smiling flirtatiously at her granddad while she's making his plate. Naquawna just stood there looking at the whole situation with one hard; glare thinking to herself 'it's as if, her and Mike are already married, and have moved in together with his mother! "How, did this happen?!" she mumbled to herself.

Walking back to her room with her eyebrows; furrowed in disbelief at how 'quickly; her life has changed, has her wishing now; that she had "never; lied" that day at the hospital saying, that they were engaged. And the thought of it all just made her so 'sick; until her "walking" to her 'bedroom, became a "run" to the toilet! It was so bad, that she hurled; all down the side of the toilet bowl. Mike's mother hearing her running down the hall 'knocks, on the bathroom door asking "honey are you okay?!" Are you sick?!" Naquawna throwing up again 'even louder, prompts his mom to say "do you think you have the flu?!" Naquawna still spitting in the toilet answers "yes?!" "I think I do!" Maybe you two should go home, so you don't catch it!" Ms. Ellis laughs saying "oh honey, I take plenty of vitamin C, this body is as strong as an ox!" she says as she's looking down at her fabulous; silhouette. Naquawna tosses her head back and forth while Ms. Ellis is talking to her through the bathroom door 'as if, to be mimicking "blah blah-blah, blah, blah!" Ms. Ellis finishes with "well, call me if you need me sweety!" Naquawna looking in the bathroom mirror with a smirk on her face thinks to herself "not"! So while granddad, Mike and Ms. Ellis eat, laugh and play cards in the dining room. Naquawna crawls back to her bedroom and sleeps for what seemed to be 'like, two whole days.

But, sleep time; who...?"! 'Sleep time; where?!" Not, down in Vegas! And not for these guys! It is back to the city, where there is 'no; need for sleep! The guys get ready to go to their first 'strip club, which Rafee'al had to Google on his smartphone to find, since none of them had ever been to any strip clubs before, and they figured; that would be the best way to find a good one. Vinnie all drunk says "hey, guys?" I think we would be considered 'strip club, virgins right now!" They all chuckle and Steeli'o looking handsome to himself, in the mirror answers back "yess, but not for long!"

They all get in the elevator and drop floor by floor, down to the lobby. When the guys get outside they get in a Town Car which is waiting for them courtesy of the Casino. They tell the driver to take them to the address in Rafee'al's phone, which was called: Bah, Bah, Black Sheep. And outside on the sign it has a beautiful black sheep with a woman's figure and long eyelashes all lit up in lights up on top of the roof. The Casino's Town Car driver is named: Myron and when they pull up to the Club he tells them "it's a nice place and that he's been in there on many occasions on his days off."

The guys give Myron a cheerful fist pound telling him "what a lucky man he is, cuz he lives here!" Myron laughs proudly; cheering "have fun guys!" "And I'll be out here waiting for you!" They all say "alright!" and head into the club all pumped up. There is a line outside but once they pay and get in the door, they walk through this dark curtain and can see all the women walking around in the club. "Wow!" said Vinnie as he looks around the room at all the beautiful women half dressed. They grab a seat away from the bar and the girls working the floor can tell when it's a man's first time there at the club, so they give those men all--, of their attention!

Not only do the girls want to show them a good time, but they also want to keep them coming back for more. One beautiful blonde walks over to Steeli'o and starts to give him a pre, lap dance, and without complaining, he lets her rub all over him as Rafee'al and Vinnie watch. Rafee'al orders them around of shots and the party gets; crackin! "Yo?"! "Man...!" "It, is, hot up in here!" blurts Vinnie in a Jamaican voice. Chuckling he starts loosening up the two buttons, on his buttoned up shirt. Vinnie even has to pull his shirt out of his pants so the people around him couldn't see how hard his 'erection, was standing up at attention! The guys laugh and flirt with most of the women in the club and place money on every beautiful lady they 'liked, that 'gave; them a rise. Steeli'o even felt like a sleaze-ball for a minute saying "how he could be spending this money on his "real; woman!" "I know, man!" said Rafee'al. Adding "but this is so--, much, more, fun!" "And--, without the nagging!" retorted Vinnie.

They all laughed out loud, and Vinnie all excited said "let's hit up; all the Clubs tonight!" "I want to see what this City "really" has to offer!" He finishes with a slurred "and, I want to gamble all night, too!" Rafee'al grunts out a laugh saying "slow down my friend, we've got one more whole day to play!" Vinnie doesn't respond back because he starts to get a lap dance from this big breasted black chick and he's liking it; a lot! Steeli'o looks over at him and has to tell him repeatedly not to spend all of his dinero in one place. As they're watching Vinnie getting played with by this black chick; out of all the people for Rafee'al to run into, he sees his old highway patrol buddy who moved to Vegas when he retired named: Hank. Hank comes over to their table saying "hey my friend!" What are you doing in here; you old scallywag?"! Rafee'al jumps up and gives him a big hug and whispers in Hanks ear, "I'm U.C, which is code for 'undercover.

Hank hears Rafee'al loud and clear and plays it cool asking "so how long have you and your 'pals, been up here in Vegas?" "We just got here today" said Rafee'al as he introduces Hank to Steeli'o and Vinnie. After everyone gets acquainted Hank tells them "about one of his favorite strip clubs up here in Vegas, and how the lap dances are much more; longer and more private; like in private rooms; even." Vinnie is so happy to hear about a private room until he stands up right then and there, spouting "let's go!"

Hank, grinning, asked "you sure?!" I don't want to interrupt you guy, because I know you just got here!" Vinnie looks at Steeli'o and Rafee'al and replies "I'm down!" What do you guys think?"! The guys shrug looking at each other, than Steeli'o says to Vinnie "it your call!" Vinnie gets a big grin on his face and looks at Hank shouting "lead the way; my friend!" Hank smiles back saying "okay," I'll show you where it is!" The men stand and Hank walks them outside. When Hank gets in his car he tells the driver of their car to follow him. Traveling close behind Hank, they pass two stone walls way outside of town on this one lit up road. Then, in this one spot surrounded by trees they see this particular strip club way off in the back. The place looks packed and they can barely find a place to park. The guys end up parking on the side of the club in a red zone since they had a driver, and Hank parked off road because he was in a Range Rover.

Vinnie gets out the car and fixes his clothes and sprays his mouth with a blast of peppermint. Rafee'al is excited about the new club too, but after seeing so many cars in the parking lot in such a 'small place, makes him 'think, this place couldn't "possibly" be up to code! And then the more he sees all of these "pimped; out"!" dressed up "looking; guys" hanging around in the parking lot, like they're dealing something other than cards, makes him also want to make a few arrests. Then, there's Steeli'o, who for some reason, was kind of cool, calm and collected as he got ready to walk in the joint; like he owned it! 'Steeli'o, acted cocky like that sometimes, because he knew he had so much money. Hank swings open the door shouting "welcome to my second home; fellas!" They all chuckle while they are showing their I.D's to the bouncer's on the door. And after the pat down and the wand was swiped over their bodies the guys; happily follow Hank inside the club since he's a regular there. The men look around the place as Hank walks them over to sit down at a favorite side table of his. "This place is classy!" said Hank to the guys as they sit down and order drinks.

A whistle sounds and then a slow 'choo-choo, train song starts playing real softly and then as the song gets louder and louder a stunningly tall female comes out on the stage with a big, caboose. Vinnie sighs "she looks like an Islander!" Everyone goes wild as she swings her caboose from side to side as she comes, into view. She takes her time 'gradually; taking every stitch of clothing off, while she's playing with the trains; tracks, by moving then all around her; tunnel. The guys at Hanks table go; crazy, telling him "now we see; why this is your second home!" Hank nods his head laughing as he orders around of beers. When the beers come to the table they all make a cheesy toast then continue to watch the women working the poles, and walking around on the floor giving lap dances as needed.

Vinnie, getting an eyeball full of the beauties, couldn't wait any longer to ask Hank "to show him where those so called; "private" rooms were". Hank with his head moving up and down with a nod and a sly look on his face stands up and slams his beer back saying "let's go Vinnie my man!" "I'm going to take you to paradise!" Vinnie gets up off his stool and goes with Hank back to where all of the private rooms are lit up in soft red lights. Once the guys get over by the rooms Hank asked "what's your type of woman?" Better yet he continues "what do you have a taste for" he laughs.

Vinnie laughs back saying "surprise me!" Hank nods and then pushes Vinnie into going inside the room where this gorgeous Japanese girl is standing up against the wall holding a whip in one hand and hand cuffs in thy other. The young lady grabs Vinnie by the hand and takes him back so he can have a private dance; in her private; room! When the young lady has him behind the curtain feeling all up on him, Vinnie gets as happy as a snowboarder who's about to fly down a hill, of fresh powder. Hank smile, pleased with Vinnie's 'luck, in finding a good choice, and as he's looking over his shoulder he sees that one of his favorite girls is working tonight; this fiery; red head! So he gallops over to her like a silly boy in 'child's play, and while playing horsy he picks her up off her feet and kisses her. It is against the 'rules, to play with the women in this manner, but not for Hank! He has spent so much money on this 'woman, to the point that he 'thinks, they should be living together!

Over the intercom 'you hear up; next and coming to the stage!" says the common tatter. "Is our very own; Tantalizing Tammy!" Tammy has all the boys in the bar throwing money up on the stage as usual because she really knows how to work those legs of hers. She could throw her legs up and down and all around on that pole. Even as far as placing them on the back of her neck as she lies there on the floor doing her routine. Steeli'o gets up and goes to the bathroom after Tammy is finished with her strip; dancing; show! He watches her leave the stage and notices that she's dripping 'sweat, from her 'naked body, which looked like hot oil was all over her. 'Tantalizing; Tammy, had Steeli'o and Rafee'al hard as concrete to the point where Steeli'o wasn't even sure he would be able to take a piss when he got into the bathroom.

Rafee'al is left at the table alone when a beautiful Puerto Rican girl comes up to the table and sits down by him, saying "you sure are handsome, muscle man" then she prompts him for a light of her cigarette. He lights it with the matches left on the table and the girl who has told him her name' which is Sage asked him "would you like a dance?" Rafee'al smiles a big smile and without hesitation he says "yeah...! "Sure!" Thinking to himself, why not, and as his high grows bigger, so does his erection! Sage straddles him right there, where he sits. And he trips at first because he didn't think she was going to be so forward and straddle him, right there at his table because he didn't see anyone else getting that special kind of treatment. He thought at first she was just going to dance for him in front of his chair, like the other girl did Steeli'o. So while he's getting played with Steeli'o comes from the bathroom and can see that Rafee'al has found himself a piece of; "pie"! So Steeli'o, smiling hangs back and lets him have his fun.

Rafee'al, being the faithful kind of guy Candis "thinks" he is, starts to feel kind of bad, because Candis has called him four times now and he has not returned any of her calls. He would never intentionally want to do Candis like this but..., he's a man, and he's liking the feeling that he's getting from Sage, who is now grinding him on his lap. In his mind drug case or not, he really does like Candis a lot, but he has to play this night to the fullest so he can really keep up with these guys. So to him, if the job calls for him, to have a pretty lady on his lap, then Candis will just have to wait for him to call her back.

But then when his phone goes off for the fifth time and it is Candis, his mood drops, along with Sage's bra! And as she shimmies her breast in his face, ending her lap dance, he politely gives her two $20.00 dollar bills saying to her "thanks for the dance, it was great!" She beams "we don't have to stop now" she said. But Rafee'al is not the type of guy who women can play out of his money. He pauses to long so she says "what's wrong honey?"! "You married or something?"! "Something like that!" he says. "It's complicated" he adds as he takes the last shot of his drink. She walks away sighing "too... bad... because I had a private place waiting just for you." He blows out a breath of air through his whistling lips 'thinking, if 'only, he wasn't working this case! Even though "technically" he wasn't "married!" he still needed Candis so he could fit in with this group of guys because without her the case could die out, if she was to find out what he was doing at the club and wanted to break up with him because he knew she would be that type to break up over something like a lack of trust.

The announcer comes on the mic while Steeli'o is getting a drink from the bar. He says "up next!" is everybody's favorite girl!" Ms. Foxy; and her name is muffled from a bad mic connection. But then out comes this long legged sexy woman with fox furs wrapped all around her body from head to toe. "Boy is she stunning" thought Steeli'o, looking at her though the smoke; filled air, and dim; dirty lights. But he could still tell she was gorgeous. He takes a drink of his drank as the beautiful woman starts to take off her fur pieces one by one. All the regulars love her and they try to rub on her fur as the pieces of fur 'fall, on to the stage floor.

With her body picture perfect she does a slow strip tease, with a few pieces still left on her body, she dances around the pop-up trees that are manmade 'props, which are spread out on the stage. The shades she has on her face, and the fur hat she has on, are the last things to come off of her body. And as Steeli'o is walking slowly up towards the stage he finds himself becoming more mesmerized by the beauty of this young woman. She looked like a tall glistening water fall, that he was 'dying, to get wet from.

He couldn't remember what her name was because it was so loud up by the bar when the announcer said it. But he knew he wanted to put some money on her body or on the stage and possibly get a lap dance from this particular woman because she was just his 'type, more than the other girls were. The closer he got to the stage the harder his 'heart; beated, down in his pants and up in his chest. When she finally throws her hat off into the crowd and shakes her; long extension hair; out of it's tied; up bun. He is right up next to the stage 'hoping, to make eye contact with this furless; sexy woman is shades. When she finally stops; dancing and twirling on the stage. She slides down from the pole and he catches her eyes and she freezes! As she inhales a deep breath her lips and her hands begins to shake. He doesn't think anything of it at first, about her reaction to him, other than him thinking she got caught by surprise when she seen his handsome face. Roxy, all in a panic reaches down to pick up her furs off the floor so she can run off the stage before he realizes it's her.

It takes him a minute but then he spots her very unique 'birth mark, which is in the shape of a Chinese dragon on her right leg. He yells out; "Roxy?"! "A drunken older man standing next to him replies "yes!" isn't she great?!" Roxy still trying to cover herself tries to run off the stage, but Steeli'o grabs her by the arm saying "are you f^*king; kidding me?!" He snatches off her shades saying "you mean to tell me; you're ah, f*^king; stripping; whore!" That same drunken guy standing next to Steeli'o yells "hey!" That's not nice!" "Don't you listen to him; honey!"

Steeli'o real angry; pushes the man out of the way and he falls into a nearby table. Then he grabs Roxy forcing her to get down off of the stage. And in return, she than has a panic attack because she doesn't know what he's going to do to her next. Then her over protective; boss 'Burt, comes running over from the bar when he sees all of the commotion going on over by Roxy. When he gets over where Roxy is he tells Steeli'o "to back off and leave her alone!" Steeli'o disregards anything that Burt has to say while he's still trying to pull Roxy out of the club with him, so he can talk to her further. She tears up; immediately shouting "I wanted to tell you!" "But I didn't know how!" He yells "I took you home to meet my mother!" "My sister!" "My family!" "And this whole time you were 'nah-thing!" but a whore!" who takes her clothes; off for money!" He balls up his fists looking at her angrily. And as she continues to sob uncontrollably, he's yelling repeatedly saying "ain't this some; sh*t!"

Steeli'o so mad pulls out his wallet shouting "how much do you need?!" 'Yelling; he throws twenty dollar bills at her face. She shakes her head to dodge the money from hitting her in thy eyes as she stands there 'crying, with her head down. Repeatedly she sobs out "I'm so-o-o--; sorry!" I'm so-o-o--; sorry!" Without accepting her; plea for forgiveness; he spits at her feet; like she's; trash! And with his brokenhearted eyes, as green as a red ‘fireball, he shouted “now I can see; why!” you didn’t have sex with me!” It’s obvious; because you were so, “busy” ‘f*^king!” all of these guys; up in here; for money!” Roxy screams “no…!” It’s not like that!” she cries. “I love you; Steeli’o!” Please; believe me!” she begs “Hah!” he blurts. And with an angry look on his face and a breaking; heart he yells “love”! “Thy only thing you “love” is money!” He looks at her so… evil; into her ‘eyes, as the pain he felt poured out, and in that ‘moment, she ‘knew, right then and there; that he hated her!

‘Vinnie, now done getting his jollies; off comes back out to where Steeli’o is arguing by the stage and then he sees; Roxy. He’s ‘drunk, but it finally registers that; that is Steeli’o’s ‘girl, and she’s “not” the cocktail waitress! Rafee’al looking at the whole thing going down knew that if he didn’t get Steeli’o out of there he would be going to jail tonight. Steeli’o is still yelling and screaming at Roxy’s boss, and is all up in his face! While Steeli’o is all up in ‘Roxy’s, face! So when Rafee’al sees Vinnie he tells him “to go get to the car so he can tell Myron to pull up to the side door. Once that’s handled Rafee’al goes and grabs Steeli’o by the arm saying to him “let’s go man!” “You know we’re not trying to go to jail down here in Vegas!”

And just when Rafee’al thinks he has it all under control because Steeli’o is starting to back off and walk away. Roxy’s boss pushes Steeli’o ‘hard, saying “you better get out of here; punk!” And that’s when Steeli’o; snapped and hauled off and punched Burt square in the nose; knocking him out; cold! When he falls to the floor Roxy can’t believe it, she bends down to make sure her boss is okay! And Rafee’al grabs Steeli’o and pulls him out of the club’s ‘side door, before the bouncers could get to Steeli’o and hold him, until the police got there. Everything happened so fast. Steeli’o is so drunk, and mad that he wants to go back into the club to get Roxy so he could finish questioning her on how she lead him to believe, that she was a “wholesome; woman!”

They ended up hauling ass out of there though; just as the cops were pulling up. Even their driver ‘Myron, was laughing at how ‘lucky, they were to get out of there on time. He laughed adding “Vegas; P.D!” “Them; boys; don’t be play-in!” As they are driving away ‘quick, fast and in a ‘hurry, poor… Hank; stood at the door with his hands up like; why are you guys leaving so fast?”! Mainly because… at the ‘time, he didn’t see the whole fight go down, just the tail end of them exiting the club with the quickness!

When Roxy walks her boss back to the office to get him cleaned up, she keeps telling him "how sorry she is that this had happened at work." Her hands and lips; quiver because her nerves are; shot! Even Tammy came to the back with some of the other girls to comfort her, saying "that it was not her fault!" and that 'Steeli'o, is the "real; jerk!" in this situation!" Roxy just cries in her friend's arms and then her boss tells the other girls to get back to work. They all scatter back to the front, where all of the men are at waiting for their services. Roxy gets some ice cubes from the mini fridge in the back office and puts them in a towel and places it on Burt's nose. He holds her by the hand squawking "I should have 'kilt, that bastard when I had the chance!"

'Roxy; sniffling said "no, don't say that!" It's not his fault!" "I should have told him long time ago!" she said crying hysterically. Her boss holds her tightly voicing "everything is going to be just fine!" you'll see! Roxy rubbing across her nose with her hand says "it's kind of good this happened though, because now he knows and he can move on" she said crying even harder. In her mind she's believing 'how could he possibly; love someone like her anyway? Burt looks at her and shouts "you deserve better!"

He wipes his nose; sharply, with thy icy cloth yelling "he's a 'scum bag, drug; pusher, anyway!" "No, yells Roxy in a shaky crying; voice. "He's a realtor!" she says as she's balling her eyes out of control. "Not with all those fancy clothes and them expensive, cars!" He shouts "he hasn't been honest with you; either!" "Really?!" sighed Roxy. Adding "you think?" she said; all naive like a school girl, who had no 'real, street game; when it came to love. Her boss, who is so-- in love with her, holds her a little too long and she starts to feel uncomfortable so she says, "I need to get another tissue."

She walks across the room to get the tissue so he can take his arms from around her waist, and while blowing her nose one of the bouncers comes into the back office saying "the cops want to talk to you, boss!" "They want to know if you want to press; charges?"! Roxy shouts "no!" Burt!" Please!" Don't!" Her boss with no remorse says "I'll be right back doll, you get cleaned up." Roxy nods saying "okay" as she reaches for another tissue.

Tammy runs back to the office when she sees that Burt is out speaking with the police. Slowly opening the office door she walks in saying "you okay Rox?" Roxy shaking her head 'no, holding back more tears hugs Tammy. Tammy hugs her back saying "let's go home." "I'm tired as hell!" "Burt will understand" said Tammy kicking off her heels. "And I'll tell him, I'm taking you home because you are so; distraught over what just happened!" Roxy sighs "I am." "This is so terrible!" "I really do 'love, him, Tammy!" Tammy sighs "I know girl, it will work out!" "I mean, look at what happened to me and Marvin!" and I gave him a second chance!" "So you never know what's gonna happen!" Momma always said "if it's meant to be!" it will be" said Tammy putting on her flat shoes.

Roxy still sniffling says "I don't know about my situation though." "You should have seen the way he looked at me, Tammy!" "Like he could have just; killed me!" right where I stood! "Well..., that's just the passion he has for you, because he really 'does, love you too, and he's hurting." "Just give him some time to miss you, and realize he can't live without you." Roxy blows her nose, nodding; saying "okay, as she gathers up her belonging saying "you are such a good friend to me Tammy." "Oh, now; now!" "You are always there when I have my short comings, too" smiles Tammy. She continues "so I'm glad you're my friend too; chil!"

They both hug and walk out closing the office door behind them. The two girls pitifully walk out to the front of the club while Tammy is holding Roxy by the arm like she will just 'fall, to the floor, if Tammy doesn't take her home right this, instant! Burt looks at Roxy with love in his eyes as he falls; hard for her every wish, and 'need, of her leaving the club! Her boss 'Burt, tells her "to call him tomorrow when she's feeling better and if she needs to take some time off, he's okay with it." Tammy looks at Burt and looks back at Roxy and thinks to herself 'he would 'never, say that to her!" or the other girls for that matter!

Roxy smiling halfway, says "thanks Burt, for understanding and for always being there for me." "I really do appreciate you" she says as she rubs her hand down the side of his right arm softly." Burt flinches back a little when she touches his right arm like he got injured when he fell from Steeli'o's punch. Roxy asked "is your arm hurt?" He returns "I'm fine" as he gives her a flatteringly; convincing smile. Before she leaves the club he gives her a big hug because he is so happy to hear those words of appreciation coming from out of her mouth. In his mind their relationship just got stronger and it is just a matter of time, when the two of them will be together 'now, that Steeli'o is out of the picture.

Tammy says to Roxy as they are walking out of the club "Rox, you better watch what you say to Burt, because he's starting to think that you two could be a couple!" "Funny!" retorts Roxy as she frowns her face up voicing "he knows he's 'just, my Boss!" Tammy opens up the car door 'locks, saying "well, even the other girls are starting to take notice; how Burt looks at you, and treats you better than the rest of us!" They get into the car with Roxy shouting "what..?"!

"Burt doesn't like me, like that!" and you know it Tammy! "He's like a dad, or an uncle to all of us!" "That's; "kind of true!" said Tammy. Adding "but daddy's liking 'you, a little "more" than the rest us!" With a laugh Tammy starts up her engine while Roxy cracks on Burt, saying "well..., Burt can hang it up!" "Because I'm, in love with; Steeli'o!" Roxy sits back in her seat and closes her eyes all the way back to Tammy's house to try and clear her mind from the monstrosities of thy evening. So while her mind, is trying to; clear! Steeli'o's 'mind, is on a ramping; rage! He and the guys get back to the hotel where Steeli'o is pacing back and forth and all he can talk about is; Roxy!

Vinnie and Rafee'al try to tell him "that it is just a job!" "And that they 'know, that Roxy really loves him, and only him!" But Steeli'o is "not" trying to hear all that! All he keeps saying is "let's just go back and wait for her in thy parking lot!" "So when she gets off work, I can talk to her then!" Vinnie and Rafee'al both say "no!" That's a bad idea!" Steeli'o turns his face looking crazy saying "and didn't she say, she was at her sister's place because she just had her baby?"! Vinnie answers "I don't know!" Steeli'o returns "I know; I'm; not; 'fu*king; crazy?"! Rafee'al answers "yep, that's what Candis confirmed." "See!" shouts Steeli'o. "So she's 'also; a 'fu*king; liar; too!" said Steeli'o holding his bottle of beer firmly in his hand wanting to throw it at the window; just talking about her!

His mind is all over the place thinking; back and forth on all the days leading up; to this moment. Then turning to look at Rafee'al he says "so--; that means; that Candis 'knew!" all along; that she was out here; in Vegas; stripping!" "Well... I don't know man!" said Rafee'al not wanting to put Candis in the middle of their fight. Steeli'o shouts "call Candis!" "I want to see if she 'knew, her friend was a stripper!" Rafee'al says "naw..., man!" because then she'll trip with me; for not calling her back all day!" Steeli'o blurts "so what; man!" "Roxy already seen you; remember?"! "So thy gig is up, for you too; bro!" "Call Candis, because she's going to find out anyway; that you are here!" "Damn...!" frowns Rafee'al. "So now I'm going; down with "your; ship!" said Rafee'al looking at him shaking his head saying "you know you're wrong for this, man!"

He stands there and dials up Candis's number. Candis picks up on the third ring because she's sleeping by now. With her eyes closed she answers "hello?" And before Rafee'al can say a word, Steeli'o snatches the phone from him saying "Candis?!" why didn't you tell me that your friend; was an f^*king; stripper?"! Candis wide awake now, answers "what?!" "Who?"! Steeli'o says "don't play dumb with me!" "How many friends do you know that, strip?"! Candis retorts "huh...?" Because she 'knows, this is not her place to say, what Roxy does, or does not do! 'You know; girl's code! Her other line starts to ring and its Roxy. Steeli'o says "you said..., she was at her sister's house!" "Yeah," said Candis. "That's what she told me." "He yells "ah-ha!" You girls are all sticking together!" Candis repeats "ah-ha!" what?"!

He says "so you're telling me, you never heard her say she 'works, at thy strip club?"! Candis says "why?!" did you see her out there or something?!" Steeli'o snaps "answer thy question; Candis!" She yells "I, am; trying; to answer the question!" But, I'm 'trying, to find 'out; did you 'hear, this from someone?!" Or did you 'see; her, with your 'own, eyes?"! Steeli'o yells "that's; not!" thy question! "Hold on!" shouts Candis, then she clicks over to answer Roxy's call. "Girl...!" What, is, going; on?!" asked Candis. Before Roxy, could even say "hello, she starts crying all over again and with a 'high; pitch, in her voice, she sobs out "he knows!" He knows!" He came to the club tonight!" He knows!" she cries.

Candis sighs, saying "I know--!" "He's on the other line call-in himself; chewing; me out!" Roxy still crying; cries "it's over, between us!" And with a wipe of her nose as tears are streaming down her face she says "I should have told him long time ago!" It's all my fault!" Candis says "dang..., girl!" "This is messed; up!" Roxy, blowing her nose says "you didn't tell Rafee'al where I worked at; did you?"! "No!" said Candis. "Why would you ask me that?!" Is Rafee'al with him?!" Roxy answers "yes...!" Candis shouts "in; Vegas?"! "Yes!" He was in the strip club too!" said Roxy. Candis belts out "really...?"! And with a big frown on her face she tells Roxy "hold on a minute!" Candis clicks over and by passes all... of Steeli'o's questions and says "where's Rafee'al?"! "He's here with me." She yells "in Vegas?"! Her lips grow tight just saying those words again. Rafee'al can hear her 'pitched; up voice through the phone when Steeli'o gives him the phone with a (she's your problemo now bro, look on his face). Candis says "hum...!" now I see why you didn't pick up your phone!" Or call me back!" Hope you had a good time!" And I hope she was 'worth; it!" Bye!" she said. Rafee'al yells "naw--!" Naw--!" "It ain't like that; babe!" It was a last minute decision from Steeli'o and Vinnie!" I didn't even want to go to; Vegas!" he said, looking at Steeli'o and Vinnie with a wink. "Plus... when we were on the plane, I couldn't get a proper signal to call you back!" So when we landed, I was going to call you but all this stuff went down with Steeli'o and Roxy so...; Candis smacks her tongue on the roof of her mouth with a tisk; and hangs up in his face. She clicks over and tells Roxy "Rafee'al is trying to tell me some "lame; ass; story!" about how he was "going" to tell me, that he was going to Vegas!" grunting she adds "and then he 'said, he was going to call me as soon as he got a better "signal!" He can miss me with that;

crap!" I don't know who he thinks he's talking too!" said Candis. "I am "not" boo-boo the fool!" And he needs to; know!" You can't play a player; foo!" So I hung up on his ass!" Her, and Roxy laughed so hard, even though, Roxy 'still, had a broken heart.

Tammy listening in as well to the conversation, laughs hearing Candis telling Roxy the same advice "which is, to just give Steeli'o some time." Candis finishes her statement with "it will all work out, because you two are meant for each other." The girls talk for a few and then she hangs up with Roxy. Candis now mad at Rafee'al walks around her apartment waiting on him to call her back, with the truth. Steeli'o did try to call Roxy back several times during the night to see if she would talk to him. At first when he called she picked up her phone to talk with him, but he was still way too angry, and when every other word out of his mouth became "you're a lying; ho!" She decided "not" to talk to him until he calmed, down.

Rafee'al also called Candis back a couple of times after she hung up on him. After three tries though, Rafee'al just lied back in his bed shaking his head because she 'wouldn't, pick up her phone anymore. Candis went back to sleep mad but 'somewhat happy, to see that he cared enough to call her back several times. She decided when she hung up on him, that she would not talk to him until tomorrow 'if, he called her back. Her logic of thinking was no need in letting him get away with lying to her this early in their relationship because he 'might start, making it a habit! So she wanted to 'nip, this in the butt because she 'knows, that guys play way to many games and she 'ain't; haven it! 'Snap!

The guys stayed up in their room, talking about the strip club and what had happened to Vinnie in the private room. Vinnie was all smiles but he didn't want to hurt Steeli'o's ego any further because Roxy was one of those "same; girls" he was talking about when describing all the things that they would 'do, in the back rooms. So being polite Vinnie played it down like it was just lap dancing, because he didn't want to tell them 'all, of the things he got 'done, for his 'money, after seeing the hurt on Steeli'o's face. Steeli'o sitting around moping; within himself, is still so very mad. He couldn't even get to sleep that night. He kept going back and forth in his mind, on how he just couldn't see; that she was playing him; like one of her; tricks! He talked about Roxy all night long! And Vinnie and Rafee'al 'tired, of hearing it, tell him "to give it a rest!" Vinnie even said "just call her back because you are truly in love with this chick; cousin!" "Hell, yeah!" said Rafee'al. "Don't let your pride, stop you from being with her, man!" voiced Rafee'al. Vinnie plops down on the couch adding "if you didn't really like her, you wouldn't keep talking about her!" Vinnie even puts a pillow over his face and lies back on the couch trying not to hear anymore of Steeli'o's 'whining, about Roxy.

Steeli'o then gets a big lump in his throat and exhales saying "you guys are right!" "Forget her!" He then stands up straight and with his hands running through his hair he says "to be honest with you guys!" "I've only really loved one woman in my 'lifetime, and she's dead!" A tear makes its way up in his eye but he refuses to let it fall.

"I open up my heart again, to try and love someone, and just when I feel 'like; I'm being loved back, I find out it's with this; whore!" Shaking his head and taking another drink he groans out "she has portrayed me!" and played me for a fool!" He throws his glass into the fireplace, and Vinnie and Rafee'al are somewhat startled from the loud shattering. Vinnie quickly takes the pillow from his face yelling "what the hell; cuzen?"! "You need to go to bed and sleep that shit off; dude!" yells Vinnie all pissed. Rafee'al agrees; offering "bruh, tomorrow will be a better day!" But there is no getting through to Steeli'o he is; crushed! He talked about Roxy until everyone fell asleep on him. But the detective side of Rafee'al heard Steeli'o loud and clear when he said, he loved someone before Roxy, who had died. He wanted to pry into it some more, but he was just too tired. So Rafee'al plans on talking to him about it, at another time, as he drifts into a sexual dream about Candis. The next day is Sunday, and 'excitement, is in thy air, and everyone around; can feel it; over at Naquawna's house!

Chapter 31

It's early Sunday morning, like I said, and Mike has falling asleep on Naquawna's couch unbeknownst to her. Ms. Ellis and Naquawna's granddad have gone to the mall so he can buy some new shirts for himself, at the request of Ms. Ellis because she wants to take him to bingo with her tonight. Well, after hearing the front door close, Naquawna thought she was home alone when she started to call her doctor's office to leave an audio requested appointment. Mike over hears her conversation when she says "hope Friday will be fine for me to come in for my checkup?" "And I might need to get some prenatal pills too because I'm pregnant."

Mike jumps up off the couch and runs back to Naquawna's room and grabs her by the waist shouting "we're having a baby?!" "Aw; man...!" "This is the best news; ever!" "We have got to move our wedding date up!" Naquawna shouts "what?"! "Hold; up!" "We are moving way to fast!" she says as she sits down on the bed ending her call. Mike all excited says "Naquawna, you know I love you." "And my mom likes you too." "She really does." Naquawna says "that's great; and all." "But you can't tell anyone; I'm pregnant; 'especially, your mom!" because she will tell my granddad and it will just kill him to know that I'm pregnant without a husband!" Mike answers "awe..., come on Naquawna he'll understand!"

"No!" she said in a stern voice. "He can't; know!" "Plus, I could--; miscarry and then it would just be a mess him knowing I was pregnant and all!" "So; no!" He looks in her eyes with joy, all happy knowing that he could be a father soon, so he says "okay, anything you say baby." Mike reaches for her hands and pulls her close to hold her in his arms, and Naquawna hugs him back but deep down she knows that this is Rayshawn's baby and she will have to find a way to tell Mike before it's too late.

Days go by and it is Christmas Eve, Steeli'o's family flew in from Italy on the 23rd after his sister found out that Steeli'o and Roxy had broken up. Steeli'o never told his family "why?" they broke up because he was just too ashamed to tell them the details. Instead, he told his family, that they 'both, just didn't see eye to eye on some things." His sister tries to pry but he tells her "to let it go, and that it's been over between him and Roxy." Gi'la has never been one to give up on, true love. And since she really likes Roxy and considers her to be 'family, and like the sister she never; had, on Christmas Eve she finds Roxy's number in Steeli'o's phone and calls her. Roxy is outside at the time in her garden pulling tomatoes from the vine when she hears her phone ring. She runs inside and sees that it is Steeli'o's number calling. She pauses... but can't wait to talk to him because she has missed him so much. She drops the tomatoes on the table and all but two, fall to the floor. Nervously she picks up her phone saying "hello? And in her most; happiest voice she wait to hear his voice. It's a girl's voice though, on the other end of the phone, and at first she thinks 'it's a joke, like some girl is calling to say "why, is your number in my man's, phone?"!

But then she hears this sweet familiar voice say "Roxy?" it's me Gi'la. The smile on Roxy's face is so big, like her heart just started back to beating for the first time. Even though she wished; it was Steeli'o calling her, she was somewhat relieved that it was his sister instead. She says "hi...!" Gi'la!" how have you been?"! Followed by "happy holidays to you and your family." Gi'la says 'the same to her, and tries to hurry and talk before her brother comes back down the stairs. She talks quickly saying "I was calling to invite you for dinner tonight." "Oh," says Roxy hesitantly. "Well..., I don't know if you 'know, but--, me and your brother broke up." "Um, yes..., he did say you two had; had some differences, and that you didn't see eye to eye on some things." "But this is what makes for a relationship; right?"! Gi'la continues to say "I told him, you don't just leave!" You work things out" she says to Roxy in her cute Italian accent.

Roxy smiling through the phone says "you are so-- sweet-- Gi'la." But I don't think your brother wants to see me anymore." "How do you think, I got your number?" said Gi'la. "Of course he wants to see you!" He's been moping around thy house since we've got here!" Dinner is at 7:00 o'clock and we don't want you to bring nothing, but yourself!" Roxy sighs "umm--, I don't know." Gi'la says "I won't, take no for an answer!" see you soon!" bye for now!" said Gi'la, and she hangs up the phone when she hears her brother running down the stairs. He says "what are you doing with my phone?" And who were you talking too?" she says "oh, just a friend." Let's go get the food now" she says with a grab of his car keys.

Roxy just stands there in her kitchen holding her phone staring at it; like "what just happened?"! She is so confused, but happy as her mind; contemplates; if she should go?" or, just 'not, show up at all! And then of course she calls Tammy who yells "girl--, it might be an ambush!" But then laughing Tammy says "just, go!" she adds "his sister invited you; so he "must" know about it!" because she called; you, from his phone!" Then Roxy calls Candis who is over at Naquawna's house cooking because the Christmas Eve dinner is over there this year and Rafee'al is even going since they've made up, due to Rafee'al promising 'not, to lie to her again about going places with the guys. When Roxy tells Candis and Naquawna that Steeli'o's sister called her and invited her to dinner, they both are so happy for Roxy because she was not doing so well after their big; break up. Roxy took it so--; hard that she wasn't even eating much, and she even had stopped, working at the club. All she was doing was taking long showers and staying in the bed. Candis and Naquawna tell her "to go to the dinner saying, you need this time to talk to him and tell him how you really; feel!"

"You're right" said Roxy. Then she adds "but what if he's just having me come over so he can tell his family all about me, face to face?" Candis says "he wouldn't do that; would he?"

Naquawna says "huh..., you never know!" These guys are; ruthless!" these days, because "I bet Rayshawn would do something like that!" Have me come over and then tell everyone all--; my business!" 'Roxy, thinks on it; hard for a few minutes. And then she says "well..., I'm gonna go because Gi'la wouldn't do me like that!" And she sounded like she really wants me to come." So maybe-- he did tell her to call me." "Okay, miss "optimistic" said Naquawna laughing. "Speaking, of, optimistic!" Ms. Bun--, in thy oven" says Roxy. "What did the doctor say?" "How many months are--; you?" asked Roxy. Naquawna says "chil... I am two and a half months."

Roxy says "really--?" so you got pregnant a while back then, huh?" Naquawna pauses for a second then says "yep. "I guess so." Candis adds "and all that partying and drinking." What did the doctor say about that?" "Umm..." moans Naquawna as she's rubbing her stomach; sympathetically. He said "as long as I 'discontinue, my drinking and partying the baby should be fine!" Roxy says "so are you going to tell Rayshawn; the great; news?"! Candis looks at Naquawna with a half-smile on her face like; that's what I've been asking her for days; now! "I'll tell him in time...!" Like maybe after my second trimester" she said.

"Why so long?" asked Roxy. "Are you afraid he's going to want you to terminate the pregnancy?" Naquawna gets all defensive shouting "no!" I'm not worried about that!" Can't nobody make me do; something!" I don't want to do!" She continues to say "and you two need to stop worrying about me; and mines!" And concentrate on your own affairs!" And that goes for you too; Candis!" Cuz 'yaw's; men ain't all that; either!" Candis and Roxy both clown saying "why you got to get all mad and stuff?!" We were just wondering why "you" who loves... Rayshawn so... "Much" wouldn't be the first to run and tell him the good news!"

Naquawna puts her oven mitts on voicing "I'm not trying to sit up here and argue with you two about my baby!" I'll tell Rayshawn when I feel like it!" So just mind yo' business!" Candis jokes with Roxy saying "she's just 'scurred, to tell him!" And the two laugh on the phone. Naquawna gets even; madder; shouting "no! I'm; not!" And then the door swings open and it's Mike bringing back the brownie mix they forgot to get, from the store. Mike comes in all smiling with his headphones on and grabs Naquawna by the belly softly and gives her a kiss on the cheek. She pushes his hand away from her stomach, so Candis won't think, that she's told Mike about the pregnancy first. But Candis is not that slow, she catches Mike's expression and when he leaves out of the kitchen Candis whispers to Roxy on the phone "mmm... but she's told Mike already about the baby; though!" And he's probably thinking; that it's his!"

Naquawna looks at Candis saying "shhhh... be quite!" My granddad is going to hear you!" He's up now!" Roxy's on the other end of the phone laughing says "then that means..., she was sleeping with the both of them!" "And telling "us" it was all about her and Rayshawn!" "Oooooh...!" retorts Candis. "You are so right!" "Right about what?!" asked Naquawna with a guilty look on her face knowing that they are talking about her. Candis looks at Naquawna smiling; saying "somebody's been getting there 'sausage, from two different; venders!" "No...!" said Naquawna. "I know whose 'sausage, this baby's from!" Candis and Roxy are laughing out loud because they "do; not" believe her at all! Naquawna knows they don't believe her, so when she puts her Christmas ham back into the oven she blares out "whatever!" You two can't talk about; nobody!" Then, all, sassed; with her mouth Naquawna shouts "and you go on ahead Roxy, and go over to Steeli'o's house and get laughed at!" because he's probably 'already, got men over there waiting on you!" so they can make it; rain!" on; yo' ass!" And as for you Candis!" you keep on think-in; that Rafee'al is being "true; tah, you!" with his sneaky ass! "He probably sneaks off to 'Vegas, every chance he; gets 'just, to get a lap dance!" because you; ain't, let him bone!"

"Dang...!" shouts Candis and Roxy. "We must have "really" struck a nerve!" Candis and Roxy bust up laughing some more when Naquawna says "no!" Not a nerve!" More like a hormone; heffa!" Yaw keep playing with me hear?" and I'm ma hit Candis over the head with this rolling pen!" The girls were laughing so hard that Mike's mom even came into the kitchen saying "It is so good to hear you girls laughing." Especially you Naquawna, being that you've been so; sick these last couple of weeks." Candis blurts "I know, right?!" That flu was rough; wasn't it?!" she said snickering into the phone. Roxy on the other end of the phone laughs out "flu my ass!" Naquawna gives Candis a funny look, as if to say "don't even; get Ms. Ellis started!

Even though Naquawna didn't want Ms. Ellis, to be all up in her "pregnancy; business"! She really has; started to warm up to Mike's mom because she can see now, that she is 'somewhat, a kind hearted woman. Also, Naquawna likes Ms. Ellis, because she spends a lot of time with her granddad 'even more so, than Naquawna lately and for that reason Naquawna is really digging her. 'Although, from time to time Naquawna would fantasize how she wishes that Ms. Ellis was 'really, Rayshawn's mom instead of 'Mike's, thinking then, everything would be all; gravy! Speaking of gravy! Way down on thy other side of town Gi'la is complaining to her brother how they forgot to get the flour when they went to the store, so they could make homemade gravy for dinner. But the gravy is the 'least, of Steeli'o's problems!

Chapter 32

Down on the other end of town in the Valley, Gi'la is asking her brother to go back to the store to get the flour, and after Steeli'o hearing her whining about it he says "he'll go get it." Grabbing his keys from the table, he puts on his jacket and goes back to the store for her. A couple of minutes later the doorbell rings and Gi'la walking towards the front door thinking it's her brother says "what happened?" Did you forget your wallet?" But when Gi'la opens the door to her surprise it is one of her favorite people; Roxy! And for a split second Roxy had thought she had seen Steeli'o drive right past her as she turned the block but wasn't sure. Gi'la says "you made it!" Come in!" come in!" she said hugging her, taking her coat.

Roxy says her 'hello's, with a friendly kiss to Gi'la's cheeks asking "did I just see Steeli'o leaving?" "Yes." But he'll be right back, we forgot the flour." Roxy smiling says "oh..., at first I thought you told him, I'd be here soon, so that's why he hurried up and left!" Gi'la laughs "no silly" then she takes Roxy into the kitchen to greet her mother. Her mom dries her hands off on her apron when she sees Roxy and gives her the biggest hug which almost brings tears to Roxy's eyes because she is so glad that she decided to come after all. When Roxy first met his family she knew that she 'so... much, wanted to be a part of his world, because she felt like she had known them all her life, the way they all connected on a real level.

Vinnie is in the hallway when he sees Roxy walking into the kitchen. Caught by surprise, his sip of cognac and seven-up goes down the wrong pipe causing him to cough; repetitiously after seeing Roxy at the house. He just couldn't believe "Roxy" of all people, was over at Steeli'o's house for dinner. And before he could call Steeli'o and tell him the "bad; news!" when he pulls out his phone he can't get a signal. 'By then, Gi'la had already taken Roxy into the living room with a glass of wine. They visited with one another on the couch talking about "what is new?" and what's now in style?" in the fashion world."

Gi'la also asked about where all the best shopping malls were at?" that they could go to, out here in Treeberry?" And Roxy couldn't wait to show her where they all were. Roxy all happy to be at the house with his sister drinking wine and talking with her, tells her about all of the great malls in their area and in other cities, further out. She even mentions some places over in Tree Berryville's mall district and goes on to say "that; they can go to the Outlets, 'or, fly down to Los Angeles to really gets some "real" girl; time; in" shopping down there too!" Roxy is so relaxed with Gi'la and feels really welcomed by the family. Even Spartique, Gi'la's husband gave her a warm hug when he came out of the bathroom and saw her sitting with his wife chatting. After slammin back the first glass of wine, Gi'la gets her a second glass of red wine figuring the way she slammed the first one back, she must need another. Her mom calls Gi'la into the kitchen to help her take the turkey out of the oven so she could baste it, and Roxy went with her to see if she could help with anything as well. Her mom says "you just relax, you are our guess." But Roxy won't hear of it, so while she's standing in the kitchen she hears keys opening up the front door and her heart just 'drops; to the bottom of her feet.

She turns her head to take a quick, glance out, of curiosity; to see if it is, Steeli'o and then she turns back towards the sink. Steeli'o is holding a bag of flour in his hand like he just saved the world when he walks towards the kitchen voicing "I tried to hurry back as fast as I could mom." And then he spots her long beautiful legs standing in the kitchen by his mom, but can't see her face. Roxy's front was turned toward the sink because she insisted on washing out the serving trays. Steeli'o walks up closer and puts the flour down on the counter and looks dead in Roxy's eyes as she's turning around to acknowledge him.

They haven't seen one another or talked to each other since that night at the club. His mom kisses him on the cheek saying "thank you son, for going back to the store for us." Still looking at Roxy he says "what is she doing here?" Gi'la answers "she came by to have dinner with us." "Us!" said Steeli'o. "That would mean "we; all" invited her!" he shouted. His mother says "it is Christmas Eve; be nice!" He frowns "you mean to tell me, she doesn't have to work tonight?"! He looks at Vinnie who is holding back a laugh. Roxy; stunned, at the accusations coming out of his mouth in front of his family, feels like she could just 'die, of embarrassment, not knowing 'now, what he has told them about her.

But she still manages to stand there looking more beautiful than ever. Roxy is, a little uncomfortable because now she can tell that he 'really, didn't; know she was, coming. So she looks at Gi'la saying "maybe I should go." Gi'la in Italian says "no!" Then she tells her brother "to take her somewhere in the house so he can talk to her in private because dinner won't be ready for another hour." 'Protesting, his sister says, "and she is... staying for dinner!" In other words, "so, make; it work!" Steeli'o has always listened to his baby sister's advice but this time he 'wasn't; budging!

Gi'la calls him a "stubborn old fool, in Italian and grabs him and Roxy by the arm and tells them both to go upstairs to his room to talk it out!" She adds "and don't come down until you two are friends again!" Steeli'o says "I'm a man!" so I don't need 'you, to tell me what to do!" In my own house!" Gi'la; snaps, voicing "this is true; brother!" But you have been moping around thy house ever since we got here!" Roxy smiles; inwardly and Steeli'o can see her gloating. So he looks at Roxy saying "it hasn't been because of you!" "That's fine!" she said as her smile fades from her face. "I don't blame you for hating me" she said. Gi'la says "now... we are getting 'somewhere!" she said pushing them both up thy stairs adding "at least you two are talking to each other!" Gi'la pushes them both in the room and closes the room door saying "dinner will be ready in an hour or so, but no rush."

When Gi'la leaves, Roxy slowly walks around the room remembering how much she wanted to make love to him in his bed with the snow falling down all over her body, under the warm lights. But now all she can see is that; that will never happen now. She rubs her forehead because now the wine has gone straight to her head. Looking at him she says "okay--; Steeli'o." I know I was wrong for not telling you, I was a dancer." He corrects her "you mean a stripper!" Just saying those words in reference to her "profession" left a dirty taste in his mouth. "Okay; fine!" she says picking up one of his bottles of oil. Walking around his room she could barely look him straight in his eyes because he was so; attractive. It's like he's gotten just that, much; more; sexier; only, so he can 'torment her, on what she's going to be missing out on!" which is him!

He's kind of uncomfortable as well when looking at her because he can feel his 'fantasizing pecker; peeking through his pants. He rubs his hand, over his other hands; knuckles to stay focused as he's repeating the words, "you played to me!" You played me!" And--; you lied about your job!" She says "well--, not exactly!" I just didn't tell you what kind, of 'dancer, I was!" "No shit!" he shouts. "And that's why it's 'not, gonna work!" because you are a very; deceitful woman!" Just like you coming over here to my house!" "No!" she shouts. "Your sister called me!" I was just fine, with you hating me!" she replied. "I had learned to live with it!" He frowns "so you've moved on?" "No." she answered.

When glancing at him, she looks at him like she can't 'believe, he would 'think, that she had moved on already. Then her eyes shift to looking back down at the floor. He groaned with disbelief, after hearing her statement. Then he grunts out a breath of air, because he's not wanting; to still like her. She can tell he's still on the fence about her, so she adds "I just learned to cope with the fact, that I had lost my best friend" she said looking back up at him sadly. While he's looking at her she sighs out "and it was totally my fault!" If I had just told you the truth, when we first met at Jake's party..., then you would have known straight up about me!" But then again; that's not the type of thing you tell a guy like 'you, when you first meet 'him!" especially when you 'know, he could have just about have any woman in the room he wanted!" And I just didn't want to mess up my chances of getting to know you better!" He stands there listening to her, and she finishes with "I know it was selfish of me, and I totally understand if you 'never, ever, forgive me!" she says as she's looking into his pretty eyes holding back her tears.

He exhales a deep breath through his mouth saying "I 'don't; hate-- you!" I just don't know how to 'trust, you anymore!" Or even know how to love you anymore!" Roxy looks at him nodding, then in a meek voice she says "I know... I know... "And I'm so-- sorry--, for that" she says as she starts to cry, and cry, and all he can do, is put his arms around her because he did still love her. He was just still so mad that she had ruined what they had; had together; and--, in front of his friend, and his family member that night at the club. But he held her anyway, stroking her head full of hair, telling her "it's alright, and repeatedly; saying to her "it's okay, just so she would stop; crying.

She starts telling him about "how much she will always remember the good times they shared." And that she's "never; ever!" not once, made love to anyone of those men at the club or anyone else since they were together!" And that; it's 'him, and only 'him, that she's in love with!" "Shhhh..." he says. "It's okay!" They sit down on his bed and as she's looking in his eyes she says "I will tell your family that I have to go, so you don't have to pretend with me here." He grunts out "Roxy, I never have to 'pretend, for no one!" I'm not a perfect man, but I do expect my woman, a woman that I wish to marry, someday to be perfectly honest with me, no matter what!" Roxy wipes her eyes; purring out the words "I know, I know, I blew it!" I better go, it's almost time for you and your family to eat dinner" she says in a crackling voice, trying to stand up from his bed.

He finished what he was saying by talking over her "trying" to leave 'speech, and he says "and the woman; I want to be with and marry can't be taking her clothes off for other men!" That is for me, and only me to view!" She holds her head down still sobbing and he lifts it up saying "you are worth 'more, than that to me!" And that is why, I have been so angry!" he confessed looking into her eyes. She stares back at him; nodding her head in agreement and he stares back at her, trying to read the "truth" once again from her crying eyes. Although he has missed her and she has missed him, he still can't bring himself to let down his guard. 'He's open, but defenseless at this time and she doesn't want to lose him again, so she just stares at him, just in case this is the last time she will ever be this close again to his beautiful face. Seeing how she's looking at him, he gently pushes the hair away from her eyes and her mouth and then he moves his face closer to hers and with his eyes; still looking in hers; he kisses her.

Roxy is still crying but 'not, from sadness; these are tears of joy and in the 'hopes, of forgiveness. By Steeli'o kissing her and wanting her, after all she's done, made her feel so loved inside and it was a feeling that she didn't think would ever be possible due to her life style; choices! So the crying also in her mind was because she 'knew, now; that 'this, was what they called unconditional 'love, in its; rawness! And this time was there's 'right now, and no 'dinner, or no phone 'ringing, was going to ruin this love and passion that the two were feeling in that moment.

He lays Roxy back on his bed and as she's kissing him and running her fingers through his hair he grabs her by her waist and pulls her over so she can; rollover and lay on top of him. And while they are kissing he slowly starts to unzip her dress. He can tell that she wants him to hurry up and take off her dress because they start to move more; quicker once her zipper is down and her arms are out of her dress. Impatiently he unsnaps her bra with his hands; fidgeting to get it off as fast as possible. She's down to her panties when he flips her back over and she lands on her back. Steeli'o, stretches his arm over her head to reach for one big black button, on the top of his head-board, and then the whole room goes pitch; black! And as the shades fall from all sides of the room, in the dark, he slides down her panties very slowly with his index finger, and whispers to her, "to push the glowing red button above her head."

She turns her head with excitement looking for the 'button, so she can push it! Gradually, a soft spark of light comes into view. The glow starts off like a sunrise as it lifts to a sharp yellowish, orange, with hints of red and purple peeking through the more dominate color of dark orange. And with the lights changing color he starts to kiss in her inner thighs and rub down her legs softly with his hand. The glow goes in and out giving them just the right amount of light and warmth. Roxy starts to get an 'elevated, heartbeat because she is so... turned, on, as he's softly; licking her, and rubbing her, in all of her, sensitive areas. He has always 'fantasized, about making love to 'her, in his 'room, in his 'bed, in the dark! And he never forgot that she said she wanted snow. So when the room gets to just the right temperature and the water bed is heated to keep her warm. With all these things happening she begins to 'squirm, out of her mind! And Steeli'o all anxious, pushes the blue button on his remote control and as she's lying back about to climax for the first time in his 'room, on his 'bed, the snow starts to fall, down, slowly, and softly; all over her body. His walls become an audio movie theater, and they are suddenly, out in the wild as the room becomes alive. Roxy is climbing the wall as the snowflakes are landing on her body, her breast, her face, and in her mouth. She starts to cry out with pure ecstasy from Steeli'o's every; touch! And as the snow is falling on her body, the feel of the hot, dark, lights and the cold snowflakes, make her start to 'hum, as her "crystal; pearl" is being "polished; royally" by his tongue!

She is jerking her 'body, back and forth like a wild woman towards the end of her pleasuring 'spike, and Steeli'o can't wait to 'pounce on her, when she is finished; 'releasing; thy endorphins; throughout her body! When she's done hollering his name, her face is a glow of red when Steeli'o climbs up on top of her. She looks into his eyes while she is calming down her awaiting body and he says to her "can I 'come, inside of you?" as he's holding her close. The sounds in the room starts to grow louder when he turns up the volume with the remote, and that is so, no one will hear her; howl, while he's making love to her. He plays nature sounds out of his speakers 'like as if, they are in a real forest, along with pictures showing on his walls and she can hardly hold back a smile when she tell him "yes, to making love to her after looking at the life-like motion pictures on the walls and hearing all the sounds in the room like they are in a wintery; type of snow forest.

She looks at him but this time more; deeper into his eyes 'so he knows, he's the only one she wants. 'While hoping, that she's the only 'woman, he's ever wanted to making love to; too, this; badly in his room. Roxy has waited for this moment, and is so... in love with 'him, for loving her; no matter what! And although, she didn't need too 'prove, her love for 'him, in that moment 'sexually, she just wanted too, because he is the kind of man she's always dreamed of being with, that she's prayed for. And without saying a word she reaches down and unzips his pants and pulls out his 'stiff; pistol, and slides him inside her; holster. He looks into her eyes while on top of her and they make love as the tears dry down the side of her face.

As things heat up he kisses her aggressively and licks her chest so he can place his mouth on her awaiting areolas. The love that they feel is so--, beautiful that Steeli'o slowly let's down his guard, and so does she, and as he's going deeper and deeper inside of her; loving her; and holding her; with all his 'might, she starts to 'cum, again and again and with all of that emotion pouring out of her body she says to him "I love you; Steeli'o!" I really do; love you!" And as he's starting to 'release, after hearing those words from her lips, he doesn't cower away from his own true feelings as he squeezes her tightly with one arm and while 'flowing through her, he says "I love you too" in her ear, in Italian. He stays on top of her for a while as the snowflakes fall on his back, cooling his body down, and she giggles a little as the cold flakes land on her face, her legs, and her body.

It is such a peaceful feeling in the room and all is back on track with the two lovers and just when Roxy couldn't be any happier as she's lying there thanking God for a second chance at love, he kisses her and then his private phone in his room rings and he doesn't 'move, from on top of Roxy for they are now at peace in one another's arms. She rubs his back and kisses his shoulder as the snow falls on the two of them ever so softly. He figures it's one of his relatives calling to wish the family a Merry Christmas; early so he just let it go to voice machine. Beep...!

"Hey?" Steeli'o?" Happy Eve; Christmas!" This is Claudia!" We need to talk!" Remember our last love session in Tahoe?" Well... I'm pregnant!" Call me; lover boy!" I'll be waiting!" After hearing that message Roxy's mouth is as wide as a leaf's blower's hose! She blinks; so hard that her lashes covered in mascara stick together when she tries to open her eyes back up to see his face. She couldn't believe what she was hearing coming from his answering machine. Lying there she goes breathless, because speechless is an understatement! She literally, couldn't even breathe, this was a panic attack times ten! Her whole body starts; shaking and she goes into hysterics! Roxy is furious when she tells Steeli'o "get; up!" Off of me!" she shouted pushing her way out from underneath him. Steeli'o is just as shocked as she is as he too was lying there in 'real; disbelief' at the phone call he just got. He almost sort of 'chuckled; thinking; "this is another one of Claudia's, practical jokes!" which; isn't funny! Or..., even worse, this stalker 'b#^ch, has 'really, lost; her f*cking; mind! Leaving a serious message like that, on his machine; especially with his family in town! All of this went through his mind. But Roxy on the other hand wasn't laughing.

In fact she was putting all of her clothes back on, and cursing him out at the same time! She blurts out "I can't believe, that I sat up here, and spilled out; all of my guts to you!" And how I..., was made to believe!" That, I..., was this "terrible; person!" Who "danced" for; money!" Oh...; no!" Let me correct; myself!" Who; "stripped"! "For money!" But, come to find out!" It's was you!" Who was the biggest; fu^king; liar!" "Steeli'o stands there, trying to calm her down by shouting "no! "This is a joke!" Trust me!" he said pushing the black button on his bed post to stop all of the snow from falling and the sound effects; from sounding. He then says "Claudia, jokes a lot!" Believe; me!" Roxy cracking on him says "jokes; my ass!" She yells "did you really have sex with her while we were up in Tahoe?!" And don't you fu*^king; lie to me!" She says with tears peaking up in her eyes. He answers "um... not; technically!" Roxy puts down her shoes saying "what does that, mean?"! He says "she took advantage of me!" Roxy blurts out "oh; sh*t!" Give me a break!" She tilts her head to one side saying "so you're telling me, she "raped" you?!" Is that what you expect me to believe?"! Then she adds "and where was I at?!" When all this was taking place?!" No, let me guess!" I was at the Cabin looking like 'Dumbo, the dummy!" He couldn't even get a word in, over her rage. She ends with "so tell me something, did you sleep with her before?!" Or after I went down on you in the room that night?"! He stands there 'thinking back, with a dumb look on his face. Disgusted she says "wow!" You are really going to stand there and think back on it?!" You are truly; an asshole!" But, hey!" she shouts, "stupid me!" Right?!" For believing I had someone who 'really, loved me?!"

He yells out "well, shit!" join the club!" Because you don't exactly have a squeaky clean, track record, yourself; sweetheart!" She shouts "yeah..., but I didn't sleep with anyone else, either!" He yells "how would I know that?"! He throws his hands up in thy air shouting "you are "naked" on stage; nightly!" Roxy stops what she's doing and glares at him, trying not to cry again after he said that. He grabs her by the hand saying "sorry!" We are supposed to be passed that." But now, you have to trust me!" when I says "you are getting mad over nothing!" And I'm telling you, that it's a joke!" "She is not pregnant!" he says. "Yes, Claudia likes me" he adds. "We've known each other for years, because of our family ties together". But she 'knows, I, am, with; you!

Roxy still angry and in her saddest voice she says "if you really loved me, you would have never slept with her." He returns "you can "not" 'tell me, what I'm 'feeling, for you!" he said She talks over him saying "and I can't believe I was up in the Cabin posing as your woman!" "While being; played in front of all our friends!" "Played!" he yells. "Don't even talk to 'me, about getting; played!" in front of friends! "You wrote 'thy; book!" on how to play a 'muddafuckar!" "So don't; Eeben!" come at 'me, with that sh*t!" Roxy returns "yeah...! Okay...!" And all you were doing, was telling me lies, about how you and your "boys" were out there doing business; up in Tahoe!" But now I know what kind of "business" you and your freelancing penis, were really doing!" He waves his hand pass her face shouting "ahhhh... come off it!" with that bull-sh*t! Angry he adds some other choice words, in Italian that she didn't understand but 'knew, that they "weren't" nice words!

She gets her dress zipped up and her shoes on and shakes her head, slowly and with a smirk on her lips, needing to have the last word, she looks at him saying "and here I thought you might have had; just a slight 'gambling, problem you didn't want me to know about, and that's why you kept leaving with your "friends"! "But I never dreamed you would be cheating on me and right under my nose!" "In a loud voice he yells "you keep making; me!" out to be thy bad guy here!" So-- if that makes you 'feel; better to blame 'me, for everything that's gone wrong in 'our, relationship; than fine!" Because I forgave you for your shit!" So I don't know what 'else, you want from me!" He looks at her with a confused face. And her, with nothing else to say reaches for the bedroom door but he presses his hand on the door so she can't leave out of his room. "Desperate not to have things end this way he says "okay!" Wait!" We can call her back, right now!" I swear; she's playing a Christmas prank!" He pleads for Roxy not to leave. Then she agrees saying "okay, call her!" She stands there with her arms folded not wanting to leave without him proving his argument.

He dials Claudia's number, not knowing what the outcome might be, but he needs Roxy to trust him in his belief that; it's "really" a joke. When Claudia picks up the phone flirting, she says "hi, baby." I've been missing you." Roxy gets really pissed off and starts to talk sh*t in the background; voicing things like "well he hasn't been missed you!" "In fact, we just got done, making love, you b#^ch!" Claudia laughs an evil laugh saying "I'm not use to being called; "b#t$h!" But...trust me, if I was one, Steeli'o can tell you; I'm ma damn; good one!" Claudia lights up her cigarette saying "and if you know, what's good for you 'little stripping; whore!" You will address me; correctly!"

Roxy looks at Steeli'o 'like as if to suggest, he's told her 'all, about her stripping; job. But he hadn't. Claudia finishes with "and as for you Steeli'o; tisk, tisk, tisk" she motioned with the suction of her tongue on the roof of her mouth, shouting "you invite 'trash, to your house, for thy Holiday's!" How sweet!" Momma must be; proud!" Steeli'o takes the phone off speaker and yells "Claudia?!" Don't you!" and your man!" have better things to do; than call and harassing me on thy Holidays?"! He adds "you; know... you're not pregnant!" You just want to start some sh^t!" between me and my woman! She just chuckles. He blurts out "what's wrong Claudia?"! "He's not d*cking you down; properly?!"

Claudia laughs at his calm, yet angry demeanor when she says "no darling!" He's; not!" You; f*ck me; better! She chuckles some more because she knows she has him by the balls because he needs her for business and she needs him as well. He yells "Claudia!" Cut thy crap!" and tell Roxy you were just joking around, so I can get back to having dinner with my family!" Claudia smiling on the other end of the phone replies "Steeli'o...?" Steeli'o...?" You know you love me and only me!" She continues to say

"Roxy, she is 'just, play; toy!" Just like all thy rest, of your 'Barbie's, from your past! "You know, like I 'know, she will; "never" make you happy!" She can't even get into thy 'family; because, she is garbage!" "Watch your mouth!" he shouts 'Claudia; exhaling her cigarette smoke in a tauntingly; high voice shouts "remember, we are 'together; 'forever; sweety!" From thy cradle; to thy grave!" He yells out "Claudia!" We will "never!" be a couple! "Get that through; that thick; scull of yours!" I, love, Roxy!" And she loves, me!" She talks over his jibber about Roxy and yells back "tell Roxy to enjoy you, while she can!" And as for me and thy baby, that is growing inside my; womb!" We will be waiting to see 'you, in about a few weeks, when we meet up for business; no?!" And then she hangs up the phone in his face after saying "ciao!

He throws his phone against the wall while Roxy is already making her way down the stairs in tears, because she could hear every word Claudia was saying through the phone and not only did it; hurt 'to hear; but it also resonated some of the things she felt about herself on her 'worse, days! Downstairs, Steeli'o's family is already sitting at the table waiting to begin their feast. So when Roxy gets to the bottom of the stairs and walks past the dining room area, Gi'la has a big smile on her face 'but, it is cut short, because she can see by the look on Roxy's face that something is wrong; like, she's been crying. So Gi'la excuses herself from the table and goes up to Roxy asking her "what is wrong?"

'Steeli'o, running down the stairs to find her, sees her with his sister; so he blurts out "everything's fine!" He said that because he didn't want Roxy to tell his sister about the baby allegations. Roxy standing there sadly; holding back more tears says "why don't you ask your "brother!" what's wrong?"! He seems to have it all "bundled; up!" Referencing a baby joke that only he and her know about. Gi'la looks at Steeli'o puzzled asking "what is she talking about?"! She reaches for Roxy's arm in concern and while looking at her brother she asked "what have you done to make her?"! Then before he could respond Gi'la looks at them both saying "momma is waiting for you to come, so we can eat."

She tries to get the two of them to come sit down at the table and stop their foolishness. But Roxy all on edge and feeling unhappy after everything that happened up in his room, starts to feel; 'clouded, in her thoughts and as she's running her fingers through her hair she begins to say "I don't think I can stay Gi'la." I'm so... sorry" she says in an almost 'faintish, voice. She turn from them both and like a drunk caricature; she walks into the dining room to give her regrets of having to leave to the rest of the family sitting at the table. His mom stops what she's doing 'which is arranging the glasses on the table and says "che c'e'?" Meaning "What is wrong?" She then turns her attention to her son asking "Steeli'o; che cosa succede'?"! (Meaning) "What is going on?"! She adds in broken English; "why is she so, upset?"! He answers "mum, everything es fine." Steeli'o looks over at Vinnie saying "you guys go ahead and eat while I go talk to Roxy. While he was telling them that; Gi'la was pleading for Roxy to please stay, as they are standing over by the entryway. But Roxy feels she can't hide the fact that she is so, hurt and confused about some other woman "claiming" to be having Steeli'o's child. And how Claudia said that "she is nothing but some, "blow-up; Barbie, toy!" Or, some tricks; ran down stripping; trash!" Well at least; that's what she, got out of it! And while all of that stuff swirled around in her brain, her self-esteem, and her confidence took a big; hit and Roxy loses it and bolts out of the house heading straight to her car. Steeli'o runs behind her yelling "don't leave!" Come on bay'be, don't listen to Claudia she's a crazy; wack-o!"

By the time Roxy reaches her car, before she can get into the driver's seat, Steeli'o rushes up to her and grabs her by the arm. With dark circles around her eyes she cries out "what kind of hold; does this Claudia girl have on you?"! "It's like she controls you, or she has something weighing over your head!" "Nah... nah... you got it all wrong!" She shouts "you talk to me about being honest!" But that's all it is; just talk!" When she opens up her car door he won't let her close it; just yet. He says "come on Roxy, come back down to the house." You know, it will just break my sister's heart, if you don't come back." "See, you didn't hear a word I said about honesty" she said. "It's all... about you!" "Right?!" Steeli'o?" "You just don't want your sister to be mad with "you!" because I'm leaving! "Yess...!" But no!" That's not thy only reason why" he confessed.

She sits down in her car toiling with her keys and doesn't look back up at him because she's so disappointed in the way things have gone. Not only is she disappointed with him, but more 'so, with herself for sleeping with him. He puts his hand on her hand, on top of the steering wheel, still pleading for her to stay. Clearing her throat and looking up at him she says "you know; 'all, about me!" So call me, when you're ready to be honest; about you!"

Looking down she starts up her car and drives away, leaving him standing in the middle of the street with his hands clasped together on top of his head 'thinking, about what she just said. Roxy drives home with tears falling on her face like a rain storm. She's crying so hard, that the tears are clouding up her vision. While crying she talks to God out loud at the same time asking; "why can't she be happily in love with someone?!" And why does she always have such bad luck with men?!" Then she tells God "that she knows; she's not living the way he would want her to be living". And so on, and so on, as she's driving and crying, talking to God about everything she's feeling inside.

When she finally gets home and no one is there, it makes it even worse! Tammy is in Vegas with Marvin and her other girlfriends are coupled up at Naquawna's house so all she can do is get into the shower and sob, all over again. 'She just figures, she is just 'meant, to be alone and that no one will ever love her. 'In her mind she thinks; who would ever love a stripper like her anyway? 'And, that Steeli'o would be better off; without her! She tries to think positive thoughts though too 'like, God has someone in the distant future for her. She goes back and forth on the subject but all she can hear the 'loudest, in her mind; is, that she's only here, to take her clothes off for 'men; and get paid!

Out loud she says to herself "what kind of wife or mother would she make 'anyways, dancing in clubs for money?" Sobbing even harder she convinces herself that she will just have to learn to be alone again. And while she's crying she doesn't even wanna think about calling the girls right now, because hearing Naquawna say "I told you so!" And having Candis confirming 'how dumb; she is, for sleeping with him 'so soon, after their; big break up, would prove to be; too 'much, for her right now! So she just sits on the shower floor in a fetal position rocking back and forth crying herself sick; yet again! And then she hears the doorbell ring. At first she hopes they will just go away but then she remembers how her mom and dad sometimes come over on Christmas Eve before they go to Church, when she's in town, and how her dad could always cheer her up; no matter what! And right now; she really 'doesn't, want to be along tonight, so she wipes her face with a towel and puts her robe on to greet her parents at the front door.

Once her robe is tied, she blows her nose and clears her throat, so they won't suspect she's been crying. Roxy always puts up this hardcore exterior in front of her parents. She makes them 'think, she's got it all 'together; like a strong independent woman and all, who has her own house and her own money. But Roxy is starting to see that; that is "not" what makes; for a happy; soul! "Money" that is; without love! Fixing her hair she looks out the peephole which is being covered up because someone is holding something in front of it; which is something her dad always 'does, so she smiles out a laugh saying "oh dad!" and then she opens up the door. 'But then, to her 'broken; 'hearted; 'surprise; it isn't her dad at all! It is 'Steeli'o, standing there looking more handsome than ever as he hands her a bouquet of long stemmed yellow roses. And in his other hand he is holding a bottle of the most expensive champagne he could fine in his wine cellar, with her coat that she left at his house; draped across his arm. He smiles saying "you didn't think I would let you spend Christmas Eve 'all alone; did you?" She smiles, a pleasantly 'happy to see him smile, and with one eyebrow up she replies "what makes you think, I'm alone?" His eyes dilated as he's looking around her living room like he's being played for a fool once again. But then she chuckles; voicing "just, kidding!" and then reaches up to give him a big hug. She looks up towards the ceiling while in his arms, and silently she says "thank you God!" He closes her door and holds her tight and they kiss all the way to the kitchen.

Roxy gets out two glasses and is smiling from ear to ear, while Steeli'o pops the cork. They both laugh when it hits the ceiling because it almost accidently, put out one of her kitchen lights. Looking in her eyes he says "what should we toast too?"! Roxy smiles out "I don't know, but let's make it something good though" she says as she's looking him back in thy eyes. He looks at her while thinking of something and as he lifts up his glass he says "okay." I know!" To you and me, and a new start!" with love, respect, and Roxy yells out "and; honesty!" Roxy taps her glass against his, saying "here; here! After his drink he says "so... show me your place!" I never got thy "grand; tour!" he said with a sly smile. "Let's start with where you sleep" he said. She chuckles "no, the tour starts here in the kitchen and then the living room and so on and so on!" He grunts out a sound while putting down his glass. And with a big smile he starts walking towards the back of the house saying "well..., I guess, I'll just have to find thy boom, boom, room; all by myself!"

He darts for the hallway and she grabs him by the arm pulling on it laughing out; "no...! "You need to do the full tour before we get to the boom, boom room!" But he's not listening. He laughs and picks her up and drapes her over his shoulder like a damsel in distress while giving her a bad girl 'spanking, on her 'buttocks, and she laughs because it's funny. And as he is spanking her, running back to her room, he is laughing a wicked laugh while carrying her. At the doorway of her room he shouts "ah-ha!" "So this is the princess's palace?!" he said as he plops; her down on her bed. She can't stop smiling when her head lands on her pillow. And with all the Getty-laughter coming out of her mouth, he slowly tries to untie the knot on her robe so he can really get a full view of her beautiful silhouette.

'Ding-dong! Her doorbell ring again. He grins voicing "ah-ha...!" Who is that?!" Thinking that it must be one of her "backup" lover's! But Roxy assures him that; that is more than likely her parents stopping by for a few minutes with gifts and food. She keeps kissing him saying "I'll just talk to them tomorrow." "No," he says as he holds her face with both of his hands looking her in thy eyes saying "come on, I want to meet them!" She returns "Steeli'o; you don't have to do that." He says "remember?" You said; honesty!" "Right?!" Roxy says "okay...!" Don't; say, I didn't warn you!" Because they are pretty; religious and they probably 'won't, approve of you dating a "stripper," because they 'know, what I do!"

He corrects her saying "no...! "They 'know, what you "use" to do! She smiles at him because he really does; believe in her. She yells out "coming!" But first she puts on some clothes telling him "she doesn't want to greet them in her robe, making it 'too; obvious, that they are 'fornicating, with each other." So she grabs some sweats and a tee shirt and Steeli'o looking tells her how hot she looks as he playfully hits her on her rear. They walk out to the living room hand in hand and when Steeli'o opens the door with a big smile he says "hello?"! My name is Steeli'o!" I've heard nothing but great things about you two!" Her parents are 'astonishingly; 'surprised; at first because; one, a man is answering her door! And second; because he's caught them off guard.

Her parents look him up and down and then her mother replies "hum-- you don't say!" Well, we haven't heard a thing; about you!" But it's nice to meet you all the same!" Roxy spouts out "that's not true!" Even Vanessa told you about Steeli'o when she was having her baby; remember?" Her mom says "well... it's so hard--, keeping track of all these things that you have going on." As if to say, Roxy has 'so many men, in and out of her life; until they can't seem to keep up! Steeli'o doesn't trip off of her mother's "negative; accusations" he just kept killing them with kindness. They all sit down on the couch and her dad asked "so... what do you do for a living son?" And as her dad is waiting for him to answer, he's looking down at Steeli'o's nicely pressed slacks and expensive accessories. It's almost like he's waiting on Steeli'o to say "he's her pimp!" Steeli'o smiles; proudly answering "I'm in Real- Estate." "And I'm hoping to bring Roxy into the business very soon" he adds as he squeezes her hand in front of her parents.

Her mom's face lights up when she hears Steeli'o's comment. But Roxy knows that 'look, all too well on her mother's face, and she's probably thinking "thank the Lord!" now she can "finally" stop taking her clothes off for men!" Roxy could always read her mother's face, so she smiles; smirkishly when she offers her parents a drink of juice; asking "or perhaps some tea; mother?" Which her mother bitterly; declines saying "well... I don't really like to eat or drink before I take communion and since we are on our way to 'church, she pauses looking at Roxy saying "you two should come with us, to midnight mass!" Her mother adds "we're going to the 9:00 service though" because Lord 'knows, we just can't stay up that late, like we use to, when you and Vanessa were younger." Steeli'o laughs "yess-- I can relate to that, because my mother 'says thy same 'thing, about midnight mass as well." He takes a drink of the juice that Roxy has brought out to him and then says to her parents "by the way, did Roxy tell you we went to thy Cathedral in Rome?" Her father coughs in his hand answering "I remember your sister saying something about it, but we didn't think you really went!" But I guess we stand corrected" said her father. He continues to say "you must be; loaded!" Roxy yells "dad!" Her dad looks her way voicing "I'm just saying!" "For you two, to be able to go on such an "expensive; trip" at the drop of a hat!" I might need to get into the "real-estate" business; myself!" said her father with a sarcastic look on his face like he's "not" believing that he makes all his money from just doing real-estate.

Roxy felt a slight jab from her father, to Steeli'o's character. But Steeli'o didn't miss a beat when he sarcastically responded with "yep--, I guess you could say; that 'God, was in the details; on that trip!" Her father and mother smiled but seemed to be a little jealous at this; point! Happy for their daughter 'but yet, jealous to see that, although in their eyes; she was viewed as a "sinner" more so, than; them! Yet; "God" seemed to still be blessing; her! Her dad grabs his hat and stand up from the couch saying "whelp--, we better get going!" "We don't want to be late to God's house!" He extends his hand to shake Steeli'o's hand saying "it was nice meeting you lad." You two have a very Merry Christmas" said her father. He hugs his daughter and his wife kisses her on the cheek with a hug as well. Smiling, Steeli'o and Roxy walk them to the door saying "thanks again, for the gifts and food" and then wave good-bye as they both got into their car. Steeli'o closes the door saying "now see, that wasn't so bad!" I even think they liked 'me, more-- than they liked you!" Roxy pops him on the arm laughing, saying "I don't think so; pal!" He laughs back and grabs her saying "now where were we?!" She breaks free from his hold and starts running and he chases her all the way back to the room while she's laughing and giggling.

Roxy runs and flops down on top of her bed, and he jumps on top of her bed with both feet standing over her with her in between his legs and then he falls down to his knees with her still in between his legs as he commences to kissing her all over her face. Roxy still wants 'truthful, answers, about his “secret; life”! As well as the Claudia thing. But, it can all wait till morning; because she’s “not” ‘about, to lose this happy feeling, and neither is he! Over at Naquawna’s house the feelings aren’t the same, as at Roxy house, and you are about to see just why!

Chapter 33

"**Good**" and "not" so good; singing is coming out of Naquawna's apartment because her granddad and Candis are singing on this 'new, karaoke machine that Mike's mom has gotten them as a family Christmas gift. Naquawna and Candis's mom are the two background singers at the moment and everyone is having a great time taking turns singing songs on Christmas Eve. It took Mike a while to warm up to Rafee'al but it worked out great, after Mike beat him in a game of basketball on the PlayStation. Once Mike beat him at one of his favorite basketball games, then he felt like he was a real; basketball pro! And that's when he had loosened up and became much more; friendlier.

Rafee'al wasn't tripping when he lost the game to Mike because he 'knew, where his strengths were; and it wasn't playing games on the PlayStation! Not that there's anything wrong with that, Rafee'al just preferred live action! 'Plus, Rafee'al didn't really care to make best friends with Mike anyway, because he liked Rayshawn better. Before Rafee'al and Candis had went over to Naquawna's place, Candis had already "clued" Rafee'al in, about Mike. And she also told him not to talk about the trip they all took to Tahoe; at all! Rafee'al hated to be on a "none" slipping slop, with these people, meaning (not to slip and say the wrong thing). But he still replied "anything, to make you happy Candis" as he kissed her before Mike had come to answer the door.

"Dinner is served!" said the ladies as they bring out all of the food to the table. Granddad, Mike and Rafee'al were treated like 'kings, that day. So when everyone sat down to eat granddad did the honors of saying "grace. He even boasted to the ladies saying "it shows that this food was cooked with love!" 'Mike's mom can really cook her 'butt off, in the kitchen! That was all Naquawna's granddad seemed to talk about the whole time, forgetting the fact that all of the 'other women, had cooked; great dishes too. But in granddad's eyes Ms. Ellis had the best of everything from her smothered pulled pork, to her homemade peach cobbler.

Candis's mom seemed to be getting a little jealous over all of the 'compliments, to 'Ms. Ellis's food. And it was more than likely, because he was acting like she was the "star; cook"! When before that was always the way he use to talked about 'Mrs. Tomson's; cooking! So when the two ladies start to fight for granddad's attention by asking him "who he thought, made the best banana pudding; pie?" Naquawna and Candis took notice and kicked each other under the table as they listened to the bickering; chatter from Mrs. Tomson and Ms. Ellis as they hovered over granddad with their pieces of pie on a spoon. The two women put a taste from each one of their pies into his mouth one by one; wanting him to say; which one he liked the best between the cobbler and the banana pudding pie?

But granddad was no fool. Plus, he loved the attention. And being that he was no rookie when it came to flirting with women. He went on ahead and told them 'both, how much he loved both of them. "Their; pies that is!" he concluded with a chuckle from his own settled joke. But then when Mrs. Tomson turns her back to give Rafee'al a slice of her pie, granddad gave Ms. Ellis a wink of his eye and held up 'her, piece of pie on his fork letting 'her know, he liked her pie the best.

Candis smiles when she catches all of the action between Ms. Ellis and granddad. So after dinner Candis secretly asked Naquawna as they were doing the dishes "if she thinks her granddad and Mike's mom would ever hook up?" Saying to Naquawna "because you 'do know; they like each other; right?" Naïvely; Naquawna replies "no girl..., they are just bingo buddies!" "Okay, if you say so" said Candis answering with a look on her face 'like, she ain't buying it! Rafee'al comes into the kitchen and grabs Candis by the waist and gives her a big kiss saying "what a great meal it was, and how he is just stuffed right now."

Naquawna looks at them both asking "are you two staying, so we can all sing some more and play spades?" Candis looks up at Rafee'al smiling because she has her own Christmas Eve plans, then she looks back at Naquawna saying "nope." Not tonight, we're going to go play a few games of our own; at his house" she says pulling Rafee'al in closer for another kiss. "Umm--; really?!" said Naquawna with a big smile on her face. Naquawna is kind of envious because she wishes she could be saying the same thing about going over to Rayshawn's house; if, he lived alone. 'Or, was really available for more than just; sex! Especially after Candis and Rafee'al anxiously said good-bye to everyone and rushed Candis's mom out of the house with her plates of food, so they could drop her off at home.

When they drive up into Candis mom's driveway she waits for her to get inside the house and then her and Rafee'al wave good-bye to her as she closes her front door. Rafee'al toots the horn and he and Candis head over to his place. When they finally get to his house Candis gets out of the car looking around his neighborhood, saying "you live in a nice area." He answered "thanks." Yeah, it's not too shabby." And it's actually pretty quiet" he said. She nods listens to him as he opens up his door to let her inside his place. Trying not to seem too eager she walks inside and immediately notices how nice his place is. "It is very structured" she would say. He replies "structured!" "What does that mean?" She smiles "you know, nice, clean, 'very; 'bachelorish; like! He laughs saying "bachelorish!" "Is that even a word?" She laughs back voicing "I don't know!" But probably somewhere in the world; it's a real word" she adds smiling. He grunts looking at her and she smiles even harder saying "so... this is where all the "date; nights!" go down at, huh?!" He chuckles with one hand rubbing his chin thinking should he lie and say "no." Or lie and say "yes." Because "technically" he's been working this case and hasn't; had much time for other woman. So he decides to tell her what he "thinks" she would want to hear; which is "naw... you're the only one I've trusted enough to bring to my crib since I've moved here." She gets a big cheesy smile on her face, loving his answer but, still not knowing if he's pulling her leg or not. So she replies with; "anyways!" Just to let him know, she's not that "naïve" but loves his answer.

Shyly looking at him; adoringly she tells him how much she likes his place. Then she walks over to his couch and makes herself comfortable on it. Candis grinning inwardly knows in her heart that she and Rafee'al are meant to be together, because she is so-o-o relaxed in his arms as they sit on his couch listening to music and talking. Rafee'al takes her by the hand and pulls her up and they dance in the middle of his living room. He kisses her and holds her close and then he pulls out this cute little box. Candis is amazed because she had no clue. "Awh...!" she purrs. Saying "Rafee'al..., you didn't have to get me a gift!" She smiles a sweet smile looking into his beautiful eyes then she kisses him. "You know I had to get you something" he said. "It's not a diamond ring or anything like that, but I hope you like it." 'Candis, kind of figured it wasn't a ring because of the size of the box, it looked more to be like, for a bracelet or necklace. But never the less she was happy to have gotten something from him; that showed; her, he was thinking of her.

She opens up the box and it's a beautiful, beautiful necklace in the shape of a heart with diamonds all around the outline of the heart. Candis gives him the biggest; most; longest; kiss she had every given him, and when the kiss is finished he tells her to turn around so he can put the necklace on her neck. Once it is on her neck she goes over to the mirror in his hallway to see how pretty it looks on her. They both stand there for a few minutes admiring the necklace and then Candis anxiously says "well..., I got you something too!" She rushes over to her purse, which is on the chair to get his gift. Rafee'al gets caught blushing a bit because he really didn't expect for her to have anything for him in that tiny little purse of hers. She walks up to him with a kiss saying "here babe." I would have given it to you over Naquawna's house but I wanted to be alone with you, when I gave it to you." He takes the box saying "thanks sweetheart."

He opens it slowly as he's looking down at her smiling and when he gets the last piece of wrapping paper off he sees that it is a watch. But not just any watch, it is a Rolex limited edition. Rafee'al had told Candis a while back how his father had given him a watch for Christmas one year and how he had lost it, and never told his dad or bought another one because his father had left by then to make a new family. So when he seen that Candis had gotten him a watch, memories of his dad came to the surface. It was kind of bitter sweet when he grabbed Candis and hugged her saying "thank you," because 'now, the watch will make a 'good, new memory from him and her now."

He held her for a long time so she couldn't see in his eyes how emotional he was getting. And in his mind he had lost his relationship with his dad, but gained a loving woman who wanted to share her life with him, and who listened to him, when he spoke from his heart. His sister who died also came to mind when one of her favorite Christmas songs came on his stereo being sung by Justin Bieber; called: Someday at Christmas. Candis is so moved by the song and his hug, and she can feel that the relationship has moved up a 'notch, for the 'better; so she just stands there letting him hold her, with all of his emotions ricocheting; off of her heart.

After the song is over he pulls back from her slowly and they both walk back over to the couch and sit down and he puts his watch on. She sits there looking at him latching up his watch, while she's rubbing on her neck touching her new necklace. Candis, suggested that they order a movie to watch on his t.v but he wasn't feeling it. He wanted "to hold her in his bed and watch t.v in there" he said. Candis gives him an innocent look like; we are not in Tahoe anymore as she sits there fiddling with the t.v remote looking for a movie for the two of them to buy.

She is thinking; very 'clearly, about staying over his house alone, and yes--, she does trust herself and she is very aware of the temptation of staying overnight with him 'with; 'no; other friends around. And granite she might be considered a "late; bloomer" in the love making department! But she is "definitely" a "veteran!" when it comes to making men fall in love with 'her, without!" having sex with them! And Rafee'al on thy other hand just "knows" in his heart of 'hearts, that 'this, is going to be the night that he 'plucks; Candis's flower for the first time. But what he doesn't know is; that she is not going down; without a ring on her finger and the papers to go with it! She smirks thinking "the necklace is beautiful!" But "not" for the price of her virginity! And now, thinking back, she can remember her mother warning her about 'accepting, expensive gifts, from men, because 'sometimes, they expect, something; back, in return!

So while the music is playing she says "let's dance" avoiding his room idea for now. They danced some more and slow danced 'a lot, to the point that Candis was almost falling asleep on his shoulder. He asked "you getting tired?" You can stay over if you want?" I'll be a complete gentleman" he said sincerely. She smiles thinking "he is really trying to get me back to his room." So with confidence she says to herself; she'll play his game. 'Sleepy-eyed, as she was, she looks at him saying "alright, and the two walk back to his 'very, masculine; room. His room was the true meaning of a man cave; 'compliments, of his two partners Lenny and Kitpatrick who helped Rafee'al lay out his pad when the case first began; knowing that Rafee'al would eventually be bringing Candis or some other lucky ladies to his room.

His walls were filled with sports memorabilia and pretty posters of sexy women. Candis not really caring for the pictures of the girls on his wall, loved his bed though. It was a king size sleep number bed, which she was more than happy to climb into for a goodnights sleep. Rafee'al takes off his shirt as Candis stands there looking at his nice abs. He tells her to make herself comfortable as his pants fall to the floor. She swallows with a dry throat asking "do you have an extra t-shirt I can wear?" He returns "why?" are you cold?" because I can warm you up, come on, get in the bed, I won't bit you, unless you want me two" he said; patting on the bed with his hand' where he wants her to lay.

Candis chuckles because she's not afraid to get in his bed, she is just 'nervous, for some crazy reason, and she doesn't know why?" because she has slept in the same bed with him before in Tahoe. But this time, it feels different 'more, grown up; like! Almost like when you feel bigger and badder when your friends are around, but now you're by yourself, so you feel more venerable. Crossing her legs she sits down on his bed in her clothes. He pats his bed and fluffs her pillow and then she lays down next to him. While watching video's; on M-TV she is feeling the closeness of his hold, and when the video's he likes, come on; he squeezes her even; tighter, making her feel more loved by him. She loves seeing this side of him too, because she wants to see how he's going to make his next move, almost like a chest game. It's what turns her on the 'most, about him.

He grabs her by the hand and kisses her and as he slides her hair back, to get a good look at her face she takes a deep breath and closes her eyes and kisses him 'like as if, time will just stop; right there; in his room. Candis smiles, but knows she is pushing thy envelope by lying down in his bed with him, while he's in his boxers. Her religious side of her brain tells her 'no! This is "not" 'wise, and way too soon! While her other side of her brain; the "torching" hot; side, is saying "to just let him rub his body up against hers" just so she can see what it would feel like to be real close to him.

She swallows hard again and he kisses her. Candis holds him tight and when he pulls on her pants, wanting them to come down she stops him; saying "Rafee'al?!" You know I like you, a lot!" He lays back on top of her answering "yep." And I like you too; a lot" he says as he's kissing her with every word. On her leg she can feel his hard; 'hammer, on top of her; begging to get inside her; "tool box"! But still telling him once again how she can't go all the way. Somberly she says "sorry, if I'm leading you on." Maybe we should just go to sleep" she adds sympathetically.

But then he kisses her endlessly; again while she's saying on his kissing lips "I want too, but--!" He pleads "well then, come on; come on; Candis!" I won't hurt you!" I'll go really; slow." She bites her bottom lip then kisses him saying "I know you won't hurt me." It's not that; it's just---." I want to really be in a committed relationship" she says. "Not, wanting to scare him off too soon; by using the "marriage; card" once again. But still letting him know that she's sticking; to her guns. He rubs her face saying "we are in a committed relationship." I'm with you, and only you." And you are my woman and I'm your man" he said holding her hand. "Unless you have someone else" he said? "No," she said. "I've only been dating you."

Smiling up at him she says "okay, so we are 'officially, together as boyfriend and girlfriend?" He kisses her again saying "yes, we are." "Alright, then" she said. And with a smile on her face she kisses him back again but slowly this time, saying "well then, {kiss}! "You won't mind; waiting, {kiss}! "To see how this; {kiss}! "Committed relationship develops, {kiss}! "Before we "do" {kiss}! "Go all the way" {kiss}! He wasn't expecting that 'twist, to come 'out, with all of those 'sex; driven; kisses! But he knows her game by now and so he makes his own game fall into play with hers by kissing her all-- the way-- down, to her belly button saying to her "I totally understand and I respect you." On his way back up, leading with his kisses he says "but now; no more talking." Now, I'm gonna let you see how much I really; like you" he whisper in her ear. She smiles and while he kisses her on his lips she voices "you're gonna make me lose my wings boy!" And I like fly way too much for that!"

She was referring, to getting into trouble with 'God, if she crosses the line. He grunts and kisses her back with a smile on his face. Still kissing him she says "I know you have needs being that you're a man, she keeps kissing him while talking. And to you--; she pauses looking at him saying "it's probably not fair to you; either she says while 'panting, over his mouth, saying "so maybe we should just stop!" He looks at her seriously 'thinking, how he thought, they were having a moment, a good moment, until she said; stop! He says "stop!" were not doing anything but kissing." She; breaths hard while looking into his eyes trying to take him all the way down to her soul from her eyes. And while looking at him she could hear the frustration and the disappointment in his voice as well as her heart racing in her chest because the feeling between them is so; intense!

He falls back on his back and lays there and then turns to face her he says "so what do you want to do; Candis?" lie here, and hold each other?" She's thinking "yes!" that would be; nice!" He looked so-o-o fyne to Candis with his sad face and his still hard; 'rock, up against her leg as he's talking to her in her ear, wanting her and saying anything to have her. She knows what temptation sounds like, and as she's looking him in the face, she pauses along pause 'thinking, as he's rubbing his fingers in her hair. And then she kisses him again and he kisses her again and he starts to rub his hands on her body and they get all hot and heavy again and then she stops' to catch her breath; with her lips so numb she can't even feel them anymore!

She sits up in his bed to clear her mind and then he kisses her again. "Gosh, he's such a good kisser!" she says in her mind. So as they are kissing and he's rubbing his middle leg on top of her body; gasping she says "I know, I can't go all the way" {kiss}! "But we can still 'play, without doing it; right?!" She smiles, then {Kiss}! He smiles back when she says that; thinking of all the other 'things, he could be doing to her and 'she, be doing to him! She grabs him by the face and kisses him; hard, breathing heavily she says "just rub your body up against mine" she says as she's pulling off her pants; slowly kissing him intensively.

She adds "I just want to feel you up against me!" But that was "not" what Rafee'al was thinking; that he was going to hear 'or, be doing! He was wanting a little more "action" than that from her!" after getting all those; steamy; kisses she was giving him! But, he went along with it anyway!" even though; he hadn't rubbed up against a girl like this; since high school. But he wasn't about to complain because he wanted Candis anyway he could have her. He unbuttons her shirt as they are kissing so he can feel her skin up against his chest, but she wouldn't let him take off her bra, though, feeling like that would "really" push her over the limit if he was to be all on her breast. He kisses her and kisses her and as he eases his body in between heirs' he starts to grind up against her. And with every press of his body she gets so--, wet as he's slowly kissing and grinding up against her, until she begins to moan slightly; over his mouth.

He is so hard because he can feel every drop of her, even though her panties, which are slightly moving over to one side because she is moving so-o-o, wildly underneath him. The louder she gets the more he presses up against her. Rafee'al turns; up his 'motor, after seeing how much 'higher, Candis is climbing. He couldn't even lie about how great she felt as he rubbed his 'paint brush, up against her; canvas! He could feel more than he ever thought he would, because she was going so 'crazy, on his "Mr. Goodbar"! So crazy that her undies begin to slide to one side revealing more 'skin, then panty. And with all the excitement; her 'clitty-clitty; 'bang-bang; grew harder and harder; and as she's moaning in his ear and moaning over his mouth while he's kissing her, one of her favorite video's by Keyshia Cole: featuring Tyrese called: Love! Comes on and when the song says "never knew what I was missing!" But I knew once we start kissing!" I found-oud... oud... oud!" "I..., found..., you!" While they are kissing she feels like that video 'came on, just for them, and that fate has brought them together as she's feeling; her heart; beating into his!

He starts kissing her so--- hard as she is moving real; seductively up against him; loving every bit of him as much as she can. And as Rafee'al; feels, what she's feeling, it is becoming harder and harder for him "not" to be able to stick his "gear" inside her "barrel"! But oooooh... just thinking about it; makes him start to "churn"! And oooooh—how—he-- creamed! He was so into what she was doing to him, until she started to slide off the bed; even! But before, she could fall to the floor, with her legs wrapped around his back, he held on to her as he 'shot, his "hot-pocket" all over her stomach and up on to that pretty bra of heir's, that never made it off of her body! Candis got her cup filled; and even chuckled when one of his "squirts" made its way 'all, the way up to her cheek.

When the two were finished; pleasing each other, Candis went to the bathroom to wash off her bra in the sink with soapy water and then she hung it up to dry. Then she climbed back into bed with one of his t-shirts on, that he left hanging on the bathroom door. Rafee'al after cleaning off, laid there in bed with his arm around Candis and a big smile on his face chuckling "you're a little freak!" Candis, with flushed cheeks laughs back answering "what?!" No, I'm not!" You are" she adds. He returns "I've heard about you Catholic girls!" She chuckles and nudges him in his ribs with her elbow. He grunts out a laugh sighing; "awh--, and you're violent; too! Continuing to laugh even harder he blurts out "the priest, isn't going to like that; either!" Candis laughed so hard, while replying "oh, come on!" You know that didn't hurt you" she retorted as she rubbed his ribs with her hand. The two of them lye in his bed looking up at his ceiling and then back at each other, as they talk and joke around with each other, until they both fall asleep in each other's arms. 'Now--, Naquawna's Christmas Eve, wasn't as fulfilling as Candis's was, because she couldn't sleep. She was up at her place, trying to get some, and we are "not" talking about Christmas; cookies!

Chapter 34

After everyone had left Naquawna's house and Mike's mom 'finally, went home, and granddad 'finally, went to bed. Naquawna and Mike stayed up to watch Scarface on channel TV-one. Naquawna knew she was not going to see Rayshawn on Christmas Eve because he had texted her earlier saying 'that his dad and his lady friend were coming down for Christmas Eve; dinner and would be spending the night at his place'. So Naquawna had figured she was not going to be alone that night either and since Mike was good company he stayed with her.

After the movie goes off Mike tries to get a little "action" by saying "let me rub your feet for you." Naquawna looks at him like 'boy, I'm already knowing; what you're trying to do! Stroking her hand he says "you've been up all day on your feet cooking that good food for us, so I'm gonna rub your feet for you." Naquawna was always a sucker for flattery, so she soaked it up like a sponge and went back to her room to go get the foot lotion he had bought her earlier, for her Christmas stocking. She sits back down on the couch with the lotion and he rubs her feet while he tells her "how glad he is that they are spending Christmas Eve together." And when he looks up at her smiling he tells her "how beautifully; glowing she is and that being pregnancy really agrees with her."

She smiles back thanking him then closes her eyes as he's rubbing on her feet real slowly with the lotion. He goes a little further up her leg than he was 'supposed; to, but she lets him anyway because her hormones are raging and he can tell. Mike is the kind of man who reads a lot of books. And the books that he finds to be most intriguing are the ones about loving women. He takes a lot of things from those books he reads and puts them into the songs he writes, as well as in his poetry. His art work always seems to center around making women feel good with his touch or with his lyrics.

With the lowering of his voice he suggested to Naquawna to lye back on the couch and relax, as he start to rub up her leg while her eyes are still closed. Then he pulls her long skirt up, gathering it up around her waist, she opens her eyes saying "wait!" my granddad might come out!" He answers her saying "his door is close." And we can hear his bed creek if he gets up." Now, lay back and be quiet" he said. He then starts to kiss Naquawna from head to toe, and when he gets to her big toe he puts it into his mouth.

She sighs in a low voice asking "is that edible lotion?" He looks up at her smiling; replying "is there any other kind?" She holds back her giggles when saying to him "you are so kinky!" He then licks in between her toes and with a grinning, smile he says "I know." And then he dives into her "Milky Way" head first; licking her; like he's replaced his tongue; with a propeller. Naquawna loving it, tells him just how much she does; love it, as he's doing her. After he finished making her into 'whipped, cream; from his tongue she climbed up on top of him and slowly road his ship; 'like as if, she was on, the seven seas. When they are done playing with each other, Naquawna quietly goes back to her room like a little church mouse, while Mike crashes on the living couch.

It's about an hour later into her sleep when Naquawna thinks she hear a pebble hitting her bedroom window. She figures it's just the wind, so she rolls back over and goes back to sleep. Then she hears it again. She gets up all sleepy and groggy and peaks out her blinds and can't she believe; it's Rayshawn outside! He points to the back door, wanting her to come let him in. She stands there like "oh shit!" 'Like, what should I do?!" So instead of going to let him in she opens the window saying "I can't!" My granddad's up!" Rayshawn knows this isn't that big of a deal because she's; snuck him in the house on many occasions with her granddad sitting right there in the living room.

So he gets a peculiar look on his face saying "cut the jokes!" He voices "you can sneak me in!" Naquawna feels like she is so--; busted right now, so her conscience won't let her weaken, to his request. He sees she's not budging so he says it even louder "what's up?!" is someone in your room?!" "No--; it's just late, and I'm already in bed!" 'Plus, not to mention;

her cup has ‘already, runneth ‘over, she thinks to herself. With anger in his voice he answers “so….!” It’s Christmas Eve!” And I want to spend some time with you!” Looking up at her he smiles adding “and…, I got you something” he said as he pulled a gift box out of his jacket pocket. Naquawna starts to bit on one of her fingernails, like she always does, when she’s trying to figure out what to do, in a very difficult situation. When she sees the gift in his hand, she weakens saying “well… maybe I can meet you outside, go to the back” she replied. He walks to the back door where the kitchen is, while Naquawna puts on her shorts and the jacket to match. She sneaks past the couch, where Mike is at ‘snoring; loudly, and she ‘gloats, because he is so… passed; out, do to all of her; “good lovin”! She quietly opens the back door full of herself, because she’s got two men; wanting her. Rayshawn grabs her immediately and kisses her saying “what took you so long?!” it’s cold out here!” he said. She smirks at him saying “how did you get out of the house; anyway?” on Christmas Eve.

“I snuck out, is that alright with you?” She just looks at him with a cocky smile on her face not trippin off him, like she normally would. So he says “naw, I just left because my pops heard me and Se’anna arguing, so I told him, I was going to go turn a few corners, to cool off.” But I really did it, so I could come see you” he said with a touch to her face. She smiles saying “so where’s my gift?” He returns “where’s mine?” “Right here” she says as she runs her hand down the middle of her body towards her feet indicating that she ‘is, the gift!

He reaches to open up her jacket by pulling on her zipper, but she pulls back from him and looks behind her to make sure no one is coming out of the house. Rayshawn says “why do you keep looking back?” like someone’s coming. “I don’t know.” It’s just a force of habit.” He says “then let’s go in the house, so you don’t have to trip so hard!” With a touch of the door he tries to walk passed her as he reaches for the doorknob, but she stops him shouting “no!” He’s on the couch!” He retorts “who?!” She slipped a little, but recovers quickly answering “my granddad!” Who else?!” He says “well…, if you want your gift, it will be in your room” he said pushing passed her, opening up the door and making his way into the kitchen.

She pulls on his arm saying “no!” No!” We can’t tonight!” He stops and notices the pie sitting underneath the dim stove light and he says “yum…, cut me a piece of that pie. She blurts “no…; for real!” This is not a good time!” Tripping on how she’s acting he asked “why?!” Don’t tell me you’re on your rag again?!” All out of sorts she shouts “yes!” As a matter of fact, I am!" Not believing her he says "you lying, come on; and bring the pie!" A voice in the next room says "Naquawna?"! "Who you talking too?"! Her eyes expand when she says "umm…, no one!" Rayshawn looks at her like 'no-one, and her eyes dilate even more, when Rayshawn asked "who's that?!" She clears her throat answering "my in-laws are here!" That's why I said; it wasn't a good time!" "Awh; damn…!" Why didn't you say so?!" We could have gotten a room and kicked it for a little bit" he claimed. She tries to hustle him back out the door, but then the light comes on in the kitchen and its Mike shouting "I thought I heard a man's voice!" "Who's this?!" asked Mike looking at Naquawna with a frown. Rayshawn holds out his hand thinking he is one of Naquawna's relatives so he says "I'm Rayshawn; man, nice to meet you." Mike, looks back at Naquawna; mean-mug-style, and doesn't even shake Rayshawn's hand. Call Rayshawn 'naïve, but he really didn't catch on, until Naquawna put her head down in shame. Then Rayshawn said "what's up; man?!" You and her; f^#ken?!" What's up?"! Naquawna yells out "no! "Not; even…!" she said looking at Mike to confirm, what she was saying. But Mike was "not" having it!" because she is having his baby and he wanted to make 'sure, that Rayshawn was 'totally; out of the picture! Mike answers "naw--!" I'm not; f*cken her!" I'm making love to her; dawg!" And she's caring my baby!" if you must; know! Rayshawn looks at Naquawna; mad, asking her "is that right?!" She shakes her head answering "no!" It ain't even like that!" Rayshawn blurts out "then what is it like?!" You playing us both?!" 'Naquawna, avoiding direct eye contact answers "no!" I'm not!" Then she looks at Mike asking "can you go back in the living room?" please…!

Rayshawn looks at Mike crazy waiting on him to leave, but Mike doesn't budge. Mike says "dude; aren't you the one who's playing; her?"! Rayshawn answers "naw!" I ain't play-in her; man!" Mike adds "but don't you have a woman and a baby at home?!" But yet; you're over 'here, trying to be all up on my; woman!" and soon to be child! Rayshawn looks at Mike and yells "man, you don't know nothing about; me!" And--; that could be 'my, baby; dawg!" adds Rayshawn staring at Mike while he's balling up his fists. Naquawna now 'uncomfortable, because she is in the middle of this love triangle blurts out "Mike, why are you still in here?!" I got this!" Let me talk to him real quick!"

'Mike, standing there with his hands ready to swing on Rayshawn says "I wanna hear what you two have to talk about! Rayshawn yells "it's not yo' business; what she wants to talk to me about! She shouts "you two are going to wake up my granddad!" She huffs "Mike, maybe you should just leave!" she adds. "Yeah man, you heard her; just get on!" said Rayshawn all bad ass and angry. Mike blurts out "I ain't going anywhere!"

Her granddad 'knows, I'm here!" but can you say the same?!" Mike continues to say "he probably doesn't even know you; bruh!" And I'd bet money; he's never met you!" Naquawna shouts "Mike, just; leave--!" Mike talks over her saying "that's because dudes all about; a booty call!" Look at what time he came over to your house!" said Mike looking at the clock on the stove pointing. "That's not what a man 'does, when he's trying to be with you on a real; level!"

Rayshawn clicks on him yelling "you need to stop speaking on me man!" You don't even know me; part'nah!" Rayshawn gets all up in Mikes face, but Mike doesn't; flinch! 'Naquawna thinks, it has something to do with his head injury; this bolder, aggressive; new Mike. "Just get on man!" said Mike not impressed with Rayshawn's; puffed; up, chest. He adds "she don't want you dude!" She's with me now!" Mike grabs Naquawna by the hand saying "we're trying to make our; own family now!" So why don't you get on, and go be with yours!" Rayshawn gets mad as hell, after hearing him say what 'he, should 'do, about going 'home; to his "own; family"! So; pissed; Rayshawn halls off, and punches Mike dead in his jaw. Mike doesn't fall, but the pie on the stove does, after Mike throws Rayshawn up against the stove and punches him back in his face hitting his nose. Naquawna tries to break them up but gets pushed up against the refrigerator and hits her stomach in the process. With all of Naquawna's 'screams, and the guys yelling; knocking over stuff in the kitchen! Her granddad makes his way into the kitchen with a bat in his hand yelling "what the hell is going on in here?!"

Mike and Rayshawn's; scuffling, slows down but they keep on fighting. The pie on the ground catches Mike's foot and he almost falls to the floor but manages to grab on to the counter while Rayshawn gets another hit to his stomach. But when Mike hits Rayshawn back, they finally stop fighting and notice that Naquawna is hunched over, holding onto her stomach crying. Mike comes to her aid asking "are you okay?!" as he touches her stomach, but she pushes his hand away so her granddad won't ask what is going on with her stomach. Rayshawn trying to stop the blood from his nose yells "I'll see you in the streets; bruh!" Mike yells back "no!" See me now!"

Rayshawn answers "come outside then!" But her granddad shut it down quickly; saying to Rayshawn "son, don't be bringing no trouble over here!" You go on now; here?"! Rayshawn nods saying "okay...; sir! Then he gives Naquawna one last evil look and nods Mike's way 'like, this ain't 'over,

and he leaves out, slamming the back door. Naquawna quietly gets some ice out of the freezer for Mike to put on his jaw, and his busted lip. All; pumped up from the fight he says to Naquawna "that fool thought he was gone punk; me!" that's why I hit that chump; hard, in his nose!" said Mike putting his arm around Naquawna as they walk back into the living room.
Her granddad was about to head back to bed but before doing so, he says to Naquawna "first of all granddaughter!" you know you; wrong!" for playing both those; men!" and having them fighting over you!" Someone could have really gotten hurt!" Even kilt!" And you; young lady; would 'have had, to live with that; as 'well, as the perpetrator!" Naquawna feeling terrible about the situation lowers her head sighing "I know, you're right; granddad. She tries to save face by saying "but he came over here on his own!" I didn't call him!" I was in my bed sleep!" She looks to Mike for support, but he lets her handle; this 'much, needed; discussion with her granddad on her own. Mike replies "well..., you should have stayed in bed; then!" You didn't have to answer the door!" And, look at how late that fool came over here!" And Mike went on and on about it; until Naquawna said "okay...!" Mike"! I get it!" She looks at his face with a smirk, and then she checks his face, on all side to make sure he's okay before she goes back into to the kitchen to clean up the pie. She can't express it enough to Mike "how sorry, she is that he got in a fight because of her." But he tells her "it's cool." But adds "now-- I hope you see, that 'dude, is a simp!" who only comes over for sex! Naquawna answers "no; that's not always the case!" 'She still tries to defend Rayshawn; believing that he really does love her.

But to avoid arguing with Mike she says "you're, right!" She finishes with "well...; goodnight...!" I'm going to bed!" she said. And then she goes back to her room and closes the door. While lying in her bed, her ego side 'smiles; just a little, because two guys fought over her tonight. Then she gets a text from Rayshawn; calling her all kinds of bees! And they weren't; the flying kind! She smirks sadly and doesn't even respond to his madness. He ends his last text with "you dirty hoe!" I guess he thinks she's into gardening; too! Crack; up!

Chapter 35

When poor little Sherry's plane landed earlier that day on Christmas Eve her sister greeted her at the airport with a big hug and a smile. Sherry had told her sister she had found out through her Doctor that Bruce had given her Chlamydia. And she just couldn't find it in her heart to forgive him yet. She wasn't even going to tell him at first; hoping he would find out on his own after his d*^k fell off. But her Doctor convinced her to be the bigger 'person, so no one 'else, would contracts, the disease. So when she called his job and he picked up the phone, he 'hoped, that her call was for 'reconciliation, of their relationship.

Sherry ended up; bursting his bubble; yelling out "your d*ck is going to fall off, if you don't get to the clinic!" You gave me Chlamydia!" You; dick!" And she slammed down the phone in his face. He didn't even bother to call her back to apologize because he 'knew; it wouldn't matter! And she probably wouldn't pick up anyway. Sherry told her sister that she will be 'swearing off men, for her upcoming; New Year's, resolution. Her sister Keyera laughs replying "so does that mean you'll be clam; bumping, now?!" Sherry cracks up laughing "I'm giving up on 'men, for a while; not d*ck!" bee-itch!

They both laugh out loud and get drunk as skunks; off of a big bottle of Earl Stevens, Moscato that Sherry had brought with her on the plane. While drinking and laughing with her sister; Sherry felt much better, as the night went on. She even went on-line to one of those dating websites to see if she could be hooked up with a match. "And the pickings are looking promising, too!" said her sister laughing. So while the girls are on line looking for Sherry a new man. A lullaby flashes across the screen saying "all the kids were snug in their beds! While all the grownups; had liquor 'dancing around; in their heads! Merry Christmas! It; read.

It's a cold Christmas morning and little Ray junior is up trying to open up all his gifts. Rayshawn is up helping his son, but still not saying too much to Se'anna. He really isn't that mad at Se'anna anymore, it's mostly the anger from what took place last night at Naquawna's house that keeps wearing; on his nerves. Zailda and Big Ray are in the kitchen making a big brunch; type Christmas breakfast for the family. Se'anna keeps going into the kitchen begging; to help, but they 'insist, that she take it easy because she has been such a 'great, daughter in-law for letting them stay at her house instead of having them; closed up in a hotel, with no kitchen. 'Brandy, wasn't with them; believe it or not, because she was spending time with her mother at a women's recovery house.

After Bonnie found Bubba dead in his house, she took it very hard. She even smoked crack that very night, until she thought her brain was 'literally, on fire. The nice people who were at the crime scene earlier on that day, had given Bonnie a card saying "if she needed to talk to someone or get help; that they could help her get into a program." So that following week after she smoked herself sick, she called to get help. Her reason for calling to get help was also because she wanted to use his death as a way of honoring his love and friendship for her 'remembering, that no one else 'cared, about getting her off the streets, or, getting her off of crack, like Bubba did! Plus, she knew he always had her back.

Bonnie also remembers Bubba telling her that weed is better for her to smoke, then crack is. And he even stopped selling rocks to her and anyone that smoked with her, months before he died. Bonnie was getting clean, and for the first time, big Ray felt comfortable about letting her take Brandy 'alone, for the Holidays. Brandy calls her brother's house and wishes everyone a very Merry Christmas and tells her father she will be back home, after New Year's. Her father smiles and in his heart, he is glad that she is spending time with her mother, which makes him feel that there is hope after all; even for Bonnie.

So while they eat breakfast and open up gifts Rayshawn and Se'anna slip off to the room to make up. The song 'Jingle bells, jingle bells, jingle; all the way, is playing over at Roxy's house on Christmas morning. Roxy is fixing Steeli'o a breakfast fit for a King. He walks over to her stereo to change the station at her request, and he stops when he hear Nat King Cole's beautiful voice; pouring out of her speaker box. The two are so in love as they sit there eating at the table looking into each other's eyes. They didn't have gifts to exchange for one another because they were broken up. But as far as they were 'concerned, they "were" each other's gifts. The two just sat around her house all hugged up together on her couch after breakfast. Their agenda for today, will more than likely; consist of them watching movies in their pj's and making love throughout the day.

Roxy finds the movie "God's of Egypt" for them to watch and couldn't be more; happier when hearing Steeli'o profess his love to her and 'how, he wants to be with her forever! She even stopped asking questions about Claudia, feeling like 'he's, with 'her, for Christmas!" so it must not be too serious between the two of them; after all! As for 'Steeli'o, he's over her past too!" for now anyways, as long as she never goes back to that life; again! 'Now, speaking of going back, a sad and depressed; Naquawna has been playing the song: All I want for Christmas is you. By Mariah Carey over and over again on her iPad. It was a quiet morning when she first got up, with a bitter taste in her mouth. And as the depression set in, over the fact that she didn't want to lose Rayshawn, she ended up crying while laying across her bed. She even wanted to call him or text him and say "that it's; his baby!" not Mike's! And tell him "how much she loves him." And that Mike was just lying about the two of them 'ever; having sex!" But even she couldn't bring herself to talk to him when she called his phone.

Naquawna sat there on the other end of the phone just listening to his voice as the song played in the background for him to hear. He could hear the song playing so he kept saying "hello?!" Hello?!" But after the third time she called him he busted her out on it; saying "I know it you!" Stop calling me!" You go on ahead and make your new family!" and I'll stick with mines! Before he hangs up she hears Se'anna in the background saying "come here; babe!" Come see what your dad got us for Christmas!" Then the phone goes dead and Naquawna sits back down on her bed teary-eyed playing the song.

She ends up calling Candis for some sisterly support and tells her the whole story about last night while Rafee'al is taking Candis home because he has to go to work, but says "he would come by Candis's house later on that night." Naquawna wanted Candis to come over today and hang out and talk, but Candis said she needed to go home and wash her hair and get some things done at home, but offered for Naquawna to come over to her place and hang, but Naquawna didn't feel like leaving the comforts of her place either. So--- Naquawna becomes even sadder; knowing, that she will be home alone for most of the day because Mike and his 'band member's, had promised to play music at a Christmas party for some under privileged kids in the park this year.

And her "partying; granddad" and Mike's mom are out trying to win some money up at a nearby Casino in the Bingo Hall. So as Candis is getting out of Rafee'al's car, Naquawna starts walking into her kitchen still on the phone talking with Candis as she's pulling out a pint of pineapple sherbet ice cream walking with it into her living room, where she plops down on the couch and turns on the t.v to watch NCIS while eating it. Candis is still on the phone listening to her talk when she gives Rafee'al a long kiss goodbye. The kiss from his lips was so succulent and warm until she forgot all about her friend on the phone. Which prompted Naquawna, to just hang up the phone, and continue to stuff her face with ice cream.

Rafee'al heads to work after his moment with Candis, and when Officer Mahavez, goes into work everyone on his team is so glad to see him because; like it or not; he is, for the 'most part, the life of the party! His fellow Officers are having a small Christmas party but it's 'nothing, like the Christmas party at his auntie's house. He stopped by her house before he went into work after dropping Candis off at home. Luckily he had put all of the gifts, his gun and his holster in the trunk of his car the night before, because Candis might have started asking a bunch of questions if he had put everything in the trunk, that morning. So when he got to his auntie's house she had hot apple cider simmering on the stove and homemade croissants filled with dark; chocolate. She also had some of the croissants filled with ham, eggs and cheese. His aunt always made the best brunches on Christmas morning.

And as usual all of the kids were there opening up presents on the living room floor. Even his niece Jasmine was sitting on the couch, all hugged up with her new boyfriend, taking selfies. The only person missing was his mom and his sister. Rafee'al picks up an old photograph of him and his deceased sister from off the mantel, and his auntie comment's on the picture saying "she was a beautiful girl wasn't she?" He nods laughing "she was alright; making light of it. Then his auntie asked "how old would she be by now?" Rafee'al just shrugs "I don't know, maybe 31 or 32, I think?" "Yep..., she replies in a sad voice. His aunt changes the subject to "your mom called." She really wanted to be here; but you know." Rafee'al says "yep, I know, she called me as soon as I pulled up to your house." Mom has always been psychic like that" he laughs. Adding "she probably knew I was on my way over here" he grunts. His auntie smiles "I know--- it's just so hard for her to come back here after your sister died, and your father left, she just can't handle living in this area anymore; it just brings up to many bad memories."

"Yep---, I know---," he said exhaling a deep breath, saying "I'll go see her sometime after the New Year. "Good---, you should; she would love that" said his aunt. She continues to say "I don't know how she deals with all that 'hot Arizona, weather though" said his aunt. He laughs saying "yeah I know, then he lightens up the mood saying this chocolate stuffed croissant reminds me something--, and he started laughing looking over at Jasmine and her boyfriend saying "remember that time auntie when my mom told me and my sister, that when you two were about 7 or 8 years old, and you auntie, told my mom that the dog poop on the ground was a piece of chocolate and you told her to taste it?" His aunt yells "not that story again!" He keeps on talking with Jasmine; laughing in the background. "But she didn't believe you, so then, you told her to smell it." And my mom told you to go first since you were the oldest." "Then, when you bent down to smell it, my mom pushed your nose in the poop and ran!" he said laughing. Of course his auntie still denies it to this day saying "that it was the other way around." But Rafee'al and Jasmine always laugh so hard about it when the two sisters are together bickering about the story that happened when they were kids. Jasmine laughing from the living room couch says "yeah---; little sister, let big sister know early on; that she was no; dummy! His auntie laughs out "boy---, you better get out my face and go on in that kitchen and make yourself a plate!" and hush! She shakes her head saying "I can't believe your momma is still telling people that; lie!" Yo' momma's a lie!"

The devils a lie!" Hell, yaw; all lying!" she said cracking herself up.

Rafee'al and Jasmine laughed the hardest while he ate a few bites of the food off his plate standing in the kitchen. He looks down at the watch Candis had gotten him and sees that he's got to get to work. But then he puts down his plate abruptly; almost forgetting about the gifts in his trunk; saying to them "he'll be right back!" Licking his fingers he runs outside to get the gifts out of his car. With his hands full he comes back inside and gives everyone their gifts. Smiling his auntie gives him a gift as well. He says "thanks auntie" and gives her a big hug.

Smiling she replies "next time you come by, bring your girlfriend with you." I would love to meet her." His eyes go cock-eyed as he looks Jasmine's way. Jasmine scoffing at him says "what?!" Everyone knows you go out with Candis!" Remember, we live in a small town, and everyone knows---, everybody's business!" And you ain't no; different, just because you 'just, moved out here!" He laughs saying "you don't know all of my business; little girl!" Jasmine laughing back at him takes a bite of her cupcake saying "okay!" Mr. delusional! He plays it off but the big grin on his face is a dead giveaway that he "does" like a girl named; Candis.

He doesn't even want to go further into it; with Jasmine about Candis so he ends the conversation with "okay auntie." I'll see yaw'll, I got to get going!" Merry Christmas yaw'll" he yells as he walks out to his car, still eating food from off his plate. So when Rafee'al finally got to work and saw that the, little party like "pot-luck" was going strong the guys pull him to the side and tell him that they have a match on the baby's DNA. But before Kitpatrick and Lenny could tell him who matched up; with the baby; his Captain calls him into his office. The Captain says "sit down son". "I don't know how to say this; but, we may have to take you off this case." "What?!" "Why?!" asked Rafee'al as he stands up from his chair thinking maybe they know he's getting to close to Candis. Rafee'al voiced out "come on!" Captain!" I'm getting real close, to solving this drug case!" "And the bigger shipment is getting closer to being revealed!" I just know it!"

His Captain says "it's not the drug case!" I'm worried about!" It's your sister's murder case! "What?!" says Rafee'al, asking "what about it?"! "Well, apparently!" says the Captain, Officer Jackson, and Officer Frankel; have taking a special interest in your sister's "case" for some reason!" After; I, could---; have sworn!" I told everyone; included you!" that the 'case, was closed!" But for some reason; no one seems to be listening; to me!" So now, that's why I have 'no choice, but to pull you off of this drug case!"

Rafee'al just stands there with his mouth open in a state of 'W.T.F, just happened?"! He looks at his Captain while trying to wrap his head around what he is "really" saying, and while looking at him; hard he says "sir." I'm confused!" What does the 'drug case, have to do with my sister's murder case?!" said Rafee'al, adding, "the two; are two different cases! "No son; the baby's DNA; matches one of your "fellow" drug; dealing; compadres!" Rafee'al shouts "What?!" Are you Fricken; kidding me?!" He stands there with his hands slowly running down the sides of his head, as he's looking straight into the Captain's eyes. Then he says "who is it?"! Gasping out some air through his mouth his Captain answers "I don't think I should tell you that right now!" But, we still need you to just 'ease; out of this case! "Captain!" shouts Rafee'al. "Tell me who it is?!"

The cops in the office outside the door can hear Rafee'al's voice go up an octave, so they look in his direction. Rafee'al sits back down so he can calm his anxiety and then he calmly repeats "Captain?" I need to know that information, and if you can't trust me, then what good is my badge?!" His Captain stares at him for what seems to be 'like, 5 whole minutes to Rafee'al. Then, the Captain walks up to him and he puts his hand on his shoulder and in a seriously sad; voice he says "it's Steeli'o!" Rafee'al's head; drops!

To be continued...

Thank you so much for reading the first half of my book!

CPSIA information can be obtained
at www.ICGtesting.com
Printed in the USA
BVOW03s2144140817
492064BV00001B/61/P

9 780998 564500